The Pie Man

Gerry FitzGerald

BookLocker.com, Inc.
2009

Dedicated to my mother

Mildred H. Johnson

who always made everything possible.

Foreword

When I began writing *The Pie Man* in 1999, the practice of mountaintop removal coal mining appeared to be on life support. A courageous federal judge, Charles H. Haden II, sitting on the U.S. District Court for the Southern District of West Virginia, in Charleston, sided with the West Virginia Highlands Conservancy and other environmentalists who had challenged the practice of mountaintop removal strip mining through a suit brought under the Federal Clean Water Act. Judge Haden agreed that burying streams and hollows under hundreds of feet of sand and rocks did in fact violate the environmental standards of the Clean Water Act. On appeal, his ruling was overturned in 2001 on the grounds that federal courts had no jurisdiction, but in avoiding a decision on the substance of the matter, the US Court of Appeals for the Fourth Circuit in Richmond, Virginia left the door invitingly open for state litigation, which was not the outcome the mining industry was looking for.

Judge Haden's ruling in March of 1999 had an immediate effect on MTR with the layoff three days later of 380 miners at the huge Dal-Tex surface mining complex of Hobet Mining, in Logan County, West Virginia. The layoffs and the subsequent work stoppage at Dal-Tex's 3,100 acre Pigeon Roost Hollow surface mine, sent an immediate and unequivocal message of the seriousness of the ruling (and the dire consequences the State and the local economies would pay). The most telling impact of the ruling came several months later with the beginning of the dismantling of Hobet's monstrous, $100million drag line and the closing of the entire Dal-Tex complex. The environmentalists and the mountain-keepers had reason to cheer.

Going back now to try to piece together the events that brought about the re-emergence of mountaintop removal mining in the last ten years entails a frustrating search through a long list of agency rulings and opinions, backdropped by suits and counter-suits, appeals and over-rules, the sum total of which is much more easily described as the *Bush Administration.*

The energy companies, their lobbyists, and their local politicians found a willing and powerful ally in George W. Bush, and while it took a few years to get the game plan installed in all the pertinent agencies, like a cancerous tumor, mountaintop removal coal mining returned with a vengeance to West Virginia. King coal continues to rule Appalachia -- as it has for the last 120 years. If I'd waited a few years for the Bush administration, the process of securing a MTR variance would have been much easier (and consumed fewer pages) for the Ackerly Coal Company of my story.

Today there are dozens of mountaintop strip mines operating in West Virginia that were permitted and opened during the Bush years. The mines are burying hundreds of miles of streambeds under rock, sand and timber, leaching sulfates and selenium into the ground water, fouling drinking wells, cracking the foundations and walls of nearby homes, producing irreversible flooding perils, and rendering nearby communities all but unlivable. And the once-beautiful, majestic, lushly forested mountains are reduced to barren wastelands, dusty scabs that would only be tolerated in Appalachia, where the population is thin, the people powerless and poor, and where the coal industry has been sucking out the wealth since the beginning of the last century.

Environmentalists and residents of the coal camp communities had much reason for optimism with the onset of the Obama administration. The new President said all the right things during the campaign and in the early days of his administration, to the point of giving the impression that the permanent eradication of mountaintop removal was a done deal as soon as Barack could get around to it after dealing with several higher priority issues. But the collapse of the economy and the financial system, along with the coaching of the powerful and deep-pocketed-campaign-contributing energy lobbyists, along with the simple realities of *big government, high unemployment, soaring energy cost* priorities have reaffirmed the irrefutable fact that in America, *Appalachia* is still *Appalachia* when it comes to politics.

Some permits have been suspended for further review, and much discussion has taken place with regard to interpretation of the regulations governing *valley fills* and which permitting process should the governing agencies adhere to, but after all the campaign pandering and the conviction of the stump speeches, the nearly inaudible murmuring of the administration over the issue of mountaintop removal coal mining, suggests some major league hedging, and that's an ominous sign for the opponents of MTR.

Currently there are 48 new mountaintop removal mines permitted for West Virginia. Another 105 new sites are permitted for Kentucky, and an additional handful in Tennessee and Virginia. In West Virginia, the new MTR sites permitted total 42,715 acres of land to be destroyed, mountains that will never again be mountains, surrounded by hundreds of miles of streams that will disappear, amid dozens of communities that will become uninhabitable. It could never happen anywhere but in Appalachia, and that, quite simply, is not fair to the people who live there. It never has been.

For information and to sense the outrage, spend some time on the websites listed below. To really experience the powerlessness, voicelessness and frustration of poor people from a poor state making a noble fight to try to protect their small, insignificant, undervalued, out-of-mind, piece of America from destruction, watch a film called *Burning The Future: Coal In America.*

West Virginia Highlands Conservancy: www.wvhighlands.org

Appalachian Voices: www.appvoices.org

Ohio Valley Environmental Coalition: www.ohvec.org

iLove Mountains: www.ilovemountains.org

Coal River Mountain Watch: www.crmw.net

The Sierra Club: www.sierraclub.org

Burning The Future: Coal in America: www.burningthefuture.org

Gerry FitzGerald

July 2009

Acknowledgments

The Pie Man is a work of fiction. The characters and their thoughts, actions and words are entirely the creation of the author and any resemblances found to an actual person, are coincidental and inadvertent. The corporations named in the story are also fictitious.

All of the places referred to in the story are real with the notable exceptions of the *town of Red Bone, Angel Mountain*, and *Hickory Hills Country Club*. McDowell County is in fact the southernmost county in West Virginia, located in the heart of the huge *Pocahontas Coal Field* that powered America's industrial revolution and fueled the war machines that saved the world twice in the last century. Mamaroneck, New York, is a diverse city of seventeen thousand in Westchester County. New York, NY remains the world's greatest city, and Warren, Vermont, is very close to Heaven.

The historical events referred to in the story are real, well documented from numerous sources and are described as factually and faithfully as I can determine. Hank's personal account of the *Buffalo Creek Disaster of 1972*, borrows heavily from an enthralling and heartbreaking series of stories (largely the work of reporter Ken Ward Jr. mentioned below) published in the *Charleston Gazette* on the 25th anniversary of the tragedy in 1997.

The December 6, 1907 coal mine explosion in Monongah, West Virginia, claimed the lives of 361 miners and remains this country's worst coal mine disaster. On November 20, 1968, a fire in the Consol Mine in Farmington, West Virginia killed 78 miners. The original New York production of *Les Miserables* closed on March 15, 2003, after a 16-year run on Broadway.

Hank's discourses on the *West Virginia Mine Wars,* the *Matewan Massacre* and the subsequent fates of *Sheriff Sid Hatfield* and his deputy *Ed Chambers*, are drawn from numerous sources including: *American Heritage Magazine, August 1974, "The West Virginia Mine Wars" by Cabell Phillips; "The Battle of Matewan", www.matewan.com/ History/battle2.htm; "West Virginia's Mine Wars", West Virginia Division of Culture and History, www.wvculture.org/hiStory/minewars.html;* and *"Matewan", United Mine Workers of America History, www.umwa.org/ history/matewan.shtml.*

For whatever understanding I have about the economics of the coal mining industry as well as what life was like in the coal fields during the last century, I am indebted to a wonderfully written book, *Coal. A Memoir And Critique*, by Duane Lockard (University Press of Virginia, 1998). Chapter 8, "Coal and Corporate Power" should be mandatory reading for all undergraduate business majors and fledgling politicians.

Throughout the writing of *The Pie Man* I found myself continually referring back to and rereading parts of a wonderful book entitled, *The Heritage of McDowell County, West Virginia, 1858-1999*, published by The McDowell County Historical Society and edited by Geneva Steele, Sandra Long and Tom Hatcher. More than anything else, this fascinating book was my primary resource for whatever knowledge I have attained about McDowell County and its residents. One of the unexpected benefits of the writing of *The Pie Man* was the many hours of pleasure I received from reading the hundreds of engrossing biographies and family histories of the people of McDowell County. I came by this book through a chance online meeting of my friend Geneva Steele of Bradshaw, West Virginia, many years ago when I was just starting the book. She has supplied many helpful comments on the story over the years and I am in her debt.

Lastly, I need to pay tribute to a journalist whose articles, columns and blogs I have been devouring on-line for the past twelve years. Ken Ward, Jr. of the *Charleston Gazette* must be this country's leading authority on Appalachian coal mining, the history of coal mining in West Virginia, coal mining safety and the attendant government bureaus and agencies, and the effects of mountaintop removal coal mining in West Virginia as well as the machinations and manipulations of local, state and federal politicians who enable it to continue. Mr. Ward is an exhaustive reporter and a prolific, lucid writer whose style made every story enlightening, every paragraph a pleasure to read.

The Pie Man

by

Gerry FitzGerald

Chapter 1

July 2000

This was her time. The quiet time. Before the sun and the kids and the rest of McDowell County rose up to demand her attention. When she could run, and be alone and pretend to be someone else, living a different life in a different place.

The woman slipped quietly out of bed and picked up the small pile of clothes and her running shoes that she'd set out on the low chair next to the dresser the night before. She heard her husband before she saw him. Buck's labored snoring told her he'd probably spent the evening at *Moody's Roadhouse* again, which was more routine than not these days.

The sliding door that led to the trailer's narrow hallway rumbled lowly and always squeaked at the same spots causing a furtive look at her husband to see if he'd awakened. She reminded herself for the hundredth time to oil the track with something.

The small bathroom had a folding door with its own set of noises as she carefully drew it shut behind her. It was still dark in the trailer at five-thirty, even at the end of July. She turned on the small light over the mirror and slid on the baggy khaki shorts, a sports bra, and a faded black T-shirt she'd pulled randomly from the drawer the night before. It was the Pittsburgh Steelers T-shirt that Buck had brought home for their son a few years earlier. The only gift she could remember Buck ever giving the boy; a glimmer of hope at the time.

The shirt was cheaply made, a size medium, snug to begin with and after many washings now too small for a twelve-year-old, big for his age through the chest and shoulders if not in height. She pulled it over her sandy blonde hair and leaned on the sink to find the insides of the running shoes with her toes. She never wore socks when she ran. When she was a child she rarely wore shoes and ran on rougher ground than she would this morning.

She brushed her teeth, splashed water on her face and stood staring into the mirror. Her hair was getting long, down almost to her shoulders now, the curly permanent from four months earlier that Buck hated, now hanging limp and lifeless. *Have to get it cut before school starts in the fall.* Maybe she'd just cut it all off like her mother used to do to her when she was in elementary school, where she was more often than not taken for a boy.

The woman leaned in closer to the mirror and examined, as she always did when she was alone, the faded white, two-inch-long scar that ran horizontally just above her left eyebrow. Another shorter but wider scar started at the edge of her upper lip just to the right center of her mouth. Both scars nearly invisible now, to everyone but her. The young intern working the emergency room that night, two years earlier, had done a masterful job on the sutures. The best work of his brief career. He had seen how noticeable, how out of place a scar would be on the woman's fine, delicate face with the ice-blue eyes that even filled with tears, sparkled like crystals, and had taken extra care to close up the wounds tightly.

Her broad shoulders stretched the T-shirt a little more tightly across her chest than she preferred, while it hung loose at her small waist. Two pregnancies had enlarged her breasts to a size that, in relation to her small frame, were at least noticeable. She would laugh at the idea of having what she considered large breasts after having the physical appearance of a little girl for most of her life. Now at thirty-years old, Natty Oakes seemed to have finally settled in to what she was supposed to look like.

At a hundred and ten pounds, her mother complained that she looked bony, but she felt good physically, and she was finally beginning to feel good about herself as well. She also had to admit that maybe she wasn't so *plain and ordinary* any more and that *some* men might even find her attractive now.

So why had Buck been losing interest lately, she wondered. Only once since the beginning of July had Buck visited her side of the bed. The few times that she had tentatively edged over to initiate activity, she had been rebuffed, sometimes crudely. *Probably the alcohol. Buck had been drinking more lately,* she told herself.

In the small kitchenette she turned on the gas burner under the tea kettle and shoveled two heaping teaspoons of instant coffee into a large steel mug on the counter. Bending low to look out the small window over the sink, she could see in the pale morning light that the stool at the corner of the trailer across the gravel road was unoccupied. She glanced at her watch. Still a few minutes early.

She went back up the short hallway a few steps to the smaller bedroom. The room was cramped enough without the mess of clothes, picture books, toys, stuffed animals, and the Nintendo game with its wires and controls and various game cartridges spread throughout the pile between the beds. *Damn, this room sucks,* she said to herself as she tiptoed through the mess. It was too small for one child, let alone two.

She looked down at her son, lying on his back wearing only jockey shorts that were too tight. The covers were pushed down around his feet. He was snoring lightly, mouth open, as he usually did while sleeping. Between his parted lips, she could see his irregularly spaced teeth. Beyond the scope of orthodontics she had been told, but it didn't matter, they couldn't afford it, and the Pie Man was never going to be popular for his looks anyway.

In the other bed, a small girl lay on her side with her thumb in her mouth. Natty pulled the sheet up over her, gently extracted her thumb, and brushed away the strands of matted blonde hair covering her face. She sat on the edge of the bed and ran her hand down her daughter's pencil-thin arm. Cat was a tiny girl, small for her age, scrawny some would say, but with boundless energy and a streak of stubbornness that Natty made allowances for because she knew where it came from.

Natty wet her thumb and gently rubbed a dirt mark from her daughter's forehead and thought about her seventh birthday coming up in September. *Seven.* The same age Natty was when she first came to McDowell County, West Virginia with her mother and her sister Annie. 1977, the year her father was killed in the mine up in Idamay in Marion County. The year they came to live with her grandparents at the farm on Angel Mountain because they had nowhere else to go. The year the joy went out of her mother's eyes.

Natty could still feel the icy chill of the rainy day in November when they stood all morning in front of the tall wooden doors surrounded by the miners' wives who had quietly drifted in to stand vigil, like they had for a hundred years. And then the screech of the elevator cables – a sound she would never erase from her mind – bringing her father up from two thousand feet below. And then walking back up the hill in the rain to their empty house, holding Annie's small hand, following their sobbing mother who was never the same after that day.

Sarah DeWitt wasn't from West Virginia. She didn't know coal mining and couldn't understand how a man could go off to work in the morning and be brought up the mine shaft in the afternoon, lifeless, covered with black dust and wrapped in a dirty blanket. She'd listened in the past to some of the old miners' wives telling stories about the day in November nine years earlier when the earth rumbled and the Consol Mine #9 in Farmington, just a few miles up the road, exploded in an uncontrollable underground firestorm, killing seventy-eight men, burning so hot that the mine was just sealed off with no attempt at rescue. Sarah had gone by the monument many times and always assumed that that was how men died in coal mines, in big catastrophes that only happened in the past because mines were safer now, Tom had told her, and technology was better. But her husband died like most men die in the mines, one at a time, miles down a dark tunnel, the lone victim of some relatively minor occurrence in the general scheme of things as mines go. Leaving her alone with her two girls in a strange land.

Natty stroked her daughter's moist forehead and heard the distant whistling sound of the blizzard winds piling the snow against the windows of the farm house. She looked down and saw three-year-old Annie sweating and delirious from the fever. *It all would have been different somehow . . . everything would have been different if Annie had lived. Mama had talked about moving back to Wisconsin where she grew up, to a city called Waukesha, with parks and streets with big houses and green lawns, and modern schools with lots of kids.* She could hear shouts. *Natty! Natty! They were yelling at her because it was her fault, for letting Annie play too long outside in the snow and down in the stream, breaking the thin ice with their shoes getting their feet wet. She knew it was her fault, Annie's pneumonia, and the road down the mountain impassable with the snow, but why were they yelling at her? What could she do now?*

"Natty, get that *fucking* pot! Nat, you out there?" It was Buck yelling from the bedroom. The tea kettle was whistling at its loudest pitch. *Oh Christ! How long had he been yelling to her?*

She bounded out of the children's room toward the kitchenette. "Yeah, I got it Buck. Sorry honey. Go back to sleep," she called out as she yanked the steaming kettle from the burner. She poured the boiling water over the coffee crystals in the metal cup and stood watching the dark steaming liquid swirl and bubble while she thought about her daydream of Annie. It surprised her. She rarely thought about

Annie any more, usually only when they went up to the farm. It had been years since the nightmares stopped. She reminded herself that they needed to go up and visit her mother soon.

Natty added an ice cube to the coffee, and a straw that hinged in the middle, and carried it outside. She stood on the small wooden deck that was their front porch and breathed in the coolness of the morning and the ever-present scent of pine in the air. The sun hadn't yet made it over the Alleghenies far to the east but it was light enough to see that nothing was stirring in Oakes Hollow.

She looked up the hill toward the *big house* where Buck's parents, Big Frank and Rose lived. The house was surrounded on three sides by a wide, covered porch from which Big Frank Oakes in his wooden rocker would look down over his domain where his three sons lived with their *sorry ass wives and too many kids to bother with all their names.* Under the porch one of the old coon hounds lifted his nose to Natty and barked twice before lying back down.

Natty had to giggle looking over at Ransom and Sally's house, at the carnage of overturned orange and yellow plastic riding toys, rusted bicycles, a broken swing set, a collapsed kiddy pool, and probably a hundred other toys that had been scattered about in front of the house all summer. She knew it wouldn't look much different inside the house either. Housekeeping would never be one of Sally's talents.

Natty wondered if Ransom was still working at the cement job he talked about bringing Buck onto. She'd begun to notice his truck parked in front of *The Spur*, the dingy little gin mill in Old Red Bone, most afternoons when she drove through town. She'd seen Buck's truck up there on occasion, but she knew if Buck was drinking in the afternoon, he preferred the pool room out at *Moody's Roadhouse*.

A light went on in the trailer directly across the road. That would be Amos, Natty knew. With his dead left side, it would take him a while to pull his pants and shirt on, being careful to not awaken Yancy, or especially Charlotte, who was a bear when the old man woke her up in the morning and *heaven forbid if he woke the girls!*

Natty felt sorry for Charlotte, because she was fat and dim-witted and mostly disagreeable, but still too young to be trapped in the mountains with two babies and an out-of-work miner for a husband – like so many other women in McDowell County. They had a lot in common. But Natty had never warmed up to her sister-in-law, from the first week Charlotte and Yancy moved into the trailer across from theirs and Charlotte let her know that *"that little mongoloid boy'd be better off in a home somewheres . . ."* They'd had it out then and several more times over the years. But it wasn't just about Pie. Later it was about her grandfather Amos who, after his stroke, Charlotte just considered a total burden, and beyond providing a small sleeping space and a place at the table for supper, largely ignored him. That was never fair, Natty thought. He deserved better.

She heard the old man shuffling slowly through the gravel and then watched him feel his way around the corner of the trailer. He couldn't turn his head and his eyesight was failing anyway so he wouldn't see her until she went down and stood right in front of him sitting on the stool. So she waited until he was ready for her.

Amos Ritter was a hard, wiry little man with short-cropped white hair, and a perpetual stubble of white whiskers. Up very close, you could look into the deep creases in the old man's forehead and the pockmarks of soft skin under his eyes and see the tiny, black, gritty remnants of more than four decades spent underground in the coal fields of West Virginia and Kentucky. His gnarled left hand was minus the last two fingers, taken off so long ago he could barely recall the mine he'd lost them to.

Every morning when Natty went out to run, Amos was sitting on his little stool at the corner of the trailer, waiting to see the sunrise, and waiting for Natty. As she brought his coffee over to him, his silent mouth twitched into an unsteady smile, the best he could do. He slowly raised his right arm from its resting place on the cane standing between his legs for a kind of half wave with his fingers pointed toward her, and blinked his small, cloudy eyes in an effort to tell her that *yes*, he was still alive, and he knew who she was, and that she was someone special to him.

"Morning Amos you old fart." Natty squatted down in front of him and held the mug on his knee until he could get his arthritic fingers through the handle. He'd spill some of the coffee getting the straw to his mouth. Natty stood and ran her fingers through Amos' hair and kissed him on the forehead.

"Sun's going to be hot today Amos, you'll need your hat," she said as she started down the hill to the road to begin her run. She turned around briefly, walking backwards and smiled at the old man. "I'll fix you an egg when I get back." Amos blinked and squinted and twitched his mouth and bent his head forward slightly in a slow nod and watched her until she disappeared down the road and around the corner of the woods.

If Amos could speak, he would tell Natty how much he loved her. He'd thank her for being his friend and making him feel like he mattered and for helping him forget the pain for a little while. And for being such a good mother in a hard situation. He would tell her how special she was and how beautiful she was, and that if he were just a few years younger, he'd beat the living piss out of her worthless husband until he straightened up or even better, just went off for good, and if Buck ever hit her again, he'd take a pickaxe handle to his head so bad you wouldn't know which side his face was on.

But Amos knew he'd never say any of these things to Natty or do anything to Buck. All he could do now was enjoy the sunrise and the sunsets, the breeze on his face, the smell of the woods, and his visits from Natty.

Chapter 2

Charlie Burden flexed his right hand as he drove. It didn't feel broken, just bruised a little, in need of some ice to keep the swelling down. He knew what broken fingers felt like and this wasn't it. He'd caught the kid flush with a couple of good ones he knew, probably a broken nose from all the blood. It was the first punch, off his helmet, that caused the pain.

"*Damn it,*" Charlie said under his breath as he eased the steel blue Lexus out of the rink parking lot onto the narrow road leading down to Route 1. This was turning out to be one piss poor day already and there was a good chance it was going to get worse when he picked up Ellen. He wondered when the last time was that anyone got thrown out of the summer hockey league for fighting.

Charlie shook his head in disgust, but then had to chuckle. As bad as he felt, he could still enjoy, at least a little bit, the irony of the situation – a forty-eight year old professional engineer, a respected member of several communities, a partner at Dietrich Delahunt & Mackey, one of the most prestigious engineering firms in the world, a member of several charitable boards, etc, etc, getting thrown out of an over-35 hockey league for fighting.

He thought about how his friend Duncan McCord would react to the news. *He'll have a lot of fun with this one* – Charlie could see it coming – at an important meeting in the luxurious boardroom on the 30th floor of the CanAmex Energy building in Toronto, Duncan McCord, one of the most powerful men in the utility industry in North America, would rise to his feet to address the meeting. '*Before we get into today's agenda, a round of applause for my friend and yours, Charlie Burden, my old line-mate at Michigan, the only middle-aged guy to ever get tossed from a recreational hockey league for fighting. What a dick-head aye?*' Yes, Duncan will enjoy this. Duncan, who in college was always ready to drop the gloves and start pounding away before the opening face-off.

Charlie turned onto Route 1 and headed west out of Stamford toward New York. The Saturday, noon-time traffic was heavy with the usual crush of mid-summer, shoreline tourists and shoppers and mini-vans full of kids headed for what had to be the world's busiest McDonald's. It would be faster if he went up to Route 95, but now he had plenty of time – too much time – so he'd just stay on Route 1 all the way down to Mamaroneck and then up to the country club to pick up Ellen.

A twinge of pain reminded him of the elbow he took to the face. He could feel the tenderness on his cheek just under the right eye. He pulled the sun visor down and opened the mirror lid and took a quick glance at the first stage of what was going to be a classic black eye.

"*Fuck!*" Charlie said out loud, flipping up the visor. Not only did he get kicked out of the summer league, he may have a problem playing in the big season that starts in October, which he would really miss. But he knew his anger wasn't just about hockey. He felt embarrassed, and irresponsible. *Christ! What was he thinking about? Losing his temper, losing control and beating up a kid at a recreational hockey game.* Even if he did have it coming.

Charlie replayed the incident in his mind, watching Nardi their big center work over the new guy, a skinny copier salesman from Danbury. Nardi was a lawyer in the city who had been a defenseman at Yale ten years earlier and now in this league he thought he was Eric Lindros. He'd been throwing his weight around all game, asking for it, and sooner or later this summer one of the veterans was going to kick Nardi's ass, but there was no justification for Charlie to drop his gloves, no need to beat him bloody like that. *No reason at all, except that Charlie knew, he'd been looking for a fight too. He'd been ready for a fight all summer.* This fight, he knew, was more about him that it was about Nardi. He flipped on WFAN to listen to Mike and the Mad Dog and tried to forget about the morning's hockey game.

The road to Hickory Hills Country Club ran through some of Westchester's most prized real estate, past the lush verdant meadows and white fences of the tony riding academy, through expansive neighborhoods of manicured lawns and large, stately homes. Tall hedges, century-old shade trees and stripped awnings provided cooling darkness and privacy. The homes exuded neatness and order and attention to detail, reflecting the wealth and success of their owners.

Charlie had to admit, even as he was becoming more and more uncomfortable with his own level of wealth and status, he did enjoy driving through the *old money* neighborhoods. They were beautiful, quiet and tranquil roads that had a naturally calming effect that made you slow down and feel, for a moment, that you were a part of this immense success. It was a contagious feeling, easy to catch around the country clubs of Westchester County. Ellen Burden had it, Charlie knew, and along with everything else, it was part of the rapidly growing crevasse in their marriage.

A few miles before the country club, Charlie decided to take a little detour to have another look at the home Ellen had set her sights on. He was still going to be at least an hour early and he didn't want to be hanging around the club for too long now that he was no longer a member. He switched off the radio, pressed both windows down and turned off the road onto Quail Hollow Lane. He wondered how many *Quail Hollow Lanes*, in up-scale, woodsy developments there must be in this country. Probably a few anyway, he guessed, but not too many like *this* Quail Hollow.

Quail Hollow Lane was part of a neighborhood of several interconnecting, aptly-named streets like, *Partridge Glen* and *Pheasant Run* that curved gently through thick woodlands as they made their way generally around the focal point of the community, a small pond that fed several streams that meandered throughout the development. There were no front lawns in this neighborhood; the only grass to be seen was a neatly edged, ten-foot buffer between the streets and the thick tree line. The driveways disappeared into the woods to secluded homes that could only be partially glimpsed through the trees or from higher elevations of the streets.

Charlie had to drive slowly to find the house. He didn't remember the number, but he recognized the white stone driveway that he had commented on the first time he saw the house. "For a million-six, you don't even get a paved driveway." Ellen thought the white stone was part of the ambiance, but then, she didn't have to push the snow blower over it. *Maybe they don't allow snow in this neighborhood*, Charlie mused, as he drove up the driveway. The house had been vacant for three months.

He got out of the Lexus and leaned back against the car and stood looking at the *hacienda* as Ellen had named it. It was a huge, sprawling configuration of white stucco, large wooden beams and glass. A *Spanish contemporary*, it looked to Charlie like a combination of the Alamo and a Malibu beach house. The architect had built the exact same house, its *hermana*, on a hillside in Taos, New Mexico. The house had every conceivable feature required for luxurious living, plus as Charlie recalled, far too many rooms, courtyards, fountains and skylights. It was clearly a home for entertaining and impressing. Several decks extended out into the trees from the second floor, and a partial third floor in the form of a *guard tower* stood at the back corner of the house, which Charlie noted on their first visit, *would be a decided advantage if they were ever attacked by the proctologist next door*.

It was a magnificent house and Ellen would put it to good use, hosting extravagant parties and intimate dinners, mixing and matching her country club set and fellow charity board members with their friends and associates from Charlie's firm, along with the occasional representative from their old neighborhood in Connecticut. She would renovate and decorate and buy artwork and southwestern antiques on trips to New York and Santa Fe and Monterey in an endless quest to put the *Burden House* on the Westchester society list of homes worthy of catty gossip. The house would be her full time job, a job for which she had been in training at least the last eight years, since Charlie's income as a partner at Dietrich Delahunt & Mackey had risen to a level that allowed her to pursue a loftier social position than that of an elementary school French teacher in the Mamaroneck school system.

Charlie disliked the house and what he knew would be their life-style in this house, on this street, in this neighborhood. It was everything he was trying to get away from. As a builder, he found the architecture ostentatious and phony. On a mountain in Taos it probably worked, but in the woods in the Hudson Valley it was pompous and showy. He knew they could afford it but it was wasteful, spending over a million and a half dollars on a home with five bedrooms now that Scott and Jennifer were out of the house and wouldn't be coming home for anything longer than a weekend visit. The house just wasn't *him*, but Charlie knew, at this point in her life, it was totally *Ellen*, and she was going to be pressing hard. It was just one more problem in a collection of uncertainties that seemed to be closing in around him. Maybe someone else would buy the house all of a sudden and the problem would go away. At one-point-six million, and Ellen Burden on the line, Charlie knew there was little chance of that happening.

He drove back out to Old County Road and headed north toward the country club. It was only about ten minutes from Quail Hollow Lane, which forced Charlie to confront his other *Ellen problem,* the one he'd been avoiding for the last several months since he took the call from his friend Dave Marchetti. Charlie hadn't yet been to the club this summer so he hadn't had to think about what his reaction would be if he ran into Rafael Escobar, his wife's lover.

It was the Thursday before Easter when Dave Marchetti called Charlie at his office in Manhattan. Marchetti owned an insurance agency in White Plains and he and his wife were members of Hickory Hills and close friends of both Charlie and Ellen Burden.

After all the usual small talk about golf, the kids and business, Dave tried to get to the point of his call. He stammered about how he considered Charlie a good friend and if their situations were reversed, he'd want to get a call from him, and how it really pained him to have to be the one to call, until Charlie cut him off gently.

"Dave, it's okay, whatever you have to say, just say it, I promise I won't have a coronary and die on the phone."

"Well Charlie, it's about Ellen." Short silence. "Linda, you know she's got a big mouth anyway and, well she gets all lathered up the other night on vodka tonics and tells me that Ellen ... Ellen's got a thing going with that tennis coach at the club, the pro, that Cuban guy, Escobar, the guy with the tan who wears the white sweaters all the time..."

Charlie swallowed hard and cut in, "I know who you mean Dave."

"Yeah, well if it were me Charlie, I'd want to know."

"Anything else Dave?" Charlie needed to get off the phone. He didn't want to get into a discussion with Marchetti or get any advice from him. He just wanted to catch his breath and think.

"She said it started at one of those tennis tournaments they played in last winter, in Scottsdale or Palm Springs, I forget where, and they've been getting together every once in a while since then. Kind of an *arrangement* Linda called it. Charlie, I'm sorry about this."

Charlie thanked his insurance man and hung up the phone. He turned off his computer and desk lamp and walked over and sat in one of the low-rise leather chairs that made up a casual conference area next to the floor- to- ceiling windows. The Park Avenue traffic six floors below was heavy and slow, as it always was late in the afternoon before a holiday. It was only Thursday, but with Good Friday a day that most of Manhattan took off, the weekend was already starting.

It was going to be a bitch getting out of the city and back to Mamaroneck. Charlie thought about staying in one of the apartments the company had on the second floor. He had been using the apartments more often over the past year, staying in the city overnight after an extended workday or to get an early start on some project in the morning. The call to Ellen had become routine, most often just a message left on her voice-mail.

The workday was over. Charlie pulled off his tie and tossed it on the chair across from him. Whether he spent the night, or drove home, with the traffic, he wasn't going anywhere for a while. He needed a drink anyway and a cigar. One of Lucien's big Cubans would be fitting for the occasion he thought.

The executive lounge was off one end of the large boardroom that occupied the middle section of the sixth floor. Charlie left his office and walked down the pushily carpeted hallway towards the center of the building. He was suddenly aware of the quietness of the floor. The secretarial suite was empty and only the recessed hallway lights were on. He looked at his watch. It was just after seven o'clock – passed quitting time on the partners' floor on a holiday eve. Down on the fourth and fifth floors where the staff engineers and architects worked, where Charlie had once toiled when he first joined the firm, putting in the happiest and most productive years of his career, there would still be activity. The computers and laser printers would be humming, the large matrix plotters clacking out their complex images and schematic diagrams of the thousands of components and systems that went into the many diverse projects the company was involved in around the world.

In the lounge he went behind the bar and poured a small glass of Canadian Club over ice and went out through the main conference room. As he made his way around the massive mahogany conference table, he couldn't help but stop, as he always did, and gaze at the display cases that lined the long interior wall of the room. Individually illuminated by small spotlights in the ceiling, the glass cases contained nearly exact replicas of some of the largest projects the firm had constructed. The models, some made of wood, others from plastic but all painstakingly accurate down to the smallest detail, were arranged chronologically starting at one corner of the room with a small and fairly simple looking replica of a coal-fired steam generation plant, built in 1938, that was used for many years to heat portions of the lower Manhattan subway system. It was the first major project of the company's founder Alistair Mackey, and the project that would launch the company that would become Dietrich Delahunt & Mackey. The steam generator looked puny and out of place compared to the models that followed, of long suspension bridges, sky scrapers, airports, a football stadium, and at least a half dozen complex and massive looking power plants.

The largest and most impressive display was also the most recent project – the first of two giant hydroelectric dams the firm was building in China. Shown with tiny trucks and cars, the scale of the project was immense. The two dams together were by far the largest and costliest project the company had ever undertaken. Charlie studied the model of the dam with its cutaway section showing the intricate details of the massive turbines inside the huge wall of concrete and steel that would be holding back a body of water the size of Rhode Island. After twenty-five years in the industry, Charlie was still amazed and awed by the engineering feats that man was capable of. The harnessing of the elements of nature and transforming them into electric power – for heat and light, and to power the technology of the world. Charlie Burden had a deep appreciation and respect for his chosen profession, and for the responsibilities that went with it.

While Charlie sipped his whiskey and gazed enviously at the model of the dam, a germ of an idea began to form in his head. An idea that might salvage his career, and now, maybe even save his marriage.

"Hard to believe we can build something that big isn't it Charlie?" Charlie was startled out of his thoughts by the deep, commanding voice of Lucien Mackey. He turned to find the managing general partner of Dietrich Delahunt & Mackey, coming at him around the conference table. "Working late? Saw the light on in your office. Everything all right?" Lucien extended his huge hand as he always did. He insisted on shaking hands with everyone he came in contact with, holding on for a few seconds while locked in intense eye contact, in a sincere effort to glean some instantaneous insight into the person's state of being. If Lucien detected some troubled or unsettled vibrations he was always ready to offer assistance of any magnitude that he was capable of to relieve the person's burden. He treated everyone he came in contact with the same way, from heads of state, and the CEOs of the world's most powerful companies, to the newest employee in the mailroom.

Charlie was glad to see his boss. Lucien Mackey's presence in a room was always magically uplifting. He was tall, silver-haired and even at sixty-eight, still had the physique of a linebacker.

"Lucien, hello. Yes I'm fine. How was China?"

"Got back this morning. Oh Charlie, you've got to see it, the model doesn't do it justice. It's just spectacular, and what beautiful people. Charlie do you realize that the first phase of this project alone is going to bring low-cost, *dependable* electricity to nearly a *hundred million* people, to power their homes and cities and factories, and provide affordable heating and cooking so they can finally stop choking themselves and their children on coal soot, and nitrous oxide and sulfuric acid . . . well, you know all about it as well as anyone I guess." He put a massive hand on Charlie's shoulder.

"Come on Charlie, let's go have a cigar. Not too many guys around here to have a smoke with any more. All those kids down stairs want to do is suck on Tic Tacs and drink their bottled water."

"As a matter of fact, I was just on my way down to your office to steal one of those expensive Cubans," said Charlie.

They left the boardroom and strode together down the hall toward Lucien's office at the southwest corner of the building. Charlie had to quicken his step to keep up with Lucien's stride.

"We'll have a nice cigar together Charlie and you can tell me what's been eating at you lately and why you're not on your way home to be with your lovely family for the Easter weekend."

Charlie wondered if Lucien didn't realize that Scott and Jennifer weren't kids any more, that they were out of the house now. It was like Lucien lately to misplace details like that. But *yes,* he definitely had things on his mind lately – for the last few years actually – things that were weighing him down, that had changed him, and changed his relationship with his wife, and now it was all coming to a boil.

Where do you start? he wondered. In his mind, it was all a tangled web of questions about family, career and wealth. *Why does life without children in the house feel so pointless? Why does my job and career get more and more boring as I get wealthier and more successful?* And, what had become a constant theme in Charlie's introspections . . . *Why, as I and my circle of friends and associates get wealthier and wealthier, do so many people grow poorer and poorer?*

Charlie was genuinely concerned about the continued polarization of the classes in America and where it would lead to. Every day he could see the blatantly unfair distribution of wealth that society and corporate institutions and governments all seemed to have put their stamp of approval on at least through the next generation. The rich were getting richer much quicker than at any other time in history, and the poor were still poor and their numbers growing, with little relief in sight. Life had been extra good to Charlie, but it didn't seem fair. *Who was losing because he was winning?* What family was going hungry and falling into despair and drugs to escape their poverty because his stock portfolio had nearly doubled in value in a ridiculous three years? He wasn't an economist but intuitively he knew there was a connection. And he knew that he had long been part of the *winning team,* the side that had the corporations and the politicians and lawmakers and regulators, and the lobbyists and the lawyers, bankers, and venture capitalists. The team that made the rules. The other side had the *land of opportunity, free-market capitalism,* and *public education,* but the fix had been in so long that none of it mattered any more.

Charlie didn't want to get into a philosophical discussion with Lucien about global economics or about his job and career. Lucien didn't have the answers to problems with no solutions. He decided to tell his boss, his good friend, about Ellen. He needed to talk to someone about it and of all his problems it was the clearest and now obviously, the most important, and Lucien, it was well known within the firm, had some experience with marital discord, to say the least.

When Lucien Mackey was fifty-one, after his two children had left home for college and career, he informed his wife of thirty years, that he was a homosexual, and moved out of their palatial home in Bergen County and into the apartment in Manhattan where he still resided. For many years now, Lucien's life-companion was a slender, light-skinned Jamaican named Carlos Marche owner of the extremely successful women's salon in the elegant first-floor retail shops of the Dietrich Delahunt & Mackey building. *Carlos Marche, New York and Paris* was hair stylist to the rich, famous and the beautiful.

In the den of Lucien's office suite they relaxed on over-sized leather chairs and filled the air with billowing clouds of cigar smoke. Charlie enjoyed cigars, ever since he quit cigarettes when he turned forty. Only his rule of *never buying* a cigar prevented him from being a full-time smoker. Lucien's humidor was always stocked with the best – illegal imports supplied by a friend at the UN.

They chatted for a while about the merits of traveling first-class on international flights, while Charlie debated in his mind how much he should tell Mackey. No need to worry about confidentiality. With Linda Marchetti on the case, most of Westchester County already knew more about the affair than Charlie did.

Ellen's fucking her tennis pro. A Cuban. Young stud with a great tan and white teeth, white outfits, gold chains and a Boxster convertible. No, that wasn't fair to Ellen. That's not how it would have been with Ellen. Charlie searched for the right words to tell Lucien about the phone call from Marchetti, about the revelation that he'd long suspected but without confirmation.

"Ellen has ... entered into a relationship with ... a guy she plays tennis with, the pro at her club." He told Lucien about the call and that he had no doubt that it was true, and that their relationship had changed, had been strained for some time and that he didn't really blame her. She was still a fabulous looking woman at fifty, (which Lucien agreed with whole-heartedly), and actually in her prime physically, intellectually, and socially. She had energy and drive and ambition, as she always had, all singularly focused now on her pursuit of social position within the Westchester country club set.

Charlie tried to tell Lucien how it had become harder and harder to share her interests and ambitions. The last few years, with the kids gone, had been so different from the first twenty years of their marriage. They had been gradually just growing apart, not trying to, but slowly almost imperceptibly, irrevocably, developing new interests and priorities and losing old ones, and soon they were on different paths leading away from each other. They were still husband and wife, a couple at parties, caring parents of successful children, good neighbors, happy, well off. They talked, though not as often as they used to. They discussed things, though not as intimately or intensely as before. They still had sex, occasionally, but more physical than emotional now. They never fought, about anything. But life just seemed to be happening to them separately, and now more of it was happening to Ellen. Charlie envied her. She was so certain of what she wanted, so at ease with how to enjoy life.

Lucien knew there was more to the story than he was hearing, more than Charlie was willing or able to tell. He advised Charlie not to confront his wife, to let Ellen work out what she had to and to give her some time and space and not to go to war over what probably would turn out to be a brief episode in the long history of their marriage. Lucien always made good sense, but it was the course of action Charlie had already decided upon, he knew, the moment he put down the phone after Marchetti's call.

Charlie knew that the present state of their relationship was more about him, than it was about any mid-life mutation or latent sexual fantasies of his wife. He had changed over the last few years, gradually, subtly, but he was cogently aware of it. The more successful he was, the greater their income – and it had risen precipitously since being made a partner in the firm – the less certain he was about what he wanted in life. His job since becoming a partner had changed too. Working on the new-business team as the CanAmex account supervisor was much more about money and influence and connections than it was about building things and it was affecting him. He didn't become an engineer to sit in meetings with lawyers and accountants.

He knew he missed his children terribly. His children when they were young, not the grown up, successful, self-assured, confident young adults he now spoke with on the phone and saw on holidays and the occasional ski weekends at the house in Vermont. He missed everything about the early years of parenting, especially the little five-room ranch, their first house, in Windsor, Connecticut, with the huge backyard and the flowering crab trees and the little hill that they would all roll down in the kids' over-loaded wagon, crashing in the grass at the bottom. He missed the stories – the *Roald Dahl years* – and the vacations, and the wide-eyed wonderment of so many Christmases and birthdays, and the celebration of so many excellent report cards.

His most vivid memories were of the kids' sports and the many teams Scott and Jennifer had played on. So many T-ball, softball, baseball and soccer games, he and Ellen had dragged their folding chairs to, and basketball games at the rec center in the winter, rooting politely for all the kids, pretending along with the other adults that they didn't really care about the outcome of the game.

Ellen soldiered through these years with admittedly less enthusiasm for the sports than Charlie, preferring to concentrate on the social opportunities the games offered to talk with and about the other mothers in town, always measuring their family's status, success and growth against their peers. It was an activity that Charlie had no interest in but Ellen excelled at. Later, when they moved to Mamaroneck, as Scott was beginning high school and Jennifer the sixth grade, Ellen had to recalibrate her *social radar* and learn a whole new system of values by which to measure their status. Mamaroneck and Westchester County were the big leagues of social climbing and it would take Ellen a few years to master the craft. And now she was ready.

The small sign for Hickory Hills Country Club came up suddenly, jolting Charlie out of his recollections. He turned the Lexus onto the long, winding entry road, took a deep breath and resolved to be on his best behavior. He was in a foul mood over the events at the hockey rink, but he would control himself if he ran into Rafael Escobar. This was Ellen's world now, it was *her* club, her friends, and Charlie would respect that.

For three months, Charlie had done nothing about Dave Marchetti's call. And he wouldn't do anything about it today. It was an easy decision because there was nothing to do about it. It hurt that she had been intimate with another man and that after all their years together she had a secret that she kept from him. And it hurt that he had to learn about it from someone else. But he had to accept that whatever chasm had developed in their marriage was more his fault than Ellen's. He was the one who was confused, so how could he condemn Ellen for being decisive, for knowing who she was and what she wanted out of life? Ellen was the rock. She hadn't changed in character, values, or ambitions since the day they met. Few women had Ellen's style, or her talent for equally living the roles of wife, mother, and independent woman, to the fullest, without diminishing any one. It was one of the things Charlie loved most about his wife.

Chapter 3

Natty used the downhill run to South County Road as her warm-up stretch, jogging easily until she reached the bottom of the hill and turned east toward Old Red Bone. Then she picked up the pace. Her first two miles were always her fastest, then slower for the long steep climb up to Main Street, and a comfortable pace for the trail around the long tail of the mountain that would bring her back down to the high end of Oakes Hollow. Today, she was also planning to take a detour which would add about a mile to her regular five-mile circuit, so she wanted to make good time on the flat part of her run.

Natty Oakes loved to run and she loved to run fast and hard. When she got her wind and her rhythm just right, she felt like she could run forever. After a while, she'd enter a runner's trance, conscious of every muscle and joint, feeling the inside of her rib-cage as her lungs expanded and contracted, the blood and the oxygen coursing through her body. The trance would clear her mind and allow her to enter a fantasy world of daydreams that she'd been working on since childhood, dreams that took her far away from West Virginia.

Today, Natty wasn't letting the trance take over. She didn't want to daydream, and she didn't want to miss the turn-off on the north side of the road about half way to Red Bone. She was surprised to see a pick-up truck coming toward her far up the road. It was unusual to find anyone on the road this early. The truck slowed down and made a right hand turn onto the road Natty was looking for.

She glanced needlessly over her left shoulder before crossing to the other side of South County Road and making a left turn down the road that the pick-up had taken. Natty ran down the middle of the narrow road, which, like most of the roads in McDowell County, was cracked and rutted for several feet along each side from years of use by over-loaded coal trucks. There was no sign of the pick-up but it could only be going to one place, which gave Natty an uneasy feeling. This was the road to the new electric generating plant being built by CanAmex Energy Ltd., an international energy conglomerate, based in Toronto. It was the biggest and most expensive construction project in the history of McDowell County.

Two years earlier, Natty and Buck with the kids and the rest of the Oakes clan, along with several hundred other people from Red Bone and surrounding towns, came down this road on a Saturday in late June, for a public picnic and a rare visit by the Governor of the State of West Virginia. A joint announcement was to be made with officials of the CanAmex Energy Company, regarding a project that would have a *monumental impact on the economy and the future of McDowell County.* It was a celebration and a show that the people of Red Bone would long remember. A day that Natty Oakes would never forget.

The party took place at the site of the proposed new plant, a two hundred acre plateau hidden from view by a ring of heavily wooded hills about a half-mile off South County Road. The site had been a surface-mine, leveled down to the bedrock in the early seventies, and in accordance with the federal and state surface mining laws, returned to its *approximate original contour*, which now made it more or less an open field with about a foot-deep layer of rolling, sandy soil over irregular levels of shale rock that poked through the surface in several places. In a few spots, the last vestiges of the coal seam were still in evidence where the loose topsoil had blown away.

The picnic was to start at noontime, but it was obvious that an army of people had been working since early that morning to get the site ready. Two large trailer trucks were parked off to the side of the field behind a stack of large cargo boxes with the name and address of a Charleston catering company stenciled on the sides. A huge three-masted circus tent had been set up to shelter several long buffet tables of food of endless variety. The sides of the tent had been rolled up, allowing easy access from the dozens of portable metal picnic tables that had been set up in the field.

Behind the tent was a battery of long, aluminum-framed charcoal stoves, manned by several dozen white-clad cooks wearing traditional chef's hats and white gloves. Roasting half-chickens and pork chops, along with hamburgs, hot dogs and sausages, covered the smoking grills. At each end of the tent was a complete bar and a large cooler filled with ice and bottles of several different types of Molson beer. It was a mystery why only Molson beer was on hand, but it was ice cold and there was plenty of it so no one complained. Uniformed bartenders mixed and poured while some obviously imported waitresses circulated to take drink orders. It only took a little while for the Oakes brothers and the rest of the crowd to get comfortable with the idea that the drinks actually were free.

The show really got started when a man who said he worked for a public relations firm in Charleston, got up on a stage set up at one end of the field and started talking over a huge loudspeaker system. He welcomed everyone and made a little speech about what a great day it was for McDowell County, and about how some very important people were going to be dropping in very shortly. He was still talking when he was drowned out by a deafening roar that got louder and louder as it seemed to be coming straight toward them through the woods. The ungodly noise sent the adults out of the tent and the children jumping around in circles, wide-eyed with both fright and glee. The PR man was yelling something over the microphone and pointing up in the air when suddenly the helicopters appeared, roaring in just over the treetops. One after the other, four in all, they flew over the tent and banked into a sharp left turn, forming up into a hovering position before they came in to land, one by one, in a roped-off area to the side of the stage.

The crowd burst into applause from the sheer excitement of the spectacle. The helicopters were magnificent looking, low-profile, twelve-passenger, jet-powered Bell 430's, finished entirely in high-gloss black with dark tinted windows. Silver lightning bolts adorned the lower front quarters of the cabin, and across both sides, below the passenger windows, in bright silver lettering was the distinctive logo of "CanAmex Energy".

Natty sat at a picnic table eating lunch with Sally, Charlotte, and Buck's mother Rose. Cat had scrambled up on her lap at the first sound of the helicopters, holding a bare, ketchup-covered hotdog in one hand and a can of orange soda in the other. Pie was running around with Sally's boys and the other kids, trying to get close to the cordoned-off helicopters and making frequent raids on the food tables. This would be a day the children would talk about for years to come – *the day the helicopters came.*

Buck and his brothers and a half dozen of their buddies had found a comfortable spot in the shade inside the tent. They had moved one of the picnic tables inside and had settled in for an enjoyable afternoon courtesy of the CanAmex Energy Company. A dozen or so other men eventually joined the group that kept one of the young waitresses on a continual circle between their table and the bar.

Natty sat nursing a Molson Light, engrossed by the show unfolding before her. She had never seen the Governor of the state and she was intrigued over what it could be that would make all these important people come to Red Bone. She was listening to the man on stage and watching the people getting out of the helicopters, but she couldn't help taking a quick glance every few minutes over at Buck in the tent. He always enjoyed himself so much when he was drinking with his friends. It wasn't about being drunk, he could be plenty miserable when he was drunk. It was about the old times, old pals and old adventures that men loved to talk about with a beer bottle in one hand. He grinned and laughed and became animated, gesturing with his hands and moving about lightly on his feet, in and out, but always at the center of the group, always the center of attention, in control. Just like he was as a child when Natty first saw him, when he was in sixth grade and she was in fourth, many years before he even knew she existed. She wished he would bring some of that good nature into their home occasionally. She wished their children could experience some of it for a while.

The helicopters were unloading their passengers who instinctively hunched down and lowered their heads as they walked toward the stage, even though they were in no danger from the spinning rotors of the big helicopters. She picked out the governor right away from his distinctive silver hair, and thought she recognized a few other politicians and some county officials who must have arrived before the helicopters. They were all splendidly dressed in expensive suits, starched shirts with stylish ties, and shiny shoes. They all walked very deliberately, with a purpose, and shook hands with each other a lot, and they always seemed to be smiling.

One of the helicopters unloaded a television crew from a station in Charleston, along with a photographer and several newspaper reporters who headed straight for the tent. This was turning into a wonderful show and Natty couldn't take her eyes away from the scene. On her lap, Cat losing energy quickly in the hot sun, had rubbed her ketchup-covered face against her mother's chest and tapped her hotdog rhythmically on Natty's white tank top.

The passengers of the third helicopter were introduced as executives of CanAmex Energy. There were five men and a very attractive, professionally-dressed woman who carried a leather note book and was talking on a cell-phone. Like the others, they were all expensively dressed and attractive men. Unlike the politicians, these men didn't find it necessary to smile continually and shake hands with everyone they saw.

One of the CanAmex men was obviously more important than the others. He looked to be in his mid-forties and was short and trim with jet-black hair combed straight back from a hairline that had receded far up his forehead. His luxurious charcoal suit was perfectly cut to his athletic build. He had deep-set, penetrating dark eyes that were very close together under thick, black sinister looking eyebrows. The Governor made his way through the throng of people to greet him and shake his hand, probably not for the first time that day, and lead him to the stage. The woman with the notebook followed behind at a short distance.

The man at the microphone quickly welcomed the passengers from the last helicopter, introducing them only as representatives of an engineering company from New York, and a law firm from Charleston. Natty forgot the names of the companies as soon as she heard them but she watched avidly as another group of well-groomed, expensively dressed men joined the others milling around near the stage, setting off another round of hand-shaking and smiles.

The Governor was at the microphone now, thanking lots of people, getting ready to make the big announcement as Sally returned from the bar with a half a dozen bottles of ice cold Molson beers. Sally was attracting a lot of attention in her skin-tight halter-top and short shorts. The tall red head wiggling her way through the crowd with an arm-full of beer didn't go unnoticed by a few of the men near the stage.

The Governor made the announcement about a huge, new *billion-dollar* coal-fired power plant to be built on the site and talked about all the new jobs that would be available and about how hard he and his economic development team and all the local politicians had worked to bring this project to McDowell County. He received a polite but not overly enthusiastic applause from a crowd that had been let down before by smiling politicians and knew well, the history of abuse the counties of southern West Virginia had suffered for so many years at the hands of outside companies that had come for the coal.

The short man in the dark suit was introduced as Duncan McCord, president and CEO of CanAmex Energy. He thanked many of the same people the Governor had, and then talked about how big the power plant was going to be and how important it was to his company. The plant was to be the third largest coal-fueled generator in North America. He had a clear, strong voice and spoke with the same lilting accent that Natty and Sally had mimicked for months after seeing the movie "Fargo" at the Cineplex in Bluefield.

As he spoke, Natty watched the other men near the stage, the ones from Toronto and New York and Charleston, so expensively dressed, so successful and smart. She wondered if they even knew where they were. They may as well have been astronauts that just got off the space shuttle on a foreign moon, they were so different. She looked back at McCord and wondered what his wife looked like and what she was doing today, and what a magnificent house they must have, and guessed that their children would be going to any college they wanted to, and she'd bet they didn't have to worry about how *they* were going to pay for their health insurance.

After McCord, there were a couple of other politicians that nobody paid too much attention to. The Governor was being interviewed by a blonde TV woman off to the side of the stage and a photographer was taking pictures of different groupings of CanAmex people and politicians. Some of the outsiders were venturing through the crowd headed for the tent for a drink or something to eat. People were moving around now, socializing and discussing the project. The open bar was having the desired effect, putting a good part of the crowd in an optimistic frame of mind regarding the project.

The last speaker was Kevin Mulrooney, an executive of Ackerly Coal of Pittsburgh, the largest mining company in West Virginia with dozens of surface mines and a few deep mines in operation, mostly in Logan, Mingo and Wyoming Counties.

Mulrooney was a huge man, well over three hundred pounds, with a red face and a large head that sat directly on his massive shoulders without the assistance of a neck. He had a booming voice with an Irish accent that commanded attention as he spoke quickly and enthusiastically. He enthused about the quality and purity of McDowell County's environmentally friendly low-sulfur coal, and how national *utility deregulation* was finally handing McDowell County the *long end of the stick* after nearly a hundred years of getting the short end of the coal mining stick. Some of the old miners in the crowd agreed, on that point, *Mulrooney should know, as he was one of the ones rammin' the short end of that stick up our butts for so many years!*

Finally the Ackerly man got to the point he was there to make, and he got the attention of the audience when he announced that Ackerly Coal had just signed a contract with CanAmex Energy to supply the coal for the new power plant. The amount of coal the new plant would require when it was fully operational ... he paused to heighten the effect of the number . . . a minimum of *eight thousand tons* a day. He talked for a little while more about the *hundreds* of new mining jobs and *millions* of dollars to the local economy that the plant would be producing over the next decade. Mulrooney received about as generous an applause as a mining company executive was going to get in McDowell County, no matter how good his news was.

To most of the people in the crowd, the amount of coal to be consumed by the power plant was a meaningless number. But to the miners on hand, some employed, more unemployed, mostly retired, *eight thousand tons a day* was a very significant number. Nearly three million tons a year of *new output* would require a big operation or the rechanneling of a great deal of Ackerly's current output from surface mines in Logan and Mingo Counties. It made for good discussion among the many small groups around the field and in the tent.

Cat ran off to find the other kids and Natty opened another Molson and started to think about taking a pee. She looked around for Pie and saw him up on the stage with his two short arms upraised, jumping up and down, waving to her with a big *happy face* on. She stood up and was waving back when she noticed the small man in the dark suit walking lazily down the pathway between the tent and the picnic tables. He was walking with another man whom she hadn't seen before. The second man was tall, and like the CanAmex man, had a lean, athletic build. He had a rugged, handsome face, with a thin, crooked nose that made him look like he might be a boxer. Dark sunglasses covered his eyes. He was wearing a tan, summer suit with pleated pants, a brilliant white shirt and a maroon tie.

Both men were holding a Molson in one hand while they talked casually, strolling down the path in the direction of Natty's table. She sat down quickly, suddenly feeling a pang of self-consciousness, inadequacy. She didn't know why. It was stupid she told herself. *They were total strangers, in her town. It must be the beer.*

She didn't want to stare at them but she couldn't keep herself from watching them out of the corner of her eye. They were having a friendly talk, she could tell, and they seemed more like friends than business acquaintances. The tall man didn't defer in any way to the status of McCord like most of the others did. They appeared as equals. The woman with the notebook who was following a few yards behind, cell phone to her ear, came up quickly to over-take her boss. She held out the phone to McCord. Almost imperceptibly, with a quick shake of his head, he declined the call and the woman fell back immediately, handling the call herself.

McCord would stop to shake hands and say a few words with the local people who came up to him but he didn't seem to mind. He smiled and was cordial and relaxed, calm and self-confidant. At one table of older men, McCord and his friend stopped for a little chat, smiling, then laughing over somebody's quip, and both came away smoking fat brown cigars they'd begged like a couple of street people.

Sally had just turned her head and noticed the two men getting closer. She inspected the taller man unabashedly, then turned back to Natty with her eyeballs rolling. "Get a load of this one coming, he is *beautiful!*" She turned for another quick look as Natty pretended not to know whom she was talking about. "Wouldn't I like to wrap my legs around that one just about any night of the week." Sally said out of the corner of her mouth as the men got closer.

Natty looked back at the stage to see if she could engage Pie in another wave so she could avoid any eye contact with the two men who were almost beside the table. She wished she hadn't just pinned her hair up hastily. She must look like she had a pile of straw sitting on top of her head. Natty was moving her head back and forth with squinting eyes looking for her son in the crowd when she felt the men stop at the end of the table. Sally was saying something about having a good time in West Virginia, and then the CEO of CanAmex Energy was standing directly in front of Natty on the other side of the picnic table. The man who could make a decision to spend a *billion dollars,* was saying something to her. She was forced to turn her eyes to him, and saw a look of concern on his face.

"Are you all right there miss?" he was saying.

Natty wondered how he could tell. "Well, I'm a *little* buzzed I guess. I don't usually drink in the – " he cut her off with a smile. "No, no, I mean that," he said gesturing toward her chest. Natty looked down at the front of her shirt and gasped at the sight of the bright red stain left by Catherine's ketchup-covered face. Red blotches on her skin above the dip of her shirt-line looked just like dried blood.

"Aw *fuck!*" she cried without thinking, reaching for a napkin. She looked up quickly. "Oh I'm sorry, I shouldn't have said that. Sorry. It's just ketchup from my daughter's hotdog."

McCord smiled. "Good. I'm glad you're not bleeding to death."

"Yeah, me too." Natty thought about pouring some beer on the stain but it was obvious that there was nothing to be done. She'd already made an ass of herself so she just shrugged and smiled at McCord. "Well, thank you, thanks for being concerned, but I'm okay . . . still a little *drunk*, but – "

"I'll get you something to wear," McCord said as he turned to find the woman with the notebook. At his gesture, she was instantly at his side. She listened intently as McCord gave her instructions and then left at a quick pace toward the helicopters.

He turned back to Natty. "My assistant will get you something to put on."

"Naw, there's no need for that, really," Natty protested. "I look like this all the time."

"It's nothing, really, it's my pleasure. I'm Duncan McCord," he said, holding out his hand.

"Natty Oakes." She said, quickly wiping her palm on the thigh of her blue jeans before reaching out to take his hand. "Thank you," she added, "thank you for coming to West Virginia and building your . . . *thing,* in Red Bone."

"You're welcome Mrs. Oakes." He let go of her hand and smiled. "You know Natty, you have *very* beautiful eyes." Before she could say anything, he added, "it was a great pleasure to meet you." Then he turned and walked off to rejoin his friend who had moved a little farther down the path and was talking with one of the politicians.

Natty just sat still, then smiled weakly at Sally who hadn't missed any of what had gone on with the CanAmex man. Normally, Sally would have a sarcastic comment for a situation like this, but this time, she let it pass and just looked away, having seen the drop of moisture in the corner of Natty's eye.

The woman with the notebook came back carrying a package wrapped in plastic. "I hope this will do," she said as she handed it to Natty. Up close, she was very attractive, wearing a lot of make-up perfectly applied. She wore a very subtle perfume that, even on a hot summer day, smelled wonderful to Natty and reminded her of the mall department store at Christmas time.

Sally watched the woman walk away as Natty pulled open the plastic covering the soft package. "I wouldn't mind wrapping my legs around that little muffin sometime either," Sally said with a laugh, taking another swig of Molson Light.

"God, you're a pig Sally." Natty had more to say but was distracted by the contents of the package, as she unfolded a beautiful and obviously very expensive jacket that was exactly like the jackets the pilots of the CanAmex helicopters were wearing. It had a jet black nylon shell with silver rings at the ends of the sleeves and at the waist, and had a soft tan lining. On the left breast embossed in silver was the CanAmex logo, with the words "CanAmex Energy" around a circle, crossed by a lightning bolt, and under it, "Toronto, Canada."

"Holy shit," she said softly. "I was thinking maybe a T-shirt. Wait 'til Pie sees this." She was startled by the high-pitched sound of the jet helicopters firing up their turbines, the big rotors beginning to spin.

A few minutes later, the four helicopters were airborne, quickly becoming distant specks, as they gained altitude to rise over the mountains before they roared off toward Charleston. Natty watched the helicopters until they disappeared in the deep blue sky to the north, carrying all those rich, beautiful people, the smiling politicians and the businessmen in their handsome suits with the pleated trousers, the TV crew and the fine-smelling lady with the note book and cell phone.

She thought about Duncan McCord and his handsome friend who seemed so nice and so natural and much more genuine than the politicians. She wondered if it was true, what everyone said about big utilities and coal companies always screwing the common folk like you find in McDowell County. Probably it was true. They were just so good at it. The big company men were never what they seemed to be, never what showed on the surface. McCord and his friend were probably headed straight for the airport and then home to be with their families and their beautiful wives in their expensive homes and wouldn't even remember their afternoon in Red Bone, West Virginia.

A noise from the tent reminded her about Buck. One of the men had fallen off the edge of a picnic table and was having trouble getting up – the rest of the group laughing hysterically in the typical drunken over-reaction to any alcohol induced mishap. The group was loud and rambunctious and getting more physical by the moment. Natty could pick out the harsh rasp of Buck's liquor-soaked, gravel-throated voice. She hated it when he got this bad; he was unpredictable and uncontrollable. Better to leave him be and take the kids home, batten down the hatches and wait for the coming storm. This was going to be a bad one. She'd seen the warning signs before.

Near the end of the road, Natty could see the framework of steel girders rising beneath a huge crane that soared skyward from a monstrous green tractor. Around the CanAmex site was a newly paved road that was said to be an after-hours racetrack for the teenagers.

Up ahead of her she could see where the paved road branched off, running through the large sliding gate that was the main entrance onto the grounds. Just inside the fence beyond the gate was a long, low building with a dozen windows. This was the main administration building, the object of Natty's search.

As she got closer, her fears were confirmed. "Damn," she said under her breath as she ran past the main gate. In front of the building, several dozen cars and pick-ups were parked helter-skelter in the unmarked parking area, and at least forty, maybe fifty men were lingering outside the building. *The ad in the paper for construction workers said apply in person at nine AM. Hell, by nine o'clock there'll be 200 men lined up. Buck won't even get out of his truck when he sees that mob.*

Natty darted into the woods down a narrow path she knew that led to an old logging road that went back out to South County Road about a quarter of a mile east of where she'd left it.

Still, Buck had a good shot at getting one of the real jobs, working at the plant, because he'd gotten in tight, bending elbows down at the Roadhouse, with that guy Hugo Paxton, the General Manager of the construction company. That would be ironic, Buck getting a break because he spent so much time in a saloon. Well Lord knows, Buck is due for a break, even if he ain't looking too hard for one any more.

Natty flew out of the woods and hit South County Road in the high gear she liked to use for the flat mile and a half stretch until you reached the up-hill climb into Old Red Bone. Today she'd run this section at a little faster pace than usual, not quite a sprint, but for this distance, a pace that brought out a good sweat and made her thin legs sting and her lungs start to burn.

Halfway to Old Red Bone, Natty saw another runner far up the road coming toward her at a good clip. She knew instantly who it was from the dark hair and the graceful, erect running style. She had seen Emma Lowe run before, many times. Natty slowed her pace in preparation to stop. She smiled to herself and wondered how many other thirteen-year-old girls were out doing roadwork at six-thirty in the morning in the middle of the summer.

They walked toward each other without speaking, both catching their breath, and then hugged in the middle of the road.

"Damn Emma, you've grown about three inches already this summer. Look at you, you're taller than I am now." Natty stood close with an arm still around the girl's waist and a hand on top of her head. The girl was at least an inch taller.

The girl just smiled self-consciously, her thin arms crossed in front of her chest, while her feet fidgeted on the road. "I guess I growed some, but I needed to, mamma says." Emma Lowe was painfully shy and spoke in a barely audible whisper, even to Natty, who, outside of her family, was the one adult in the world that she was the most comfortable with.

The girl had thick, coarse black hair tied in a long ponytail and heavy eyebrows that would someday join in the middle. Her eyes were small and dark, set closely together. A wide nose and thick lips were the most visible gifts from her black grandmother, Ada Lowe, who raised Emma's father, Gus, without benefit of a husband. Gus Lowe's father was a Hungarian miner, one of thousands of immigrants that flooded the West Virginia coal fields in the early 1940's to supply coal to fuel the war effort of the great steel mills of the Ohio River Valley. Just prior to Gus's birth, his father whose name Ada could scarcely pronounce, determined that marrying a fifteen-year-old, pregnant black girl, was not in anyone's best interest and abruptly departed for parts unknown.

When he was eighteen, Gus joined the Navy and spent twenty years as a machinist's mate before returning to West Virginia and opening an auto repair shop and gas station, still the only one in Old Red Bone. At the age of forty, he married a local woman of Italian descent in her late thirties, who had resigned herself to life as a spinster until she met Gus. The fruit of their marriage was Emma, their only child and the center of their universe.

"How's mama and papa and Ada doing?" Natty inquired. It had been at least a month since she had seen Emma.

"They're all fine, 'cept papa's shop ain't doing too good he says, 'cause a that new gas station out at the crossroads. But mama's okay and mawmaw Ada's real good."

"Yeah? And how about you? What are you doing out here so early in the morning pounding down this road? Getting in shape already? Season don't start 'til September you know."

"Naw, I ain't worried about that. I just like to run once in a while, couple of times a week, sometimes more. Makes me feel good. It's like, you know, the only thing I'm good at." Emma spoke so softly that she always sounded sad.

Natty understood how she felt. "Well we both know it's not the only thing your good at, but I know what you mean, it does feel good." She gave Emma a long hug, and told her the first practice would be sometime during the last week in August, she'd send out a schedule. She watched as the girl loped off down the road, her strong legs gobbling up the pavement in long, graceful strides with so little effort.

Natty saw so much of herself in Emma – the insecurity and shyness and self-consciousness of adolescence, the need to withdraw into physical exertion to hide for a while. For a moment Natty could feel her small legs aching and hear the exhausted panting from her lungs as she ran up Angel Mountain one more time, the song from Annie's music box in her head, the taste of salty tears on her lips.

But Emma, Natty knew, was much different from herself. Because Emma had a gift, an immense talent that would transport her out of McDowell County one day and make up for any shortcomings she may have in the way of looks or intelligence or personality. Unlike Natty, Emma would never be considered pretty nor anything more than an average student, but at thirteen, Emma Lowe was without argument, the finest soccer player for her age that anyone in southern West Virginia had ever seen, boys included. Not just an excellent player, the best on the field at any one time, but an extraordinary player with near magical ability at every facet of the game.

Natty let out a perceptible giggle when she thought about how good Emma would be this year. She was noticeably taller and looked stronger, and Natty knew that Emma continued to practice her soccer skills as she had been doing for many years. Natty had stopped her car one day in April the previous year, going up Coal Road, around the north side of Red Bone Mountain, and watched Emma kicking soccer balls in an old quarried-out gash that ran fifty yards or so into the side of the mountain. The small quarry provided a natural amphitheater with high walls and a floor that sloped gradually back toward the road where Emma, with a half dozen, beaten up old soccer balls, would kick ball after ball towards a six-foot high iron pipe that rose vertically out of the rock about thirty yards away. The old rusted pipe must have been used somehow in quarrying operations years ago. The balls would eventually roll back down the gentle incline and back toward the kicker. Emma would kick, she said, until she hit the pipe ten times left-footed and ten times with her right foot, but Natty suspected the girl would stay out practicing much longer than that on some days. From thirty yards out Emma could easily drive the ball on a line past the post with both feet. The shortness of the pipe meant she had to keep her shots low and forced her to practice putting a hooking topspin to the ball, which she applied with vicious perfection. It was a rare week in which Emma didn't visit her kicking range three or four times.

Emma first played organized soccer when she was seven years old, on the first team coached by Natty Oakes, who at that time knew as much about soccer as most of the first and second graders on the team. Natty had brought Pie down to Center Field in old Red Bone on the first Saturday morning in September for soccer tryouts. Natty wanted Pie to have a sport and be able to play on a team with other kids, and soccer seemed like the best possibility. Baseball and basketball required too much coordination, she thought at his point, and football was advised against. Soccer was good exercise and it also didn't require buying a lot of equipment. Plus, it seemed to her that at this level, it didn't really matter how bad a player was, that Pie's physical shortcomings wouldn't prevent him from at least trying the game and having fun.

That first day there were twelve first and second graders on the field, plenty for a team but no coach, which Natty learned, was not an uncommon occurrence in kids' soccer. None of the other parents could or would take the job, and Natty got the distinct feeling that if she didn't volunteer to be the coach, the team just wouldn't happen.

So Natty became a soccer coach. She continued as coach of Pie's team every year, because it was her team, and she never really came up with a good reason to give it up. This would be her seventh and final season, along with the kids who would turn fourteen after the beginning of the season like Emma and most of the other kids on the team. Next year they would have to play for the high school team.

Natty came into old Red Bone and slowed down in anticipation of the steep, uphill climb to Main Street. She looked over at the soccer field off to her left, which was located in the flat valley at the bottom of the hill. What grass there was on the field was at least a foot high, surrounding large patches of crabgrass, weeds, dandelions and bare patches of earth where not even the weeds wanted to grow. It was a mess, as always. The worst field in the league by far. Before the season started, Natty and Pie would have to come out and fill in some of the holes and ruts in the field.

Beyond one end of the field, higher up the hill, was a small L-shaped, cinder block building with an old gray shingled roof. A plain white sign attached to the end of the building facing the road, said *Red Bone Children's Library*. As she jogged slowly up the hill, Natty inspected the top of the building and saw that the sagging roof had gotten worse. She made a mental note that very soon, before any serious rain came, she'd have to go in and move the rest of the books into the little storeroom at the dry end of the building. After that, she didn't know what would happen with the Library.

Laboring her way up the hill almost to Main Street, she was jarred out of her thoughts by a familiar, voice from above. "Morning Mrs. Oakes. Little late this morning. Sleep in did we?"

Natty looked high up, toward the back porch on the fourth floor of the old, brown stone building that stood on the corner of Main Street. She found P. J. Hankinson, where he was most mornings, leaning over the porch railing, wearing only his boxer shorts and a wide-brimmed straw hat, binoculars slung around his neck, his tea cup resting on the wooden railing.

"Hey Hank. Just getting slow in my old age is all." Natty gave the old man a little wave before she disappeared from his view going up past the building and turning right onto Main Street.

On the first floor of the building was *Barney's General Store*, which was actually a hardware, grocery, bakery, liquor store, hunting and fishing outfitter, gift shop and video store rolled into one. Natty looked through the big windows of the restaurant section to the right of the front door and waved to Buck's sister Eve, who was sweeping the floor. The widow of the late Barney Brewster, Eve grinned broadly and waved enthusiastically as Natty ran by.

Down Main Street a quarter of a mile, Natty left the road and picked up the trail that ran through a hundred yards of thick woods and then west along the south side of the long flank of Red Bone Mountain. This section of the mountain was a high ridge that stretched for about two miles from the main mountain all the way back out to Oakes Hollow.

The trail ran through the dark woods and out into the sunlight along rocky ledges where the view was spectacular. It was rugged in spots and treacherous on some narrow cliff sides, but Natty had run it so many times before, she knew where to be careful. The solitude and the scenery made up for the difficulty of the terrain.

At around the mid-point of the trail's traverse along the southern slope of the mountain, Natty came to a stop and left the trail and began a laborious climb up a steep, narrow goat path, through the rocks and trees, that few people would even notice. She hadn't been up to her spot in several weeks, and today she thought, she deserved a few minutes on the rock.

After a steep climb, the trail ended in a thicket of pine trees on a high outcropping that dropped off precipitously on three sides. Natty walked through the trees, as she had done so many times in her youth, to a mammoth rock formation that jutted out off the side of the mountain like a huge inverted nose. The top of the rock was smooth and gently curved, like a large, inverted, saucer. She sat down and rested at the edge of the rock, her legs dangling over the edge. She leaned forward and looked down at the tops of the trees and the rocky Cliffside several hundred feet below and instinctively pulled herself a little farther away from the edge.

Next to the farm on Angel Mountain, this was her favorite spot in the universe. Looking south, the mountains stretched as far as the eye could see – green up close over on the other side of the Heavenly River, turning lighter shades of blue and gray as they ran off in the distance to Virginia. When the sky held wispy, white clouds, it was difficult to tell where the mountains ended and the sky began. Gazing hypnotically off at the hazy clouds, it was possible to trick the mind into seeing massive, snow-capped mountain ranges rising high into the sky out of the horizon.

Natty came to the rock with her friends in high school to smoke cigarettes, pot when they had some, and to drink and get silly and talk about boys and sex and share their dreams about what they were going to do when they all left McDowell County. Now, the other girls had gone – to colleges, jobs, husbands, new homes in Ohio, and Pennsylvania and North Carolina – and only Natty still came here, alone now, to enjoy the view and the serenity, and still, to daydream and visit her *if things had been different* fantasy world where she could become anything she wanted to.

But not today. She didn't have time to get into a good daydream. She stood up on the rock and looked out toward the southwest. Beyond some of the smaller hills, she could just make out the peak of Angel Mountain about twelve miles away. Somewhere over there, her mother was probably up and working at some farm chores thinking about Natty and wondering when her little girl was going to come and visit her. Natty stood on her tiptoes and cupped her hands around her mouth and shattered the morning silence, yelling at the top of her lungs. "*Hello mama. I love you mama. I'm coming to see you on Sunday.*" She laughed and wondered if any mothers living in the cabins over on the other side of the Heavenly River down below might have been cheered by her message.

Chapter 4

Charlie was feeling more uneasy as he got closer to the club. He wished Ellen hadn't asked him to pick her up after her tennis match. He wished her Volvo wasn't in the shop. He wished it wasn't a beautiful Saturday afternoon in July. The clubhouse and the patio bar would be crowded with members and he was sure to run into old friends whom, under different circumstances he would enjoy stopping and talking to, but not today.

Most of all, he wasn't looking forward to seeing Rafael Escobar. Charlie hadn't seen the tennis pro since resigning from the club two years ago. He recalled his jet-black curly hair, dark tan and trademark white outfits, an athlete's physique – a little on the short side – and always too much jewelry. He wasn't sure what he would do if he came face-to-face with Escobar. The morning's debacle at the hockey game had put Charlie in a surly mood and he knew it would be best to avoid any confrontation with his wife's good friend.

It was a gorgeous sun-drenched summer day and the course was crowded. Golfers standing around, in the fairways, along the rough, waiting patiently for the hole to open up in front of them. *Five-hour rounds today* Charlie figured. It was one of the reasons he had given up golf although he knew there was much more to it than just the time it took to play.

Some day he would take it up again. Golf was one of the few sports you could participate in for a lifetime, and he knew he wasn't going to be able to play hockey too much longer. He was already a dinosaur in his league at forty-eight.

For now, he still felt relieved by his decision to leave the club and relished the new found source of time he now had to devote to other pursuits. But more than the time he now had for running and for hockey, his *liberation* from the country club life style that had been slowly suffocating him like a weight on his chest, produced in Charlie an emotion close to euphoria. The club had become a stage-play of actors displaying for each other their wealth and status and talent for living well, with a script endlessly devoted to the benchmarks of success – stocks and the *market*, big houses and summer homes, exotic vacations, fine restaurants and trendy wines, good schools and fast-tracked children, and of course, the *politics* that supported it all. Charlie couldn't pretend any longer that these things interested him.

The country club lifestyle was something that Ellen had set her sights on from the first days of their marriage, living in the squalid little three-room apartment in Cambridge with its permanent odor of Asian cooking. It was the life she was raised in. It was all she knew of how adults were supposed to live and socialize.

Charlie played his part for many years with as much enthusiasm as he could muster and Ellen was aghast when he told her that he was resigning from the country club. Hickory Hills and its restaurants and parties, golf and tennis and their tight circle of friends had become the central theme in their lives, as Ellen had long planned it. She didn't understand it then and she still didn't get it, although by now it was a dead issue and wasn't discussed any longer. To their friends, all she could offer was a terse, '*Charlie was just too busy with his job now that he was a partner*' and left it at that.

Eventually, Ellen resigned herself to the fact that if she wanted to enjoy the *country club life,* she was going to have to do it on her own and she did, diving back into the club activities as a single member with renewed enthusiasm and energy. She spent even more time at the club now, nearly every day in the summer, playing tennis and working out on the exercise machines and in the weight room. Health and fitness had become her mantra. She changed her diet and even cut down on the late afternoon cocktail hours that had been her favorite time of day. At home they simply didn't discuss activities of the country club although she did enjoy chatting about the results of her victorious tennis matches, and Charlie was always glad for the opportunity to share in some part of her day. They'd reached a truce over the country club issue, but the fissure in their marriage remained.

The outside restaurant area was crowded as Charlie had feared. Every linen-covered table was occupied with lunching, drinking, and gabbing golfers and tennis players, eager to get on with the main sport of the club, which was watching and talking about each other.

Charlie wore only Khaki shorts, his favorite faded gray University of Michigan T-shirt, and a pair of well-worn running shoes. He left his sunglasses on to hide at least part of the shiner that had darkened around his left eye. When he was a member, walking around the grounds in this outfit would have brought a reprimand and some penalty points from the membership committee. It felt good not to have to deal with the petty aspects of the club any more.

He stood at the edge of the patio, hands in his pockets trying unsuccessfully to look inconspicuous while scanning the tables for Ellen. Charlie Burden had the muscular build of a defensive back, and the kind of rugged, permanently weathered face that women were universally attracted to. His nose, broken more times than he could remember, had a slender s-curve shape. At forty-eight, Charlie was actually ten pounds lighter and in overall better physical condition than when he played hockey at Michigan. It was difficult for Charlie Burden to be inconspicuous anywhere, and he could feel the eyes upon him.

Charlie would have to walk through the gauntlet of tables to the short wooden fence overlooking the tennis courts to see if Ellen was still playing. Some people he knew had already spied him. A few were rising up in their seats to catch his eye for the quick *wave-over.* Others were making sidelong comments to their neighbors, he was sure, identifying him to the curious as *Ellen Burden's husband.*

Just as he was about to wade into the murmuring crowd, Charlie saw something out of the corner of his eye, a familiar sight off to his right at a small table against the garden wall. He had to maneuver for a look around some golfers standing by a near table, and then he saw him, sitting alone, looking straight back at him. Charlie recognized the wide grin, the trademark black beret and the long dark cigar clamped in his teeth. He hadn't seen his friend Mal Berman in several months and instantly he regretted it. If there was one person at the club he truly missed spending time with it was Mal. Charlie postponed his search for Ellen and went over to see his old friend.

"Well hellooo Charlie," Berman cooed as he half-rose and extended his hand. "Come sit with me and have a beer like the old days."

"I'd love to Malcolm, since it will have to be on your number now, *not* like the old days. So how have you been? Break one-fifty today?"

"Hah! Oh I miss you, Burden. Golf isn't as much fun without you, and yes I damned near broke a hundred today wise ass!"

Charlie took a chair next to Berman at the small round table, his back to the garden wall, looking out at the crowded patio.

"And what brings you out to our sorry little club that you're now too good for, and by the way, I love the outfit, that'll get the dress-code boys buzzing"

"You should talk." Charlie replied, nodding toward his friend's typically showy golfing attire of a red, green and blue flowered shirt, yellow belt, bright red shorts, knee-high green argyle socks and black and white golf shoes along with the always-present black beret. "Circus leave you behind?"

Charlie and Malcolm had always shared a disdain for the dress codes that country clubs instituted to promote some measure of high-minded conformity. Malcolm liked to "tweak" the rules a little by wearing conforming, but outlandish and gaudy color combinations.

Not the most popular member of Hickory Hills to begin with, Berman's obnoxious outfits placed him on an orbit far from the center of the club's social system, making it difficult to find regular playing partners and social companions. Berman was also one of the few Jews in the club and while never experiencing any overt anti-Semitism from the members, Berman knew that being Jewish was part of his persona just like his beret, wild clothes and his high handicap, and it made a difference.

What saved Mal Berman from complete ostracism and enabled him to join up with the odd threesome, was his reputation and status as one of the smartest and most successful lawyers in New York City. He was also one of the wealthiest members of Hickory Hills, a quality rarely ignored by the membership of a country club.

Mal Berman was a senior partner in a small but extremely prestigious and profitable law firm specializing in international banking and finance issues. Dietrich, Delahunt & Mackey was his oldest and most important client. DD&M utilized another larger New York law firm for its every-day contract and litigation work, but called on Schafner & Berman for their critical assistance in the legal aspects of financing massive projects around the globe. There were few big-league bankers in London, Zurich, Paris, Hong Kong and Tokyo that Mal Berman didn't know on a first name basis and no American lawyer was more respected or feared in contract negotiations than Berman.

Semi-retired, Mal Berman loved golf and loved playing it with his young friend Charlie. He was disappointed when Charlie told him he was giving it up. Though unlike Ellen, Malcolm could empathize with his friend's decision. Malcolm wasn't a *country club* kind of guy either, but he *did* love to play.

Berman folded up his New York Times and stuffed it into a canvas tote bag by his chair, coming back up with a long, silver cigar case. "I know this is what you're really after Burden. It's the only reason you ever played golf with me."

Charlie laughed and accepted the twenty-dollar cigar. He had taken plenty of Malcolm's cigars over the years while playing golf. It had become a ritual of their friendship and he would enjoy this one. He slid the long cigar out of its silver sleeve. "I'm here to pick up Ellen, have you seen her? She's playing tennis."

"What else would the lovely Mrs. Burden be doing but playing tennis?" Berman beckoned over a young waitress, one of the attractive college girls the club was known for hiring in the summer. "Bring us two Heinekens and run down to the tennis courts and inquire as to the score of Mrs. Burden's tennis match and very quietly, at an appropriate moment, you may inform Mrs. Burden that her husband is on the patio enjoying the stimulating company of Mr. Berman and Mr. Castro, and she needn't hurry through the next set."

The girl flashed a quick, flirtatious smile at Charlie before hurrying off on her assignment, stopping in the kitchen only long enough to report to the other waitresses that the gorgeous and dangerous looking stranger in the sun glasses was none other than the husband of the *queen bitch,* Ellen Burden.

"So you gave up golf to take up boxing, or is that eye shadow you wearing?" Malcolm gestured to the darkening bruise visible from the side, behind Charlie's sun glasses.

"Rough game this morning." Charlie gave Berman a brief synopsis of the fight at the hockey game.

Before Berman could reply, the waitress arrived with the bottles of Heineken and frosted mugs. "I'm sorry, I didn't see Mrs. Burden anywhere down at the courts," the waitress explained as she put the beer on the table. At that moment, Ellen Burden and her entourage of three other women, an older man with a towel around his neck and Rafael Escobar, emerged from the far stairway that led up from the tennis courts. In spite of the heat, Escobar wore long white pants and a white, v-neck, short-sleeve sweatshirt, obviously only a spectator to today's match.

The buzz level on the patio rose as the group made their way toward one of the large tables near the center of the floor that almost by design, opened up as they made their entrance. Greetings and waves and radiant smiles were sent around the patio as the women, the older man and the club's tennis pro unloaded their equipment on and under the canopied table. This was a group with *star power* within the club's social spectrum, and the group's leader was clearly Ellen Burden.

Tall, tanned and elegant, Ellen Burden radiated confidence and charisma. Her jet-black, shoulder length hair shined as she quickly brushed it out of its competition ponytail. Her dark eyes and brilliant white smile sparkled like the jewelry on her hands as she moderated the discussion of the day's match with animated enthusiasm. Her companions coveted her attention which she would bestow by leaning forward, raising her eyebrows and the intensity of her smile as she listened to her subject's contribution, followed by a hearty, guttural laugh or clap of the hands to show her pleasure. *Compete hard, relax hard.* Few people could match Ellen Burden's intensity in the pursuit of life's enjoyments.

At fifty years old, Ellen D'Angelo Burden was easily one of the club's most attractive and captivating females. Large boned at five foot ten, with the figure of a twenty-five-year-old, Ellen, since adolescence, had become accustomed to the subtle peeks and sideways glances that large-breasted women can detect like live sonar. Now after several years of devoted physical conditioning and weight training, her rounded shoulders and taut arm and back muscles added an aura of sexual power and self-confidence. Only a very slight middle-age spread of the hips, and strong thighs, prevented her from attaining the look that she worked so hard for.

She also enlisted whatever outside assistance she needed in pursuit of her image. Several hours every two weeks at the *Carlos Marche* salon, at a hundred seventy-five dollars an hour preserved the ebony sheen of her hair and eyebrows. A visit to a noted cosmetic surgeon in Boston several years earlier, followed by a month-long recuperative stay at the *Boca Raton Club*, effectively pulled up the slightly sagging skin of the lower jaw area and erased the creases around the eyes.

Ellen worked hard at her physical appearance, but anyone who got close to her soon came to know that her dominating characteristic was her relentless *ambition.* Ellen Burden craved success and status and recognition like others needed alcohol, sex or money.

Mal Berman motioned the waitress over and pointed his long cigar in the direction of Ellen Burden's table. "Darling run over and tell Mrs. Burden --"

Charlie interrupted him. "No, no, let her enjoy her lunch with her friends. And we'll have two more on Mr. Berman's tab." Turning to Malcolm. "We don't get this chance too often, I'm in no hurry, and it looks like they're getting something to eat."

Charlie sat with his elbows on the table, hands clasped with an index finger wrapped around his cigar, concealed behind the dark glasses and the smoke, watching his wife's party from across the patio. It had been almost three months since Dave Marchetti's call about Ellen and Escobar, and still he hadn't done anything about it. He didn't know what to do or even how he honestly felt about it. He had blindsided Ellen, there was no doubt. He had been unfair to her and pushed her into decisions she shouldn't have had to make, and Escobar was certainly one of them. Confronting her about the affair would force one more decision on her at a time when he couldn't help her find the answers.

His wife was laughing, enjoying a three-way conversation with one of the other women and Escobar. For emphasis, she would reach out and touch his arm resting on the table. The tennis pro glowed in contrasting tones – a brilliant white smile against his deep, rich tan, jet black curly hair against his white shirt and slacks.

Charlie gazed across the patio at his wife's lover and let his mind drift back to the morning's hockey game. *He watched himself skate out of his own zone picking up speed with short, choppy steps at first, then long powerful strides, looking up to see Rafael Escobar, wearing his white tennis ensemble and white figure skates, a gold chain around his neck, a silver Rolex, and no helmet, coming toward him with his head down looking for the puck somewhere at his feet. The tennis pro had only an instant's warning before Charlie, accelerating through the hit with knees bent low, his shoulder pad just under the Cuban's breast bone and the top, front edge of his helmet directly into the bridge of his nose, delivered the most violent, ferocious check of his hockey career. Bones and cartilage snapped as the air whooshed out of Escobar's chest cavity while jewelry and body parts flew in all directions. In slow motion, Charlie saw Escobar's stick flying end-over-end through the air, as absolute stillness came over the ice, the only movement coming from the tennis pro's severed head, spinning slowly as it slid across the ice to the feet of one of Charlie's teammates. "Charlie, great hit," he heard the player say as he reached out with his stick and flipped the still smiling head over the boards.*

"Ellen's going to be the first female president of this club very soon, I have no doubt." Malcolm's words brought his friend back to reality. Charlie had to let out a hearty laugh over his bizarre daydream, startling Malcolm.

"And no one deserves it more Mal, no one deserves it more." Charlie slapped his old friend on the back, still chuckling over his imagined encounter with Rafael Escobar. He looked back over at his wife. She was having fun with her friends. She was enjoying her day, enjoying life. And there was nothing wrong with that.

Ellen had changed a little physically over the years but she was the same woman he had married twenty-six years ago. She had always been a woman who needed substance and craved status, and had never pretended to be anything different. This was the life she was born to, Charlie knew. It was he who had changed, who had altered the small print of their contract without warning or explanation, and he was determined to not let his confusion about life distort Ellen's clarity.

The fire of determination was lit within Ellen years earlier, on the day, during her senior year at Wellesley, when the word spread across the campus that Ellen D'Angelo's father, a Providence car dealer, had been indicted for racketeering, loan sharking, receiving stolen property and various related charges, along with a group of other Rhode Island businessmen known to reside on the fringe of the Providence underworld.

Augie D'Angelo it appeared was in a lot deeper than first reported. Years of mob activities, including old contract hits and extortion charges surfaced, leading Augie to plea-bargain his way out of a murder charge and accept a twenty- year sentence in a federal prison. His daughter's humiliation at the hands of the high-society Wellesley elite that she had so recently been a part of, was deep and permanent.

The family had enough money for Ellen to finish out her degree at Wellesley but the big house in East Greenwich with the barn and the horses was gone, along with the stocks, the condo at Sea Pines and the A-frame at Killington. After graduation, Ellen had virtually nothing but a degree, her clothes and the Karman Ghia convertible her father had given her when she left for college.

She also had Charlie Burden, the handsome Michigan hockey player she had met the previous summer at a bar in Newport. Even though Charlie came from a lower middle class background, the son of a train conductor for the New York - New Haven Railroad, he had future success stamped all over him. He was a brilliant student in engineering, an outstanding natural athlete and the most sensual lover she had ever had. Charlie Burden was going somewhere in life, and Ellen D'Angelo was determined to be there with him.

When Charlie was accepted into graduate school at M.I.T., everything began to fall into place for Ellen. Without his hockey scholarship, Charlie never would have been able to go to the University of Michigan. Now he would have to come up with a *lot* of money for two years at M.I.T., even after securing the available grants-in-aid and student loans, but he desperately wanted his Masters in Civil Engineering from the prestigious school. Ellen's suggestion that they just get married and squeeze out enough from her salary teaching school to pay for Charlie's tuition seemed like the most natural thing to do. She was a beautiful, sexy and intelligent woman and in spite of her family misfortunes, Charlie felt fortunate that she would marry a penniless graduate student like him. She was also employed and there was no avoiding the fact that Charlie needed a source of income if he was to attend M.I.T.

Charlie loved M.I.T. but they both hated living in abject poverty in the crowded building in Cambridge, no matter how temporary. They got a reprieve from their desultory existence the summer of Charlie's first year when he took a work-study job on a hydroelectric project in Wyoming that one of his professors was consulting on. Charlie spent a deliriously happy summer operating huge pieces of earth moving equipment while Ellen reveled in her free time in the beautiful Wyoming mountains, reading one novel after another and writing long letters to old friends. They lived in a hillside cabin with no electricity or running water, just a spring-fed pump in front and an out-house behind. They read to each other by the light of an oil lamp, sharing a bottle of cheap wine and occasionally a small ration of marijuana in a water pipe, and made love each night on a feather-filled mattress on the floor. It was the happiest summer they would ever spend together.

Charlie decided to make the most of the few moments he had left in the company of Malcolm Berman who was not only a smart lawyer but also a very perceptive and insightful friend.

"Mal, what did you do when the kids left, when the last of your girls was off to college and wasn't coming home?" Malcolm and his wife Nina, had raised four girls, all who attended Ivy League schools and Ivy League graduate schools . . . a doctor, two lawyers and a college professor.

"Is that what this is all about Charlie, the empty nest, is that what's short circuiting you?"

"It's just part of it Mal, it's complicated, hard to explain." He chuckled at sounding pathetic. "But the kids *are* a big part of it. I really miss them, when they were babies, when they were toddlers, in grade school – every age it seemed, just kept getting better. They were so much fun and great pals to us and we spent so much time with them, on their reading, and school and sports and social activities. Ellen and I, our lives were so much about the kids for so long . . ." Charlie drew on his shrinking cigar and glanced back at Ellen's table. "And then . . . they're gone, and all of a sudden, life seems, you know . . . kind of pointless," he said, almost to himself.

"Well I can't help you much with that one because I was a shitty father, gone most of the time when my girls were growing up, off in Europe or Latin America or China, and I hated all that little league crap anyway. So when each of the girls would leave for college, Nina would cry and I'd have another Manhattan and we'd get through it. But we still see them, all the time. Too much we see them! So you miss your kids, call them up, go see them."

Charlie smiled at his friend's inability to grasp what he was saying. "Malcolm, I don't miss my kids *now*. They're grown up, they're adults. Course I still love them but I don't miss them. Christ, they bore me to tears now. They're *too* perfect. Both just in their twenties and their major concern in life is *retirement*. Scotty's working for Fidelity up in Boston, a stock picker, and he's planning on retiring at *thirty-five*. Jennifer's in grad school at Northwestern and she spends all her free time managing her portfolio on-line. She's getting married next summer to a *dentist* and they've got it all laid out, a schedule for their incomes and investments, kids, the houses, the country club, retirement." Charlie took a long pull on his cigar. "Both of them, all they do is plan for the *perfect life*. I wish one of them would one time do something *irrational, inefficient,* be *spontaneous* about something, think about something besides success and themselves and the *good life*."

"So what you want are some new kids, that you can steer more towards alcohol, drugs, violence, pre-marital sex, that sort of thing." They enjoyed a laugh at Malcolm's sarcasm but Charlie continued thinking about his children. It bothered him that he and Ellen had raised two seemingly perfect children, but children of privilege who had never known any of the adversity or the hardships faced by most of society, had little interest or capacity for concern for anyone outside of their social stratum, and were rapidly becoming as adults, the kind of people that Charlie was beginning to detest. He often wondered what they might have done differently. It bothered him that neither Scotty nor Jennifer, to his knowledge, had ever had a friend or even casual acquaintance who was black, or Hispanic . . . or just a *lower-class kid from across the tracks in the poor section of New Haven*.

He flashed back to the sour memory of three summers earlier when he'd invited his life-long best friend Cecil Thomas, to play in a Wednesday member-guest at Hickory Hills. The events of that day festered in Charlie's mind for some time, and it became a catalyst in his decision to leave the club.

Charlie couldn't remember a time before he and Cecil were best friends. Their mothers had brought them home from the hospital only weeks apart to the old house on Western Boulevard in New Haven. The Thomas's lived on the second floor, one of several black families living in the handful of three-decker houses that remained standing on the street that was gradually giving way to the encroaching concrete and asphalt of an expanding industrial zone. Across the Boulevard, beyond the barren fields where other houses once stood, six widths of train tracks guarded the warehouses and storage tanks of the city's gasoline alley.

That Cecil was black or in any way different from himself, was never a concern to Charlie. He knew Cecil long before he'd ever met any other white children. From elementary school through high school, the best friends were a curious pair; Charlie, strong, athletic and only marginally interested in school; Cecil, over-weight and uncoordinated but gifted academically. Cecil was often called on to help Charlie with his homework, and more than a few times, Charlie had to put his fists to work to protect his black buddy.

When Charlie went off to college at Michigan, Cecil went to work, and to night school, eventually getting a degree from the University of New Haven, and then several years later, a law degree from Fordham. But Cecil never fit the profile of the fast-track minority candidate that the prestigious law firms coveted. He was too old, too fat and too black, and there were plenty of Ivy League minority graduates to pick from. So Cecil went on to a career as a lawyer in New Haven's system of public agencies that variously dealt with the housing, welfare, medical, and aging problems of the poor. Thankless, frustrating work at an income level that would forever place him at the bottom of the scale for practicing attorneys.

Charlie and Cecil had stayed in contact over the years and got together often when the Burdens moved to Windsor, Connecticut, and then, less often after they moved to Mamaroneck. Cecil had told Charlie that he'd taken up golf, and was in a group that played regularly at a little nine-hole public course and that he would soon be able to beat his old pal. For several years though, Cecil had been declining Charlie's invitations to play at Hickory Hills, always with some excuse about not having the time.

Then one day, Cecil finally accepted the invitation to a member-guest in mid-August. Charlie had no reason to suspect that Cecil wasn't ready to play in a real tournament, on a real golf course, or that Hickory Hills wasn't ready for Cecil.

But Cecil knew it. The moment he stepped into the dining room for the luncheon and looked around for Charlie, into the sea of white faces staring back at him, staring at the overweight black man in the basketball sneakers and the long out-of-style Bermuda shorts and the Izod sports shirt a size too small. Cecil had been there before.

It didn't help that they played with a member with a five handicap and his guest with a Westchester CC bag tag, both who would have had little patience with a white man's whiffs, shanks and wild slices, let alone this clearly out-of-place black man who looked like he could very well be picking up their trash next week. After a few holes they played as a twosome, standing well off to the side of the green, or heading to the next tee while Charlie and Cecil finished the hole. Playing slowly, Cecil always had too much of a gallery on every tee as the group behind pressed in to watch the show.

It took Charlie a while to fully grasp Cecil's nervousness and discomfort at being the only black man on the course, the only black man on the grounds not working in the back of the kitchen. Then he began to notice the sideways glances and rolling eyeballs and the cupped-hand-to-mouth comments followed by the quick turn-away chuckles of the other players and it dawned on him what a horrible mistake he'd made in subjecting his friend to this kind of test.

If Cecil had been the white CFO of a Fortune 500 company, he could have shot 140 and everyone would have joked and had a good time with it. But the standard for a middle-class black man to be accepted at Hickory Hills was much tougher, and crueler, and it gnawed at Charlie's gut every time he played after that day. He and Cecil had talked on the phone only a few times in the last two years, occasionally exchanging e-mails, as their friendship dissipated. His estrangement from Cecil continually gnawed away at an empty space in Charlie's gut.

"Hey I've got an idea." Malcolm's voice brought Charlie's attention back to the table. "Why don't you and Ellen have another child? Adopt one I mean, it's much easier than it used to be. You're both still young enough." Malcolm's question raised an issue Charlie had pondered many times over the last few years. But he knew his wife very well. Adoption wasn't in their future.

Looking across the patio at Ellen, Charlie wondered for a moment if he should tell Malcolm about their *third* child, the child they never had, the child that just wouldn't have fit into their life style. No, that was ancient history, done and gone. Nobody's business but his and Ellen's.

Instead, Charlie decided to sound out Malcolm about an idea he'd been developing in the back of his mind for some time. "Malcolm I've been thinking about getting away for a while, working in the field." He paused to choose his words carefully because talking to Malcolm was in many ways like talking directly to the Executive Committee of Dietrich Delahunt & Mackey.

"I need to *build* something, get back to engineering, to get away from *new business* for a while. I've been thinking about asking to be assigned to the China project, the second dam." Charlie knew that Malcolm was closely involved with the project and knew as much about it as anyone outside of the San Francisco office and Lucien Mackey.

"That's a tough one Charlie. It technically belongs to San Francisco, which has half its people in Beijing already. Plus it's not the kind of post a partner is often considered for." Charlie knew Malcolm was referring to the fact that most of the partners, although highly educated and experienced engineers, generally arrived on the partners' floor through their business and political acumen, not their engineering talents. The real ability to manage the complex construction projects of a company like Dietrich, Delahunt & Mackey, lay with a small cadre of experienced engineers who had spent their entire careers in the field, building mammoth structures around the globe, working for a fraction of the income of a partner. They were the kind of engineer that Charlie Burden had once set out to become, had dreamed of becoming, before he became a rainmaker and had to come inside.

"I could build that dam Malcolm."

"You should talk to Lucien, Charlie. Lucien will know what's best. Trust his judgment."

Trusting Lucien's judgment was always good advice thought Charlie. He'd go and see Lucien next week. Charlie turned away from his friend and looked up to see Ellen standing at the edge of the table, equipment bag on her shoulder, smiling down at them.

"Hello Malcolm. Nice outfit," Ellen said, before turning to her husband. "Shall we go Charlie? Wouldn't want you to get too comfortable here. You may want to become a member again and spoil all my fun."

Chapter 5

The steering of Natty's Honda felt a little wobbly as she turned onto Heaven's Gate, which after a short, winding climb through Angel Hollow would lead to Angel Mountain·Road. Another mile through alternating dark woods and sunlit green meadows would bring them up to the DeWitt Farm. The 1980 Accord at one time was red, but now was mostly a dull shade of faded maroon. She hoped the wobble in the steering was maybe just a tire needing air. Even with Gus Lowe's garage always giving her a break, she couldn't afford any car repairs right now.

Natty loved to come back to the farm, but not without some anxiety about what she always had to face there. She looked forward to seeing her mother and grandpa Bud, Alice, and Uncle Pete. She loved the smells and the colors and sounds of the farm and the coolness of the air on Angel Mountain. Even the pungent aromas of the pig pens and the chicken house brought back nostalgic flashes, and the greens of the trees and the corn stalks and the fallow pastures always appeared deeper and richer and greener than anywhere else. On the farm, food tasted better, the water colder and purer, and the air smelled fresher. Natty liked to walk barefoot in the fields and feel the hot, soft earth between her toes, and then sit on the warm flat rocks in the stream with her legs, up to the knee, numbed by the ice cold water that ran down from the pond farther up the mountain.

But the farm was also the source of Natty's greatest sadness, and she couldn't walk through the house or the barn or the fields, or sit on the porch for very long without thinking of Annie. Twenty-three years later, she could still hear her voice, and feel her small hands and her downy cheeks, and see her running across the dirt yard with her arms upraised, the sign for Natty to hold her.

The melancholy of old memories was supplanted by the unbridled joy the children experienced at the farm, and Natty enjoyed sharing their excitement as they explored the world of her childhood. After the obligatory hugs and a suitable interval of fawning by their grandmother and great grand parents, Pie would always beg for his release to run off with Uncle Pete to see the animals, and – his single favorite activity in life –sitting on Pete's lap and driving the old tractor around the farm. Cat, after a hand-in-hand walking tour with great grandmother Alice, to see the newest piglets, would invariably sneak off to the warm floor of the sun room, surrounded by the tattered, yellowing picture books from Sarah's library. She could sit for hours, cross-legged, reading the stories out loud to herself, just as her mother had done with the same books twenty years earlier.

Natty was always struck now by how much smaller and lately, how run down the farm seemed when she first arrived. The gray clapboards of the house needed painting, the roof was worn and patched in a dozen places and the long boards of the porch now sagged noticeably. Sarah still had her flowerbeds around the house but not as full or as neatly edged as they once were. The farm, like its occupants, was looking tired.

In truth, it never was much of a farm – a small one-story house, a barn, and several sheds, the pig sties, one large field for growing feed corn, two smaller fields farther down the hill running along either side of the stream, and at the lowest end of the farm, the long chicken house. But it was where Natty grew up and it was the safest place she knew.

As they pulled into the yard in front of the house, Grandpa DeWitt and Alice were getting out of their chairs on the porch to greet them. While the children were hugging their grandparents and Uncle Pete, Natty's mother drifted quietly through the screen door and stood unnoticed on the porch, arms folded in front of her, a serene smile on her face as she awaited her turn. This was her manner – never impatient, never demonstrative or in any way calling attention to herself.

Sarah DeWitt was several inches taller than her daughter and only recently had she started to put some middle-aged pounds on her thin frame. She was fifty-three but looked older, the weathered skin of her face and arms showing the effects of more than twenty years of farm life. Her hair was prematurely white, the color of thick smoke. It hung down her back reaching almost to her waist. Today it hung loose and with her faded cotton dress and well-worn sandals, she gave the appearance, as she often did, of a Native American.

After the children had run off – Pie scrambling up onto the tractor with Pete, Catherine pulling mawmaw Alice toward the big barn – Sarah DeWitt turned her attention to her daughter. She pulled Natty close for a long hug then ran her hands over her shoulders and slowly down her arms and held onto her wrists while she looked closely at her face, inspecting her eyes and her cheek bones, her lips, looking for a telltale sign. Natty knew what she was doing. It was their usual routine since the night Buck had beaten her.

"So, he's been leaving you alone then." Sarah had a soft, unhurried way of speaking, a mannerism inherited by her daughter.

"*Yes* mama." Natty was irritated. "You don't always have to *do* this. Buck ain't like that anymore, he's fine."

"Of course he is. Of course he is. And he's given up drinking, and he spends all of his free time now with his children."

"He's getting better, mama. He's trying anyway. He'll be fine when the new power plant opens in another year, maybe sooner. He's made good friends with the head man from the construction company, a *big* company from New York, and he's promised Buck a job for sure when the plant opens. And those are *good* jobs too."

"Yes, I'm sure Buck will be very much needed at the new power plant," Sarah said.

They'd reached the point they always reached very quickly, when Sarah was making her usual inferences about Buck, where Natty had to resist the instinct to throw her mother's own lifestyle back at her. But she always knew it would just make things worse and she didn't want to argue with her mother. And, she had to admit, it also wasn't fair. Her mother never hurt anyone with her addictions.

They strolled slowly toward the barn, hand in hand, her mother bringing her up to date on the insignificant details that make up the news on a small farm. They sat down on an old bench in the shade of the barn where they could watch the pigs cooling themselves in the wet mud.

"You look very thin Natty. Are you still doing all that running?"

"Every day, unless the weather won't let me. It's the best thing I do for myself mama. And I feel fine, I feel great."

"And your nursing job, how are all your patients?"

"I ain't a nurse mama. I'm a *home health aide.*"

"*Aren't* a nurse Natty. You don't always have to *sound* like a hillbilly."

"I know mama. I *aren't* a nurse." Her wisecrack was ignored. "Anyway, I haven't lost any this week, but I got a few going to be on the wrong side of the grass pretty quick. They just keep giving me more."

"No, I don't think we'll be running out of *old people* in McDowell County very soon," Sarah replied pensively. "And you'll be working at the school again in the fall?"

"Yeah, in the mornings, for a few hours. Still gives me time to make my rounds and I'll be able to see Cat once in a while. Make sure she's doing okay."

"Yes, that'll be good for her. And Pie, he's ready to go back to school?"

"Well he's going in seventh grade, about where he's supposed to be and there ain't too many retarded kids can manage that." Natty reflected for a moment about her remarkable son. "He still has his problems with the numbers, arithmetic confuses him some, but it sure as hell confused me a lot in school too. You know that. But damn, if he ain't the most entertaining and funniest little boy." Natty smiled at some humorous memory. "He makes me laugh like we got no troubles in the world at all."

"You've done a good job with that boy Natty, a great job, all by yourself."

Natty ignored her mother's subtle jab at Buck. Sarah didn't like Buck as a child, liked him less as the husband of her daughter, and now despised him as the father of her grandchildren. It had been several years since Buck had been to the farm and years since Sarah had been to Oakes Hollow, holding the rest of the Oakes clan in about the same regard she had for Buck. "Not just me mama, mostly Mabel Willard at the school. Thank God for that woman being there. She's been teaching Pie since kindergarten, putting in extra time all these years."

"And with all your work, you'll still be having your football team again?"

"Hell mama, that's about the only fun I have in life, that and my running. And it's *soccer*, not football." Natty thought about the coming season and had to admit that her enthusiasm for coaching was waning. She was tired of being undermanned and out-gunned against the all-boy teams from Bluefield, Princeton, and Welch. Even with Emma Lowe, her *Bones* had always lost more than they won. She wasn't sure if they would even be competitive this season having lost a couple of capable players, but she knew she had to run the team for one more season, the last season, for Emma's sake anyway.

Sarah's attention had drifted away as it often did after a few minutes of conversation. She would appear transfixed in deep thought as she gazed off in the distance at nothing in particular. Natty was used to her departures. She sat by her side looking over the old farm, content to let her mother have "her own time" as she called it when she was young.

Natty shielded her eyes and looked up toward the cornfield, the green stalks yet only three feet high in mid-summer with the lack of rain. By mid-September they'd be seven feet tall with fat, heavy ears a foot long. She scanned the field to see if she could detect where Pete had hidden this year's "weed patch." It wouldn't be detectable from down in the yard Natty knew. Pete was an expert at hiding a stand of marijuana plants.

The pot was only for their own use, Sarah had told her, Pete having learned his lesson by spending his twenty-second year in the Southern District Correctional facility in Beckley after a conviction for trafficking. But Natty knew that Pete grew a lot of marijuana and had a suspicion that while he may not be selling it, he could probably be persuaded to barter a little bag of it now and then to people he knew.

It had been over a dozen years since Natty last smoked marijuana, with Buck in the back seat of his father's Chevy Blazer in the parking lot of *Moody's Roadhouse,* a week before she learned she was pregnant with Pie. But Natty didn't begrudge her mother or Uncle Pete the small pleasures they took from the drug. They led an isolated existence on a dirt farm in the mountains with a lonely and hard future, and the need for some relief, whatever the source, was understandable. She knew that not long after she and Pie and Cat said their good-byes and drove off down the Mountain Road, Sarah and Pete would be in their rocking chairs on the porch with their pipes and a small bowl of weed on the little plastic table between them, Sarah with a glass of wine and a book, and Pete watching her and watching the sun set over the hazy gray mountains to the west as the heavy night air swept in over Angel Mountain.

Natty knew that it was a too late in life for Sarah to *just say no.* Drugs and the search for spiritual and psychological independence had been a part of Sarah's life too long for her to become somebody else's notion of a middle-aged grandmother. Her life had been uprooted during a tumultuous time in the country's history and like a lot of other young people, she had lost her way and a lot of her spirit during the 1960's. It was more coincidence than anything else that she had finally found much of what she had long been seeking, on Angel Mountain, West Virginia.

In the afternoon, while the children went down to play in the stream with Petey and Sarah, Natty decided to take a quick run up to the cemetery to see Annie and her father. It was only about a mile and even with the intense afternoon heat, she knew it would be an easy run. Afterward she'd race downhill all the way to the stream and plunge in, running shoes and all.

The DeWitt Farm was about half way up Angel Mountain Road. A little farther up the mountain, the road split. The right fork continued to climb, going around and up the south side of the mountain, eventually running out at a rocky promontory just down from the top of the mountain. The left fork continued along the gently-sloped north side for another half mile until it came to the small cemetery.

In a corner of the cemetery, looking out of place among the antique markers, were three identical polished marble stones, lying flat, about four feet apart, surrounded on three sides by a well-manicured bed of flowers. Natty walked up and stood looking down at the three plain markers, without any epitaphs, engraved only with names and dates. On the left, her sister, Annie DeWitt, b.1973 – d.1976, then her father, Thomas A. DeWitt, b.1949 – d.1977, and on the right, the uncle she never knew, Earl J. DeWitt, b.1951 – d.1970.

Natty dropped to her knees between the stones and began pulling up the weeds that had escaped the attention of Grandma Alice who at least once a week made a long, slow hike up to the cemetery to spend a few minutes with her two oldest boys and her granddaughter. *'There's a lot of heartache in these mountains'* Alice was prone to lamenting, and nowhere was it more evident than at the little cemetery on Angel Mountain.

Her weeding done, Natty squatted on her haunches and said a short, silent prayer for her father and sister before the tears came as they always did, splattering on the cool, smooth marble. Natty wondered if the sadness over Annie would ever leave her. A good hard, sweaty run in the afternoon heat would take care of today. She thought about Cat sitting in the stream and just wanted to get down to her and hold her and splash around in the cold water and make her laugh.

Natty ran hard down the gently sloping road until, a hundred yards before where the road split, a white pickup truck sped across her view going up toward the south side of the mountain. Running into anyone on Angel Mountain was a rarity. No one lived on the mountain beyond the DeWitt farm any more, and there was something *official* looking about the truck that made her curious.

At the fork, she stopped and looked up the road where the truck had disappeared. A short run up the hill would give Natty a vantage point from which she could see long stretches of the road as it weaved its way up the mountain. Adopting an innocent jogger's pace, Natty made her way up the curve to investigate. As the south side of the mountain came into view, she was surprised to see not one, but two white pickup trucks, one parked at the side of the road about a hundred yards from the curve, the other, farther up the mountain and still moving. She was more surprised to see several men, who she could tell, were not on the mountain to enjoy the scenery on a Sunday afternoon. Two of the men stood in the road by the first white pickup, looking up the mountain, talking, and occasionally pointing out some spot higher up on the jagged, rocky slopes above them. Twenty yards off the road, another man stood peering through an instrument mounted on a tripod. Next to him an assistant stood with a black walkie-talkie and a clipboard on which he was making notations. All the men wore hard hats, blue jeans and construction boots.

One of the men in the road saw Natty approaching and nodded toward her to alert his partner who stopped talking and turned to watch the little woman jogging slowly toward them. Natty slowed to a walk fifty feet from the men, pretending to need a rest to catch her breath. The afternoon sun was beating down on the hot side of the mountain with no breeze at all for relief. The men had sweat stains down the front of their work shirts.

"Hey, how you boys doin' today, hot enough for ya?" Natty got no reply beyond a polite nod and half a smile from one of the men who held a walkie-talkie and looked like he was in charge.

"Don't see too many people up here on this mountain, let alone on a Sunday, and *working* to boot." Still no response. As Natty came even with the men, she stopped and wiped her brow with the bottom of her shirt, exposing her thin waist. Behind the men, Natty could see the white pickup truck, a late model Dodge with an extended cab. On the side of the door a company logo was painted in dark green. It read, *Southern States Geological Surveys,* and under it, *Huntington, West Virginia.*

She didn't recognize either of the men, and it was a good bet they weren't from McDowell County. It was clear that she wasn't going to get much information out of them unless she got more direct. "So," Natty said as she looked around at the other men at work on the mountain, and then directly back at the man in front of her, the one she assumed was in charge. "What are you all doin' up here?"

The man avoided her eyes and looked up the mountain, still not saying anything. After an awkward few seconds, the other man came to his aid. "We're just doing a little surveying ma'am, couple of days of readings and we'll be done and off this mountain."

"It's for the road project." The man in charge had a deep, authoritative voice and he sounded irritated. "There's some federal money available for rebuilding mountain roads, and this road may qualify." He took off his hard hat and wiped his forehead with his sleeve, heading for the door of the truck. It was obvious that his conversation with the inquisitive jogger was over.

Natty felt like she'd been dismissed by a teacher in school and her anger started to grow. "Well sure, that makes sense. A new road." She talked louder as the men walked away from her. "Could sure use a new road up here, what with all the traffic runnin' up and down Angel Mountain. Like a damn freeway up here." Both men were climbing into the truck now. She raised her voice. "What we really need up here is a couple of stop lights and maybe a McDonald's." Her sarcasm was lost in the roar of the big truck as it left Natty standing in a cloud of hot dust. She watched it drive up the road toward where she'd seen the other truck drive off.

"*Road project,* what a bunch of bullshit," Natty said to herself as the truck pulled away. She turned and began her run down the mountain curious to see if Bud and Pete knew anything about what was going on.

Natty helped Alice set the table and put out the dinner, as she had so many times in her youth. The children came in still slightly damp from their dip in the stream, followed by Sarah and Petey who had changed out of their wet clothing. Bud was the last to be seated.

While she was cutting up Cat's chicken, Natty brought up the strange events she'd witnessed that afternoon. "Saw a whole bunch of men working at some kind of surveying job up on the south road this afternoon. Two big white pickups too, with the name of some *geological survey* company on the door. I ran over that way to see what they were up to but they were tighter than a new jar of pickles. Gave me some phony story about building a new road which is . . ." Natty looked up and saw that Bud and Petey had both stopped eating and were staring at her with grim looks on their faces. It was apparent that they knew something.

"So what's going on?" Natty asked softly.

Sarah too was curious. It was obviously news to her. "Petey, Bud, do you know something?" Bud had taken up his fork and was picking at his food, reluctant to comment.

After a few moments Petey broke the silence. "The-they was up there a c-couple a w-weeks ago. Seen one a the trucks go by th-this morning." Pete had stuttered all his life and it pained him when he had to speak to more than one person.

Suddenly, Bud DeWitt's soft but deep voice filled the small dining room with a sense of authority. "They're comin' for the coal."

Sarah reacted immediately. "Coal? What coal, Bud? There's no coal up here." Sarah didn't want to hear about coal. Coal had meant nothing but heartache to her and the idea that coal may again enter her life was cause for concern.

But Angel Mountain was Bud DeWitt's mountain more than any other person alive. Seventy-two years he'd lived on the mountain, fifty-three of those years with his wife Alice. He'd buried his parents, two brothers, a sister, two sons, and a granddaughter on the mountain and planned to be buried there himself when his time came. When Bud DeWitt talked about Angel Mountain, it was time for everyone else to just listen.

Bud put down his fork and took up his napkin, readying himself to tell the family what they had a right to know. He spoke softly which made even the children pay attention to his words.

"There's coal up here. A lot of coal. Big seam, about twenty foot thick through most of the mountain about half way up. The mineral rights to Angel Mountain was owned for years by a little company from down in Tazewell County. Family business, Ferris Mining it was called. Ran a couple dog-holes a few miles south of here, and over in Virginia and Kentucky, and a deep shaft as I recall somewheres over near Jolo. Never much of a company, always non-union, lot of safety problems and such. Well they went bankrupt about the mid-sixties but it got tied up in the courts for years by some technicality or another and everyone just forgot about it for years and the coal business I reckon just lost track of Angel Mountain."

Bud paused to take a drink of his ice water, then wiped his mouth before continuing. "Well then at the end of the seventies, early eighties, you know, the coal business was going bust and they was closing most of the deep mines. Most of the coal taken then was from the surface mines in Logan and Mingo Counties, not much from McDowell. I figured Angel Mountain was safe then, that nobody'd ever be coming up here for the coal. But . . ." He stopped and turned toward the dining room window with a grimace on his face as he looked out at his farm.

Natty could see in Bud's demeanor that there was something serious about all this that she couldn't quite figure out. "But *what,* Grandpa? Why is this a problem now."

Bud looked across the table at her. "Well, about two and a half years ago, I'm looking at the Welch Daily and I glance at the legal notices and something catches my eye. I see the name Ferris Mining in there, so naturally it grabs my attention and I read all that small print you can hardly see, and it says that all the assets of the Ferris Mining Company was purchased by the Ackerly Coal Company of Pittsburgh."

The name *Ackerly Coal Company* immediately sent a shiver of recognition through Natty as she recalled that day, two years ago, when the helicopters came, the day of the picnic and the big announcement, and the speakers up on the stage, including the big red-face Irishman from Ackerly Coal Company. It was the day when the Canadian man gave her the CanAmex jacket. The night that Buck beat her.

"Now that bothered me some, Ackerly getting the mineral rights," Bud continued, pulling Natty's attention back to the present. "Because Ackerly's a big company, does a lot of mining in the southern counties, mostly at them big mountaintop mines in Logan and Mingo."

Natty had now put it together and understood Bud's fears, but she could see on her mother's face, an inquisitive scowl, still trying to understand how a seam of coal on Angel Mountain could possibly affect their farm.

"Well, I didn't think anything more about it 'til I read about that circus down in Red Bone, with the picnic and the Governor and all them politicians, and," Bud paused for dramatic effect, "the fact that it was clear as day, they'd *already* made the deal with Ackerly to supply the coal. That smelled a little fishy to me, 'cause there's a number of coal companies operating in the southern counties where you find the low-sulfur, soft coal they need for their power plant, but okay, Ackerly's a big company and maybe this CanAmex, which is a lot bigger company than anything we ever been involved with around here, maybe that's how they like to do business."

Sarah had calmed down and started eating her dinner along with the children. "Well Bud just because this Ackerly company's got a contract to supply coal for the new power plant doesn't mean they'll be opening a mine on Angel Mountain. You said yourself that they've got lots of mines already operating, they don't need to come up here."

"Well Sarah, there's a little more to it," Bud continued. "You remember that about a month after the picnic they had some hearings about a number of permits and such the company would need from the county and from the town of Red Bone. Well them permits was what that whole picnic show was all about and it worked like a charm with nary an objection to anything the company wanted to do, which I guess is understandable when you're holding all the cards and offering all them jobs and tax dollars and whatnot. But I'm reading the story in the paper about the permits and there's somebody there from the Governor's office, I guess still trying to grab all the credit for bringing the power plant here, and as part of the story, the Governor's guy says, 'and we're also pleased to announce that the CanAmex Energy Company has agreed that all of the coal burned in the new plant will *have to come* from McDowell County.'" Bud put his fork down and started to talk a little faster. "Now just for a second, don't think about *where* the coal is going to come from, just think about *whose deal it is.* This ain't something that the county commissioners negotiated down at the permit hearings at the Red Bone High School. Those fellas are good men, and meaning well, but this is *way* out of their league. This business about the coal coming from McDowell County, you can bet was a deal made in Charleston a long time ago, right at the beginning of this whole thing, and you can bet there was some serious negotiating going on 'cause Ackerly Coal and especially the CanAmex Energy Company ain't about to let the poorest county in just about the poorest state in the Union, tell them where to get their coal from."

Sarah was starting to get impatient with Bud's explanation. "So Bud, what are you saying, that . . ."

He cut her off softly. "I'm *saying*, that the negotiating went something like, 'okay, Mr. Governor, we'll guarantee that the coal comes from McDowell County, *and* guarantee a couple of hundred, good-paying, union mining jobs to residents of the county, *and* we'll pay so much in taxes to the county and the town, etcetera, etcetera, but *you guys* have to guarantee us that the Ackerly Coal Company will get a brand new *surface mining permit* for the piece of land known as Angel Mountain 'cause there's plenty of coal up there and we need to be able to get at it quick and cheap like in order to get enough coal from McDowell County to run a power plant of this size,' and *that's* why surveying crews are running all over this mountain."

Bud paused to take a drink of water and to calm himself a little before continuing. "Sometime before the end of the year they're going to come up here and take down all the trees for lumber, and then they'll start blasting the top off this mountain, pushing it into the valleys, filling in all the hollows, and covering the streams, and sure enough, covering this farm under about a hundred feet of rock and sand." The room was silent as they tried to absorb the meaning of Bud's words before he continued, his voice getting softer with helplessness now. "There's enough coal up here to run that plant for *years,* good *low-sulfur* coal, the kind they got to have for their power plant. And it'll mean a lot of good jobs, and the politicians and the union and every out-of-work miner in McDowell County will support the project."

"But Bud," Sarah protested, "there's a *ban* against new mountaintop-removal permits, I remember signing a petition last year for *Save The Mountains,* remember?"

Her father-in-law looked at her irritably. "Sarah, *you ain't been listening*! A *deal's been made* I'm telling you. They'll find a way around that injunction nice and quiet, probably get another judge or a magistrate to suspend it temporarily, just long enough to get Ackerly a permit for Angel Mountain, then put it back in place again. They'll make a deal with the environmental groups 'cause nobody really cares much about what happens down here. Ain't nobody living anymore on Angel Mountain, 'cept some no-account hillbilly family running a dusty little pig farm."

Natty was also skeptical. "Grandpa, I just don't know that it's going to be that easy to get a surface mine permit for Angel Mountain."

Bud wiped his mouth and pushed his plate away without having eaten much of his dinner. "Natty, you're too young to know it, but this is the way it's *always* been. It's the history of West Virginia. The big companies come here and they make a deal with Charleston, and they take the coal, and the timber, and the gas, and they get rich, and the people get poorer and the land gets tore up, and the water gets fouled, and it's okay 'cause there ain't hardly anybody left living in the coal counties, and besides, they're all just old and poor and uneducated and don't matter to no one!" When he finished, he was almost shouting. Bud took in a deep breath to calm himself. "Way it's always been," he said softly getting up from the table letting his napkin fall to the floor. He went through the kitchen and out the door, headed for the barn to get back to work.

Alice DeWitt watched her husband leave with a pained expression on her face. She rarely spoke out on her own so she immediately had the attention of the room. "Some men come up here a month ago and wanted to buy the farm," she said softly. "Bud told me they offered him a hundred thousand dollars for the farm, cash money."

"Wow, that seems like a lot of money for this place," Natty said. "What did Bud say?"

"He just told them the farm weren't for sale, for any price, which the men couldn't seem to understand, but Bud just said that's the end of it and he weren't going to discuss it. So we give 'em some lemonade and corn bread out on the porch there, and sent them on their way. They wasn't too happy about it I suspect from the way they moped off and such but . . . they was lawyers from Charleston . . . tall, good looking men with nice suits. Never said what they wanted with the farm, but now it seems it must have been about the coal."

Alice gazed out the window and watched the man she had been married to for fifty-three years, trudge up the hill one more time, moving more slowly and with more effort than he used to. "Where would we go?" she asked softly. "This is the only home Bud's ever had. He was born right here in this house. We could never sell the farm. No, Bud and me are going to live out the few days we got left right here, and then lay down together up in the cemetery. Then it will be Petey's farm."

With the children finally in the car, having said their good-byes, Natty started to back the Honda out of the front yard and onto Mountain Road. Normally, she wouldn't have given a thought to looking for any other cars on the road but something made her stop, not an instant too soon, as the white Dodge pickup trucks, going much too fast on the narrow road, raced by her rear fender. The side windows of the trucks were tinted black, but through the windshield of the second truck, she caught a glimpse of three men in the front seat, still wearing their white hardhats. As she watched the trucks roar down the mountain road and go out of sight, Natty suddenly realized that everything Bud said was true. The men in the hard hats were going to destroy Angel Mountain and everything on it

Driving up the gravel road into Oakes Hollow, Natty could tell that something was going on. It wasn't unusual to see the residents of Oakes Hollow sitting around shooting the breeze and drinking beer, especially on a hot summer evening, but there were *too many* people about for there not to be some news in the air. Natty could see Ransom and Sally standing in the driveway and Yancy sitting up on the hood of his truck. Charlotte occupied Amos' stool at the corner of the trailer. Across the drive, next to Natty's trailer, Drew Merrill and Roy Hogan were leaning against Roy's truck.

Suddenly, Natty realized that she didn't see Buck anywhere. *Something must have happened to Buck!* He had been gone for three days working for a crew that ran an illegal timber operation up in Monroe County. Every so often, when he really needed some cash, Buck would go off for a few days at a time and cut trees for the timber pirates. It was hard and dangerous work but he'd get paid two hundred dollars for a twelve-hour day, all the beer he could drink afterward and a tent to sleep in. Natty knew that Buck was strong and he knew what he was doing, cutting trees down, but she still worried about him getting hurt or getting arrested when he was off working for the timber pirates, and now something must have happened.

Natty's panic subsided when she saw Buck's truck parked just beyond Roy Hogan's. Then she saw him. On the small deck outside their trailer, Buck lay on his back, unmoving, looking at the sky, one foot on the top step of three leading to the ground, his other leg just falling limply down the stairs almost reaching the gravel. One hand rested on his stomach, the other around a beer can at his side. He was wearing denim overalls and a long-sleeve white tee shirt, both filthy with dirt and tree sap. His tall boots, coated with dried mud, lay at the bottom of the stairs, his feet covered by well-worn gray wool socks.

The parking area around the trailers was getting crowded so Natty pulled the Honda off the driveway to the right, just below Yancy's trailer and walked the few yards up to the center of the group. She was glad to see Buck home safe after three days in the woods. "*Hey* Buck! How'd it go?" she offered without really expecting much of a response. Buck just lay still on the deck.

She exchanged greetings with the rest of the family and Roy Hogan, and helped herself to a beer out of the cooler at the bottom of the stairs. "So what's going on here, somebody *die* or something?"

Sally had lifted Cat up for a hug and was lowering her to the ground. "Well, as a matter of fact Nat, somebody *did* die. That guy, Hugo Paxton, you know, the power plant boss?"

She knew Paxton well enough from the *Road House*, but she wasn't friendly with him like Buck and his brothers were, and she didn't like the way the fat man always had to find some way to rub against her whenever he passed by. "*Course* I know who he is. Seen Mr. Paxton in action." She took swig of beer, relieved that it wasn't somebody in the family or a local person. "So what happened to him?"

Roy Hogan took up the story. "Last night, down at the *Fat Cat's,* Hugo goes and has a big T-bone at the *Road House,* and then goes into *Fat Cat's.* Ransom and I was in there having a beer and saw the whole thing." Natty glanced at Sally who made her smile as she made a contorted face to the back of Ransom's head. "Well, Hugo's all fired up and ready for action, getting himself a lap dance from that big girl. Doreen? You know, the one with the *huge* melons?"

"I'll have to take your word for that Roy," Natty responded.

"Yeah well, Paxton's shuckin' and jivin' and really getting into it and he's got a fist full of twenties ready to fly, when *boom,* he hits the floor like he fell out of a damn airplane. *Dead,* dead as a mackerel. Heart attack it looked like. Ransom jumped down there and pounded his chest and blew some air into him for a while but he's so fat, nothing's going to work on him."

"Well you should have had Sally do the mouth-to-mouth part," Natty said, with a wink to her sister-in-law. "That would have got Paxton's heart pumping again. He *sure* was hot for Sal."

Buck sat up slowly on the deck and tossed his empty beer can toward a box next to the stairs. He hadn't shaved for several days, and his black goatee was a little longer than he normally kept it. At the front and top of his head, his jet-black hair shot straight up like short porcupine quills. At the sides, it was longer and slicked straight back. Black wrap-around sunglasses with the flared wings covered his eyes. As always, whenever Buck did *anything,* he commanded attention.

He spoke with a low, gravelly, tired voice. "Well I'm glad you think this is so damn funny Nat. After all the time I spent with that fat asshole. Getting close to him. Drinking with him. Introducing him to my buddies. Making him feel like maybe he wasn't a *complete fucking dork*, just so's he'll put in the good word for me to get a decent job at the power plant, and I got him to the point where he says 'no problem Buck, you're in, *guaranteed',* and then . . ." Buck stood up pulling his tee-shirt off over his muscular chest and shoulders. Tossing it down on the deck, he slowly, achingly, shuffled toward the door of the trailer. "So now they'll send some new asshole down here and he don't know me from Jack-shit-out-a-luck and I get fucked again." The metal screen door slammed behind him.

Sally broke the silence that followed. "So how's your mama Nat?"

Natty immediately thought about the Angel Mountain problem. She decided to leave it alone for now. This wouldn't be the most sympathetic audience to enlist in a crusade against a mountaintop-removal mining project for Angel Mountain. In fact, with the possible exception of Sally, Natty knew that on this issue, she would be standing alone against the entire Oakes clan. Maybe the whole thing would just go away, she hoped. She didn't need any more friction in her relationship with Buck.

"Mama's fine Sal," Natty answered. "We had real nice visit. It was just beautiful up on Angel Mountain, really beautiful."

Chapter 6

The July heat shimmered across the yard in waves from a merciless afternoon sun. It hadn't rained in the northeast in weeks and a dusty haze hung in the air. Not the best day to be working on the stumps, Charlie Burden concluded as he sat down to rest on the edge of the hole he'd excavated around what remained of a large maple. The project was at one time to be Ellen's tennis court, but over the years, as their involvement with *Hickory Hills Country Club* became more extensive, her desire for a backyard tennis court waned. Now it was just an enjoyable project, and a good physical workout that Charlie could return to with no set timetable.

He wiped the sweat from his face with his balled up T-shirt and looked down the hill toward the pool and the house. It was a beautiful house, and a wonderful home, though from a practical standpoint, much too big now for just he and Ellen, but still not as large as the *hacienda* that Ellen had her eye on.

Charlie saw Ellen come out the back door and through the garden with the cordless phone in one hand and in the other, a tall plastic cup he knew would be filled with ice water. She made her way around the pool and up the grassy slope.

"It's Scottie. He's in his car somewhere." Ellen smiled down at Charlie as she handed him the phone and the ice water at the same time. Charlie rested the phone in his lap and took a long drink.

"Thanks. Anything important? he asked, gesturing to the phone.

"Just something about business, you know Scottie." Ellen sat on a nearby stump to eavesdrop while Charlie spoke to their son.

"Hi Scott, how are you?"

"I'm driving up to Nahant to look at some property, investment property on the water. You may want to get into this, I'll let you know." Scott was speaking quickly as always and loudly into the car phone. Charlie could hear the air rushing by. He could picture his son speeding up Route 128 in the Porsche twin–turbo Carrera, with the top down, his lap-top opened in the seat next to him. "Dad, real quick. What's Duncan up to, do you know? Lots of buzz late Friday and all day yesterday. CanAmex in another big tender. Word is it's CES. What do you know?"

Charlie disliked it when his son treated him like just another one of his many sources of financial intelligence. He'd also been through this before regarding Scott's squeezing him to supply inside information about CanAmex, which under Duncan McCord's stewardship had been a very active and aggressive force in the world of global acquisitions. Hundreds of millions of dollars could be made on the knowledge of CanAmex's intentions. And Scott, Charlie continually had to remind himself, was not just some hack stockbroker looking to make a few points on a hot tip. He was a stock analyst for Fidelity, a front-line player in the big leagues of international investments.

Charlie couldn't confirm that CanAmex was going after Continental Electric Systems, but he knew it was probably true. He recalled Duncan talking about CES two years ago. And now it fit the profile for a CanAmex takeover like a glove. Continental was a huge utility conglomerate in its own right that had been on an aggressive merger and acquisition schedule for several years. Most of Continental's growth had come in the last few years during the acquisition frenzy caused by deregulation of the nation's electric and natural gas utilities. Like many other publicly held utilities, Continental responded to the challenges of open market competition by getting bigger. Much bigger. It was now big enough to be of interest to CanAmex.

"Yes Scott, I'm fine, how are you? Your mother wants to know when you're getting married." Ellen flashed Charlie a quick smile.

"Sorry Dad, but I've got a call holding here I have to take. Listen, just tell me if it's CES, okay? Can you do that?"

Charlie could see that his son was beyond any small talk on this call. "No Scott, I can't confirm that. I don't know anything about CanAmex going after CES. I haven't heard anything. I haven't talked to Duncan in over a month."

"Okay Dad, fine. That's all right." Scott was unable to hide the irritation in his voice. They'd been over this ground before. "Say bye to Mom for me, I really need to go now. I'll let you know about this Nahant property. We may want to get you out of the pharmaceuticals for a while and put it into this. I'll let you know."

"Yeah, let me know what you want to do. I'll see you." Charlie and his son clicked off at the same time.

If Scott wanted to sell some stocks and buy real estate, it was fine with Charlie. His son had complete control of Charlie's investment portfolio. In just a few years, Scott had transformed Charlie's investments from a conservative collection of venerable blue chips worth around six hundred thousand, into a diversified selection of international holdings with a value of over one and a half million. In the last year alone, Scott had increased the value of Charlie's portfolio by a third with his keen insight and superb timing in the buying and selling of high-flying Internet stocks.

The increase in value of his investments seemed like an obscene amount to Charlie. To be able to make that much money so quickly without benefit of any constructive labor or even a creative idea worried him. *Should it be that easy? Is there a payback coming down the road?* And most problematical to him, *is somebody else now paying the tab so he can live on easy street?* The economics at work in the creation of his wealth puzzled Charlie. Along with his annual income that, with bonus, averaged between three and six hundred thousand a year, and his 401K that was currently worth around a million, Charlie knew he didn't have to worry about their financial security. But when he dwelled on it, he couldn't help thinking about his old friend Cecil, who he knew, was smarter than he was, had about as much education with law school, but had always struggled financially and whose only hope of attaining the kind of wealth that Charlie had, came from the hand-full of *Power Ball* and *Big Game* tickets he purchased religiously each week. *Was it just that Cecil was black and fat and unlucky? Or was it only because Charlie had gotten a hockey scholarship to Michigan and happened to play on the same line and room with Duncan McCord? If not couldn't he very easily be Cecil's neighbor in North Haven? Maybe that wouldn't be so bad,* Charlie thought on some days.

"Scott just called to say hi and say that he loves his mother very much," Charlie joked as he put the phone down. Ellen smiled and looked down at the house but stayed seated on the stump. Something was on her mind.

"Charlie, we need to talk." Ellen sounded forceful but not confrontational.

Charlie had come to hate hearing those words over the years. It always meant that Ellen was serious about something and wanted Charlie to know it before the conversation started. He particularly didn't want to hear those words now. He didn't want to talk about Rafael Escobar. He didn't want to, for the first time in their marriage, have to talk about infidelity or falling out of love. Women, he guessed would always be better at these conversations and he didn't want to hear what he was afraid Ellen was going to say.

"Actually there are two things I want to talk about. First, is the house. Martha's pressing me about Quail Hollow. Said there's some new interest, who she's afraid will put in a bid, and she wants us to get it of course." Martha, Charlie knew, was a real estate agent, a good friend of Ellen's and a member of Hickory Hills.

"I'm sure she does." Charlie answered trying to sound more matter-of-fact than sarcastic.

"And if we are going to move, we need to list our house very soon. It's already the middle of summer. Martha thinks it would sell quickly if we priced it properly."

Priced it properly. Thanks very much Martha. A smile flickered across Charlie's face. *Typical real estate agent. A quick commission beats a big commission every time.*

"What's the second thing you wanted to talk about?" Charlie asked, still wondering if there was a more personal issue on Ellen's agenda.

"It's nothing, A minor thing." Ellen paused before going on. "Jennifer needs a new car. That's all. I want to surprise her when she comes out at the beginning of September, Labor Day weekend."

So these were Ellen's pressing issues – buying a house, buying a car. Charlie was both relieved and disappointed that his wife didn't have any weightier concerns on her mind. "Jen *doesn't* need a new car," Charlie said. "Her Camry is fine, it's only five years old. Those things last forever." *Plus in less than a year she'll be graduating from one of the finest MBA programs in the world, and then marrying a fucking dentist, and their household income will be in the stratosphere for two people in their twenties, so let them buy their own damn cars!* "But if you really have your heart set on continuing to spoil your children long after the job's been so well done, then it's all right, I don't mind. But don't get too exotic, okay? What did you have in mind?"

Ellen smiled thinly at Charlie's obvious ploy to give in reluctantly on the car before taking up the more important issue of the house. "Oh I think a new Saab would be fine. She'd like that.

"Charlie, lets talk about the Quail Hollow house. It's something that I really want to do, want *us* to . . ." She was interrupted by the shrill buzzing of the cordless phone sitting on the ground next to Charlie.

"Saved by the bell." Charlie gave Ellen a mischievous smile.

Lucien Mackey's deep baritone even at a normal tone sounded louder than most men. "Charlie? Charlie we need to talk"

"You sound just like Ellen," Charlie answered.

"How is the gorgeous Mrs. Burden?"

"She's fine. She says hello."

Lucien was anxious to get to the point. "Listen Charlie, CanAmex is coming to town later tonight. Jack Torkelson called me this morning. They'll be in tomorrow. There are some important issues we need to address. They're making a play for Continental and we've also got some problems in West Virginia. Somehow they're all related. Torkelson was a little vague, but he's bringing the whole crew in, plus some lawyers up from West Virginia, so we have to get ready. It's a different bunch we're dealing with now that your friend Duncan and Red Landon are above all this."

"So it's true. They're going after Continental. Scott called me a few minutes ago looking for confirmation."

"Tough to keep one that big under wraps. Official word will be out in London in a few hours. Doesn't really affect us but Torkelson's got some issues we need to get ready for."

"That's fine Lucien, I'll be in early. There was actually something I needed to talk to you about too."

"You mean that thing you mentioned to Mal Berman last week, about getting out into the field for a while?"

Charlie was surprised. "Mal talked to you about that? Is that okay that I brought it up with him?"

"Course it is Charlie. We have no secrets from Mal. He and I and Carlos had a nice dinner together in the city last night. Mal's looking out for you. He told me about your, lets call it *professional angst,* and I think we have some good news for you, and CanAmex will approve also. But we can talk about it all tomorrow, seven AM, we'll have breakfast brought in."

Charlie was elated and excited, but puzzled at the same time by Lucien's remarks. What would CanAmex have to do with Charlie's going to China to build the second dam? It wasn't a CanAmex project - one of the few big power generation projects under construction anywhere in the world that CanAmex didn't at least have some interest in. Going to China would mean that Charlie would be leaving *new business* and leaving the CanAmex account entirely. Is that what they were approving? Getting Charlie off the account? Charlie didn't get along well with Jack Torkelson, CanAmex's *Director of U.S. Operations,* or his staff, and Charlie was embarrassed that Torkelson would call Lucien directly to set up an important meeting with Dietrich Delahunt & Mackey. But this wasn't the first time in the past year that Torkelson had gone around him, sending a message to the DD&M hierarchy that Torkelson didn't necessarily approve of

Duncan McCord's hand-picked CanAmex account manager. Even so, Lucien and Torkelson both knew that of the three of them, only Charlie had the number to Duncan's personal cell phone and his private e-mail address.

"Now Charlie, I've got some bad news I'm afraid, but it's part of our situation. You of course know Hugo Paxton, our Lead Engineer down in Red Bone."

"Sure I know Hugo. Spent a lot of time with him going over the project. He's a little strange but a good . . ."

Lucien interrupted. "Paxton died last night Charlie. Massive heart attack. Drunk. In a strip bar down there somewhere. They tried to revive him but he never even made it to the hospital."

"*Oh God,* Lucien, I can't *believe* that. He was a young man, just in his forties. He was . . ."

"He was a *liability* Charlie. A good builder but a time bomb ready to explode and we both know it. But it is a shame, such a damn waste. His deputy, that young fellow, Summers, Terry Summers is coming up tonight. He'll brief us on the project. There's a problem with the project, potentially a pretty expensive one, but Summers will fill us in."

Charlie remembered Terry Summers. He'd interviewed him several years earlier when he was joining the firm. An impressive, capable young engineer from southern California—prep school, undergraduate at UCLA, Masters from Cal Tech —although a little cocky and arrogant. "Yeah, I know Summers. Very sharp. Very capable."

"But still a little young, a little green. Let's see what he has to say tomorrow." Lucien signed off.

Charlie thought about Hugo Paxton. He knew Paxton was divorced and had spent a lot of his career in Asia. In fact he only took the West Virginia project so he could get back to China. It suddenly dawned on Charlie that Paxton's untimely demise was probably fortuitous for himself. That's what Lucien's *good news* was referring to.

Ellen jarred him out of his thoughts about Paxton. "Charlie, the house, it's important to me. You know we can afford it. We don't *need* to live here any more." She was pressing hard.

Charlie knew he couldn't avoid this discussion any longer. "Ellen the timing isn't right. That phone call, it was Lucien. Some things are happening at the company, some changes are happening."

"Involving you?" Ellen had leaned forward with her eyes narrowed, sensing something serious was about to surface.

"Yes it involves me. Because I've requested a change." Charlie grimaced slightly, knowing that the hard part was coming. "I need to get away for a while, away from New York. I need to be an engineer again, off of *new-business*. I want to *build* something Ellen. That's important to me. I'm tired of the politics and the meetings and all the contracts and financial bullshit. It's strangling me. I need to *build* something, something to be proud of, that I can look back on and say that I put that up and the world's a better place because of it. It's what being an engineer is all about." He looked directly at his wife and continued. "I also need a change *personally. We* need a change. We need to figure out what our *life-after-kids* is going to be about."

Ellen saw her opening. "I *know* that Charlie. That's what the house is all *about.* A change. Something different for us now that the children are almost on their own."

"No, that's not what I'm talking about. I'm not talking about *material possessions* and raising our standard of living another notch to impress the Hickory Hills crowd."

"Oh Charlie, that's not fair," she interrupted. Ellen shook her head irritably. "So what does all this mean, what do you want to do Charlie?"

"I've asked to be transferred to China, to work on the second dam project. And Ellen, I want *us* to go. Both of us, together. Sell the house and when we come back we'll figure out what we want to do, where and how we want to live."

She looked at him blankly for a few seconds, trying to digest the meaning of his words. "*China,*" Ellen said softly looking away.

"Lucien just gave me his approval," Charlie added.

"*China,*" Ellen repeated a little louder. She turned her gaze out toward the house and spoke in a calm, level voice. "Charlie, have you lost your fucking mind? Sell the house and move to *China,* the two of us, like we're in the *goddamn* Peace Corps or something. You want me to pack up and move to China, so you can play in the mud with your steam shovels and bulldozers and . . ."

"I'll go without you Ellen. I love you and I want you to be with me but this is important to me. I'm suffocating in this job now." After a pause he decided it was time get it all out. "And you know things aren't right with us." He hesitated. "I know about Escobar." He watched her carefully for her reaction to his revelation but she remained expressionless.

She sounded weary, tired of the entire conversation when she looked back at him. "I know you do Charlie, I know you know." She stood and brushed the dirt off the back of her skirt. "I'm sorry you found out about that Charlie. It would have just passed. It was . . . an aberration, something I had to do, I needed to . . . well I don't expect you to understand. But it doesn't mean anything, it never did. It's nothing now. In the past."

Ellen took a few steps down the hill before turning back to face Charlie once more. "Charlie, *you* go to China. Do what you have to do, build what you have to build. We'll be okay. I'll still be here when you get back. I'll fly over a few times a year. We can meet in Tokyo or Singapore or someplace. But Charlie, I *can't* go to China. I'm just . . . I'm just too *busy* to go to China." She took a few steps down the hill before Charlie stopped her.

"Ellen, what color is it?"

"What?

"The Saab, what color is it?"

She smiled up at her husband. "It's white Charlie, a convertible with a black top and a tan leather interior."

"Jen will love it."

"Yeah, she will," Ellen replied, turning back toward the house.

* * *

Turning south onto Park Avenue, the building that was for so long the Pan American Building looming over the street several blocks ahead made Charlie think about actually going to China. He'd have to check his passport and shots and talk to the guys in the San Francisco office, and what else? He'd have Nina Matlin, the head librarian/researcher at DD&M, brief him on traveling to China. Nina would know everything there was to know about a DD&M project locale. If everything worked out right, he would be able to hand off his projects and be ready to go in as little as eight weeks, around mid September. It was a much simpler undertaking with Ellen not going.

The sixth floor was already humming with activity when Charlie got off the elevator. Several strange faces were sitting in the waiting area, and a waiter from the catering company was pushing a cart with three coffee urns and a large platter of bagels and muffins covered by tight clear plastic. The door to the main conference room was open as Charlie passed by. He looked in and saw Jack Torkelson and his right hand man, Larry Tuthill, the director of CanAmex's U.S. power generation facilities, along with four or five other CanAmex managers and several men he didn't recognize. They appeared ready to commence their meeting.

In his office, Charlie put his briefcase on the glass coffee table, hung up his jacket and quickly checked his e-mail. He only had a few minutes until he needed to be in Lucien's office. A pair of quick soft raps on his open door made Charlie look up from his computer. Warren Brand, a partner and member of the executive committee came through the door, his hand extended, a disarming smile on his face. Brand, a consummate office politician was the youngest partner in the firm and undeniably, the most ambitious. Warren Brand liked to get up close and speak in low tones that made every conversation seem of vital importance. "Charlie, I think congratulations are in order here. Getting back out into the field. That's *laudable*. It's brave, courageous and bold is what it is my friend!"

So the word was out, Lucien must have already tested the waters with some members of the executive committee. Still, it came as a surprise that Brand seemed to be signaling the executive committee's approval of Charlie's transfer to China. "Thanks Warren, yeah it's what I need to do. So the word is already out?"

"Not officially, 'til after the exec meets, but yeah a few people know. Charlie listen, I know this may seem a bit opportunistic, but I wanted to be the first to talk to you about the *tickets*." Brand was moving in even closer and talking more softly, as he usually did when he was closing in on his real objective.

"Tickets? What tickets?" Charlie was genuinely baffled.

"*The* tickets Charlie." Brand was almost whispering. "Your *New York football Giants tickets.* I'll pay you for them of course, whatever's fair, you know that. I'm not looking for a gift here. It's just that you probably won't be using them this season, and you know I'll put them to good use."

Charlie had to stifle a laugh. *Typical Brand, like a vulture, after his Giants tickets.* He hadn't given any thought to the upcoming football season or the tickets that had arrived by certified mail only a week ago. The season tickets were a gift from Ellen's father, Augie D'Angelo who after a few years in federal prison finally accepted the fact that he'd be an old man before he'd ever see another Giants game.

"I'll have to let you know about the tickets Warren, but thanks for reminding me. I need to run right now but I'll get back to you." Charlie ushered Brand toward the door so he could get to his meeting with Lucien Mackey. He knew right away whom he'd be giving his tickets to and it wouldn't be Warren Brand. Plus, he'd still be around for a few games if he didn't leave for China until late September. It would be fun to get out to the Meadowlands for a couple of games before he left. Charlie still enjoyed watching football, the last of the major sports that he was still enthusiastic about. Greed and free-agency, over-expansion, too much hype and too many games, had spoiled baseball, basketball and even hockey. Football suffered from many of the same ills, particularly its meaningless exhibition season, but at least the regular season games meant something and the season was short enough to enjoy. Charlie liked to have a team to root for but after the Giants, Michigan hockey, football and basketball, it was hard to generate any real passion for a team any more. He still tried to follow the Yankees and Rangers, occasionally using DD&M's tickets, but it was a struggle. More and more he saw major league sports as just another glaring example of the polarization of the classes. Sports had become a big money, big-ticket business where the best and truest fans - the working class to whom a sports team's success or failure really meant something - were now priced out of the market, relegated to a seat in front of the TV. On the other end, Charlie had friends, who he knew would only go to a game if they had *exclusive- class* tickets in a corporate or luxury box, or attended only *playoff games* or marquis event*s* – *The Super Bowl, The Masters, U.S. Open, The Final Four,* or *The World Series* – *ego-fans* that used sports as a trophy of personal success. Warren Brand was definitely a *corporate box* and *marquis event* guy. Charlie suspected that Brand wouldn't actually use the Giants tickets himself but wanted them to give to his butcher or the starter at his country club or whomever else he wanted to impress. *Brand could buy his own Giants tickets from a broker.*

Charlie put on his jacket and started down the hall to the corner office of Lucien Mackey. Meetings with the managing partner were always illuminating and inspirational experiences. Charlie had a feeling that this one would be the start of a new chapter in his career at Dietrich Delahunt & Mackey.

Chapter 7

Finally it rained. A hot summer rain, lightly at first but enough to force Natty to roll up the driver's side window almost all the way. With no air conditioning, it was hot and muggy in the small car. And Natty was tired. She'd already seen five clients and covered a lot of miles. She was glad the day was over and wouldn't be doing any more blood pressures or sponge baths, or wrapping any more varicose legs. A cold shower and a beer on the porch would be heaven, but she needed to make one more stop, an unscheduled stop, before heading home.

Natty had been thinking about Birdie Merkely since the previous Thursday night when Birdie had called and told Natty not to come by on Friday, that some of the church ladies were coming to take her out for lunch, and anyway, she was feeling better and Natty could skip her for this week. Something about her call didn't settle just right with Natty. Birdie sounded maybe a little too chipper about the whole affair.

Natty had been taking care of Birdie Merkely for the past year and a half since her broken hip and Birdie hadn't been doing well lately. Her arthritis had gotten worse and her hip was healing slowly, leaving her in a fairly constant state of discomfort and often, intense pain. She had also become more and more sullen and withdrawn, a distinct change from the always cheerful, optimistic personality that gave rise to her life-long nickname.

At the turnoff to Ledger Mountain Road, a dirt and gravel path that led several miles up to Birdie Merkely's cabin, Natty pulled into the small gas station and market on the corner. She parked next to the single gas pump, the needle of the gas gauge resting menacingly on the E.

As the rain began to ease up, Natty reached into the back seat and brought up her knitted handbag and counted her money. *Sixteen dollars,* to buy gas and the groceries she always brought up to Birdie. *Damn, where did the money go all the time?* She'd buy Birdie's food first and save a little bit for gas, just to get her up to the cabin where Birdie would reimburse her for the groceries like she always did.

Inside the store, Natty took a hand basket and walked about the cramped aisles picking out the items that she knew by heart after shopping for Birdie so many times before, leaving out the nonessentials. The *Ritz Crackers,* grape jelly, half dozen eggs, quart of milk, quart of cranberry juice, quart of ginger ale, a small can of Spam, small can of *Bumble Bee* tuna (which Natty would have to open for her and leave in the refrigerator), the sliced turkey, loaf of dark bread, were all definites. She'd leave out the soup, the *Oreo Cookies,* ice cream, and sliced ham, and the lettuce was too expensive anyway. The total still came to $15.11. Natty gave the clerk the sixteen dollars and told him to put the change towards her gasoline. "The *whole eighty-nine cents*?" he asked.

On her way out, Natty noticed a small gray-haired woman coming into the store that she recognized as a Mrs. Petrie who was a friend of Birdie Merkely and a member of her church.

"Hello there Mrs. Petrie," Natty called over to her.

The woman looked up puzzled, straining her memory to identify the thin girl with the friendly voice who knew her name.

Natty came to her aid. "I'm going up to see Birdie. I look in on Birdie."

The woman smiled with recognition. "Oh yes, that's right, you're Birdie's nurse. We met once up at her house."

"Yeah, that's right. Listen, Mrs. Petrie, have you seen Birdie recently, did you take her out to lunch last Friday?"

"Oh no, no dear, not for lunch. But I did see Birdie, yes, it was Friday. She called in the morning and wanted to get her hair done, she said," Mrs. Petrie chuckled, "which was a queer thing for sure, as I can't ever remember Birdie having *anything* done to her hair before."

"So you didn't have lunch with her?"

"Lordy no, just picked her up and took her down to that little beauty parlor in Gary, went and did my errands and brought her back up the hill later on. Didn't even invite me in for tea or nothin'." With that, the old woman turned to go about her business. Natty watched her for a second and then started out of the store. The sound of the old woman's voice stopped her. "Honey you be careful of that dip in the road 'bout half ways up where the water runs through that gully. Sometimes with quick storms like this, the water can come running down real sudden like through there."

"Yes ma'am, that's right. Thank you. I'll watch for it," Natty answered. Mrs. Petrie probably worried about flash floods more than Natty did, simply because she was older and had more experience with the havoc that could result when millions of gallons of water, gathered quickly in a storm by the wide arms of the mountains, were sent ripping down narrow streambeds into the valleys. But Natty had seen enough to have a healthy fear of fast moving water.

It was still raining while Natty pumped the gas into the Accord's empty tank. In the car she found her blue baseball cap with the red *Spider-man* logo on the front, that kept the rain out of her face a little, but after a few seconds she was pretty well soaked. The pump clinked off almost as soon as she'd started it. It read *$.89. Right to the penny.* Not much more than a couple of ounces of gas. Enough she figured to get her up the mountain and down.

Ledger Hollow was one of the many isolated pockets of poverty that were hidden away in the rugged landscape of McDowell County. Most of the inhabitants of the ramshackle huts and cabins along the lower portion of Ledger Mountain Road lived well below the poverty line. Natty had had two other clients in the hollow a few years earlier so she was familiar with the area even before taking on Birdie Merkely.

A hundred yards beyond the railroad tracks running behind the store, on the left side of the road stood a line of sprawling shacks more or less connected by the additions put on over the years. Between the cabins and the road, a huge puddle had formed in the hard bare ground and a dozen or so children of various ages were playing, splashing each other and throwing mud balls. Natty pulled the car over to say hello to one of the older children that she recognized. The boy knew who she was but was shy in front of the other children and had little to say so Natty just told him to "say hey to your mama for me."

Pulling slowly away from the edge of the road, Natty noticed a woman standing in the doorway of one of the cabins, leaning against the doorframe, holding an infant to her breast. The woman, who was about her own age, eyed Natty dispassionately, without any sign of emotion or recognition. Natty had seen the blank look of despair before, the glassy stare that said she was too tired, too spent, too beaten down by life to care any more. Natty smiled and raised her hand in a small wave to the woman who nodded almost imperceptibly, moving only her eyes to watch as the stranger in the faded red car drove off.

The home that Birdie Merkely had lived in for the past thirty-seven years, sat in a small clearing in the trees about fifty yards up a deeply-rutted dirt driveway. The house was bigger than it looked from the outside, being a little longer front to back than it was wide. To the right of the front door sat two metal chairs, the kind found in front of old motels or rental cabins. At the side of the house, beyond the end of the driveway were two rust-stained propane tanks.

Natty stood next to her car with the bag of groceries, looking at the house, knowing something wasn't right. The front door was shut, which was rare in the summer. The mountain rising from the rear of the house blocked out the late afternoon sun, but there were no lights on in the dark house. There was no sign of life anywhere.

Out of habit, Natty had taken her small suitcase-like equipment bag out of the car and it stood on the ground at her feet. She pulled the strap over her shoulder and readied herself for what she hoped she wouldn't find inside. Natty closed her eyes and whispered to herself, *'oh Birdie, please don't do this.'* She went up on the porch and opened the front door.

The small house was cool and dark. The front parlor and dining room were neat and spotless, as always. Even the kitchen was cleaner than Natty had ever seen it. Usually, she had to spend her first few minutes at Birdie's washing up several days worth of dishes and silverware. Today the sink was empty, and the counter top and even the floor, shined from a recent scrubbing.

There was a slightly acrid smell in the house that was noticeable even with a steady breeze wafting through the screened windows. From the rear of the house Natty could make out the sound of soft music. She could see down the hallway that ran through the middle of the house, to Birdie's bedroom at the rear. The door was closed, which was also odd. That was where she knew she would find Birdie. Natty noticed the old rotary phone on the small table in the parlor and wondered if she should just call the Sheriff's office first . . . *look pretty stupid if Birdie was just off visiting for a few days.*

But she wasn't off visiting. Natty stood in the doorway of the bedroom and saw Birdie Merkely laying face up in the middle of the bed, her favorite quilt pulled up to her waist. There was an unmistakable odor of death in the room but not yet overpowering. Moving next to the bed, Natty touched the old woman's forehead and then her cheek with the back of her fingers. She felt briefly for

Birdie's carotid artery for a pulse that she knew wouldn't be there. Finally she just stood at the side of the bed and looked down at Birdie.

The old woman was dressed in her favorite blue silk dress. Her gray hair had recently been set in a tightly curled permanent, and her face had been carefully made-up with red lipstick, a faint smear of rouge on her soft, wrinkled cheeks, and even eyeliner and mascara. She wore a simple strand of yellowing pearls, and gold, scalloped earrings. The makeup and the jewelry made her look much younger than seventy-six and revealed a woman that Natty had never known, a woman who had once enjoyed a life before loneliness and constant pain defined her existence.

Under Birdie's clasped hands, under the fingers gnarled by years of crippling arthritis, Natty could see the faded, yellowing back of what she could tell from the serrated edges, was an old photograph. She pulled it out gently and turned it over to see a young couple sitting on a park bench, squinting slightly from a bright sun that appeared to be directly overhead. Behind the bench was an iron railing and in the distance was a stretch of sandy beach and then deep blue ocean and a pale blue sky. On the bench was a young Birdie Merkely leaning seductively against the young man seated next to her, her bright eyes focused on the face of the skinny but rugged looking man in his twenties wearing some kind of military uniform, his billed cap pushed back jauntily on his head, a khaki tie loose at his neck. Both had a look of spontaneous laughter on their faces as if they were responding to a funny comment by someone, maybe the photographer. In the bottom border of the picture in faded blue ink was written, *Pensacola, Fla, 1946.* Natty recognized a young Everett Merkely from his later pictures on the living room wall. Birdie, she calculated, would have been twenty-two in the picture – the image she chose to take with her to the hereafter.

On the table next to the bed, Natty saw a familiar looking plastic prescription bottle. She knew without reading the label that it was Birdie's Darvocet, a sixty-day supply, more than usually prescribed at one time because of the remote location of the patient. Also on the table was an empty wineglass, a trace of dried residue at the bottom. Natty walked over to the far corner of the room where the old Victrola was playing the Mozart Clarinet Concerto album that Birdie loved. The perfect music to go to sleep to. She turned off the machine.

In the parlor, Natty called the Sheriff's department and told the dispatcher what she had found. "Do you know who it'll be, which officer will be coming up?" Natty asked

After a short pause the dispatcher replied. "That would be officer Lester, Wayne Lester will be responding ma'am."

"Yeah, great. Thanks." Natty couldn't hide the disappointment in her voice. The one Deputy Sheriff she *didn't* want to have to deal with was Wayne Lester. She had known Lester since high school where he was an obnoxious, over-weight pervert who liked to cruise the halls feeling the backs of girls' blouses while announcing a "bra check." Lester had for a short time in the tenth grade, focused his attentions on Natty, assuming that due to her youthful, undeveloped appearance, and lack of boy friends, she would be a little more receptive than the other girls were. He didn't take rejection by the *"flat-chested little hillbilly"* too well.

Lester's disdain for Natty intensified later, after her marriage to Buck Oakes. His long-standing hatred for Buck was rooted in the unmerciful beating that Buck had administered to the bigger boy one summer afternoon at the baseball field when they were in their early teens. It was a fight, one of many that Buck soon forgot about. But Lester carried the painful memory of being permanently embarrassed in front of a large gang of jeering and cheering kids as Buck's superior boxing skills, strength, and an innate instinct for cruelty, turned Lester into a bloody, staggering, hulk, whose cries for mercy just made the punches come faster and the crowd yell louder.

For years, the memory and the desire for revenge smoldered deep within Wayne Lester, unfulfilled. Until one night during the third year of his new career as a law enforcement officer, working the overnight shift, Lester and another deputy, got the call to respond to a *domestic disturbance* in Oakes Hollow. It was the day of the big announcement about the new power plant to be built in Red Bone. The day the helicopters came.

It wasn't clear from the call *who* was beating *whom*, but Wayne Lester knew who it would be as he went into the trunk of his patrol car to get his heavy, lead-filled riot stick. It was the call that Wayne Lester had been waiting for since becoming a Deputy Sheriff.

Drunk and out of control, Buck could be counted on to resist arrest, especially with a little provocation from Lester as he and the other deputy tried to get Buck into the patrol car in the early morning darkness of Oakes Hollow. The darkness and confusion provided sufficient cover for Lester to administer some solid shots with the heavy stick to Buck's ribcage and a few to the calves and knee caps, but it wasn't until they got Buck to the underground garage of the county lock-up that Lester went to work with a vengeance.

Buck ended up with several broken ribs, a collapsed lung, a broken clavicle, broken nose and jaw, and a fractured tibia. He ended up staying in the hospital two weeks longer than Natty.

Turning on a table lamp in the darkening parlor, Natty's attention was drawn to the several framed photographs that decorated the main wall of the sparsely furnished room. There was a pastel tinted wedding picture, both Birdie and Everett gazing slightly upward and off to the photographer's left, looking young and scared and serious. Another color portrait of Everett in his tan marine uniform. The largest picture on the wall was a grainy, black and white photograph of a group of coal miners, loosely arranged in three rows to get everyone in the picture. Behind the men, a sign on a wood-planked building identified the mine as, "U.S. Steel Number 9." In the dark foreground of the picture, written in script in white marker, was *"November, 1954, Everett, 2nd row, #4.* Natty knew all about Everett Merkely even though he had died in 1985, five years after retiring from thirty-three years in the coal mines of McDowell County. Everett was Birdie's singular interest in life while he was alive and her number one topic of conversation afterward. Everett retired from the mines with emphysema and black lung. His last years, with Birdie at his side, were not pleasant as he gradually suffocated in his own fluids.

Natty thought about the *Pensacola* picture that Birdie had chosen as her final memory of life on earth. She tried to recall the few pictures she had of her and Buck together. None revealed anything like the love and pure joy experienced by the couple in Birdie's picture. She and Buck didn't have a *Pensacola picture*.

Natty went back into Birdie's bedroom and sat in a tall straight-backed wooden chair against the wall a few feet from the end of Birdie's bed. She would stay with her friend while waiting for Deputy Sheriff Lester to arrive. Natty put her head back, folded her arms in front of her chest and gave in to the exhaustion of a long day, closing her eyes, for just a few minutes.

A booming voice a few feet away from her face, startled Natty out of her half-sleep. "Well if it ain't Natty *De*-nit-*Witt* sleeping on the job!"

She looked up to see the hulking figure of Deputy Sheriff Wayne Lester filling the doorway of the bedroom. Six –four and closing in on three hundred pounds, most of it gathered around the huge girth of his waist, Wayne Lester was an intimidating figure dressed out in his police equipment belt with holstered pistol, dangling handcuffs, billy club and mobile radio-phone. Hooked onto his breast pocket was a pair of wire-rimmed, aviator sunglasses. A pencil thin, black mustache adorned a flushed and pockmarked face that widened around the jaw to blend smoothly into a fleshy double chin. The deputy wiggled a toothpick between his crooked teeth and puffy lips as he stood in the doorway, alternately eyeing Natty and the figure on the bed.

Natty resisted the urge to come back with a *Lester the Molester* crack and decided to try to be civil and not get Lester riled up so she could just get out of the house and get home. "Hey Lester, how you been?" Natty answered softly.

"I'm fine Nat, just fine." The deputy was clearly encouraged by Natty's tone. "How you been? I see you running down the road real early sometimes when I'm going through Red Bone headed up to Eve's for breakfast. You lookin' good these days Nat, *real* good. Lookin' like a real woman now."

Maybe it was always a mistake to be civil to a slug like Lester, Natty thought. "Yeah, thanks for noticing Wayne."

Wayne Lester turned and walked toward the bed. "So what have we got here then, *Bye Bye Birdie,* like the movie, right?" Lester chuckled as he leaned over for a closer look. "So what do you think happened here Nat?"

What happened here? God, what do you think happened here Lester? Natty just wanted to go home. She didn't want to talk about Birdie, but she knew she'd be able to leave quicker if she helped Deputy Lester do his job. She got up and stood at the end of the bed.

"What *happened* here Lester," Natty snapped a little too brusquely before catching herself and slowing down and lowering her voice, "is that Birdie got tired of always feeling the pain from her arthritis, and tired of limping and hurting on her bad hip and using a walker." Natty's voice became softer as she looked down at her friend Birdie on the bed. "And she got tired of being alone all the time, having nobody to do things for, nobody to share with, no one to love any more.

No one to love her." Natty paused for a moment. "So she went out and got her hair done, came home and gave her house a good cleaning, got herself all made up pretty as she could, put on her best dress, put on her favorite music, and lay down on the bed with her nice soft quilt there, and had a glass of wine and a bottle of Darvocet pills."

After a few moments of silence signaling that Natty was done, Lester replied. "Yeah, that's probably how it went down alright." He bent over to look at the label on the pill bottle on the table. "She don't smell too bad though for being dead up here a few days. Not like that big nigger we found last summer, dead in his shed a couple weeks. Stunk so bad they had to burn that shed ... "

"Lester, don't use that kind of talk around me. I mean it. Now can I go? I need to get home."

"Well not so fast there Nat. Why don't you go out and sit on the sofa for a bit while I do my investigation in here. Then, I'll come out and you can give me your statement." Lester put his fleshy palm to Natty's back and gently pushed her toward the doorway, taking his hand away with a very subtle sideways rub with his fingertips.

After a few minutes, Lester came out of the bedroom and wandered through the parlor and into the kitchen. Natty saw him take off his equipment belt and pistol and lay it over the back of a kitchen chair.

"Hey, looks like the old bird left some groceries here on the table before she kicked off," Lester called in to Natty.

"I brought that stuff Lester, for Birdie, and she owes me fifteen dollars. You think if we found her purse I could see if she had some money
    and ..."

Coming back into the parlor, Lester cut her off. "No can do Nat. Uh, uh. No can do." he said emphatically shaking his head. "Cannot remove *any* property, especially monetary funds from the scene."

"Aw cut the shit Lester, I need the money for gas. I spent my last dollar on them groceries and I ain't got even a quarter on me."

"That's okay Nat, maybe I'll give you some money for gas, later on." Lester took his beaked sheriff's department cap off and dropped it on one of the rocking chairs as he maneuvered his way slowly around the low oval coffee table to the sofa where Natty was sitting. He reached out and put a spiral notepad and his pocket tape recorder on the table as he sat down in the middle seat of the sofa, right next to Natty.

She went to stand up, but Lester shot his right arm around her back and had a heavy paw on top of her right shoulder pulling her back down. "Now just hold on there Nat, don't be getting jumpy here. I'm just going to take your statement here." The man had edged forward on the couch a little closer to Natty and had turned slightly towards her so that his left leg was now in front of her to block her escape.

Natty was nervous now, suddenly realizing the predicament she was in, alone in a very isolated cabin with a man like Wayne Lester. "Lester you can get my statement sitting at the kitchen table, now why're you doing this?" she pleaded, once again trying to get off the couch.

The policeman tightened his grip with his right arm and slid his left hand over onto Natty's left thigh. Her white poplin pants were still damp from the rain. "You ought to take off these wet clothes Nat and let 'em dry some. We got some time, more than an hour before the M.E. gets up here." He pulled Natty closer to him and started to slide his hand farther up her thigh. Her left hand went to his massive wrist to try to push his hand away with no effect.

Lester leaned in toward Natty's face and did his best to affect a soft, intimate tone. "And I know you could use a little lovin' Nat, stuck with that shit-heel, wife-beating husband of yours."

"Lester, stop this right now!" Natty yelled.

He nuzzled her neck as Natty turned her face away from his. "How is old *Bucko* these days Nat? I hear he's back to visitin' that big gal up in Northfork again. One with the extra ripe melons. You hear that Nat?"

Natty stopped struggling with the stronger man. She knew she wouldn't be able to get away from his grip and she realized that Lester had given her the means to her escape. He'd reminded her of one of his deepest fears.

"Lester, you keep up with this, you take this *any* farther than it's already gone, then I'm going to have to go home and tell my husband everything that's happened here. And what do you think Buck Oakes is going to do after I tell him Wayne Lester tried to rape his wife?" She could feel a slight relaxing of his grip on her shoulder.

Natty went on. "What he's going to do is come and find you, and in front of anybody who wants to watch, cause he ain't going to care that you're wearing a badge Lester, cause he's been just *waiting for an excuse,* for two years now, you know that, and he's going to give you the absolute worst beating of your life. Worse than that beating he gave you when you were kids when Buck beat you with his fists 'til you cried and begged for him to stop."

"Aw fuck you Natty." Lester pushed away from her as he got off the couch. "I ain't afraid of *him*. I ain't afraid of Buck. Fuck him too." But Lester didn't sound convincing as he gathered up his notebook and tape recorder. "Plus he's still on probation. Get in big trouble, assaultin' a law enforcement officer," he added more softly. Then, looking at the floor, "but I guess I made a mistake here. Just takin' a shot Nat, you know, hoping that … well, you can take off now Nat."

"Yeah okay Lester, that's good. That's over. You made a little misjudgment is all." Natty offered as she straightened out her clothes.

The deputy was relieved by the peace offering. "Okay, yeah, thanks Nat. Just got a little carried away for a minute. You're lookin' real good these days Nat, so I was just hoping, you know."

Natty smiled sympathetically trying to ease the large man's embarrassment. "Thanks Lester. But I *am* a married woman." She was relieved the episode was over. Buck didn't need any trouble with Wayne Lester. And, she also didn't need trouble with Lester, who was on the county's Youth Sports Coaches Board that she had to answer to as a soccer coach.

Natty walked past Lester into the bedroom and stood for a minute next to the bed and said good-bye to her friend Birdie. She reached down and squeezed Birdie's hand for a few seconds, then picked up the *Pensacola picture* and stuffed it into her pocket. She wanted some remembrance of Birdie, and her friend's last image of life on earth seemed as fitting as anything else in the house.

In the hallway she stopped to pick up her equipment bag. "Now I got to *go*, Lester. Take care of Birdie for me." She left the grocery bag where it was on the counter and was almost to the front door when she heard Wayne Lester's voice behind her.

"Say Nat, there's something come up you maybe would want to know about. Has to do with your mama and your grandpa Bud's farm up there." Lester was standing in the hallway with his hands in his pockets looking contrite. He had her full attention.

"About three weeks ago, up at the station house, these three lawyer types from Charleston, driving a big *Town Car*, well they come in asking to see the sheriff, no appointment or anything, but Earl's in his office not doing much so he invites 'em on in. Well he always leaves his door open and my desk is right there so I can't help overhearing that these fellows are asking all about Bud and Alice DeWitt, and about Petey and your mama, and all about the farm and everything."

Natty lowered her equipment bag back down to the floor and turned toward Lester, her eyes squinting in rapt concentration. "Go on Lester."

"They was specially interested in knowing if Sheriff Mullins ever had any kind of trouble with the DeWitts, ever had any complaints from anyone or had to arrest anyone up on Angel Mountain. Well of course the sheriff had a good chuckle over all that and tells these boys that the DeWitts and your mama are about the nicest, least troublesome people in McDowell County. Course he did recall to 'em about Petey taking a pinch there for selling the dope and for growing it back when Petey was, what, twenty or so? But that was a long time ago and wasn't hardly anything to talk about anyways, so I don't think they was too interested in that."

"They say anything else Lester? You sure they were lawyers?"

"That was about it. Well two of them were lawyers anyway, one, a big fellah with silver hair, sharp looking guy, did most of the talking, and a younger guy with him had a big silver briefcase like lawyers got sometimes. The third guy, he looked more like a private dick to me but I can't be certain."

"Okay thanks Lester. I'm sure it's nothing." Natty headed out the front door.

"Yeah, okay Nat. Probably nothing. See you around," answered Lester as he watched Natty go through the door. But the deputy knew it wasn't *nothing*. Something was brewing up on Angel Mountain, and he could sense opportunity in the visitors from Charleston. They would be coming back to McDowell County, Lester was certain of that.

Halfway to her car, Lester called out to her again, from the doorway. "So we're okay Nat, right? You ain't going to say nothin' about . . . you ain't saying nothing to Buck or anyone?"

Natty turned her head to reply as she walked to her car. "Yeah, we're okay Lester. Take care of Birdie. I'll see you." She put her case in the back seat.

But there was something else out there, hanging over her now, that she couldn't leave without knowing. She stood with her hands on the top of the open door and looked back at Wayne Lester who was watching her from the porch. "Lester, what you said in there, about that woman in Northfork. You just bringing up old news, or you knowing something?"

The deputy shrugged his shoulders and looked off in the distance through the trees at the view of the valley to the northeast, a new toothpick bobbing between his teeth. "Well Nat, I can't personally vouch for anything, but, you know, cops hear lots of stuff, some true, some ain't." He looked back at Natty. "So, you know, maybe there's nothin' to it at all."

Natty pursed her lips in a tight smile and gave Lester a brief nod of understanding. She turned the Honda around in the tall weeds in front of the house and drove past Lester's shiny white police cruiser, down the long driveway and onto Ledger Mountain Road feeling as empty and alone as she had in a long time.

Natty ran out of gas a mile from Oakes Hollow. The Honda's engine went quiet and then chugged a few times as she pulled onto the sandy shoulder of the road. Natty sighed and let out a sarcastic chuckle at what was such a fitting end to the day. She pulled off her white nursing shoes and knee-high nylons, tossed them into the back seat, stuffed her purse under the front seat, and sprinted home running barefoot down the middle of South County Road, finally allowing the tears to flow freely for her friend Birdie Merkely.

Just after midnight, a dark blue Crown Victoria with a spotlight mounted on the driver's side door, made the sharp turn onto Angel Mountain Road. Tinted windows would have concealed the two men in the front seat even in broad daylight. A half mile below the DeWitt farm, the big car pulled off the road into the well-hidden driveway of a cabin that had long ago been destroyed by fire. The driver turned off the ignition and looked at his watch.

"We wait," he said quietly to the other man. The passenger just grunted and stared straight ahead at the still standing, lower half of the cabin's chimney, illuminated by the light of a nearly full moon.

"Tell me again why we gotta do this tonight, with a full moon?" The passenger asked, breaking the silence in the car.

"You want to clomp around up there on that farm with flashlights? Shit, the lights'd wake up everybody in that house. You'd be pushing through them corn rows with your flashlight, and *bam,* you run smack into that old pig farmer with his shotgun ready to blast your balls off, and he probably would."

"Yeah, okay. But I still don't like all this moonlight," the passenger replied.

"Gotta be able to see what we're looking for. And I want to do this quick, with no trace. We find what we're looking for, if it's there, then we get out with nobody knowin' we were up here. Cover your tracks."

At one-thirty, the men left the car and started walking up Angel Mountain Road toward the DeWitt farm. They were dressed entirely in black and had smeared their faces and hands with black camouflage cream. The driver wore a black lightweight nylon jacket, zipped up to cover his shoulder holster and silver-finished forty-five caliber automatic. Both men carried small garden-size bamboo rakes.

Two hundred yards below the DeWitt house the men left the road and went through the trees and over the short stone wall that marked the road-side boundary of the farm. They found the dirt road that looped around the circumference of the farm and followed it first down to the chicken coops and then back up along the far side of the corn field. The route they chose was the long way around, but it was entirely out of sight of the house.

They split up as they entered the field. The passenger went quickly up to the end of the field and searched in a back-and-forth pattern as he made his way back toward the driver, who was doing the same from the lower end. They would meet somewhere around the middle of the field.

The cornfield was only about four acres, which they calculated should take them less than thirty minutes. What they were looking for would be very evident, even in the dim light of the moon. They each moved methodically down the rows between the towering corn stalks, dragging the small rakes behind them to obliterate their tracks. If they found nothing, evidence of their tracks wouldn't matter. If their search was successful, it would be imperative that they left no trace.

After covering what seemed like half the field, the driver stopped to listen for signs of his partner. He heard nothing, and began to worry. *Had the farmer been awakened and sneaked out and got the drop on him?* He pushed carefully through another row of stalks and traversed the field slowly, stopping several times to listen. *Where the hell did he go? They should have met up by now.*

At the middle of the next row, near the center of the entire field, the driver heard a soft *pssst* from through the next row of stalks, only a few yards away from him. He reached inside his jacket for the thick handle of the forty-five and pushed through the corn. He found his partner squatting on his haunches, amid a distinctly different looking section of the field covered with dozens of shorter, weedier looking plants. The smaller man looked up at him with a wide grin shining through his black-smeared face as he broke off a branch of a marijuana plant to take with them. "Bingo," he whispered to his partner.

Chapter 8

The door to Lucien Mackey's corner office was open, as it usually was. Charlie Burden rapped a knuckle as he walked in. The senior partner of Dietrich Delahunt & Mackey was hunched over a large conference table that dominated one end of the massive office. "Well we fucked this up pretty good Charlie." He was peering intently at a set of charts that covered every inch of the worn mahogany tabletop that had seen its share of blueprints and maps over the years. His jacket was off, a troubled look on his face that Charlie recognized as the warning sign that this was going to be a bad day for someone at Dietrich Delahunt & Mackey.

Moving closer to the table, Charlie recognized the layout of the CanAmex plant in West Virginia. "What's the problem down there?"

"Well Charlie, it's pretty simple. The goddamn pond is in the wrong spot. Can you believe that? After all this time? Two years we've been building this thing down there, with Paxton and a battalion of contractors, surveyors, engineers and environmental people crawling all over it and nobody notices that the cooling pond is situated on a hundred foot thick ledge of solid bedrock that a *fucking nuclear bomb couldn't blast through deep enough to . . .*" Lucien stopped and took a deep breath to control his anger. He tossed a pencil down on the chart and stood erect, offering his hand to Charlie, smiling thinly, embarrassed that he'd forgotten his manners. "Good morning Charlie. Thanks for coming in early."

Mackey gestured toward the black leather couch with two matching chairs, separated by a massive glass coffee table. "Come on Charlie, sit down, we need to talk and we don't have a lot of time." Charlie sunk uncomfortably into the center of the couch as Mackey took one of the chairs.

"Terry Summers will be along in a few minutes and, well, we need to come to an agreement here, you and I Charlie, before he gets here."

Charlie had known his boss long enough to know when he was having trouble getting to the point. "Lucien, what's up, what is it you want me to do? You know we'll come to an agreement. We always agree on whatever it is you want." Lucien smiled at Charlie's attempt to loosen him up.

"Charlie, about this China thing, well, you're a valuable asset here Charlie, you know that. You've brought in a lot of business with CanAmex, a *hell* of a lot of business, and we want to accommodate you, and hopefully we'll be able to." Lucien stopped to take a sip of his green tea before going on. "But right now Charlie we've got a problem, and it's not in China, it's in West Virginia, and we've got a problem right here, with CanAmex. They're not happy with this thing with the pond. It's potentially a very expensive problem for them because they okayed all the plans as you know, but understandably, they're not too thrilled with this. Torkelson's on the warpath, and Tuthill, you know, he just takes Torkelson's lead so he's got a hair across his ass too. So what we need to . . ."

Suddenly it all came to Charlie like a brilliant spotlight being snapped on. *Christ, how dense can you be? Lucien's call. Paxton's death. Torkelson and*

Tuthill in town. Terry Summers. Even Warren Brand after his Giants tickets. They want him to go to West Virginia, not China! He wasn't going to be working on one of the engineering marvels of the millennium. They wanted him to baby sit a half-built coal-burner in the back woods of Appalachia.

Lucien was still talking when Charlie came out of his thoughts and interrupted his boss. "You want me to take over the West Virginia project, is that it Lucien?"

"That's it Charlie. CanAmex wants a senior level person down there to straighten this mess out." Lucien paused to reach out and pick up some notes off the table. Without looking at Charlie he continued. "And, Torkelson wants that person to be you Charlie. He thinks you're perfect for the job. It was just a coincidence that at the same time, you happened to bring up your desire to get out into the field for a while, so it's good timing. This would be good for you Charlie."

Charlie rolled his eyeballs. "Lucien, come on. It's West Virginia. The plant's half built already. It'll be on automatic pilot now. I need to *build* something, to create something, something new, that's mine –"

"A year Charlie, maybe less," Lucien broke in. There was a pleading quality in his voice that sounded strangely out of place. "You go down there and help Tuthill with the local politics and fix the pond problem, and you get the turbines in place. They're scheduled to arrive in the spring. Then we'll let Summers mop up and we'll see about China." Charlie noticed that Lucien averted his eyes when he mentioned China.

"Just fix the pond problem and get the turbines in," Charlie was half thinking out loud.

Lucien hesitated. "Well, there is one other issue that Torkelson will brief you on, something they're real concerned about because they think it could have some impact on this take-over of Continental."

Charlie's radar lit up at the mention of the Continental deal. This was big time stuff that you didn't fool around with. Mergers that went bad were serious, expensive, litigious, and career-ending occurrences. Once you made the announcement, the clock was ticking and billions of dollars were at stake, the kind of money that made individuals, companies, politicians and regulators sometimes do curious things. Whatever was happening in West Virginia that could have any effect on the takeover of CES was a lot more serious than a site plan with a cooling pond in the wrong place.

"Okay Lucien let me have it. Before I decide on West Virginia, I want your take on this problem with the CES merger. I want the straight dope before I listen to Torkelson's version."

Lucien got up slowly from his chair and walked over to the door and gently closed it. "Fair enough Charlie. Here's where we stand. Torkelson's ass is hanging out a mile here, Tuthill too. They've been in charge of the whole West Virginia project from the beginning. And they've done nothing illegal, mind you, it's just that they got a little too inside on this deal, did a little too much maneuvering, too much conniving, simply because that's their nature, I think. They can't just do things straight up, like McCord and Red Landon used to. Well, anyway, three years ago Torkelson made a deal with this coal company down there, Ackerly Coal, which is owned by CES, to supply all the coal for the new plant, which as you know, is going to require a hell of a lot of compliance coal. At the same time, they're negotiating with the Governor's economic development people about the taxes and access to the power grid and getting more land adjacent to the property and all that business, holding out that billion dollar carrot your friend Duncan loves to beat people over the head with." Lucien paused for a sip of tea and glanced at his watch before continuing.

"So, someone in the Governor's office, responding to some local politician no doubt, comes up with a condition that all the fuel for the plant should come from mines in that county, McDowell County, a real depressed area of the state. But, the Ackerly guys tell Torkelson that that isn't a problem at all, in fact, it presents a good opportunity to really lower CanAmex's fuel costs for quite some time. Seems that Ackerly owns the rights to a huge seam of good coal down there in McDowell County, enough coal to supply all the fuel for the plant for the next fifteen years, and it's only about ten, twelve miles or so from the plant. An easy trucking operation. Eliminates the need and the expense of putting in a new track spur to the site." Lucien paused to get up and bring a tray of bagels over to the coffee table and place it in front of Charlie.

"So what's Ackerly's problem with the mine," prompted Charlie, anxious to get to the heart of the matter.

"Well the problem is that the coal isn't down in a mine, it's *up*, halfway up a mountain. And, the best way to get the coal out, the most economical way, which of course is what Ackerly and CanAmex are both acutely interested in, is through a surface mining operation."

"So they need some permits."

"More than just permits." Lucien frowned as he thought about the situation he was about to describe. "Charlie, are you familiar with term *mountaintop-removal mining*?

"Vaguely. It's a surface mining technique. But I thought it had been outlawed in most places." Charlie recalled reading about the process in some engineering journal.

"You're right. And more specifically, a State judge has issued an injunction barring the EPA from giving out any permits in West Virginia, where, as you might expect, it had been doing the most damage." Lucien paused, reluctant to put himself and his company so at odds with an important client.

"It's an insidious practice Charlie, mountaintop-removal. It's an environmental crime that for years was rationalized in the name of jobs and local economics. The mining companies would hold a gun to the head of these depressed coal mining areas and say, in effect, if you want us to continue mining operations here and you want the jobs and the taxes, then you have to let us destroy your mountain and fill in your valleys and stream beds." Lucien shook his head ruefully. "It all started out west with those huge surface mines, which brought about the creation of the draglines and all the big earth-moving equipment that we're so familiar with in our industry. The environmental requirements placed on strip miners simply say that after you've exhausted a surface mine, you're required to return the land to its *approximate original contour*."

Charlie interrupted Lucien. "But in Montana and Wyoming, you're basically digging a big shallow hole. When you're done, you fill it in as best you can and contour the land a little and the environment is just reshaped a bit."

"Right, but in the mountains of the east it's not that easy," Lucien continued. "Because of the way the seams run in the big Pocahontas Coal Field of West Virginia, Kentucky and Virginia," Lucien ran his flat hand through the air in an up and down wavy pattern to demonstrate, "there is a lot of coal up in some of the mountains, usually at right around the mid-point of the elevation. So the coal companies, back in the seventies, said, since we've got all this big efficient equipment, let's do surface mines on these mountains just like we do out west. But the whole thing is just a ruse Charlie, it's semantics. These mountain sites aren't surface mines! In no way can they be returned to their original contour, so the famous variance was created which gave the state and the politicians and the EPA and Bureau of Surface Mines an out which basically says, well, just do your best and return the land to a condition that's in *harmony with the natural habitat*." Lucien grimaced in an expression of disgust. It didn't surprise Charlie that Lucien held strong feelings for the subject. He was after all, a consummate environmentalist.

"So they go up in the mountains and they blast away, on a huge scale we're talking about. Charlie, there are mountaintop sites down there in Logan County that have used more explosives than both sides used in the Civil War! Two hundred, three hundred feet or more of overburden, covering an area sometimes as large as ten square miles, and they push it all over the side - everything, the trees, the vegetation, the animal habitats – down into the valleys, covering the streams and the meadows and all the natural growth with rock and sand and mineral deposits to expose the coal seam."

A knock at the office door interrupted Lucien and gave him the welcome opportunity to curtail his tirade that was becoming more of a lecture than a briefing. He took a deep breath and smiled at Charlie. "That would be Summers."

Lucien opened the door and welcomed Terry Summers. He was tall and thin with straight blond hair slicked back in the fashion favored by young professionals. The young engineer wore a very chic light gray summer weight suit with a black shirt and a dark gray tie. He had a wide, classically handsome face with dimpled cheeks and brilliant white teeth that he revealed often with a practiced smile that he flashed on and off as a kind of visual emphasis to his words.

Lucien gestured toward the couch where Charlie was rising. "You remember Charlie Burden of course."

Summers turned and fired a broad smile before moving with slow deliberation toward Charlie's outstretched hand. "Yes. How are you Charlie? Congratulations. That's great, you'll be taking over in West Virginia."

So Summers had already been told. Charlie wondered if Summers comment was another subtle show of arrogance. Or did he really think that the West Virginia post would be a promotion for Charlie? No, he wouldn't be that naïve. Summers had been around a bit. He knew the way up the corporate ladder, and down. He would have figured out that Charlie had been chosen to be Jack Torkelson's sacrificial lamb in case the situation in West Virginia led to the blow up of the Continental merger. And he would have figured out with whom he was going to align himself in order to come out of West Virginia in an advantageous career position.

"Hello Terry. Nice to see you again." They shook hands and Terry Summers took a chair at the end of the coffee table.

Lucien continued the discussion. "Of course not everyone agrees with my position on mountaintop-removal," he said, an obvious invitation for Summers to join in.

With a quick smile at Lucien, Summers unbuttoned his jacket and sat back in the soft leather chair, his arms resting casually along each armrest, legs folded comfortably in front of him. Charlie thought his demeanor in the presence of the chief executive of the company was a little too informal. He was still a cocky young man who had the world by the balls and it wasn't in his makeup to show professional deference even to senior partners of the firm.

Summers turned his attention to Charlie when he spoke. "If you took a poll today of every person living in McDowell County, you'd have a tough time finding a half dozen who would oppose a surface mining permit for Angel Mountain. It's just a big lump of earth with hardly anybody living anywhere near it, and inside it lies enough coal to produce three hundred good mining jobs and millions of dollars of family income and county taxes for the next fifteen, twenty years. It's crazy to take that away from those people just to save an otherwise worthless mountain. They've got plenty of mountains in West Virginia. What they need are jobs and some level ground to build on."

Lucien spread his arms out wide. "And *that* Charlie, is our official position on the matter. We are in support of our client CanAmex and the Ackerly Coal Company in their efforts to get a surface mining permit in West Virginia." Then, with his voice tailing off, rising slowly out of his chair, he added, "no matter how distasteful that prospect is to some of us personally." Lucien Mackey looked drained and tired. He had obviously had a contentious meeting the previous evening with Torkelson and Tuthill.

Charlie suddenly realized the tremendous strain that Lucien was experiencing over this issue. He was being forced to subjugate his own ideals to the needs of a powerful client. With almost any other client, over an environmental conflict, Lucien would find a way to prevail, but CanAmex had become too big, too important to the firm to stand up to. So now he was just trying to wash his hands of the whole West Virginia mess, and he was looking to Charlie to bring DD&M through it with as little damage as possible. As he watched Lucien walk over and sit at his big desk, it occurred to Charlie that he hadn't officially accepted the job as Lead Engineer at the Red Bone site. That's what Lucien had wanted to settle on before Summers arrived but he'd gotten sidetracked. Lucien would be in a fix now – after telling CanAmex and the Executive Committee that Charlie was going to be the guy – if he turned the job down, which, as a partner, he could very well do. He knew he would be taking the job as soon as Lucien asked – he could never refuse his boss, his great friend. But how Lucien must now be agonizing over his decision.

Charlie watched Lucien at his desk as he spoke firmly to Summers. "Terry, first of all, give me our options on the pond problem, then we'll talk about the surface mine issue before we meet with Torkelson and Tuthill." There was suddenly a new sound of authority in the room. Charlie was taking charge of the Red Bone project. He saw Lucien look up at him almost imperceptibly. Charlie flashed him a quick wink across the room that was filled with meaning for the two men.

"There have been a number of scenarios discussed . . ." Summers sounded like he was ready to occupy the floor for a while.

Charlie interrupted the young engineer. "Give me the top two."

"Okay, well there's fast and cheap, and slow and expensive. Fast and cheap is that we just relocate the pond up to some open acreage on the site that we own just inside the northern border of the property, marked by Cold Spring Road. We'd have to make the pond a little deeper and build a levy along the road for about a hundred or so yards but it would be easy excavation and the levy would be nothing to build. That's the way to go. That's what Paxton was going to recommend."

"Sounds easy. So what's the problem with fast and cheap?" Charlie knew there had to be a catch or the problem wouldn't have reached New York.

"Well, the problem is the unknown," Summers continued, "in the form of the town Planning Board. To move the pond we'd have to get a variance to the site plan from the Planning Board at their next meeting, which isn't until September. Anyway, up until now, we haven't had to go before the board for anything. The whole project, as you know, was laid out in Charleston between CanAmex and the Governor's people. That's the way they like to work, at a high level. CanAmex doesn't like to screw around with the locals, and they're big enough, you know . . . when you're ready to spend a billion dollars in a state as poor as West Virginia, you can sidestep a lot of the local crap."

Charlie knew better than anyone how CanAmex liked to operate. To say they preferred to work at a high level was a vast understatement. He recalled Duncan McCord telling him five years earlier that CanAmex that year would spend a hundred and twenty million dollars on lobbyists, political donations, well-connected law firms and public relations companies in Washington, Ottawa, Mexico City, and state capitals throughout the country, to facilitate the CanAmex vision of the future of the electric utility industry. That figure may well have doubled in the last five years.

Terry Summers got up to pour himself a cup of coffee as he continued. "So the problem is, now we go before the board for the first time, and we don't know what they might be thinking, or if they've got some beef with the whole project, like maybe one of our cowboy iron workers ran over one of their dogs or something, and we go in there with our Charleston lawyers and our PR guy and our Power Point show and tell them that we need to move our pond, and these hillbillies just look at each other and laugh and say, '*hell no*' and get up and high-five each other, drop the gavel and go fishing. It could happen."

"And then we've got a real problem," Charlie added. He knew enough about rural politics versus utility companies to know that Summers' scenario wasn't far-fetched.

"And then we're on to option two," Summers continued. "Slow and expensive. We stick with the site plan and blast through the bedrock." Charlie knew what was coming and almost didn't want to hear the gory details.

"All work on the plant stops for four months minimum, all the subs leave and we have to reschedule all the work and all the deliveries until the springtime. We blast away the rock and move it all to who knows where. We postpone delivery of the turbines, which is going to cost a fortune, plus, when it's all done we've got the biggest problem still ahead of us, the . . ."

Charlie finished his sentence. "The structural integrity of the plant that's already been built. It would be a mess no matter how careful we were, all that blasting that close to the main building. We'd be lucky if we didn't have to tear down the whole thing and start over. No, that's not an option." In his mind, Charlie quickly did a rough estimate of the cost of slow and expensive to be a minimum of a hundred million dollars.

Both men knew that simply acquiring more land abutting the site wasn't an option either. The property was located on a strip-mined plateau that was surrounded entirely by steeply sloped, mountainous terrain. There wasn't another suitable site for a man-made cooling pond within ten miles of the site. Plus, for security, safety and environmental compliance reasons, the pond had to be located on the site.

"Okay then," Charlie said quietly, "our only option is we make sure we get the variance from the Planning Board, then we *take* them fishing. Now, tell me how Torkelson's planning to get a variance for a mountaintop-removal permit."

Summers squirmed a little in his chair before answering. "Well as I understand it, they've got a Superior Court judge who's going to lift the injunction, just temporarily, on some technicality that will allow the EPA to issue the variance. It's all being handled out of Charleston and Washington. The EPA, the Bureau of Surface Mines – they've already told their West Virginia people what's going on. The Governor's office is handling the environmentalists – the Appalachian Conservancy – and the DEP. The State is going to cancel a big road project through some forest land up in the northern part of the state that the environmentalists have been fighting for several years. It'll be a major victory for them, plus a couple of big developers get it stuck up the ass, which the tree huggers always love. In return, the Conservancy is going to look the other way on the Angel Mountain variance. Ackerly already has a surface mining permit they got two years ago when this all started. So, the judge lifts the injunction, a few minutes later, the EPA issues the variance, and bam," Summers clapped his hands together for emphasis, "everybody's happy. A few weeks later, the court issues a statement saying the technicality has been cleared up and the injunction is back and force and the environmentalists are satisfied. It's all about this one mountain."

Charlie sat listening, making a few notations on a blank page at the back of his Day-Timer, a list of the parties involved in the plan. He could envision all the hushed, low-tone conversations that had taken place in unofficial venues in Washington and Charleston to put this deal together. CanAmex would have put all their lobbyists, lawyers, and politicians to work on it. There would be no memos, no paper trail. There would have been a lot of cash spread around, plus some dinners, tickets and junkets for the bureaucrats, and more contributions, hard and soft money to the politicians and their phony foundations, and both parties. That's how CanAmex worked. They would have taken care of everything at the high level. So the problem must be on the ground locally, in Red Bone.

"And the best part of the whole initiative Charlie," Summers continued to sell the plan, "is that everyone involved, from the West Virginia delegation in Washington on down, plus the EPA, the Corps of Engineers, and even the environmentalists, all agree that a surface mining permit for Angel Mountain makes a lot of sense. It benefits everyone involved. It's good for the locals who get the much-needed jobs and a huge boost to the local economy. It's good for the State and the County, which reap the tax benefits, and it's good for the environment, now and for the long run. The environmentalists, as I understand it, don't think too much of Angel Mountain to begin with, and they also don't care too much about McDowell County. It's not a real hot spot for hiking and kayaking and mountain biking, and all those things the Granola-heads like." Charlie glanced over to see a look of disdain on Lucien's face.

Summers continued. "You have to understand that the coal that's up there in Angel Mountain is the purest, lowest sulfur coal anywhere in the eastern United States. That coal is going to make the Red Bone plant the cleanest, and most efficient, high-output, coal-fired generator in the world. And it will be for many years."

Charlie recognized the influence of Duncan McCord's long-range vision for CanAmex, on Summers' sales pitch. The environmental card. It was the heart of CanAmex's strategic plan. Be the low-cost producer of the cleanest electricity in the world, and produce more of it than anyone else. And the way to do it was to build huge new generating plants like the one in Red Bone that incorporated massive, state-of-the-art smoke scrubbers, utilizing the latest in selective catalytic reduction technology to reduce nitrogen oxide and sulfur dioxide emissions far below the EPA requirements of the Clean Air Act. It was an expensive strategy. The scrubber unit alone, for the Red Bone plant came with a three hundred million dollar price tag. But how many small, 100 to 500-megawatt coal-fueled power plants will be forced to close over the next ten years by the ever more stringent requirements of the Clean Air Act that CanAmex had had so much influence in drafting. Antiquated facilities, the limited availability and rising cost of low-sulfur coal, and the economics of scrubber technology, would spell the end of hundreds of coal burning plants across the country. Combined with the shut-down of fifty percent of the nation's remaining nuclear capacity over the next ten years and the entire nuclear energy industry within twenty years, the volume of electricity generation that would need to be replaced in the coming years was staggering. At an operating capacity of 3000-megawatts, the Red Bone plant, and several dozen others of similar size, were going to be important weapons in Duncan McCord's vision of the future of the electric industry, but the plants had to produce clean power, and above all, they had to be efficient.

Terry Summers spread his arms wide in summation. "Charlie, the Angel Mountain coal makes the Red Bone plant the cleanest *and* most efficient coal-fired generator in the world, and it brings economic prosperity to the families of McDowell County." He flashed a high wattage grin. "And what CanAmex wants, CanAmex gets."

Ten minutes later, Charlie, Summers and a young lawyer from DD&M's legal department were seated at the boardroom table for their meeting with CanAmex. Jack Torkelson sat quietly at one end of the table, separate from the rest of the CanAmex team lined up across from Charlie and Terry Summers. Larry Tuthill was in charge of the meeting. He introduced two men from CanAmex's legal department that Charlie had never met before.

Tuthill then introduced three lawyers who were principals of Kerns & Yarbrough, "the most prestigious law firm in Charleston, West Virginia." Three of the firm's principals, up from Charleston, Charlie mused to himself. He wondered how much Kerns & Yarbrough was soaking CanAmex for. Fifty thousand a month anyway, plus expenses. In the legal business, there's nothing quite like having a deep-pocketed utility for a client.

Vernon Yarbrough was broad, tanned and distinguished looking with silver hair, a large silver pinky ring and a gold Rolex that he revealed as he reached a big hand across the table at Charlie. "Hara you mister Bur-dan. Anything you need in West Virginia, you just call us and we'll git it done." Charlie wondered if sometimes southerners didn't pack on a little extra accent when they came to New York. He knew though that if they were working for CanAmex, Vernon Yarbrough and his firm would be pretty powerful forces in Charleston.

Terry Summers recounted the problem with the cooling pond but there were too many lawyers present and soon the discussion ground to a near halt over some arcane issue of who approved the first draft of the site plan and when. The lawyers went painstakingly back over their notes and made new notes to look for old notes, and noted that they would memo each other when they found them. Losing interest in the discussion, Charlie glanced over at Jack Torkelson, who hadn't said a word to anyone so far, sitting by himself at the end of the table sipping bottled water. He had a stern expression on his face, his brow furrowed in concentration on some thought that would not be about the location of the cooling pond.

Charlie wondered why Torkelson was in the room. He knew Torkelson and the other CanAmex people were meeting later with some New York financial writers about the Continental Electric Systems merger, but why was he bothering with this pond issue or even about the Angel Mountain surface mining issue? It was out of character for him. Normally he'd let Tuthill handle operational matters like these.

Jack Torkelson was in his early sixties. Completely bald with a neatly trimmed gray beard and wire rimmed glasses, he had the appearance of a college professor. A Harvard grad, justice department lawyer and a former commissioner of the Federal Energy Regulatory Commission, Torkelson was Duncan McCord's handpicked architect of CanAmex's strategy for managing the deregulation of the utility industries. Together they recognized the immutable power that the lure of lower utility rates held over state and federal politicians, a power that could be used to craft and manipulate legislation favorable to powerful companies with vision and the boldness to determine the make-up of the utility industry of the future.

This was Jack Torkelson's mandate. Not the method of coal mining used by an insignificant vendor in West Virginia. He must have real concerns that CanAmex's involvement in Ackerly's mining permit for Angel Mountain could somehow interfere with the CES merger. If that were in fact the case, there was no doubt in Charlie's mind that Torkelson's career with CanAmex would be over. The merger was friendly – at the premium CanAmex was offering, possibly too friendly - because Duncan McCord didn't have time or the energy to waste on a hostile takeover. It was supposed to be a slam dunk. If Torkelson screwed it up somehow, he would be gone.

So the potential problem must lie in the state-by-state regulatory approvals process. The West Virginia Public Utilities Commission would have to approve the deal because CES operated several electric utility companies within the state. Suddenly it came to Charlie. *That was it.* Torkelson would have greased the rails all the way from Washington to McDowell County on the mountaintop-removal issue but nobody would have paid any attention to the PUC because they had nothing to say about it. But they'll have a lot to say about the merger with CES. Two years ago Torkelson couldn't see the merger coming but now, the CES deal was a lot more important to CanAmex than the price of coal in West Virginia, and the PUC must be giving off some bad signals about Angel Mountain.

When Charlie refocused his attention on the meeting, the lawyers were droning on about a liability clause in the master contract. Enough was enough. Charlie raised his open hand slowly to gain their attention and spoke a little more loudly than the lawyers were used to. "We will go before the planning board in September and get a variance to the site plan to build the pond on the north end of the property and on schedule. Now let's move on. I've got packing to do."

Across the table, Larry Tuthill came to life with a big grin, slapping the table with an open palm. "*God damn straight Charlie!* That's the attitude we need here. You go on down there, you and Vern and take *care* of this. Do what you have to do, but just get it done. He glanced sideways at the Charleston lawyers who were nodding in unison their enthusiastic agreement.

"And we've got this to help you prepare." Tuthill slid a manila file folder across the table to Charlie. "It's the bios and some other info on the three Planning Board members. We had a private investigator do some homework down there, just to leave no stone unturned so to speak. Some interesting stuff on these boys in there."

Charlie slid the folder unopened into his notebook. Typical Torkelson and Tuthill. Hire a private investigator. Find some dirt to use. Nothing was ever simple with CanAmex anymore. It was more fun when he worked directly with Duncan McCord and his right hand man, Red Landon, the big affable Canadian who never took himself as seriously as his replacement, Jack Torkelson. Landon moved up to the executive suite along with McCord and was now too immersed in CanAmex's mergers and acquisitions activities to be aware of the day-to-day management of company operations.

"I'll read it when I get down there." Charlie didn't want to get into a discussion about the personal lives of the Red Bone Planning Board.

"When *are* you going to West Virginia Charlie?" Tuthill asked. "We got a pretty expensive ship down there with no captain at the helm right now."

Charlie hadn't thought about it until Tuthill brought it up. He was right. There were a lot of things that could go wrong on a big construction site with many different subcontractors and unions at work simultaneously, and deliveries of materials arriving daily. Plus there was a lot of work to be done very quickly on revising the plans for the cooling pond. If Charlie was going, he should go right away.

"I'll be going down on Friday, spend the weekend getting acclimated, and be on the job Monday." It seemed like a reasonable timetable. He'd have his computers with him and could hand off his current projects from West Virginia.

Before Tuthill could respond, Jack Torkelson spoke his first words of the meeting. He spoke softly to force the rapt attention of his audience. "Charlie, it's good that you are going to West Virginia and taking over the project. We see that as a symbol of the importance that Dietrich Delahunt & Mackey places on this project and this account, and we appreciate someone of your stature taking over on such short notice. Now about the Angel Mountain issue. I'm sure Lucien has given you his synopsis of the situation, but I'm afraid Lucien doesn't understand the state of affairs in rural West Virginia. There is nothing nefarious or underhanded about this project. Everyone involved agrees that the judge's injunction against variances for mountaintop mining was misguided and unfair – to the mining industry, the miners and their families, and to the people of West Virginia." The skilled lawyer, Torkelson was ably pleading his case.

"The injunction never should have happened. It was just a lazy, knee-jerk concession by a liberal judge to the environmentalists. And now, even the environmentalists are with us on the Angel Mountain issue. Everyone involved, from Washington to Charleston, agree that this is a good thing, a wonderful thing for the people of McDowell County, and when Ackerly and the Union start hiring miners – McDowell County miners – you won't find hardly a soul down there to voice any opposition to the project."

Charlie knew that someone had to be against the project, but he decided to let Torkelson make his case without interruption. Sooner or later he had to get to the real problem.

"Charlie, we're not talking about creating some flunky jobs at the

Seven/Eleven or hiring a bunch of stock boys for a new Wal-Mart. Within a year Ackerly will be up to a level of two hundred and fifty miners at work on Angel Mountain – Union miners, making up to fifty-two thousand a year with full medical benefits. Do you understand how significant that is for the economy of McDowell County?"

Torkelson looked at his watch. He reached down for his brief case and stood up as he resumed speaking. "This is a big project. It's important to a lot of people. It's important to us. The Angel Mountain Coal will make Red Bone the most efficient non-nuclear generating plant in the world. There's a lot riding on this, too much to let one old hillbilly farmer screw it all up. Larry and our lawyers from Charleston here will fill you in on the details. You get down there Burden, figure out those people and spend some money if you have to, but make sure this thing goes our way." Torkelson turned away and strode for the door without saying anything more.

An old hillbilly farmer. Charlie almost let out a laugh. *Some old hillbilly farmer in West Virginia had Torkelson by the nuts. Going to be hard not to root for the farmer.*

Torkelson's abrupt departure left a vacuum of silence in the room. The Charleston lawyers started fidgeting with their notes and stealing glances at Tuthill, eager for the opportunity to start earning their generous retainer.

Charlie broke the silence. "So, who's the farmer"?

After a short hesitant pause, Tuthill dismissed all the lawyers except the three from Charleston. He waited until they left the room and reached into his briefcase and brought out another thin manila folder and slid it across the table to Charlie. "A farmer, his wife, their son and his girl friend . . . woman who was once married to the son's older brother. Nice cozy arrangement. That's how they do things down there."

Charlie added the folder to his notebook on top of the one about the Red Bone Planning Board. Some private investigator was having a pretty good year on CanAmex too. "And where is this farm in relation to the mountain?" Charlie asked no one in particular.

Vernon Yarbrough was eager to join the discussion. "Why it's right smack on the side of the mountain, about half way up the Mountain Road."

Charlie glared at Terry Summers. "I thought you said there was nobody living on the mountain?"

"Well, I meant hardly anybody. It's just one family and a worthless old pig farm with a house and a barn ready to fall down. There isn't another house within three miles of the mountain." Summers was scrambling to justify his earlier statement. "Charlie, you have to understand, at some of these other mountaintop sites over in Logan and Mingo Counties, there were usually dozens, sometimes fifty or sixty houses or trailers, that were displaced by the mining operations, plus a lot more that were affected by the blasting. One little derelict farm is nothing in this kind of thing."

The lawyer Yarbrough eagerly supported Summers' description. "That's right Mr. Bur-dan. In our experience, if we have to go the eminent domain route, one little farm would be much easier than some of the other mining projects we've been involved in."

"So the farm is in the way? The mountain can't be mined without taking the farm?" Charlie was trying to take things in an orderly progression to fully understand the situation he was about to involve himself in.

Tuthill let out a soft chuckle. "Charlie, when Ackerly starts blasting the top off that mountain, it's going to be like the siege of fucking Khe Sanh on that farm. That part of the mountain, the whole farm would end up getting covered over."

Charlie went back to Yarbrough. "What's the problem with eminent domain?"

"Well there's two things, Mr. Bur-dan. First is when you take up an eminent domain petition, either by the state or the county, you have to state your reason for taking the property, which in this case," he glanced around at Tuthill and the other lawyers in a show of unanimity, "nobody is too anxious to put out on the table either in Welch or in Charleston. See the politicians are on our side but they'll get a might squeamish about going into a public proceeding and justifying why they want to evict a family from their land they been living on for a hundred and thirty-one years so some big coal company, with the help of a Superior Court judge, can all of a sudden do a mountaintop-removal mine on Angel Mountain." Yarbrough lowered his voice as lawyers do to emphasize a sensitive point. "You can see the PR problem some of our friends have here."

Yarbrough leaned back in his chair and continued. "But more importantly, we probably won't have time for an eminent domain proceeding. Because if DeWitt – he's the farmer – if DeWitt gets a lawyer to fight it, which he surely would if it got that far, then the case could stretch into next year, and this whole thing has to happen this year. They have to be off the land so Ackerly can start mining operations before the end of the year."

"What's the hurry? Why does everything have to happen this year?

The lawyer leaned forward on the table as if to accentuate the importance of this issue. "Well now, you see Mr. Bur-dan, there's new state legislation going into effect on January one, which says in effect, for any new coal mining operation started after the first of January, you can't put any mining waste or residue of any kind into a stream, river, or any body of water in West Virginia." Yarbrough cut the air with his hand for effect. "And that Mr. Bur-dan will eliminate any new mountaintop-removal operations, with or without a variance. With or without a judge on your side. "

One of the other Kerns & Yarbrough lawyers added, "and that's legislation, not a court ruling like the injunction. Much tougher to do something about."

Yarbrough took over again. "But we're all right as long as the mine gets started before the end of the year. The new law was just too tough on mining so the industry and the Union got a grandfather clause put in that protects current mines."

"You couldn't mine Angel Mountain without affecting a stream?"

Yarbrough grinned broadly. "Mr. Bur-dan, you can't take a piss off a mountain in West Virginia without it ending up in a stream. That's what mountains *do*, they make streams. In the case of Angel Mountain, there's a stream running right down through the middle of the mountain. Pond about two thirds a the way up, and streams running through most of the length of the valleys on either side of the mountain."

Charlie made a note in his book to get a copy of the legislation, and then looked up again at Yarbrough. "So what does the farmer say? I assume we've made him an offer."

One of the other Charleston lawyers joined the discussion. "Yes sir, we did. Mr. Yarbrough and I went up to see him, beginning of summer. Offered him a hundred thousand, which was just our opening number you understand, but a real good price for that kind of property which isn't really worth anything as a farm or a homestead."

"Turned us down cold," Yarbrough added. "Wasn't interested in selling, and wouldn't discuss it. Went back up a few weeks later, increased the offer, but still no interest."

Yarbrough clasped his hands together behind his head and leaned back in his chair, gazing toward the ceiling. "This farmer, this DeWitt's a hardboiled character. A real hillbilly. Probably hasn't been out of the state of West Virginia more than a couple of times in the last sixty years. Born on that farm and poor as a church mouse his whole life. Don't really know what money can buy."

"So what's the real number? How high are we willing to go for the farm?" said Charlie. He was looking at Yarbrough since it now was apparent the lawyer was to be the front man in negotiations over the farm.

Before Yarbrough could answer, Larry Tuthill slapped the table lightly with the palm of his hand for emphasis. "One million," he said softly. "You guys can go to a million for the farm but we need a deal by the end of October. Our judge is going to vacate the injunction against mountaintop variances in mid –November." Tuthill's voice was down to almost a whisper. "But he wants to see that we own that farm before he does anything. We've got to get our variance and blasting permits and be in operation by December, and we're not going to get *dick* if that farmer isn't long gone from Angel Mountain."

Tuthill sank back in his chair and looked at Yarbrough then back at Charlie and Terry Summers. "So the number is a million. You guys can split whatever you don't have to give to the farmer but nobody gets anything if we don't have a deal by October thirty-first. 'Cause then, if we have to, we'll do an eminent domain petition and just deal with the PR problems, and we'll see if a million bucks can't speed up the process a little. Hey, the thirty-first, that's Halloween. Maybe you can dress up like the headless horseman and scare him off the mountain."

Yarbrough had a big grin on his face. "Well that's a shit-pot full of money Larry, and the best thing is, I don't think we're going to need anywhere near a million to make a deal with that farmer."

"Why is that Mr. Yarbrough?" Charlie asked.

"Well let's just say we got a secret weapon, at least a theory that our investigator is working on down there that may make this whole thing easier than a two-inch putt. But that's all I can say about it right now."

lie was content to let Yarbrough's secret weapon theory drop without
discussion. The whole issue of evicting the farmer, and now the bounty
t. anAmex was willing to put up to get this done in a timely fashion, made him
uncomfortable. He accepted a lot of what Summers and then Torkelson had said
about the mining project. It would undoubtedly be a huge boon to the economy of
the county and make the Red Bone plant a fabulous asset for his client. Yet, he
couldn't shake the nagging feeling that he was lining up on the wrong side of this
issue. *The rich get richer and the poor get thrown off their farms.*

Behind Tuthill, in the showcase against the long wall of the boardroom,
Charlie noticed the replica of the China dam project. How quickly his fortunes had
changed. From going to a professionally fulfilling assignment like the second dam
project, to what was more and more sounding like a career-ending quagmire in
West Virginia. He started thinking about the run he'd be taking that evening
through the Mamaroneck countryside. He wondered if it would still be light out
when he got home. He needed a run.

"All right," said Charlie, "in a few weeks or so, after I get settled down
there, Mr. Yarbrough and I will go up and visit this farmer and find out what he
needs." Charlie wanted to move on the merger problem.

"Yeah we need to do that Charlie, the sooner the better," responded
Yarbrough. "And we'll take Kevin Mulrooney, the head of Ackerly up there with
us. Show of force, you know. We'll let this farmer know what he's up against."

"Yeah, sounds like great fun," Charlie said, making a note in his book to
schedule their visit to Angel Mountain. "Now somebody tell me how this whole
thing is going to affect the Continental deal."

Tuthill pursed his lips hard and looked at Vernon Yarbrough who gave him
a quick, almost imperceptible nod, like a predetermined signal. Tuthill rose to his
feet, gathering up his briefcase. He looked toward Terry Summers and then, the
other Kerns & Yarbrough lawyers. "I think we'll leave the room to Charlie and
Vernon now boys." Then facing Charlie. "Vernon will explain it to you Charlie,
you don't need us for this." He reached a hand across the table. "I'll see you in
West Virginia in a few weeks. Glad to have you down there."

It was obvious that Yarbrough, the lawyer, didn't want any witnesses to
what he was about to relate to Charlie. He waited until the conference room door
shut, then got up and came around to Charlie's side of the table and took the chair
next to him.

Charlie took the initiative. "It's the Public Utilities Commission, right
Vernon? Is that what Torkelson's worried about?"

"That's it Charlie. Except it isn't so much the PUC as it is the *process*, you
know, the settlement process they have to go through to approve the merger. Now
the head of the PUC is a good boy, friend of mine, member of my club. Couple of
weeks ago, Larry gives me a heads up about the CES deal and tells me to go ahead
and bounce the Angel Mountain initiative off my PUC guy to see if there's any
worms in the oatmeal there. Well he'd already got wind of something happening
with a variance being issued for an Angel Mountain surface mine – these
regulators and government guys are all wired in together you see – but he tells me,

he and the rest of the commission are all for it. Got no problem at all with a little finagling with the feds to get a big mining project going in McDowell County. He thinks the injunction against mountaintop variances was all bullshit too. Wants to see McDowell come back and he knows low sulfur coal is the salvation of southern West Virginia, the *only* salvation. Ain't any Indian casinos or Jap car makers moving into McDowell County any time soon, so he's all for it even if it is Ackerly, which he isn't too fond of, but shit, everyone hates the coal companies."

"Then what's his problem with the merger?" asked Charlie.

"The settlement hearings will be scheduled for sometime in the spring. Going to sail through. They'll go ahead and rubber-stamp all the PR bullshit, you know, all the usual crap about the merger being good for customers and increasing competition, and being just peachy for the environment and all that boilerplate stuff. But, as you know, as part of these things, the public, anyone – a business, another regulatory body, friend or foe, the man in the fucking moon – can file a complaint with the commission about any little picayune aspect of the merger, and it would have to be officially investigated and discussed in public session before it can be dismissed.

"So, here's what's going to happen," Yarbrough lowered his voice and leaned slightly forward toward Charlie. "If someone files an objection, based on say, some improprieties, between the two companies with regard to the issuance of a variance for a mountaintop-removal permit for Angel Mountain, my guy tells me that the commission will have to launch a complete and thorough investigation of every aspect of the deal. Got no choice. He's got no way around that."

Charlie knew they were finally getting to the heart of the matter. "So, what are they going to find there Vernon? What is it that's got our friend Torkelson so worried?"

"Well most likely nothing comes out of such an investigation, but . . . you know, you talk to the wrong person, at a weak moment somebody says something, and you never know what kind of story just might come bubbling up to the surface."

Charlie just waited silently, staring at the lawyer seated next to him.

Before he spoke again, Yarbrough's demeanor seemed to change. He stared coldly back at Charlie and the smile disappeared from his face and from his voice along with most of his accent. "Now Mr. Burden, you make a clear mental note to yourself right here that I am using the word *hypothetically*, as in, hypothetically, if the investigation were to show that someone connected to CanAmex Energy Limited, in the course of the Angel Mountain project, were to have possibly *bribed* a high court judge in the course of these events, then the PUC of West Virginia, and probably a whole bunch of other states, would have a big problem with the merger between CanAmex and Continental Electric Systems. All of which is not very pleasant for our client, let alone the shit storm of judicial activity that would no doubt ensue."

The lawyer held up his hand, not to be interrupted, as Charlie started to speak. Yarbrough continued. "Now I, of course, have no knowledge that this may be the case, but it has been relayed to me by knowledgeable sources that, *hypothetically*, this kind of accusation could possibly come out of a PUC investigation. So, Mr. Burden, our job down there, yours and mine, is to make sure that no one has any interest in filing anything regarding Angel Mountain with the Public Utilities Commission or any other regulatory body in the state of West Virginia. What that means Mr. Burden, is creating as little fuss and muss as possible in displacing that disagreeable old pig farmer off that decrepit little mountain, 'cause he my friend, is our only loose end down there." Yarbrough rose up out of his chair.

"Mr. Yarbrough . . ." Charlie wanted more information.

Yarbrough put his index finger up to his lips, asking for silence. He gathered up his notes and smiled broadly at Charlie. "Now Mr. Bur-dan, you make sure you bring your clubs down and we'll have you up to my club on a weekend real soon. Send the chopper down and have you on the first tee before you can finish your cold drink." The lawyer gave Charlie a quick nod to signal the end of the conversation, picked up his briefcase and left the boardroom.

Charlie sat at the conference table going over in his mind what he had just heard. *Bribing a State judge.* If that were the case, then Torkelson had a lot to worry about. A PUC investigation of Angel Mountain would have to focus on the judge and his ruling, and it would be pretty obvious that he was carrying the water for some interested party, which could only be CanAmex or Ackerly Coal, and with the pending merger, most likely both. It must be true or Torkelson wouldn't be so worried. But bribery of a judge just didn't seem to fit. It wasn't CanAmex's modus operandi. Unless it was the only way. Maybe Yarbrough already had the judge in his pocket and representing both CanAmex and Ackerly, he put the deal together and just gave Torkelson a number. Nice and clean, easy and quick. But then the merger came along and muddied the water. And now they were involving him because they needed help in West Virginia, and Torkelson was counting on Charlie's loyalty to Duncan McCord and CanAmex, to make sure this didn't blow up in everyone's face.

It would be bad for everyone, Charlie had to agree, if the PUC had to launch a formal investigation of Angel Mountain. Especially bad for Torkelson and Tuthill, who would definitely lose their jobs and could end up serving some jail time. But it would be almost as bad for his friend Duncan in the long run. His company's name would be dragged through the mud and a huge, expensive merger would go down the drain. The stock price would be battered and Duncan's image would be forever tarnished with the Board of Directors and the financial community. Most likely his spectacular career in the utility industry would be over. Yes, Charlie would do all in his power to prevent that. Torkelson knew what he was doing when he brought Charlie into the fold by letting him in on their dirty little secret. And now, everyone's fate, as Yarbrough said, lay in the hands of a pig farmer on Angel Mountain, West Virginia.

Back in his office, Charlie shut the door and started in on a list of the things he'd need to get done, postpone or cancel, if he was to leave for West Virginia at the end of the week. The list got longer and longer as he went over his schedule for the coming months but he also began to get a sense of relief at the prospect of being unburdened of so many of the tasks that had made his job nearly unbearable the last few years. Going to West Virginia to build the CanAmex plant, in fact, would certainly simplify his life, in spite of the cooling pond and Angel Mountain problems. But it wasn't China. In the end, it was a relatively insignificant coal burner in the back woods of Appalachia, an area that Charlie had no particular zeal to see or to live in and would no doubt be departing at the first opportunity. He also knew it was probably the end of his career at Dietrich Delahunt & Mackey. The vultures were circling. The Warren Brands and Terry Summers of the firm. Young, ambitious and impatient, who smelled opportunity in the form of Jack Torkelson and Larry Tuthill who had been sending out subtle signals that Charlie Burden's position on the CanAmex account might not be as impregnable as it had been for the past fifteen years under the wing of Duncan McCord. Of that, Charlie had no delusions. McCord had been moving up and up, to global heights and away from the operational details that involved Charlie, while Torkelson gained more and more power in the tactical decisions of the company. Now Torkelson was dragging Charlie into a no-win situation in West Virginia. If Torkelson went down over the Angel Mountain issue, the vortex would swallow everyone involved, most particularly, Charlie Burden and Lucien Mackey. If Torkelson were successful, his stature and power within the company would be guaranteed to the point where not even his close friendship with McCord could save Charlie.

He called down to the library and gave Nina Matlin the news she already had, and asked her to download all the Red Bone plans and status reports onto a clean laptop, and to send along her background file on the local area.

"Whole file on McDowell County and the town of Red Bone is about two pages long," Nina replied. "Not too much going on there."

As he hung up the phone, Terry Summers opened the door a crack to peek in. Charlie waved him in.

"Got some presents for you," had said, flashing his trademark smile. "I'm headed back to West Virginia tonight so I wanted to get this stuff to you." From his jacket pocket he took out a ring of keys to the Red Bone site, a pager that had been Hugo Paxton's, and a set of car keys. "Hugo's Navigator. We leased it down there. It's parked at the condo."

"Hugo had rich tastes I guess. Did he really need a Navigator?"

"Well, the roads are a little rough down there, and you need a four-wheel-drive in the winter. You know, Charlie, there isn't a four-lane road anywhere in McDowell County."

"Really?" Charlie was surprised.

"Land that time forgot," replied Summers. He handed Charlie another key ring with a yellow plastic fob in the shaped of an old gas lamp. "These are the keys to the condo. It's in Bluefield. Nice little town. The "naturally air conditioned city" they call it, or something like that. The condo's about an hour from the site, but the only decent housing around. Nice places. Modern enough. Pool and a tennis court and all that. We've got four of them and CanAmex is renting a couple. I'm right next door to you. Some of the contractors are there.

Few of the locals moved out and jacked the rents up but they're still cheap. Anyway, nothing available to rent around Red Bone that you'd consider living in. We had the place all cleaned up for you."

When Summers had gone, Charlie picked up the phone and made the call he'd been dreading all afternoon. Ellen would be on her way to Vermont with Linda Marchetti, headed for Mount Snow and three days at the golf school, and then up to the house at Sugarbush for some more golf and tennis. He would be leaving for West Virginia before she returned on Sunday night. He reached her on her cell phone. They were in Linda's Ferrari, just outside of Brattleboro on Route 9.

"*West Virginia*? What is that? That's like down next to Mississippi, right? What the hell is a Red Bone? *You agreed to go down there*?" Ellen was more upset over the news than Charlie had anticipated. He'd underestimated how much of the corporate culture of Dietrich Delahunt & Mackey she had assimilated over the years. She knew immediately that, unlike a posting to China, West Virginia was not a positive career move for a partner of the firm. There was something afoot and it didn't bode well for her husband, or for her ambitions and status within the social hierarchy of Westchester County. This move was going to affect her right away, she told him, and Charlie was on a downward spiral – it was all part of this *affliction* that had come over him the last few years – and he'd better figure it all out soon. She masked her disgust only slightly, in deference to her friend sitting in the car next to her, but Charlie could feel it over the phone. And he had no answer, again. She was right, and he couldn't explain why he was doing what he knew he had to do. He didn't want to bring Lucien into the discussion, how he needed to do it for Lucien, and now for Duncan. She knew it was a bad career move for him, and she didn't even know anything about the worst part – the Angel Mountain issue. The story was too complex. He told her not to worry. Ellen told him to call her next week then she clicked off abruptly.

Charlie Burden sat at his desk and thought about his wife. He wondered if they were still in love or had they just been through so much, so many years together, that they just pretended they were. They were on such different tracks now, always at odds about so much it seemed. Charlie knew he had to get away for a while, to postpone the inevitable decisions they would be forced to make that he wasn't ready for. Maybe Lucien was right. Maybe West Virginia would be good for him.

He looked at the picture on the wall next to his desk. It was one of those collage frames with nine small holes for family photos. It had been a father's day present from Ellen and the kids many years ago. Now it was old and outdated, but for years it had been next to Charlie's desk in several different offices. He enjoyed the instant nostalgia that engulfed him when he looked at the pictures of the children when they were small; Scotty holding up an old brown baseball, wearing a glove that was far too big for him; Jennifer, four years old, sitting on the grass holding a puppy, their first dog, *Mr. Pips*; a picture of him and Ellen in front of their house in Connecticut. They look liked they'd been doing yard work. Charlie, wearing a dirty tee shirt and work gloves, had an arm around Ellen bending her close to him, their laughing faces cheek-to-cheek. His hair was a little darker then, hers a shade lighter. Charlie stared at the picture. It was so long ago it seemed like a former life to him now. He couldn't remember the last time he and Ellen had looked so happy together.

On his way out of the building, Charlie carried his briefcase, a laptop in a case slung over his shoulder, and the white envelope containing his New York Giants season tickets. He took the main elevator in the front of the building down to the Park Avenue entrance. On the street a white limousine with tinted windows pulled up at the curb. An older woman wearing a Florida tan, large brown sunglasses and a stylish beige pantsuit exited from the back seat and strode confidently into the Carlos Marche Salon. *Upper East Side, or maybe West Central Park, serious money anyway*, Charlie mused as he followed her through the door.

The slim, super-chic receptionist winked at Charlie and waved him through as she turned her attention to the older woman. In his expansive private salon, Carlos Marche was working on an attractive woman that Charlie thought he recognized from the local news on one of the New York stations.

He gave Carlos the tickets and told him about West Virginia. Maybe he'd be back in town sometime during the season to go to a game with him. Carlos knew about West Virginia and he was very appreciative of the tickets. He knew how good the seats were and how hard they were to come by, but he was most appreciative of the fact that Charlie chose him to give the tickets to. With his considerable wealth, Carlos Marche could easily buy good tickets to any Giants' game from the ticket services, but it wasn't his way. This was better. He insisted on writing out a check to Charlie for the tickets, which Charlie refused.

"Just take good care of Lucien while I'm gone Carlos, he may be having a rough time in the company."

They shook hands and Carlos watched his friend leave without telling him that Lucien had used nearly the same words the previous evening, talking about Charlie.

Chapter 9

The construction site was entirely deserted. Charlie knew there was supposed to be a full-time watchman on duty but he didn't see any sign of life as he peered through the twelve-foot high, chain link fence. *Late in the afternoon on a Friday. Should have expected it.*

The site was bigger than he'd imagined. The massive shell of the main building dominated the landscape, rising five stories high on a footprint of several acres about a hundred yards in from the fence. To the right just inside the fence was the long, flat-roofed administration building. Visible behind it were a dozen trailers and a few small shacks of the type that pop up unnoticed at large construction projects. Beyond the stacks of pipes, iron beams, cinder blocks, and rolls of cable, Charlie could see a huge, yellow and green earth mover, a power shovel, a massive dump truck and road grader. Huge piles of dirt, sand, stone and other debris were spread throughout the vast site that was entirely enclosed by two and a half miles of fence topped with several strands of barbed wire.

The project looked awesome to Charlie as he gazed slowly around the interior, resigned to the fact that he wouldn't be getting onto the grounds tonight. He slumped heavily against the fence, resting his weight on his arms stretched out over his head. He was hot and tired from the ten-hour drive from New York. The late afternoon sun threw down daggers of white heat on his bare neck and the back of his black golf shirt. He could feel the rivulets of sweat running down the middle of his back to gather at the waste-line of his khaki Dockers. There was dust in the air from the open scars of the construction site. Behind him, the steel blue Lexus sat with the engine running, the driver's door open, the air-conditioner's compressor and the cooling system fan were racing madly trying to adjust to the heat.

As he took in the complexity of the project that he was now in charge of Charlie was consumed by a sinking feeling of inadequacy. *Was it all a colossal mistake? Maybe he did belong behind a desk, on the phone, having luncheon meetings at Four Seasons. Maybe he'd been away from it all for too long.* And now here he was, in the middle of nowhere, at his project, and he couldn't even get through the gate.

When Charlie turned around, the boy was sitting on his bike next to the car. Charlie smiled at him. "Hey, how ya doing buddy?" he said.

The boy just sat on his bike, a beat-up old banana-seat model with no fenders and plenty of rust. He wore a dirty white T-shirt that the sleeves had been cut from, long brown shorts with big utility pockets that extended to just below his knees, black high-top sneakers, and white athletic socks that were now light brown from a covering of road dust. On his head he wore a dark blue cap, turned backwards like kids everywhere. His skin was fair with a good coating of summer freckles. As he rocked slowly forward and back on his bike, observing the tall stranger, the boy could have been just an average ten or eleven year-old, Charlie guessed, except for the mongoloid features of the head and face, and the short, thick legs and arms. Charlie instantly flashed backed to his brief but intense research effort into the affliction of Down Syndrome, some twelve years earlier.

The boy looked at Charlie through squinting eyes, the tip of his tongue protruding through tightly pursed lips. It was a hard face to read. Charlie moved away from the fence toward the boy. "Can you speak son?"

The boy's face relaxed, his eyes widening with some amusement. "Of coth I can thpeak. You think I'm thum *dummy*?" He had a hint of hoarseness in his voice and a lisp.

"Well no, I didn't, I wasn't sure, that's all."

"You locked out?" The boy was looking past Charlie toward the fence gate.

"Yeah, I guess I am. You ever see a man inside the fence, a security guard?"

"Thumtime. He go out in hith twuck a lot. You want to get inthide?"

"You can get in? You've been inside here before?"

"Lotth of time. Want me to thow you?"

Charlie got into his car and turned off the ignition. "Okay. Why don't you show me how you get in." He closed the door of the Lexus and locked it with the remote-entry button. The car beeped twice.

"Nobody thteal you caw heah mithter," the boy said as he laid his bicycle down on the pavement.

Charlie knew the boy was right but with his luggage and computers and everything else he had brought with him from Mamaroneck still in the car, he would feel uneasy about going off and leaving the car open. "I know. It's just a habit I guess. I'm from New York."

"New Yowk Yankeeth."

"Yeah, that's right. You play baseball?"

The boy had started out on the path along the outside of the fence headed to the left of the gate. Charlie followed.

"No. No batheball. Can't thwow. Can't catch. Louthy at batheball. I am thocker player. Good thocker playah. My mama ith the coach."

"Well that's good. Soccer's a great game." Charlie tried to picture the chunky little boy with his short, thick legs, playing soccer. "As long as you have fun playing."

"My daddy wath a football playah. A thtar football playah. He play football in cowlege."

Charlie could see that it meant a lot to the boy. "Wow, that's great. What college did he play for?"

The boy stopped abruptly and squinted his eyes in thought so he could get it right. "Play football for Wetht Vooginia Univoothity . . . the *Mountaineath*!" He continued along the path.

After traversing the fence for a short distance, they came to a deep gully where the fence dipped down abruptly and up on the opposite side. At the bottom of the gully a thick growth of bushes and vines concealed a gap of about a foot between the bottom of the fence and the ground. Pulling up on the bottom of the fence, the boy gave Charlie ample room to get down and slither under the fence. On the other side he stood up and brushed the dirt off his pants and shirt. He felt like a kid again having an adventure, like the times when he and Cecil would sneak into the Yale Bowl or the New Haven Coliseum to watch a game. It had been a long time since he'd crawled under a fence to get into anything. He made a mental note to notify security about the breach in the fence.

Outside the fence, the boy stood with his hands in his pockets watching him. Charlie thought he'd play a little game with his new friend. He turned without a word and started walking away. After about ten yards he stopped and turned back to the boy. "Well, aren't you coming?" Charlie asked with mock impatience.

The boy's face scrunched up with a huge smile as he dropped to his belly and scrambled under the fence like an alligator. He ran to catch up to Charlie who had started off at a good pace toward the huge generator building. It felt good to have a companion to explore the grounds with and this little retarded boy with the easy-going self-confidence, was very likeable. It was good just to have someone to talk to after ten hours alone in a car. Charlie realized the boy was the first person he'd met in West Virginia. He stopped walking and turned to the boy. "Hey buddy, you know what? We haven been introduced." Charlie held out his hand. "I'm Charlie Burden."

The happy look of inner laughter came over the boy's face again. He took Charlie's large hand in his short chubby fingers as best he could. "Hello Chowly. I am the Pie Man."

Charlie smiled down at him, watching the boy's face. "The *Pie Man*," he repeated slowly. "That's your name, the Pie Man?"

The boy nodded his head affirmatively. "Yeth, I am the Pie Man," he said proudly.

Charlie chuckled and shook his head. *This is definitely not Westchester County.* "Well I guess you *are* the *Pie Man* then." Charlie replied. "I'm very happy to meet you Pie Man. Now let's have a look around."

Charlie could only imagine the number of OSHA violations he was committing by walking through an open construction site after hours with a child, neither of them wearing hardhats. He'd have to keep a close eye on the boy. If he got hurt at the site after sneaking under the fence with no security guard on duty, *everyone*, most particularly Charlie, would be in deep shit.

They ventured into the cavernous main building that was cool and dark on the ground floor. A steel stairway led to the second level where there was more available light from the numerous openings in the walls and through the floors above. Charlie showed the boy the huge cavities that would be filled by the three giant turbines that would be arriving by train in a few months. They walked inside the massive boilers that would burn the pulverized coal to turn purified water into steam. The boilers were bigger than any Charlie had seen before. He thought about the huge amounts of coal that they would be consuming, reminding him of the Angel Mountain problem, which he knew, was the primary reason he was in West Virginia.

Charlie pointed out the three exhaust portals that would lead to the scrubber assembly and tried to explain briefly without getting into the chemistry involved, why and how they cleaned the smoke produced by the burning coal. The boy was a more than willing student. He soaked up everything Charlie had to say and had a question for every answer. Sometimes Charlie had to just laugh and tell the boy 'we'll cover that next time.' Up on the third level, he showed him where the plant's control room, currently being assembled at a sub-contractor's facility in California, would be reassembled after traveling across the country on flatbed trailer trucks. The boy was mesmerized by the stranger's endless knowledge of the huge, complicated building, and was elated at the amount of attention the man was paying to him. No one except his mother, and his teacher Mrs. Willard, and maybe Auntie Sally once in a while, had ever talked *directly to him* like this for so long.

They clambered noisily down the stairway to the first floor and back out into the sunlight. Around the outside of the plant the ground was rough with large gouges and muddy trenches left by the heavy machinery. Charlie had forgotten how much standing water is indigenous to large construction sites and made a mental note to get a pair of high rubber boots. As they made their way toward the center of the big field, he and the boy both got their sneakers covered with mud.

Charlie stood at where he judged the center of the cooling pond was originally planned to go. He could see several places where the hard, brown rock pushed through the sandy soil like the back of a long, subterranean whale lurking just beneath the surface. *Christ, anyone could see that this was going to be a horrible place to build a damn pond. What the hell were the site architects thinking about?* Charlie chocked it up to arrogance, a quality available in great supply to today's mega-project engineers like those employed by Dietrich Delahunt & Mackey, who considered themselves *masters of the universe* and wouldn't worry too much about an insignificant detail like the location of a cooling pond.

He turned northward in the direction of the alternative pond location at the far end of the site. It looked to be about a ten-minute walk up to the spot that they would now have to get approved by the planning board. He'd skip it for today. He wanted to see as much of the project as he could but he also wanted to get into Bluefield to find the condo and unpack and take a shower.

He started out toward the admin building, the boy by his side. "Tell me Pie Man, when you sneak in here at night when the guard isn't around, what do you do here?"

The boy just pursed his lips tightly and scurried along next to Charlie with his hands thrust into his pockets. Charlie laughed, understanding that the boy thought he might be getting in trouble for admitting what he did when he went under the fence. "C'mon, you can tell me," Charlie cajoled. "It'll be our secret."

With that, the boy came to a stop, turned to his left and lifted his right arm and pointed past Charlie toward the collection of Caterpillar bulldozers, dump trucks, power shovels and several enormous earth movers, which were neatly parked for the weekend. Charlie stopped and followed his gesture. *Of course! What kid could resist monster toys like those?*

The Pie Man had a big happy face on, his eyes just narrow slits as his face scrunched with inner glee, the pink tip of his tongue sticking through his tiny mouth. With both hands, he pretended to be turning an imaginary steering wheel.

"Pie Man dwive the twucks. Make woads. Thumtime play awoplane owa play Awmy."

Charlie smiled at the boy. "Yeah, I don't blame you Pie Man. That's what I'd be doing if I was a kid around here I bet." He pushed down on the top of the boy's head playfully, pulling his cap down over his eyes. "But, I've got a feeling the security guard may be paying closer attention in the future. C'mon, let's see if we can get into the administration building."

As they walked toward the building's main double-door which was on the opposite side from the fence, Charlie noticed that the main gate had been rolled open and the boy's bicycle was lying in the weeds at the side of the entry road. At the end of the building, in the paved parking area, sat a black Chevy Suburban with the unmistakable CanAmex Energy logo with the silver lightning bolts on the side.

"Well it looks like our security guard has finally turned up," Charlie said as much to himself as to the boy.

When he noticed the black truck, the boy slowed down noticeably and Charlie could see him glancing between the truck and the gate and his bike, as if measuring the distance to his escape route.

"It's all right Pie Man, don't worry about it. You're with me. It's okay," Charlie reassured him.

As Charlie walked toward the double door, the boy lingered behind, preferring to stay within sight of the open -gate and his bike. "I wait out heah Chowly. I wait heah," he called from the end of the building.

"Okay, I'm just going to see if he's inside," Charlie answered as he tried the locked door. He pulled the ring of keys from his pocket. He half expected the boy to be gone when he came out anyway and that was okay. Maybe he'd run into him again sometime. Then he heard a deep, heavy voice from around the end of the building.

"Hey, you, *kid!* What the fuck are you're doin' on my property? Get over here!"

The boy was sidling nervously away from the voice, to get a look around the side of the building to see if he could find Charlie who was striding toward him.

"Hey kid, you deaf or wha . . ." The security guard stopped talking abruptly when Charlie came into view around the corner of the building. The guard was tall and powerful looking with a thick gray mustache and the look of an ex-military man or state trooper. He wore a dark blue CanAmex shirt with the name Hicks on a tag sewn in over the left pocket, and a black baseball cap emblazoned with "CanAmex Security".

"The kid's with me, he's okay," said Charlie.

"*Okay huh.* Yeah? And just who the hell are you, and why are you and Charlie Brown here trespassing on my property?" The security guard, who was several inches taller than Charlie, leaned forward in an intimidating posture and bellowed louder than he had to.

Charlie tried to maintain his patience. He offered his hand. "Hi, I'm Charlie Burden. I'm the. . ."

"How'd you assholes get in here anyway?" Hicks continued, ignoring Charlie's hand. "I want you to show me, *right now!*"

This was getting ridiculous, Charlie thought, his patience draining out of him. He could sense the boy's nervousness as he tried to edge away from the two men to get a little closer to the freedom of the gate. *This wasn't fair to the kid. He didn't deserve to be frightened over this.* Charlie had had enough.

He gritted his teeth, the veins standing out on his neck as he moved up closer to get into the guard's face. "All right Hicks, that's enough!" Charlie's voice had lost any tone of cordiality. "If you want to keep your job beyond the next thirty seconds, you'll shut up and listen."

The security guard blinked a few times and his face softened as it came to him . . . the expensive car with New York plates parked at the gate, the name *Burden . . . the new guy! Hugo Paxton's replacement.*

"I'm Charlie Burden and I'm in charge of this site, and you may be getting paid by CanAmex but now you work for me and your first day on the job isn't going well. Now if you were doing your job, you'd *know* how we got in here. So when I come in to work on Monday morning, you'd better be able to show me how we got in and you'd better have had it taken care of."

Charlie moved away from the now docile Hicks toward the boy who was standing a few yards away, wide-eyed with amazement and apprehension at how his new friend had spoken to the guard. Charlie put his hand on the back of the boy's neck to reassure him that everything was all right and started walking him toward the gate.

"Hey, Mr. Burden, I'm sorry. I didn't know it was you, you know, and all I saw was that kid there, and . . ." Hicks' tone showed real concern over the prospect of losing his over-paid job.

Charlie stopped and turned back to the guard, turning the boy with him. "Mr. Hicks, this is my good friend the Pie Man, and any time he wants to come on the grounds to see me when I'm here, he's welcome. Okay?"

"Yessir, Mr. Burden, I'll see to it. I'll see you then on Monday morning, and we'll start fresh."

Charlie ignored the guard as he and the boy walked out through the gate. He didn't want to deal any more with security guard Hicks. He was tired and hot and sticky and the sun was getting lower and he still needed to get to Bluefield and find the condo. A cold shower and eight hours of sleep was what he needed now.

The boy had picked up his bicycle and stood with his legs straddling the front wheel as he straightened the loose handlebars.

"Should have your daddy put a wrench on that and tighten it up for you Pie Man," Charlie said as he unlocked the Lexus. The boy just shrugged off the suggestion. He seemed a little subdued. When he looked up at Charlie, he squinted one eye closed and turned his head at an angle to avoid looking directly into the sun over Charlie's shoulder.

"Chowly, am I weally youwa good fwend, like you tell that man?"

Charlie chuckled at the expression on the boy's face as it contorted around the flat nose with the tip of his tongue showing through the small mouth. Charlie stepped forward and turned the boy's cap around so the bill shielded his eyes from the sun. Then he tapped him gently on the top of his head.

"Pie Man, you're the best friend I have in West Virginia."

The boy looked away, as if he were somehow embarrassed. Then he turned back to Charlie as he jumped onto his bicycle seat. He had on his scrunched up happy face with the smile so tight it closed his eyes and pushed the little pink tip of his tongue out even farther. He rode his bike a few yards down the entry road, unable to talk, then he circled around slowly and came back toward Charlie and stopped.

"Thank you fowa thowing me waya the towabins and the contwol woom will go Chowly."

"You're welcome Pie Man. Thanks for showing me how to sneak in." Charlie grinned at his new friend.

As the boy started to ride off, Charlie called after him. "Hey Pie Man." The boy stopped his bike and turned back to Charlie, his feet on the pavement. "How old are you?"

The boy held up ten fingers. "I am twelve yewas old," he said concentrating on his fingers. Charlie had to laugh at the expression on his face along with the discrepancy of his statement. The boy grinned back.

Charlie watched as his new friend pedaled off toward the logging road that ran through the woods to South County Road. Twice, he turned back to see that Charlie was still watching him and he waved. Charlie could see that he still had the queer, happy look on his face even as he rode into the woods. As he watched him, Charlie tried to recall when he last spoke to a twelve-year-old, or any child. *Why couldn't he remember? Had it really been that long since he'd had any contact with a child?* It seemed like a very strange realization after all the years he'd spent among children when his kids were growing up. It was fun being with a child again, showing him things, being his friend. And there was something about this little boy that was very likeable. Retarded or not, he was just a real neat kid. Charlie wondered if he would ever see him again.

On the way out to the CanAmex site, Charlie had passed through the center of Red Bone – an old-time Main Street with a few side streets running off of it and half a dozen or so old, dark stone buildings of three and four stories. He remembered a place called *Barney's* that looked like a general store with a restaurant on one side. It was in a four story building on a corner at the center of the town. He would stop there on the way back to get directions to Bluefield and a cup of coffee to go.

Charlie drove leisurely east on South County Road back toward Old Red Bone taking in the sights now that he was in no particular hurry. He went past a boarded up motel with a heavy growth of weeds pushing up through long-neglected cracks in the parking area in front. Several other abandoned buildings that could have once been small manufacturing companies or warehouses. A two - story red brick building with hundreds of small windows, mostly broken, that had to have been a school at one time. There was very little along the road that seemed to be currently functioning. It appeared that nothing new had been built on South County Road for many years.

Yet beyond the road, on both sides and to the front and rear as Charlie drove into Red Bone, there was tangible excitement to the land as it rose up in all directions from rolling hills and ridges and craggy rock formations, to larger hills and higher ridges, on up to the mountains beyond. In every direction the land rose, covered with the deep green of dense woods occasionally broken by the lighter shade of a rolling meadow. The sheer magnitude and rugged grandeur of the topography seemed to minimize the effect of the derelict structures along the road rendering them irrelevant. The landscape reminded Charlie a lot of Vermont but more concentrated, as if someone had pushed all the hills closer together.

But it wasn't Vermont, not this part of West Virginia, not McDowell County. Charlie thought about some of the facts and figures contained in the economics brief that Nina Matlin, DD&M's librarian, had given him before he left. *McDowell County*, lowest per capita income of the 55 counties in West Virginia, the 48th ranked state in the country in personal income. County population in 1960: 100,000. Population in 1980: 49,000. Current population estimate: 25,000. And another statistic that Charlie remembered . . . the percentage of children living below the poverty line: 53%. *So much for the war on poverty in Appalachia.*

From a long way off, Charlie could see the old buildings of Red Bone etched against the mountain by the light of the sun setting in the west behind him. He drove up the long, steep hill to Main Street and pulled around the corner and stopped in front of Barney's General Store. The lights were out on the store side on the left, but in the restaurant he could see a woman sweeping the floor. Probably closing up, too late to get coffee, Charlie assumed. But he still needed directions.

Inside the vestibule, Charlie peeked into the darkened store through a large plate glass window. It looked like a cross between a grocery and a hardware store. Toward the rear he noticed a sign designating the "shoe" department. Maybe they would have the rubber boots he would need. Better to buy local if he could.

The restaurant could have served as a set for a fifties movie. Wooden booths with individual jukeboxes ran along the front windows. The counter snaked out and back in the typical, space-saving, U-shaped pattern. At the counter were the standard round steel-rimmed stools covered with red naugahyde. Overhead, large ceiling fans turned slowly, and above them long fluorescent lights bathed the restaurant in near daylight. On the floor, black and yellow checked linoleum was worn through in spots in front of each booth and around the counter stools.

The floor creaked as Charlie entered the restaurant. The woman looked up from her sweeping as if she were expecting him. She was a heavy-set woman who looked to be in her late fifties, with short gray hair and a round, fleshy face that sagged to jowls connected to a wide neck. She had a tired, end-of-the-day look about her.

"Let me guess," the woman interrupted, leaning on the top of the broom with both hands, studying Charlie intently. "White-water guy, down here for the rafting on the New River and you missed your exit and got lost and now you need directions up to Fayette County. Right?" She smiled at Charlie, enjoying her little game.

"Well you got part of it right. I do need directions. I'm looking for the best way to get to Bluefield." Charlie took a few steps into the restaurant, looking around, enjoying the nostalgia the place brought back. It reminded him of several long-gone New Haven diners of his youth. "A lot of people come down here for the rafting?"

"Sure, it's a big deal up on the Gauley and the New River, which is actually the oldest river in North America I read somewheres. Anyway, they tell me kayakers and rafters come from all over the world for the rapids up there though it beats me why anyone'd want to be doing that kind of thing.

"Now, was that all you wanted when you come in here, directions? Or were you looking to eat? Cause, I can't turn on the grill again but I got some cold stuff if you're hungry."

"No, that's okay. I *was* looking for a cup of coffee to go but that's all right."

The woman leaned her broom against one of the booths and went behind the counter. "Well you sit down for a minute then and I'll make you coffee," she called over her shoulder as she ran water into a clear coffeepot.

Charlie protested to no avail as the woman waved him to a stool at the counter. While the coffee brewed, she told him how to get to Bluefield. He asked about the condo development and she drew a little map for him. It would be easy to find she said.

"So, you must be a power plant guy then. A lot of them live over there in Bluefield."

"Yeah, that's right. I'm here to work on the CanAmex project."

"Well then, welcome to West Virginia. I'm Eve Brewster," she said holding out her hand. "This town really needed that project, more than you can imagine. Really been good for my business I'll tell you."

Charlie shook her hand over the counter top. "I'm Charlie Burden, Eve, and I'm very happy to meet you, but I do wish you hadn't made coffee just for me. It wasn't that important."

Eve Brewster just looked at him with a wry smile on her face. "So you're the new *big mule* then. Charlie Burden, from New York."

Charlie laughed. "What am I? The big *what?*"

"The big mule. The boss. It's an old coal mining expression."

"Word travels fast."

"Your man Summers, young guy with the white sports car? He was in tossing your name around to the construction guys the other day. Saying you were on your way down here. Couldn't help but take note."

"I'm surprised anyone would care," Charlie commented.

"Well the big mule at the power plant is pretty important stuff around here. You're kind of like a celebrity here. Just like poor Mr. Paxton was, rest his soul."

"You knew Hugo?"

"Just from coming in here. He was about my best customer. Man could eat cheese omelets like he just got out of a Japanese prison camp. Good tipper too." Eve poured coffee into a tall styrofoam cup and brought it over to Charlie.

"He'd stop in on his way out some evenings and buy his beer and liquor here too. And his cigarettes." Eve Brewster's eyebrows curved upward as she let out a hearty laugh. "*God damn,* if it don't sound like I killed that man single handed."

Charlie grinned. "Yeah, it must have been the omelets that did it."

Eve looked out the window as a car pulled around the corner. Charlie glanced over his shoulder long enough to see a red Honda, then heard the squeak of an emergency brake being applied and the thud of a door.

"Mr. Burden, you feel free to sit there and enjoy your coffee. I think I'm going to have to open the store for my sister-in-law here," Eve said as she came through the counter and moved toward the front door.

"No, that's okay. I'll be hitting the road," Charlie replied as he stood up and reached for his wallet to pay for the coffee. But the woman had moved off toward the darkened store.

The little bell over the front door tinkled and a new voice filled the vestibule between the store and the restaurant. "Hey Evey. Got to open up the store for just a minute, please. I'm runnin' late and I got to bring the boys their medicine."

"Yes, Natty. I know, it's Friday, and you're in a hurry like always." The lights went on in the store side. "How you been Nat? Everything okay in the hollow? Hey, I'm sorry about your friend Birdie. That was a shame."

"Yeah thanks Eve. It was a shame, but even so, you and I should go like Birdie Merkely did when our time comes."

Charlie looked in his wallet and found nothing smaller than a twenty, but he couldn't leave without paying for the coffee. Plus he did want to say goodbye to Eve and thank her. While he waited he sipped his coffee and wandered over to the bulletin board on the wall just inside the door of the restaurant. It held a few yellowing business cards, several ads for various items for sale and some notices of upcoming church events. One notice caught Charlie's eye. It was headlined "New York Trip" and contained information about a bus trip to New York in November to 'see the sights' and the Broadway play *Les Miserables.* The trip included two nights at the Milford Plaza, and the total cost was $321, which seemed pretty reasonable to Charlie. The trip was sponsored by the Red Bone Baptist Church Social Club and anyone interested should call Ada Lowe at home. Reproduced in the upper right hand corner of the flyer was the haunting image of the waif wearing a beret, the famous icon of *Les Miserables.* It was Charlie's all time favorite show. He'd seen it three times, but not for several years now. *What a treat these people are in for,* thought Charlie, *those who would be lucky enough to go.*

"Gimmee a pint of Jack, carton of Marlboros, and a six-pack of Bud tall boys."

Charlie couldn't help overhearing Eve's sister-in-law's voice. She had a nice sounding, slow voice with just a hint of a southern accent. Even in her obvious hurry she had a controlled, gentle quality to her voice.

"And, oh yeah, a can of Red Man for Woody."

"Damn, still chawin' at his age. Surprised that man can still spit," Eve replied.

"Not a pretty sight. Gets a lot of it on him, but he enjoys his chew and he ain't got much else to enjoy these days."

Standing at the counter, Natty looked out the front window and only then realized that there was another car parked in front of the store. An expensive car that surely didn't belong to anyone in Red Bone. Then she realized that the lights were on in the restaurant. She lowered her voice. "Eve you got a customer over there, or'd you go out and get yourself a fancy new car?"

Eve leaned across the counter and told her sister-in-law about the handsome new boss of the power plant who had stopped in for directions and a cup of coffee. With a twinkle in her eye, she offered to take her over and introduce her. Natty absentmindedly felt for the faded green bandana she'd tied her hair back with. "No, I can't now, I've got to get across the street and take care of the boys," she said smoothing out a lock of hair that hung limply across her left eye.

Charlie could hear Eve ringing up her sister-in-law's purchase on an old time cash register and was about to wander over to the store side when he noticed one more item on the bulletin board. A hand-written, three by five card wedged into the wooden border. It read: *Alva Paine's apartment for rent. Clean, furnished, spacious, porch with spectacular view of sunsets. 4th flr. Barney's Bldg., no elevator. Utilities included. Cable and phone extra. See Eve.*

"Damn Eve, *thirty-two bucks for cigarettes!* Every time I come in here they cost more," Natty said as she counted her money out onto the counter while Eve bagged her purchase.

"Generics are cheaper." Eve replied.

"Yeah, but you know Mr. Jacks, got to be Marlboros." Natty curled one arm around the bag and started toward the vestibule. "Well anyway, I'm stealing these pork rinds here," she said flashing a wide grin back at Eve as she grabbed a bag off the wire display rack at the end of the counter. Eve smiled back and shrugged resignedly.

Natty turned her head back toward the front door just in time to avoid running into Charlie Burden standing in the entryway holding his Styrofoam coffee cup. She came up with a start.

"Oh, excuse me, I'm sorry," she said as she looked up quickly at the tall stranger and felt her heart pound for an instant as she immediately recognized the ruggedly handsome friend of Duncan McCord. For two years she'd held the picture in her mind of the two sophisticated, successful men walking toward her at the CanAmex picnic, and then, her embarrassing and exhilarating moment with McCord. She wanted to say something else but she couldn't talk.

"Save a lot of money if you just quit." Charlie tried to sound friendly but his comment sounded like a lecture.

"Yeah, thanks a lot. That's a great idea," Natty said as she just put her head down and moved around him.

He'd only gotten a quick glimpse of the woman's face which was partially hidden by a shock of sandy brown hair but he was surprised by the beauty of her pale blue eyes. For some reason he wasn't expecting Eve Brewster's sister-in-law to be in any way attractive. He immediately wished he hadn't made the comment about the cigarettes. He tried to amend the situation before she got to the front door.

"Sorry," he said to her back. "I know it's not easy. I used to smoke. I quit when I turned forty."

Natty stopped at the door and readjusted her package in her arms while she tried to take a breath before turning back toward the man who, she knew, now held one of the most powerful jobs in McDowell County.

"Yeah, well, I quit when I was in high school. About the time I got pregnant the first time. So I guess we both quit a long time ago." Her voice was slow with a soft, easy drawl, but her irritation with the stranger was clear. She went out the door and went down the wooden boardwalk headed away from her parked car.

Charlie watched her through the front window of the store as she skipped down off the walk and headed diagonally across the street toward a large, dark stone, three-story building. Above the wide, recessed front entryway of the building, a horizontal black sign with lettering now almost completely faded away, read in a classic script, *Pocahontas Hotel*. There didn't seem to be any lights on at the *Pocahontas Hotel*.

'*So I guess we both quit a long time ago.*' Nice dig. Charlie watched her disappear into the old building, then turned back toward Eve, still standing behind the counter of the store, watching him. "I think I insulted your sister-in-law," he said with a sheepish look on his face.

"She'll get over it," Eve replied with a laugh. "Nothing bothers that girl for too long, everything she's been through."

"So does anybody buy anything but booze and cigarettes in here?" Charlie joked, walking into the store.

Eve laughed. "Nat takes care of a couple old colored gentlemen got a room cross the way. Friday afternoon usually, she stops in for their "medicine" she calls it, before going up." Eve looked out the window toward the old building. "Nice men. Old coal miners. The two been together for years and years. Ain't got much time left so Nat does what she can. Ends up paying some outta her own pocket, which she can't afford to do, but she won't say nothin', won't ask . . ." Eve's voice trailed off as she turned back to Charlie.

"Here, I didn't pay you for the coffee yet. That was very nice of . . ."

Eve cut him off as he was pulling out his wallet. "No need for that. It's my treat Mr. Burden, besides I already put the restaurant cash away."

Charlie protested but Eve just waved him off as she shut off the lights to the store.

"Well I'll probably be back in tomorrow to look for some water-proof boots. Then I'll pay you for the coffee too," Charlie said on his way to the front door.

"I'll just overcharge you for the boots like we do to everybody from New York," Eve said with a wink over her shoulder as she continued toward the restaurant. "Good night Mr. Burden."

"Good night Eve, thank you."

Inside the front door of the former *Pocahontas Hotel,* Natty Oakes slumped against the door frame and peeked through a once-frosted window back across the street. She watched as Eve moved from behind the counter and saw the lights go out in the store. Natty closed her eyes and grimaced as she replayed her embarrassing meeting with Charlie Burden. *Damn! What was she thinking about? Copping an attitude with the new power plant boss! The only person around who could give Buck a break and get him a decent job finally. Maybe even save their marriage. Christ, he was just trying to be friendly. And that crack about getting pregnant, jeez, what a dope!* She shook her head in bewilderment as she went down the dark center hallway of the old building, passed a long-out-of service elevator cage, to the wide staircase for the hike up to the third floor. Today, she'd probably have a little glass of *Jack Daniels* with the boys before she left.

Eve Brewster's directions to Bluefield and the condo development were easy to follow. Fifty-five minutes after leaving Red Bone, Charlie found the turnoff to what was unmistakably the entrance to an up-scale, modern condominium community. The entryway was marked by short stone pillars on either side of the road, which had been freshly paved to a darker, smoother look than the county road. Neatly edged belts of grass and mulched flowerbeds lined the road that wound its way through the development in a long meandering circle. Faux gas lamps stood at the corners of brick sidewalks that ran around and into the dozen or so individual buildings.

It all felt suddenly familiar to Charlie. He could have been in New York or Connecticut or New Jersey where similar buildings, each with four or six units with small wooden decks on two floors, had been punched out like cookies, in the seventies and eighties to house the young professionals not ready to give up the carefree life for a heavy mortgage in the suburbs. The look and feel of the place surprised Charlie after his afternoon in Red Bone.

He drove passed a community building next to a large swimming pool that even in mid-evening still had a dozen or so young men and women around it. Beyond the pool he could see two lighted tennis courts. Yes, this is the kind of place that the well-paid young men working for the various contractors employed at the power plant would choose to live.

When he found his building, Charlie pulled in next to a new white Corvette convertible with California plates that he knew would belong to Terry Summers. From the trunk of the Lexus he took out a tennis duffel bag that held most of his casual clothes and his shaving kit and locked up the car. A few units down, a group of three men and two women all in their early thirties, relaxed on a second - floor deck drinking deep red wine from long-stem goblets. They murmured lowly as they noted Charlie's arrival. Scanning the parking area, Charlie noticed more out-of-state cars . . . several from Texas, Ohio, Pennsylvania, one from Ontario.

Charlie dropped his bag on the chocolate leather couch in the spacious living room, and tossed his keys on the credenza in the hallway leading to the dining room and kitchen area. Along one wall of the living room was an expansive entertainment center with a wide-screen television. It was all as he'd expected. Sumptuous and comfortable. Dark and cool. Somewhere outside an air-conditioning unit hummed. Cool air circulated from ceiling vents. The place had undergone a thorough, professional cleaning. The furniture shined and smelled of lemon scented polish. Charlie could find no evidence of Hugo Paxton until, in a small cupboard over the refrigerator, he found half a dozen liquor bottles, several unopened.

Upstairs was a large master bedroom suite with a private dressing room with skylight, and a bathroom with a separate Jacuzzi. The bedroom furniture was heavy and dark. Facing the bed was a hotel style television cabinet with doors that slid back out of sight to reveal another large screen television and VCR.

Charlie went back down to the kitchen and pressed the red, blinking button on the answering machine next to the telephone. There was a message from Terry Summers telling him he'd stop by at nine on Saturday morning and drive Charlie in to take a look at the plant. On a hook over the phone there was a set of car keys with a plastic key fob from a leasing company in Charleston. The keys were adorned with the luxurious looking *Lincoln* logo. Through the large window in the living room, Charlie could see Hugo Paxton's black Lincoln Navigator parked a few spots away from his Lexus.

Charlie took another slow tour of the apartment, but he had known what he was going to do even before he'd come through the front door, maybe as soon as he'd driven through the gate and seen the manicured lawns. He didn't want to be in West Virginia. The assignment had been forced on him, by Lucien, by CanAmex, by his own situation. But if he had to be here, he wanted to be part of it. He wanted to experience McDowell County, experience Red Bone. He'd already gotten a little taste of it – the boy at the construction site, Eve Brewster and her hospitality, even her harried sister-in-law, the little woman with the blue eyes – and it felt good because it felt different. It really was a different world, which was what he needed for a while.

In the small phone book in the kitchen he was surprised to find a listing for Eve Brewster. Her address was the same as Barney's General Store, on Main Street in Red Bone. She must have an apartment in the building. Charlie looked at his watch, hoping that ten-fifteen wasn't too late to call, but he didn't want to wait until morning.

"Hello, this is Eve." She answered in a low voice after several rings.

"Eve, this is Charlie Burden. I met you earlier tonight. I came into the ..."

Eve Brewster chuckled as she cut him off. "Yes, Mr. Burden, I remember. It wasn't that long ago. Are you all right? You didn't drive off the mountain did you?"

"No I'm fine Eve. I hope I didn't wake you up. I hope it's not too late to call."

"No, it's okay Mr. Burden. I had to get up to answer the phone anyway."

Charlie smiled at the old joke.

"Listen Eve, that apartment you have up on the bulletin board. Is it still available?"

"What?" Eve sounded genuinely baffled.

"The apartment. The one on the fourth floor. It's on a little card on the board in the restaurant."

"Oh *God*, Mr. Burden. That apartment's not for you. It's old. This is an old building. Plus it's up on the fourth floor and there's no elevator."

"That doesn't matter. Is it still available?"

"*Available?* Hell, that place'll be available 'til the building falls down. Ain't but a handful of people in all of Red Bone could make it up them stairs without an oxygen bottle."

"Could I take a look at it? Tomorrow morning?"

"What happened to that place in Bluefield? You get lost?"

"No Eve, it's fine. It's a beautiful place. It's just not what I was looking for."

Eve didn't answer for a moment. "Well Mr. Burden you can sure look at it if you want to."

"Tomorrow morning?"

"I'll be here. I'm always here. Goodnight Mr. Burden."

Chapter 10

Buck Oakes' twelve-year-old Chevy pickup always had a distinctive sound as it accelerated up the steep, stone-covered road to Oakes Hill. The engine would whine in first gear as Buck spun the tires through the well-worn ruts, sending stones flying off into the woods like machinegun fire. He tended to drive too fast even when he hadn't been drinking.

The sound of Buck's truck had become both a comforting and frightening signal to Natty over the years. So many nights she had lain awake in the trailer with the windows open to the night air, waiting for that first, distant sound of the truck far down on the lower road – on a still night she could pick it out nearly a half mile away – before he made the final, noisy run up the hill. She would be relieved at first that he had finally come home and then, apprehensive about his condition and state of mind. After he parked his truck at the end of the trailer, she would listen with a trained ear for the tell-tale signs – how hard he slammed the truck's door, whether he was shuffling his feet through the stones in the road, the sound of his boots on the deck – to determine how drunk he may be and if he'd reached that critical stage at which it was best for Natty to just hunker down under the blanket and feign deep sleep.

Tonight, Natty had fallen asleep and woken up several times to find Buck's side of the bed empty. She had many things on her mind that wanted to keep her awake, but it had been a long day and she'd stayed a little later than usual at the *Pocahontas Hotel* having a glass of *Jack Daniels* with Woody and Mr. Jacks. The sound of the truck accelerating up the hill, the beam of the headlights bouncing madly up and down the window screen, awakened her one more time. She automatically shot a glance at the digital clock on the nightstand. *Three-fifteen AM*, the large red numbers glowed in the darkness of the room. *Damn you Buck. Why are you doing this to us again?*

Natty lay awake on her back with the sheet pulled up to her neck, listening, and debating, as she had so many times before, whether to say anything when her husband entered the room. Usually silence ruled. She waited with her eyes open thinking about what Deputy Sheriff Wayne Lester had said up at Birdie Merkely's cabin. She waited with a hollow, anxious feeling in the pit of her stomach, thinking about the woman in Northfork, an old high school girl friend of Buck's. The woman that Buck had gone to live with for six months right after Cat was born. Natty took in a deep breath and waited.

She could hear him rooting around in the refrigerator, and then in the bathroom taking a long pee, splashing water on his face, and finally shoving open the squeaky sliding door to the bedroom. He pulled his T-shirt over his head and sat heavily on the side of the bed to take his boots off. Natty could see him from the faint light of the small nightlight plugged into the hallway outside the children's room.

"So where you been Buck?" The sound of her own small voice startled her in the dead quiet of the dark bedroom. Her husband showed no reaction, pulling off a second boot and tossing it loudly to the floor.

"It's past three o'clock. I been worried," she added a little more softly, apprehensive about Buck's silence.

Buck stood and unzipped his blue jeans. In the dim light Natty saw him stagger slightly causing him to reach out for the corner of the dresser to steady himself. Natty could smell a mixture of sweat and liquor and perfume, coming from her husband as he worked to kick his pants off into the corner. Suddenly a rush of anger enveloped her and she sat up in the middle of the bed determined to make her husband respond.

"Buck where the *fuck* have you been all night?" she demanded in a louder voice. "Tell me. I deserve an answer."

Her husband had turned back toward the bed and had one knee on the mattress as Natty sat up. In the darkness she couldn't see his large left hand as it snapped out and slashed across her face. The blow was landed more with the fingers than the palm of the hand but the suddenness of the slap and the sting of Buck's Red Bone High School ring as it caught the corner of Natty's mouth caused her to see stars as she recoiled to the edge of the bed.

"Don't give me any of that shit Natty." Buck's deep, gravelly voice had a cruel edge to it causing Natty to retreat a little farther in the dark. "It's Friday night. I been out. Pourin' cement all day for forty fuckin' dollars, I deserve some time away from this dump. So don't be givin' me that lip when I come in." Buck rolled heavily onto his back as Natty got up from the bed. Tears ran down her cheeks to mix with the trickle of blood from her upper lip.

"Goddamn you Buck, you prick! You swore you'd never do that again!" Natty forced the words out between clenched teeth. She made her way around the bed, stumbling on one of Buck's boots. "I try so hard Buck. I try so damn hard," she said angrily as she fled the bedroom.

At first light, Natty went back into the bedroom and got her running shoes and shorts. She couldn't wait to feel the fresh cool air of the dawn and lose herself in a long, hard run. Later she'd take the kids and Amos into town for breakfast at Barney's and some of Eve's famous blueberry pancakes, then, maybe to the mall in Bluefield. Anywhere to get away from the hollow for the day. She longed for the refuge of Angel Mountain. But not this day. Not with a new red welt on her cheek and a cut on her lip. Natty couldn't go home today. Her mother might finally persuade her to stay.

Eve Brewster chuckled as she looked out from behind the counter, through the huge plate glass window and saw Charlie Burden's blue Lexus pull into one of the angle-in parking spaces in front of the restaurant. "*Damn,* he really is serious," Eve said more to herself than to any of the dozen or so customers eating breakfast.

The restaurant had a different feel to it in the morning, populated with customers, all local people who had known each other for years. Charlie could feel all eyes on him as he walked in, nodded to Eve and took a seat at the counter.

Dressed in Saturday morning casual – khaki shorts, his faded gray Michigan T-shirt and well-worn deck shoes – Charlie looked more like a misplaced tourist than the new boss of the power plant project.

"Morning Mr. Burden," Eve said as she came over to him with a mug in one hand and a pot of steaming coffee in the other.

"Good morning Eve."

"Still interested in the apartment, or did you come to your senses yet," she asked quietly.

Charlie laughed. "Yeah I'd like to see it. And I want to look at some boots too."

"Well the store don't open 'til nine, so why don't you have some breakfast, then go up and take a look at the place and see what you think. Fourth floor, there's two apartments. Mr. Hankinson's on the right, other one's to the left. Door 'll be open. If you want the place, we'll find a key somewhere, though I don't think Alva Paine ever locked the door in thirty-one years up there."

Charlie's eyebrows went up. "*Thirty-one years* he lived there?"

"Yeah. Long time," she said gazing out the window as if at some distant memory. "He was a wonderful man, Mr. Paine. Hank's ... Mr. Hankinson's closest friend for a long, long time. Still misses him a lot. I can tell. Ain't been the same with Hank since Alva Paine died. He won't admit it but he's been real lonely this past year."

She looked back at Charlie and handed him a menu. "Anyway, you go take a look at it if you want to, and no hard feelings if you decide not to take it, okay?"

"It's a deal," Charlie answered, looking at his watch. He'd left a message on Terry Summers' machine telling him to meet him in front of Barney's General Store in Red Bone at ten o'clock. He wasn't very hungry but thought it would be friendlier if had breakfast. He ordered *"Eve's Specialty,"* the blueberry pancakes.

The hike up the four flights didn't bother Charlie anywhere near as much as Eve Brewster warned, although he had to concede you wouldn't want to be making too many unnecessary trips up and down. At the top of the stairs to the right, a door held a small plastic sign hung from a white pushpin that read: "Dr. P.J. Hankinson" and under it, the word "Principal." To the left there was an identical door with a white pushpin in the middle, but no sign.

The apartment opened into a wide living area dominated by three large windows along the outside wall that stretched from two feet above the floor, to just below the ten-foot ceiling. The windows provided a spectacular, unimpeded view of the southernmost reaches of West Virginia and then, the mountains of Virginia beyond. Charlie walked over to the center window and enjoyed a full view of the scenery.

The place had a musty smell – it had probably been closed up for some time – and an old, lived-in feel about it, but it was clean and bright. Charlie was pleasantly surprised. The high ceiling, antique windows and polished hardwood floor reminded him a little of a tony Tribeca loft he had once been to a party at.

The living room was furnished in a potpourri of old but sturdy furniture. Along the entire length of the interior wall, starting at the door, was a built-in bookcase crammed full of books of endless variety including a very old Britannica Encyclopedia set and dozens of old high school textbooks on math, science and mechanical drawing. Mr. Alva Paine it seemed, must have been a school teacher.

Toward the back of the apartment was a small dining area and a kitchenette. Big enough thought Charlie, for cooking for one. Through the kitchen, another door led out to a large covered porch that extended out twelve feet from the back wall and ran the entire width of the building. The porch yielded another stunning view, looking down the hill westward from Old Red Bone. Charlie could see that the sunsets beyond the seemingly endless stretch of mountains would indeed be spectacular. Looking straight down South County Road, the porch also offered a bird's eye view of the athletic field at the bottom of the hill.

At the other end of the porch, there was another door from the adjoining apartment. Halfway between the doors sat a small, square, cherry table between two identical, high-backed wooden chairs that looked to Charlie like the chairs the teachers always had in school. On the table was a small, wooden cribbage board from which nearly all the surface paint had been worn away. Next to the cribbage board, a wooden cigar box held several well-used decks of cards held together with a rubber band, and under them, a black notebook, an inch thick, also held closed by several rubber bands. Charlie slid the notebook out from under the cards and removed the rubber bands. It was an appointment book for the year 1979. For the first three quarters of the book, every page, front and back was completely covered with columns of minutely printed numbers and dollar signs, mostly in black ink, sometimes blue, and occasionally several pages in pencil. At the top of each page the names Alva and Hank, were repeated to produce three different scoring columns. Under each name there was a list of plus and minus amounts followed by a horizontal line and what looked to be a running total of the cumulative score in dollars. The book held the results of what had to be thousands of games. Charlie thumbed to the last page of entries. The last entry showed Hank +$1,192. Charlie put the book back into the cigar box.

Through the living room, on the front side of the building, was the bedroom, another oversized room with a high ceiling. Like the rest of the apartment, the bedroom was furnished with a mismatched variety of different pieces, but it was clean and spacious.

Charlie knew right away he'd be taking the apartment. It had a beautiful view and a lot of personality. It felt right, more like what he needed than the urbane condo in Bluefield. He was about to go down to find Eve Brewster when he heard something from the bedroom. It was a low droning, like humming, coming from a door in the bedroom that Charlie had assumed was a closet.

Charlie opened the door to find a large bathroom, brilliantly lit by a round skylight in the roof. In the center of the white tiled floor, sat an antique tub with brass fittings and ornate claw feet. Sitting in the tub, staring at him with wide-eyed surprise, was an elderly man with shoulder-length snow white hair, a classic, white handlebar mustache that flowed down well below the man's chin on each side, and a matching goatee that reached to the middle of his chest.

In an instant, the old man recovered, the look of fright replaced with an angry glare. He lifted a long, bony arm out of the bath water and gestured a sarcastic welcome to Charlie. "So just barge right in on an old man's bath why don'tcha? Don't knock. Don't announce yourself. Just come right on in."

Charlie was taken by surprise. "Er, no. I'm sorry, I ..." he stammered.

"So you're the one Eve called me about this morning then. Says you're thinking about renting Alva's place. From New York, the big *goddamn apple,* hot shit new boss of that silly power station." The old man reached over the back side of the tub and brought up a glass jelly jar half filled with a brown liquid. He spit another generous addition of the liquid into the jar. Charlie winced involuntarily at the sickening sight of the tobacco juice.

"Ain't got a problem with chawin' tobacco do ya? Better get used to it down here boy. West Virginia's number one state in the country for chawin' tobacco. Know that? Least it used to be." After a pause he added a little more softly, "back when we had enough people livin' around here to qualify for such things." He reached down and placed the jar on the floor. "Can't light up down in the mines is why."

"You were a coal miner?" Charlie took the opportunity to enter the conversation.

"*Sure* I was a coal miner. For *one goddamn month* I was a coal miner," the old man nearly shouted. "Worst job ever was. Seventeen years old and I cried like a baby every day walkin' up to that mine. Crawlin' around in the dark all day on your hands and knees cuttin' coal, waiting to get buried alive or blown to little pieces or suffocated by the gas. Came out of the mine after one month. Hitchhiked off to Huntington and worked my way through Marshall University just to stay out of them damn holes. So you writin' my goddamned biography or lookin' for an apartment?"

The old man suddenly rose up out of the bath water and climbed slowly out of the tub dripping water across the tiled floor. His skin had a reddish hue with many brown liver spots and hung in loose folds where the flesh was losing the battle with gravity. He had narrow shoulders and a pear-shaped body that was once probably around Charlie's height but had lost a few inches to a hunched back. He covered himself with an old terrycloth robe that was hanging on a rack next to a second door on the opposite side of the bathroom.

Charlie stepped forward and offered his hand. "Charlie Burden," he said.

The old man hesitated as if he were sizing Charlie up before finally taking his hand while nodding his head as though he had reached some decision in his own mind.

"Pullman Hankinson," he offered grudgingly. "But all anyone ever calls me now is Hank." More to himself than to Charlie, he added in a low voice, "Alva Paine used to call me *Doctor* Hankinson, but, well that was a different . . ." His voice trailed off.

In his bare feet, Hankinson shuffled over to the door to his apartment. With his hand on the knob, he turned back toward Charlie. "So you going to take the place or ain't ya? Got to let Eve know if it's okay, if you're okay, with me, cause now I'll have to share the goddamned bathroom again. I'll have to call her."

"Yeah, I'd like to take it. If it's okay. If it's okay with you."

The old man sniffed and shrugged as he mulled it over. "Well, Eve can use the rent money, for sure. So, no, I don't mind. It's alright with me." He took his hand off the doorknob and pointed a bony finger at Charlie for emphasis. "But don't you let her go jackin' the price up cause you're from New York. Next thing, she'll be lookin' to dicker with my rent."

"No, I'll bargain hard with her," Charlie replied sincerely.

As Hankinson opened the door to his apartment, Charlie stopped him. "Hey Hank?" The old man looked up, raising his eyebrows in answer. "How long have *you* lived here?" Charlie asked.

Hankinson tilted his head back in thought, as if the answer might be written on the high ceiling. "Twenty-one years I been here. Six months after my wife died, I moved in here. Twenty-one years," he said as if it were the first time he'd ever thought about it. The old man closed the door behind him, and then opened it again suddenly. "Hey Burden!" he called out as if he'd expected Charlie to be gone from the bathroom.

"Yeah Hank," Charlie answered softly still standing in the doorway of the apartment.

"You play cribbage?"

"Yeah, I play."

"Maybe we'll have a game then. Play for a little something just to keep it interesting."

"That'd be good, Hank. We'll play some cribbage."

The old man was nodding his head affirmatively as he closed the door once more.

Charlie found Eve Brewster behind the counter of the store. She was hanging up the phone as Charlie entered. She smiled and raised her eyes upward indicating that she had been talking to Mr. Hankinson.

"Forgot to tell you about sharing the bathroom."

"That's alright. I don't mind," Charlie replied. "He's quite a character isn't he?"

"Hank? He can be a pain in the ass but he's about the smartest man in McDowell County. Anything you need to know about history or anything else around here, Hank will know it." Eve talked while she went about her business of opening the cash register.

"Taught school at Red Bone High for forty-four years – even after he was the Principal, he kept teaching. Still goes in and teaches a history lesson now and then, though they can't pay him 'cause he's retired."

She turned her attention to Charlie. "So'd Hank scare you off or you going to move in with us Mr. Burden?"

"No, he's fine. I like Hank. We're going to play some cribbage together. But I told him I'd bargain hard on the rent so you wouldn't be raising his side."

Eve laughed. "Well up until about three years ago, Mr. Paine was paying two sixty a month which was the deal he and my late husband Barney made a long time ago. Told him I had to get more, so we settled on two seventy-five. That's what Hank pays. Think you can afford that?"

Charlie pursed his lips, pretending to be struggling with the figure. In his mind, he was shocked at the ridiculously low rent. He paid his landscaper in Mamaroneck more than two seventy-five a month.

"It's worth more than that Eve. You should be getting more," Charlie answered sincerely.

"Yeah, I guess. But old school teachers around here," she glanced upwards again, "they don't get the greatest pension around. So, we all try to get by with what we need. You understand Mr. Burden?"

"Yes Eve. I think I do."

Over Eve's protestations, Charlie wrote out a check paying for the apartment for a year in advance. "If I don't stay a year, you just keep the balance and we won't tell Hank." Charlie still had all his bags in his car and they agreed he would move in that day. He told Eve that if Alva Paine didn't need a key, than neither did he.

When they'd concluded their business, Charlie browsed through the store, slowly making his way to the shoe section in the rear. A lower shelf in the back corner was crammed with a dust-covered selection of tough black leather boots with steel toes. Some of the miners boots looked like they had been there for years. Above them were the more traditional construction boots and the knee-high waterproof boots Charlie was looking for. He sat on a low stool to try on a pair of boots he'd found in his size.

Looking down at the floor as he pulled on one of the boots, Charlie was suddenly aware of someone directly in front of him, blocking the morning light from a rear window. He first recognized the black, high-top sneakers and the same road – dusted white socks. Then, the thick, pale, down-covered lower legs beneath the baggy shorts. The boy was wearing the exact same outfit he'd had on the previous day at the construction site. Charlie looked up to see the scrunched up look of silent laughter on the face of his new pal. The boy's eyes were narrowed to slits by the tightness of his round cheeks. The point of his tongue protruded from the tiny mouth. His short stocky arms hung straight down as he leaned forward toward Charlie in an expression of surprise. The boy was obviously overjoyed to see his new adult friend.

"Hello Chowly. I am the Pie Man!" He held up his open palm for a high five from Charlie.

"Well you sure are the Pie Man," Charlie chuckled as he slapped his palm firmly against the boy's small hand. "How *are* you pal? What are you doing here?"

"We have bweakfast. We have pancakes. Me and mama and Cat and gwandpa Amos. Vewy delicious pancakes." Charlie noticed a maple syrup stain on the boy's shirt.

Suddenly the boy's eyes grew wide with excitement as he focused on Charlie's T-shirt. He pointed a chubby finger at Charlie's chest. "Mithgan, Mithgan. Thath my favowit team. The woovaweens!" Charlie didn't immediately grasp what the boy was saying until he looked down and saw that he was wearing his old University of Michigan shirt. He laughed.

"So you're a Michigan fan. I knew you were a sharp kid as soon as I met you. Hey, Pie Man, try this on." Charlie took off his large blue Michigan ring and held it up for his little friend to see. The boy's eyes widened again.

Suddenly, the boy turned and darted back around the corner of the shoe aisle, still holding the ring. He was calling out excitedly as he scampered toward the front of the store.

"Mama, mama, Chowly go to Mithgan. My fwend Chowly go to Mithgan!"

Charlie pulled on a second boot, wondering if he'd ever see his college ring again. Sitting on the low stool again he looked up to see the tiny face of a small girl with long, golden blonde hair peeking around the corner of the shelving. She had an expressionless face and stared at him with intense curiosity. As she pulled her head back around the corner, Charlie heard the boy's voice again and footsteps coming toward him down the wooden-planked floor.

"Chowly ovah heah mama. My fwend Chowly ovah heah."

Charlie readied himself reluctantly to meet the little retarded boy's mother and probably to do some explaining as to how he and Pie met. Without thinking too much about it, he had a less than complimentary vision in his mind of what he assumed a little retarded boy's mother would look like in rural West Virginia. Then he heard a voice from the next aisle that sounded vaguely familiar.

"Well whoever he is Pie, you have to give him back that ring . . ." The boy, with a look of excitement on his face, reappeared around the end of the aisle with his mother in tow, his chubby fingers wrapped firmly around the small wrist of Eve Brewster's sister-in-law.

Charlie rose to his feet from the low stool, concealing his surprise at seeing the small woman with the pale blue eyes from the night before. She was not what he was expecting.

"Oh *God,* it's *you,*" Natty blurted as she half turned away in an expression of embarrassment that Charlie didn't quite understand. Maybe it was her outfit. She was wearing baggy, faded blue jeans that looked to be several sizes too big for her, loosely tucked into a pair of well-worn, untied tan construction boots, an overly-large man's white, long-sleeve dress shirt that hung loose at the waist, the sleeves rolled up to the elbow, and on her head, a blue baseball cap with a red Spider-man figure on the front.

"I'm sorry," she continued. "I didn't mean it like that. Pie's been talking about his new friend all day yesterday and this morning, and I . . . I was just surprised. That it's *you.* From last night I mean."

Charlie was studying the woman's face as she prattled on. She had a small thin nose, a sharply defined but delicate chin and a wide, sensual mouth. He liked the way she blinked in a slow, drawn out manner – almost in rhythm with the cadence of her speech – and then had a tendency to shift her gaze as she reopened her eyes. But there was something different about her this morning. Her eyes, still a stunning ice blue, but now they seemed glazed, a little bloodshot maybe. As if she might have been crying. And a small cut at the corner of her mouth. *Had that been there yesterday?*

When she stopped speaking suddenly, there was a moment of awkward silence between them before the boy thrust his hand up toward Charlie with the big ring around his index finger.

"Heahs yaw wing Chowly."

"Oh, thanks Pie." Charlie put the ring on his finger and looked back at the woman.

The woman seemed to relax a little. "I'm Pie's mother. Natty Oakes," she said. With Pie between them and Catherine peeking around her from behind, it seemed awkward to offer her hand, so she didn't.

"It's a pleasure to meet you Mrs. Oakes. I'm Charlie Burden," he replied also deciding to skip the handshake part.

"So, are you?" Natty asked quickly.

"Am I what?" Charlie was puzzled.

"A burden."

"Oh. yeah. Well I hope not," Charlie replied to the old joke.

"Sorry. Pretty stupid joke. Probably heard that one before, huh?" Natty shook her head and rolled her eyeballs at her own embarrassment.

"Been a while." Charlie smiled as he looked down at Pie, beaming with pride, intent on not missing a word of the conversation between his mother and his new friend.

"I met Pie at the power plant site yesterday," Charlie said as he playfully pushed down the back of the boy's cap over his forehead. "He showed me around."

"That's right, you're the new boss . . ."

"I'm the *big mule*," Charlie added, at which Pie let out a shriek and then gasped for air as he bent over in spasms of silent laughter. Natty then, had to burst out in laughter at both Charlie's comment and her son's contagious reaction. The sight of the chunky little retarded boy staggering down the shoe aisle, convulsed in a high-pitched squealing laugh, and his mother, covering her mouth, trying unsuccessfully to control herself, caused Charlie to involuntarily join in the laughing. He laughed harder and harder until his stomach hurt and he had tears in his eyes. Even little Cat had a big grin on her face as she watched her brother and the two adults howl irrationally. Just as their laughter started to subside into giggles, Pie rose up, pointing to Charlie, saying, "Chowly a big mule!" and off they went again into another round of convulsions.

Finally, Charlie had to sit back down on the stool in an effort to control the involuntary laughter. The appearance of Eve Brewster at the end of the aisle helped them all gain some composure.

"What the hell's goin' on back here?" Eve also couldn't suppress a wide grin as she watched the three of them wind down from their laughing fit.

"Oh, it's nothing Eve," Natty answered. "Pie said something funny, that's all." She didn't want to embarrass Charlie. "Come on Pie, we got to get going. Amos is waitin' in the car."

Charlie sat on the stool still giddy from the laughing. He tried to remember when he'd last had such a laughing attack. It was the boy's fault of course. *Damn, that kid is contagious.*

On the wooden boardwalk in front of the store, Natty saw Sally Oakes's orange Camaro pull around the corner and take the spot between Natty's Accord and a gleaming white Corvette convertible with the top down. Pie and Cat had run over to take a closer look at the sports car they had seen several times before, speeding along South County Road with a young blonde-haired man at the wheel. Sally had to maneuver carefully between the children and the open front passenger-side door of Natty's car. In the front seat, Amos Ritter sat sideways with his feet on the ground, hands on his thighs, unmoving except for an occasional slow turn of his head and blinking eyes, happy to be away from his stool on Oakes's Hill for short while.

Across Main Street, Emma Lowe was walking hand-in-hand with her grandmother Ada. When they saw Natty waving to them they started across the street toward *Barney's*. Emma broke off to say hi to Pie and look at the fancy car with him, while Ada stopped off at Natty's car, leaning in close to speak to Amos.

Sally bounded up onto the boardwalk wearing her trademark tight shorts, a revealing halter-top and purple horn-rimmed sunglasses. She was smoking a thin, brown cigarette and working over a large wad of gum.

At that moment, Eve came out the front door of the store. She smiled at Natty. "So I see you met our Mr. Burden, Nat." Eve winked a hello to Sally.

Natty shook her head disgustedly. "Christ, Eve. I talked to that man twice now and I made an *asshole* out of myself both times."

"Seems like he was enjoying himself alright," Eve replied.

"Aw that was all Pie's fault. He got us laughing, you know, and ..."

Sally had perked up to the reference to a man. "Who's this? What man you all talkin' about?"

Eve supplied the details. "The new power plant boss. Down here from New York. His name's Charlie Burden. Come in yesterday." She nodded her head sideways at Natty. "Our sister-in-law here almost knocked him down on her way out of the store last night. All she could come up with for conversation was to tell him that she got herself pregnant in high school."

Natty scowled at Eve. "Wasn't like that Eve..."

"So what's he look like?" Sally wanted to get to the point.

"Aw he's *ugly*," Natty answered quickly. "Not your type at all Sal. Fatter than Hugo Paxton and shorter too."

"Yeah. I'll bet," Sally said softly as she eyed the tall stranger wearing a Michigan T-shirt who had just come out the front door.

Before the women could say anything, the Pie Man had Charlie's attention. "Chowly, Chowly," he called out excitedly as he pulled the dark-skinned girl up onto the boardwalk and came between Charlie and the women. "Thith my fwend Emma. Emma on my thocka team. Emma betht thocka playah inna whole wold." Charlie said hello and shook hands with the shy girl who could only shrug and smile nervously in response.

Natty then introduced Charlie to Emma's grandmother Ada Lowe, and then to Sally's consternation, she brought him down to the street to introduce him to Amos sitting in her car. Charlie squeezed the old man's hand firmly as Amos twitched his mouth and blinked his greetings.

As Charlie turned back to the store, Natty was just about to finally introduce Sally, when Terry Summers strode aggressively through the front door of the restaurant and out onto the boardwalk. He stopped short when he saw Charlie and the collection of locals. With sunglasses hooked onto the front of his white polo shirt, tan slacks and brown Italian loafers, Summers, as always, was the picture of Southern California chic. A broad smile came over his face revealing a set of perfect white teeth that gleamed in the morning sun as he looked over the scene.

"Well there you go Charlie," he held out his two arms expansively, palms up, presenting the group before him. "Welcome to West Virginia."

Natty bridled visibly at Summers' comment, her eyes narrowed as she stepped forward from the car a little closer to the wooden stairs. But Sally beat her to a response. "What was that crack Summers? What was that supposed to mean, that '*welcome to West Virginia*' thing?"

Summers knew he'd made a mistake and tried to laugh it off. "Nothing, Sally. Didn't mean nothing Sal. Just a little joke. That's all." He flashed his highest-wattage smile around the group.

Natty wasn't going to let him off so easily. "Sal, I think Mr. Summers was just trying to warn Mr. Burden here about what a backward place he come to so he'll know not to expect too much out of us hillbillies."

"Yeah and probably a good thing too." Sally caught on right away. "With all these retards and crippled old people we got around here . . ."

"And cheap lookin' women," said Natty firing a mischievous eye at Sally who made a quick face back at her before she took over.

"And *ignorant* too. Why Mr. Burden you come to about the most ignorant place in America. Ain't that right Summers?"

"Come on Sal," Terry Summers pleaded, "I didn't mean . . ."

"It sure is *that*," Natty interrupted. "Why you remember that movie *Deliverance?* That kid with the banjo . . . why he'd a been the *damn superintendent of schools* up here."

Sally took her turn. "And the people here're *so* ugly . . . that guy *The Elephant Man,* he coulda moved to Red Bone and taken that bag off his head and nobody woulda even noticed."

A quick wink from Eve told Charlie that the women were just having fun. He stood with his arms folded enjoying the skewering that Summers was taking. He'd deal with the insensitivity of Summers' remark later.

"Course you know what our state flower is don't you Mr. Burden?" Natty continued. "It's the satellite dish."

"And they just raised the drinking age in Red Bone to twenty-eight," said Sally. "Tryin' to keep alcohol out of the high school."

Natty and Sally were both having trouble acting serious about the situation and were starting to laugh at the jokes they'd heard so many times before.

"Hey Summers, you're a single guy," Natty called out, "so you probably know what the best pick-up line is down here." She paused for effect. "Nice tooth!"

Sally went next. "You know folks around here still think the last line to the national anthem is *'gentlemen, start your engines!'*"

As the carnage continued, Summers taking it all in good humor with a broad grin, Charlie used the opportunity to take a closer look at Natty Oakes. When she smiled, as she was doing now, she glowed, and in spite of the unflattering clothing, the boots and the goofy looking hat, Charlie could see that she had a slender, attractive frame. Her broad shoulders and thin legs gave her an athletic appearance, and she had an easygoing self-confidence. She also had a disarmingly alluring way about her. And she was the Pie Man's mother, which also intrigued him.

Finally Sally and Natty ran out of material and Terry Summers came off the boardwalk and greeted his new boss. "Well, welcome to West Virginia anyway," he said glancing at Sally Oakes who shot him a flirtatious look over her shoulder as she headed into Barney's.

Charlie told him about taking the fourth floor apartment. Summers leaned back and squinted upward toward the top floor. "Check out the fire escape," he advised. "I think the closest fire department's in Charleston. Good idea though, moving into town. Get on good terms with the locals."

Charlie watched as Pie and his mother walked down the wooden boardwalk toward the corner to greet a huge black woman who had just lumbered up the steps from South County Road.

"Terry, speaking of the locals, it doesn't help anyone to make insulting comments like that." Charlie turned his eyes back on Summers.

"Yeah, that just kind of slipped out," Summers said without any remorse as he slid on his sunglasses. "But it's true Charlie. What you see is what you get. You'll see. People are fucking weird down here," he said softly. He flashed Charlie a smile and popped a stick of gum in his mouth.

Charlie told him he'd meet him out at the construction site after he took care of a few things. He watched Summers lower himself into the Corvette and rumble off around the corner and down South County Road.

Charlie wanted to move his things from the car up to the fourth floor apartment and thought that he'd ask Pie to help him. The boy would get a kick out of that, plus he'd give him a few dollars. He saw Pie at the corner of the boardwalk, standing with the girl Emma a little ways away from Natty and the large black woman. Farther down the street, a gangly looking black boy in blue overalls with no shirt, and a baseball cap on backwards, was slowly sauntering toward them.

Charlie went up on the boardwalk and walked toward the group. As he got near Natty and the black woman, Natty and the woman stopped their conversation as Natty pulled her friend toward Charlie to introduce her. The black woman was as wide as a door with huge arms, the rolls of fat straining the circumference of the short sleeves of her purple flowered dress.

"Mabel, I want you to meet Mr. Burden," Natty said as he approached. "Mr. Burden's the new *big mule* out at the power plant." She flashed a quick smile at Charlie, then looked around quickly for Pie, relieved that he hadn't overheard her. "He's just come down here from New York City. Mr. Burden, this is Mabel Willard. Mabel's the special ed teacher at the elementary school, and she's the reason your little friend the Pie Man is such a wise ass."

The black woman shrugged off Natty's comment and reached out two huge paws that engulfed Charlie's hand in a firm, warm handshake. "Well let me welcome you to West Virginia, Mr. Burden, and to our little town of Red Bone. That's just a wonderful thing you all are doing out there, putting our boys to work and all. And that's so Christian of you fellows to leave your families and come down here and do that *dangerous* work." She leaned in a little closer, still squeezing Charlie's hand tightly, and tilted her head slightly. "You *do* have a family Mr. Burden, a *wife, children,* back there in New York City?" She fixed on him a huge smile filled with brilliant large white teeth accented by several shining gold caps.

Natty poked the woman's massive left arm with little impact. "Mabel, don't be asking Mr. Burden such personal questions." The woman ignored Natty and continued to hold on to Charlie with her hands and her large brown eyes.

Charlie had to grin at Mabel's thinly disguised inquiry. "Mrs. Willard, it's a pleasure to meet you, and yes I have a family. A wife and two children . . . one in college and one now living on his own in Boston. And I actually live in Mamaroneck, New York. My office is in the city. And please, call me Charlie."

Mabel Willard finally leaned back releasing Charlie's hand seemingly disappointed by his story. "Well that's fine, that's fine. Very nice to meet you Charlie," she added sincerely. Suddenly she became energized again as she turned toward the end of the boardwalk pulling Natty with her as she lumbered past Charlie. "Now where is that boy?" she bellowed. Then quietly to Natty, "Sammy got somethin' *real important* he got to ask you."

The black boy loped up the steps from the street. He touched knuckles with Pie. "Sup Pie Man? Hey Em," he said as sauntered past the other children. He was a little taller than Emma Lowe and had a lean but muscular build.

"Sammy get on over here. Miz Natty ain't got all day to wait on you," Mabel thundered.

Natty smiled at the slender boy as he came up to them. "Damn Sammy, you've grown a foot this summer, just like Emma."

"Now Sammy, you go ahead and ask miz Natty what you wanted to ask her," instructed Mabel.

The boy fidgeted with his hands thrust deep into the pockets of the denim overalls. "Well, miz Natty I was wonderin' you know, if I could, ah, play on your soccer team this year, you know, get back to playing soccer." The boy shot a quick glance over at Pie and Emma who were listening intently.

Natty was clearly taken by surprise. She tilted her head inquisitively. "Soccer? You're not going to play football this year?"

"No ma'am, I ain't playin' football this year," he said softly as he looked toward Mabel who remained silent.

"But Sammy, you're one of the best football players in the county. You haven't played soccer for what, three years?"

"I can still play," Sammy said with a little more cockiness in his voice. "And also, I'm supposed to tell you, Zack wants to play soccer on your team too."

Natty was speechless. Sammy's twin brother Zachary was the football team's star quarterback. The two Willard boys had played on Natty's soccer team for a few seasons when they were younger, before they started playing football. Both were wonderful athletes and Natty knew that what they may lack in polished soccer skills, they would make up for with blazing foot speed and competitive drive. Zachary especially was an extremely gifted athlete who hated to lose at anything. Even after several years away from competitive soccer, Natty knew that the brothers would very quickly become two of the best players in the league. This was like a gift from heaven after all the worrying she had been doing about this year's team.

Natty looked to Mabel for an explanation. "So, what's up?"

Mabel folded her arms across her massive breasts, her chin rising slightly to indicate her consternation. "The boys ain't playing for that coach this year is all. That new coach Lester come in at the beginning of last year and the boys was on the team, committed, you know, so they stuck it out. But no more, not for that man. They can play football again when they get to the high school. So this year they can play soccer, if you'll have 'em."

Deputy Sheriff Wayne Lester. Of course. He became coach of the football team the previous season. Natty knew first hand, that he was pretty much of a bigot but it must have been worse than she thought for him to lose the Willard boys. *Christ, he'd have it in for her now when he finds out that she took his two best players.*

"Well Sammy, of course you can play, and Zachary too. I'm thrilled to have you back." Natty could see Pie and Emma grinning with excitement. She smiled at Emma. This was especially good news for her. Not only would they probably have enough players to make up a team, but now with Sammy and Zack on the team, opposing teams would have to worry about more than just Emma. The Willard boys were well known around the athletic fields of McDowell County and news of their joining *The Bones,* would spread very quickly to the other teams in the league.

Natty turned her attention back to Sammy. "Now Sammy you and your brother are going to have to start brushing up on your soccer skills real quick then. First practice is in couple of weeks and then we got a game right away, so come on, we'll walk down to the library and get you a couple of balls you can take home and kick around." Natty looked at Mabel for consent.

"Well you kids go ahead. I can walk down there fine, but I *ain't* walkin' back up that hill. No way," said Mabel. "Ada and me'll be sittin' right here on this porch with this little Cat on my lap," she said wrapping her large arms around Catherine making her giggle. Then she added quickly, "say Natty, why don't you take Mr. Burden down there and show him that poor roof on your library. Maybe his big company might be able to plug up that hole for you."

Natty looked at Charlie, but before she could say anything, her son had leaped at the suggestion. He ran over and grabbed Charlie's hand and started pulling him toward the corner. "C'mon Chowly. I show you owa thocka field."

Natty protested "No Pie, I'm sure Mr. Burden is too busy to be . . ."

Charlie cut in. "No it's okay. I'll take a look at your roof." Then he added, to Pie, "and, I'd love to see where my little pal plays soccer." If Charlie had been watching Natty's face, he would have seen, for just an instant, a look of surprise and puzzlement over this stranger's affection for her son.

Pie was beaming as they all went down the stairs to the street and started walking down the steep hill. Emma and Sammy had run on ahead and Pie soon dropped Charlie's hand to try to catch up to them. Natty and Charlie crossed the street and walked together down the cracked, crumbling sidewalk. They both felt a little uneasy about being left together. Natty spoke first.

"So what's this, punishment for you? Getting sent down here? New York City to Red Bone, West Virginia . . . *man*, that's got to be serious. Get caught diddlin' the boss's wife or something?"

Charlie laughed. "No, no. I volunteered, sort of. The company needed someone here and CanAmex, our client, they wanted me. It's an important project and ..."

"I was just making a joke. I didn't meant to insult you or anything."

"Yeah I know," Charlie assured her. "Plus, I'm not going to be here that long, maybe nine months. Then I'm going to China, to work on a big hydroelectric project."

"Wow, that sounds exciting. *China.* Jeez, I'm hoping to go to *Myrtle Beach* some day," she said with a chuckle.

They didn't say anything more until they got near the bottom of the hill and approached the small building at the end of the soccer field.

"This is a library? This little building here?" Charlie asked.

"Well it's supposed to be a children's library, but a lot of the books got ruined by the water leaking in. Had to throw them away. I packed up the rest in a couple of boxes and moved them to a dry part. But you can't have kids sitting around in a wet, leaky building reading books, so it's just closed now. I don't know what we'll do with it. Probably nothing. Just wait for it to fall down." Then she added softly, "just like everything else around here."

"How come Mabel called it *your* library?" Charlie asked.

Natty laughed. "Everyone calls it *my* library, cause it was my dumb idea and I got the town to let us use the building, so then I had to make it happen, get the books and all."

On her tiptoes, she reached up over the metal doorframe and brought down a key. "Kids'd come in and read the books here or take em home for a while if they wanted and it was nice. Then the damn roof started leaking and, well you can see what a mess it is."

Natty pushed open the door and flipped on the lights. A small puddle of water remained in the main room but Charlie could tell from the watermarks at the base of the walls that the water had at times, covered the entire floor several inches deep. There was mildew on the walls. A drop ceiling had several panels missing and most of the other panels were stained brown from rainwater.

"If we could just get the roof fixed, then we could get some new furniture, get some more books and we'd be back in business," Natty said hopefully. "I was going to get a computer that we could hook up to the Internet, so the kids could . . . well, that ain't going to happen anyway."

Natty went into an adjacent room crowded with old maintenance equipment, a portable blackboard, and several wicker baskets of old athletic equipment. Hanging on a wall was a mesh-net bag of white soccer balls. She took down the bag and brought out two balls.

In the center room, Charlie had found an old wooden flagpole and used it to push up several ceiling panels to get a better look at the roof. Standing on the back of a long, green plastic-covered couch, he pulled himself up through the hanging ceiling and up into the rafters of the building to take a closer look. Natty came back into the room with the soccer balls and heard him climbing around in the roof trusses. She went outside to the back of the building and threw the balls down to the kids on the soccer field and went back inside the building. Charlie was just coming down out of the ceiling.

"Mr. Burden, you didn't have to do that. I'm not expecting you to do anything about our roof. It ain't your problem." She watched him while Charlie used some paper towels to wipe off his hands. He had strong, muscular arms and a hard looking chest under his T-shirt, a lot like Buck, but Charlie's stomach was flatter. Buck was maybe an inch taller and his legs were thicker than Charlie's.

"So, can it be patched up then?" She was curious about his evaluation.

Charlie finished cleaning his hands and threw the towels in a cardboard box on the floor. "No, it's a problem," he said. "You need to rebuild the whole roof structure. The trusses are rotting and the whole thing is sagging. Foot of snow up there in the winter, and it'll cave in."

"Damn," she said dejectedly. "That sounds expensive."

"Well it's more than a patch job anyway."

Outside, they went around to the back of the building and down a long flight of crumbling cement stairs to the soccer field. Emma and Sammy were playing keep-away from Pie who was running around like a madman as they dribbled and kicked the ball back and forth. The boy had a big *happy face* on and every few seconds he would look up to see if Charlie was still watching him.

The field was overgrown with weeds, dandelions, and large patches of crabgrass. In front of the goal was a large indentation in the dirt that was certain to be a foot-deep pond after a rainstorm. Across the field Charlie could see several more depressions and some ruts made by water run-off. In Mamaroneck, the parents wouldn't have used the field for a parking lot.

"Don't look like much now." Natty was reading his thoughts. "But it'll be okay when we mow it down and fill in some holes. Worst field in the league. But it's okay," she added unconvincingly. "You'll have to come down and watch one of our games. Do you like soccer Mr. Burden?"

"Yeah, I do like soccer. I'd like to watch your team play sometime," said Charlie, thinking that it *would* be nice to have a team to root for.

Going back up the hill, Emma took off at a quick sprint pursued closely by Sammy Willard encumbered by the two soccer balls. Pie ran after them for a few yards but soon gave up the chase, his short legs no match for the hill or the other children. He fell into a labored hike a few yards in front of the adults.

Natty thought about asking Charlie about Angel Mountain and if he knew anything about plans to mine the coal up there, but she thought better of it and kept silent. She reminded herself that Charlie Burden was on the other side of that whole issue. It was probably why they sent a big shot New York guy down there, to make sure that they got a surface mining permit for Angel Mountain. Best to just let it go.

Then, for a moment, she considered asking Charlie about his friend Duncan McCord, the powerful leader of CanAmex who had been so nice to her at the picnic two years earlier. But then she'd have to explain how she knew who Duncan was and how she knew that he and Charlie were friends, and admit that she had remembered Charlie from that very brief encounter so long ago now and maybe even have to admit to how many times since then, while she was running or laying in the sun with her eyes closed on her rock up on the side of Red Bone Mountain, she had thought about Charlie and his friend Duncan. And she certainly wasn't going to do that.

Half way up the hill, Charlie broke the silence. "Say Pie Man," he called out. The boy stopped and turned back toward Charlie. "How'd you like to make ten bucks, helping me move my stuff from my car up to the fourth floor?" Charlie gestured with his thumb up toward the top of the building next to them.

Natty stopped and looked at him with surprise on her face. "You're moving in here? Alva Paine's apartment, on the fourth floor?"

"Yeah, I looked at it this morning. It's fine, and a lot closer to the project than Bluefield. The price is right too. Is there something wrong?" he asked.

"No, no. I'm just surprised is all. That's good. That's very good for . . . well, Hank needs someone up there. I'm *glad* you're moving in here Mr. Burden." She resumed walking up the hill.

"You know Hank?" Charlie asked.

Natty laughed and smiled at him. "Damn, you still don't know where you are, do you Mr. Burden? *Everybody knows everybody* in Red Bone." She looked up toward the fourth floor porch where she often saw Hank when she was running in the morning. "Mr. Hankinson was my history teacher, two years in high school, before I got . . . before I left. He was the principal for a long time too. Tried his best with me, but, I guess I was beyond hope," she said with a laugh.

"Why did you . . ."

Natty cut him off. "And, Pie would be more than happy to help you move your stuff upstairs, and don't even think about giving him any money. That right Pie Man?"

Continuing to trudge up the sidewalk without turning around, the boy plunged both hands into the pockets of his shorts and pulled his pockets inside out, showing that he was penniless. "Yeth mama," he called over his shoulder, "I help Chowly."

Charlie and Natty both had to laugh at the boy's antic. They could see from the movement of his shoulders that the boy was chuckling over his little joke and knew that he had his happy face on.

A few yards from the top of the hill, Natty winced when she heard the unmistakable sound of Buck's truck as it whined in low gear to make it up the hill behind her. She didn't turn to look. She didn't want to see the truck and didn't want Buck to be there. Most of all she didn't want this moment with the kind, considerate man from New York to end. It had been such an enjoyable morning starting with their laughing fit in the back of the store and meeting up with Ada and Emma, and Mabel and Sammy, and then the walk down the hill with Charlie Burden. It had been a perfect morning. She wanted it to continue. And she certainly didn't want a scene with Buck, not here with this outsider present. *Maybe he'd just drive right by without stopping.*

The white pickup truck came to a rough stop a few yards farther up the hill, the front right tire jumping over the short stone curbing. Charlie was startled at first but he could see from Natty's reaction that it was someone she knew. Buck fixed Charlie briefly with a cold eye before turning to Natty and leaning over toward the open passenger window.

"C'mon Nat. We need to talk. I gotta talk to you Nat. C'mon, get in." It was the apologetic voice that Buck could summon up when he needed it, but he was never able to mask the look in his eyes that said there was trouble rumbling just beneath the surface.

Natty knew the look and didn't want to provoke any trouble. She stood still for a second, looking down at the ground and then shrugged her shoulders resignedly and walked toward the truck. She turned her head back to her son. "Pie, you go help Mr. Burden move his things. I'll get you at Eve's later." She got into the truck and stared straight ahead as Buck roared away from the curbing faster than he had to.

Charlie watched the boy stare after the truck as it climbed the hill, took a left on Main Street and accelerated noisily away. The Pie Man didn't say anything. He just trudged more quickly up the hill staying a little ways out in front of Charlie.

After a long afternoon with Terry Summers, touring the construction site until seven o'clock, Charlie declined the younger man's invitation to dinner and a few beers with some of the other construction workers at a place called *Moody's Roadhouse*, and returned to the apartment in Old Red Bone. The store and the diner were closed and Main Street was deserted. Charlie suddenly felt quite alone as he hiked up the four flights of stairs in the center of the old building.

On the kitchen table, wrapped in aluminum and still warm from the oven was a large turkey pot pie with a note from Eve Brewster that read simply, "Welcome to West Virginia." and under it in parentheses, "P.S. this is Hank's favorite." In the refrigerator, there was a homemade apple pie from Mabel Willard. Charlie rapped on the back door to his neighbor's apartment and invited Mr. Hankinson over for dinner and afterward, some cribbage.

After devouring a good portion of the turkey pie, the two men went out on the porch and took their chairs at the card table. Hank went over the stakes as Charlie admired the orange sunset which cast a warm, comforting glow across the table and against the red brick wall.

"Okay. We play for twenty dollars a game, plus a dollar a point, ten for the high hand, double for a skunk." He looked up quickly to see if Charlie had any objections. The stakes seemed a little steep to Charlie, then he remembered the score book with the thousands of games and the running total.

Charlie won the first game and lost the next three, finishing as the light faded with the sun falling behind the mountains of southern West Virginia. On a piece of scratch paper, Hank totaled up the damage.

"That's eighty-two dollars my friend," said Hank sounding pleased with himself. "Pay up."

The demand took Charlie by surprise. "What about the book?" he said pointing to the old appointment calendar.

"Oh no," said Hank gruffly, shaking his head. "Last time I did that, the guy stiffed me for eleven-hundred bucks!" He sat staring at Charlie unflinchingly.

Finally, Charlie reached for his wallet. "Well okay," he said, a little bewildered. "I guess we can do it like this." He was thumbing out four twenties when he looked up and saw Hank grinning through his white mustache.

"Gotcha there Burden," the old man said, slapping the table loudly. He reached for the score book. "We'll put it on account and see how things go. We may have to lower the stakes if you're as lousy a player as you showed today."

"Don't worry about me Hank," Charlie said, relieved that they wouldn't be playing for cash. He watched P. J. Hankinson write in the book that only he and Alva Paine had shared in for twenty-one years. Charlie thought he saw Hank sigh when he looked at the last page of scores and wrote Charlie's name in place of Alva at the top of the column. "You two played a lot of games, huh Hank?"

Hank didn't answer. He seemed distracted, lost in thought. Finally he looked up and saw Charlie, then looked away. "Yeah, lot of games," he said softly.

Charlie got up to relieve the moment and leaned on the porch railing. He looked down at the decrepit soccer field and the children's library with the leaking roof. Across the field from the South County Road side, there was a grassy bench area and behind it a gravel parking lot accessed by a dirt road which looped around the west end of the field. Next to the parking lot, there was a field that looked like it was once a baseball field with a rusted backstop and a crabgrass infield. Beyond the baseball field were several acres of boulder-strewn, rolling meadows, and then woodlands. Between the soccer field and the overgrown baseball field, on a small patch of high weeds sat a rusted frame of an old swing set.

Looking down at the whole area, Charlie had a glimmer of an idea. He stared down at the road and the field and the woods and the contours of the land and visualized the possibilities.

"Say Hank," he said softly over his shoulder.

The old man rose from his chair with effort. "Yeah Burden." He came to the railing next to Charlie.

"Who owns all that land down there?" He drew the parameters of his query with an open hand. "The land next to the soccer field and that baseball field."

Hank spit tobacco juice over the side of the porch onto an area of brown rocks far below. "Well that land and pretty much everything else that ain't built on in Red Bone is owned by a company called Ackerly Coal. Own all of Red Bone Mountain and the mineral rights for anything they don't own outright."

"*Ackerly Coal* huh. That's interesting," Charlie said.

"Course, your pals at CanAmex going to own it all soon's they take over Continental Electric." Hank watched another gob of tobacco juice make the long trip down to the rocks below.

Charlie looked at Hank, surprised that the old man was aware of the takeover. "Yeah, that's right Hank. If it all goes through."

Charlie and Hankinson stood side by side at the porch railing, without talking, watching the last of the orange sun as it was slowly extinguished by the gray mountains to the west.

That night Charlie called Ellen at the house in Vermont. Ellen and Linda Marchetti were making dinner for some people from the tennis tournament. Charlie could hear loud voices and sporadic laughter in the background.

"Darling, how's everything in Arkansas?" Ellen said grandly as if for the benefit of her guests. She sounded full of life and in command as always.

"West Virginia. Red Bone, West Virginia," he corrected. He told her about the drive down, and about the apartment and shopping for boots. "They have a *Barney's* here," he told her without elaborating.

"Oh that's good. You'll have somewhere to shop then."

She and Linda were playing in the finals of the tennis tournament in the morning, then driving down to Manchester for some high-level outlet shopping, staying over at the Equinox.

"So, you'll be up for Columbus weekend, darling, the foliage is going to be spectacular this year. And I've made the reservations in Aspen for Christmas." Ellen enjoyed playing for the crowd. Charlie could visualize her waving a wineglass like an orchestra leader's baton, head tilted back to air out her words.

"Yeah, that's fine Ellen, shouldn't be a problem," said Charlie.

Ellen needed to attend to the dinner. Charlie wished her luck in the tennis tournament and Ellen said something in reply that Charlie didn't catch, but brought a laugh from her dinner guests. Then she clicked off.

Chapter 11

Eighteen thousand feet over central Pennsylvania, a silver and black Gulfstream V leased to CamAmex Energy Ltd. flashed across the evening sky on a heading for Toronto's Lester Pearson International Airport. Alone in the small, luxuriously appointed cabin, Jack Torkelson sat in one of the four beige leather captain's chairs staring at a laptop open on the fold-out table in front of him. To his right was a communications console with two telephones and a fax machine. CanAmex's Director of U.S. Operations sipped a mineral water and studied the rows of figures on the computer screen while he waited for the conference call operator to buzz him back when she'd connected all parties.

After a weekend at home in Georgetown, Torkelson was headed to Toronto for his bi-weekly schedule of meetings with upper management, before heading back to the Washington office on the same jet on Wednesday. Torkelson disliked the time he had to spend in Toronto with the headquarters people. He found dealing with the bright-eyed, simple-minded Canadians to be tedious at best, and the time he spent north of the border to be an inefficient use of his time which was better spent in Washington, the vortex of the global energy industry, among the legislators, regulators and lobbyists who would determine the winners and losers of the new energy economy. This was where he belonged, where he was most at home. Not in the CanAmex boardroom facing the over-achieving Duncan McCord who just happened to be in the right place at the right time, and his chief lieutenant, the roughneck, Red Landon.

The phone buzzed softly and Torkelson waited for the other conferees to come on the line. Larry Tuthill first, from his hotel at O'Hare, then Vernon Yarbrough, the lawyer, from his home in Charleston and finally, from his apartment in Bluefield, West Virginia, Terry Summers of Dietrich Delahunt & Mackey.

After the obligatory salutations, Torkelson got down to business. "So, Mr. Yarbrough, how is our judge? How did your meeting go?"

"It went just fine Jack, couldn't be better. He'll make his ruling in November and we'll have our variance for Angel Mountain within a week. All according to plan. As long as Ackerly Coal has a deed for that pig farm." While the others waited, Vernon Yarbrough kissed his two daughters good night, before returning to the call. "But, if DeWitt hasn't sold out by mid - November, the whole thing is off. The judge isn't going to do *anything* unless DeWitt sells and he isn't going to make this an open-ended deal. If it isn't done in early November it's all moot anyway, cause of the legislation."

"Okay, well that's good," said Torkelson. "All we need is his ruling. Everything else is taken care of."

Larry Tuthill broke in. "Now tell Jack the good news Vernon."

"What news?" Torkelson asked quickly.

The others could hear the tinkle of ice in Vernon Yarbrough's cocktail glass before he spoke. "Well Jack, seems that we've got ourselves some *leverage* now with that old pig farmer should make him a little more receptive with regards to the magnanimous nature of our offer."

"What leverage?" Torkelson asked softly, trying to hide his impatience. He held southerners in about the same regard as he did Canadians, and southern lawyers, with their sham degrees from country club law schools like Vanderbilt and Duke, were just barely tolerable.

The lawyer had a smile in his voice. "Now Jack, what would you say if I told you that we've established first hand, that our favorite pig farmer, or more likely, his grown son – *Petey* they call him – has about a third of an acre of three-foot-tall, commercial grade, swat-team-ready, early-news-quality cannabis plants growing smack in the middle of his corn field?"

Larry Tuthill let out an audible chuckle. He enjoyed Yarbrough's facility with words.

The lawyer continued. "*And*, that son Petey, during his early adulthood, did a year-long stretch at one of our fine penal institutions for a previous felony, which would be child's play compared to the time he'd now be faced with for a second offense of this magnitude, *if* that is, someone were to bring the illicit herb garden to the attention of our county and state law enforcement agencies."

Jack Torkelson, alone in the cabin of the Lear jet, couldn't repress a wide smile. Finally they had the advantage over that unreasonable old pig farmer who didn't care about money. This was better than money. This was family. "They're growing *pot*? In the corn field?" Torkelson sounded genuinely amused.

"Yessir, and a nice healthy crop it is too," Yarbrough responded. "Getting plenty of good sunshine up on that mountain."

"Alright, that's good. But we don't use it unless we have to. Still much cleaner if DeWitt just sells out and goes away happy. So go down there and make him another offer, a good offer he can't refuse. If that doesn't work, then we'll play hardball," said Torkelson.

"My thoughts exactly," replied Yarbrough. "Our judge is going to want to see that the pig farmer got a nice pay day for the farm, so he can feel good about the whole thing. But now we got a mulligan to use if we need it."

"And gentlemen," Torkelson had a serious edge to his voice now, "we keep this new development strictly to ourselves, no leaks, to *anyone*. Is that clear Summers?"

The reference to Charlie Burden was obvious to Terry Summers. "Yeah, I understand. No need for anyone else to know," Summers answered. Inside, he was elated that Torkelson was taking him even further into his confidence while at the same time, continuing to ease Charlie Burden out the door. Summers' plan to become CanAmex's man at Dietrich Delahunt & Mackey, with a commensurate partnership and place on the Executive Committee, was becoming a very realistic goal.

"Terry, what's happening with Burden? Larry Tuthill asked. "He get down there all right?"

"Yeah, he's here. Saw him yesterday. Took him around the site. Funny thing though, he didn't take the condo in Bluefield. Moved into an old fire trap in the middle of Red Bone."

"Why would he do that?" Torkelson asked suspiciously.

"I don't know. Get in good with the locals I guess. Looks like he's already made some acquaintances there," answered Summers.

"Well you need to keep an eye on him Summers. A close eye. I need to know if he has any suspicions at all. And above all, I need to know if he has any contact with Toronto, any contact at all with McCord or Landon. Is that clear?"

"Yessir, Mr. Torkelson. I'll stay on it."

Jack Torkelson wasn't at all comfortable sharing his anxieties publicly with this brash junior engineer but he was Tuthill's man, and Torkelson needed someone watching Charlie Burden. The last thing he needed right now was Burden bringing McCord or Red Landon into the situation. Torkelson could control things as long as it was solely about the Red Bone project but anything that hinted of a problem with the CES takeover was something else entirely. McCord and Landon would be all over him like a couple of pit bulls if they got wind of a possible problem with the merger, and then the game would be over. He was depending on Burden's loyalty to McCord to keep him quiet and to enlist his needed assistance on the Angel Mountain initiative. And, to take the blame if it all blew up in their faces.

"Good," said Torkelson, "now what about our cooling pond problem?"

Yarbrough was again the professional lawyer. "We've got a date before the town planning board for the third week in September. We'll be putting together a first rate presentation, plus we'll have representation from the Governor's office, couple of state Senators and reps and probably some county politicians too."

"Don't worry Jack, we'll get that done," added Larry Tuthill.

"Don't screw it up," Torkelson responded calmly. "Then, take care of the pig farmer. Larry keep me informed. Good night gentlemen."

Late in the afternoon on Thursday, walking back across the open field from the generator building to his office, Charlie happened to glance toward the main gate and saw a familiar figure riding his bike slowly in circles on the entry road just outside the gate. Occasionally the boy would look up and scan the site quickly before the lazy circling of the bike turned his head away again. He didn't see Charlie or maybe he didn't recognize him wearing his white hardhat and shorts.

Charlie changed his direction and headed for the gate. He could see that not Hicks but one of the other security guards was on duty in the little house just inside the gate. As he neared the fence the guard, a bored looking older man, put down his magazine and pulled himself laboriously from his stool to see what the boss man wanted. In response to the activity of the security guard, the boy started to ride off down the short hill to the encircling road. Charlie took off his hardhat and let out a shrill whistle.

"Hey Pie Man," he called out. "Get over here!"

The boy jerked his head around when he heard the familiar voice. His round cheeks tightened, squeezing his eyes nearly shut as the tip of his tongue waggled between the tightly pursed lips of his small mouth. He wheeled the bike around and pumped the pedals up to the open gate where he slid off the banana seat letting the bike slide to the pavement.

"Hello Chowly!" he said loudly. "I am the Pie Man!" He walked toward Charlie quickly, his small hand up in the air for a high five. Charlie squeezed his hand and pushed the back of his baseball cap down over his eyes.

"Well Pie Man, you finally came to visit me."

"I came befowa one time Chowly, but . . ." The boy glanced at the security guard unsure if he should continue.

Charlie nodded to him knowingly and introduced him to the security guard. "This is my friend Pie. You can let him in to see me whenever he comes by."

"Okay, Mr. Burden, whatever you say," the guard answered, anxious to get back to his stool and his magazine.

Charlie took the boy up to the administration building and introduced him to the few people working at the computers in the main engineering room. The boy was wide-eyed with wonderment upon seeing the sophisticated electronics arrays and the complex images dancing across the large-screen monitors. A young engineer for one of the contractors put him up on a stool in front of a computer showing the layout of the site and showed him how to manipulate the mouse to move trees around the screen. The boy was completely mesmerized by the computer and incredulous as the engineer clicked them through a three dimensional tour of the interior of the main generator building. Charlie stood by watching the boy's face, so incapable of concealment or deception, as it alternately scrunched up with glee or went slack with open-mouth awe. As a new image came up on the screen, the boy pointed at the monitor and looked up at Charlie with obvious pride. "Towabins," he said.

Charlie laughed as he looked down at the screen. "Right you are Pie Man, that's where the turbines are going."

The young engineer added his approval, patting the boy on the back. "Kid, you're a born engineer."

"Pie Man is an engineewa," he said sliding off the stool. "I will be an engineewa, like Chowly."

Charlie glanced at his watch. "Hey, I've got an idea Pie. C'mon, let's go outside," It was near the end of the day anyway, a good time for what he had in mind. On their way out, Charlie ducked into a storage room. After a few seconds, he came out with a brand new shining white hardhat that, after adjusting the fitting band, he placed ceremoniously on Pie's head. The boy's face couldn't have lit up any brighter as he and Charlie, with matching hardhats, walked through the interior yard of the site, headed for the collection of mammoth yellow and green vehicles lined up in the huge, dusty, "parking lot" of the project.

They finally stopped next to a huge, complex looking yellow Caterpillar bulldozer. The top of the heavy metal tread was over the boy's head. Pie was gazing up at the open-air cab at the extreme rear of the monstrous piece of machinery when he heard Charlie's voice and saw him halfway up the narrow stairway at the rear of the bulldozer.

"Well c'mon Pie. Let's go!"

There was plenty of room for them on the wide seat, which was one reason Charlie had selected the large bulldozer. Another was the incredible noise it made when Charlie activated the choke and hit the starter button. Charlie laughed as he watched the expression of fear and excitement on the boy's face as the engine clacked and belched to life, puffs of black smoke exploding from the tall exhaust pipes behind them.

"Hang on Pie," he yelled over the noise as he squeezed the handgrips and pulled on the levers that sent the heavy treads into action. The boy pressed in closer against Charlie and squeezed the bar in front of him as the giant machine shuddered and jerked forward. His eyes and mouth were open wide with amazement that Charlie was actually going to move the incredible machine.

They left the equipment yard and headed toward the large open area at the northern end of the site. With the eastern boundary fence on their right they followed a well-worn dirt road, gradually picking up speed that from high up in the cab seemed much faster than they were actually going. They bounced along steadily, the heavy shovel in a vertical travel position. As the road entered a long, smooth straightaway, Charlie reached an arm around behind the boy and prodded him forward to a position on the edge of the seat directly in front of Charlie.

"Okay, Pie Man, you take over," he said into the boy's ear. He showed him how to put his foot on the accelerator and how to grip the control levers. The machine slowed until with Charlie's gentle coaxing, the boy overcame his wariness of applying the accelerator, and off they went again. Charlie held onto the levers over the boy's hands, gradually letting him get the feeling of how the treads responded. As he overcame his initial anxiety and realized that he was actually driving the huge machine, the Pie Man had on a happy face that closed his eyes to near slits.

Nearing the northern boundary fence that ran along Cold Springs Road, Charlie took over the levers again in preparation of making the left turn. He coached Pie to ease back a little on the gas, and together they negotiated a smooth left turn and continued on a path along the fence.

Charlie noticed a white pick-up truck coming up quickly from their right headed west on Cold Springs Road. The truck slowed sharply as it came abreast of them, and then came to a complete stop in the middle of the road a short distance beyond the slowly moving bulldozer. As they drew even with the truck on the other side of the fence, Charlie recognized the cold stare from the angry looking driver with the black goatee. Then he recognized the truck.

Charlie looked down at the boy who was looking over toward the truck. His happy face was gone. He didn't wave or nod. He just watched.

After a few seconds, the driver turned away and the white truck accelerated noisily out of view as Cold Springs Road disappeared into the dark woods. Pie relinquished control of the levers to Charlie and pulled himself over to the end of the seat. He sat looking out pensively at the scenery without speaking as Charlie drove them back to the equipment yard.

When he turned off the engine, the sudden cessation of the noise and the vibration engulfed them in stillness. Charlie sat still, looking over at his little friend who had a pensive look on his face that Charlie hadn't seen before.

The boy turned to look at Charlie. "That wath my papa in the twuck," he said.

"Is he going to be mad at you, for being here, for ridding up here with me?"

The boy thought about the question for a moment before answering. Then, he shrugged. "No, papa won't be mad. He won't be anything."

Charlie let it go. He liked the boy a lot but he didn't want to push his way into a family problem he didn't know anything about. Better to just stay out of it.

"How's your mother Pie?" he said, taking the opportunity to inquire about the little woman that he'd laughed with so uncontrollably in the store, and then shared a nice walk with down the hill to the soccer field, before she left in the white truck. Actually, she hadn't been too far out of his thoughts since that day. He was intrigued with her. There was something about her openness and sharp sense of humor that made her very alluring, along with, he had to admit, a look that seemed to camouflage a much more attractive woman than she presented to the world.

"Mama wowk all the time. Mama alwayth wowking."

They sat in silence for a few moments before Charlie stirred to get up off the seat. The boy stood up in the cab facing Charlie. There were tears in his eyes.

"Hey, c'mon Pie Man. What's that for?" he asked. "I thought you'd enjoy going for a ride. Didn't you have fun driving the dozer?" Charlie implored.

The boy looked down at his feet embarrassedly. Finally, he looked up at Charlie and wiped his nose with the back of his hand. He glanced around at all the trucks and tractors that he had played on so many times alone at night after sneaking under the fence, and then turned back to Charlie.

"Chowly, thith wath the betht day of my whole life."

Then Charlie understood. "Okay Pie," he said softly. "Okay." He ran his fingers through the boy's hair, then placed the hardhat back on his head, knocking it down tight with a rap of the knuckles, making the little boy laugh. "C'mon, let's go get a soda."

Driving back into Old Red Bone as the falling sun cast its warm, comforting glow over the red stone buildings far up the hill on Main Street, Charlie had an idea. On his cell phone, he called Hank and invited him over for dinner. Then he called Eve in the restaurant and asked her to pick up a box of spaghetti and some meat sauce, grated cheese, a loaf of bread and a bottle of red wine from the store before she closed up.

"Sounds like a hot date." Eve was curious.

Charlie laughed. "No, just Hank, and I feel like spaghetti. That's all. Hey Eve, why don't you come up too?"

"No, you'd probably make me do the cooking," said Eve. "But thanks for asking Charlie. I'm going out tonight, but some other time, that would be nice, to have dinner with you and Hank. I'll leave the food on the stairway."

Charlie and Hank sat out on the porch having a glass of wine, enjoying the view of the setting sun, while letting the spaghetti sauce simmer. The two men sat in silence for some time. Hank was a talkative man by nature but when the occasion called for it, he was very content to enjoy the silence in the company of a friend.

Charlie was preoccupied with the afternoon's curious episode with the boy and then his father in the white truck. It bothered him, the exchange between the boy and his father, or rather the lack of any exchange, and then Pie crying with happiness, so receptive to his hug, so needing of affection. He felt sorry for Pie and wanted to help him but he could sense trouble ahead if he went any farther than just a casual friendship.

Hank interrupted his reverie "Everything going okay down at your power plant Burden?"

"Oh, sure. Yeah everything's fine Hank," Charlie said, snapping back to the present. After thinking about the question for a moment, he decided to broach the subject of the cooling pond with Hank. He might have some insight about how the members of the Planning Board may react.

"We do have one problem coming up though that we're going to have to go before the Planning Board for. We're going to have to move the cooling pond to another area of the site because of the underlying rock strata."

"So that's a problem?" Hank inquired.

"It's a significant change to the site plan. The Planning Board has to okay it."

"Planning Board, huh,"

"Yeah," said Charlie. "You know those fellows?" Charlie immediately remembered the thin manila file folder with the information about the planning board members that Larry Tuthill had passed across the table to him at their meeting in New York. The file was still tucked away, unread, in one of his briefcases on the floor next to the old roll-top desk in the living room. He would have to dig it out soon and see what was in there.

"Yeah, I know 'em," said Hank. "Miserable pricks, all of 'em." He rose out of his chair and went to the porch railing to spit a large gob of tobacco juice over the side. He watched it fly down and splat against the brown boulders far below. "Be lucky to get out of that meeting with your balls still in your pants. Disagreeable old hillbillies, and dumb as rocks too."

"Really?" Charlie was alarmed at Hank's assessment. "This is a real important variance we need. It's potentially a very expensive problem. The project could get shut down for months or even a year if we can't move the pond."

Hank shook his head ominously. "Well, good luck with that bunch," he said discouragingly.

Eating their spaghetti dinner at Charlie's small round kitchen table, Charlie's thoughts returned to his little friend the Pie Man. He couldn't leave it alone.

"Hank, there's a kid I met out at the project the first day I got here, a retarded kid ..."

"The Pie Man," said Hank with a wide smile coming across his face pulling up the ends of his sauce-stained handlebar mustache.

"Yeah, that's him. The Pie Man. You know him?"

"Burden, let me tell you something," said Hank shoveling another forkful of spaghetti into his mouth. "That kid's going to be governor of this state some day. An amazing kid."

"Yeah, he sure is," Charlie agreed

"A course, to my mind he won't be the first retarded governor we ever had, by a long shot."

Charlie laughed. "He came by the site today. I took him for a ride on one of the big machines. He had a good time." After a pause, he added, "so did I."

"Yeah he's a pistol alright."

After a few moments of eating in silence, Charlie spoke again. "I met his mother too, last weekend, down in the store."

"Natty Oakes," said Hank.

"Yeah. She's got a funny sense of humor. Nice woman it seems like."

"*Nice, hell.* Woman's a damn saint. The best. Works like a dog too, takin' care of the old people all over McDowell County. Home nurse kind of job. Takes care of two old colored boys across the street, she don't even get paid for any more."

"How's that?"

"Well I guess they used to be on her list, Woody and Mr. Jacks. You've seen them probably, down in the restaurant – always take a booth by the window – having breakfast. Eat breakfast every morning in the restaurant. Takes 'em so long to crawl down the stairs from the third floor over there and then hobble back, by the time they get back up there from breakfast it's already *lunchtime.* Well I guess at one time they qualified for getting the service, and then, they wasn't. Got taken off the list by the government I guess. But Natty stills goes in and sees 'em and does what she can for 'em. She's got a few other ones like that I understand."

"The boy says she works a lot," said Charlie.

"All the time. Always on the go. Always doing something," Hank replied. "She's a runner too. Like you."

Charlie was surprised. "Is that right? She runs?"

"Every morning. Comes up this hill out here about six-fifteen every morning, rain or shine. I'm surprised you ain't seen her at all when you go running."

"I go a little later than that. That surprises me. She doesn't seem like a runner."

Hank broke off a piece of bread, leaned back in his chair and focused on Charlie with narrowed eyes. "Ain't a *bad* lookin' woman either."

Charlie didn't comment.

"When she cleans herself up and does something with her hair," Hank continued. "And don't dress like some Raggedy Ann doll, she ain't a bad lookin' woman. Little too skinny though."

"Well she's got pretty eyes anyway," said Charlie trying to avoid the subject.

"Beautiful eyes," said Hank.

Charlie refilled their glasses with wine. "What about her husband, Pie's father? We saw him today and he and the boy didn't even wave to each other, didn't say a word. It seemed strange."

Hank pushed his plate away and made a long process of wiping his mouth, mustache and beard with his napkin. Finally he looked up at Charlie. "He's a bum. Drunk most of the time. He's bad news, Buck Oakes. Stay away from him."

"The kid said he played football. Said he was a football star in college."

Hank shifted around in his chair to where he could gaze out through the open back door and see the last vestiges of the orange sun dropping behind the mountains to the west. The small kitchen was darkening quickly, lit only by the thin golden panels of sunlight that ran across the small refrigerator and the wall.

"Yeah, Buck played some football alright," Hank said, taking a sip of wine and pausing as if he was recalling some far off memories that he hadn't thought about for a long time. "Source of all his problems, football.

"Buck Oakes was about the most famous football player there ever was at Red Bone High. Set all kinds of records as a running back. Played linebacker too. I was still principal at the High School then, back when Buck was there. Near the end of my time.

"He was fast and strong . . . and cocky. Handsome devil too, with black curly hair and a smile like a damn movie star. The girls were crazy about him. Dumb as a goddamn fence post though. Don't think he ever read anything but the sports page and probably only looked at the pictures at that. But he was quite an athlete. Played baseball and basketball too, but football was his sport." Hank pulled out his tobacco pouch and squeezed a wad into his cheek.

"Football was also his daddy's sport. Big Frank Oakes, one of those blowhard Notre Dame fans, made it known to everyone that Buck was going to get a *full scholarship* to play for the *Fighting Irish*. Played it up so big that everyone believed it, including the kid. It was Notre Dame for him, and then the pros. Everyone around here believed it.

"You see, Buck had a real unfortunate thing happen to him toward the end of his junior season. He had one of those rare games that becomes a legend, you know? A game so big that it distorts reality. It was against a team from up in Wyoming County, kind of a weak team as I recall, but it didn't matter. Buck scored six touchdowns, couple of 'em on kickoff returns, and ran for about three hundred yards. Had a few interceptions on defense. You know, one of those once-in-a-lifetime kind of games. Well it was a big deal in the sports pages all over the state. Charleston TV stations sent crews down here. Buck even got his picture in that little column in *Sports Illustrated*, I forget what it's called."

"Faces in the Crowd," said Charlie.

"Yeah, that was it. But the game was a fluke. It happens sometimes. He was never as good as that game. Well anyway, his last couple of games, college scouts were all over Red Bone, and Buck did okay. Had a couple of decent games and got a lot of interest from the recruiters. Started getting letters from all over the country. He'd bring 'em into school and toss 'em around and talk about Notre Dame being the only team good enough to get him and all that cocky rubbish."

Hank looked around and found only his empty wineglass to spit his tobacco juice into, making Charlie wince, as Hank knew he would.

"So Buck spends the summer before his senior year drinking and partying and sleeping and eating, and he puts on some weight and slows down a little. Then he has an okay season, not great, but still has some good games, 'cause he's naturally strong and a gifted athlete. But the scouts stop coming around about half way through the season 'cause they seen enough, and Big Frank he goes into a panic 'cause there's nothing from Notre Dame, and nothing from Penn State, which would have been their second choice. In fact there's hardly no interest at all from any of the big time schools. No Ohio State or Michigan. Big Frank calls up Notre Dame and they tell him they never heard of his son.

"Finally Big Frank, who had some political connections 'cause of his county job, and the football coach at the High School, they get together at the last minute and get to somebody at West Virginia University, and Buck gets a one year scholarship, renewable if he makes the team.

"So Buck goes up to Morgantown, still cocky as ever, thinkin' he should really be at Notre Dame or Penn State, and everything's going to be that much easier at a place like W.V.U. 'cause it's a couple of pegs down from where he belongs."

From his experience with college athletics, Charlie could guess what was coming. "And Buck found out it was a little tougher than he thought, right?" said Charlie.

"As I heard it, first week on the practice field, Buck got run over like he ain't never got run over before. Welcome to big time division one football. Those boys up there were all bigger and faster and stronger and hungrier, lifting weights all summer long while Buck was lifting sixteen ounce Budweisers, and Buck took a beating, physically and psychologically, that he ain't never recovered from. Buck never had a chance at making that team, hell, he didn't belong in college anyway. Never even went to a class. Just hung around up there 'til they finally threw him out, sometime in November I guess it was.

"Come back down here and been a fuck-up ever since. Permanent chip on his shoulder about football. Still telling some story about getting injured at practice and the University screwing him by tossing him out 'cause he couldn't play. Pure *bullshit*," Hank said spitting into the wineglass. "Been nothing but trouble for a lot of people ever since."

Hank rose to his feet in the dark kitchen. "Thanks for the spaghetti Burden. Too late for cribbage now. I've got some reading to do." He went to the rear door, limping slightly on his stiff legs. With his hand on the screen door, he turned back to Charlie. When he spoke again there was sadness in his low voice.

"Buck Oakes never wanted a kid. He didn't want to be *married*, but he got her pregnant and Big Frank was disgusted with him so he made him marry her. He *sure* didn't want a retarded kid, so Buck's just pretty much ignored him his whole life. Buck thinks it's all unfair, all this *undeserved* misfortune that's come down on him. Thinks everything's always about *him*."

Hank stood in the doorway, silhouetted by the light gray evening sky. He shook his head slowly back and forth. "*Ignorance*, Burden. That's what you're seeing between the father and the kid. Just ignorance." He started out the door before stopping once more. "You know, Buck Oakes's 'bout the luckiest man in McDowell County and he . . . he don't know a thing about it. *Damned ignorance,*" Hank growled. "Good night Burden."

"Night Hank."

Charlie sat in the dark, sipping his wine, thinking about Hank's story about Buck. It had reminded him of a brief period in his life when he was feeling cocky and confident about *his* future in sports. During his junior year at Michigan, playing on a good team with a lot of seniors, scoring goals on a line with Duncan McCord, feeling fast and tough and invincible, dropping their gloves at the slightest provocation, a brawl a game or there was no sense playing, and between periods getting high on a fat bone in the locker room shitter. Take no prisoners hockey, just like the big leagues.

Halfway through the season he started thinking about the NHL, that maybe he *was* going to be good enough, that if he scored a few more goals he'd start to get noticed because more and more American kids were getting drafted than there used to be, and then he could bag his engineering courses.

The dream was still alive when Charlie went back to New Haven on a leave of absence for his mother's funeral in February. A bitterly cold week without snow, just icy wind. Two days after the burial, after the cousins and aunts and uncles and well-wishers had all gone, after spending the day inside the big lonely house keeping his father company, Charlie went by himself down to the Coliseum to see the Nighthawks play the Springfield Indians, always a powerhouse in the American Hockey League.

He hadn't been to a professional hockey game in several years – he was always playing. This was an opportunity he relished – watching the game with an insider's eye – to see how his vision of himself measured up to these professionals, many of them not far removed from the college ranks. He bought a ticket on the glass in the corner, to be as close to the action and the speed and the intensity of the players as possible. He knew a few of the names and one player that he'd played against the previous year from Lake Superior State.

From the opening face-off, the mayhem on the ice knotted his stomach and dried his tongue as he stared transfixed at the moving blurs sailing past and into the Plexiglas panel a few inches from his face. It wasn't college hockey. It was all out war between large, muscular men with broad shoulders and beards and black dots for eyes. The hitting and the digging and the elbowing against the glass was ferocious and serious, like their careers depended on it. But most of all it was the sheer speed of the game that forced upon Charlie, like a cold sweat, the realization that his daydreams were just that. The forwards flew up and down the ice and handled and passed and shot the puck at a tempo Charlie couldn't fathom. With reflexes like cobras, they picked flying pucks out of the air and redirected them toward small openings in the goalie's defense that would snap shut in an instant. They played a game that Charlie was unfamiliar with. And worst of all, Charlie knew, these were *minor leaguers!* The National Hockey League, he had been told, was *two steps faster* than the American Hockey League. The player he knew from Lake Superior State – who had been the best player on the ice in every game he'd ever played in from pee wee through college – never got off the bench.

The game confirmed what deep down, he already knew. Charlie left the New Haven Coliseum that night relieved by the certainty and the finality of his assessment of his prospects of a professional hockey career. When he got back to Ann Arbor he re-immersed himself in his studies and began to investigate the admissions requirements of the best engineering graduate schools.

After cleaning up the dinner dishes, Charlie decided to get to bed early. But there was something nagging at him, as the result of Hank's less than optimistic appraisal of their prospects before the Red Bone Planning Board. Something he needed to do before he turned in. Hank's assessment worried him in spite of the optimistic assurances of CanAmex's Charleston law firm.

He snapped on the small lamp within the roll-top desk and sat down on the old, lumpy executive chair that Charlie suspected had come from the law firm that once inhabited the office on the second floor. On his lap he opened one of his over-stuffed brief cases and searched through the folders and reports for the manila folder marked only in pencil, in Larry Tuthill's nearly illegible handwriting, *Planning Board.* The file was in the middle of the briefcase, next to another thin folder that Charlie had forgotten about. It was similarly marked in penciled script, *DeWitt.* It was the background information on the pig farmer. He placed both folders on the desk and returned the briefcase to the floor.

Charlie opened the *Planning Board* folder and then sat, unmoving for several seconds, staring incredulously at the first document in the folder, an eight by ten copy of a black and white photograph. It was obviously an enlargement of a picture cut from a newspaper. Charlie looked at the caption at the bottom of the picture for confirmation of what he was looking at. *The Red Bone Planning Board convened its quarterly meeting last week at the High School.*

Charlie's eye went back to the picture of three men seated at what looked like a school cafeteria table, each with a name-plate in front him. He stared at the picture for a few more moments and then shook his head slowly, and smiled, and then, holding the picture up to the light as he slumped back in the large chair, he burst out laughing. Charlie laughed harder as he focused on the center figure in the picture and the familiar white handlebar mustache and long goatee and the penetrating dark eyes staring back at the camera as they had stared at Charlie across the table in the kitchen a few minutes earlier. The sign in front of Hank read, "Pullman J. Hankinson" and under his name, "Chairman." Charlie looked at the caption again . . . *seated are, Earl Fitch, P.J. Hankinson, and Jimmy Hagerman.*

"*Miserable pricks, all of 'em,*" Charlie said out loud, still chuckling. He looked over the very brief bios of the three men; Earl Fitch, 64, barber; Jimmy Hagerman, 72, retired railroad worker; Pullman J. Hankinson, 76, BBA-History, MSE-Education from Marshall University, PHD from West Virginia University, retired teacher, Principal, Red Bone High School. *Seventy-six years old.* That surprised Charlie. He glanced again at the picture, then closed the file. *Welcome to West Virginia Burden* he said to himself with a chuckle.

As he reached for the small chain to turn off the light, Charlie noticed the second file, the one labeled *DeWitt.* Curious, he opened it to find another grainy enlargement of a picture from a newspaper. It was a picture of three people -- an older woman, a man in the middle, who was obviously the farmer Bud DeWitt, and next to him, a tall, gangly looking younger man. The caption beneath the picture read, 'Alice, Bud and Petey DeWitt of Angel Mountain, enjoying the McDowell County Fair.' All three had taciturn, smileless expressions on their faces. Bud DeWitt had the hard, weathered look of a man who had engaged in physical labor his whole life. He wore what looked like a brand new baseball cap with a 'Peterbilt' logo on the front. It was a stark picture of three very plain looking people.

The second sheet in the folder was another picture, an enlargement of a graduation picture from a yearbook. In marked contrast to the black and white newspaper picture, this one was a glossy color print of a well-lighted, obviously professionally done photograph of a stunningly beautiful young woman. She had pale blue eyes and a relaxed, natural smile that showed her perfect white teeth. Long blond hair, parted in the middle, split at the shoulders and hung straight down the front of her white blouse. The girl's heavy eye make-up and pink lip-gloss had the unmistakable look of the sixties. On the back of the picture, a typed label read, *Sarah Carlson DeWitt, b. 1947, Waukesha, WI. wife of Thomas DeWitt (deceased, 1977). High School Graduation picture, 1964.*

Charlie turned the picture over again and stared at the face that seemed so familiar to him. *Where had he seen her before?* It was just a vague notion. He shook his head and tossed the picture back into the file, reminding himself that the photo was thirty-six years old. It was probably just a *composite recollection* of all the girls of his youth when long, straight hair was the style of the day. He quickly scanned the spare biographies of the DeWitt family, closed the file and went to bed.

Chapter 12

It was nearly six-thirty when Natty finally pulled up in front of the "Olander Legal Clinic" in Welch. Through the large storefront windows she could see the lawyer pacing with his hands in his pockets waiting for her. He had agreed, reluctantly, to stay until six o'clock, the earliest she could get into Welch after seeing her last client of the day. On the seat next to her was the small yellow pages ad she'd torn out of the phone book that morning. *"Free initial consultation"* it promised, *"Specializing in personal injuries, family law, and real estate matters."* Close enough she thought.

Ted Olander greeted Natty with a quick, impatient smile and ushered her into his cramped office. The lawyer was in his mid-forties, slightly overweight and well dressed in a blue shirt with a white collar and a charcoal suit with suspenders. He glanced at his watch as he took his chair behind the desk and pulled a yellow legal pad in front of him.

"Now Miss . . . Mrs. Oakes? What can I do for you?"

"It's Mrs., and I need some legal advice about coal mining."

The lawyer looked at her blankly. "Coal mining," he said, dropping his pencil on the pad. He had made a quick assumption, watching her get out of the car, that the woman's concern would be of a domestic nature.

"Yes sir. Coal mining, specifically mountaintop - removal mining on Angel Mountain." She told the lawyer about her grandparents' farm and the recent activity of the surveyors on Angel Mountain and about Bud DeWitt's conclusions regarding the CanAmex deal with the Ackerly Coal Company, the company that owned the mineral rights to Angel Mountain. She told him about the lawyers visiting Angel Mountain and offering to buy the farm for considerably more than it was worth. At this, Olander showed a flicker of interest and picked up his pencil to make a quick notation on the legal pad. Then she was done. "So, Mr. Olander, what can we do to stop this if they really are planning to do a surface mine on Angel Mountain? And what would it cost, the legal work I mean, your fee?"

The lawyer didn't say anything for several seconds. Finally a thin smile crept across his face and he let out a series of soft chuckles. Trying not to be rude, he put his hands over his face and rubbed his eyes until he could address the question seriously. "I'm sorry Mrs. Oakes. I don't mean to make light of your situation, but let me give you some advice. Let me tell you what's going on here." Olander leaned forward, his elbows on the desk in front of him, using his hands for emphasis. "The Ackerly Coal Company is a huge company, one of the largest coal producers in the world. It's owned by a company called Continental Electric Systems, which is even bigger, probably fifty times bigger than Ackerly. It's monstrous. And the CanAmex Energy Company which, incidentally, is in the process of buying up Continental, is probably a hundred times bigger than Continental. It's a global conglomerate. One of the biggest energy companies in the world." He sat back to let his words sink in.

"Now Mrs. Oakes, if these companies want to mine coal on Angel Mountain, there's nothing you or your grandpa or anyone else down there is going to do about it, because CanAmex and Ackerly will have the County, the State, and the Federal Government, securely in their corner before they do anything. You see, this kind of thing is all done in Charleston and Washington. And this CanAmex plant over there in Red Bone, well this is big time stuff for the State and McDowell County. It's a *billion-dollar* plant, with *millions* of dollars in tax money and *millions* worth of spin-off economic activity. The State lobbied real hard to get CanAmex to build here instead of over in Kentucky or in Virginia, so you can just bet that the CanAmex Company got everything they wanted as far as cooperation on such things as fixing the price of coal down here."

The lawyer looked at his watch again and saw that he needed to get going. "Now, in answer to your second question about cost, about what would it cost to fight them . . . well I wouldn't and couldn't do that. No, you'd need one of the big Charleston firms – New York or Washington would be better – but one of the Charleston outfits could do it. The cost would probably be in the area of three to five million over the two, three, four years it would go on, somewhere in that ballpark." After a moment of silence, the lawyer stood up indicating that he needed to leave. As he put on his suit jacket he added, "and in the end, Mrs. Oakes, you'd lose. You could win all the legal battles, but in the end, they'd still carve up Angel Mountain and take their coal." He looked down at Natty and shrugged his shoulders. "Way it's always been here," he said softly.

Natty sat for a few seconds looking straight ahead, then looked up at the lawyer. "So what you're saying is that we got a *real good case* here." She stared at the lawyer's blank face for a few seconds and then grinned as she got up from the chair. The lawyer smiled with relief when he saw she was making a joke. He walked her toward the front door.

"Well thanks anyway for waiting around for me," Natty said. "Thanks for your help."

They stood just inside the front door. The lawyer spoke in a softer voice as if he didn't want to be overheard. "Mrs. Oakes, the thing you have to realize is that these utility and coal company guys . . . well, they're a tough bunch. They're not like just regular business people. They're cutthroats in fine suits. They've been fighting the unions and the regulators and each other for so long, well you know, they're used to it, *hell*, they *enjoy* it. It's what they do . . . hire big law firms, buy politicians, and run over people, and mostly they get their own way. You don't want to go up against a company like Ackerly, or especially CanAmex. So tell your grandpa to just sell. Get a good price and sell, 'cause in the end, those boys aren't going to play fair. They'll find a way."

Natty pursed her lips and nodded her head in recognition of the soundness of the lawyer's advice. "Yeah, you're probably right Mr. Olander. Well thanks anyway."

The lawyer held the door open for her and watched as Natty drove off in the Accord. When she was gone, Ted Olander relocked the front door and went back into his office. He'd done his best for the little woman from Red Bone . . . given her some damn fine legal advice – *gratis* to boot. Now maybe he could score a few points for himself he thought as he thumbed through the large Rolodex on his desk. He pulled out the small card for the Kerns & Yarbrough law firm in Charleston and got the name of the junior associate that he had dealt with a year earlier on a minor real estate deal involving the Charleston firm's major client, Ackerly Coal. He didn't expect to reach anyone in the office at seven o'clock but he wanted to leave a voice mail for the associate to see what kind of interest it might generate in the morning . . . *"have received an inquiry from the granddaughter of a farmer on Angel Mountain in McDowell County, concerning a possible surface mine by the Ackerly Coal Company on Angel Mountain. Call me in the morning at . . ."*

Natty was discouraged by her visit to the lawyer. She hadn't thought it would be such an impossibility to wage a legal battle to save Angel Mountain, but she knew the lawyer was right. Win or lose it would certainly take a lot of money to fight the coal company. *Three to five million dollars.* She laughed when she thought about how naïve she was regarding the cost of legal services. *Coming up a little short with just $139 in her checking account!*

Driving as fast as she dared with the front end of her car shaking noticeably, Natty headed south out of Welch on Route 103. She would cut over Cold Springs Road and take the short cut on the new road around the power plant. *Be lucky to get home by eight o'clock. Damn, now Buck would be pissed and have another excuse to bitch at her.*

It bothered her that she'd be the one getting home late, because Buck had been good all week – about as good as he was able these days – working at the temporary cement job and getting home early without stopping off anywhere. She knew it wouldn't last – they'd been through these *make up* periods before – but she needed to make it last as long as possible. They had such little good time together.

Thinking about Buck reminded her, once again, of the previous Saturday, the day that had started out so enjoyably in Eve's store laughing to tears over that silly little joke with Pie and Charlie Burden, the man who was so nice to her son. Then the walk down to the soccer field with Emma and Sammy, and Pie – so proud of his new friend – and Charlie Burden and her chatting like two teenagers who had just met, and him taking an interest in her library. And then the, irresponsible, exhilarating, depressing, erotic episode in Buck's truck that filled her with a level of guilt she hadn't felt for a long time.

She hadn't wanted to get into the truck – she was still livid with Buck, but more than that she had to admit to herself that it was nice being with the kids and the man from New York, and she didn't want their walk to end – but she had no choice. She was afraid of the violent scene she knew Buck was capable of, especially with another man being present.

Buck had accelerated away quickly from the curb. In the truck's right-side rearview mirror Natty stole a peek at Pie and Charlie Burden still standing on the sidewalk watching the truck leave. They turned left on Main Street and drove for a mile before Buck broke the silence. He tried to sound contrite but it was a hard role for Buck to play. Natty knew he felt bad about hitting her, it wasn't really the way he was. It only happened when he was drunk and in a foul mood about life in general, but he was never very good at apologizing. Natty sat with her arms crossed staring out the side window while Buck talked.

"Nat, I'm sorry about smackin' you last night. I wasn't thinking, you know. You know I'd never want to hurt you. I was drunk and I was pissed off about stuff, you know, about everything, and, well that ain't gonna happen again, *never*." Natty remained silent.

"Nat, you okay?" Silence. "Nat? C'mon Nat, help me out a little here."

Buck drove north out of Red Bone on the Mountain Road, and then turned off on an old logging road that ran for miles through the dense forest.

"So who was that guy you and the kid was walking with? Huh? Never seen him before. Nat?" She didn't answer. He looked over at her sternly. "Nat, I *asked* you, who was that guy?"

Natty could feel his anger growing. "He's nobody Buck. He's just the new power plant guy. Took Hugo Paxton's place. He took a look at the library . . . see how bad the roof is, that's all."

"The guy from New York? The construction guy?" Buck shot a glance over at her. "That's good Nat . . . you gettin' friendly with that boy. That's *real* good."

They rode along in silence for several minutes before Natty spoke again. She turned toward Buck and spoke softly and evenly. "Buck that was the *last time*. You can't hit me no more, *ever*."

"Nat, I swear..."

Natty cut him off. "And you can't see that woman in Northfork. You got to choose, but if you go again, don't you *ever* come back to me. I mean it Buck."

"Aw Nat, that's done with. It's all over. That gal was just an itch I had to scratch a little that's all. She don't mean nothin' to me."

Natty winced and drew in a quick breath to combat the sick feeling that engulfed her with the confirmation of Buck's latest infidelity. She knew it was true the moment Deputy Sheriff Wayne Lester said it, but it felt different, like a kick in the stomach, when it came from Buck's own lips. Tears crept into her eyes as she tried to think of something else to say. *What else was there to say? What the hell was she even doing here, going through all this stuff again, still trying to make this work, after all these years. Did she really love Buck this much, or was she just another ignorant hillbilly with nowhere else to go?* She blinked her eyes rapidly and leaned over toward the open window to let the breeze dry her eyes.

"Remember this place Nat?" Buck had made a sharp turn off the logging road and they were bumping down a smaller dirt road just wide enough for the big pickup. She looked up, wiping her right eye with the sleeve of the white shirt, and recognized the road they'd come down so many times the year after Buck came back from Morgantown.

"Yeah, I remember Buck," she breathed softly. They would come down this road to where it ended in a small clearing surrounded by thick trees where no one would ever find them. They'd drink a six-pack or a pint of something harder and smoke a few joints, making out with the radio playing softly. Then they'd climb into the back of Buck's father's Blazer and take turns exploring each other's body. This was where Natty learned about sex. Where she learned, at first, to bear the pain and the embarrassment and pretend it was good, and later, to enjoy it without reservation and to take pride in her ability to satisfy Buck.

They'd come to their spot two or three times a week, sometimes more often in the summer following Natty's junior year. Usually at night but sometimes during the day in the summer. In the beginning they'd come here after going to the movies or a dance or a party. Later on, as Buck began to lose interest in doing those things and hanging around with Natty's friends, he would pick her up and they'd just come straight to the woods. Usually he'd already have had a good deal to drink before he picked her up, and gradually their time spent in the front seat got shorter and shorter. Toward the end Buck would just turn off the truck and they'd both crawl over the seat and get right to it. It wasn't how she wanted it but she treasured every moment with Buck and if sex was all they had, that's what she would take.

It all ended in September, when she went back to school for her senior year and found out she was two months pregnant. They only came to their spot one time after that – a year after their son was born, after having a few beers at *Moody's Roadhouse* and feeling a little adventurous. The thought of coming back never seemed to come up after that.

The clearing was still there at the end of the road, after all those years, but the trees and the bushes had grown and filled out and now left just barely enough room to squeeze into with the wide pickup. The green covering was dense all around the truck as Buck turned off the engine and pulled on the parking brake.

Natty sat still, gazing through the windshield at the light green canopy that enveloped them like a bubble. The sun beat down on the outside of the canopy but inside the bubble it was cool and dark and protected. Through the open window, Natty could smell the fresh, earthy aroma of the woods, filling her with nostalgia for that brief season thirteen years earlier when she had Buck so completely to herself.

And now they were in the truck, in the woods, alone again. *She shouldn't be here, not today, not now with Buck, after what he did. Why didn't she say anything? Why was she letting this happen? She knew where he was going when he turned down the logging road. She hadn't protested. Just like when she was in high school. Now they were in this green bubble where no one could see them. No one would ever know.*

Natty turned her head away from Buck and looked out the side window and stared at the shimmering green foliage and let her mind drift back to the morning, and thought about Charlie Burden. *Then they were alone in the library with Charlie dropping out of the rafters after checking the roof. The children had gone back up the hill and the door was locked. They were only a yard apart in the dimly lit room as Charlie wiped his hands and face with a paper towel.*

Buck pushed the long bench seat back as far as it would go, then he slid over to the middle of the seat next to Natty. She felt his arm go over her shoulders pulling her closer to him. He tossed her *Spider-man* baseball cap onto the dashboard and reached up with both hands to take the elastic out of her pony tail, letting her hair fall straight, partially covering her face. He ran his fingers through her hair and over her face as he brought his mouth to her cheek and whispered. "Nat, I ain't been much of a husband lately. I'm gonna make it up to you."

She closed her eyes and leaned her head back against the seat. Buck's left hand was on her thigh rubbing gently up and down from her knee. She could feel the deep stirring inside and took a deep breath.

She moved forward and reached both hands under Charlie's T-shirt, feeling his ribs and then the muscles on his chest and shoulders as Charlie pulled the shirt off over his head. He caressed her neck and then held her face gently with both hands as he looked down into her eyes and smiled. He kissed her forehead lightly and then, slowly, warmly, he kissed her left cheek. Very softly, he said 'Natty' and then pulled her chin up and kissed her fully on the mouth. He guided her down to the long green, plastic couch in back of him.

Natty turned her face to Buck and opened her mouth to his, their tongues pressing warmly against each other. She put her left hand on top of Buck's hand and pulled it over to her crotch as she slid down in the seat, stretching her legs out in the spacious cab. Buck pulled her to him with his right arm behind her back and massaged the crotch of her blue jeans as she spread her legs limply on the floor of the truck. With her right hand she unhooked her belt and the button of her baggy blue jeans.

She rolled over to face Charlie, kissing him wetly on the mouth and then pushing him down on his back on the couch. She ran her hands through the hair on his chest as she worked her way down to the button on his Khaki shorts and then the zipper. His hands fell away and his head went back on the couch. His eyes were closed and his mouth open in deep breathing as Natty pulled off his shorts. She straddled his hips with her knees on the couch and straightened up as she pulled the still buttoned shirt up over her head. Charlie's hands went around her small waist and then up her rib cage and under the front of her bra releasing her breasts.

Natty felt herself being lifted and spun, her left shoulder glancing hard off the bottom of the steering wheel as Buck pushed her down on the hot seat that was wet with his sweat. She opened her eyes to see Buck, his blue jeans rolled down to his knees, working at pulling down his shorts, releasing himself. He put both hands under her small buttocks and pulled her up toward him. The contrition was gone from his voice when he spoke.

"This is what you like Nat, huh," he groaned. "This is what keeps you coming back," he whispered as he pushed himself deep inside her.

Natty reached over her head with both hands and held onto the frame of the door as she closed her eyes again and buried her face in the cloth seat back. "Yeah Buck," she finally managed to breathe out softly, "that's what I like." She bit her lower lip and hid her tears.

On the ride back into Red Bone, Buck prattled on about some new scheme that he and Roy Hogan were cooking up about building a hunting camp and working as guides for wealthy sportsmen during the hunting season. Natty had heard it all before – the enthusiasm for a half-baked idea that would soon turn to nothing – and remained silent. She was preoccupied with what had just happened and was trying to rationalize the guilt she felt. Certainly it wasn't about the sex. Lord knows, she was feeling randy enough to deserve a good lay from her husband, even if she was pissed at him. No, it was about fantasizing about another man when she was with Buck. That had never happened to her before and it was a strange, uncomfortable feeling. And it was about Charlie Burden, a stranger she'd only met the day before. *God, it was all so stupid! Here she was fantasizing about an almost complete stranger who most likely didn't even remember her name, who would only recall her as the 'retarded kid's mother.' And in a short time he'd be gone, back to New York or off to China . . . imagine that, going to live in fucking China! . . . and he sure as shit wouldn't be remembering much about the little bit of time he spent in Red Bone, West Virginia. But Buck would still be here. He'd always be here. And so would she.*

Buck slid to a stop in front of Barney's General Store. Natty tucked the ends of the white shirt into her blue jeans and tried to brush back her unruly hair with her fingers. She tucked the Spider Man cap into the front waistline of her jeans as she opened the door.

"So Nat, we're okay right? I'll see you at home later on? We're good right?" Natty shut the door of the truck and gave her husband a thin smile through the open passenger side window. "Yeah Buck," she said softly, "we're just great." She turned and walked toward the steps up to the boardwalk in front of the store with the familiar sound of Buck's truck accelerating away behind her.

From the vestibule, she could see Cat in the restaurant sitting on a counter stool with an ice cream cone, swinging her legs back and forth while she watched Pie and Charlie Burden in a nearby booth. They were playing some kind of game on the table and by the wide smile on Charlie's face and the animated actions of her son, she could tell, even with his back to her, that Pie had on one of his great happy faces. As she stood by the edge of the door to watch without being seen, she could hear the glee in her son's voice and see on Charlie's face the genuine affection he had for Pie. *Damn, he makes it look so easy,* she thought.

"Oooh, Chowly almoth get a touthdown." Pie was on his knees on the bench, moving about excitedly. His baseball cap was turned around backwards, facing Natty. She moved into the doorway and leaned against the frame, content to just watch for a few moments. They were flicking a bag of sugar back and forth across the slippery table. Pie apparently scored as he leaped up suddenly. "Touthdown Mithgan!" he shouted as he put his short arms straight up over his head for the touchdown signal. Charlie laughed and was giving him a high-five as he looked up and saw Natty in the doorway. He smiled at her and said something to the boy who wheeled around excitedly.

"Mama, Chowly and me play thugabag football with the thugabag. Mama, come thee."

Cat jumped off the counter stool and ran over to her mother. Natty stayed leaning against the doorframe. She didn't want to go into the restaurant. She suddenly felt exhausted and emotionally numb and didn't want to get into a conversation with Charlie Burden or get any closer to him, not right then.

"Come on Pie, we need to get going. We've already imposed on Mr. Burden enough," she said.

"Oh Mama . . ." Pie started to protest. But Charlie said something to him and he slowly climbed down out of the booth. The boy gave Charlie another high-five, turned and skipped toward his mother, the happy face restored as he thought about the stories he had to tell her about helping Charlie move his things up to the fourth floor and about learning how to play sugar-bag football. The ten-dollar bill in his pocket that Charlie insisted he take, he would keep quiet about.

Charlie stayed seated in the booth as he watched Natty in the doorway. If she wanted to keep her distance, for whatever reason, he would respect that. As Pie walked over to her, Charlie noticed how different she now looked from the first two times he'd seen her. The baseball cap was gone and her hair was down, falling to her shoulders unevenly like a wavy mop, an unruly shock rakishly crossing her left eye. The man's white dress shirt was now tucked into her blue jeans, the belt pulled tight at her small waist, the ends of the pants were pushed sloppily into the high, untied construction boots. As she leaned lazily against the doorframe, gazing back at Charlie with a tired smile, her arms crossed at her chest, the effect was dramatic. Without any effort or awareness, she could have been a professional model Charlie thought, posing for some sort of rumpled chic leisure clothing collection in a Vanity Fair ad.

As the children went out through the doorway, Natty lingered for a moment in thought, still looking at Charlie. Finally she straightened up and mouthed a silent "thank you" and smiled. Charlie nodded to her and watched her walk out through the vestibule toward the store where Eve had been watching them from just inside the doorway.

In the dusky twilight, darkness came earlier in the shadows of the steep, tree-covered slopes that surrounded the power plant and Natty almost drove past the turnoff from Cold Springs Road. It was cool and dark on the smooth new road that ran along the western boundary of the CanAmex site, while far up on the hills on the eastern side of the property, the tops of the trees reflected the deep orange glow of the setting sun. Natty had to turn on her headlights to follow the edge of the road. Drainage ditches ran along each side of the road, which had no guardrails or painted lines to navigate by.

Still trying to make good time, Natty leaned forward and concentrated on staying in the middle of the road while she held a firm grip on the shimmying steering wheel. Going around a bend, the shimmy in the front end stopped and Natty suddenly felt the steering wheel go slack as the Accord bucked, listed forward, then screeched along the pavement out of control, headed for the right side drainage ditch. Sparks flew up around the right fender before the car finally slid to a stop a few feet from the ditch. Still shaking and afraid the car may be on fire, Natty quickly turned off the ignition, gathered up her purse and client files and yanked her equipment bag from the back seat. She put her things down on the road about ten yards in front of the car, then went back to inspect.

On Cold Springs Road, Charlie Burden was about halfway through his second lap around the perimeter of the power plant. There was more light when he'd started out thirty minutes earlier but the road was easy enough to follow and he was confident enough of his footing to maintain a moderate pace on the fairly level ground. He turned onto the new power plant road and ran another two hundred yards before he heard what sounded like a car door slamming on the road up ahead. He slowed down to a walk, catching his breath as he turned his head to the side, listening for another sound. After walking a short distance, he heard something again, clearer this time, from just around a sharp bend in the road a few yards ahead. As he got closer, he could identify it as a woman's voice.

". . . damn piece of shit car. Fucking cars! Mother-fucking cars." Then a door slammed.

When he rounded the bend, the car came into view in the dusky stillness of the woods, an odor of burnt metal and rubber hanging in the air. The old Honda was parked on the shoulder of the road, listing awkwardly forward to the right. Not seeing anyone, Charlie stopped and listened.

"Hello. Is anyone there?" he called out.

He walked toward the car, and saw a head pop up in front of the hood and then the rest of the person climbing up out of the drainage ditch. He didn't recognize Natty until she spoke.

"That you Mr. Burden?"

"Oh, hello Mrs. Oakes. I heard someone, uh, yelling, but I didn't recognize your voice."

"Yeah, nice mouth, huh." She laughed. "I didn't know anyone was around."

"So what happened to your car? Smells like something's burning," Charlie said as he passed by her and walked around to the front of the car.

"Think maybe I got a flat tire."

Charlie leaned out over the drainage ditch and saw that the right front wheel had broken off at the axle and was lodged under the frame of the car. Metal shards were visible at the end of the axle and brake fluid was leaking into the sand next to the road. Charlie couldn't help letting out a laugh when he saw the extent of the damage. Natty Oakes, he was beginning to understand, had a most amusing gift for understatement.

"So what's funny? It's a flat tire right?" she asked, smiling.

"No, it's a lot worse than that," Charlie answered. "The whole wheel came off. It broke right off at the axle."

"Aw man, that doesn't sound good. Shit. I don't need this right now." A troubled look came over her face as she realized she was now facing another bill she couldn't afford.

Charlie saw that she felt bad and wished he hadn't laughed about the broken wheel. "You're going to need a tow truck. Is there a garage you can call? We can use the phone in the office," he said gesturing toward the power plant.

Natty stood in the road looking at her car, shaking her head disgustedly. "Damn. I got a lot of clients to see tomorrow," she said softly. "Friday's always a busy day for me."

She sighed resignedly and started toward her things lying in the road. "Yeah, I can call Gus Lowe. He's got a tow truck. If I can use your phone I can call home and get a ride."

Charlie took Natty's equipment bag from her and slung it over his shoulder while she gathered up her files. They started off up the road toward the main gate, three quarters of a mile away.

"Car's only got two hundred and fifty thousand miles on it," Natty said with a quick glance back at the Honda. "You'd think you'd get at least three hundred before the damn wheels started falling off." Charlie smiled in the darkness. He enjoyed Natty's sense of humor. Eve Brewster was right – nothing bothered her sister-in-law for too long.

"If you're stuck, you can use my car for a few days," Charlie offered, looking down at the little woman walking beside him. He could use Hugo Paxton's Navigator, which was still parked at the condo in Bluefield. "The company has a truck that I can use," he added.

The offer didn't seem to register with her right away. "Huh? I'm sorry. What did you say?"

"I said you could use my car for a few days if you need to," Charlie replied.

Natty looked up at him with a curious look on her face. "You'd let me use your car? To go to work in, to do my rounds in tomorrow? Why would you do that? You hardly even know me."

Charlie laughed. "Hey, don't you know, everybody knows everybody in Red Bone?"

Natty smiled at Charlie's imitation of her. "Well, thanks anyway, but I couldn't do that. I'll find another car somewhere," she said softly. "But, thank you." Charlie let it go and they walked on together in silence for a while.

"Pie came by the plant this afternoon," Charlie said. "He comes by every day, late in the afternoon usually."

"Yeah, that's all he talks about now. I heard all about the ride you gave him last week on the tractor."

"Bulldozer," Charlie said.

"Hey, if he's being a pest, getting in your way and all, I'll tell him to stop going over there," Natty said earnestly.

Charlie chuckled a little to himself. "No, he's not a pest. Everyone in the office loves it when he comes in. He's funny. We're teaching him how to use the computer, and the Internet. He's a great kid. He really is." Charlie wanted to tell her just how much he looked forward to the visits from the Pie Man, that it was the highpoint of his day now that he'd gotten to know the boy so well. He wanted to tell her about the vacuum in his life that had been gnawing at him the last few years without young children to father anymore and how good it felt to have Pie want to spend time with him.

"Computers, wow, that's great. Maybe that'll help him with his math. He's terrible with his arithmetic, just like I was too. He's only, like a grade level or two under on the reading and verbal stuff, which is pretty good they tell me, but he's got a tough time with the numbers. You think that computer stuff will help him with math?"

"Yeah, maybe. I'll see if I can get him a math program, one of those tutorials he can work at on his own. That would work I think," Charlie said.

"Jeez, that would be super. I think Pie would like that. That's very nice of you Mr. Burden," Natty said sounding a little embarrassed. "You've been real nice to Pie."

"He's a nice kid," Charlie said.

"Had him tested a couple of years ago and they said he's just mildly retarded. So he can learn stuff, he ain't stupid," she said softly.

"Hank thinks he's going to be the Governor some day," Charlie said. Natty just smiled in the darkness.

They walked along at a leisurely pace on the dark road for a short distance before Charlie decided to bring up a subject that he had been wondering about since the first day he'd met Pie. "You know, I was wondering about, well, how Pie got that name, the Pie Man. After you get used to it, it seems very natural. It fits him well, but . . ."

"But still, a pretty stupid name for a kid. Yeah I know. Well it ain't really much of a story," she said.

"If I'm being too nosey, just . . . it's not really any of my business," Charlie interrupted.

Natty thought for a moment before she responded in a soft voice. "Christ, Mr. Burden, you're all Pie talks about now. You're like the only adult man that's ever given that boy the time of day, including his father. Course it's your business."

"Well, I was curious."

"First, it probably helps to know that his real name is Boyd," Natty said with a chuckle. "How's that for a handle? Boyd . . . makes Pie Man sound pretty smooth don't it?"

Charlie laughed along with her. "Boyd," he said, trying out the name.

"Yeah, it's a family thing, with the names. Buck's father – Buck, that's my husband – his father, Big Frank, he's got this thing about naming his grandkids, and, well anyway, that's where Boyd came from.

"So when Pie's almost four, I asked Buck one day to read to him a little bit from the big nursery rhyme book that Pie liked, which was probably a mistake 'cause back then, Buck was pretty much in a shitty mood most all the time and that day was no different. But Buck surprises me and says 'okay' and it was like the first time he ever put Pie on his lap and tried to read to him, 'cause Buck, he don't read too well for one thing and second, he never paid much attention to Pie from the beginning, 'cause . . . well that's another story entirely. Anyway, Buck opens the book to that story about Simple Simon, which Pie knows about by heart 'cause we read it so many times and Buck starts reading, 'Simple Simon met a Pie

Man,' and he stops, and he points to the picture and he says to Pie, 'that's you kid, the simpleton, Simple Simon, the retard' and he keeps saying it, 'that's you, Simple Simon, Simple Simon the retard, that's you . . .' and he gets mad and keeps saying those things, even though Pie don't know what the hell he means. Then I'm telling Buck to quit it, and he's yellin' back at me and I'm yellin' at him, and then all of a sudden, Pie jabs his finger at the other picture and yells, 'no, I am the Pie Man, I am the Pie Man' louder and louder 'til Buck and I shut up, and he says again, 'I am the Pie Man, I am the Pie Man.' Then Buck pushes him off his lap onto the floor and stomps out and Pie's just sitting there with that stubborn look on his face . . . I'm sure you've seen it."

Natty took a deep breath and walked for a few seconds in silence to control her emotions. She'd never told this story, the real story, to anyone else before. Previously, it had always been the "sugar coated" version – Pie just really liked the picture of the Pie Man in the nursery rhyme book and for no other reason started saying 'I am the Pie Man, I am the Pie Man going to the fair' and the name just stuck. Now here she was telling it all to this near stranger, although she'd leave out the part about Buck just coming in and her not knowing he was stone drunk in the middle of the day when she asked him to read to their son. Damn, why hadn't she just given Charlie Burden the 'story book' version?

Charlie was wondering if she was going to continue the story, when she spoke again. "So I picked him up and put him on my lap, and he looks at me and says again, 'I am the Pie Man.' And it was strange because it was like the first time he'd ever made some kind of decision . . . the first time he'd shown that he was really thinking about something, you know. It's a weird name and everything but it was his decision, and it was the first sort of intelligent thing he ever said, you know, after the usual baby talk stuff. So I said to him 'yes, you are the Pie Man', and well, that's what he's called himself ever since, and that's all anyone around here has called him, even in school. I don't think he even remembers the name Boyd."

They rounded a bend in the road and were now on the southern side of the site. A light was visible on the administration building. In another few minutes, they would be at the front gate.

"Pretty pathetic story huh Mr. Burden. Welcome to West Virginia, right?"

"No," Charlie answered. "It isn't at all," he said trying to sound understanding.

Natty stopped walking and half turned toward Charlie who had continued another few paces before he realized that Natty wasn't next to him. He turned back to her and saw that she had something to say.

"Listen, Mr. Burden, don't think too poorly about my husband. I probably shouldn't have told you that story, but you've been real special to Pie and . . ." Natty looked up at the hills surrounding them as she tried to arrange the words in her mind. "This is a hard place. It's not an easy place to live. I mean, I love it here and I could never live anywhere else. But, 'there's a lot of heartache in these mountains,' that's what my grandma Alice says, and it's true. I know it's true," she said almost to herself. "And it's harder I think, for a man. It's not an easy place to make a living, with the coal mining mostly gone, and that takes a lot out of a man around here . . ." Her voice faded. ". . .getting trapped here and not being able to make a living and support a family . . . takes a lot out of a man."

"Yeah, I understand," said Charlie. "I don't know your husband, so I don't . . . I haven't been here long enough to be making judgments about people, except I really like the ones I've met – Eve, Hank, Pie of course, Mabel Willard, the guys working on the project."

Natty laughed as she started walking again. "Hey what about me? Don't I make that list?" she teased.

Charlie pretended to mull it over for a few seconds before answering. "Well, based on Pie's recommendation, I guess I'd put you on the list too."

"Well that's good to know," said Natty. They were nearing the main gate. "Hey, I'm sorry to spoil your run. It's a nice night for a run too."

"That's okay. I already did one lap around the plant. I usually run in the morning but I had an early meeting."

"That's when I run," said Natty. "In the morning."

"Yeah, that's what Hank said. He said you run up the hill to Main Street every morning."

"About six-thirty or so I run through Old Red Bone . . . see Hank out on your back porch most days, having his cup of tea." Natty wondered to herself as to what occasion Charlie and P. J. Hankinson might have had to be talking about her. "Where do you run, in the morning?" she asked.

"I've been going out Main Street and over North Mountain Road a ways and back," Charlie replied. "It's a nice run."

"Sometime I'll show you my course. It's about five and a half miles, up to Main Street, and then through the woods on a trail along the south side of Red Bone Mountain. It's beautiful in the morning."

"I'd like that. That would be great," said Charlie. "How about Monday?"

"Um, Monday?" She hesitated. Natty knew she'd made a mistake and now she was stuck. She hadn't meant to invite Charlie Burden to go running with her. That was crazy! What was she thinking about?

"Yeah, I'll watch for you from the porch around six-thirty or so, and I'll meet you out in front of the store. You can show me the trail along the mountain, and then just point me back toward South County Road when you're all done. Don't worry, I won't hold you up too much," Charlie added with a laugh.

Natty couldn't find a polite way out. "Sure, we could do that. I'll look for you on Monday."

Once they were inside the gate, Natty conceded that it made more sense to let Charlie drive her home than for her to call someone for a ride. Plus, she wasn't sure who would be around and she knew she didn't want to ask Buck to come and get her. Gus Lowe wouldn't be towing her car tonight anyway, so she could wait and call him from home. While Charlie went into the admin building to get his keys, Natty waited next to the low-slung Lexus sports coupe. This would be exciting anyway, getting a ride in a fancy sports car, Natty thought as she peered down through the moon roof trying to see into the dark car. She was startled as the door locks clicked and several small lights came on in the interior of the car. She looked up to see Charlie approaching with an athletic bag. He'd put a sweatshirt on over his T-shirt. He opened the trunk lid and deposited Natty's equipment bag.

Natty was mesmerized by all the lights and the gauges on the dashboard, the soft leather seats and the overall feeling of quiet luxury in the car. She'd never before ridden in a car so new or so expensive.

Charlie drove slowly on the dark, narrow access road that ran from the plant through the woods back out to South County Road. When they approached the intersection, Natty said, "you take a right here, and go about a half mile . . ." She stopped talking when Charlie abruptly stopped the car in the middle of the road just short of the intersection and pulled on the emergency brake. He left the engine running, opened the driver's door and got out. He leaned his head down into the car and instructed Natty to get out.

"What are you going to do now, kill me?" she asked with a chuckle.

Charlie laughed. "No. I'm going to run home, and you're going to take my car until you get yours fixed," he said while pulling tight the Velcro on his fanny pack that held his wallet and keys.

"No, c'mon, I can't do this," Natty protested over the top of the car.

"You know you need a car tomorrow, I don't," Charlie replied as he started backing away toward South County Road.

"But I can't drive this. Please Mr. Burden, I don't – "

"It's just like a Honda. Put it in gear and go. Don't worry about it. I'll see you Monday." He loped off at an easy gait and disappeared into the dark, heading for Old Red Bone.

Natty watched until she lost sight of the reflective tape on the heels of his running shoes. She glanced at her watch. It was past nine o'clock. She went around the car and got into the driver's seat and shut the door. It took her a few seconds to figure out how to use the electric seat adjustment to raise the seat and move it up to where she could reach the pedals. She pulled the steering wheel down to a comfortable position, then played with the accelerator slightly to get a feeling for the smooth, powerful engine. She giggled at the thought of her driving a car like this. As she looked over the gauges and the luxurious interior of the car, she bit on her lower lip and shook and head. *How the hell was she going to explain this one to Buck*, she wondered as she moved the console shift into drive, pulled out onto South County Road and headed west toward Oakes Hollow.

Chapter 13

A late-summer heat wave had settled on the mountains like a hot blanket over the weekend. Even in August, temperatures in the eighties were rare in McDowell County, the locals working at the plant told Charlie. The air conditioners in the administration building were humming at full power at nine o'clock in the morning.

Charlie would spend the first couple of hours reading and answering his e-mail as he usually did on Monday mornings. He reviewed the long list of messages, deleting the junk first before going back and prioritizing the remaining e-mails for attention.

There were two messages from Ellen. One from Friday night saying that her realtor had called to tell her that the owner of the Quail Hollow Lane house had dropped the price to 1.4 million, and that there was some new interest in the house and that she didn't think it would last too long at this price. Ellen added that Jennifer would be home from Evanston the last week of the month and would be leaving to go back on Labor Day weekend, and she hoped Charlie could get back to Mamaroneck for a few days to see her. The new Saab Ellen had purchased for their daughter was also going to be delivered that week and she wanted Charlie to be part of the surprise.

Before replying, Charlie clicked on the second e-mail from Ellen, which was sent on Sunday. It was a very brief note saying that her realtor had a "very good prospect" who might be interested in buying their present house if it were to go on the market soon. The buyers were "very motivated" to get their children situated into the Mamaroneck school system for the beginning of the school year. Ellen hoped they could make some decisions if Charlie could get home sometime during the week before Labor Day. Charlie could feel the wheels in motion back in Mamaroneck. The noose was tightening. Ellen would be pushing hard to close the deal when he went home to see Jennifer. He replied that he would try to get home for the last week in August.

He skipped over a dozen messages from the office in New York that he knew would be long and involved inquiries about the projects that Charlie had been working on before leaving for West Virginia. He went instead to a message entitled "Angel Mountain," from Larry Tuthill at CanAmex.com. It said tersely that Vernon Yarbrough with another Kerns & Yarbrough lawyer, plus Kevin Mulrooney from Ackerly Coal Company, would be arriving by helicopter at the Red Bone site on Thursday morning to accompany C. Burden to a meeting with B. DeWitt to reach an agreement on the purchase of the Angel Mountain farm. It was followed with the notation, "this is a highest priority meeting." He responded to all that he would be available to attend the meeting on Thursday.

Charlie started going through the company emails but made little progress. After a few minutes of reading, his mind would invariable drift back to earlier that morning and his exhilarating run along the side of Red Bone Mountain with Natty Oakes. It was an experience he couldn't wait to repeat again the following day.

In the middle of the street in front of the store, Charlie was stretching as Natty came up the hill and rounded the corner. "Morning Mr. Burden," she said without slowing down. Charlie noticed that she didn't seem to be breathing overly hard from the run up the hill. A light coating of perspiration covered her skin but the morning's humidity didn't seem to be affecting her.

"Good morning Mrs. Oakes," Charlie replied as he fell in beside Natty at a pace he thought was a little quick for five miles.

In the still dark restaurant, Eve Brewster, filling the salt shakers, stood at a booth by the front window and watched her sister-in-law and the new power plant boss jog off together down Main Street. Leaning closer to the window, she watched them until they disappeared from view. Wiping the outside of a salt shaker with her towel, Eve shook her head slowly. With a sigh she whispered to herself, '*oh Natty, be careful.*'

"How's your car?" asked Charlie.

"I got rid of it." Natty looked up at Charlie with a mischievous twinkle in her eyes. "I don't need it anymore. Got a new Lexus," she added, smiling at Charlie. "It'll be ready tomorrow. Is that okay?" *The car would be ready, but how she was going to handle the five hundred and eighty-dollar bill at Gus Lowe's garage was another story.*

"Sure it is. That's fine," Charlie answered.

Before he could say anything else, Natty veered to the right and left the road, headed for a field of high weeds and scrub bushes. "Come on. I'll show you what heaven is like for a runner," she said turning her head back toward Charlie.

He followed her up a narrow dirt path across the small field, over a set of railroad tracks that looked like they had been out of use for a long time, and then into the woods. They ran single file for a hundred yards along a narrow path until suddenly the tree line ended revealing a spectacular panorama of the rugged southern slope of Red Bone Mountain, the undulating, tree-lined valley of the Heavenly River far below them, and off to their left a sweeping vista of endless blue and gray mountains. The view was breathtaking, as was the sheer drop-off of several hundred feet just a few yards now from the edge of the trail. Natty looked back to catch the reaction on Charlie's face when they came out of the woods and he didn't disappoint her. She smiled as his eyes suddenly went wide with amazement and probably a little terror as he looked over the rugged cliff that was now just a stumble away.

"Great isn't it?" she called back, partially to alleviate his anxiety.

"Yeah, it's beautiful," he answered.

"The trail's fine, but you have to watch your step in a few places. Just follow me."

"I'm right behind you," replied Charlie, feeling a little skeptical that this trail would be suitable for anything but hiking.

But the trail quickly turned out to be much more level and sure-footed than he'd anticipated. It was an absolutely first-rate running course with some nice long, gentle climbs and downhills, and the scenery continued to be more spectacular as they went along. The trail alternated between peaceful glides through dark woods and thrilling jaunts along the edge of rocky precipices looking down at the tops of trees that grew out of the ruggedest, most inaccessible topography Charlie had ever seen. He was awestruck at every turn, stunned that such a manageable course could be found running along the side of a mountain, taking them right up to the edge of such a remote and breath-taking landscape.

They ran single file all the way along the mountain trail, Natty leading the way and forcing the pace, which was beginning to tell on Charlie. It was a strenuous pace for five miles and Charlie wondered if the little woman in front of him was just trying to show off a little until he remembered that she had already run over two miles.

Following her along the trail gave Charlie a good chance to again study Natty Oakes who was now a genuine enigma to him. He smiled to himself as he wondered if she owned *any* clothing of her own. She was obviously an experienced and accomplished runner, yet she wore a pair of over-sized khaki work shorts that extended down to her knees, and a navy blue, man's golf shirt that must have also been an extra-large. The sleeves of the shirt went down past her elbows, the ends of the loose shirt hung down almost to mid-thigh. On her head was the familiar Spiderman hat and on her sockless feet were a pair of well-worn Reebok running shoes – the only part of her outfit that seemed to fit the occasion.

Yet beneath the camouflage of the ill-fitting clothing, Natty Oakes moved with the economy and grace of a thoroughbred, without any outward display of strain or fatigue. She never wavered in her pace or breathing or adjusted her arm swing. Whether going up-hill or down, her slender, muscular legs maintained their long, powerful strides. Beneath the over-sized shirt and baggy shorts, Charlie could discern the broad shoulders, straight back and narrow hips of a natural athlete and knew that there was no 'show off' in the pace she set.

At the mid-point of the mountain trail, Natty's eyes glanced up at the large boulder jutting out over the trail a hundred feet above them. They ran past the entrance to the steep goat path that went up to her special place. It would have been a wonderful morning to lay on the rock for a few minutes, enjoying the warmth and the stillness of the air, and catch up on her daydreams. But she wouldn't be visiting her spot today, not with this man she hardly knew.

A mile past the boulder, they reentered thick woods on a generally downhill plain, leaving the spectacular view to the south behind them. Natty led them through a stand of tall pine trees where their footfalls seemed to echo in the stillness of the forest and the sound of their rhythmic breathing was amplified.

Just as Charlie's lungs and thighs were screaming for a rest, Natty suddenly slowed her pace quickly to a walk and then stopped dead in the middle of the path. Following her lead, gratefully, Charlie came up beside her, breathing heavily and started to speak, but she quickly put a finger up to her lips and pointed down the path with her other hand.

Charlie stood with his hands on his hips breathing deeply and tried to see what Natty was pointing at. He peered through the trees and didn't see anything, until the deer moved – a good size buck, not twenty yards from them. It walked slowly but confidently out of the trees and across the path immediately followed by a doe and then, three smaller deer. They moved through the trees like smoke with hardly a sound and in a few moments they were gone from sight.

Natty started walking down the trail. "See a lot of deer around here this time of year," she said. "Then in the fall, my husband and his brothers, they come up here and bow-hunt 'em."

"Your husband likes to hunt?" asked Charlie.

"*Lives* to hunt is more like it. He's a real good hunter. Been doing it his whole life."

Natty looked up at Charlie. His face was flushed, the sweat dripping down his forehead. She smiled at him. "You okay Mr. Burden?"

"Yeah, I'm fine," he answered, thankful that they were still walking. "We almost done?"

Natty laughed. "Well I am, but you still got the hardest part ahead of you, running back up to Old Red Bone."

Then she walked to the right edge of the path and stopped. "This is where I get off," she said. She pointed down the hill that was covered with rugged outcroppings of boulders, a few thin stands of birch trees and thick short bushes. "This is the top of Oakes Hollow. That's where I live, down there."

Charlie came over to the side of the trail and looked down the hill. He could see the top of a house about a hundred yards from where they stood, and farther down the hill, two smaller houses and two trailers.

"You keep going down the trail a little ways and you'll come to a dirt road. Go right, and it'll take you down to South County Road. Then you got a nice run ahead of you back up to Main Street," she said with a chuckle. She glanced at the small watch on her wrist. "I got to go," she said as she moved off the trail through the bushes along a narrow path that only she would know existed.

Charlie watched her disappear into the bushes and then reappear briefly a little ways down the hill. "Hey," he called out softly to get her attention. "Thank you. Thanks for showing me your trail. It's beautiful." She just smiled back at him and nodded her head.

Before she started out again, Charlie said, "will you be running tomorrow?"

Natty looked back up the hill at him and shrugged her shoulders. "I run every day," she said, then dropped out of sight as the path went behind a large rock formation. Charlie finished the last two and a half miles of his run at a much more leisurely pace.

After several hours of work at the computer, Charlie was interrupted by a rap on his open office door. He looked up to see one of the young sub-contractors' engineers who had been working in the main computer workroom.

"Some guy here wants to see you. Old guy, says his name's, ah, Nickerson or Hankerson or something."

"*Hankinson*," Charlie corrected him. "Send him in."

Charlie and Hank had played cribbage several times in the evening since Hank had duped him about the Planning Board, but Charlie hadn't let him know that he knew Hank was on the board. Charlie wanted to wait for the right occasion. He had an idea that the occasion was close at hand as Hank walked through the door.

Pullman J. Hankinson was wearing a brown suit so old it was almost back in style. He wore a white dress shirt that had long ago gone to a shade of pale yellow from years of starching, and a black string tie. His cloud white hair was pulled back and tied in a short pony tail. Under his arm he carried an ancient looking brown accordion file, tied shut with black string.

"Morning Hank," Charlie said looking up from his computer. They were by now close enough friends to dispense with the ritual of shaking hands every time they saw each other.

"Burden," Hank answered through the white mustache that covered most of his mouth, looking around the tiny office. He put the file down on the edge of the desk and sat in the sole visitor's chair facing Charlie.

"So what are you up to today Hank?" Charlie asked.

"Working," stated Hank flatly.

"Working? On what?"

"We need to take a look at what plans you got to move that cooling pond of yours."

"*Cooling pond?*" Charlie tried his best to look puzzled. "Oh yeah, moving the cooling pond, because of the rock formations. That's right, I remember telling you about that. Well, it's not a problem anymore. We decided to just go ahead and keep the pond where it is." Charlie leaned back in his chair with his hands clasped behind his head. "After you told me about those guys on the Planning Board, we did some research, and *boy* were you right. *Miserable pricks*, all three of them you said, and that's about the nicest thing anyone had to say." Charlie did his best to put a disgusted scowl on his face. He shook his head back and forth. "We asked around, all over town and everyone said the same thing, '*forget about it,* those boys on the Planning Board are just too *stupid* and too *ignorant* to know what you're talking about.' *Plus*, they're too belligerent and mean and disagreeable to reason with, and they're all pretty damned *ugly* to boot.' That's what they said. So we're just going to leave the pond where it is." When he was done, Charlie folded his arms and stared across the desk at his neighbor.

After nearly a half a minute of silent staring, Hank's mustache started moving up at the sides, signifying a smile growing under the thick white wall of whiskers. He reached out and slapped the desk with an open palm. "Ha! You got me Burden," Hank said with a loud laugh. "When'd you find out?"

"I got a file on the Planning Board. They gave it to me in New York. I looked at it that night. Got your picture in it."

Hankinson nodded his head as he mused over the fact that CanAmex had gone to the trouble of assembling a file on the Planning Board. At least Charlie was good enough to tell him about it. He'd have to look at the file sometime.

"Let's go take a look at your cooling pond," said Hank rising out of his chair.

Charlie deliberated for a moment about the efficacy of meeting informally like this one-on-one with the Planning Board Chairman about such a serious issue. He knew that the lawyers at Kerns & Yarbrough would have a problem with it. Also, w*hat if Hank was looking for a payoff?* He decided to just trust his friend and to trust Hank's judgment as the Planning Board Chairman. Charlie also had a feeling that Hank was doing him a huge personal favor by coming to talk to him like this about the pond.

They took Charlie's Navigator out to the original site of the cooling pond, roughly in the middle of the entire development. They walked over the hard rock strata that was laid bare in several wide expanses where the loose soil had eroded away. Charlie pointed out the close proximity of the planned pond to the main building that was now a gigantic structure of iron, steel, cement, and glass, towering over them fifty yards away. He began explaining to Hank how the shock of blasting the dense rock would easily reach the sub-foundation of the main plant, weakening the entire structure beyond permissible limits. Hank waved him off with a knowing nod of the head.

"Too late for blasting here," Hank said. "No telling how far down you'd have to go. The main building'd have to come down for sure." With his brown leather boot, Hank kicked away the soil in a few places revealing the hard rock just a few inches beneath the surface. He turned to Charlie. "You boys really fucked up here didn't you?"

"Yeah we sure did Hank," Charlie answered, wondering if he should be admitting that to the Planning Board Chairman.

"Okay, let's go see where you want to move it to."

They drove up to the north end of the property just inside the fence along Cold Spring Road. Charlie reached into the back seat and brought up a scrolled blueprint of the revised pond design and gave it to Hank. The old man studied it carefully as they drove around what would be the perimeter of the new pond. Charlie stopped at what he estimated would be the center of the pond. Hank continued to study the revised engineering drawing, occasionally squinting his eyes at some detail and then looking up to study the topography of the land around them. After ten minutes of intense review of the plan, Hank rolled it up and got out of the Navigator. He walked directly north toward the boundary fence and stopped where the land suddenly fell away going down a slope to the fence and Cold Spring Road. Then he walked along the edge of the hill parallel to the fence for a hundred and fifty yards, stood still for a few moments gazing around as if visualizing the future pond, and then to Charlie's surprise, Hank suddenly sat down on the ground. He took out a pen and began writing something on the back of the plan, occasionally looking up at the land in front of him and then going back to his writing. After about twenty-minutes, he arose again and walked back slowly to where Charlie was waiting for him at the edge of the property looking down at Cold Spring Road.

When Hank got back to where Charlie was standing, he again sat down on the sandy ground. Pulling the fat ballpoint pen from his inside pocket again, he gestured to a spot on the ground in front of him. "C'mon Burden, let's make a deal." he said.

Charlie sat down and crossed his legs Indian style. "What'd you have in mind Hank?"

Hank rolled out the blueprint of the pond on the ground between them. "First of all, you got a problem here with the plans. You need 300 million gallons, right? And you've got fifty-two acres up here you can use, so your pond is a foot too shallow. Here, I'll show you."

Pointing to his figures on the back of the plan with his pen, Hank proceeded to amaze Charlie with his knowledge of advanced calculus. He worked out the complex formula for computing the volume of the asymmetrical pond while taking into consideration the height of the sides and the angles of the pond's sloping bottom. It was obvious that Hank had taught mathematics somewhere along the line in his career in the Red Bone school system.

Charlie followed along as Hank explained his calculations. The arithmetic seemed to confirm Hank's contention that the pond would need to be a foot deeper than planned, but Charlie wasn't ready to concede the point without putting it through the computer.

"We'll go back and check our math," said Charlie.

"You bet your ass you will, and you better have it right when you come before the board in September," answered Hankinson. "Now everything else is up to standard for water impoundments – the pumping and release systems, and the levees – your boys can read the regs as good as we can, but you're going to have to make a couple of changes you probably ain't going to like too much." Hank reached into his suit jacket pocket and pulled out his tobacco pouch.

Charlie put his hands on the dusty ground in back of him and leaned back on his stiff arms. He was apprehensive about what was coming next. If Hank was looking for a bribe, this is where it would come.

"What kind of a change Hank?"

Hank put a plug of chewing tobacco in his mouth, put the pouch back in his pocket and took off his jacket. The mid-day sun was beating down on them without any breeze. Hank was sweating through his white shirt. He held his arm out and pointed around the perimeter of the future pond as he spoke. "Around this northern half of the pond, where the land goes down away from the mountain here, you're going to have to make that containment dike two feet higher than you got it laid out. And, you're going to have to reinforce it with steel."

"Two feet higher? Reinforced with steel? That's way beyond the code Hank. You said yourself everything met the requirements of the regulations." Charlie was perplexed more than disappointed or angry. He did a quick calculation in his mind and estimated that the cost of Hank's requirements, most particularly for the cost of steel framing to reinforce the dike, would be around a hundred thousand dollars. Still a very affordable solution. Hank remained silent.

"You know Hank, that would cost us about a hundred thousand, maybe a hundred fifty," Charlie said, looking around at the site.

Hank turned his head and spit a gob of tobacco juice in the sand. "Tough shit," he said. "Your client can afford to build a safe pond."

"Wouldn't a pond built to code be safe enough?" Charlie asked.

Hank's mustache bounced up and down as he vigorously massaged the wad of chewing tobacco. After a long pause, he spoke in a low voice. "Safe enough for the State and for the County. Safe enough for the board too, legally, 'cause I can't *make* you go beyond the code." Almost to himself he added, "not safe enough though for families that may be living along Cold Spring Road someday, years from now, when you and I are long gone and other people got the responsibility for . . ." He stopped and turned to Charlie with a pained look on his face. "The levee needs to be higher, and it needs to be reinforced. It's something *I* need you to do."

Charlie was relieved that Hank wasn't looking for a payoff. He'd only known him a short time and while he'd concluded that Hank was a man of integrity, you couldn't be sure until the moment of truth came. It had now come and gone, and Hank, it was obvious, had concerns about the project that were at a much higher plane. Hank's concerns, Charlie could see, were also very personal.

"What's it all about Hank? There's more to this than code requirements, right?" Charlie said softly, sensing his friend's reluctance to elaborate.

Hank gazed around at the surrounding hills with a far away look in his eyes as his mind resurrected the painful memories from twenty-eight years earlier. After a few moments, he nodded his head slowly, as if telling himself that it would be all right to share these memories with Charlie Burden.

"It was a lousy day," he started in a low voice. "Been raining and drizzling for three days straight. February twenty-sixth, nineteen seventy-two. It was a Saturday." Hank paused to gather his thoughts. "I was a school teacher here in Red Bone, and assistant principal at the time. Well about noon time I get a call at home from a good friend of mine, a deputy sheriff here and he tells me he just got a call that a dam let go up in Logan County – a coal-waste dam the mining companies build to make water impoundments to clean their coal with. A hundred years they been doing it like that in spite of all the problems they cause. Anyway, he tells me it looks like there could be some damage and maybe some injuries, and he was heading on up there to provide assistance. Reason he called me was he knows I got a cousin living up there in a little coal camp town called Lundale, couple miles down the creek from the dam. Cousin was married to a miner – all miners livin' up there – and had a little girl." Hank took in a deep breath and let out a sigh. "So, he picked me up out at the house and we drove on up there. Up to Buffalo Creek."

For the next twenty minutes, Charlie didn't utter a sound as Hank told him the story of the Buffalo Creek disaster, the worst dam failure in West Virginia history. It happened on the morning of February 26, 1972. After a week of snow and rain, a series of three coal-waste dams breached, sending 120 million gallons of water crashing down the narrow valley of Buffalo Creek in southeastern Logan County. When the twenty-foot high wall of black water and coal-waste sludge had finished its eighteen-mile path of destruction, five towns had been totally obliterated and nine others severely damaged. Four thousand were left homeless. Seven hundred homes were destroyed along with fifty house trailers, thirty businesses and 900 automobiles and trucks. After weeks of searching through the rubble and debris by the National Guard and the State Police, the death toll ended at 125, including seven whose bodies were never recovered.

"We drove up as far as we could before the road just disappeared, just below Amherstdale, and then we started walking. There was some state police there and you could see they were pretty shaken. Told us we wouldn't believe how bad it was." Hank would often pause and shake his head slowly as if he were fighting off the horror of the memories that came back as he was telling the story.

"Above Amherstdale we came to a railroad trestle across the creek and on the other side of it there was this huge pile of rubble – must have been thirty feet high covering forty or fifty yards of the creek bed – all packed in so tight you couldn't even pull a board out of there. Looked like a pile of matchsticks with a bunch of toy cars thrown in. But they weren't toys. It was what was left of most of the houses and buildings from all the towns for the next eight miles up to the where the dam broke in Saunders.

"We kept walking up the valley and pretty soon there was nothing left . . . houses gone, road and the top-soil all washed away, even the railroad tracks were gone. People were wandering around with that dazed look on their faces looking for people . . . mothers calling out for their babies, children looking for their parents . . . it was horrible Charlie. Worst day I ever had to live through." Charlie could see tears rolling down the sides of Hank's mustache.

"Anyway, we get up to Lundale, and there's nothing left, nothing there. Ground is scraped down to the gravel. Wouldn't have known there was once a town there if you didn't know the hollows and the shape of the hillsides. Total devastation from there all the way up to the dam." Hank turned to spit tobacco juice in the sand. "Cousin's house was gone. They found her body the next day and then her little girl about a week later. Her husband was early shift down in one of the mines when it all happened. Later on he gets his settlement check . . . pathetic little retribution payment – about twenty-eight hundred dollars as I recall – and he turns into a drunk and drug user, and then moves away. Never heard from him." Then he added softly, "can't blame him though.

"Next day the National Guard moves in and takes over and shuts everything off. No volunteers, no media, no nothing allowed into the valley. Damn governor's in bed with the coal companies you see, and they're scrambling right away to cover their ass, calling it an *'act of God'*, just another *natural* disaster. *'Too much rain'* they said, and they don't want people snooping around up there and taking pictures of the dam or the destruction they caused . . . or the bodies of kids lying in the mud." The sadness in Hank's voice had now been replaced by the sound of bitterness. Charlie could see the firm set of Hank's jaw and the look of anger in his eyes.

"They *knew* the dams weren't safe. State inspectors had been up there and cited them a year earlier for not having any emergency spillway and told them to reinforce the dams. But they never did anything – *nobody* did anything – and the state didn't give a shit. They *all* just let it happen. The *motherfuckers!*" Hank slammed an open hand against the ground sending up a cloud of dust around them while the tears streamed down his cheeks onto his white whiskers. "They knew the night before that the dams might collapse but they didn't warn *anyone!*"

Hank shook his head in frustration and wiped his eyes with a shirt sleeve. "Lot of 'em were little *kids* Charlie. *Forty-three* of the dead were under the age of *fifteen . . . forty-three,*" Hank pleaded. "Had all these little bodies piled up in the cafeteria down at the middle school in Man. Whole families wiped out. *Jesus,*" Hank said, closing his eyes.

The anger was back in his voice and in his dark eyes when he continued. "A *hundred and twenty-five* good people died at Buffalo Creek, Charlie. Wasn't any act of *God*. God had nothing to do with it! Was an act of *man! A*nd corporate *greed*, and *arrogance* from a hundred years of *taking and taking* and keeping the people poor and dependent and powerless . . ." Hank stopped to take a deep breath and calm himself down before continuing in a softer tone. "Three of the bodies they found were little babies that no one could identify. Think about that Burden. Three kids with no name, no identity."

Hank was quiet for a few moments, shaking his head as if he was still trying to make sense of it all. "You know, in 1971, the year before Buffalo Creek, the coal company was cited for *five thousand* violations at their mines all over the country – back then, they were the nation's second biggest coal company – and they got fined *one point three million dollars* for those violations. Well they challenged *every* violation, and you know how much they ended up paying?" Hank paused for effect. "*Two hundred and seventy-five fucking dollars!* That's what they paid in fines." He turned and spit a gob of brown tobacco juice for emphasis.

"'Bout a year after the flood, the state's Attorney General goes after them for damages and sues for a hundred million dollars, and ready to go into court and put them bastards out of business too. So what happens? *Damn coal companies.* Two days before his term is up, the Governor settles the case for *one million. One million dollars* they got off with. It was *nothing* to them. *Pocket change!*"

Hank pulled out a handkerchief and blew his nose quietly and rubbed his eyes. He sat quietly for a moment in thought. "You know what gets me the worst Burden?" The old man turned to Charlie with sad, imploring eyes. "*No one* from the company, or from the state, or the federal government . . . *no one*, ever said they were *sorry* for what happened. No one ever apologized to the survivors of Buffalo Creek for their years and years of nightmares, or apologized to the relatives for their lifetime of heartache. And surely no one ever apologized to the people of West Virginia for making us look like . . . like backward, hillbilly fools livin' in flimsy shacks where we shouldn't be . . . like the flood was the fault of the people living there. *Goddammit.*"

Listening and watching Hank relate the story of Buffalo Creek, Charlie felt as close to Hank as he'd gotten to anyone in many years. He was gratified that Hank had shared such a painful memory with him. He could see that it wasn't a story that his friend enjoyed telling or one that he told very often.

Charlie also had a newfound appreciation for his neighbor's strength of character, and his sensitivity to the plight of his fellow West Virginians. *What was it Natty Oakes said her grandmother always said? . . . 'there's a lot of heartache in these mountains.' Hank would surely agree with that,* thought Charlie. He chastised himself for even considering that Hank may have been looking for a payoff. Maybe it was the New York mentality or just the nature of the business that jaded your outlook.

"So Burden," Hankinson had turned back toward Charlie, the customary gruffness back in his voice. "When it comes to water impoundments, like we got here, when I got something to do with it, I go beyond the code. I make it as safe as I can. Safe as it should be for now, and forty, fifty years from now. Cause I can't bring back any of those kids from Buffalo Creek, but maybe I can help save . . . well, you know what I'm saying Burden. Maybe it's just a symbolic gesture, who knows. But that's the way it is and right now I got the gavel, so that's the deal."

Hank started to get to his feet, laboring to push himself up on stiff legs. Charlie bounced up quickly and extended a hand to help pull the old man erect. They stood facing each other a few feet apart.

Hank spoke first. "So we got a deal Burden?"

Charlie smiled at his friend and offered his hand. "Yeah Hank, we got a deal. We'll reinforce it with steel and build it two feet higher." He gripped Hank's bony hand firmly and looked into his dark brown eyes. "We'll build a safe pond Hank, for now and for years to come. I guarantee it."

"Okay Burden. Okay. That's good," said Hank. "You revise the plan and you'll get your permit."

The men turned and started walking back to the Navigator. "What about the other two board members?" Charlie asked. "Will they be okay with this?"

"Oh them? Miserable pricks, both of 'em," Hank laughed. "But they'll be okay. They'll listen to me. What about your client? What are they going to say?" asked Hank.

"CanAmex? Well they're mostly miserable pricks too, except for a couple of them. They'll approve it on my recommendation. Actually Hank, they'll be thrilled with the deal. A hundred thousand is a cheap price to pay to keep the project on schedule."

Hank laughed. "Should of asked for more then," he said jokingly.

"Well Hank," Charlie said as if he were thinking aloud, "maybe you'll get a little more. I've got an idea I need to work on a little. We'll talk about it before the Planning Board meeting."

They drove back to the administration building and parked next to Hank's beat up old Chrysler. Hank refused Charlie's invitation to buy him lunch out at the *Roadhouse,* but they agreed to meet that evening on the porch for some cribbage and a shot or two of some local moonshine one of Hank's former students had dropped off for him.

Charlie watched Hank drive out through the gate, the rumbling exhaust of the Chrysler belching white smoke as it accelerated away toward the access road. The big car rode low on shocks and springs that had given up long ago. In a few days Hank could be rid of the Chrysler and driving a brand new car, any make he wanted, Charlie mused, if he were at all interested in such things. One phone call to Vernon Yarbrough in Charleston and the next day Charlie would have a gym bag full of cash for the Planning Board Chairman, he had no doubt. But Pullman Hankinson didn't care about cars, or about owning things or living high, that was clear. He cared about people, his neighbors, and his town, and certainly about West Virginia. And he cared about the injustice – most fervently about injustice – of poor people dying because they were poor enough not to matter.

Even after the Chrysler disappeared around the corner of the dusty access road, Charlie stood watching, thinking about Hank. He suddenly felt a rush of pride in having Hank for a friend. It was a rare episode he'd experienced out in the field, a demonstration of selflessness and emotional exposure that didn't seem to exist any more in Charlie's world. Hank had opened himself up and allowed Charlie to see into his inner core in an unconditional expression of nobility. *Maybe that's what he had been searching for these past few years. Personal nobility. Was that the corollary to the unceasing pursuit of wealth that everyone around him seemed to be infected with?*

A hazy cloud of dust hung in the air in the Chrysler's wake. Charlie smiled and whispered out loud, "you're my *hero* Hank." He went back inside, into the main computer room and went to work rechecking the calculations on the depth of the cooling pond.

The next morning Charlie was on the porch watching for Natty when he saw his blue Lexus coming up South County Road. Natty flashed the headlights and waved to Charlie through the open moon roof. She was standing in the middle of Main Street, ready to go, by the time Charlie got down stairs. The Lexus was parked between the Navigator and Hank's Chrysler in front of the store.

"Keys are over the visor," Natty said, as they started out at slow jog. "Thank you. Thanks for the car. It was a big help."

"You're welcome," said Charlie.

It was then that he first noticed that Natty's appearance had changed. The long baggy shorts were gone, replaced by a very short pair of lightweight red running shorts. On top she wore a black T-shirt that fit snugly across her back and shoulders and hung loose at the waste. The shirt was short enough to occasionally reveal her small waist as it flapped in the breeze. In place of the customary Spiderman cap, her hair was pulled back in a dark green bandana that covered the top half of her forehead.

Charlie smiled inwardly as he watched Natty's small hips and strong thin legs churning confidently in front of him. *She could be a New York model running through Central Park,* thought Charlie. *Or was she just a hillbilly mountain girl from the backwoods of Appalachia?* Charlie wondered if she knew how good she looked in *normal* clothing.

When they exited the woods and hit the mountain trail, Natty gradually picked up the pace and was soon twenty yards in front of Charlie. He made no effort to catch up to her as it seemed obvious that Natty wasn't interested in idle chatter while they ran this morning. Charlie surmised that she was probably a little uncomfortable, as was he, with the idea of running together two days in a row, as if they were establishing a routine. He only had to glance up ahead at Natty's slender hips and thin legs to know that this indeed was a bad idea.

They ran through the dark woods above Oakes Hollow and down the logging road without slowing their pace a step and when Charlie finally crossed the wooden foot-bridge to South County Road, Natty was fifty yards ahead of him and his lungs and thighs were burning.

A half mile from Old Red Bone, Charlie watched Natty stop running and walk toward a man walking his dog on the other side of the road. Relieved, he slowed down himself, and then came to a walk as he approached them. Natty hugged the man and then dropped to her knees to scratch the dog energetically behind both ears.

As Charlie came abreast of them, Natty arose and waved him over to them. Charlie used the front of his T-shirt to mop up the sweat that was still pouring from his head as he crossed the road.

"Mr. Burden, this is Earl Fitch," Natty said. "Earl, Mr. Burden's the new power plant boss, down here from New York." The two men shook hands. "Earl owns Red Bone's only barber shop."

Earl Fitch looked to be in his mid-sixties with a white crew cut and a large belly. He had a round, pinkish face and a bulbous nose that reminded Charlie of W.C. Fields. In the breast pocket of his white shirt, several fat cigars stood at attention.

"Sure, I know all about Mr. Burden. From Hank. Says you ain't a bad cribbage player, which is pretty high praise coming from that old coot. Don't generally have much good to say about anybody." Earl Fitch eyed Charlie's hair, which he hadn't had cut since leaving New York. "Looks like you could use a little trim there, son." He fished a business card from his pocket and gave it to Charlie. His shop was on Main Street next to the vacant United Mine Workers office. Charlie assured him that he'd be in for a haircut soon.

"Maybe we'll have a cigar together," Charlie said, eyeing the cigars in Earl Fitch's breast pocket.

"You bet," said the barber as he tugged gently on the leash to get his dog up on her feet. "Good to meet you Burden," he said. Then he added, "Hank's real fond of you Charlie, and that goes a long way around here."

Earl Fitch winked at Natty and gave her a fatherly pat on the shoulder as he resumed his walk down South County Road. Natty and Charlie began walking toward Old Red Bone. They'd run hard for over four miles and there was no way to start up again now that they cooled down.

"Shouldn't be smoking cigars Mr. Burden. Not good for your wind you know," Natty said.

"Well, I like smoking them, but I don't buy them," Charlie answered. "It's a rule, to keep me from smoking regularly. So once in a while, I find someone to bum one from."

Earl Fitch . . . there was something about the man with the dog that was familiar to Charlie. *How do I know that name?* He was sure he'd heard or seen it before.

After a few minutes of walking, they reached the soccer field, now thick with end-of-summer weeds, the bare earth patches cracked from dryness. Natty stopped to assess the work ahead of her in getting the field ready for their first practice in a little over a week.

"God what a mess. Have to get it mowed down pretty soon. Got our first practice the Saturday after next," she said.

"How's your team going to be this season?" asked Charlie.

Natty laughed and shrugged her shoulders. "We'll be fine if we can find enough players. Won't win any trophies but we'll win some games. We do okay against the other teams from McDowell County 'cept for Welch, and get beat up pretty good by the teams from Bluefield and Princeton. But I think we at least may have enough players, which is our biggest problem every year." They resumed their walk up the hill. "We got the Pie Man of course," she laughed. "And a few other decent players who should be back. Plus Sammy Willard who you met and his brother Zack. They'll be terrific players once they practice a little. Got a good goalie – girl named Brenda Giles. And of course, we got Emma Lowe. You met her in front of Eve's place."

"Oh, yeah. Pie says she's a pretty good player."

"Emma Lowe's the best thirteen year-old girl soccer player in the country," Natty said matter-of-factly.

"Whoa, that's a pretty big statement," Charlie said with a chuckle. He'd been around the sport of kid's soccer enough years to have heard many times, the exaggerated praise of individual players by parents and coaches. Invariably the praise fell somewhat short of reality.

"I know. Well, you'll just have to come a watch a game and make up your own mind," First practice is Saturday after next and then the first game's a week later. We could use a few fans and Pie would love it if you were to come to a game."

"Yeah, of course I'll go to a game. Been a few years since I had a reason to watch a kids soccer game. That'd be a lot of fun."

Natty nodded her head and flashed an uneasy smile, nervous at the thought of the new power plant boss attending one of their rag-tag soccer games.

"Probably miss the first game though. I have to go back up to New York for a while, probably a week, maybe longer."

"Business?" Natty asked, happy to change the subject.

"No, not really. My daughter's coming in from Illinois for a few days so I want to see her before she goes back to school. She goes to Northwestern. And also, my wife's going to force me to make a decision on a house she wants to buy."

"Doesn't sound like you're crazy about the idea," Natty said looking up at Charlie to see if she could read anything from his face.

After a pause, he replied, "No, I'm not too excited about it." He sounded like he was thinking out loud instead of talking to Natty. "But she really wants it, and she deserves it too. So . . . I don't know. It just seems so wasteful to me. The house is too big and it's over a million bucks."

Natty swallowed hard and blinked her eyelids rapidly trying to hide the shock and the sudden wave of insecurity that swept over her like nausea. *What was it he just said? Over a million bucks. Not just a million, like a rough estimate or a generalization for an expensive house. It was "over" a million, meaning a real specific number that they were actually considering to spend for a house.*

"That's a lot of money alright. Must be a pretty nice house," Natty said, recovering enough to sound politely interested. *What kind of world did this man live in? 'Forced into making a decision' about buying a million dollar house that 'his wife deserved.' What was he even doing here, in Red Bone, West Virginia, this tall, beautiful, sensitive, super successful man, walking up South County Road with a plain looking, no-account hillbilly girl, talking about kid's soccer, and being so nice to her son and everybody else in town. Christ!*

"Oh it's a beautiful house, but it's also Westchester County, which is one of the most expensive real estate markets in the county. Million bucks doesn't buy as much house as it used to in Westchester," Charlie said with a grin.

Natty's thoughts drifted back to the little ranch style house with the *for sale* sign, she'd stopped in front of on one of her quick detours through the neat little neighborhood near her company's office in Bluefield. The seventy-four thousand dollar price seemed like so much money, even if Buck would ever consider moving from Oakes Hollow, which he wouldn't, but she could still dream about getting out of the cramped trailer and living in a regular house on a street with neighbors. *A million dollars for a house!* "Yeah, must be tough trying get by up there," Natty said, playing along. *God, they were like two people from different planets who just looked to be of the same species and spoke roughly the same language. This was one daydream that would never make any sense.*

Natty got her purse out of Charlie's car and walked up Main Street to Gus Lowe's garage to pick up her Accord with the new front axle, wheel bearings, brake fluid, and right rocker panel. The new rocker panel was black, the color it would stay. She wrote out a check for eighty-dollars which, she told Gus, was all she had until payday when she might be able to give him another hundred. Gus Lowe just nodded and accepted the check without comment. Natty knew Gus needed the money and couldn't afford to be financing her debts. She told him that she'd try to clear it up as quickly as she could, but they both knew that Gus's bill would soon cease to be a priority in the growing pile of debt in the Oakes household.

She drove home feeling sick to her stomach thinking about the money she owed Gus and how he hadn't uttered a word of protest. The Accord felt old and noisy compared to Charlie's Lexus, which Natty had just been getting used to.

Chapter 14

The dull *whump, whump,* of the helicopter blades announced the arrival of the lawyers from Charleston. Charlie glanced at his watch – ten A.M – right on schedule. Vernon Yarbrough had called him from the helicopter twenty minutes earlier to announce their arrival. Charlie leaned back in his chair to look up through his office window to see if he could spot the helicopter. The gleaming black Bell - 430 with the silver lightning bolts under the CanAmex Energy Company logo, roared in over the trees from the Northwest, pulled up sharply over the middle of the site and feathered gently down onto the landing pad adjacent to the parking lot for the administration building.

As Charlie arose from his desk to pull his sport jacket from the rack in the corner he was surprised to see Terry Summers appear in the doorway. "Ready boss? Looks like it's show time." Terry Summers flashed Charlie one of his trademark smiles. He was dressed in an elegant looking beige summer-weight suit, white shirt and an expensive looking brown tie.

"Hey, Terry," Charlie answered. "You going up to see the farmer with us?"

"Wouldn't miss it for the world. Plus, I know the way up there so it'll be easier if I drive."

Charlie was surprised that Summers had been included in the visit to Angel Mountain. He hadn't noticed his name on the E-mail distribution of Larry Tuthill's message. It made some sense that he was included, but Charlie thought Summers was leaving that day for a long golf weekend with a few of the other young engineers working for sub-contractors.

"Thought you were on your way up to *The Greenbrier.*" Charlie said, on their way through the computer room.

"Later on. After we get back. We'll take the chopper up there. Take about ten minutes the way these CanAmex pilots fly."

Vernon Yarbrough came across the parking lot like a candidate for the U.S. Senate, arm outstretched, his big hand searching for Charlie's, a smile across his face as if he was greeting a life-long friend. "Well Mr. Bur – *dan.* How the hell are *you* sir? *God-damn,* you're looking *fine,* just *fine.* Our mountain air must agree with you." The silver-haired lawyer gave Charlie the two-handed shake, his left hand at Charlie's right elbow.

Yarbrough introduced Kevin Mulrooney from Ackerly Coal Company. Charlie remembered Mulrooney from a couple of years earlier when they were all down for the original announcement of the Red Bone plant. Mulrooney was red-faced and sweating from the heat. Already he had loosened his tie which, after it wrapped around his huge neck, had only enough length left to reach halfway to his belt. His waist was hidden by a massive stomach that threatened to pop the lower buttons of his shirt. An uncomfortable scowl on his face said that he really didn't want to be here. But, technically, Charlie knew, Ackerly Coal was to be the purchaser of the farm, even though it had now become an imperative for CanAmex due to the CES merger.

Following behind Yarbrough and Mulrooney was a tall young man with black glasses who was obviously a lawyer, carrying two briefcases. Yarbrough introduced him offhandedly as 'that's Leonard over there, from my office.' Charlie nodded to Leonard, thinking that it probably wasn't too pleasant being a junior associate at Kerns & Yarbrough.

Charlie tossed Terry Summers the keys to the Navigator. Vernon Yarbrough took the front seat. Charlie sat directly behind the lawyer, with Mulrooney to his left. Leonard climbed into the rear seat with the brief cases.

"Take us about forty minutes to get up there," Summers announced as they drove through the gate.

"That's fine, just fine," Vernon Yarbrough answered, pushing back the sleeve of his suit jacket to reveal the gold Rolex. "Put us up at the farm about eleven o'clock."

Yarbrough turned halfway toward the passengers in the rear seats. "Talked to farmer DeWitt last night. Told him we were coming up today to give him some real good news. 'Course he protested. Said he wasn't interested, wasn't selling, and all that, but I told him I'as bringin' up some pretty important folks to meet him," he nodded toward the back seat, "and wasn't taking *no* for an answer. So, farmer DeWitt says, well if y'all are coming up, may as well come around lunch time, around eleven o'clock they break for lunch and that'd be the only time he might have for *jawin'* around with us, even though we're still wasting our time he says.

"Don't think we're wasting our time, aye Kevin?" Yarbrough said loudly with a laugh as he shot a knowing glance at Mulrooney. The lawyer seemed to be in a pretty positive mood, thought Charlie, for getting so little encouragement from the farmer.

"What we're doing here today gentlemen," Yarbrough continued, "is giving farmer DeWitt one last chance to make a good deal and save his ass." He turned back around to face front. "Cause next time I have to come back up here, that fucking pig farmer ain't going to be inviting us to lunch. You can bet your ass on that." The lawyer, Summers and Mulrooney joined in a short, knowing laugh. Charlie got the feeling that he was missing something the other three were in on. He wasn't sure he wanted to be in on it, and remained silent.

They drove along in welcome silence for twenty minutes. Charlie used the opportunity to study the rugged landscape, which had become fascinating to him. He was beginning to understand the magnetism created by the beauty and quiet serenity of the mountains, how it could grab hold of someone and not let go.

Kevin Mulrooney's nasally voice jarred him from his reverie. "So, hear about any more noise from the granddaughter?" He was addressing Yarbrough.

The lawyer turned again toward the back seat. He shot Mulrooney a quick glance that may have had some displeasure in it for bringing up the subject. "No, nothing more from her. And I don't think we will. She took her shot, I think, and that's probably the end of it." Then he turned farther around to bring Charlie up to date.

"What happened?" asked Charlie.

"Well, it seems the farmer's granddaughter, got a little inquisitive all of a sudden and went to see a lawyer in Welch, asking questions about *mountaintop-removal* mining on Angel Mountain. Looks like they put two and two together and figured out some things. *How the hell* they ever got to *mountaintop-removal* . . . well I don't know why she'd be talking like that, but we got to make sure she don't start making any *serious* noise. Think we got it pretty well contained though. Lawyer in Welch is a nobody – shitty little practice, divorce, custody, probate crap and like that – but we got him on our side now case she tries to stir things up. So we're okay." Yarbrough turned back to the front. "We're okay. Just got to wrap up this farm business sooner than later, like *today*, and then we don't have to worry." He glanced at his watch again. "Five hundred thousand. That's our number today. As high as we're going," said Yarbrough as he sliced the air with a short karate chop with his left hand. His diamond pinky ring looked huge on the big hand suspended in air for emphasis. "Five hundred thousand, or we move on to *Plan B*," added Yarbrough.

"What's *Plan B*?" asked Charlie, wondering what happened to the *million dollar* figure that Larry Tuthill had authorized in New York.

In the front seat, the lawyer from Charleston seemed to shift a little uncomfortably and glanced around at the scenery in an effort to avoid Charlie's question. "Well let's just say we got some other avenues to take with this boy. Some legal remedies we can pursue." He let it drop for a few moments, then added, "But five hundred grand's a huge number for that place, so . . . we'll be okay. We won't need to go anywhere else."

It was obvious the lawyer didn't want to go into any of the details of what *Plan B* might be, so Charlie just let it go. Mention of the money though, reminded him of the meeting in New York and Larry Tuthill's offer – '*a million dollars, and you guys split whatever you don't have to pay the farmer.*' Charlie hadn't thought much about it at the time – he hadn't yet gotten over the fact that he would be going to West Virginia instead of China – but even then, at that moment, he recalled thinking that there was *something off* about that part of the meeting.

Tuthill's offer just didn't make any sense. Charlie could understand that Tuthill and his boss Jack Torkelson were in a bind over the CES merger because *someone* – according to Vernon Yarbrough – *may have bribed a superior court judge,* to set aside a court ruling against *mountaintop-removal* variances, and now they needed to purchase the farm quickly and quietly. It was the reason Charlie was in West Virginia. To help CanAmex, and in doing so, protect his friend Duncan McCord. But Tuthill's *million-dollar deal* was a *small time* maneuver for a high-level CanAmex manager. Larry Tuthill was a senior executive for an international energy conglomerate. What was he doing screwing around with offering bonus payments to guys like Charlie Burden and a big-time lawyer like Vernon Yarbrough who were already on the payroll? Did he think they were going to work more diligently at the task of displacing the pig farmer because of an incentive payment of a few hundred thousand? Yarbrough was already on retainer for a good five figures a month, and Charlie, Tuthill was quite aware, was in West Virginia, only because of his loyalty to McCord and to Lucien Mackey.

The money and the offer just didn't fit the players or the situation thought Charlie. *Maybe Tuthill was just panicking, envisioning his career going down the toilet in a messy PUC hearing in Charleston over the CES merger, and wanted some kind of insurance.* That was the best rationale Charlie could come up with. His nagging doubts about the whole Angel Mountain issue made him less than enthusiastic about getting involved. He hoped that Yarbrough could close the deal, nice and neat, with farmer DeWitt today, so Charlie could forget about Angel Mountain, *and* about *Plan B,* whatever it was, and just concentrate on building the plant.

"Goddammit," exclaimed Terry Summers as he pulled over to the side of the narrow road. "Think I missed the turnoff," he said as he pulled a section of a map from his inside pocket.

After studying the map and driving another half mile to find a road sign as a landmark, he pulled the big SUV into a U-turn and raced back in the direction they'd come from.

"Fucking roads all look the same down here." Summers drove back a little too impatiently. "Too many forked turns," he said to explain his mistake.

"Slow down son," Yarbrough said with a chuckle. "Remember, this is the south. It's okay to be a little late."

After a few minutes, Summers found the turn he was looking for and slowed down almost to a stop to make a sharp turn onto Heaven's Gate. An old wooden sign with an arrow pointed them in the direction of Angel Hollow. Immediately, they started a gradual, winding climb through a dark forest, the road barely wide enough in places for the big Navigator to ride without scraping the tree limbs that reached out at them from the woods. Charlie buzzed down his window and leaned close to the door to drink in the cool, moist smells of the forest. The aroma had a sweetness that was foreign to him, unlike the fresh cut grass scent of Mamaroneck or the strong, dairy farm smells of Vermont that he was familiar with. It reminded him of the fragrant pipe tobacco aroma of his grandfather's house when he was a boy.

Gradually the thick woods gave way to thin stands of birches and maples and small rolling meadows of wild grasses sprinkled with white and yellow flowers. Formations of large boulders and smooth, flat rock surfaces pushed up through the ground to tell them that this was a rugged piece of land they were traveling through. In places, the old road inclined precipitously as it snaked its way up through the unyielding topography, causing even the Navigator's big V-8 to whine for a distance in a lower gear.

Soon they came to another sharp turn, almost a hairpin, that Summers was ready for. He eased the big vehicle nearly to a stop as he cut the wheel hard to the left and then accelerated up a steep incline onto Angel Mountain Road. "Almost there," he announced. "'Bout a mile or so up this road on the right."

After a long gentle curve, the road straightened into a steady climb up the northern side of Angel Mountain. The trees fell away quickly on the left side of the road revealing finally how high they had already come. On the right, they passed sections of old stone walls, a few caved in wooden shacks and then, an isolated brick fireplace and chimney surrounded by underbrush that concealed any trace of the slab foundation now covered with years' worth of dirt and rotting vegetation.

A minute later, Summers announced their arrival. "Here we are boys," he said as he slowed suddenly and then pulled the Navigator into the hard-packed earthen front yard of the DeWitt farm. He parked in the shade of a huge oak tree and the five men exited the vehicle in a noisy succession of slamming doors. Acorns crackled under their feet as they stretched their legs and put on their suit jackets. Only Charlie Burden wasn't wearing a tie.

There was no one in sight and no sound came from the house through the screen door and open windows. The silence and serenity of the scene were broken only by the birds chirping in the trees above them and from the gentle summer breezes that came in from the open valley on the other side of the road. The only sign of recent activity was a picnic table set up in front of the small house. It was covered with a yellow plastic table cloth, a large glass pitcher of ice water, and a stack of brown plastic cups.

Right away the farm reminded Charlie of the tired old farms you run across on the back roads of Vermont. The real farms, not the renovated, antique-filled farms taken over by the wealthy gentlemen farmers from New York and New Jersey to raise horses and hay as a tax dodge, but the real working farms that year after year survive, just barely, to reward their owners with a poverty-line existence. The patches in the roof of the house, the sagging porch, and the ominous lean of the walls of the barn, told a familiar story.

"Hello in the house. Mr. Dewitt, hello," Vernon Yarbrough called out loudly. There was no answer. Terry Summers leaned inside the Navigator and pushed on the loud horn for several seconds. The rude sound pierced the quietude of the mountain farm. Charlie flashed Summers a look of disapproval, which he returned in the form of a wide, amused smile.

At that moment, the front door of the house swung open quietly as an elderly woman backed through it carrying a tray covered with a red checked cloth. Carefully, she made her way down the short flight of steps, placed the tray in the middle of the table and stood up stiffly. "Bud'll be down in a minute," she said looking up toward the cornfield and the road that ran along it. "I'll bring out the coffee," she said turning back toward the house.

"Mrs. DeWitt," Vernon Yarbrough stopped her. "Nice to see you again ma'am. Let me introduce my associates," he said as the old woman looked back at them nervously. Yarbrough introduced Mulrooney and Charlie. Summers, she'd met before, he said, although the woman showed no sign of recognition. He ignored Leonard.

"Fellows, this is our hostess for today," said Yarbrough grandly, "Mrs. Agnes DeWitt."

The men said hello and in turn came up and shook hands with the woman, who said nothing. She hesitated for a moment as if she had something to say, but then just turned and went slowly up the steps and into the house.

Mulrooney stepped forward and pulled back the cloth covering the tray and helped himself to a chicken salad sandwich. "Imagine living way the fuck up here," he said as he stuffed a large part of half a sandwich into his mouth. "Have to go nuts after a while, wouldn'tcha think?"

Before anyone could offer an opinion, the sound of a tractor caught their attention. A few seconds later, the green tractor, clacking loudly and churning up a cloud of dust behind it, came slowly down the farm's interior road. Bud DeWitt parked the tractor next to the barn and walked over to a wooden bucket sitting on a shelf on the barn wall and washed his hands and face. He dried himself with a small white towel as he walked down toward the men at the picnic table.

Charlie recognized him from the picture in the folder. Medium height, a weathered face creased by years of squinting into the sun, and a thin, wiry build. Except for a slow, stiff-jointed gait, he looked younger than seventy-two. DeWitt was wearing the same *Peterbilt* hat that he wore in the picture. He nodded toward Vernon Yarbrough as he got close to them. "Mr. Yarbrough," he said as a way of a greeting.

"Mr. DeWitt, nice to see you again sir," said Yarbrough as he applied the two-handed shake on the farmer. "We appreciate your lettin' us come on up here and I think we're prepared to close this deal today sir. And we sincerely do appreciate this fine lunch that your lovely wife has put out for us," Yarbrough said as Bud DeWitt sat down at the picnic table and reached for a sandwich.

"Got only a half hour," said DeWitt pouring himself some ice water. "Better get started."

Yarbrough introduced Kevin Mulrooney, the head of the Ackerly Coal Company and then, Mr. Charlie Burden, recently down from New York, *the big mule* of the construction project of the CanAmex power plant. Charlie reached across the table and shook hands with Bud DeWitt. The farmer had a naturally strong grip and clear gray eyes. As they shook hands he studied Charlie's face for a few seconds as if trying to discern what part this newcomer might play in the negotiations. Terry Summers and Leonard sat at the end of the table. Mulrooney remained standing as he ate rather than risk trying to squeeze onto the table's bench seat from which he may not be able to extricate himself.

"Well sir, looks like you got yourself a bumper crop of corn coming in," Yarbrough said glancing up the hill to the field of corn that was a bright green forest of stalks seven feet high. "Bet that's some real sweet tasting corn up there."

DeWitt poured himself a glass of ice water. "Hogs like it," he said dryly. He looked up to see Charlie smiling. The farmer gave him a quick wink as he took a drink. After a few minutes, Yarbrough reached for a napkin and wiped his mouth signaling that he was ready to get down to business. He folded his hands in front of him and stared intently across the table at Bud DeWitt. The lawyer leaned forward almost imperceptibly into a more aggressive posture.

"Now Mr. DeWitt, you know why we're here. Last time we came up, we offered you a hundred thousand dollars for your farm, a more than fair price for this place as you well know." The farmer just sat still and stared back at Yarbrough knowing it wasn't his turn to speak.

The silence didn't throw the skilled negotiator off a bit. "But today sir, and today only, I am authorized to extend to you one more offer for your farm. And

I'm sure you'll agree that it is a pretty astounding offer. An offer that's so crazy you'd have to be insane to turn it down." Yarbrough was speaking in a low, earnest tone.

"My associate here," Yarbrough pointed at Leonard without taking his eyes off of the farmer, "has all the necessary paperwork, *and a check,* in his briefcase there to make this happen today." He leaned forward another inch. "Now Mr. DeWitt, what would you say if I told you that the amount that I'm authorized to offer you today is *two hundred* and *fifty thousand dollars* ... that's a *quarter of a million dollars* ... for this little farm." Yarbrough leaned back from the table with a triumphant smile on his face. "What would you say to that sir?"

Bud DeWitt stared off at the ground trying to arrange the words in his mind as he drummed his finger tips on the table. It appeared to the others that he was mulling over the offer. Yarbrough tried to speed the process along. "But I have to remind you, that an offer of this magnitude can only stay on the table for a short time, for today only. After today we – "

"I understand Mr. Yarbrough," Bud DeWitt said holding up his hand to interrupt the lawyer. "You don't have to play that game, 'cause it don't matter. Like I told you on the phone, the farm ain't for sale, for any price. It don't matter. We ain't selling. We ain't moving."

Yarbrough stared at the farmer through narrow eyes for a moment, then reached out and slapped a heavy palm on the surface of the picnic table. "Goddammit man, that's a lot of money! A *hell* of a lot of money. Do you know what you could *do* with that kind of money?"

The farmer didn't flinch at the lawyer's outburst. "It ain't the money Mr. Yarbrough," DeWitt said in a slow, strong voice. "I know you gentlemen will never understand it, but this has been my home for seventy-two years. I was born on this mountain. I grew up here. Raised my family here. My parents and grandparents are buried up there," he gestured up the mountain, "along with my two oldest boys. My granddaughter too," he added softly. "This is the only home I ever known. It ain't for sale. Now fellahs, I got to get back to work," DeWitt said swinging his legs out from under the picnic table.

Then it was Mulrooney's turn to explode. He moved quickly to the end of the table and slammed both of his huge hands down startling everyone present. "Just what the *fuck* is wrong with you DeWitt? You're going to turn down a quarter of a million bucks so you can go on living in this shit-hole pigsty? I don't get it. I don't get this game you're playing. What's your price? Stop fucking around with us!" Mulrooney's face was beet red and spit flew with every word.

Charlie scrambled up off the bench, shocked at Mulrooney's rude outburst. "Mulrooney, knock it off! What's the matter with you?" Charlie said as he moved quickly to get the large man away from the farmer.

Vernon Yarbrough stepped in between Mulrooney and Charlie. He pulled Mulrooney away from the table toward the Navigator. "Kevin, sit in the truck for a while and let me handle this," he said.

Mulrooney turned and glared angrily at Charlie as he shuffled slowly toward the Navigator. But he wasn't done. Suddenly he wheeled around, shaking

Yarbrough's hand off his arm and came back toward the farmer. "Listen good you fucking hillbilly. We're going to take this farm one way or the other. Don't you *get* it? Don't you know who you're dealing with here?"

Yarbrough tried once more to silence the coal man. "C'mon Kevin, this isn't the way," he said trying to get in front of Mulrooney who just brushed him aside with his huge arm.

"We go into court, we got a judge that'll take this place in twenty minutes," Mulrooney said with a snap of his fingers. He was roaring now. "Then we pay you market value for this place, which is going to be a long way from a quarter of a million bucks, I'll guarantee you that." Mulrooney was flushed and sweating and breathing hard. He paused to catch his breath and seemed to calm down a little. When he spoke again it was in a lower voice.

"You're not a kid DeWitt. You know what's going on here. There's coal up here, and we're going to get it. Like we always do. Coal's still king here. So take your money while it's on the table . . . else you and your family get fucked in the end." He turned and walked toward the Navigator.

The veins on Charlie's neck were dilated with anger. He had to fight back the instant urge to stride over to Mulrooney and knock him out cold. *Damn! How did he become part of this bunch?* He was embarrassed by the way they had treated the farmer.

Yarbrough was talking lowly to Mulrooney as he coaxed the big man into the Navigator. DeWitt was walking back toward his tractor.

"Mr. DeWitt," Charlie called out to him, causing him to stop and turn. "I'm sorry. I apologize for the rudeness of my colleague. There's no – "

DeWitt held up his hand and shook his head. "Wasn't rudeness Mr. Burden. It was a history lesson."

Vernon Yarbrough came toward Charlie while holding his index finger up to the farmer. "Just hold one second there DeWitt. I've got one more thing I need to discuss with you if I could." Then, close to Charlie, turning away from the waiting farmer, he said quietly, "Burden I'm going to take a little walk with our farmer and up the ante to five hundred grand – see if I can close this deal. Why don't you go in the house and work on the old lady a little. See if you can get her on board at that number, okay?"

Charlie glanced over at Mulrooney sitting in the truck, who glared back at him. "What the hell's wrong with Mulrooney," Charlie said angrily to Yarbrough.

The lawyer put his hand on Charlie's arm as he came in closer. "Hey, don't worry about it," he said softly. "Kevin's got some pressure on him is all."

Before Charlie could say anything, Yarbrough did an abrupt about-face and with a confident smile on his face, went off to re-engage Bud DeWitt. Charlie watched as the lawyer swung an arm around the farmer's shoulders and ushered him slowly up the road away from the house.

Charlie looked toward the house. He had no intention of *working on the old lady*. He'd had enough of this charade, even if buying the farm *was* crucial to his client and to his friend Duncan McCord. This wasn't his kind of work. Yarbrough and Mulrooney would just have to get it done without his participation. But right then, he needed *something* to do and he wanted to get away from Summers and Leonard who were still sitting at the table enjoying the show.

"You guys done?" Charlie said, motioning toward the tray of uneaten sandwiches. Without waiting for a reply, he picked up the tray and carried it up the steps and into the house.

The front door opened into a narrow hallway that led to the rear of the house where another screen door was visible. On the right, a large opening revealed the living room, and through it, a door to what appeared to be a closed-in porch or sunroom. To the left was a small dining room furnished in plain but obviously very old furniture. The room reminded Charlie of the many antique shops along Route 100 in Vermont that he and Ellen used to frequent right after they bought the house in Warren. Diagonally across the dining room was a doorway that led to the kitchen, where, Charlie could see from the moving shadows against the wall and counter top, he would find Mrs. DeWitt.

As he entered the dining room to bring the tray into the kitchen, Charlie was about to call out to the elderly woman so his presence wouldn't startle her, but he stopped when he noticed that the two interior walls of the room were covered with photographs. The wall between the dining room and the hallway held mostly color pictures and a few black and whites of fairly recent vintage. What drew Charlie's attention was the wall to the kitchen that was covered with mostly sepia-toned, formal portraits of what must have been Bud DeWitt's parents and grandparents and various relatives taken at a time when everyone, even working farmers, were made to look like the Astors in the photographer's studio. There were several, now light brown prints of stern-faced couples – the men wearing mustaches and bowler hats, the women, uncomfortable looking woolen dresses – in oval matting and ornate metal frames. As you moved to the right on the wall, the pictures became more recent and the subjects seemed to get poorer or at least poorer looking. The formal poses and bowler hats disappeared along with the fancy picture frames. Charlie peered in close to examine a photo in which he recognized Bud DeWitt and his wife posed on the front porch of the house with three boys standing reluctantly in front of them on the ground. One of the children appeared to be about three or four years old. The other two, fairly close in age, in their mid - teens probably. As in the other pictures on the wall, the faces were stern with no indication of happiness.

The last two pictures on the wall were two eight-by-ten, color photographs of two very handsome young men in military uniforms. Charlie glanced back at the teenagers in the family picture to confirm that the soldiers were indeed the boys in the picture.

"Can I take that from you Mr. Burden?" Charlie almost dropped the tray of sandwiches at the sound of the old woman right behind him.

"Oh, jeez," he stammered in shock, and then laughed when he saw who it was.

"I'm sorry Mr. Burden," she said with a thin smile. "I didn't mean to scare you."

"No, that's okay. I was just bringing in the tray when I noticed the pictures. I hope you don't mind me looking at them," Charlie said.

The woman looked at the pictures thoughtfully before answering softly. "No, no, it's fine. They're nice pictures aren't they?"

"Yes they are," said Charlie. "Are these your sons here Agnes?"

"Alice," the woman replied.

"What? I'm sorry."

"It's *Alice*. My name is *Alice*."

"But I thought Mr. Yarbrough said your name was – "

"Well he's pretty much of a horse's ass now, isn't he?" said the woman with a twinkle in her eye.

Charlie paused with surprise at the old woman's expression, and then let out a hearty laugh and nodded his head. "Yeah, he sure is Alice. He sure is."

Alice DeWitt looked over at the two pictures of the men in uniform and the smile left her face. She reached a hand out and made a very subtle adjustment to one of the frames. "Yes, these are my boys Mr. Burden," she said softly. "This is Tommy, my oldest. And that's Earl," she said touching the next picture. "Earl was a Marine." She paused for a few moments in thought before continuing. "He was killed in Viet Nam," she said. She looked back at the other picture. "Tommy, he went to Viet Nam too. But he came home. Then he died in a coal mine, up north. He was twenty-eight." Alice DeWitt turned to Charlie and took the tray from his hands.

Charlie looked down at the small woman's face and swallowed hard. "God, that's got to be hard to take," he said softly. "Losing two sons."

She shrugged and flashed a tight smile that said that she'd dealt with it and had long ago come to terms with the loss of her boys. She started toward the kitchen. "There's a *lot* of heartache in these mountains, Mr. Burden," she said as she went through the doorway.

Charlie had turned toward the other wall of pictures, and suddenly it all hit him at once. The old woman's words were ringing in his ears . . . *'there's a lot of heartache in these mountains,' my grandma Alice always says* . . . and there she was, in front of him in a small color picture with a simple frame, when she was a child – probably ten or eleven – but unmistakably her, skinny as a rail with the wide bony shoulders and thin neck and the delicate face with the ice blue eyes and the full, soft mouth. Her blond hair, much lighter then, bleached by the summer sun and cropped short like a boy's crew cut that had grown out for a month. But Charlie recognized Natty immediately. Even in the young girl, Charlie could see the face that had been on his mind so much lately.

Standing next to her in the picture was the woman from the DeWitt file that Tuthill had given him in New York – *Sarah Carlson DeWitt*. Natty's mother looked much older than the high school picture in which Charlie had recognized something without realizing that it was Natty's eyes he had seen. In this picture, the natural cockiness and joyful optimism of the teenager was gone.

Charlie quickly scanned the other pictures on the wall, trying to sort out in his mind the implications of Natty, and also his little buddy the Pie Man, being so intimately connected now to the Angel Mountain issue. Yes, there he was, in several pictures – Pie with his grandparents; with his sister Cat up on the green tractor; with another man who must be his uncle, Peter DeWitt, the third son – always with the big *happy face* on. *Yes, Pie would always be excited in front of a camera.* Charlie had to smile at the familiar look on his pal's face.

And then, moving to the right on the wall, to a group of more recent pictures, another picture of Natty with her mother that must have been taken within the last year. Natty had her arm around her mother pulling her close and making her laugh, like Natty was tickling her with her hidden hand. They were both laughing. It was a nice picture that from the color of the trees, must have been taken in the fall. A moment of unplanned foolishness between mother and daughter. Charlie couldn't help staring at the young woman in the picture. His heart beat faster as he leaned in close. Natty was wearing her ever-present faded blue jeans and a loose-fitting blue sweater. As she pulled at her mother, twisting her body slightly, her blue jeans were drawn snug, accentuating her small hips and thin legs. Her hair hung like a dried mop, almost down to her shoulders, with a long shock nearly covering one eye. *Only Natty could care so little about her hair and her appearance and still look so great,* thought Charlie. But it was her face that kept drawing Charlie's eye back to the picture. Back to the broad, soft smile and the sparkling eyes that could light up a room even from a five-by- seven print on the wall. It was the face of innocence, so incapable of duplicity or guile, so unconcerned with herself, so unaware of how attractive she was. *God, she could look so plain and so beautiful at the same time.* His concentration was broken by a sound in the kitchen. It was Alice DeWitt washing some dishes.

Charlie quietly left the dining room and went out the front door. Terry Summers and Leonard were leaning against the Navigator engaged in low conversation with Mulrooney who was smoking a cigarette in the back seat. Yarbrough and DeWitt were nowhere in sight. Rather than join the men at the truck, which he didn't want to do, Charlie went down the porch steps and wandered across the road to better enjoy the panoramic view of the valley through the thin trees. It seemed to him that he must be looking in the general direction of Red Bone Mountain but he was uncertain of which one it might be.

Turning to come back across the road, a movement at the back corner of the house caught his eye. From the movement of the bushes at the corner of the house, it looked like someone was back there doing some kind of gardening work. Out of curiosity and to kill time until Yarbrough returned, Charlie strolled to the back of the house. As he came around the corner, Sarah DeWitt was just coming to her feet, a bundle of long weed grass in each hand. She stood up with some effort to straighten her back and came face-to-face with Charlie, about four feet apart. She smiled politely and fastened on him the sparkling blue eyes that he'd seen in her high school picture – Natty's eyes – but didn't speak.

Charlie offered his hand even though she still clung to the weeds. "Hello Sarah," he said, "I'm Charlie Burden."

She slowly turned away from him, with some noticeable effort, and dropped the weeds into a small wicker basket. Wiping her hands on the side of her gray smock, she turned back to Charlie and slowly offered her hand as if she were consciously thinking over every movement she made.

"You know my name," she said softly.

"I've met your daughter, Natty," Charlie replied, not wanting to tell her that he knew her name from a private investigator's file that he'd brought with him from New York. "And Pie and Cat too," he added.

Sarah DeWitt smiled at the mention of the children's names and nodded lightly as she digested what he had said. She had a dreamy, introspective quality about her, as if she were having difficulty focusing on the idea at hand.

"You must be one of the coal men," she said finally.

"Well actually, no, I'm here to build the . . ." Charlie was cut off by the loud blare of the Navigator's horn, repeated three times in quick succession. Yarbrough must have returned, anxious to get going. " . . . to build the power plant," he continued. "Up in Red Bone."

Sarah blinked her eyes rapidly and smiled at Charlie. "Looks like your friends are ready to go Mr. Burden." She thrust her hands into pockets hidden in the sides of her smock.

"Yeah, sounds like it," said Charlie looking toward the front of the house.

It didn't look as if Natty's mother cared to shake hands again, so Charlie just took a step backwards and then turned to go. "It was nice meeting you Sarah," he offered. Sarah just nodded to him.

Charlie had nearly rounded the corner of the house when she spoke again. "Mr. Burden?" Charlie turned to face her, then took a step back toward her.

"Yes, Mrs. DeWitt?"

"Are you going to take our farm Mr. Burden?"

"Well, Sarah, I think that . . ." Charlie stopped himself. The words were right there on the tip of his tongue, the pat answer about how it would be good for everyone, how it was inevitable, and the best thing the DeWitts could do was to take the money – now up to a *half a million* – and stop fighting a losing battle . . . because, *of course they were going to take their farm!* But something made him stop. He looked down at the ground at his feet, unable to speak.

Charlie didn't want to give the answer because it wasn't *his* answer. He didn't like the answer. It was the answer the rich gave to the poor. The answer the corporations spun to the media. The politicians to the voters. It was the answer that he'd grown so sick of over the last few years.

He looked up past Sarah at the green meadows higher up on the mountain behind the farm, and thought about the issue of taking the farm for what seemed like the first time. He turned and looked out across the road at the spectacular view of the mountains to the north and breathed in the cool clean air. He listened to the silence of the mountain, accentuated by the music of the birds and the rustle of the trees in the breeze. *God! No wonder DeWitt doesn't want to move from this beautiful place. Seventy-two years. His entire life spent of this mountain, with his family.*

The horn blared again impatiently and Charlie half-turned his head toward the front of the house and thought about the people he was with: Yarbrough and

Mulrooney, scheming, filled with greed, rude and vulgar; Summers and Leonard, following in their footsteps. He looked back at Sarah DeWitt who had a politely inquisitive smile on her face as she watched Charlie Burden having such obvious trouble with her simple question. He thought about Bud DeWitt and Alice, and now Sarah, thoroughly likeable and genuine people – like Hank, and Eve Brewster – people he respected and enjoyed being with. And then, he thought about Natty, the woman he couldn't get out of his mind. The woman that he now realized, as soon as he saw her picture on the dining room wall, he was rapidly falling in love with. This was her home too. *How did he get on the opposite side from these people? The kind of people he'd been searching for – so unconcerned with status and egos and the accumulation of wealth. And here he was, as always, on the side of the big money trying to get bigger by taking this little farm away from the only people on earth who could truly appreciate its beauty and its legacy. Wasn't this exactly what he'd been trying to escape from?*

"Mr. Burden, are you okay?" Sarah DeWitt had taken a step closer to Charlie and leaned over to look into his face.

Charlie smiled at her and nodded his head as he seemed to reach some internal decision. "Sarah, I don't know if you're going to lose your farm or not," said Charlie. He turned to the front of the house to see the Navigator pull up to the edge of the road waiting for him. Yarbrough glared at him impatiently from the front seat. He looked back at Natty's mother. "But, I'm going to do whatever I can to prevent it. I don't know if I can stop it, but I'll try." He took a step toward Sarah and offered his hand, more as a show to Yarbrough in the truck, and said quietly, "but this has to be our secret, okay?"

"I understand," she said as they shook hands once more. Then she added, "thank you Mr. Burden."

Charlie left her and walked slowly back to the Navigator and climbed into the second seat next to Mulrooney.

As they turned onto Angel Mountain Road, Yarbrough twisted around in the seat to look at Charlie. "So, any luck with the old lady?"

Charlie shrugged and shook his head. "No, she's just like her husband. No interest in selling."

"Yeah, I didn't figure she'd have much of a say in this," Yarbrough said as he turned around to get comfortable for the ride back to Red Bone.

"Hey Yarbrough," Charlie called up to the front seat.

Yarbrough's head went up and to the side a little. "What?"

"Her name's Alice," said Charlie.

"Huh?"

"DeWitt's wife. Her name is *Alice*, not *Agnes*," Charlie said a little louder.

The lawyer shrugged his shoulders unconcerned. "Well whatever. We gave 'em a chance. Can't say we didn't make 'em a fair offer. Seven-fifty I went to with the farmer. *Seven hundred and fifty thousand bucks* that boy turned down." Yarbrough laughed and shook his head in disbelief. "Well Mr. DeWitt," Yarbrough said, more to himself than to the other passengers, "I'll be back. I'll be back real soon."

Chapter 15

The first soccer practice of the season was an event that Natty looked forward to with mixed emotions. She was anxious to see the kids again – a few of whom she hadn't seen all summer – and she enjoyed the practice time and looked forward to the excitement of the games, and also to the additional time she got to spend with Pie. But the beginning of soccer had come to be the dividing line between summer and fall and there was a sadness attached to the passing of another season. The sun would remain hot for another month even as the air became cooler, but it wasn't summer any more after soccer started.

Walking down the long flight of cracked and crumbling cement steps from the library, the large mesh bag of soccer balls over her shoulder, the small blackboard and easel tucked under her left arm, Natty watched Pie carrying shovelfuls of dirt from a pile in back of the goal to fill in the holes in the field that she had missed. He was dressed in his complete soccer outfit from the previous year – black shorts and a red T- shirt, along with his shin guards and knee-high socks that used to be white but were now a dingy gray.

Next week, the kids would go back to school and Natty would go back to her second job as a teacher's aide for three hours each morning at the elementary school. She wasn't looking forward to rescheduling many of her home nursing clients to the afternoon and early evening. It would be more difficult this year with the additional cases she'd taken on – *be lucky to get home before eight o'clock most nights* – but she knew she couldn't afford to give up the job at the school. The hundred twenty dollars a week was important, especially now that she had another good size debt to Gus Lowe for her car repairs.

Natty dropped the bag of balls on the grass and set up the blackboard in front of the bleachers. She looked at her watch. Still a little early. Most of the kids wouldn't show up until around *nine-fifteen* for the *nine-o'clock* practice. That's just the way it had always been and there wasn't much Natty was ever going to do about it. She absent-mindedly took another look up the hill toward Old Red Bone, up to the back porch on the fourth floor of the *Barney's* building, as she had several times already that morning. Natty had to squint into the sun but she could see that the porch was unoccupied and there was no light on in either of the apartments. Of course she didn't expect to see him up there. Hadn't Charlie told her he was going back up to New York – for at least a week – *to give his daughter a car and argue with his wife about the million dollar house?* Anyway, she knew he was still gone because Pie came home every day with a long face and told her. *'Chowly gone away. Gone to New Yowk. My fwend Chowly go home.'*

On her morning run, several times during the week, Hank had been out on the porch in his underwear and straw hat, with his cup of tea. She'd waved to him and called up a 'good morning' and resisted the impulse to ask about Charlie. And toward the end of the week, even though there was no reason to think he might be back and out in front of the store in the middle of Main Street waiting for her, Natty would take a deep breath to still her beating heart and swallow hard to clear her throat in nervous anticipation as she came to the top of the hill and rounded the corner. *Her anxiety was nothing personal,* she told herself. She got a little nervous because Charlie Burden was an important man now in McDowell County and when the opportunity presented itself, she was going to use their friendship to try to get Buck a job at the power plant. *That was all there was to it.* Each day the street had been empty.

Of course maybe now there was another opportunity for Buck beyond the power plant, she had to admit as she recalled the excited announcement made by Yancy Oakes earlier in the week. Yancy had spent the afternoon over in Mingo County looking into the remote prospect of a job in one of Ackerly's deep mines, and came back with a rumor, confirmed by several sources including a UMWA union steward, that *'Ackerly was going to be doing a big surface mine on Angel Mountain to feed the new power plant, and the union was going to be supplying 200 miners in the first six months of the project and more later, and that McDowell County men would get first crack at the jobs!'*

Natty had slipped quietly out onto the deck when she'd heard Yancy mention Angel Mountain. *So it was true, and the word was out.* Buck, Ransom, Big Frank and Roy Hogan were sitting on the deck surrounded by empty beer cans when Yancy came back with his exciting but implausible news. Buck had spun around to face her. "You know anything about this Nat? Your mama or Bud say anything about a mining project up on Angel Mountain?"

How much should she tell them? How much did she really know? It was all just speculation really. Until now, with Yancy's information. If the Ackerly people and the Union are letting it out it must be true, and like the lawyer in Welch said 'you don't want to try and fight these companies.' "Well, maybe they had some lawyers go up there and offer to buy the farm few weeks back," Natty said, "but, they didn't say nothing more about it than that." Buck stared at her for a few seconds as if determining whether she may be holding back information, before he turned back to the conversation.

Natty listened for a while as Buck and the others talked about how important the new power plant was to McDowell County and to West Virginia, and how powerful CanAmex Energy and Ackerly Coal were, and if anyone would be able to get a mountaintop-removal variance, it would be those two companies. They convinced themselves that the story was probably true, and got more excited as they went along over the prospect of getting high-paying, long-term jobs at the surface mine. No one expressed any concern over the destruction of Angel Mountain or the DeWitt farm.

Natty went back inside the trailer, disheartened that her first instincts about the Angel Mountain issue were correct – that her husband and the rest of the Oakes clan, and indeed just about everyone in Red Bone, would be in favor of the project. She, and her mother, and Bud and Alice DeWitt would be a small, powerless minority in the fight to save Angel Mountain. *Except . . . how did her mother put it when she called a few days earlier?* "I met your Mr. Burden today," Sarah had said. *'Your' Mr. Burden. I wonder what she meant by that.*

"He came up with the lawyers to try to buy the farm again . . . Bud had some words in the yard with the coal man. Later, Mr. Burden came around back of the house just before they left, and told me right off, that he knew you and he knew the children . . . 'Pie and Cat' he said . . . he used their names. You must have mentioned something about us to him?"

No, I've never said a thing to him about Angel Mountain or about the DeWitts . . . have I?

"Well I asked him straight away if we were going to lose the farm and he seemed to think about it for a long time and then he said, 'I'm going to do everything I can to prevent it'. That's what he said after thinking about it for a while. Now why would he say that Natty? Does he have any say in this? Have you talked to him about this?"

Natty went back over in her mind the few brief conversations she'd had with Charlie Burden. She'd never mentioned anything about Angel Mountain, or her mother or grand parents, she was certain. *He had to be on the other side of the Angel Mountain issue. Why else did he go up there with the lawyers? He was working for CanAmex wasn't he? Why would he tell her mother that he 'would try to prevent it'? It was crazy. It made no sense at all.*

A car door slammed in the street behind the bleachers, and Natty heard children's voices but she struggled to concentrate on the most perplexing part of the conversation with her mother. She stood up from the bench and took another quick look up the hill toward the fourth floor apartment. *How did Charlie Burden know that Sarah DeWitt was her mother? And, was there more to their Mr. Burden than a chance meeting with a little retarded boy and a friendly relationship with his mother?* She shook her head and laughed. *God, it was so stupid! Thinking that there might be some intrigue involved between Charlie Burden and a little hillbilly, backwoods nobody like Natty Oakes. Somebody, probably Hank or even Bud, must have told him that Sarah was her mother. And that was that.* She turned to greet the first arrivals for soccer practice.

A group of five boys, who lived in the trailer park out near the crossroads, were the first to arrive. Natty turned around in time to wave to Gladys Steele, pulling away from the sandy shoulder of the road in an old brown station wagon. She'd dropped off the bunch, including her twin boys, Gilbert and Hardy Steele, two habitually over-weight, freckled-faced red heads who tended to tire easily but had fairly strong kicks that made up somewhat for their slowness afoot.

Arriving with the Steeles, were Jason Bailey, a tiny boy with a good competitive attitude but who tended to get knocked down a lot by the bigger boys, Matt Hatfield who next to Emma Lowe, had always been the team's best all-around player, although his foot speed was usually a couple of steps behind the better players on the other teams, and Billy Staten, an uncoordinated, timid black boy who never seemed to enjoy the games that much, but came back year after year and did his best.

Natty was happy and relieved to see the *crossroads gang*. She didn't see too much of them outside of soccer season and was never sure if they were all still living in Red Bone and were going to show up each year. Pie was greeting them all with his customary high fives and *whasup knuckle touches.* Natty gave each boy a hug and a few words before they escaped to kick balls around the field.

As a pick-up truck pulled up behind the bleachers, Natty noticed Emma Lowe and Brenda Giles, the team's goalie, running down the hill from Main Street. From the back of the truck leaped Jimmy Hopson and George Jarrell, two of the mainstays of the team every year since the beginning. Although neither was a gifted athlete, Jimmy and George found soccer to be the only sport they had been able to develop some skills at and had become technically solid and strong players, and due to their outgoing personalities had become the team's leaders. They were also the players most discouraged by the team's chronic inability to be competitive with the powerful teams from Welch, Bluefield and Princeton.

"Hey Miz Oakes," said George. "We gonna have enough this year? Hey, where's Emma? Ain't Emma playing?" he asked looking around with a look of concern on his face.

"She's coming George," Natty laughed, pointing at the two girls jogging down the hill. "Don't worry, Emma's playing."

"Damn good thing too," chimed in Jimmy Hopson, looking around the field. "Wouldn't win one game with this rag tag crew without Emma. See the fat-boy twins are back," he said with a grin referring to the Steele brothers. "Hey Gilbert," he yelled out to the field, "have another doughnut."

Gilbert Steele looked over at Jimmy with a big smile on his freckled face and stuck his middle finger in the air. "Suck my dick Hopson," he called back.

"Gotta find it first," yelled George as he and Jimmy ran out onto the field.

Natty just shook her head and pursed her lips. *This could be a long season,* she told herself. She glanced at her watch. Almost nine-twenty and still no sign of the Willard boys. *Maybe Mabel had changed her mind about not letting them play football, which it was plain as day, both boys would rather be doing than playing soccer.* She blew her whistle to start practice.

As she did every year, at the beginning of the first practice she assembled the team on the bleachers and set up her blackboard with the chalk outline of a soccer field. First she would go over the basic rules again, covering things like free kicks, goal kicks, corner kicks, throw-ins, and offsides. Then she would diagram the positions and the field responsibilities of each position, before going on to talk about offensive and defensive strategies that the team would employ. The initial "board talk" took about a half hour, which the kids, itching to start playing, hated since they'd all heard it every year, but Natty knew it was important, to set a foundation for all the things they would be practicing on the field, and it was necessary to impress upon the kids again each year that soccer was a *team* sport. She also knew from experience that the only reason her under-manned, under-talented teams were ever competitive with the better teams in the league was that they played disciplined, positional soccer.

Just as she was about to start the "board talk," Natty noticed out of the corner of her eye, someone standing across the field on the edge of the far parking lot. She turned and saw that there were two people, a heavy-set woman in a long brown dress and heavy black shoes, and a thin boy with a short, blonde crew cut

Gerry FitzGerald

dressed in a strange looking soccer outfit. He wore a light blue shirt with black pinstripes and a black collar – a *real* soccer shirt, not the cheap T-shirts worn by the Bones – and dark blue nylon shorts and white stockings over his shin guards.

As Natty looked over at them, the woman waved and they started to walk slowly across the field toward her. She put her chalk down, told the team to stay put and started off toward the center of the field to meet them. Natty recognized the woman as they got closer. Her name was Helen, with a long unpronounceable last name. She and her husband were from Poland and had come to Red Bone several years ago, moving into one of the large old double-decker row houses just off Main Street, not far from where Emma's family lived. Natty had run into the woman a few times at *Barney's* and said hello but little more.

"Helloo, helloo," the woman called out as they met in the middle of the field. "Mrs. Oakes, I like to see you again. I am Helen, do you remember?" The woman had a heavy European accent.

"Yes, of course I do Helen, how are you?" Natty answered shaking hands with the woman who had a large powerful grip. "And who is this handsome young man?" she asked, smiling at the boy who had a blank, nervous look on his face. "A soccer player for our team?"

"Yes, yes, Mrs. Oakes. This is *Pawel.*" She spelled his name. "But here he is just *Paul.* He is the son of my sister who comes to live vid us. He could play football on your team if you can. Okay? He play much football in Poland. Is good player my sister say. Okay?"

Natty laughed. "Of course he can. Paul can play on our team. If he's under fourteen. How old is Paul?" she asked looking at the boy. He just shrugged and looked at the woman.

"Yes, yes, he is only *turteen,*" she said. "But Paul speak not much English. Okay, he can play?"

Okay? Thought Natty. *You're damn right it's okay.* After so many years of coaching and watching kid's soccer, Natty knew a soccer player when she saw one, and she knew right away that *Pawel* was a gift from heaven. The boy was thin but his neck and arms were well muscled. He had the sloping shoulders of an athlete and wide, powerful thighs. His uniform and his cleats, she noticed, had also been through many a game. *Yes, this was going to be an interesting season.*

Natty led her newest recruit back to the bleachers where the rest of the team was watching the approach of the new kid with the real soccer uniform with rapt attention.

"This is Paul, the newest member of *The Bones*," Natty announced. "Paul is from Poland and doesn't speak much English."

After a silent interlude in which the team just stared at Paul and he, nervously back at them, Pie jumped down from the second bench and hopped over in front of the new boy.

"Hello!" he said, holding up his hand for a high-five. "I am the Pie Man."

Paul peered down at the strange looking little boy before him and slowly a smile grew on his face and he pushed a gentle high-five onto Pie's chubby hand. With a wide *happy face,* Pie took a hold of the new boy's wrist and led him up on the bleachers to a seat next to him. Natty looked up at Emma Lowe in the back row and gave her a quick wink. *Now, if the Willard boys ever show up, we might actually have us a pretty decent team.*

As if on cue, Sammy and Zack Willard appeared far up the hill sauntering slowly down the middle of the road. Sammy was about ten yards ahead of Zack who was carrying a large paper soda cup with a straw. Natty could see from where she was that there was an *attitude* about the boys that was going to be a problem. Taking up her chalk, she blew her whistle loudly, startling the children who were sitting just a few feet away from her, their eyes riveted on the Willard brothers moseying down the hill almost thirty minutes late for practice.

"Okay," Natty said loudly. "Pay attention. I don't want anybody on the field who doesn't know the rules and doesn't know their position."

Totally ignoring the Willard brothers as they finally reached the bleachers and took seats on the back row, Natty started her lecture. She went through all the rules. Then painstakingly, described the responsibilities and range of movement of each position on the field. Natty had always used a very simple formation of three forwards, three mid-fielders, three defenders, a sweeper and the goalie, because it was easy for the kids to understand and as the lines adjusted to the play on the field, it actually brought more players into the proximity of the ball. Occasionally, against some of the teams that were too strong for them, she would have to take Emma off the front line and put her on defense to try to hold the score down.

Natty went through each player on the team by name and assigned them their *primary* and *secondary* positions. Most of them had been on the team so long now that everyone knew where they would be playing, even though *everyone* wanted to play forward. She appeased them by giving nearly everyone a secondary assignment as a forward. "Matt Hatfield, you're a mid-fielder, but sometime we'll use you at forward. Jimmy Hopson …defense and fill-in at forward. Pie, you and Gilbert are forwards with Emma, and you'll fill in on defense."

When she got down to Paul and the Willard brothers, Natty thought about it for a few seconds and then decided. "Paul," she said seeking out the new boy. When she had his attention she went to the board and said, "center mid-fielder," as she circled that position on the board for him to see. She raised her eyebrows in question to see if Paul understood what she was saying. "Yes?" she said. The boy shook his head up and down to indicate that he understood. Then he flashed a quick smile that told Natty she was right in her hunch that Paul was a player who understood the importance of the center mid-fielder position and would feel honored by receiving the assignment. If it didn't work out she could make a change later on but she had a feeling that Paul at center mid-fielder would be sending a lot of nice balls up to Emma and would also have some good chances of his own as defenses collapsed around her.

Finally, Natty looked up at the Willard brothers. "Sammy, you'll be a mid-fielder and some forward. And Zack, you're our new sweeper, the most important position on a soccer team."

Zack Willard sat for a moment and glared at Natty. "Aw Miz Natty, what kind a booshit is that? I's a *scorer*, not a damn sweeper."

"Well Zack, we don't need any more scorers. What we need is a damn sweeper so that's where you're going to play, unless you can't handle it. Then we'll move you somewhere else. Okay," she concluded with a hand clap, "let's play some soccer."

As the team emptied from the bleachers, Natty waited for the Willard brothers to come down from the back row. "Sammy, Zack, c'mere," she said moving off toward the end of the bleachers. The boys kind of sidled up to her slowly, knowing they were in for a scolding.

When they reached her, Natty moved in closer and grabbed the neck of their T-shirts and pulled the boys in close to her so they could see the anger in her eyes and the hard set of her jaw. "Don't you boys ever, *ever, disrespect this team again by showing up late for practice or a game!*" Natty could see the shock and trepidation in their eyes. The Willard brothers had never before seen Natty Oakes show any anger about anything. She had their attention. "You want to play soccer, you come and play soccer, but you get here on time and you don't mope and whine about not playing football. You ever show up late again for practice or a game, you're off the team. Is that clear?"

The Willard brothers both mumbled a soft 'yes ma'am,' and looked down at their feet.

"Okay then," Natty said softly, releasing her grip on their shirts. She stepped back and smiled at the two boys. "Your grandmaw's finest woman ever lived, you know that don'tcha? I don't want to disappoint her by chuckin' either one of you off the team. So don't make me."

For the next half-hour they practiced short passes, trapping the ball, and throw-ins. Then, Natty decided it was time for the Willard brothers to get a taste of what they were going to be up against. She called for a full-field scrimmage, six against six, with Sammy and Zack on a strong team with Matt, Jimmy, George, and Brenda in goal. Emma would play with the new boy Paul, the Steele brothers, little Jason Bailey and Billy Staten in the goal. Pie would be a sub for whoever got tired and needed a break.

As soon as she blew the whistle to start the game, Natty could see that she had not been wrong about Paul. He was a skilled and experienced player who could dribble the ball like it was glued to his foot, had powerful accurate kicks with both feet, and had tremendous acceleration. It was evident right away that he was accustomed to a much higher level of competition than was presently on the field with him. It didn't take him long though to figure out that Emma Lowe was a player you should get the ball to.

Just two minutes into the game, Paul and Emma worked a series of give-and-goes up the right half of the field before Emma took off and Paul feathered a perfect lead over the head of a defender. Emma gathered in the ball, easily juked past Zack Willard who had rushed at her too quickly, and took the ball in alone on Brenda Giles. Instead of just firing the ball into the net, Emma drew Brenda toward the near post and then with the outside of her left foot, neatly flicked a perfect pass across the goal box to an onrushing Paul who just guided the ball smoothly into the open net. Natty was impressed that Paul didn't feel the need to slam the ball high into the back of the goal as most of her players would have, (often times popping it over the cross bar). It was obvious that he'd scored goals before.

In the next few minutes, Emma scored an easy goal from close in, and then Paul, passing up another scoring chance of his own, set up Hardy Steele for a tap-in goal that lit up the chubby boy's face like a jack-o'lantern. Natty could see that Paul was a natural leader on the field and that he understood the game so well that even without speaking he just naturally made his teammates better players. By pointing out a spot or gesturing with his eyes he got the Steele brothers and Jason Bailey to fill in open spaces and create passing lanes and he always rewarded them with beautifully paced passes. After only a few minutes on the field with an experienced and unselfish player like Paul, the Steeles, and Jason were playing better soccer than they ever thought they could, cutting toward open areas, anticipating, and most of all, playing with a new sense of confidence.

Natty noticed that Emma, who rarely showed any emotion on the field, was actually smiling as she watched the other players react to Paul's silent coaching. With a three-goal lead, Emma following Paul's lead, stopped trying to score and concentrated on setting up the other boys for good shots on Briana. When Natty put Pie into the game in place of Gilbert Steele, Emma and Paul focused on getting the ball to Pie in an effort to get him his first-ever goal in any kind of game. Even Pie's play improved as he sent a pass from a crowd in front of the goal, back to a wide open Paul twenty yards out in the center of the field, who buried a rocket into the high right corner of the net. Pie was thrilled when Paul immediately pointed at the little boy and ran toward him for a high-five in recognition of his assist

Before Natty could put the ball in play again after Paul's goal, she heard Zack Willard call out. "Miz Natty, time out. Time out here." Then, motioning his teammates toward him with his hands, "c'mon, everyone get the fuck over here. Right here." He looked up quickly at Natty to see if she'd overheard him. "Sorry 'bout that Miz Natty."

Natty just rolled her eyeballs and shook her head.

Zack Willard had a fearsome look on his normally handsome face as his teammates closed in around him. He dropped to one knee and scratched in the dirt as he continued to chastise his team with an angry voice. "Dat new boy is killin' us, just killin' us. Hopson you get all over dat boy like a fuckin' tattoo. And Sammy," he poked his brother's chest for emphasis, "you get up on Emma so's she can smell dat ugly breath a yours, and don't let her *touch* the ball. Hatfield, you're a forward. Get up the field and we'll get you the ball. George and me is on defense."

Natty, standing ten yards away holding the ball, could hear Zack's tirade clearly, and in spite of his foul language, she was enjoying it immensely. Zack's lackadaisical attitude toward soccer was disappearing and he was very quickly becoming the leader she knew he would, and it was happening now because he hated to lose, *at anything.*

"Okay, c'mon, lets go," Zack said, with a clap breaking the huddle, as he'd done so many times as a quarterback. "Stay spread out. Pass the ball. Use your heads. Let's kick some ass here!"

Natty just shook her head at the language, wondering to herself if maybe she had just known all these kids too long for them to think of her as an adult.

When the game resumed there was a noticeable difference in the intensity level of both teams. Zack's team responded to his leadership and Emma's team, with Gilbert back in for Pie, could see that they were now playing a different opponent.

Jimmy Hopson and Sammy shadowed Paul and Emma closely, forcing the Steele brothers and Jason Bailey to play more with the ball. Zack and George Jarrell hung back on defense, eliminating the easy break up the field that Emma's team had been feasting on.

After a series of exchanges in the middle of the field, Paul finally got control of the ball with some space ahead of him and Emma headed up the wing. He raced the ball across mid-field with only Zack Willard fifteen yards in front of him. As he looked over to find Emma, Paul let the ball get just a few feet too far out in front of him and Zack pounced with the kind of acceleration he had used so many times to cut through the line off tackle on a quarterback keeper. He used a sliding tackle to poke the ball away from Paul, and in one motion he was up and on the ball and racing down the field. Paul was ten yards behind him and Emma was on the other side of the field, leaving only the Steele brothers and little Jason Bailey to stop Zack who was racing down the field like a runaway train. He kept the ball a good distance out in front of him so he could use all of his blinding speed. Gilbert Steele slowed him up for a step with an attempt at a sliding tackle but he didn't get the ball and Zack just jumped over him and resumed his run. He cut directly toward the goal and Jason Bailey in the middle of the field who froze in his position as Zack bore down on him. With a quick fake to the left, Zack put Jason out of the play when he pulled the ball back to his right and went in alone on the goalie. Seeing that he was one-on-one with Zack, Billy Staten came racing out of the goal to try to catch him by surprise before he was ready to shoot. He slid along the ground length-wise in an attempt to corral the ball but Zack was too quick. He pushed the ball deftly to his left toward the center of the field, avoided the goalie at his feet and regained the ball, all alone ten yards in front of the goal. Just as Paul and Hardy Steele came sliding through the grass in desperate attempts to poke the ball away, Zack blasted a left-footer straight into the back of the net.

Zack whirled to glare at the three opponents lying on the grass around him, and did a long, slow fist pump, accentuated at the end with a loud, "yeah!" Then he ran back up field to distribute high-fives to all his teammates.

Natty was stunned by Zack's run. She new he was fast but she'd never seen any kid move down the field with the ball at that speed. And his skills with the ball were far beyond what she'd thought they'd be after not playing organized soccer for several years.

Because of his power and his drive and leadership qualities, Natty knew that Zack was going to make a great sweeper, but she couldn't help formulating a plan to put Zack up on the forward line with Emma sometime when they really needed a goal. The two of them together were going to scare the daylights out of some poor kids on defense.

Each team scored again before they settled into an evenly matched positional battle with the ball staying mostly in the middle third of the field. Even though they were dead tired from covering the entire field with so few players, both teams played with an intensity and skill level that Natty had never before seen at practice. The Willard brothers brought speed, power and desire. Paul was a consummate player who could kick the ball a mile. Emma was Emma and she wasn't really trying to score. And everyone else on the team played better because of them. She refrained from blowing the whistle to let them battle it out and even get a little rough if they wanted.

As she observed the speed of the game, the good passes, sound positional play and the great individual skills of a few of the players, it occurred to Natty the she was now watching unquestionably, one of the best teams in the league at work. *Was this really her team? The team that struggled every year to win a few games . . . to field enough players.* Natty laughed to herself inside. *This season was going to be fun.* She started thinking about a few teams and a few opposing coaches she couldn't *wait* to play this year.

When Gilbert Steele went to his knees at mid-field and threw up what must have been a very large breakfast, Natty blew the whistle to end the game. The players were beat but there was a palpable excitement on the field as many of the players dared to believe that, finally, they might be on a pretty decent team.

George Jarrell and Jimmy Hopson came straight at Natty. "Miz Oakes," said George with an excited look on his face. "We got a good team now, don't you think?"

Hopson edged in front of him. "Yeah, coach. With the Willards and that new kid, we'll be winning some games, right coach?"

Natty just smiled at the boys as she looked over at Zack Willard who was approaching Paul. He put up his hand for a high-five from Paul, then threw his left arm around the new boy's shoulders. "Man, you is a *soccer player*," Zack told him. "You can play da game. On dis team, *you* gonna be da quarterback." Paul smiled and nodded his head even though he couldn't understand what this powerful black boy was saying to him. Zack laughed and ran his hand roughly through Paul's bristly crew cut. "Das okay, we be teachin' you all da words you gotta know," he said, flashing his brilliant white smile and a mischievous look at Natty. The idea made Natty shudder.

She looked back to George and Jimmy who were waiting for her opinion. "Yeah, boys," she said softly. "We're still a little short-handed but, yeah, I think we may have a team this year."

She reminded the team about the Wednesday night practice, and then, their first game next Saturday. "Playing Welch, right here Saturday morning so we got to be ready."

Packing the balls back into the mesh bag, Natty noticed Pie sitting quietly on the bench. She instantly felt badly that he hadn't played much in the game. "*Hey* Pie Man," she called over to him. "I'm sorry, I should have put you back in the game. I forgot . . ."

"Thath okay mama," he said getting up from the bench and walking slowly over to her.

"I don't mind. I wath tired anyway." He had a sad look on his face.

"So what's the matter Pie Man? Why the long face? she asked, slinging the bag of balls over her shoulder.

The boy just shrugged his shoulders and kicked at the dirt with the toe of his cleats, delaying his answer. Finally, he looked up at Natty. "Mama, when will Chowly come back? Did Chowly go away fowevah?"

Natty stood still and smiled down at her little boy. She put her hand on the back of his neck and affectionately pulled him toward her. "No Pie," she said. "Charlie's coming back. He'll be back in a few days, I think."

Pie looked up the hill toward old Red Bone. "I mith Chowly mama. Chowly ith my good fwend."

Natty tucked the blackboard and easel under her arm. "I know, Pie. Charlie *is* a good friend," she said starting the trudge up the hill to the library.

*   *   *

There were coins in the fountain. In the late afternoon sun they glistened like small copper and silver lights in the rippling water. Charlie had to laugh at the pains Ellen and her realtor had taken to set the stage. Just having the fountain turned on was a nice touch, without the several handfuls of coins that they had added for effect.

A geyser of water shot four feet into the air from an alabaster cherub at the center of the fountain, sending a cooling mist into the air. After two hours in the hot sun on the patio at Hickory Hills Country Club, Charlie welcomed the moisture on his face and began thinking about a nude swim in the pool when he and Ellen got back to the house.

The cocktail party in honor of the outgoing president of the country club, wasn't as excruciating as Charlie thought it would be. He felt out of place and uncomfortable with all the typical country club chatter about golf, the stock market, the successes and failures of mutual acquaintances, and the outstanding accomplishments of everyone's children. But he did enjoy seeing some of his old friends from the club.

Plus, it was important for Ellen to go, as one of the candidates in line to become the next president of the club. And it helped that Charlie went with her. Together, they made a very handsome and powerful looking couple – still a valuable attribute within the country club *milieu,* even for a very independent woman. Ellen would be the first female president of the club, which worked in her favor everyone told her. The club was *ready, the time was right* for a woman they said. Plus, Ellen was Ellen and she was hard to beat at anything she put her mind to. Charlie didn't envy the two male candidates vying for the position.

Charlie took off his linen sport jacket and laid it over the back of a wrought iron chair at one of the three small glass-topped tables that accented the central courtyard of the *hacienda*. The courtyard of the Quail Hollow Lane house was designed to replicate a Mexican street café. Charlie sat down on one of the hard straight chairs and looked around at the second floor balcony ringing the courtyard on three sides. He could imagine *Zorro* from the old TV show, a band of Mexican soldiers in hot pursuit, swinging across the courtyard on the ever-present rope to a waiting horse.

The new house would undoubtedly help Ellen's candidacy too, although Charlie couldn't pinpoint exactly why. Maybe it was just that successful people liked to associate with successful people, and *this* house and *this* address reeked of success. Yes, that would be important to the people at Hickory Hills, ever mindful of the club's *second tier* status in relation to Winged Foot and Westchester CC. They would be proud of Ellen Burden's *star power* and her growing status in Westchester society.

Charlie reached over and fished his cell phone from the pocket of his jacket to check his messages. Ellen had gone off to the kitchen to get her "little surprise," and the messages wouldn't take long to go through. On a Sunday afternoon he didn't expect anything of an urgent nature from either West Virginia or the New York office but you could never be sure.

There was a message from Larry Tuthill calling from CanAmex's Washington D.C. offices to set up a conference call with the Charleston lawyers to discuss "strategy and logistics" for the presentation later in the month, to the Red Bone Planning Board regarding the cooling pond. Charlie smiled at Tuthill's serious tone when he mentioned the planning board. This was one conference call, Charlie would be looking forward to.

The only other message Charlie chose to listen to was from Carlos Marche, inviting Charlie to attend the Yankee game with him and Lucien Mackey on Monday night. The Red Sox were in town. Charlie called and left an affirmative message for Carlos. *Yankees and Red Sox at Yankee Stadium in a September pennant race . . . baseball doesn't get much better than that!*

The message about the cooling pond reminded Charlie of Hank, and of the apartment in Red Bone and the spectacular view of the mountains from the porch. After being back in New York for ten days, it all seemed so long ago and far away. He'd put West Virginia out of his mind when he got home to the noisy, fast-paced excitement of the city and the richly manicured landscape of Mamaroneck, still lush with summer greenery the first week of September. He'd taken a run each morning through the bucolic Westchester countryside, and forgotten about the Red Bone Mountain trail.

After a few days, he'd been able to put Natty Oakes out of his mind too. This *infatuation* he'd had, was just the sort of thing that happened when you moved alone to a new place, he told himself. *She's a nice person, and Pie's mother. That's all it was. He'd thought a lot about her when he was down there, but now that was over. Thankfully! Getting involved with some girl in West Virginia was plain stupid, and dangerous too. He didn't need any of that.*

As if on cue, to second his thoughts, Ellen breezed through the hand-carved teak doorway out into the courtyard carrying a bottle of champagne in one hand, and in the other, two long stemmed, red champagne flutes. Stopping abruptly, with an evil smile, she kicked off her high-heels, sending one flying without even watching where it landed in a small island of thick green plants in the center of the courtyard. She'd taken off the jacket to her elegant white pant-suit, revealing a very sexy, sleeveless, satin blouse. The definition of her shoulders and arms clearly showed the result of her twice-weekly session with the free weights, and the muscles of her back pulled the blouse tight against her breasts.

Charlie felt a visceral stirring deep inside him as she placed the champagne on the table and leaned over to plant a long, warm kiss on his mouth. She sat down across from him while he worked the stopper out of the bottle.

"Now that wasn't so bad was it?" Ellen asked.

"The kiss?" Charlie joked.

"The party."

"No, it was fine. How did I do?"

Ellen smiled. "The perfect trophy husband."

Charlie poured the champagne. They touched glasses. "To the next president of Hickory Hills Country Club," said Charlie raising his glass. Ellen just smiled and turned toward the fountain.

"Do you think you'll get it? asked Charlie. "Club president?"

Ellen smiled wryly. "Of course I will."

They sat in silence watching and listening to the hypnotic rise and fall of the water into the stone fountain a few yards away from them. It occurred to Charlie that with Jennifer around most of the week, he and Ellen hadn't had too many opportunities to be alone like this. Of course this one had been well planned, by Ellen and her realtor – Ellen having the keys to the house, the Champagne in the refrigerator, the coins in the fountain – the scene had been set, and Charlie knew what was coming. He'd decided to make Ellen's job easier – he didn't want her to have to beg him about the house . . . that wasn't fair – they both knew what she wanted. Before he could speak, she interrupted his thoughts.

"Charlie, you haven't told me much about Virginia. About the people down there. Have you made any friends in . . . what is it?"

"Red Bone," said Charlie. He thought about the question for a few moments before answering. The *Virginia* thing, he'd let go – close enough. Ellen was much keener on European geography.

"Yeah, I've met a few people," he answered. He thought about Hank, and Eve Brewster, and of course Natty Oakes, and a few of the guys working on the project. Who should he tell her about? He leaned forward with his elbows on his knees, staring into the fountain, and smiled at the thought.

"There's a kid. I met him the first day I was down there. Showed me how to sneak under the fence to get onto the site." Charlie chuckled softly as he pictured in his mind, the contagiously funny *happy face* of his little buddy, the Pie Man.

"He's quite a character," he continued. "Comes by the site almost every day. Lot of fun to be around."

Charlie stopped to take a sip of champagne.

"What's his name?" Ellen sounded genuinely interested.

Charlie smiled at his wife as he thought for a second. "It's Boyd," he answered. "Boyd Oakes." He turned back toward the fountain before continuing. "He's, uh, retarded . . . Down Syndrome."

Charlie could feel Ellen's concentration on the side of his face. "How old is he?" she asked softly.

"He's twelve," Charlie answered. He turned to Ellen and their eyes locked as they shared a distant memory in silence. Finally, Ellen smiled and turned away. Charlie started to say something and then stopped. That wasn't why they were there, Charlie knew, to dredge up old memories. This was to be a happier occasion.

He'd thought about the house a lot over the past month and now he wanted this to be a special day for Ellen. Putting his wine glass on the table, Charlie stood up and stretched his arms over his head, then pulled off his tie. With his hands in his pockets, he did a turn around the fountain before coming back next to the table where Ellen was sitting. He looked down at her and smiled. "Well, this is quite a house we're buying here, isn't it?"

Ellen blinked with surprise, and then smiled a broad, joyful smile and nodded her head. "Thank you Charlie," she said rising out of her chair and going to him. "Thank you," she said softly, putting her arms around her husband's neck and pressing against him.

Charlie kissed her and held her close. Then he whispered into her ear. "I seem to remember the master bedroom having a nice thick carpet," he said suggestively.

"Yes, yes . . . no, wait," she said excitedly, turning away from him. She looked toward the house and bit the end of a manicured fingernail in concentration. "I have to make some calls, right away," she said, reaching for her handbag. She flashed Charlie an embarrassed smile as she pulled the phone from her bag. "I need to call Martha, and, and a couple of . . . just a few minutes darling." She walked quickly toward the teak doors and the quiet of the house, squinting at the small phone as she squeezed out the tiny beeps with her thumb.

Charlie poured himself a full glass of champagne and wandered out the back of the courtyard and through the attached pool house and cabana. Clear blue water was circulating in the kidney-shaped pool that was fed by a waterfall cascading down a high rock formation that made up part of the back wall of the house. Charlie knew that the waterfall would be turned off and the pool covered soon after they were gone this afternoon. Twenty yards beyond the pool, a tall brown stockade fence guarded the rear perimeter of the property.

Charlie sat down on the first of three wide marble stairs that led down to the pool area and gazed off at the thick green tree-tops visible over the stockade fence. A warm beam of late afternoon sunshine sliced through the trees to where he was sitting. Closing his eyes, he was back on his back porch aerie in Red Bone.

His eye went from the rolling green of the westward flank of Red Bone Mountain, to the egg-crate landscape of Virginia to the south where the mountains and the sky melded in swirls of blue and gray. Then he looked down at South County Road directly below him and followed it down the hill until he saw her, the bouncing dot, coming toward him up the hill at a good pace – running, not jogging – wearing the goofy blue hat and the over-size khaki shorts. And then, at the bottom of the hill, she looked up at him and waved and smiled the smile that made his heart skip. He opened his eyes to dismiss the vision, drained his champagne glass quickly and went back into the house to find his wife.

Chapter 16

The black Bell 430 rose off the tarmac of the Chuck Yeager Airport, did a quick spin in the air as it gained altitude, and roared south out of Charleston on a heading for McDowell County. Terry Summers was right, thought Charlie – these CanAmex pilots knew one way to fly ... aggressively! ... the way the company did everything. It was part of the corporate culture at CanAmex.

Charlie settled into the soft leather window seat and watched as the buildings and parking lots, warehouses and busy roadways of greater Charleston receded quickly behind them as they gained altitude, giving way to the heavy blanket of rolling green forest that would rise and fall beneath them all the way down to Red Bone. They quickly crossed the Kanawha River and Route 60, the only major highway they would pass over on their way south. Occasionally the green carpet would open up to reveal brown, gray and black scars that sat like open sores on the otherwise tranquil landscape. They reminded Charlie of pictures he'd seen of Army and Marine bases carved out of the jungles of Viet Nam.

Ahead of them and above, huge cumulonimbus clouds rose like frozen cotton candy against the deep blue sky, the detail of every curve and fissure highlighted by the bright sun still high in the sky to the west in the early evening. Charlie reached into the pocket of his sport jacket lying on the seat across the small aisle from him, and pulled out his sunglasses. As he glanced at his watch, the pilot's voice came over the speaker next to Charlie's seat. "About an hour – twenty now down to Red Bone, Mr. Burden. Put down about seven-thirty."

The timing was fine. He'd pick up his car at the construction site and get back to the apartment in time to get some dinner at Eve's restaurant and then stop in and see Hank. Maybe even get in a game of cribbage on the porch. It was going to be a nice evening to spend some time on the porch.

After being gone for ten days, Charlie was looking forward to getting back into the mountains and back to work on the project, and to seeing the Pie Man again. He'd missed the boy. More than he would have ever thought. Charlie reached down and unzipped the middle section of his large tennis bag to make sure it was there – the white plastic bag drawn tight around the official, dark blue, wool New York Yankees cap with the unmistakable white logo, along with the official program that Charlie had purchased at the game he'd attended on Monday night with Lucien Mackey and Carlos Marche.

From the liquor cabinet just behind the front bulkhead, Charlie poured himself a Canadian Club and then settled back into the soft leather seat. He took a sip of the liquor and gazed off at the luminous clouds and then finally, allowed himself to think about *her. What was he going to do about Natty Oakes? He couldn't just avoid her, not in the small environment of Red Bone, not with his relationship with Pie. No, he'd just have to deal with it, as an adult, as a man who had always been faithful to his wife and wasn't about to get involved with a woman down here. He'd treat her like any other acquaintance or friend he'd made in West Virginia. Nothing more, nothing less. Friendly and cordial but not personal. That was how adults handled situations like this.*

"We've got a nice little tail wind tonight sir, be on the ground ahead of schedule I think." The soft voice of the pilot in the speaker next to his ear brought Charlie's attention back to the present situation. In a few minutes he'd be back in her world and the closer he got to Red Bone, the more she crept back into his thoughts. In New York, in a different environment, he'd been able to put her out of his mind, but down here it was different. It would be harder.

He knew the moment he saw her picture on the dining room wall in the farmhouse on Angel Mountain that he had serious feelings for her and she hadn't been out of his thoughts much since then. And soon he would see her again, face to face, and speak with her and see her smile and hear her laugh and say something funny.

Charlie clenched his teeth and shook his head. *Shit! This wasn't going to be easy.*

And the Angel Mountain issue complicated things. Why the fuck did he ever tell Sarah DeWitt he'd try to save their farm? He should just stay out of it and let Vernon Yarbrough and Mulrooney do their thing. He wasn't going to be able to do anything anyway. The DeWitts were going to lose their farm and he was going to get his balls cut off by CanAmex if he did anything to try to prevent it. This whole thing – his infatuation with Natty Oakes and switching sides on the Angel Mountain issue – was nothing but trouble for him, personally and professionally. The best thing he could do was go back to New York right now and tell Lucien he wanted out, that he wasn't the man for the job in West Virginia. That's what he should do.

Charlie finished his drink and got up to throw the plastic cup into the waste chute next to the liquor cabinet. He leaned down and peered over the pilot's shoulder through the front windshield of the helicopter at the rugged landscape of mountains to the south and had an idea. Stepping down to the front compartment, Charlie squeezed past the pilot and sat down in the unoccupied co-pilot's seat.

"How's it going up here?" asked Charlie. He'd flown several times before with this pilot who he now remembered was a cigar smoker when he saw the box of Garcia Vegas sticking out of the breast pocket of his jacket hanging on a hook behind the pilot's seat.

"Real good Mr. Burden. Have you on the ground before too long."

"Mind if I steal a cigar?" Charlie asked reaching for the pack.

The pilot laughed, remembering that they'd gone through this routine before. "No, not at all. Help yourself," he answered handing Charlie a Zippo lighter with an Army Air Corps insignia on the side.

"Officially though," said the pilot, "you can't smoke up here."

Charlie puffed on the cigar to get it going while the pilot reached under his seat and pulled out a bean bag ashtray he placed on the console between them.

"How about unofficially?" asked Charlie as he handed back the lighter.

"Enjoy your cigar sir."

After a few moments of watching the scenery from the front of the helicopter, Charlie got to the point of his trip up front. "Listen, down south of here a little ways, there's a place called Angel Mountain. It's about twelve, fifteen miles from Red ..."

"I know where Angel Mountain is sir," the pilot cut in. "Been down there a couple of times."

Charlie was surprised. He looked over at the pilot. "You've been to Angel Mountain?"

"Yessir. 'Bout three, three and a half, years ago. Made a *couple* of flights down there. Landed right on the road up on the south face of the mountain. Mostly sand and gravel and rocks over on that side as I recall."

Charlie was intrigued, and curious. "Do you remember who you took down there?"

"Sure," the pilot answered without hesitation. "Took Mr.Torkelson, Larry Tuthill and that lawyer from Charleston, Yarbrough – had to stop in Charleston to pick him up. Second time, 'bout six months later, was those three plus the big guy from the coal company, the Irish guy ..."

"Mulrooney," Charlie prompted.

"Yeah, Mulrooney. He was a load. Haven't been back there since."

Charlie held the cigar up to the side of his head as he thought about what the pilot had just told him. *Why two trips down there, and so long ago – back when the whole project was still in the planning stages? And why Torkelson? How would he have even known of the existence of Angel Mountain so long before the project broke ground?*

Charlie glanced at his watch and then over at the pilot. "We're a little early. Would you mind taking a ride down there? Just a quick fly-over, that's all."

"Sure, that's no problem. Just a couple of minutes down there and back," said the pilot as he threw the powerful helicopter into a hard bank to the southwest and picked up the speed.

From the air Charlie could see that Angel Mountain was much larger than he'd perceived on their drive up to the DeWitt farm. The mountain was roughly in the shape of a long, obtuse triangle with its western slope – where the DeWitt farm was located – making up the short side of the triangle. The two longer sides ran in a generally east-southeast direction for about a mile until the mountain gradually lost its shape in a collection of rugged foothills. It was a long and massive structure. As Charlie peered down at it, he tried to imagine a thick seam of coal running through the middle of the mountain and envisioned how massive a job it would be to uncover it by removing the entire top third of the mountain.

They flew in low over the farm, low enough to clearly see the house and the barn, the several fields of solid green and the circular road that ran down past the chicken house and up along the corn field again. But they saw no sign of life in the quick pass over. From the air it looked even more remote and more idyllic than it did from the ground.

What a beautiful, wonderful place to live and raise a family, thought Charlie, *so isolated from all the crap, totally unconcerned with the corporate world and success and status and all the rest of it . . .*

The farm disappeared behind them as the helicopter heaved up and over a craggy peak to reveal the long, rocky south face of the mountain. The pilot pointed out the spot where he'd landed on his earlier trips to Angel Mountain and asked Charlie if he wanted to traverse the whole south slope of the mountain. But Charlie had seen what he wanted to see. It was the farm he wanted to look at again and its position on the mountain.

"No, that's enough. Let's head back up to Red Bone," he told the pilot.

It was still just eight o'clock by the time Charlie approached Old Red Bone driving up South County Road. The stone buildings high up on Main Street, bathed in light from the falling evening sun behind him, had the surreal quality of an old oil painting. It was a beautiful sight at this time of day and Charlie never failed to appreciate it. He also enjoyed the quiet of the scene. As usual, there were no other cars on the road and he hadn't seen a soul on the way in from the power plant. It was a stark change from the fluid movement of the never ending traffic flow of Westchester County, and the cacophony of Manhattan. McDowell County was much easier on the senses.

As he approached the soccer field at the bottom of the hill, a movement off to his left caught his eye and he instinctively slowed the Lexus. Drawing even with the field, Charlie pulled quietly to the left side of the road and stopped. Through the open window he sat and watched the boy in black soccer shorts, red T-shirt and shin guards, playing an imaginary game with himself, running and kicking a well-scuffed white paneled soccer ball, passing to himself and sidestepping invisible defenders, always hopping and moving and making his way up field toward the far goal. Finally, about ten yards in front of the goal, he rolled a slow pass toward the middle of the field and then encircled the ball quickly and attempted to blast it into the goal. He left foot slipped and he only brushed the top of the ball, which rolled lazily toward the goal as the boy sat watching from his seat on the ground. When the ball crossed the goal line, the boy scrambled up awkwardly and leaped a few inches into the air and threw his short arms up in celebration.

As he spun around in his celebratory dance, Pie noticed the car parked at the side of the road, and saw the grinning face of Charlie Burden looking directly at him. Pie dropped his arms by his side and his mouth fell open as he leaned forward to make sure he was seeing what he thought he saw. "*Chowly,*" he whispered to himself, and took a few steps forward.

Charlie climbed out of the car holding the white plastic bag. He walked onto the field and stopped as he watched the boy still creeping forward. He held his arms out wide.

"Well c'mon Pie Man, get over here!"

"Chowly!" the boy yelled. "Chowly ith back," he said as he broke into a lumbering sprint.

When he got to Charlie, he stopped abruptly. He had on an extreme happy face, his eyes mere slits, the tip of his tongue waggling excitedly between tight lips. But he wasn't sure of what to do next.

Charlie stepped forward and reached under his arms and heaved him up high over his head and spun him around as the Pie Man squealed with delight. Then he brought him in close to his chest and hugged him and spun him around again several times before depositing him on his feet. The boy continued his breathless giggle, the happy face closing his eyes completely, as he bounced up and down on his feet in front of Charlie.

Up the hill, in the small parking area next to the library, Natty Oakes stood next to her red Honda with her arms crossed on her chest. She'd put the soccer balls and her blackboard away after the evening practice and had come out of the library in time to see Charlie Burden get out of his car and to see Pie race across the field to him. She watched as Charlie lifted her son and spun him around. She could hear Pie's glee from up the hill. Then she watched Charlie hug her little boy with the kind of affection Pie had never gotten before from a man, and she blinked her eyes rapidly but couldn't prevent the tears that ran down her cheeks and rolled off onto her breast. She took deep breaths so she wouldn't sob but the tears came freely because there was no stopping them as she watched her son enjoy the kind of moment that he had been so long cheated out of.

Charlie sat down on the grass, still holding on to the bag that he could see Pie was now curious about. "C'mon Pie Man, sit down here and tell me what you've been up to."

Pie fell to the grass in front of Charlie, bubbling over with the news about their soccer team. He told him all about the Willard brothers and the new boy named Paul who came from someplace else and couldn't speak but was almost as good as Emma. He told him about the practice that had just gotten over and about the game that was coming up on Saturday morning. When he was out of soccer news, a pensive look came over his face and he looked down toward the ground.

"A couple of timeth I cwied, becoth I thought Chowly would nevah come back to Wed Bone." He looked sheepishly up at Charlie.

Charlie looked at his little friend for a few moments before speaking. This wasn't where he'd wanted this relationship to go, but it was inevitable he guessed.

"Well I came back Pie Man. I told you I was coming back, so you shouldn't have worried." He reached out and knocked Pie's backward baseball cap off and made the boy laugh. "Here, I got you something in New York," he said to change the subject. He reached behind him and brought forward the white bag and put it in the boy's lap.

Pie's eyes went wide with wonder as soon as he saw the bag, with the New York Yankees logo on the outside. "Thith ith fowa *me* Chowly?" He pointed at the logo. "*New Yowk Yankeeth*," he said softly.

Charlie laughed at the boy's reaction. He would have been thrilled to get just the *plastic bag* with the Yankees logo. "C'mon, Pie, open it up," he prodded.

Pie closed his eyes and reached inside the bag and pulled out the hat. When he opened his eyes, again his mouth fell open in wonderment. He stared at the hat for a few moments and ran his chubby little fingers over the white embroidered Yankees insignia. Finally, he said softly. "Oh Chowly, thith ith a weal hat like New Yowk Yankeeth batheball playahht wayah."

"Yep, it's the real thing Pie Man," Charlie said. "The same hat that Paul O'Neill and Derek Jeter and Bernie Williams wear." He could see that the names meant nothing to the boy. "C'mon, try it on," he said taking the hat from him. He adjusted the band in the rear to fit Pie's head and pulled it onto him tightly.

Immediately, Pie jumped up. "I have to thow mama," he said with the happy face coming back over him. "I thow mama my New Yowk Yankeeth hat!"

"Wait Pie, there's something else in here," Charlie said, holding out the bag to him.

Pie pulled out the thick program with the picture of Yankee Stadium on the cover, and his eyes again became as large as saucers. He turned the pages slowly, staring intently at the all the pictures, including the advertising. "Oh, Chowly, I *love* thith book," he said looking up at his friend. Then he closed the program suddenly, turned, and started to run toward the hill. "I have to thow mama. I have to thow mama my New Yowk Yankeeth hat," he yelled back at Charlie.

About ten yards away, the boy stopped running as abruptly as he'd started. He turned around and walked back toward Charlie still sitting on the ground. When he reached him, Pie held up his hand for their usual high-five. "Thank you Chowly. Thank you fowah my Yankeeth hat and fowah my Yankeeth book," he said softly.

Charlie pressed his hand against Pie's and held onto it for a moment. "Pie Man, thanks for being my best friend in West Virginia."

The boy stood still for a moment with pursed lips and nodded his head as if thinking over what Charlie had just said. Finally, he said, "Chowly?"

"Yeah Pie Man?"

The boy smiled broadly and pointed down at the white plastic bag in Charlie's left hand. "Chowly can I have the Yankeeth bag?"

Charlie laughed and poked the boy in the stomach with the plastic bag. "Of course you can Pie." The boy grabbed the bag with a huge happy face on again, and darted off once more. Again, he stopped abruptly and turned back to Charlie.

"Chowly? Will you come to owa thockah game on Thatwaday? Pleathe! You have to come Chowly," the boy pleaded.

"Well yeah, of course I'll ..." Charlie stopped in mid-answer as he looked up at the boy, and over his shoulder, up the hill next to the library, standing next to the red Honda, he saw Natty Oakes looking down at them. He felt the now-familiar pang of emptiness or longing or whatever it was, inside him, whenever he was near her.

Natty watched Pie turn around and go back to Charlie and get something that looked like a white bag. Then he started out and stopped again and turned back and spoke to Charlie. And then, Charlie was looking up at her, unmistakably, he leaned a little to his right to see clearly around Pie, then he got to his feet and waved up to her. *That was typical of him – to wait until he stood up to wave – being courteous even a hundred yards away.*

Her tears had stopped and she wanted to rub her eyes and wipe her cheeks but she didn't want to give anything away so she just smiled and gave him a wave that might have been a little over-enthusiastic, but that was okay, it was a *"welcome back to Red Bone, Mr. Burden"* wave. She didn't call out to him. It was a little too far and she was afraid her voice might not work right. *No, the wave was sufficient.*

Natty wondered to herself if Charlie Burden even remembered her name. He'd never addressed her as anything but "Mrs. Oakes," and even though he'd loaned her his car for a week and they'd gone running together and had several conversations, nothing he'd ever said was of a personal nature at all. Mostly just being kind of *professionally friendly*, and always courteous, and usually about the Pie Man. *Christ! What was she thinking? Of course she was just another backwoods nobody to him, like everyone else in town. If it wasn't for Pie they wouldn't have said word one to each other.* But now Pie had come all the way up the field and was clambering up the cement stairs toward the library, and Charlie Burden was still standing there on the field, looking up at her, with his hands in his pockets and a look on his face that said he was thinking about . . . *or maybe he was just watching Pie run up the steps.*

"Mama, mama." Pie was out of breath from excitement and the exertion of running up the long flight of steps. "Look what Chowly got fowah me in New Yowk!"

Charlie walked back to his car and drove up the hill. Natty and Pie were just pulling out in the Honda as he went by. He tooted and waved with his left hand out the window.

Pie sat up on the seat and swiveled around to see out the side rear window to follow the blue Lexus up the hill. "Chowly say he will come to owa thockah game on Thatwaday, mama."

"Yeah, that's good Pie Man, that's good," said Natty as she finally rubbed her eyes with the back of her hands before pulling out of the library parking lot and heading down the hill away from old Red Bone.

*　*　*

Larry Tuthill was already on the line from a hotel in Los Angeles when Charlie dialed in the code to join the conference call.

"Hi Larry, how's everything?" asked Charlie.

"Great Charlie, great. Everything's moving ahead, on schedule. Couple of more rolling blackouts out here and the feds'll be *begging* us to build more plants and the EPA will be working for *us*. And these Enron guys are just un-fucking-believable. Deregulation is beautiful Charlie. You know, it's amazing, you can lobby the shit out of these assholes, but nothing gets results like pulling the plug for a while. These tree huggers out here are against *everything* in the utility business, but you turn off their air conditioners and their cappuccino machines for twenty minutes and they're ready to build a nuclear plant in the neighborhood school yard. It's like *heroin* Charlie, America is just *addicted* to electricity."

"Yeah, you're right Larry, and you guys do a terrific job pushing it," Charlie said, trying to sound at least a little upbeat over the thought of America's insatiable appetite for electric power.

A few seconds later, they were joined by Vernon Yarbrough and with him in his personal conference room, the other Kerns & Yarbrough lawyer known only as Leonard, along with a public relations man from a firm in Charleston.

"Alright then," Larry Tuthill started the meeting. "Week after next, on Thursday, we're scheduled to go before the Planning Board down there to petition for the site change plan to move the pond. As you know gentlemen, this is a critical issue and we need it to go smoothly and in our favor. This is one of those thorny kinds of issues where we're stuck dealing with the locals and can't rely on our people in Charleston or Washington to take care of it. This is the kind of crap we try to avoid, but sometimes . . . well, sometimes you just have to pucker up and kiss some local asses to get the job done."

Vernon Yarbrough took over at this point and described the presentation that he and the PR firm had put together, including a series of large charts they were going to use to show the severe economic impact on the project and on the county if the plan wasn't approved.

"Plus, we got a bunch of good people comin' down, from the Governor's Office, the EPA, some local politicians and so forth, to do a little intimidating for us if we need it, a real show of force," continued Yarbrough, "so I think we'll be in good shape."

"Yeah, it sounds good Vernon," replied Tuthill. "Charlie what do you think?"

Charlie Burden looked down at the notes he'd made on the yellow legal pad on his desk. Then he leaned back in his chair, put his feet up on the desk and paused to get the moment right..

"We got a problem," said Charlie.

"What? What do you mean?" asked Yarbrough before Tuthill could say anything.

"Well, I had a little talk with the Planning Board president . . ."

"You had a meeting with Harkinson, *on your own, without counsel?*" Yarbrough's voice was loud and he was clearly perturbed. "You shouldn't have done that Burden, you should have waited for . . ."

"*Hankinson,*" Charlie interrupted. "His name is *Hankinson,* and he lives in my building, and, well, I ran into him one day and mentioned the pond problem and next thing you know he shows up out at the site and wants to take a look at the whole thing."

"So what's his problem Charlie," asked Tuthill in a quieter tone. "What did he say?"

"Well the problem's not really with him. He wants a couple of things that are going to raise the cost of the plan a little."

"Like what?" snapped Yarbrough.

"Well, he wants us to raise the height of the retaining levee on the northern border of the pond by two feet and to reinforce it with steel framing."

"Two feet? That's way beyond the code requirements," said Leonard quickly. Leonard was obviously more into the details of the building code statutes for containment levees than was Yarbrough. "And steel framing, that's not required either."

"Well that's what Hankinson wants. He's got a personal thing about these water impoundments. Wants the pond safe," said Charlie, "and it's not negotiable."

"What's this going to cost us?" asked Tuthill.

"About a hundred, hundred-fifty thousand, at the most."

Tuthill snorted audibly. "That's nothing. What's the problem? We'll do that in a second."

"What else does he want Burden?" Yarbrough asked. Charlie noticed that the lawyer seemed to have less of an accent when he was vexed.

"Well, Hankinson told me that the other two planning board members, Fitch and Hagerman, along with a few of the townspeople, well they've been griping that CanAmex and the project have been real good for the state and the county but they haven't really done much for the town so far. And they kind of have a point. You know most of the contractors have brought in their skilled labor from outside the area, and those guys have been spending their money over in Bluefield and in Welch. There have been a lot fewer local jobs than was originally promised."

"So what's his point, this *Hankinson,* what's he want?" asked an obviously irritated Vernon Yarbrough. Charlie could picture him stealing glances at his big Rolex as he talked on the phone.

Charlie continued his story. "Hankinson says that Fitch and Hagerman aren't going to approve *anything* for CanAmex, especially if someone gets up at the meeting and voices some complaint about the project, which is about guaranteed, he says. Probably be a lineup of people looking to speak out at the meeting, he says, because it's the first one since the original permitting."

"So how do we get to these boys, Fitch and Hagerman? What do they need?" asked Larry Tuthill.

Charlie took a sip of coffee to let Tuthill suffer for a moment before answering. "Well Larry, Hankinson feels that we need to find some local project to put some money into that will make the townspeople feel good and get them off the backs of the Planning Board so that he and Fitch and Hagerman will be able to vote with the company and approve the plan. That's what it'll take he says."

"Well shit, that's just a minor PR problem, right Dave?" said Yarbrough.

Dave the PR man came to life. "Well sure, Vern. I think with a little time on the ground down there, we'll be able to identify a suitable cause-related issue that we can cost-effectively address that will position us as a socially conscious . . . "

"Excuse me, uh Dave," Charlie interrupted, "but I think I have a solution to the situation that may kill two birds with one stone."

"Let's hear it Charlie," said Tuthill.

"Well, it has to do with DeWitt's granddaughter – that woman who went to see the lawyer in Welch about Angel Mountain?"

"What about her? How does she fit into this?" asked Yarbrough, obviously now more interested with the mention of Angel Mountain.

"She's got a project that would be perfect for us," Charlie said. "Seems that she's tried to open a children's library in a small building up near the town, next to the athletic fields. But the roof is leaking badly. Needs a lot of work. And she could use some new kid's books to replace the ones ruined by water too. Make, a nice high visibility project, and that woman – Natty Oakes is her name – is a real pistol, as you know. She'd probably be leading the lynch mob against us, especially with the Angel Mountain issue also concerning her. So if we could neutralize her a little by taking care of her pet project, well, it could quiet her down a bit on the Angel Mountain thing too."

"Charlie, I *like* that. It's great," replied Tuthill. "What do you think Vern?"

"Could work, if Burden can pull it off," the lawyer answered cautiously. "You sure you can get her to pull in her horns if we take care of this library?"

"Well I don't know what her plans are on the Angel Mountain thing, so I can't guarantee anything. But I don't think she has much recourse other than trying to make some noise in the media, so I think fixing up her library might make her back off a little," said Charlie.

"Good. That's it then," announced Larry Tuthill. "You orchestrate it Charlie. Talk to the girl and to the Planning Board guy and set it up. Spread a little cash around down there if you need to. Let's put that town to sleep so we can get some things done. Vernon, you'll go through your whole show and then when the shit starts flying, Charlie and the DeWitt girl . . ."

"Oakes," said Charlie.

"Huh, what?"

"He married name is Oakes."

"Yeah, right. So you and the girl put on a show about the library and everybody's happy and those boys vote it through and we move on. Is that about right?" asked Tuthill.

"That's it," answered Charlie.

"Vern?" queried Tuthill.

"Yeah, sounds okay to me," said Vernon Yarbrough sounding less than enthusiastic about the plan.

"Okay, that's it then. Thanks everybody. I won't be able to get down there for the meeting so Charlie, you and Vern will be speaking for CanAmex," said Larry Tuthill. "I'll see you guys. Vern, call me right after the meeting."

"Yeah, will do Larry, so long. Charlie, I'll see you week after next," responded Yarbrough.

"Goodbye guys," said Charlie.

Charlie clicked the hold button on his phone and covered the speaker section of the phone with his hand. Then he gently pressed the hold button once more. He could hear the hollow sound of an open phone line and what sounded like someone moving around in a conference room and then a door closing. Then he heard Larry Tuthill's voice again.

"Oh, I almost forgot, Charlie, you still there?" Tuthill asked innocently.

Charlie remained silent.

Tuthill's voice had a more serious tone when he spoke again. "Vern, you there?"

After a few seconds, Vernon Yarbrough's voice came on again, but now on a handset instead of a speakerphone. "Yeah, Larry, I'm here."

"We're alone. When you gonna move on the farmer?"

"Well, I'm thinking now, that we should wait until right after the Planning Board meeting, based on what Burden said about the state of mind of those old hillbillies on the board. Don't need any repercussions affecting the pond thing."

"Yeah, I think you're right," said Tuthill.

"So we'll go up the week after the Planning Board meeting. Need a little more time anyway to find a local boy to put on the team. That sheriff down there's a real straight arrow, but I got a line on another fellow – a deputy, named Lester, Wayne Lester – supposed to be willing to play ball a little."

"Everything else all set?" asked Tuthill.

"Planned out like the invasion of fucking Normandy. The staties are all set, and the D.E.A., and our judge. We'll have warrants up the ass, search, inside and out, seizure of property, everything. It's a done deal. That hillbilly pig-fucker'll be wishing he grabbed that seven-fifty was on the table last time I had to go crawling around that dump eatin' his shit."

"So as soon as the pond issue is out of the way you move on the farm," said Tuthill.

"Right. I'll give you a call when it's going down."

Larry Tuthill and Vernon Yarbrough clicked off the line. Charlie Burden sat still with the phone in the air. He quickly replayed the conversation in his mind to ascertain what he had just overheard. *Staties, D.E.A., search warrants. What the hell was Yarbrough planning to do? Have DeWitt arrested? For what? What were they going to find at the farm?* This was obviously the secretive *Plan B* that Yarbrough let slip in the car on the way down to Angel Mountain, and it didn't sound good for Bud DeWitt.

But what, if anything, could he or should he do about it? This was the dividing line between the two camps that Charlie would have to cross if he was to make good on his promise to Sarah DeWitt. Talk was cheap. Now, when he was faced with having to take action to '*do whatever he could to save their farm*', he knew it wouldn't be that easy.

This was serious business now. If he in some way sabotaged CanAmex's effort to acquire the farm, and was exposed, his career would be over and Dietrich Delahunt & Mackey would be devastated by the loss of it's biggest client. His friend Lucien Mackey would have to give up control of the firm. And it could get worse. With Duncan McCord's blessing, CanAmex would probably sue DD&M and Charlie personally for breach of contract and who knows what else and wage a protracted legal battle that in the end would go nowhere but would eventually bankrupt him with legal fees. Ellen's dream house would again be just a dream. Even if Charlie could live with the consequences, it wouldn't be fair to her. *No, he'd have to go slowly on this and see how it played out. Maybe Plan B would fall apart on its own somehow.* He quietly hung up the phone.

*   *   *

The sweat poured off his forehead in rivulets, running down to his already soaked T-shirt. Charlie looked at his watch to check his time . . . five minutes until his seven o'clock target finish time and he was still a good mile from Main Street with the dreaded uphill climb looming ahead. He'd push on as hard as he could, and even though he wouldn't come close to making his time, it had been a great run, a wonderful workout. He'd missed the exhilarating scenery of the run along the side of the mountain, as well as its awesome and somehow, unnerving serenity. There was something very lonely and even dangerous about the trail that made it more alluring, kind of like a roller coaster ride at an amusement park. He wondered how many times Natty Oakes had run the trail alone and if it ever intimidated her. *She was a strong woman,* he thought, *and god, how she could run!*

Charlie was totally unaware of the car that had crept quietly up behind him and when the horn blared he leaped in fright to the shoulder of the road. He turned to see the grinning face of Natty Oakes behind the windshield of the red Honda. She accelerated past him and stopped about fifteen yards up the road and got out of the car. She stood by the open door with her arms on the top of the car and smiled back at Charlie.

"Need a ride sailor? Don't look like you're going to make it back to town."

Thankful for a reason to stop running, Charlie slowed to a walk and wiped the sweat from his face with the front of his shirt.

"This part of West Virginia politeness? Whenever you see someone you know, you pull your car over?"

"No not for everyone," Natty said, squinting into the falling sun, "just the men with nice legs."

Charlie smiled at her and again wiped the sweat still running down his face.

"Hey, thanks for getting' Pie that hat. He really loves it. Wore it to bed the last two nights."

"Yeah, I knew he'd like it," said Charlie.

"And he hasn't put that magazine down since you gave it to him. I think he's memorizing it," she said with a chuckle.

And then they were both at a loss for words. Charlie wanted to mention the Planning Board meeting and his plan to fix the library, but he needed to discuss it with Hank first to see if it would really work. No need to get her excited about it when there was still a good chance it may not happen.

Then he remembered something else. "I got Pie a program. One of those math-tutoring programs I mentioned to you. I ordered it on-line and it was on my desk when I got back. I'll install it on one of our spare computers and get Pie working on it when he comes by the office."

Natty swallowed hard to hide her emotion. Her voice was softer when she spoke. "Yeah, he'll be excited about that. Good for him too. School starts next week." She looked up the hill to avoid his eyes for just a second. "That was very nice of you Mr. Burden to do that. You let me know how much that program cost so I can pay you back, I mean it."

"No, you don't have to – "

"Really now. I mean it. I want to pay you for it," Natty protested, looking back at him with a serious look on her face.

"All right," said Charlie. "It was seven hundred dollars," he fibbed. He stared at her blankly, not giving anything away.

Natty drummed her fingers on the roof of the car for a few seconds, then her face lit up with her trademark smile. "Well then, how about I just buy you a cold beer at the store whenever you finally make it up there?"

Charlie laughed. "It's a deal," he said as he turned and began running again with very short, quick strides to get started. The Honda passed him and he noticed how the exhaust pipe swayed back and forth, suspended on a twisted coat hanger.

It took him another ten minutes to make it up the hill to Main Street. He rounded the corner and slowed to a walk, catching his breath and cooling down in the gentle mountain breeze that always seemed to be floating through the town.

Natty Oakes was sitting on the bench in front of the store. Next to her was a small plastic bowl full of ice with a 16oz. Budweiser can stuck in the middle.

"Hot night for running," Natty said pulling the beer from the ice and offering it to Charlie. "It's better in the morning."

"Yeah but you can't have a beer in the morning," said Charlie. He sat down on a bench across the porch from Natty, facing the store. As he pressed the ice cold can to his forehead, he noticed Eve Brewster looking out at them through the large window. He waved to her but she just nodded quickly before disappearing into the store. He wondered if Eve might be having a problem with him sitting having a beer with her sister-in-law. *Maybe she thinks there's something going on between him and Natty. He'd have to dispel that notion real quick, if that's what she thought.*

Charlie opened the beer and took a long, satisfying drink, the icy coldness stinging his hot throat. He looked over at Natty. "Thanks," he said gesturing with the beer can.

Natty finished the beer she had been drinking and tossed the can in a cardboard box on the porch next to her bench. She edged forward on the seat and Charlie expected her to get up and leave. Near the steps down to the street, he noticed her suitcase-like kit that he carried for her the night her wheel fell off near the power plant. Next to it was a small brown grocery bag from the store from which he could see protruding the unmistakable shape of a Jack Daniels bottle and a carton of Marlboros. Friday night, she must be on her way over to tend to her "two old colored gentlemen," as Eve put it.

He wondered how he could get her to stay for a few more minutes . . . an hour . . . all night long he could sit there with her in the peaceful quiet of the porch and listen to her talk, and find out everything there was to know about her.

"Been meaning to ask you something, Mr. Burden." Her voice had a more serious tone than usual.

"Sure," Charlie said, "what is it?"

"Well, I been tryin' to figure out . . . uhm, went you went up to Angel Mountain and you talked to my mother, well how'd you know she was my mother? I never said anything about her or being a DeWitt and you know, it ain't the kind of thing that pops up in conversation much. So, I was just wondering."

The question surprised Charlie, but now that he thought about it, he could see how she and her mother might find it curious. His mind went back to that day and to the small dining room of the farmhouse and the pictures on the wall, and the picture of Natty and her mother that he couldn't take his eyes away from. The picture of Natty in her blue jeans and the baggy sweater, and the wild hair with the shock hanging down across her forehead, uncaring about any of it, concerned only with the hug she was squeezing her mother with. The picture of Natty with the ice blue eyes so alive with fun, and the broad, white smile so genuine and natural . . . the face of absolute beauty that Charlie couldn't erase from his mind.

He looked over at her and there it was, the same face, the same woman wearing the customary camouflage – the baggy blue jeans, construction boots and the long-sleeved, man's white shirt, only the *Spider-Man* cap was missing – but still the same woman from the picture. It was then that it suddenly dawned on him. Natty wasn't wearing any make-up. He thought about it and couldn't remember ever seeing her with any makeup – on her eyes, or lipstick – nothing. Then something else occurred to him as he looked at her. She never wore any jewelry. No earrings, necklaces, bracelets. He checked her hands quickly – no rings of any kind, just a small, white-faced watch with a brown leather strap on her left wrist. *Christ, how could she always look so . . . great . . . with no makeup or jewelry?*

"Course you don't have to tell me if you don't want to," Natty interrupted his thoughts.

Charlie smiled at her. "No, I'm sorry. I was thinking about something." He refocused on the question. "I saw your picture. On the dining room wall. I was bringing in a tray from outside, for your grandmother, and I saw the pictures in the dining room. Pictures of Pie and Cat, and you and your mother. And your father. Alice showed them to me."

Natty smiled and looked across the street toward the Pocahontas Hotel. "The pictures on the wall. Yeah, I forgot about them," she said softly.

A few moments of silence passed. Charlie took another long swig of beer. Then, Natty spoke again. "So, how are you going to save our farm, Mr. Burden? Like you told my mother."

It was the question Charlie didn't want to hear. It was the issue he needed to avoid. He squeezed his beer can flat and tossed it into the box with the other empties.

Natty didn't want to make him uncomfortable but this was important. She pressed him. "All of your friends are trying their damnedest to take that farm, but you tell my mother that you're on *our* side. How can you do that? How can you be working for them and prevent them from taking the farm at the same time?"

She was relentless. It was another part of her that Charlie found attractive. He knew she was a tough, competitive woman from the way she ran, but now he could sense her courage as well. When it came to her family and fighting for the farm, she would be like a pit bull. He leaned forward with his elbows on his knees and looked down at the wide planks of the porch. She deserved an answer. The real answer, not some corporate spin.

"Natty, I'm not sure I *can* save your farm," he said softly. "If I can save it, I will, but you have to understand that there are a great many powerful people who at this point will stop at nothing to take that farm." He thought about the conference call and *Plan B*.

Natty watched him and listened as he labored over his answer, but all she could think about was how, for the very first time, he had called her *Natty*. He said it so naturally, as if they had been friends for years, like he had said it before in his head many times. He really did know her name.

He looked up at her. "I told your mother I would do what I could, and I *will*, to a certain point. But this is serious business, to a lot of people and several companies, and there is a lot of money involved. Trying to save Angel Mountain could mean the end of my career and the financial ruin of my company and many of the people who work there, so I have to be careful because I won't let that happen." He reached down and loosened the laces of his running shoes. "I'll do what I can, but your grandfather is most likely going to lose his farm."

The cold fear of reality replaced the giddiness Natty had felt from hearing her name come from Charlie Burden's lips. She nodded her understanding. "Okay. That's fair enough. You'll do what you can and we'll just see what happens," she said trying not to sound too discouraged.

She looked at her watch. "Got to go take care of my boys," she said standing up.

Charlie stood up as well, anxious to get upstairs and into the shower. He watched her sling her case over her shoulder and pick up the grocery bag.

"Want to come over and meet a couple of old coal miners?" she said with one foot on the step down to the street.

Charlie looked over toward the old building across the street. He would enjoy meeting the two old black men he'd seen a couple of times in the restaurant, and more than that, he'd love to spend some more time with Natty Oakes, but no, he needed to avoid that.

"I really would like to meet them sometime, but not tonight. Tonight isn't –"

"Yeah, that's okay. I understand. Some other time. They'd get a kick out of meeting the *big mule*."

They both smiled. Then Charlie took a step toward her, the levity draining from his face. "Natty, this has to be our secret, about Angel Mountain, you understand that."

She took a step back up onto the porch. The sun had almost gone down and they were both hidden in shadows. "Yeah, I know," she said softly. "I can see the fix you're in. Wouldn't do to have that too public. You're like the only friend we got in this thing."

Through the darkness, she could see him standing still, just looking at her.

"Yeah, you're probably right about *that*," he said after a few moments of silence. "Good night Natty, thanks for the beer," he said , moving toward the front door.

"Hey Charlie," Natty said, stopping him with his hand on the screen door.

"Yeah?"

"Thank you. Thanks for everything." She turned and went down the steps and headed for the Pocahontas Hotel across the street. She could feel Charlie watching her for a few seconds until she heard the familiar crack of the screen door closing. In the darkness she smiled to herself.

Inside the Barney's Building, in the pitch black basement, Eve Brewster stood silently on an old wooden packing crate that lifted her head up to one of the two basement windows that had long ago been hidden by the construction of the wooden boardwalk in front of the building. The window, which opened inwardly on hinges at the top, was just two feet below the bench that Natty had been sitting on. Eve remained still, her face resting in the crook of her arm on the window sill, thinking about the conversation she had just listened in on. When she was certain that Natty had made it across the street to the Pocahontas Hotel, she quietly closed and locked the small window.

Chapter 17

A noise awakened him. Charlie lay still in the darkness of the big bedroom trying to figure out where he was, as he often had to do when he woke up in the apartment. Then he heard the toilet flush in the adjoining bathroom, and Hank, standing at the sink, hacking up his morning ritual. It was the apartment's only drawback, but Charlie could live with it.

He looked at the foldout travel alarm on the table next to the bed. *Five forty-five.* Too early on a Saturday morning. Rolling over and pulling the covers up over him, Charlie suddenly realized how cool it had gotten in the apartment overnight. The large windows in the living room were always open, as was the back door to the porch, and now the cold air made it feel almost like winter.

After fifteen minutes of squirming under the cool blankets with too many thoughts running through his head, Charlie abandoned his attempt at going back to sleep. He lay in the bed looking up at the ceiling and concentrated on the random thoughts that were clamoring for his attention.

He thought about Ellen and the house in Mamaroneck that was now on the market. She was going to be having an open house both days this weekend to try for a fast sale, and knowing Ellen and her realtor, that's what they would get. Now that he'd given the okay to the Quail Hollow Lane house, Ellen would be focused and driven to make it happen as soon as possible.

Charlie found that he was now more uneasy about the sale of the old house than he was about the purchase of the new one. He had an empty feeling inside as he thought about losing another part of the life he desperately wanted to hold on to. They had spent so many years and created an album of family memories in the old house and now it was all being wiped away too quickly, and soon it would all be gone – the house where their children had grown into young adults, the backyard where he and the kids had spent so much time playing catch and kicking soccer balls, and his tennis court project with the few trees still to be cut and the stubborn stumps, victoriously, still in their holes. He wondered if the new owner would continue the hand-to-hand combat with the stumps. Probably not.

He thought about the power plant, and the scheduling, and the weather, and the timetable for the delivery of the turbines and the control room, and what could go wrong – things he went over in his mind almost every day. And the pond problem, and Angel Mountain, trying to figure out some way to make that work out right for everyone – which just didn't seem possible – or how to extricate himself from the situation while doing the least amount of damage to himself and Ellen and Lucien and also the DeWitts.

Then, inevitably, *she* came into his thoughts. He smiled to himself when he thought about Natty standing next to her car the previous day ... *'Need a ride sailor? Don't look like you're going to make it'* . . . Natty made him laugh. *She could be a real ball-buster when she wanted to.*

Charlie looked again at the clock on the table. He got out of bed and dug out his blue sweat pants from the bottom drawer of the bureau, and a threadbare, ancient brown flannel shirt that Ellen had been threatening to throw away for years. Going through the living room, the wood floor was cold on his bare feet. He shut the large windows, and made his way through the small kitchen and out onto the porch, anxious as always to see the morning view of the mountains.

Then he heard her footsteps. Faintly, almost imperceptibly at first if one wasn't attuned to the sound, and then more clearly as she approached the bottom of the hill, almost to the soccer field. He recognized the rhythm of a runner's footfalls, and then, in the dead silence of the morning, her short but unhurried breaths, amplified by the damp air.

Charlie retreated into the apartment quietly behind the screen door. He didn't want her to look up and see him, so obviously waiting for her – *what other reason could he have for being out on the porch at 6:15 in the morning?* – and get the wrong idea. As he leaned against the doorframe, still listening to her footsteps, he heard Hank's door clap shut and the gentle creak of the porch floorboards and the soft patter of his neighbor's slippers. Hank was up with his morning tea.

"Morning Natty," he heard Hank call down. "Air's a little thick this morning. Going to have quite a sight over the other side of the mountain."

"Yeah, gonna be like runnin' on a cloud." Natty's voice rose up to the fourth floor like she was standing out on the porch. It sounded to Charlie like she had stopped running or at least had slowed to a walk coming up the hill.

"How you doin' Hank? Everything okay?" she called up.

"I'm fine Natty, but thanks for asking," Hank replied.

"Be expecting you at the soccer game later on. Ten o'clock. Playin' Welch so we could use some fans you know."

"Wouldn't miss it Natty. Going to win some games this year?"

"Well, we're gonna try, like we always do."

From inside the doorway, Charlie could hear the smile in Natty's voice.

"Then I'll see you later on," said Hank.

Charlie continued to listen for a few moments but heard only silence. He'd forgotten about the soccer game that Pie had told him about on Wednesday. Ten o'clock – he'd take a walk down the hill and watch a little of the game, for Pie's sake. It looked like it was going to be a beautiful early fall morning, the kind of morning that was made for kids' soccer. It would be fun watching Pie and maybe having a team to root for again.

From his stool at the counter in Eve's Restaurant, Charlie saw Hank shuffle past the window, heading toward the corner. He was walking with a cane, which he probably needed to make it down and back up the steep hill from the soccer field. Charlie folded up the Charleston Gazette and placed it back on the end of the counter. He pulled out some bills to pay for his breakfast just as Eve Brewster came out from the kitchen.

"Goin' down to watch Natty's team play Mr. Burden?" she asked as she came out from behind the counter, headed out of the restaurant.

"Yeah, I want to watch my buddy the Pie Man in …" But Eve had breezed past him without waiting for his reply.

Charlie watched her go out through the front door. It wasn't like her to be so brusque, or to call him *Mr. Burden*. It could only be her suspicion about Charlie's intentions toward her sister-in-law. He made a mental note to have a talk with Eve real soon. He liked her too much to have her angry with him for no reason.

As Charlie left the restaurant, three boys in blue soccer uniforms were coming out of the store carrying plastic bottles of an orange sports drink. These boys reminded Charlie more of the kind of soccer teams his kids had played on. Their uniforms were the modern style – nylon shirts with a striped pattern and contrasting collar – not like the plain red T-shirts that Natty's team wore. They had on dark blue shorts with the Umbro logo, and light blue stockings over their shin guards. Even in Westchester County the uniforms would have been considered very sharp looking.

Two of the boys were tall and athletic looking and had the kind of swagger that Charlie knew from his years of watching kids' soccer, identified them as confident, experienced players. The third boy was shorter and stockier and was probably a year or two younger than the others.

Charlie let the boys go ahead of him through the front door and then followed behind as they all made their way down the boardwalk and down the steps to the street. The short, stocky boy fell in behind the other two, with Charlie ten yards back, but close enough to overhear their conversation.

"So their best player's a girl, we gonna kick some butt today, right Gabe?" the younger boy asked. The taller boys ignored him. "We're gonna kick ass here, right? If their best player's some girl, we're gonna kick ass, right Vinnie? Huh Gabe?" he continued.

Finally, the boy named Gabe half turned his head to the rear. "Dicky, better shut up 'bout playin' *some girl*, 'cause you ain't never played against Emma Lowe before." He turned around and walked backwards as he spoke to the younger boy, poking him in the chest for emphasis. "You playin' fullback Dicky so you better not *let* Emma Lowe get the ball, 'cause she gets the ball you ain't gonna touch it again." He spun around and walked forward, turning his head for one last comment. "Emma's best player *you'll* ever play against Dicky, girl *or* boy."

The boys broke into a trot to get down the hill and join their team warming up on the field, leaving Charlie behind. The conversation of the boys increased his anticipation. He recalled Natty's praise for the shy girl that he had met in front of the store the day that Natty and her sister-in-law, Sally, had taken off on Terry Summers. He'd discounted her words as typical adult exaggeration of a decent player's skills. But coming from other kids, especially from an opposing team, the praise took on more meaning. He was still a bit skeptical but now he was looking forward to watching the *Bones'* star player in action.

Charlie took a seat next to Hank up on the last row of the small four-row bleachers on the *Bones* side of the field. Eve Brewster was sitting down on the second row with Ada Lowe and Mabel Willard, and several other women Charlie didn't know. They all waved to him and said 'good morning' as he climbed over the benches to get up to Hank. A few other spectators, obviously parents and grandparents sat along the sideline in folding chairs or in the several cars and pick-ups that were pulled off the road onto the weedy grass shoulder facing the field.

Across the field, Charlie noticed that there were more spectators lining the sideline, and the parking lot beyond the visitors' bench area held a more up-scale looking collection of vehicles. A BMW and a Volvo were mixed in with several Dodge Caravans and Jeeps, along with a few pick-ups. The newer cars looked out of place in Red Bone.

From the look of the players warming up and the number of supporters on their side of the field, the blue team had the look of a formidable opponent. Natty's team, with their plain red T-shirts looked smaller and less accomplished than the other team, although Charlie knew it was impossible to pick out the stronger team in kids' soccer based on their appearance during warm-ups.

After a brief conversation with Hank, Charlie turned to focus on the activity out on the field as the teams warmed up. He picked out Pie right away. He was the shortest player on the field, and his short arms stuck out like wings when he ran giving him, from a distance, the appearance very similar to a penguin. Charlie smiled when he saw the New York Yankees hat backward on his little buddy's head.

Charlie was impressed with the powerful shots of some of the other boys, particularly two taller black kids, one of whom he recognized as Sammy Willard. The other boy Charlie surmised must be Sammy's brother Zack. Another boy, with short-cropped blond hair, had a very competent way with the ball and also a very powerful low shot on goal. Charlie wondered if that was the boy named Paul that Pie had told him about.

Then he remembered Emma. He looked for her in the line of players waiting for a turn with the ball, but the only girl he saw on the field was a large black girl who was wearing the dark shirt and gloves of a goaltender. He turned to Hank. "Where's that girl Emma that's supposed to be so good?"

Hank looked over the field for a second and then pointed to their right, to the near corner of the field. Charlie turned to see the girl spread-eagle on the ground, her legs straight out in the splits position, her chest and face pressed flat against the grass, arms stretched out over her head, unmoving in what looked like an impossibly painful position. She remained like that as Charlie watched her, for at least another minute, until Natty blew her whistle to summon her team to the sideline.

Charlie was distracted by a few more cars pulling up to park on the shoulder of the road just up from the bleachers. He turned to see Natty's sister-in-law, Sally, the tall redhead, get out of an old orange Camaro, accompanied by a rugged looking man of about forty, wearing a blue work shirt with holes worn through at both elbows, blue jeans and boots coated a dull gray from cement work. Natty's daughter, Cat, and two young boys, obviously twins, scrambled out of the back seat of the Camaro and immediately ran over to see their Aunt Eve. Eve Brewster waved to Sally and the man, and then concentrated her attention on the children.

A powerful looking Ford pickup pulled in front of the Camaro. The driver was short and very thin, almost gaunt, with a bushy mustache and a black baseball cap with what looked like some kind of union emblem on the front. The short sleeves of his T-shirt were rolled up to reveal several tattoos on each arm.

The woman, who took her time exiting the truck, was twice the size of the driver – at least three hundred pounds – with a pasty, white complexion that showed that she didn't get outside much.

The couple joined up with Sally and her husband, standing along the sideline. Charlie heard Sally call out to Natty. "Luck Nat," she said with a wave, as Natty waved back at her and the others. "Go get um you Pie Man," she added. The boy ran over to give his trademark "high five" to his Aunt Sally and to, what Charlie presumed to be his uncles.

Hank leaned over and gestured with his chin in the direction of the newcomers. "Ransom and Yancy Oakes . . . Eve's brothers," he said. "Big one's Charlotte, Yancy's wife."

Charlie watched as the two couples moved up the sideline a little ways. The women opened up lawn chairs to sit on while the men wandered off to talk with a couple of old men sitting on the back of a truck. Charlie wondered if Natty's husband would be joining them. He looked around behind him, up and down South County Road for the white pickup truck but saw nothing.

"Chowly! Chowly!" The Pie Man's excited voice brought Charlie's attention back to the sideline. He turned to see his little pal, with a short arm up in the air waving to him, a severe happy face closing his eyes to slits.

Charlie waved back. "Hey Pie Man," he called back. "Have a good game."

The boy was pointing out Charlie to his nearby teammates. "Thath my fwend Chowly. Chowly bwing me my New Yowk Yankeeth hat all da way fwom New Yowk Thity." Some of the boys looked over at Charlie quickly as they went by Pie, not very interested in Pie's friend in the stands.

Natty was just about to call her team together for her last minute pep talk, when she heard Pie's voice. '*Chowly! Chowly!*' the words sounded so familiar now, coming from her son. She'd seen Hank sitting alone on the back row of the little bleachers. That would be where Charlie was now sitting, next to his friend. She turned inconspicuously to the side and sneaked a look toward the bleachers and saw Charlie waving to Pie. She quickly turned back toward the field and then looked down at her clipboard and line-up sheet.

Damn, why was she acting like such a child? Afraid to even look up at the man. A week ago she would have spun around and called out a 'hey there Mr. Burden!' to her son's new friend without caring who might be looking on. But now . . . Christ! was she just imagining it, like a schoolgirl?. . . after the previous night and their beer together on the porch in front of the dark store and their little talk, and then he said her name for the first time – not like he was just trying it out or being polite, but like he'd been wanting to say it since that first day they met in the shoe aisle of the store and almost bust a gut laughing over the 'big mule' thing – she knew he had at least some little bit of a thought in his head for her. And now if she looked back at him, she'd give it away, and everyone in the bleachers would know what she was feeling.

"Morning Mrs. Oakes!" A voice bellowed from somewhere on the field.

Natty winced when she heard the voice of the league president. She looked up to see Kyle Loftus, whom she'd had several run-ins with the previous season, striding across the field toward her. The owner of the *Loftus Insurance Agency* of Welch, the largest agency in McDowell County, was wearing his customary white shirt and tie, with a bright green blazer slung over his shoulder. He was a large man who moved with a very deliberate back and forth sway as if to make certain that no one along the sidelines missed his entrance. As he made his way across the field, he talked into a cell phone pressed to his ear with his left hand, his elbow flying straight out and high to let everyone know that he was engaged in electronic conversation.

"Hey there Mr. Loftus," was all Natty could get out, not certain if the league president was paying attention to her or to his cell phone. As much as she disliked this pompous insurance man, she would try to stay on his good side so he wouldn't cause any trouble for her or her team. She knew that Loftus, a good friend of Deputy Sheriff Wayne Lester, and the brother-in-law of the coach of the Welch team, had it in for her and would love to suspend her from the league if he got the chance. Loftus and several other coaches agreed that the league would be better off without this feisty little woman coach and her *girls* playing in a boys league. Loftus' son also played for the Welch team with which the *Bones* had had some nasty confrontations the previous season. Natty had lost her temper on several occasions and had let loose with some words she probably shouldn't have used.

"Field's still pretty sub-standard, Mrs. Oakes. Worst in the league," said Loftus looking around him as he got closer. He stopped and made a show of kicking a rock toward the sideline.

"Been a real dry summer Mr. Lof . . ." Natty stopped as Loftus held up his palm to her and shifted his attention back to his phone conversation. Natty waited for a few seconds while Loftus spoke on the phone, then she noticed that the referee had finally arrived and was chatting with the Welch coach on the other side of the field. She turned around and sent her team onto the field. Pie, the only substitute, remained on the sideline. Loftus wandered off toward the end of the field, satisfied that he had made his point.

The blue team had the ball to start the game, and after the initial touch, their left forward, one of the taller boys Charlie had walked behind coming down the hill, lofted the ball down field and gave chase.

Charlie watched the action for a few seconds and then couldn't help turning his eyes toward Natty He found her on the sideline, edging down closer to the *Bones'* end of the field where her team was having trouble clearing the ball out. She'd taken off her blue sweater as the September morning sun quickly warmed up the field. From the back, in her red, *Bones* T-shirt, she could have been one of the players, she looked so small and young. Charlie admired the lines between her broad, sharply defined shoulders, board-straight back, and her narrow waist and hips. When she turned to say something to an older couple sitting in lawn chairs along the sideline, Charlie saw the smooth curves of her breasts and the white flash of her smile and felt the pang in his gut that he hadn't felt since high school, but was now experiencing quite regularly in Red Bone, West Virginia.

Directly behind the bleachers on the street, Charlie heard the double thud of two car doors closing. He looked down to see a white Taurus with a Dollar Rent-A-Car sticker on the rear bumper. Two women were walking around the end of the bleachers toward the field. One of the women, who looked to be in her mid-twenties, was tall with an athletic build and short curly brown hair. She wore an expensive looking powder blue warm-up suit and white Nike sneakers. Her companion was a little older, shorter, with medium-length black hair, and dressed like she was working, in a black cashmere blazer, gray slacks and white blouse. A black pocketbook hung from her right shoulder while her left arm cradled a leather notebook.

Charlie eyed the women with curiosity because even *he* could tell they weren't from Red Bone or even McDowell County, and most likely not from West Virginia. There was something too professional, too major league about their demeanor, to mistake them for locals.

The women stood on the sideline for a few moments watching the game before the shorter one turned and motioned toward the bleachers as a preferable place to watch from. They made their way through the few spectators on the first two rows, the well-dressed woman in charge, leading the way with a practiced, polite smile. As they reached the seats directly in front of Charlie and Hank, the men could see that the woman was beautifully made-up and very attractive. She flashed them a quick smile and gave them a polite "good morning gentlemen" in a drawl that definitely wasn't from New Jersey. As the younger woman climbed over the lower row, Charlie read the modest white lettering embroidered on the left breast of her blue warm-up jacket . . . *University of North Carolina Soccer.* She had a bored, tired look on her face that said she really didn't want to be here and she'd leave the politeness to her companion.

Charlie looked out to the middle of the field where Emma Lowe was standing perfectly still with her arms crossed, feet spread far apart lazily, as she had been for the first several minutes of the game, watching her team struggle to clear the ball. *No, it couldn't be. College scouts here to watch a thirteen-year-old? That didn't make sense, especially from the perennial number one powerhouse team in women's soccer.* Charlie wanted to stand up and yell out to Emma to look alive and get busy instead of just standing still. There were people here to watch her play.

The well-dressed woman scanned the field for a minute, then turned around to Charlie. "Excuse me," she said softly. "Is that Emma Lowe there?" She pointed toward mid-field.

"Yes," Charlie answered. "That's her."

The woman nodded and smiled a polite *thank you,* and turned back to her companion who just rolled her eyeballs to reemphasize that they were wasting their time here.

Charlie was still curious. He leaned forward and tapped the dark-haired woman on the shoulder. "Are you ladies here to, ah, *scout* Emma?"

The woman turned back to Charlie and spoke very softly. "Well we don't call it scouting when they're this young, but we're up here looking at a few high school kids, in Bluefield and Beckley, and coaches keep telling us we need to see this girl Emma play. So, we had some time this morning and we found out there was a game down here, and here we are. This is what we do," she added with a friendly smile.

Her companion, turned toward them with a wry look on her face. "Yeah, this is what we do when we'd rather take a two-hour drive in the morning than sleep."

They both turned their attention back to the field where the blue team was getting ready to take their third corner kick of the young game. Natty's team had been panicking under the pressure of the experienced Welch players and had been giving up the ball on bad passes and then just booting the ball out of bounds to regroup. Zack Willard had been trying to do too much dribbling to bring the ball out only to lose it repeatedly to double-teams and then be caught out of position. The confusion at the back line had brought the mid-fielders like Paul back too deep and as a result the blue team had wide holes in the field to maneuver and set up plays.

Natty watched as her team abandoned their spacing and the positional play that she continually stressed, and ran around helter skelter, everyone bunched up trying to make the play. But they were working hard, and Natty had to admit that the Welch team had improved a lot also. They were always a strong team and now they were all a year older too. Along the Welch sideline, the spectators were whooping and cheering and throwing their hands up with each close call, thoroughly enjoying what was beginning to look like a one-sided game. Suddenly Natty's team didn't seem like the powerhouse she had hoped it would be with the addition of the new players. They hadn't been able to get the ball across mid-field for the first five minutes of the game, and only some aggressive goal tending by Brenda Giles had prevented the blue team from scoring.

Finally, one of the Welch forwards made a mistake, trying to juke around Matt Hatfield. He gave up the ball and was going in the wrong direction as Matt started up the field with some room to run. He made a good pass to Paul in the middle of the field with some space to finally use his speed and show off his ability with the ball. He sliced smartly through two on-rushing defenders, brought the ball across the mid-field line, and then looked for Emma.

In the bleachers, Charlie had been keeping his eye on Emma while the blue team carried the play, looking for some sign of her talent, more intently now that he knew there were college scouts watching her. But she hardly moved off the center line, calmly watching the action at her end of the field. Hovering around her, some blue team defenders, obviously coached to shadow the *Bones* star, edged up and back, getting into the play occasionally, and then back quickly to not lose track of their responsibility.

When the Bones finally gained control of the ball and began to advance it up-field, Emma began walking backward, slowly not to get beyond the defenders who had been drawn far up the field to join the blue attack. As Matt Hatfield passed the ball up to Paul, Emma started to trot backwards, watching the action behind her. When Paul cut across midfield with the ball and room to maneuver, she whirled to find the defenders, gliding sideways with long, easy strides to catch up with their retreating line without putting herself offside. The defenders though, because of their assignment to shadow her, were staying too close, too far up the field, and Emma knew it. And so did Paul.

Paul waited until a blue midfielder was almost upon him before he pulled the trigger, lofting a long, high ball down the field to the right of the goal, which would land well beyond the blue fullbacks. The two defenders with Emma turned to give chase, and Emma took off. Her acceleration was explosive as she streaked past the surprised fullbacks, circling slightly to the right to put herself on a better angle to the goal. The ball took one long bounce on the rock hard ground before Emma caught up to it. Just as a third defender arrived from the middle of the field, Emma leaped into the air to control the ball before it bounced a second time. With her right leg stretched out straight in front of her, she took the ball three feet from the ground and tipped it over the head of the quickly closing defender, toward the center of the field. Emma came down on a track directly toward the ball, and the goal, with several more blue shirts racing at her from across the field. Behind her, the beaten fullbacks were digging hard to get back into the play.

In the bleachers, Charlie literally gasped when he saw Emma's mid-air move. "Oh *man!*" he blurted excitedly. "Did you see that? Did you see that?" he asked of no one in particular. Beside him Hank smiled and nodded in agreement. The women in front of them sat unmoving, their eyes riveted on the action on the field.

In the next instant, a moment before the blue sweeper reached her from the front and the fullbacks from behind, Emma took two quick, measured steps toward the ball and then one long powerful stride with her right leg, and with knees bent low and her head down, fired her left foot through the slowly rolling ball with a sharp crack. The defenders and the goalie hadn't expected a quick shot from twenty-five yards out and were taken by surprise, as were most of the spectators. The ball left her foot like a bullet, alive with vicious, hooking spin on a low, rising path to the far post The goalie, who had started to come out towards the action, favoring the near side of the goal, never came within five yards of the ball as it rocketed past him on a wide, hooking trajectory, just barely scraping the inside of the post as it buried itself high in the net. The goalie just looked behind him in disbelief and then to the sideline, shrugging his shoulders in helplessness.

The *Bones'* side of the field greeted the goal with polite cheers and clapping, while the team whooped it up on the field and ran together at midfield to share high-fives. In the bleachers, Charlie had let out a loud '*yeah*' and jumped to his feet when the ball went into the goal, but then he just stood in stunned silence as he thought about what he had just seen. He looked around him, at Hank, at the women from North Carolina, to see what their reaction had been. "Did you see that?" he muttered softly. "Did you see that kick?"

To him, it was probably the greatest goal he had ever seen scored in a kids' soccer game. Forget about the acrobatic leap Emma had made to control the ball and set herself up, it was the sheer velocity of the shot that had stunned Charlie. He'd seen kids with good hard shots before, but Emma's kick was far beyond the best he'd seen, even at the high school level. And to bury it, on a rope, into the top corner of the goal from twenty-five yards out was a phenomenal kick even for a professional player.

Next to him, Hank continued to clap slowly. The soccer women in front of him sat motionless, staring out at the field through narrowed eyes in rapt concentration. Charlie could see that the attitude of the woman in the warm-up suit had changed dramatically in the last few seconds. On the Welch sideline, the spectators sat in stunned silence, while the coach berated his defensive players right up to the whistle to restart play.

When the game resumed, there was a marked difference in the confidence level of both teams. The cockiness had left the blue defenders, replaced by looks of concern as they now hung back apprehensively and warily eyed Emma. The blue midfielders and forwards had also become more cautious as a result of Emma's incredible goal, but also from being victimized by the speed and ball handling ability of the new kid *Paul*. All of the players on the Welch team knew about the Willard boys, but now it was evident that this other new kid had played soccer before and at a pretty high level.

What the blue team lost in confidence had been transferred to the *Bones*. They had regained their spacing and their confidence in each other, and were now executing the quick moving passing triangles that Natty had drilled them on at practice. The *Bones* now played aggressively, as a team, while their opponents played tentatively and started to bunch up.

It also helped that now the blue defenders were playing much more conservatively, opening up the middle of the field allowing Paul, Matt Hatfield and Sammy Willard to control the play with their speed and ball handling. Emma also got more involved in the midfield play as the blue defense hung back.

After a few minutes of dominating the play, the *Bones* scored again, on a corner kick. Emma took it with her right foot from the left corner, sending a screaming hook toward the far post of the goal. As the ball came through the goalie's box, Paul took it out of the air with a vicious sidewinder kick that put the ball into the back of the net before the goalie could even move for it. It was another truly spectacular goal, particularly at this level, where corner kicks weren't supposed to travel with such velocity and accuracy, and balls weren't supposed to be picked so cleanly out of the air.

In the stands, Charlie again leaped to his feet and blurted out another loud '*yeah!*' which stood out from the rest of the polite clapping on the *Bones*' side of the field. Natty couldn't help turning to look up at Charlie. She squinted into the morning sun behind the bleachers, and smiled at his enthusiasm. It was nice for a change to have a man along their sideline who wasn't too old or too reticent to let out a cheer for her team. Charlie grinned back at her, gave her a quick thumbs up, and clapped a little louder.

The scouts from North Carolina smiled at each other in appreciation for the quality of the goal. Across the field, the Welch fans were silent, while the coach seethed and continued to chastise his players.

The second *Bones'* goal caused the already shaken blue team to totally lose their confidence, and the floodgates opened. The *Bones* controlled the play with sharp passing, the ball-control skills of Paul and Emma, and the domination of the middle of the field by Zack Willard. After another five minutes of near-misses and several great saves by the Welch goalie, Sammy Willard sent a beautiful, long crossing pass into the middle of the penalty area that Emma soared through the air to take two feet above several defenders and with a quick snap of her neck, headed the ball like a bullet into the back of the net past the unsuspecting goalie.

Charlie again leaped to his feet to cheer a truly incredible goal. In front of him, he noticed, the North Carolina women, had finally broken out of their trance-like observation mode and were smiling and nodding affirmatively to each other over what they were watching. They also stood to cheer Emma's goal.

This was the goal they wanted to see. Emma's foot speed and powerful shot with either leg had become very evident to the scouts early in the game, and although they didn't expect much of an air game from a thirteen year old, they had been reserving overall judgment until they could see if Emma had a feel for heading the ball, which was a major part of the game at the college level. The goal had erased any doubts. Emma's elevation, balance and timing, and the sheer power of the shot, showed that she was indeed a superior soccer player who could play the game in the air.

As they stood clapping, Charlie leaned forward, between the two scouts. "So what do think?" he asked. "She any good? Think she'll be able to play for your team some day?"

The women from North Carolina just looked at each other and smiled. Then the younger woman in the warm up suit turned back to Charlie. "She could play for our varsity right now," she said softly. The woman in the blazer didn't offer an opinion, but sat down and opened her notebook for the first time and began writing.

After the third goal, Natty put Pie into the game for Hardy Steele at right fullback. He ran onto the field, turning several times to make sure Charlie was watching. Charlie grinned and waved to his little friend who gave a high-five to everyone he came near on the field, even opposing players. When the referee made Pie get rid of his Yankees hat, the boy had an embarrassed *happy face* on as he raced over and tossed the hat to his mother, glancing up once more at Charlie before running back onto the field.

It was readily apparent that Pie was never going to be much of a soccer player but it was also clear that no player on the field would enjoy his time in the game as much as the Pie Man. With his short legs and slow foot speed, he was rarely involved in the play and his tendency to run straight toward an onrushing player made him an easy defender to go around.

On the few occasions when Pie would come across a loose ball with some room to run, he would put his head down in concentration on the ball and dribble it up the field on a line as fast as he could go before running straight into a defender who inevitably took the ball away from him with one solid kick, usually sending the boy stumbling and rolling animatedly to the ground. His delight at being such a central part of the action on the field was contagious, and his brief solo dashes with the ball became a crowd favorite, on both sides of the field.

A few minutes before halftime, Emma put on a show, dribbling and spinning magically through three blue defenders, the ball seemingly glued to her feet as she broke alone into the penalty area with the helpless goalie at her mercy. From eight yards out, she could easily have blasted the ball into the net on either side of the goalie who was frozen in his tracks on the goal line. She surprised everyone by continuing to dribble, taking the ball toward the right end of the goal. The goalie seized on this unexpected opportunity, lunging out toward Emma with a sliding tackle trying to block as much of the goal as he could with his body along the ground. With the goalie now totally committed, Emma calmly stepped past the ball with her left foot and without even a glance, using the instep of her right foot behind her, sent a firm, accurate pass across the length of the open goal to Paul standing all alone three yards from the goal post. But instead of just slamming the ball into the net, Paul waited, as a blue defender came sliding across the grass in a desperate attempt to get between the ball and the goal. Paul could have easily lifted the ball over the prone defender but instead he pulled the ball back, turned and sent a slow rolling pass out to a lumbering Gilbert Steele, eight yards from the wide open goal. Still panting and red-faced from his run up the field, Gilbert's eyes went wide with excitement as the first goal he'd ever scored in a game went skidding into the net. The chubby forward raced off on a run of celebration back up the field to high-five all of his teammates. The joy on his face revealed just how badly he had always wanted to score a goal. Natty went out on the field to give him a hug as he reached mid-field. Walking behind the rest of the jubilant team, Emma looked over at Paul and pointed her index finger at him and gave him a wink.

In the bleachers, the scout with the notebook sat with her feet on the bench in front of her, her chin resting on her clasped hands. She ignored the team celebration and kept her eyes glued on Emma. "She's incredible," she said softly to her companion without turning away from the field. "Five years from now, she's a national championship."

At halftime, Charlie talked Hank into taking a little walk with him. They walked up the hill to the children's library and stood in the small parking lot looking down on the field where Natty had her team huddled on the grass in front of the near goal. Charlie explained his plan for that Thursday's hearing before the planning board regarding the CanAmex petition to move the cooling pond.

"We've made the changes to the plan that you wanted Hank. The dike will be two feet higher and the whole thing will be framed with steel," said Charlie.

"That's good Burden. That's good" said Hank. "I already told the other fellas what was happening. You'll get your permit to move the pond."

"Well Hank, I'd like to get a little more than that out of Thursday's meeting." Charlie laid out his plan to have CanAmex fund the repairs to Natty's children's library. How he was going to have Natty testify at the hearing about how little the town had gotten out of the construction project and to offer up the library project in exchange for the board's cooperation. He related to Hank how he had set up CanAmex and the lawyers and already gotten tacit approval of the library repair project. Now it was just a matter of putting on the show.

"I'd like to have a couple of other townspeople go up before Natty and say a few negative things about the project and oppose the plan to move the pond, not too strongly, but enough to set the stage," Charlie explained.

"They won't be hard to find," said Hank, spitting a gob of tobacco juice over the cement wall and down to the weeds on the side of the hill. He stood looking down the hill toward the soccer field for a few seconds, then turned to look over at the library building with its sagging roof. Hank turned back to Charlie and motioned with his jaw to start walking back down the hill.

"This is a good thing you're doing Burden," said Hank. "But it ain't necessary, you know that. You know you're getting your permit 'cause I told you you were getting it. So tell me something." Hank stopped walking and looked up to study Charlie's face. "Is this about the library, or is this about the Oakes woman?"

Charlie smiled at Hank's directness. He knew what the old man was getting at. "It's a little of both, I guess Hank. It's a good project for CanAmex, *and . . .*" He paused for a second to search for the right words. "I do like Natty . . . a lot. And Pie too. I'd like to help her out with this, the library. It's something she worked hard at and really wants to make happen, but she needs some help. That's all."

The two men resumed their walk down the hill. "That ain't all, and you know it," Hank spit out, a little irritably, surprising Charlie. "But you're a big boy Charlie and you can take care of yourself." Hank slowed to a stop and continued in a softer voice. "But Charlie listen to me, you got to be careful in this area, 'cause Buck Oakes ain't somebody to fool with. He's a violent, unpredictable man, and he's mean-tempered."

"Like you said Hank, I can take care of myself. Don't worry about me," said Charlie.

Hank shook his head irritably. "Burden, it ain't *you* I'm worried about."

Charlie looked down toward the soccer field where Natty was still sitting on the grass surrounded by her team. "Yeah, okay Hank. I understand. Don't worry. There's nothing going to happen there."

In the second half, the *Bones* continued their domination of the game. They were just too fast and too talented for the Welch team. Emma scored two more goals in the first ten minutes of the second half before Natty put her on defense and moved Jimmy Hopson up to forward. The final score was 8 – 0, the largest margin any of Natty's teams had ever won a game by.

At the end of the game, the two scouts from *North Carolina* hurried down to introduce themselves to Natty. They thrust their business cards into Natty's hand and asked if they could meet Emma. Natty called her over.

As her painfully shy star reached the sideline, Natty put her arm around Emma's shoulders for reassurance. "Emma, these woman are from the University of North Carolina and they came to watch you play today."

Emma could only manage a tight, nervous smile and a shrug of the shoulders. The girl who could do anything on the field, was consumed by her shyness off it.

The woman in the blazer tried to put her at ease. "Emma, you're a wonderful soccer player. The best I've ever seen at your age."

Emma just hunched her shoulders a little more and blinked her eyelids nervously, as Natty smiled and squeezed her proudly.

"Someday," the scout continued. "We hope you'll think about coming to the University of North Carolina to play soccer. That's all. Just keep us in mind for a while okay?"

Natty was smiling broadly with excitement for her star player. These women were experts and they wanted Emma. This was going to be her ticket out of McDowell County, out to the real world of fame and fortune. Emma wasn't going to be trapped here in the mountains with no future and no opportunities beyond getting married and having babies.

"Ain't that great Em?" Natty enthused. "The *University of North Carolina*!"

The words brought a real smile to Emma's face, and made her let out a small chuckle. Then, the girl leaned in close to Natty and whispered in her ear. Natty smiled and looked at the head scout. "Emma wants to know if you know Mia Hamm."

The soccer women both laughed. "No," the dark haired woman answered. "Mia was gone before we got there." She reached out and shook Emma's hand. "But, I hope I'm there when Emma Lowe gets there."

Standing on one of the aluminum bleacher seats, Charlie reached back to help Hank negotiate his way over the slippery benches. As they stepped down to the next seat, Charlie happened to look over toward the sideline and see Eve Brewster standing next to her brother Yancy. His wife Charlotte, still in her folding chair was next to him, looking up, intent on hearing what Eve was saying. Eve stood with one arm folded across her breast, the other straight out holding a cigarette away from her body. Her face was canted slightly toward Yancy, as if she were speaking in a low voice, but her eyes were unmistakably focused on Charlie, as were her brother's. Yancy had a rigid scowl on his face beneath the long beak of his black cap, as he listened intently to his sister. Charlie thought that maybe the sun behind him was causing the angry looks on their faces.

Chapter 18

The morning air was finally starting to feel like the third week into September. Natty went back inside the trailer to get a jacket to put over Amos Ritter's shoulders. She wouldn't have to bother putting an ice cube in his coffee any more. He'd be looking forward to the hot metal cup to warm his brittle fingers. But he would still be there every morning, on his stool at the corner of Yancy and Charlotte's trailer, until the snow fell. Then he would stop coming out to sit on his stool.

"Gonna take my time today Amos," Natty said as she backed down the stone drive. "Feeling a little lazy this morning." The old man blinked and twitched and nodded slowly in response as Natty turned and loped off down the hill and disappeared around the corner of the trees. She headed up South County Road toward Old Red Bone at a comfortable pace but one that would at least take the chill off the cool damp air.

As she came abreast of the soccer field, at the bottom of the hill going up to Old Red Bone, a wave of elation came over Natty at the thought of their first soccer game. It couldn't have gone much better. The *Bones*, with the Willard brothers and Paul, the new boy from Poland, really was a good team now. *A great team, probably. And didn't Emma put on a show! In front of the women from the University of North Carolina to boot. And what did the woman say – the scout who was a professional and really knows what she's talking about – she said Emma was 'the best she'd ever seen at that age.' Damn Emma, you're going to be playing soccer for the University of North Carolina some day. And then probably the National Team and the Olympics!*

Natty had to wipe away the tears of joy that welled up in her eyes. She loved Emma so much and was so happy for the shy little girl who had worked so hard, all by herself, running and kicking soccer balls, to make herself into the best soccer player she could be. And it was all going to pay off for Emma. In a few years, she'd be watching Emma play soccer on television. The thought made Natty smile as she recalled how she and Emma, the previous July had driven around frantically to find somewhere to watch the women's World Cup soccer championship game between the United States and China. Buck had been hanging around the trailer, and besides, Natty and Emma wanted some place quiet where they could be alone to watch the most important sports event of either of their lives. After watching all of the previous games together including the impressive win over Germany and then the unbelievable victory over the unbeatable Brazilian team, Natty and Emma were overflowing with nervous anticipation of the final game against the powerful team from China and the great Sun Wen.

They ended up sitting side-by-side in a dark booth at *The Spur*, the old miners' saloon on Main Street in Old Red Bone, staring up at a small television suspended from the ceiling almost directly above them. They both nursed cokes for the whole game until Natty finally got herself a shot of Jack Daniels when the game went into overtime. Then they hugged and cried like babies and danced around on the old beer-stained wooden floor of the empty barroom when Brandi Chastain's penalty kick won the game.

Natty also remembered Emma's telling comment after the game. *'Brandi's goal won the game, but Michelle Akers won the World Cup.'* Emma Lowe knew soccer. *Some day she would sit in that same booth at The Spur and watch Emma play in a World Cup championship game!*

Natty was still thinking about Emma when she reached the top of the hill and rounded the corner onto Main Street and was startled to see Charlie Burden standing in the middle of the street in his running shorts and a sweatshirt, obviously waiting for her. It had been several weeks since they'd last run together and Natty had given up her anticipation of seeing him standing there when she came around the corner. She could only take one deep breath and a hard swallow to calm herself before she came up to him directly in front of the restaurant.

"Morning Mr. Burden," Natty managed. "Thought maybe you'd given up on running in the morning."

Charlie fell in beside her thankful for the easy pace Natty was at after her climb up the hill. "No, I still go once in a while in the morning, but mostly now after work," he said, glancing down at her next to him. "Fills the time. You know, not much to do around here in the evening."

"Yeah, you're right about that," said Natty.

"Do you mind?" asked Charlie. "Me running with you?"

Natty laughed. "Course I don't mind. Why would I mind? Is that why you stopped, uh, coming out in the morning. Cause you thought I minded?"

Charlie reached for a deep breath. "No, I just thought it would be … well …I didn't think it was a good idea to be running together every day."

Natty thought about teasing him a little, pressing for more of an answer, but she decided to let it go. She knew he was right.

"There's something I need to talk to you about though," said Charlie. "Before this Thursday's Planning Board meeting."

Natty looked up at him with a curious look on her face. *"Planning Board?"*

"Yeah. I think we can get CanAmex to pay to fix the roof of your library." Charlie explained his plan to have CanAmex adopt the library repair project as part of the deal to get the Planning Board's approval of the revised site plan to move the cooling pond. He told her that he'd discussed the whole thing with his client and also with Hank and had his approval. They were going to find a couple of other townspeople to also appear and give some negative testimony. All Natty had to do was go up last and offer her library roof as a worthwhile community service project for CanAmex, and he and Hank would do the rest.

"That's all I gotta do?" Natty sounded skeptical.

"That's it," said Charlie. "It'll be easy. You'll have fun."

"Yeah, fun," said Natty sarcastically.

"C'mon, you're getting a new roof on your library."

"I know. I'm sorry Mr. Burden. I do appreciate what you're doing, very much. I'm just nervous about talking in front of a bunch of people I guess."

"Don't be. You'll do fine," Charlie reassured her. "And I thought we'd gotten past this '*Mr. Burden* stuff."

Natty just smiled quickly and ran on ahead as the path narrowed going through the woods before coming to the trail that ran along the side of the southern slope of Red Bone Mountain. They ran along in single file for several minutes enjoying the scenery and the isolation of the Cliffside path. Charlie dropped back about twenty yards to give Natty some space, but he was still close enough to admire her form from the rear. He had to admit that Natty looked pretty spectacular from the back when she ran, even in her baggy shorts and the *Spider-Man* cap. Today she was wearing a long-sleeve gray jersey that clung a little tighter than her usual golf shirts. Every once in a while, she would pull up the front of the shirt to wipe the sweat from her brow, giving Charlie a glimpse of her small waist and the smooth flesh of her lower back. *Following her from behind was all the reason he needed to avoid running with Natty Oakes.*

They followed the path through a glade of birch trees and then back out to the Cliffside portion of the trail where the mountain rose up steeply on their right, and disappeared precipitously on the left side of the path, dropping off for hundreds of feet down to boulder-strewn chasms below. It was the most exhilarating and intimidating section of the run. Charlie instinctively edged over closer to the right side of the path. He looked up just in time to see that Natty had slowed down to a walk, now only about ten yards in front of him. Charlie pulled up quickly so as not to overrun her. He walked behind her, wiping his face with the sleeve of his sweatshirt, curious as to why Natty had quit running. It was very unlike her to even slow down during a run. After walking a short distance, Natty came to a stop and turned around to find Charlie.

"What's up?" said Charlie still mopping the sweat from his forehead, as he caught up to her.

"C'mon. I want to show you something," said Natty. Then she left the trail, scrambling up a narrow goat path that climbed through the pine trees and large rock formations that made up the rugged slope above the running trail. Charlie followed, trying hard to keep up with her as she sure-footedly went up the winding passageway through the trees. In some places, he found the trail so steep, he had to reach out for the smaller trees to pull himself up. Soon, he had no idea where Natty was, but just kept climbing up the path, hoping that they weren't going all the way to the top of the mountain ridge.

Then the path ended and Charlie found himself standing on a bed of pine needles amid a small grotto of fir trees. Through the trees, he had glimpses of the spectacular vista of the mountains to the south.

"Boo!" Natty suddenly appeared from behind a tree next to him, making him jump. She laughed and started off through the trees toward the light. "C'mon," she said. "This way."

Charlie followed her to the edge of the trees where she stopped and turned around to him. "Okay, now close your eyes and don't open them 'til I tell you to, all right?" she said.

"Sure. I'm all yours," said Charlie smiling as he made a show of closing his eyes tightly.

Natty reached out and took hold of his right wrist, conscious of the fact that this was the first time they had ever touched, and led him out from the trees onto the surface of the gently sloping boulder.

Charlie could feel the change in the light and a gentle breeze on his face and knew they had come out of the trees and were now on some kind of rock formation that must be near the edge of the cliffside, but he managed to keep his eyes closed, confident in Natty's grasp on his arm.

Natty led him out onto the surface of the boulder that gradually started to slope down toward its sharp edge that hung out over the trail far below. After side-stepping down the boulder a few yards, Natty instructed Charlie to sit down with his legs straight out down the slope of the smooth rock and to continue to edge out on the rock until she told him to stop. She was amazed that he was able to keep his eyes closed through it all. "You ain't afraid of heights are you Mr. Burden?" she teased.

Finally they came to the edge of the boulder where Charlie's feet were no longer in contact with the hard surface. "Okay," Natty said sitting next to him with her legs over the edge. "You can open your eyes."

Charlie's stomach rode up as if he were on a roller coaster ride when he found himself literally hanging off the edge of the earth, surrounded on three sides by open space and only a few feet of rock surface between him and a fall off the mountain of what seemed like thousands of feet. The angle of the boulder's surface had felt much less inclined when his eyes were closed. Charlie immediately felt dizzy. He closed his eyes again and lay back slowly on the boulder pressing his palms against the smooth surface of the rock for traction.

"*Oh God,*" he said breathlessly. "I'm going over the edge. I'm dead. I know it."

Natty couldn't help laughing at his reaction. She'd sat on this same spot so many times over so many years since she was a teenager that she'd forgotten how precarious a newcomer might find it.

"Relax Mr. Burden, you're fine," Natty assured him. "Just don't lean too far forward," she added with a mischievous chuckle. "C'mon now, sit up and enjoy the view."

Charlie opened his eyes and slowly sat up, his palms still pressed firmly against the rock on either side of his hips. A few feet away from him, Natty was sitting farther down the slope of the boulder, directly on the edge with her lower legs over the side, her feet dangling in open air. She was watching him with a broad smile, amused at his trepidation.

Her demeanor reassured Charlie that his situation probably wasn't as life-threatening as he first thought.

After a few moments he began to relax and was able to appreciate the incredible exhilaration of the spot. It was more than just the spectacular view. It was the feeling of being suspended in mid-air, like an eagle, with nothing above or below or to the side to confine or limit – as close to flying as one might get while still in contact with the earth.

Charlie smiled weakly at Natty and nodded his head to show that he was all right. Slowly he edged down the rock the last few feet to where Natty was sitting and inched his legs over the side as she had done. With a few deep breaths he calmed himself and began to feel confident about his perch.

"This is a pretty spectacular spot," Charlie said, peeking tentatively over the edge.

"Been coming here since I was twelve," said Natty. "Used to come with my girlfriends all the time. We'd come up here to smoke cigarettes and talk about, you know, girl talk. Then sometimes we'd bring our beer up here – lucky no one ever fell off – and then our pot when we were in high school."

"Ever do anything legal when you were a kid?" said Charlie, grimacing slightly as he peeked over the edge of the boulder.

Natty laughed. "Wasn't as bad as it sounds. Just not a lot for teenagers to do around here." She stared out at the far off hills of Virginia to the south, silent for a few moments as she thought about her teenage years.

"Those girls are all gone away now – only three or four good friends I had anyway – but they all left, like most of the young people do," she continued. "They go off to college – funny how even the poorest hillbilly kids in West Virginia can find a way to go to college if they got a mind to – or they just move on, to Ohio or Pittsburgh or down to Charlotte. Anywhere to get out of the coal fields where there's no future any more."

"But some people stay," said Charlie watching her closely.

Natty looked at Charlie and laughed. "Some people get *trapped*, and then they *can't* leave," she said. Turning back to the view, she added more softly, "and then they grow to love the mountains so much they never *want* to leave."

"So you've been coming up here *alone* all these years, since you were in high school?" Charlie asked.

"Well, I stopped when I got ... when I had Pie. Only came up a few times 'til after Cat was born, when I started running. So, last seven years I been coming up here by myself."

Natty turned back and smiled at Charlie. "You're the first person I been up here with since I told my girlfriends I was pregnant, beginning of my senior year."

"I'm honored," said Charlie.

"You should be." Natty pulled her feet up onto the rock and pushed herself back up the boulder a few yards and sat with her arms around her bent knees. Charlie gratefully followed her, crawling backward like a crab to a spot a few feet farther up the boulder than Natty.

"Now I just come up here 'bout once a week – sometimes more often – to have my quiet time and work on my daydreams."

Charlie was glad she wanted to continue their conversation. He was afraid she was getting up to leave. He loved listening to the soft, slow cadence of her accent, and he had to admit, he wanted to learn more about her.

"What kind of daydreams?" he encouraged her.

Natty laughed. "Aw you know. The typically little hillbilly girl dreams. Kind you have when you're alone a lot in the mountains."

"Tell me," Charlie said.

Natty remained silent. She stretched out her left leg and was bouncing her knee up and down on the rock as she thought. "Well I can't tell you about the big one, the one you start as a little girl and never let go of. Can't tell you about that one, cause ... well, that one's special." Natty laughed and flashed a smile at Charlie, quickly turning away. "But I got others."

Charlie didn't say anything. He didn't want to press her if she didn't really want to talk about her personal thoughts.

"They're mostly about my husband though," she said, bouncing her knee a little faster. "Ain't nothing too exciting about any of em." Natty squinted into the rising sun off to their left and bit her lower lip as she thought about the daydreams she'd been creating about Buck for years.

"Main one, is that we're living in this cute little white house with a nice lawn and some bushes in the front in a nice neighborhood like the ones I sometimes drive through over in Bluefield. It's a nice street with lots of friendly people and kids playing . . . and in my dream, I know everybody on the street of course, and Pie and Cat got lots of friends and then, at the end, I'm standing in the front doorway, and Buck and Pie and Cat are coming up the front walk and they're all smiling and holding hands with Buck in the middle . . . Buck's holding hands with his kids." Natty's voice tailed off at the end. She remained silent for a few seconds, gazing off at the distant mountains.

"Don't sound like much of a fantasy does it?" Natty said, turning her head to look back at Charlie. She twisted her body a little to the side toward Charlie and looked down at the rock. "Thing you got to realize is that, I ain't once in twelve years, ever seen my husband holding hands with either of his kids. It just ain't something Buck would do. He don't pay much attention to 'em."

Charlie recalled the angry eyes of the hard looking man with the black goatee in the white pickup truck, staring at him and Pie up on the bulldozer, and then, leaning across the seat to the open window, telling Natty to get into the truck, when they were walking up the hill from the library.

"How about this one?" Natty interrupted his thoughts. "Buck and I are sitting in a *real* fancy restaurant in a big city someplace and it's nice and cozy and dark and we're all dressed up – he's wearing a beautiful black suit with a white shirt and a shiny, red tie, and I'm wearing ... well it don't matter what I'm wearing – and we're having a bottle of wine, and then Buck pulls out this little box from his pocket and gives it to me, and I open it and it's this beautiful diamond ring, 'cause, well I never bothered to get a ring when we got married, and I'm putting it on and Buck says," Natty looked up and fluttered her eyelids playfully and smiled, "he says, 'I *love* you Nat.'"

Natty turned and leaned back on the rock resting on her elbows. "Pretty sorry dream huh? I do that one a lot when I'm running. Stupid too, 'cause I don't even like rings, never even cared about it when we got married. Still don't." Her knee stopped bouncing on the rock and she let out a sigh.

When she leaned back, Charlie couldn't help noticing the curve of her breasts under the jersey pulled tight by her high, broad shoulders. Her breasts were round and larger than they normally seemed hidden under her over-sized shirts and sweaters. As she lay on the rocks with her thin, smooth legs still shiny with a light coating of perspiration from their run, Charlie thought she looked like both an extremely sexy woman and a little girl at the same time. He felt a deep stirring and had an urge to reach over and pull her to him. He took a deep breath and was relieved when Natty started speaking again.

"Reason it's a daydream, case you're trying to figure it out, is that Buck ain't once since we been married, told me that he loves me. Oh he let it slip out a couple a times when we were goin' at it in the back of his daddy's Blazer when I was in high school. Course he was usually drunk and it was right before he … well you know…" She flashed a quick smile at Charlie. "… got carried away by the moment." Natty sat up and rested on her straight arms braced out behind her. "But, never after I told him I was pregnant."

She bounced both knees for a moment and looked down at her legs stretched out in front of her before continuing in a low voice, almost to herself. "Ain't a big deal, but a woman likes to hear it once in a while."

Charlie didn't know what to say. He hadn't expected Natty to share such intimate thoughts but he was glad she did and now he didn't want her to feel embarrassed. "So why did you ever marry Buck?" he asked, and then instantly regretted how insulting it sounded.

Natty wasn't insulted. She laughed and turned to Charlie with a broad smile. "*Why? God!* Why'd I marry *Buck?*" she repeated like it was the dumb question of the day. "Cause I'd been in love with Buck ever since I was in the fourth grade and all I ever *dreamed* about for most of my life was marrying Buck Oakes. *God, why'd I marry Buck?*" she repeated, gazing up at the clouds overhead. "Cause that was the best day of my whole *life*, is why."

Natty pulled her feet up in front of her and wrapped her arms around her knees, gazing out at the distance with a smile on her face as she recalled her first memories of Buck.

"First time mama ever brought me into Old Red Bone, I was eight years old, and while she was runnin' errands and stuff, I'd go down the hill to the ball fields. Had an old swing set back then right next to the baseball field and I'd sit there on the swings and watch the other kids playin' and, first time I saw Buck, well, my heart was gone forever. He was a couple of years older than me and later I found out he was in the sixth grade."

Natty rocked back and forth on her seat and talked a little faster now that she was on a subject she could still get excited about.

"He was taller than the other kids and real skinny, and had this mop of jet black curly hair, and those dark eyes, and he was the handsomest boy I'd ever, *ever* seen. I can still remember what he was wearing that day – black Levi's, rolled up at the bottom, white T-shirt, and some old black high-top sneakers." Natty paused as though she was picturing him in his mind.

"Buck was always laughing and talking and rankin' on everybody, and always in charge. He was the best player at everything and always seemed to be having more fun than anybody else. I could sit there for an hour on that swing just watching him playing baseball or sometimes basketball at this decrepit old hoop used to be down there, or just hanging around with his pals." She chuckled. "I was so small and plain looking, I just blended into the scenery and nobody ever noticed me."

Natty stopped rocking, and was silent for a few moments with a squint on her face as if she was looking into the past. "One day Buck and his friends are playing baseball, and these three older kids – seemed like they was in middle school I think 'cause they were bigger than Buck and his group – well they come walkin' by lookin' for trouble and they grab this kid's baseball glove and wouldn't give it back, you know, throwing it around playing keep-away with it, and then pushing this smaller boy down when he tried to get it back. Well, of course, I'm watching Buck, and he's just standing still out at the pitcher's circle there, taking it all in, then all of a sudden he throws his glove down and runs in at the kids as fast as he can and he goes after the biggest of the three and without saying anything, he just punches him in the face real hard and then he punches him again and again so fast you couldn't hardly see his hands move, and the boy falls down to the ground with blood all over his face. Then Buck goes after one of the other two boys and he gave him a real good beating too and he's kneeling on the ground spitting out blood, and Buck gets off him looking for the third kid who takes off running across the field toward the road and Buck goes running after him. The third boy was a real fast runner but not as fast as Buck and he finally catches him and tackles him in the middle of South County Road, and then beats him up too, real bad, right there in the middle of the road."

The smile was gone from Natty's face as well as the joy in her voice. "Probably should have seen the anger in him that day," she said softly. "All I saw was the hero protecting his friend. My hero."

Natty shifted her weight on the hard rock, turning directly toward Charlie and pulling her feet under her into the Indian sitting position. When she looked up, with the morning sun fully illuminating her face and her hair pulled back through the *Spider-Man* cap, Charlie noticed for the first time, the very subtle, but unmistakable, thin white scar running just over her left eyebrow. With the sunlight at just the right angle, the scar was clearly visible, which made Charlie realize that most of the times he'd seen her, Natty always seemed to have a shock of hair dropping down over the left side of her forehead. Then he noticed an even fainter scar just over her lip, barely visible.

"So I adored Buck all through school and he never even knew I was alive." Natty dropped her head slightly, shading her face with the brim of the cap as if she knew the sunlight exposed her. "Even in high school, 'cause I was two years behind him and I was just a scrawny little thing, and well, he had plenty of girl friends of course. And I'd write his name all over my book covers and I'd watch him all the time in the hallways and in the cafeteria and out in the playground, and then I'd go to all the football games and sit there and pretend that I was Buck

Oakes's girlfriend and I'd make believe that we were going to meet up after the game and that whenever he looked up into the stands, he was looking for me, even though . . ." Her voice fell away, then she shook her head, and laughed. "Wasn't as pathetic as it sounds. I wasn't nuts or anything," she said looking up with crossed eyeballs and her tongue sticking out the side of her mouth, making Charlie laugh. She smiled. "I was just a kid in love."

Charlie sat watching her, transfixed by her soft, wide mouth as she talked and smiled, and by the sharp outline of her jaw and delicately pointed chin, feeling a pang of emptiness inside and growing more and more envious of Buck Oakes with every word. *Hank was so right that night he told him about Buck Oakes . . . 'the luckiest man in McDowell County, but he don't know any of it,' Hank had said.*

"So what happened? How did you finally get together?" Charlie asked, not wanting Natty to quit talking.

The happy glow returned to Natty's face and to her voice as she recalled the night when she and Buck finally came together.

"What *happened* was... the *luckiest* day of my *life*, is what happened. Day before Thanksgiving, my junior year in high school. My girlfriend and I are out late, driving around drinking beer and talking, like we used to do a lot, and we end up out at the *Roadhouse* parking lot. Couldn't go inside 'cause we were only seventeen, but we used to hang out there in the parking lot sometimes. Well anyway, across the street from the bar there's this little store that was also the bus station for Red Bone. So about eleven o'clock that night, I take a walk over there to get some cigarettes, and I walk inside the door and my heart practically comes to a stop 'cause there's Buck Oakes sitting there in the little tiny bus station waiting room. Buck was in his first year up at W.V.U. on a football scholarship, but there he is, sitting there all by himself with this big suitcase and a big brown duffel bag on the floor next to him. And he's looking like a pile of last week's dog shit – hair all messy, ain't shaved for a couple of days, or slept either it looks like – with this sad, scared look in his eyes."

Natty turned away and blinked her eyes rapidly to prevent the tears she felt coming on. She smiled and laughed briefly at her own sensitivity as she rubbed her eyes with the sleeve of her jersey. "I could tell something was up 'cause all them bags on the floor and the look on Buck's face says he wasn't just home from Morgantown for the holiday. So, normally I'd a swallowed my tongue and run out of there, but that night I'm feelin' a foot taller from the beer and all, and there's Buck sitting there looking . . . looking real ordinary, you know, so . . . I walk up to where he's sitting there just staring at the floor, and I says *'hey Buck'* – first words I ever said to him – *'hey Buck, how ya doin'* ? Remember me from school? *I'm Natty DeWitt.'* And Buck looks up at me real slow and painful like." Natty stuck her chin out, pursed her lips and closed her eyes to slits as she imitated Buck's long face, making Charlie smile, "and he squints at me for a few seconds with those bloodshot eyes. Then the first words Buck ever says to me, he says, *'oh yeah ... little Miss no - tits.'"* Charlie and Natty both laughed.

"So anyway, Buck and I get talkin' and he tells me that they threw him off the football team 'cause he hurt his knee or something and couldn't play, and he's all done with school, 'cause he never went to any classes anyway or got any books or anything and he shouldn't of gone there in the first place." Natty sighed and a pained look came over her face. "God, he seemed so much different from when he left, like so much of the fun had been sucked out of him.

"And the reason he's just sitting there is because he's afraid to call his daddy to come and pick him up 'cause Big Frank don't know anything about him getting' tossed from the football team or leaving school, and he's gonna have one horrendous shit fit when he finds out. So I says to Buck, 'well I got some beer in the car if you want to drive around a little, and then *I* can take you home,' and Buck perks up a *lot* and says '*yeah, sure*, we could do that,' cause I'm sure that driving around drinking beer with *little Miss no-tits* still sounded a hell of a lot better than sitting there waiting for a major league ass whuppin' from his old man." Charlie laughed, but Natty just smiled thinly.

"So I run back over to the *Roadhouse* and I tell my girl friend that I *got* to take her car and the beer and she's going to have to find a ride home from somebody and *don't argue with me,* 'cause this is like the biggest break I *ever* got in life you know . . ." Natty started laughing as she told the story making Charlie laugh along with her. ". . . and I don't even have a license . . . *hell* I never even drove a *car* before. But I get it going and I drive over and pick up Buck and my heart's beatin' like a damn drum and I'm nervous and grinding the gears all over the place and driving down the middle of the road with the headlights off 'cause I don't know where the switch is, but I'm acting real cool you know, like it's my car and everything, and Buck's laughing and drinking beer and yelling about how I'm the worst driver he's ever seen and how I'm trying my best to kill him and . . ."

The smile faded from Natty's face as she picked absentmindedly at some pieces of rubber that were coming off one of her running shoes. "Anyway, we end up at this spot way back in the woods off Mountain Road – place we used to go to a lot after that – and well, one thing led to another and then . . ." Natty's voice tailed off to almost a whisper as she recollected the long ago night. "We're in the back seat, and the moment came, you know, to shit or get off the pot so to speak, and I didn't even hesitate, even though I was scared to death 'cause I never done *anything* like that before. *Hell,* I never even *kissed* a boy before that night, but I went ahead 'cause I *knew* if I didn't, I'd *never* see Buck Oakes again after that night – knew that for a fact, and it was true." Natty turned away and gazed out at the distance before speaking again in a soft voice, almost to herself. "So I'm glad I did. Worked out all right. Everything worked out fine."

After a long pause, Natty turned back toward Charlie. "Buck was right, his daddy was rip-shit. Big Frank stayed mad at Buck for a long time, for screwing everything up and embarrassing him and disappointing him about football and college. See, Buck's brothers were good athletes too but they never amounted to anything and Big Frank, he always bragged that Buck would go to Notre Dame, so then when he went to West Virginia University he was supposed to be a real . . . well anyway, he stayed pissed at Buck for a long time."

She leaned back with a far-off look in her eye as if she was trying to remember something from the past. "I always figured that had a lot to do with why Buck, uh . . . that he made Buck . . ." Natty smiled at Charlie. "Well, nothing. It don't mean nothing now," she said quickly, glancing down at her watch. "Getting late. I got to get going," she said getting to her feet quickly.

Charlie did the same. She was right. It was getting late and they'd been too long on the rock, even though he hated to see it come to an end. Charlie thought he could listen to Natty talk forever. He walked the few steps down closer to the edge of the boulder to enjoy one last look over the side.

"*Damn* Mr. Burden, I . . ."

Charlie looked back at her sharply. "Who?"

"Okay," she started again. "*Damn* Mr. *Charlie*, I brought you up here to see the view and then I go and talk your ear off like you're my therapist or something. I didn't mean to . . ."

Charlie laughed as he started walking back up the rock. "It's okay. It was interesting. I'm interested in . . ." He caught himself and stopped.

Natty looked back at him quickly with a sparkle in her eye. "You're interested in *me*? Is that what you were going to say?" she said teasingly. Charlie just smiled briefly and looked down at the rock to check his footing as they made their way back to the trees.

In the middle of the small grotto formed by the tall pines, Natty stopped and turned back to Charlie. "Look," she said pointing up to the shafts of morning sunlight that were penetrating the thick branches and illuminating the higher reaches of the trees. "It's just like a church in the morning, with the light coming through the stain glass windows."

"Wow," said Charlie softly, looking up at the beams of light. "It's beautiful."

When he looked back down, Natty was facing him about ten feet away across the pine needle covered ground with her feet spread slightly apart in a purposeful stance. The light was dim inside the lower section of the trees but Charlie could see that she had an anxious look on her face and she was twisting her fingers together in front of her

"What is it . . . *Mrs. Oakes?* he added, trying to ease her tension.

She smiled briefly, then squinted in thought as she searched for the right words. Finally she just shrugged her shoulders and let out a sigh. "Charlie, there's something I need to know," she said quietly. "Something I need to get out of the way, 'cause I don't *know* much about this stuff . . . ain't met many men in my life, as you probably already figured out," she said with a small chuckle. "But I need to ask you something personal, which I figure is all right since I just told *you* all about the first time I ever got laid and a whole bunch of other intimate stuff." They both laughed.

"Sure," said Charlie, leaning lightly against the base of a thin hickory tree, his arms crossed at his chest. "You can ask me anything." After a slight pause he added, "what *is* it Natty?"

Natty took a step closer to him and stopped. She flashed a quick, embarrassed smile and took a deep breath. "Charlie . . . is there anything, uhm, happening here?" She waggled her index finger back and forth between them.

"You mean . . ."

Natty interrupted him. "Yeah," she said earnestly, "between us," she added more softly.

Charlie smiled and chuckled lightly. "Natty, come on. I'm old enough to be your father," he said defensively.

She eyed him warily. "Hell, around here, man *your* age could about be my *grandpa*, but that ain't what I asked you."

Charlie laughed but he immediately regretted his shallow reply. It was obvious that Natty was serious and that it wasn't an easy subject for her. He'd given her the defensive *spin* when she deserved an honest answer.

But what should he tell her? Should he tell her that she was the most alluring, captivating, intriguing woman he'd met in years? As well as the kindest, most unpretentious and emotionally honest. Should he tell her that he'd never known a woman who could make him laugh so easily, or make him smile to himself at the thought of her, even when she wasn't around.

"I don't mean to embarrass you Charlie," Natty said, misinterpreting his silence and the pensive look on Charlie's face. "Maybe I'm way off base here . . ."

"No, no," said Charlie. "It isn't . . ."

"But, you've been real special to Pie – *God*, that boy loves you ..."

Should he tell her that he loves her small delicate face and her beautiful eyes and her smile, and tell her how much he wanted to put his palm against her cheek and touch her soft, wide lips lightly with the end of his thumb.

". . . and there ain't no man ever been as kind to me as you have . . . letting me have your car for that week there, and helping us with Angel Mountain, and now getting the library fixed and, you know . . ." She shrugged her shoulders. "Just talking to me like you do."

And how much he enjoyed sitting and listening to her talk, and watching her run, and seeing her coach her soccer team, and how his heart beat faster whenever he saw her . . . and that he longed to run his hands across her high shoulders and down her thin arms and around her small waist.

"Course, I never met anyone from New York before, so I'm thinking maybe it's all just *professional courtesy,* 'cause probably that's why you're down here, to be nice to people and . . ."

Should he warn her that at that moment he was just two steps and a mad impulse away from reaching out for her and pulling her against him and never letting her go?

"But then, sometimes, like that day you came back from New York, and I watched you, down on the soccer field, spinning Pie around and giving him that nice hug, and then you saw me, and the *way* you looked up the hill at me, it seemed like, you know, maybe you were thinkin' about something. And then that night we sat in front of the store and talked about Angel Mountain . . ." Natty became silent, aware that she sounded like she was babbling. She looked up at

Charlie. ". . . and you said my name," she added meekly. Natty had a pained look on her face as she suddenly felt as if she was back in school and had just given a dumb answer and now she was waiting for the teacher to embarrass her.

Charlie refocused his eyes on Natty's face and smiled thinly, trying to mask his own nervousness. "Natty, since that morning in the store . . ." He hesitated in thought, and then started again. "Since that morning, I've been thinking about you every minute of every day," he said softly.

Natty looked up at him, squinting in surprise. *"What?"* she blurted.

Charlie laughed. "I said . . ."

"No, no, I'm sorry Charlie," Natty said. "I heard you. I just . . . I guess I wasn't ready to hear you say *that.*" Natty bit her lower lip trying not to smile. Then she turned away, and looked around at the trees and then up at the shafts of sunlight, blinking her eyes rapidly. She laughed with embarrassment. *"Damn Charlie,"* she whispered, "nobody's *ever* said something like that to me before." Natty folded her arms together in front of her and started moving around in small circles. Her shoulders were hunched up as if she was getting cold.

Charlie watched her with concern but didn't know what to say next. He was nervous. His heart was beating faster. He hadn't said anything affectionate to a woman other than Ellen since he was in college, and it felt very strange, almost dangerous. He needed for the situation to be clear.

"Listen Natty, I . . ." *Christ, no excuses, no bullshit, just honesty, just be honest.* "I, uh . . . in twenty-six years of marriage I never even *thought* about another woman, until I met you." Natty was standing sideways to him next to a tree about six feet away with her head turned slightly toward him, listening. She seemed to be taking deep breaths to calm herself. "And now I hardly think about anything else," he added.

Natty smiled briefly and then shut her eyes tightly as if she was in pain. She looked a little pale to Charlie.

"Are you all right Natty?" Charlie asked.

She smiled thinly and nodded several times quickly with her eyes still closed.

"I love my wife Nat," Charlie pressed on. "She's a wonderful woman." He paused in thought about the new house in Mamaroneck, the country club, about Rafael Escobar. "But . . .well, we have had some problems the last few years that I, uhm . . . I don't know how they're going to work out."

Charlie looked back through the trees, out toward the distant mountains as he thought out loud. "We've changed a lot, both Ellen and I. Since the kids grew up. Our lives changed, without the kids around. You know, you invest so much of yourself in your children – we both did – then, all of a sudden, they're gone." Charlie paused in thought. "And, things change. Your outlook on life and your career changes. It's why I came down here . . . to get away from what my job had turned into. To get away from . . . well, a lot of things. And to *do* something, something constructive. I needed to build something . . . to be an engineer again." Charlie looked down at his feet. "So, I'm not sure what all that means, except that

I'm not as certain about things as I used to be, but . . . I'm still married and I've never done anything I couldn't talk to my wife about."

"*Oooh, Charlie,*" Natty groaned, startling him out of his monologue.

Charlie looked over quickly to see Natty bent forward slightly with her eyes closed, her hands clasped in front of her as her stomach heaved with a silent wretch.

"Natty, what's the matter?" he asked. Two quick strides brought him in front of her just as she doubled over and expelled a violent stream of orange colored vomit, scoring a direct hit on one of Charlie's new Asics running shoes. He hopped back quickly but the damage was done.

Natty bobbed up briefly before leaning forward again quickly with a second, smaller eruption. She stayed leaning forward with her hands on her knees, spitting out the residue of her *Special-K* and orange juice breakfast, breathing deeply and then wiping her mouth with the sleeve of her gray jersey.

Charlie disregarded the mess on his left shoe and leaned over to try and see into Natty's face. "Natty, Natty you okay? What happened?" he asked, resisting the impulse to put his hand on her back and feeling helpless as she remained bent over, breathing deeply and swallowing hard. After a few moments, she raised one hand to him, indicating that she was all right. She wiped her mouth again with the bottom of her jersey and then slowly straightened up.

Natty took a deep breath and wiped her mouth again with her sleeve. She looked at Charlie and smiled weakly. "So, I guess you won't be trying to kiss me this morning," she said. They both laughed.

"Oh *shit* Charlie," Natty said pointing downward and laughing harder. "Look at your shoe. God, what a mess. I'm sorry Charlie."

Charlie looked down at his vomit covered shoe with a tight grin. "It's okay, really." He shook his foot and tapped it against a tree, without much success. He looked back at Natty with concern. Her face was still a little pale. "Are you all right?"

"Yeah, I'm okay," she said. "I'm fine. C'mon, let's go," she added, motioning toward the path down to the running trail. "I'm going to be late for work."

They clambered down the path through the trees back to where they'd left the running trail and started walking. They walked along together in silence for only a few yards before Natty looked at her watch again and started into a slow jog. She didn't want to be late for school but she also felt embarrassed and confused and wanted to avoid any more conversation for the time being. After just a minute at warm-up speed, she accelerated up to her normal running pace. Charlie followed her lead, getting up to speed a little more slowly and was soon thirty yards behind her. They had a run of about a mile to the top of Oakes Hollow where Natty would leave the trail.

Running out in front, Natty could feel Charlie's eyes on her and for the first time she felt self conscious while running with him. Before, they'd just been acquaintances, or maybe even friends, but now, after everything that was said up on the rock and in the grotto, that had all changed. Now they were more than friends, even though nothing but words had crossed between them. *Goddamit! What was wrong with her? Taking him up to the boulder and telling him all that stuff, and then, coming right out and asking him . . . Shit! How much more trouble did she need in life? Then, the first time a man ever says something nice to her, she pukes on his foot!* Natty shook her head in disgust, and ran a little harder.

When the trail entered the woods, Natty slowed down abruptly and walked a few yards to catch her breath. She recalled that this was the spot they'd seen the deer crossing the trail the first time Charlie had run with her. She came to a stop and turned around to wait for Charlie, who had fallen back some distance.

Natty kept thinking about what Charlie had said up in the trees. She'd asked him a very personal question and he'd given her an answer – a beautiful, honest answer that scared her to death – an answer that she knew she would replay in her mind for the rest of her life. It wasn't fair to Charlie to just throw up on his shoe and run off without her answering the same question. If she could.

Charlie slowed down to a walk as he reached the edge of the woods and saw Natty waiting for him. He walked very slowly toward her while he caught his breath and wiped the sweat from his face. She was standing with her arms crossed on her chest, an embarrassed smile on her face as she watched him approach. He stopped about ten feet away from her.

"You okay?" Charlie asked softly. The sound of his voice seemed to be amplified by the acoustics of the closed-in woods.

"Yeah, I'm fine," said Natty sheepishly, looking down at Charlie's fouled running shoe. "Sorry about your shoe."

Charlie just nodded that it was okay, without saying anything.

After another few moments of silent thought, Natty spoke again. "Got sick 'cause I got scared. Listening to you talking and saying the words, well, that was different from, you know, daydreaming and sitting on the rock thinking foolish *girl things.*" Natty looked down at the ground and moved a small rock around with the toe of her shoe. "All of a sudden it wasn't pretend any more and it surprised me and scared me, 'cause, you know . . ." She looked up at Charlie with a pained look on her face. "For so long – long as I can remember – the only man I ever had thoughts about was Buck." She turned away and looked back down the trail toward the sunlight. Almost to herself, she said, "and Buck's the only man ever showed some interest in me, finally, 'cept maybe for a few drunks out at the *Roadhouse* once in a while. Then you come down here and next thing you know you're telling me that you . . . well, you know, what you said up there."

"Ah, I was just making all that up," Charlie with a grin.

Natty chuckled and smiled back at him. "Yeah, thanks," she said.

After a few moments of awkward silence, Natty began again. "Listen, Charlie," she started apologetically. "I need to . . . I want you to understand what – "

"Natty, you don't need to explain anything," Charlie interrupted. "We can just leave it like it is for now and – "

"No. No, Charlie," Natty said shaking her head, holding up her palms to him. "This is important to me . . . for you to understand this."

Charlie nodded his acquiescence and walked over to the edge of the trail and sat on the edge of a wide old stump that had been cut about three feet from the ground as the big trees normally were. The darkness of the stump and the rotting at the center told Charlie that the tree had been taken many years earlier and the smoothness of the cut indicated a two man crosscut saw instead of the modern chainsaw that would leave a series of irregular slashes.

Natty sat down on a wide stump next to her and rested her elbows on her knees. "Charlie, what I said up there, on the rock, about marrying Buck and everything working out all right, everything being fine. Well, that ain't exactly true. It's a little different then that. Actually, it's pretty much all bullshit. Fact is, been a pretty sorry twelve years, except for the kids. Wouldn't trade them for anything. But, living with Buck, well, that ain't been easy." Natty stared at her hands in front of her as she thought about her twelve year marriage to Buck Oakes and debated in her mind how much of it Charlie Burden needed or even wanted to hear.

Should she tell him about the maddening silence, and the disinterest, and the surliness and how Buck had generally ignored her and the kids for most of that time? About the mean, drunken late nights and, once in a while, the slaps and the pushes . . . and then, a few times – on the special occasions when Buck came home blind drunk and angry at the world, with still enough energy – the beatings, like the one two years ago – the day the helicopters came – when she first saw Charlie Burden and Duncan McCord. Or about the six months that Buck moved out and lived with the woman in Northfork right after Cat was born, and she had to get the welfare checks to live on. Charlie would have a tough time understanding all that, being an outsider. No, Charlie didn't need to hear any of that. That was between her and Buck.

So were the tears. Buck's tears, which nobody else ever saw. When he'd bury his head against her breast and let go the anguish of one more failure in life, one more disappointment heaped upon the pile of disappointments that had defined his adult life after so much unbridled success in his youth. The tears of humiliation and shame, for his mistakes and his shortcomings that Big Frank or the collection agencies or the court system or his own memory never seemed willing to let go of. Only Natty shared those moments with him – usually he was drunk, except for the time after he got out of the hospital and after his sentencing, the night before he had to report to the county correctional facility for the six months he got for beating her and for resisting arrest by Wayne Lester . . . that night he hadn't needed any liquor to allow the tears to come – and while it was only a few times, and Buck would probably deny they ever happened, these were the only moments of hope and warmth and real need they'd shared in their marriage and she held onto them tightly. Charlie Burden didn't need to hear any of that stuff either. She didn't want him to pity her or Buck.

Natty put her palms down on the stump next to her hips and straightened her arms pushing her shoulders up. She bounced her knees up and down restlessly on the balls of her feet. Charlie remained silent, watching her as she seemed to struggle with a difficult thought.

"Charlie, I'm not ready to give up on Buck just yet," she said softly. "Been working at this for twelve years now, trying to make a home, make a marriage." She looked over at Charlie with a thin, embarrassed smile. "Trying to get Buck to love me, love his kids.

"Thing is, Buck's just had one bad time after another. Mostly his own fault sure, but not all of it. Not all of it." Natty paused for a moment before adding a little more softly, "I was part of it too. Part of his bad breaks."

Charlie started to protest but decided to remain silent. This was Natty's turn to talk.

"The college football thing and Big Frank's disappointment, well that was the start of it. Then he comes home and next thing you know, he knocks up this dumb little hillbilly high school girl and finds himself getting married when he don't want to and shouldn't have to, and not too long after that, having a baby that he don't want. Then, to top it off, he's got a retarded baby with a funny lookin' head, which was something he just couldn't ever deal with."

Natty reached down and picked up a long twig from the ground and spun it absentmindedly in her fingers. "Buck was just twenty years old then. Still a kid himself practically. Wasn't fair to him. Wasn't the way it should have been.

"And then, it was one thing after another." Natty shook her head ruefully as she recalled the missteps and failures in her husband's attempts to make a living in the terminally depressed economy of McDowell County in the 1990's. She told Charlie about the Oakes brothers' ill-fated hunting lodge, and the worm farm that ended with thousands of dollars worth of dead worms, Buck's brief misguided career selling insurance for the Loftus Agency in Welch before being fired by the insufferable Kyle Loftus, and then, most painfully, the expensive foray into long-haul trucking that would continue to drain their finances for many years into the future. She omitted the dozen or so, short-term jobs, some that ended badly due to Buck's drinking or volatile personality, or for reasons she never even knew.

Natty stood up, threw away the twig and wiped her hands on the sides of her shorts. She smiled down at Charlie. "So what I'm trying to say here Charlie, and not doing too good a job is . . . that I understand what you were saying up there on the rock, about not knowing how things are going to work out." Then she added, more tentatively, "how your marriage is going to work out. 'Cause I don't know either. But right now, I can't give up on Buck 'cause I've been loving him for too long, and I know there's a chance for him, for us to be a family, you know . . . like you and your wife had for so long. I know Buck and I know there's a good man in him and a good father, if . . . if he can just get a break, just find a job and get some of his self respect back. That's all he needs, just . . ." Then she was out of words. "I'm really late Charlie. Got to go." She started walking down the path. Charlie got up from the stump and fell in next to her. They walked in silence the last thirty yards to where Natty would leave the trail at the top of Oakes Hollow.

At the break in the bushes that Natty would slide through, they both stopped. Natty turned toward Charlie who continued a few steps farther down the trail.

"Charlie," said Natty softly, "thanks for what you said up there. That felt real nice."

Charlie smiled and just nodded. It seemed like everything to be said had already been said this morning. He started backing away from her, to get started on his run back up to Old Red Bone. "Need to get going."

"Okay. I'll see you Thursday, at the Planning Board," Natty said, watching him.

Charlie turned to start his run, and then stopped. He thought for a moment and then turned to see if Natty was still there. She smiled at him and raised her eyebrows in question. Charlie took a couple of steps back to her.

"Listen, does Buck have any experience cutting wood? Big trees, commercial work."

Natty shook her head in the affirmative. "Oh God yes. He's done plenty of wood cutting. Most of it illegal. For the timber pirates, you know, but he's cut down plenty of big trees."

"Okay," said Charlie putting his hand to his mouth thinking. "We just hired a lumber contractor to cut the right of way through to the power grid connection. Big job. Several miles through really rugged terrain. About a three or four month job, using the big helicopters to take the lumber out. They're going to be hiring about thirty experienced woodcutters next week some time. I'll give them Buck's name so he won't have to go through the line. They figure there'll be a couple of hundred guys showing up for the jobs. It's good pay. I know 'cause they're really screwing us on the contract," Charlie said with a laugh. He started backing away down the trail. "Buck will have to join the union though. Everything is union work. That's all right though. He'll get some good benefits. I'll let you know what he has to do."

"Yeah, okay . . . *great*," said Natty excitedly as Charlie turned and began to jog. He waved to her over his shoulder. Natty watched him go. "Thank you Charlie," she said softly, to herself. "Again."

Chapter 19

Charlie spent most of the day at his desk revising the *Request For Variance* they would be presenting to the Planning Board that evening. He paid particular attention to the redesign of the higher containment levee and the specifications and architecture of the dike's steel framing. And once again he went over the recalculation of the size of the cooling pond, still amazed at how a seventy-six year old, retired high school principal, could sit down in the middle of a field with just a ballpoint pen and reveal a critical in-putting error in a complex computer calculation.

Late in the afternoon, the Pie Man came in. From his office, Charlie heard the two beeps of the alarm system that announced that the main door had been opened. He glanced at the clock and guessed it was the boy before he heard his trademark greeting to whoever might be working in the main room. "*Hello*, I am the Pie Man," the boy announced as he came through the door. He would go around the room exchanging high-fives with everyone present before looking up at the white in-or-out board on the wall to see where Charlie's magnet was. Pointing up at the board, he announced, "I go see Chowly."

In his office the ritual was repeated. "Hello *Chowly*," the boy said as he burst through the door with a jump stop. "I am the Pie Man." He would inevitably have on his happy face when he first saw his good friend.

Charlie found it impossible not to laugh when Pie made his entrance. The boy was irrepressible, always able to lift Charlie's spirits no matter what kind of mood he was in. They exchanged high fives. "Hey, Pie Man," Charlie said. "What's going on?" He reached out and pushed the boy's backward Yankees cap down over his eyes, making him giggle as always.

"Chowly, we win anothah thowka game yethtoday! We win the game thix owa seven to zewo, I fowaget."

"Wow, that's great Pie," said Charlie, offering another high-five. "Score any goals?"

"Pie Man not thcowa any goal, but Emma thcowa fowa owa five owa thix. Loth of goal, I fowaget," the boy said holding up a hand with his fingers spread out.

"I'm glad you came Pie Man," said Charlie getting up from behind his desk. "Got a surprise for you."

The boy's mouth dropped open and his eyes grew wide with excitement at the word *surprise*. He followed Charlie to a corner of the office where a low makeshift desk of a three-foot section of counter top had been set up on cinder blocks. In front of the small desk was a short stool, the perfect height for the boy. On the desk was an older model Compaq *Presario* with a monitor, keyboard and mouse. The system had belonged to a contractor who had abandoned it months ago when their work was finished. On the monitor, over the screen, the words "The Pie Man" had been applied printed on transparent tape.

"C'mon sit down," Charlie said as he reached around to the back of the computer and turned it on. "This is yours."

"Wooo, Chowly," the boy said reverently, as he ran his fingertips across the lettering of his name. "Look, my name ith on the compootah, Chowly."

One of the younger construction workers had installed a package of games on the computer that Pie couldn't wait to start exploring. He was adept enough by now at using a computer that Charlie left him alone to explore his incredible new gift. Working at his own desk, Charlie would glance over at the boy periodically and watch him maneuver the mouse deftly in the destruction of various space invaders. He rocked back and forth on the stool in rhythmic concentration on the game while he continually talked to himself in a low mumbling kind of chant. Charlie couldn't make out most of what he was saying, but every few minutes he could just barely hear the boy repeat several times, "Chowly, my fwend, Chowly, my fwend."

After an hour, satisfied that the revised site plan was in order, Charlie turned off his own computer for the day. He delivered the plan to the outer office to have copies made, then returned to his office and pulled a chair up next to the boy.

"Okay Pie Man," he said. "That's enough games for today. Time to start becoming an engineer." He clicked on the icon for the new math tutorial program. Charlie explained to Pie what the program was all about and got him started on an easy level and let him explore his way through the easy-to-use curriculum. He told Pie that in order to use the computer when he came in, Pie would have to spend a half-hour each day working at the math program before he played any games or used the Internet.

"Okay, Chowly," the boy conceded after a moment of thought. "I would like to be an engineewa. Ith a deal." They sealed it with a high five. Pie worked at the computer for a while and then, after exchanging a high-five with Charlie, left for home.

Pie's visit reminded Charlie that he would be seeing Natty that night at the Planning Board meeting. He hadn't seen her since their eventful run on Monday morning. He'd resisted the urge to go out early and run with her again and enjoy those glorious twenty minutes of running time along the side of the mountain when he had her so completely to himself. *No, that was a situation to avoid. He'd known that since that first time Natty had shown him the trail, but then he had violated his own rule. Was it just an excuse – the whole library roof repair plan – to run with her one more time? Whatever the reason, he'd given in, and look what happened!*

Thinking of Natty reminded Charlie about Buck and the phone call he needed to make. He went to his desk and thumbed through the large Rolodex until he found the card for the timbering contractor who had won the bid to cut the right-of-way through the forest to the power grid.

Charlie had met Jack Garvey, owner of Garvey Lumber, several times in the course of the bidding and negotiation of the timber contract. He reached him on his cell phone in his truck. After the appropriate amount of small talk, Charlie got to the point.

"Jack, I need a favor."

"Sure, Charlie, if it's something I can do, you got it," said Garvey, ever mindful of the future business that the head boss of the construction project might be able to steer his way.

"It's about your woodcutters for the project. I got a guy, experienced tree cutter they tell me, could really use one of those jobs you're going to be hiring for," said Charlie.

"Well, you know Charlie, since we got the contract, experienced guys have been breaking the door down. McDowell County guys too, good woodcutters. Lot of 'em, I worked with before. So I'm about filled up, got a full crew without having to even go looking for 'em, you know."

"You can always use one more Jack," said Charlie, recognizing the initial *hardship plea* of the experienced businessman negotiating the high end of a favor. "It'd be a personal favor to me."

"Yeah, well for you Charlie, I could probably put one more on, as a favor to you . . . but he's got to be a good woodcutter, team player, 'cause that's going to be serious work out there. Real rugged terrain, and I don't want nobody getting killed. So, who's your guy? Got a name for me?"

"Yeah, fellow's name is Buck Oakes. Lives in Red Bone."

There was silence on the phone. Charlie could hear the sound of Garvey's truck motoring down the road, and then Garvey clearing his throat.

Charlie spoke again to break the silence. "Supposed to have some woodcutting experience. Strong guy too."

Finally, Garvey's voice came back over the phone. "Yeah, Buck's cut some wood. He can cut wood," said Garvey sounding less than enthusiastic.

"So you know Buck Oakes?" asked Charlie.

"Sure, I know Buck." Garvey went silent for a few more seconds as if he was trying to think of a way out of this favor. "Listen, Charlie . . ."

"Jack," Charlie interrupted. "I know Buck's got some problems. I don't need to hear all that. I'm trying to give him a break. If it doesn't work out, it doesn't work out. If he causes any problems, you fire him, no questions asked. I'll take care of the union."

"Okay, Charlie. Okay. We'll give it a try, but Buck's a hothead you know, and a boozer. He worked for me once on small job, clearing a lot for a house. Came back from a lunch of boilermakers and beat up one of my foremen and wrecked a couple of saws on his way out. Bad tempered guy. Hard to figure out. What's your connection with him anyway?"

"I, uh, he's my landlady's brother. Trying to do her a favor. I know he's a handful but I'd like you to take him on."

"Yeah, okay Charlie, I see." Garvey paused a few seconds before speaking again, a little more softly. "You know Buck beat the shit out of his wife couple years ago, real bad. Came home drunk as a skunk one night and beat the daylights out of her . . . so bad she was in the hospital for a while. Broken jaw, and her eye and her mouth all closed up with stitches."

Charlie had to take a deep breath to stop the nausea that was overcoming him. He thought he might drop the phone. *Why hadn't she said anything about it in all that talk about Buck? Why was she even still living with him?*

"Poor kid's face was black and blue for months . . ."

Oh Christ! Those scars over her eye and over her mouth, and she's sitting there talking about how much she loves him . . .

". . . couldn't eat or even talk for a long time. Real nice girl too. Took care of my grandma for a while before she passed on, few years back."

Charlie closed his eyes and fought back the anger that tightened his neck muscles as he thought about the beautiful little woman, his good friend, getting pummeled by the ignorant brute who had glared at him from the white pickup.

"Yeah, yeah I heard about all that," Charlie lied in a soft, cracking voice.

"Buck did six months in the lockup for that one, plus resisting arrest."

Charlie just listened to the hum of Jack Garvey's truck over the phone and took deep breaths to calm himself. *Why was he doing this? Trying to get this man a job, a man he now hated without even knowing him.*

"Alright Charlie, for you, I'll give Buck a try, but he fucks up one time he's gone. Right Charlie?"

"Yeah, Jack. We'll give him one shot. We'll give him a break."

"You got it Charlie. I'll get in touch with Buck and give him the good news. Hope it works out 'cause Buck's a good woodcutter. Be the best paying job he's had in a long time, I'll guarantee you that."

"And Jack, when you call him, don't mention anything about me. Okay? Just make this your idea."

"Sure, if that's how you want it Charlie. Your name will never come up."

Charlie hung up the phone feeling drained and sick and angry. He decided to call it a day and go for a run to clear his head before the Planning Board meeting.

The Red Bone High School was a cavernous old building of huge blocks of red and brown stone, massive multi-paned windows and wide plank flooring, built in the nineteen twenties at a time when the population of Red Bone could generate the three hundred high-school age children necessary to fill the two story, H-shaped building.

Now only the front half of the building was used for classrooms – the top floor for the high school and the first floor for the middle school and the School Department offices.

The gymnasium, where the Red Bone Planning Board held its meetings, was in the middle section of the building, accessible only via a long, dimly-lit hallway from the front wing.

Charlie Burden and Terry Summers, along with Vernon Yarbrough and two other lawyers from Kerns & Yarbrough, including Leonard, plus the PR man from Charleston, strode noisily down the creaky hallway and into the empty gym. They were a half-hour early for the eight o'clock meeting. The group had just finished a run through of their presentation over dinner in a private room at a restaurant in

Welch and now wanted to set up their exhibits for the presentation to the Planning Board. Over the next half hour they would be joined by a representative from the Governor's Office, a State Senator, a State Representative, and the Director of the West Virginia Economic Development Commission, who would all give testimony in support of the CanAmex petition.

The gym was empty save for a high school boy who was setting up tables, and rows of wooden folding chairs for the audience. At one end of the gym, under a basketball backboard that had been partially folded up toward the ceiling, a long cafeteria table was set up with three microphones and the nameplates of the three Planning Board members. In the center aisle, between the chairs for the audience, stood a podium with a microphone.

The high school boy looked up in surprise as the phalanx of well-dressed, important looking men, obviously outsiders, entered the gym. Vernon Yarbrough went to the middle of the room, surveyed the arrangements and quickly took charge of the situation.

"Alright son, we're going to have to change these tables around a bit up here," he said, striding toward the front of the gym where the boy was plugging microphone wires into jacks in the floor. The silver haired attorney reached into his pocket, pulled out a thick wad of bills in a gold money clip and expertly separated a twenty, which he pressed into the boy's unsuspecting hand. "You're doing a fine job here son, a fine job," said Yarbrough, flashing a quick, low-wattage smile, commensurate with the boy's status. "Now let's make some room up front here for our guests – got some important people come all the way down here from Charleston just for this meeting – and a spot for the easels."

At ten minutes before eight, the gym was still empty. Charlie wondered if they would be giving their presentation to a sea of empty chairs. Then, as if a bus had pulled up outside, the locals began to arrive. They came in groups of three and four and five, families or just friends together, and quickly the gym began filling up. Charlie recognized a few of the people. Mabel Willard and Ada Lowe along with another couple that Charlie surmised to be Emma Lowe's parents, plus several other older women he'd seen in the restaurant. Eve Brewster came in with Sally Oakes and her husband Ransom, his brother Yancy, and a very large gruff-looking older man that Charlie guessed would be Big Frank Oakes. The Oakes family took seats in the middle of the room among a group of men that had the look of out-of-work miners. But for the most part the audience was made up of strangers to Charlie. He wondered to himself, where they all lived and why he ran into so few of the residents of Red Bone in the course of his daily activities.

As he watched the citizens of McDowell County file quietly and orderly into the rows of chairs in front of him, a sinking feeling came over Charlie, along with a feeling of guilt and anxiousness. The gym looked like high school gyms everywhere, but this group of people was definitely not from Westchester County. In Mamaroneck, a meeting such as this, would quickly develop into a chat fest of smiling, handsomely dressed couples, shaking hands and waving across the room as they exuded personal contentment while performing for each other in a group exhibition of responsible civic concern.

The faces that Charlie looked out on showed little contentment. They were faces of dire concern if not abject despair. Smiles were forced and short lived and the chatter was brief and subdued. This was serious business to these people. They were looking to the power plant and its spin-off activities for their economic salvation, the source of a family-saving job for a husband, a brother, a son, anyone who might bring home a paycheck. This wasn't a game to them, as it had become to Charlie and the lawyers and the CanAmex people – this charade they were going to soon play out about repairing the library roof. These people were genuinely concerned about the project and the jobs it might someday produce – brought out this evening, no doubt by the rumor so artfully crafted by Vernon Yarbrough and disseminated through the United Mine Workers that the project might shut down permanently if they weren't granted a variance – and they didn't know the fix was in, as it always was with companies like CanAmex.

Charlie sat still in the small chair in his twelve hundred dollar, *Joseph Aboud* charcoal suit, dark gray silk shirt and matching tie, and looked around him at the lawyers and the politicians who had joined them at the power table, all similarly dressed for intimidation, and realized again that he was on the wrong side of the room. He should be the one out in the audience grilling these assholes and making them pay, not shills like poor Natty Oakes who's got enough things to worry about in life without being a part of Charlie Burden's little parlor game.

He thought about the library roof repair proposal that Natty had probably been dreading all day long and shook his head. Charlie looked over and saw Hank settling into his chair at the center of the Planning Board table getting ready to start the meeting, and then back over toward Vernon Yarbrough to make sure the lawyer could see him. Making a little extra scrapping noise as he pushed his chair back and came to his feet, Charlie went over to greet the Chairman of the Planning Board. As they shook hands Charlie leaned a little closer and spoke very softly. "Hank, pull me away from the table like you've got something real important to tell me. And keep talking."

The two men moved together toward the back of the room and stood close for a few minutes of intense, quiet conversation. Charlie made certain that his back shielded Hank from the inquiring eyes of Vernon Yarbrough that he could feel boring into him. Finally, Charlie nodded his head several times to indicate that he understood what Hank was telling him and turned to rejoin his team at the table.

Vernon Yarbrough leaned anxiously toward Charlie. "What's going on?" he whispered.

The loud bang of Hank's wooden gavel on the aluminum table, interrupted Charlie's response. "Tell you later," Charlie whispered quickly. "I think we're still all right." Yarbrough scowled but pulled back to his seat as the crowd grew silent.

Charlie looked out and saw that the crowd had stopped coming in and that the gymnasium chairs were nearly three quarters occupied. Then the door at the back of the gym opened once more and Natty and the Pie Man came in. They made their way up the center of the room and found seats about half way back, on the aisle.

As always now, Charlie's heart beat a little faster when he saw Natty. He had to smile to himself as she walked up the middle aisle dressed in her usual baggy jeans, man's white dress shirt and the untied construction boots. On her head though, she was wearing Pie's Yankee cap, while the boy wore her blue Spider-Man hat. Probably her idea of dressing up for the meeting. Again, Natty amazed Charlie with her ability to be so inconspicuous and attract so little attention. Here she was, one of the most beautiful women Charlie had ever met, and she could walk into a room, looking so plain in her unflattering clothing with no make-up or jewelry, that hardly a man in the room would look up and take notice.

Hank started the meeting by bringing everyone to their feet and leading the assembly in the Pledge Allegiance to the flag. While they were all standing, Charlie took the opportunity to look over at the Planning Board members. Immediately he recognized Earl Fitch, the barber that Natty had introduced him to on South County Road when they'd had their aborted race. Charlie knew he had heard the name somewhere but even after he'd visited Earl's barber shop for a trim and complimentary cigar a few days later, he still hadn't connected him with the thin file on his desk in the apartment. The local barber just didn't seem like a Planning Board type.

As Charlie looked over at him, Earl Fitch turned and caught Charlie's eye. He tugged lightly on a shock of his hair and pointed over at Charlie with a grin. Charlie smiled back at him and nodded his agreement. *God, this whole thing was too easy*, thought Charlie. These people were just too nice for this.

Hank read aloud the executive summary of the Request For Variance that Charlie had written, which was the only business before the board that evening and then laid out the ground rules for the meeting. "First, the CanAmex side, represented by Mr. Vernon Yarbrough from the law firm of Kerns & Yarbrough, of Charleston, and Mr. Charles Burden of the project's engineering company, Dietrich Delahunt & Mackey, from New York City, will present their petition, and supporting testimony."

At the mention of Charlie's name, Pie leaned across his mother's lap, with an excited happy face and pointed the index fingers of both hands toward Charlie. Charlie had to look away quickly to avoid laughing.

"And after that, if anyone's got anything to say, for or against the plan, or you just want to beat the hell out of a big utility company, you can take your shot at the podium there." Then, Hank turned the meeting over to Vernon Yarbrough.

The silver-tongued litigator had announced his three objectives at dinner earlier: to make friends with the audience; extol the benefits to the local economy of the CanAmex project; and then, to scare the shit out of everyone in the room by strongly implying that the project may well be terminated if the Request For Variance was denied. This was what he got paid so much money for and he was a master of his craft.

Speaking without the need of a microphone, Yarbrough mesmerized the audience with the rich, stentorian sound of his voice, expressive use of his hands and his body language as he moved around lightly on his feet, venturing at times down the aisle into the audience, and then like a dancer, bouncing back quickly to the easel to point out a, no doubt, critical figure on one of the charts. In twenty minutes, the lawyer stated his case, backed it up with factual looking figures and charts, made his closing argument, and then rested with a gracious thank you to the Planning Board and the audience.

Yarbrough's only moment of indecision came near the end of his presentation when he tried to answer a technical question about the effect the blasting of the rock formation would have on the structure of the main building. The question was posed by a tall, gaunt miner who obviously had some experience with explosives, and didn't seem to be buying Yarbrough's amateurish rambling on the subject. Charlie rose out of his seat, to Yarbrough's relief, and dealt briefly with the man's question and noted that he would be going into more detail about the blasting problem in his portion of the presentation.

Charlie began with an explanation of how the problem was created and admitted the fault lay with a junior engineer from Dietrich Delahunt & Mackey who had worked on the original site plan several years earlier. The admission seemed to strike a sympathetic chord with the audience and with the Planning Board members.

Then he started his presentation with a large board showing a diagram of the entire site plan. For reference, using a collapsible steel pointer, Charlie pointed out the main building, the administration building and front gate. Then pointing to a spot on the perimeter fence to the left of the main gate, Charlie noted, "and right about here is a spot where I understand the local kids used to sneak under the fence before I got here." There was a smattering of knowing chuckles in the audience as Charlie took two strides up the aisle and grinned directly at the Pie Man who shrunk down in his seat, unsure if he was in trouble. The look on Charlie's face reassured him and slowly a blushing happy face closed his eyes to slits. "Fortunately," Charlie continued, "one very nice young man from your town offered to show me where the hole was, so we were able to fix it."

Natty smiled down at her embarrassed son, afraid to look up, afraid to find that Charlie may be looking at her. She waited until he started talking again before she turned back toward the front of the room. She had been nervous since the moment she came into the gym and saw Charlie sitting behind the table at the front of the room with all the other important men. Now as she watched him occupying center stage she felt like she had a hole in her stomach as she replayed in her mind for the hundredth time, the words he had said to her up in the grotto. And there he was, the same man, speaking with the same voice, up in front of all these people, sounding so professional and being so good at his job, in control of the room, and so confident.

Natty couldn't remember if she'd ever seen Charlie wearing anything but shorts and a T-shirt – except for that day two years ago when the helicopters came – and now here he was, wearing the most exquisitely tailored, beautiful dark suit and gray shirt and tie ensemble that was light years ahead of what businessmen wore in McDowell County, and it looked so perfect and natural on him. He was so clearly not one of them. He was an outsider, from a different world, like the other men at the front table . . . and it made her feel foolish for what she had been thinking the past few days.

Natty's attention was riveted on Charlie as he talked about the problem of blasting the rock formation at the original pond site. He sought out the miner who had posed the question to Yarbrough, and went into some detail, using technical terms like, seismic echoes, metal fatigue, and stress tolerances that the miner, nodding his head affirmatively, seemed to understand. Charlie didn't leave the topic until he was sure that the miner was satisfied.

Using several large boards of maps and charts, Charlie described the location and design of the new pond, and the containment dike with its steel framework, that would be several feet higher than the code demanded.

Then, because Charlie appeared to be so easy-going and knowledgeable about every aspect of the project, questions started coming from the audience. He explained to a woman how the water from the pond would be used to cool down the steam after it went through the three massive turbines, and no, the water for the steam was actually ultra-purified water in a closed system, and not the water from the pond. He patiently and forthrightly answered several other questions about the amount of water to be taken from and discharged into the Heavenly River, then a few unrelated questions about the technology of the scrubber units and the emissions from the three boilers that he admitted would be about the largest of their type in the world. Then he fielded questions about the amount of coal the plant would be burning, going into some detail, for the miners again, about the BTU's per ton and the tonnage required to produce the steam needed to generate up to 3000 megawatts of electric power.

Natty was awed by Charlie's incredible depth of knowledge of the complex technology that went into an electrical power plant. And she was discouraged at seeing this new side of him. *God, not only is he the nicest, and the most beautiful man she'd ever met, he was the smartest too! How could Charlie Burden ever have two thoughts about some pathetic little hillbilly girl who couldn't even graduate from high school.* Then a question from the middle of the gymnasium, jarred Natty's attention back to the present.

"Mr. Burden, we been hearin' a rumor for d'last few weeks about a big surface mine openin' up on Angel Mountain to fuel your new power plant, and I'as wonderin' sir if you could say whether'd ats true or it ain't, cause there's a lot a idle miners here be interested in nat."

Natty turned around to see that the questioner was a some-time miner, sitting next to Yancy Oakes. Over Yancy's shoulder, Natty noticed Eve Brewster who met her eye with what seemed to be a stern look on her face. It was disconcerting to Natty, to realize suddenly that Eve would also be aligned against her on the Angel Mountain issue, having three brothers who could all use some help from a new mining operation. Natty turned back quickly to see Charlie's reaction to the question.

There was some stirring at the CanAmex table behind Charlie. Vernon Yarbrough was in a whispered conversation with the representative from the Governor's office. Charlie stood still with his hands in his pockets and thought for a moment, how he should answer. He could hear the murmurs behind him and it flashed through his mind that the question might be a set-up in some way, though he couldn't figure out how or why. He decided to just evade the question as best he could, and then let Yarbrough address it if he wanted to. Charlie took a few steps towards the audience and the questioner.

"Well, the contract for the coal to be used in the power plant was awarded to the Ackerly Coal Company, which I'm sure you're familiar with," said Charlie. "Now it's up to them, how they meet the terms of that contract. Where, and from what mines that coal comes from, is entirely in Ackerly's hands."

"Yessir, I un'erstand nat," the miner replied, coming to his feet again. "But what I'm askin' is, is your big construction company and the CanAmex company involved in tryin' to get Ackerly a new *mountaintop-removal* permit to use on Angel Mountain, 'cause the word *is,* around the union, that there ain't no way Ackerly goin' to get it by itself without you big boys pitchin' in on the politics and such."

Thankfully, Charlie heard Vernon Yarbrough's chair scraping against the wooden floor. He turned to see the lawyer coming around the table to take the stage again.

"Thank you Charlie. Nice job. Good job," said Yarbrough loudly, patting Charlie on the shoulder as he passed him and went down the middle aisle a little ways into the audience. "Let me see if I can answer this gentleman's very important question."

Yarbrough ventured a few more steps down the center aisle and paused with his hands clasped together in front of him, a thoughtful scowl on his face as if he was having some trouble finding the words. Finally he spoke, but now in a much softer, more intimate manner then he had previously.

"This is a ticklish situation," Yarbrough confided. "Being a representative of the Ackerly Coal Company, there's some parts of your question I can neither confirm for you this evening or deny, but I can tell you this, that there's a lot of interest, by a lot of fine people," Yarbrough, half turned with a sweep of his arm toward the table of politicians behind him, "in opening a new surface mine in McDowell County. A mine big enough to supply *all* of the coal for the new plant for the next twenty years. A mine big enough to create more than 250 new mining jobs for McDowell County men." A few grunts of agreement came back from the audience. Yarbrough nodded his head affirmatively, and then continued, his voice growing louder. "Lot of interest, from Charleston to Washington, because what this county needs, is a big new mine, to put everybody to work, at good, union wages." The audience seemed to lean together and murmur as one in reaction to this excellent news.

Yarbrough, the master of timing, waited for the audience to come back to him before continuing. "But," he silenced them, "this is a *long* way from a done deal. There's legal problems – getting the ban overturned – which we are all," again Yarbrough gestured back toward the table behind him, "working at a solution. Plus, we got the always thorny problem of some . . . well, *local opposition* to the Angel Mountain site, which creates a ticklish sort of situation with regard to public relations and such and . . . " Yarbrough grimaced as he pretended to struggle for the right words, "well, could turn the tide against us in the end." The audience let out a collective groan of disappointment.

Natty felt like she had a spotlight on her as the lawyer spoke. She just stared straight ahead, taking care to avoid Charlie Burden's eye at the front table.

Yarbrough paused for a few seconds in thought, and then shook his head and smiled at the audience. "No, I guess we'll have to leave it at that for now. That's the best I can answer your question right now," he said holding his palms up to the audience.

As Yarbrough finished, Charlie glanced over at the Planning Board table and saw trouble in the face of P. J. Hankinson. Hank was staring at him with cold, hard eyes, and Charlie could tell that beneath all the white whiskers, there was a clenched jaw that signified the same smoldering anger Hank had exhibited that day sitting in the field telling him the story of Buffalo Creek. Hank, better than anyone in the room, Charlie realized, could read through Yarbrough's bullshit and know that the big companies were at it again and there was a lot more to the story than the lawyer was ever going to divulge at a public meeting. Hank's reaction took Charlie by surprise, and made him look away quickly.

After a few, mostly self-serving, comments by the politicians in support of the CanAmex petition, the presentation was over and Hank opened up the floor to public comment. The audience looked around at each other to see who might have something to say. The first to rise and move to the podium was someone who was not on Charlie and Hank's script. It was the miner who had asked the questions about the blasting.

"Well, I'd just like to say, that ," he started nervously, "that the only thing I ever knew how to do . . . only thing on this earth I'm any good at, is pullin' coal out of the ground, and I ain't been able to do that for the past four years, so me and my wife and three little ones'd appreciate the Board helping out this project any way you can, cause," his voice tailed away softly, "it's about the only hope we got."

Charlie cringed inside listening to the miner's plea. He didn't need such a sincere endorsement at this stage of the play. He looked over at Yarbrough who was smiling benignly like a priest looking out over his parishioners.

Thankfully, one of Hank's shills was next. He introduced himself as a science teacher at Red Bone High and said he had strong *doubts* about the alleged affects of blasting the rock at the existing site of the pond. He also made the point that the new pond would be too close to Cold Spring Road, and proposed a six-month delay in the granting of a variance, in which time, an independent geological study could be done. He was perfect, thought Charlie. Hank had coached him well. A six month delay in granting the variance would sound like an easy, compromise solution but Charlie knew that such a delay would be catastrophic to the project, and he knew that next to him at the CanAmex table, the lawyers would be gnashing their teeth over the teacher's proposal.

Hank thanked the teacher for his comments and then announced Mrs. Mabel Willard who was lumbering up to the podium from the rear of the gym. The huge black woman was to be their *star* witness and she didn't disappoint them. Her thunderous voice, coupled with an undaunted attitude of righteous indignation, were just what Charlie needed.

"My problem with this whole show tonight," roared Mabel, "is that this big-time CanAmex Company come to our little town with all kind of promises and prognostications and such about all the wonderful things they was going to do for the town of Red Bone in terms of jobs for the local men and boostin' the local economy and what not, and I ain't seen diddly squat of neither!" In spite of her contrary view, there was a noticeable murmur of support from the audience. "Seems to me," she continued, "that Bluefield and Welch been getting the best of the economics, and I see an awful lot of out-of-state license plates driving out of that construction site every night, and not too many of our Red Bone men put to work out there." Support from the crowd behind her was growing, causing looks of consternation on the faces of the Kerns & Yarbrough lawyers. She was perfect, thought Charlie, setting the stage just right for Natty.

"So, what I'm sayin' is," Mabel continued, "that I don't know why we should be so quick to just give in to every little thing that CanAmex wants to do out there, when they ain't really done anything for us here in Red Bone." Mabel was so good, Charlie wanted to applaud her performance.

Then it was Natty's turn. Charlie watched her as she fidgeted nervously, turning around to see if someone else, hopefully, might be rising to speak.

"Anyone else have something to say?" said Hank, looking directly at Natty over his wire-rimmed spectacles.

Natty flashed a quick, nervous smile at the Planning Board Chairman, and rose to her feet. At the podium she pulled the microphone down, cleared her throat, and put her hands on hands on top of the podium, trying to get comfortable.

"My name's, uh, Natty Oakes," she said softly, "and I live in Red Bone." Charlie glanced over at Vernon Yarbrough who gave him a quick wink indicating that the lawyer felt that everything was going according to plan. "And I agree with everything Mabel said, about the promises CanAmex made and how there ain't been much to show for it all in the town. So I was thinking that, uhm . . ." Natty glanced over at Hank, unsure of what she was supposed to propose.

Hank came to her aid. "Mrs. Oakes, I believe that you might have come her tonight to offer up some sort of worthwhile community improvement project that the CanAmex Corporation might want to undertake in order to make a meaningful contribution to the town in order to help their chances of getting' this here variance passed. Is that about right Natty?"

Grateful that Hank had gotten right to the point, Natty leaned into the microphone. "Yes sir Hank, er, Mr. Hankinson sir, that's what I'd like to do." She looked over at the CanAmex table and saw that Charlie had moved his chair out to the end of the table and was sitting back very casually, his legs extended straight out with his ankles crossed. His hands were in his pockets.

"Well what I was thinkin'," said Natty, sounding a little more relaxed now, "was that, we got this little children's library up next to the soccer field that I started a couple of years ago to give the kids some place to get books, you know, and have a nice quiet place to read. And I was going to some day maybe get some computers in there, so the kids could use them and maybe even go on the Internet and all that stuff, you know. But, well the roof started leakin' and it kept getting' worse and worse, and there was no money from the town to patch it or anything, so . . . all the books – didn't really have too many to begin with – well, they all got ruined and the floors are pretty wet most the time, so . . ." Natty looked over at Hank and shrugged, not knowing what to say next.

Hank looked over at the CanAmex table. "So what Mrs. Oakes is proposing to you folks is, that maybe you might find some way to fix the roof of her kids' library there and maybe get her some new books and maybe even a computer." He looked back at Natty. "That about right Natty?"

She smile broadly. "Yeah Hank. That'd be great."

Hank turned back to the lawyers. "And then we'd take that into consideration here when we're ruminatin' over this request of yours for a variance." Hank sat back but continued to look over at the lawyers for their response.

Vernon Yarbrough nodded his head and pursed his lips as though he was engaged in serious contemplation, then he leaned over for a hushed conversation with Leonard and the other lawyer beside him. He arose from the huddle and looked toward Natty at the podium.

"Mizz Oakes, I was wonderin' ma'am, if you might have just a ballpark figure in your mind as to the cost of fixing your roof?"

Charlie, who had sat unmoving, watching Natty at the podium, turned and squinted slightly at Yarbrough. *God, what a showman. Pretending to care about the cost of fixing the roof!* Charlie knew that the lawyers would be giddy with satisfaction that the Request For Variance would be passing, and at a cost that was nothing more than tip money to CanAmex.

"Well, no sir, I wouldn't know anything about that," said Natty. "But, I know Mr. Burden there took a look at our roof one day," Natty smiled at Charlie. "And he's such a smart man, he'd probably have a guess at the cost."

Charlie chuckled, and smiled back at Natty without saying anything.

The lawyer turned to Charlie. "So what do you think Charlie?" asked Yarbrough, playing along. "This a viable project for our client to undertake?"

Charlie sat motionless for a few seconds before bending his legs and placing his feet heavily on the floor. He looked over at Yarbrough. "No," he said in the direction of the lawyers before turning back toward Natty who blinked her eyes slowly and let her mouth drop open in bewilderment. "It's not a good project for our client."

Charlie leaned forward and came to his feet. He stood between the two tables at the front of the room. "I did go up and look at the roof of the building and it's a mess. But the building's got bigger problems than the roof. You could put a new roof on it and the building would still be unusable. The heating system is shot and there's no air conditioning, which you'd need for a library with computers in there."

Charlie turned in a small semi-circle as he spoke, alternately addressing the Planning Board table, the audience, and the lawyers' table. "The walls have been weakened by the water and the floors are warped and pushing up in spots and there's mold growing because of the dampness and poor drainage. The drainage system is a problem all the way down to the soccer field, because the water just comes running down the hill from the mountain. It would have to be fixed before you could do any improvements to the library." He shook his head, "it's pretty much a total loss."

Natty stood at the podium staring at Charlie in disbelief. *How could he do this? Ask her to get up in front of everybody and offer up the roof project, and then say no!* She didn't know whether she should go sit down or stay at the podium or what she should do.

Then Charlie looked directly at her and smiled. He crossed his arms in front of him "So, here's what we're going to do." He turned to Hank. "This is what we propose in place of Mrs. Oakes's roof project." He turned back to Natty. "We're going to demolish the present building, along with the parking lot and the stairs down to the field. We're going to tear up the soccer field and the lower parking lot and the old baseball field, and we're going to clear and level the five additional acres of abutting land that the Ackerly Coal Company will be contributing to the project." Hearing Vernon Yarbrough clear his throat, Charlie shot him a stern look to keep him quiet.

"Then, we're going to build a drainage system to channel the run-off through a culvert to the stream on the other side of South County Road. We'll build a new building on the present site with the children's library on the upper floor and shower rooms and athletic facilities on the lower floor. Then we're going to build a new soccer field, football and baseball complex on the expanded lower level with a new parking lot at the western end of the site."

It was evident to Yarbrough that Charlie had given this project some thought prior to this evening. He didn't understand what was going on and what he didn't understand, he kept quiet about. Anyway, it was CanAmex's money and Charlie Burden's neck on the line.

"Whole project should only take a few months if the winter isn't too bad," Charlie continued. He paused in thought for a few seconds looking down at the floor, then he continued, his voice lower now as he looked around the room. "This is what the town needs," he said. He looked over at the lawyers. "And this is what we're going to do for the town." He took a few steps toward Natty at the podium and spoke to the audience. "If we're going to do something here, we want to do something meaningful, that we can all be proud of for a long time, and that you and your children can all benefit from for a long time." He shrugged and nodded his head. "So this is what we're going to do."

Vernon Yarbrough rose to his feet, knowing the die was cast, eager to take some credit. "Well Charlie, I think this is going to be a splendid project . . ."

From the back of the gym, Yarbrough was interrupted by the sound of Mabel Willard slowly clapping her huge hands together. In another few seconds, the entire gym was on its feet clapping, drowning out Yarbrough's words. Still at the podium, Natty smiled broadly and clapped loudly, amazed at what Charlie had just done. The Pie Man was jumping up and down on his chair, clapping his hands over his head.

Embarrassed, Charlie turned and walked to he Planning Board table where Hank and the others were also clapping. He shook hands with Hank who pulled him closer and spoke into Charlie's ear. "Now you're fucked," he said, smiling at Charlie as he straightened up.

"Yeah, you're right about that," Charlie said with a laugh as he moved on to shake hands with Earl Fitch.

Chapter 20

P. J. Hankinson was already seated at the wooden table shuffling the cards when Charlie came out onto the porch. Charlie hadn't seen Hank since the Planning Board meeting, which he thought was a little strange, but now here he was, ready for their ritual Sunday night game.

"Hey Hank, how you doing?" Charlie asked as he took his seat across the table.

"Burden," Hank said gruffly as he cut his card for the deal.

They played the game without speaking beyond the necessary cribbage announcements of the card totals and the point counts. Charlie knew something was up when Hank skunked him and also had the high hand, without any of the usual crowing and subtle barbs he liked to use on the occasion of such a slaughter. Something was obviously troubling the old man. Charlie recalled the angry stare he'd received from Hank at the Planning Board meeting.

"Okay Hank," said Charlie, picking up the deck of cards and putting them down on his side of the table. "Let's have it."

Hank picked up the score book and recorded the financial result of their game. Posting the result to the book meant that no more games were to be played that evening. He stretched the rubber band around the book, placed it back in the cigar box and then looked up at Charlie.

"Burden, I ain't sure I can trust you any more. You're starting to look an awful lot like those lawyers and CanAmex people you hang around with."

"C'mon Hank, what are you ..."

Hank held up a hand to Charlie.

"Charlie, reason you're down here, with all them lawyers and politicians at your table is for *one* thing . . . to get a surface mining variance for Angel Mountain. It's the reason why you're building that power station here in Red Bone . . . to be within easy trucking distance of Angel Mountain."

"Hank, you got this wrong," Charlie protested.

"Do I? Do I?" Hank said as he slid his chair back and laboriously pushed himself to his feet and went to the railing. He spit his tobacco juice over the side and leaned against the post looking out at the mountains to the southwest, in the general direction of Angel Mountain. "Soon as that miner got up at the meeting and asked about Angel Mountain, it all hit me like a bucket of ice water. Ain't no way an idle miner like him knows anything about anything lest it comes from the Union. And the Union sure as hell don't know anything without Ackerly or CanAmex telling them what to know."

"Well sure Hank, there's an option that some people are working on to fuel the plant with coal from Angel Mountain," said Charlie. "But it's just one option."

Hank spit over the side again and turned to glare at Charlie. "Option, *bullshit*. It's the only reason you and your pals are here. Without the coal from Angel Mountain, that plant gets built over in Logan or Mingo County, or more likely in Kentucky or Virginia, but sure as hell not in Red Bone or anywhere else in McDowell County."

"Hank, you're speculating, and I don't know how much of your theory is real or not, but, what's it all got to do with me?"

Hank stood silently at the railing pondering his answer. "Burden, you may not know or care much about mountaintop mining, but that's why you're down here, to help make that happen, that and getting a variance for your pond," he said softly. "It's why you're here, living in this old fire trap, and making friends with an old man who happens to be on the Planning Board, and . . ." Hank limped heavily back to his chair and leaned over the table to focus his dark eyes on Charlie. "Tell me again, Burden, what's your interest in the Oakes woman? Nothing personal you told me, right? So it's just coincidence that you've become so friendly with this little hillbilly girl and her retarded son? The granddaughter of Bud DeWitt who you're going to have to move off of Angel Mountain pretty quick here to get your surface mine started before the end of the year." Hank leaned back in his chair and took a breath. "Yeah, I know a little about what's going on here Burden."

Charlie stared across the table, his jaw and neck muscles tightened with anger over Hank's accusal. He took a deep breath and forced himself to calm down before replying. He didn't want to get into an argument with Hank. He sat back in his chair and thought about what Hank had said. Then he leaned forward and put his hands on the table and spoke softly and calmly.

"Hank, part of what you said was true. One of my jobs down here is to help CanAmex get a variance for a surface mine on Angel Mountain. To do that, we need to buy the DeWitt farm and we've been trying to do that. Also, the pond problem obviously was my responsibility too." Hank sat with his arms crossed, stone-faced, listening to Charlie.

"But Hank, none of that has anything to do with me taking this apartment, or us being friends, and it's certainly got nothing to do with Natty Oakes. I met Pie the first day I was here, and Natty the next day, and it wasn't until several weeks later that I found out she was a DeWitt." Charlie shook his head sideways. "You got that part of it all wrong Hank."

Charlie sat back in his chair and looked out over the porch wall at the scenery to the west where the sun was getting ready to drop behind the mountains. "Meeting you and Natty and Pie, and everybody else I've met here is all just part of moving to a small town. There's nothing more to it than that." He turned to look Hank in the eye. "It's important to me Hank, that you believe that."

After a long, silent pause, Hank finally unfolded his arms. He put his hands on his knees and seemed to slump in his chair as his shoulders relaxed. "Okay Burden. Okay," he said softly. "I didn't really think you were that cunning. Had to know though. 'Cause this whole thing with Angel Mountain, it's like the damn history of West Virginia and I hate it in my gut." Hank turned to look out at the mountains and spoke in a low voice, almost to himself. "Big companies been coming down here squeezing the blood out of these people for a hundred years . . . takin' their land and keepin' 'em poor and ignorant and dependent, all with the help of the damn government and the judicial system 'cause they follow the money and the power, and the money and the power down here has always been the coal companies."

"Hank, c'mon, that's a little extreme here. We made the DeWitts a very fair offer for the farm."

"Fair." Hank said the word like it was the first time he'd ever heard it. He looked back at Charlie with a fiery glint in his eye. "Burden, let me tell you something. There ain't *nothin'* fair about what the coal companies done to the people of West Virginia. And nothing's changed in a hundred years, and now you and CanAmex and Ackerly are all doing it again." Hank turned away and shook his head slowly. "It'll never change. Way it's always been in West Virginia."

Charlie leaned forward to argue his case. "Hank, listen. Even if you're against mountaintop-removal because of the environment, you still have to admit it's going to put a lot of men to work making good union wages supporting a lot of McDowell County families. It's a coal mine Hank, putting miners to work." He paused for a second and leaned back in his chair. "Isn't that good for McDowell County Hank? Isn't that good for West Virginia?"

Hank stared back at Charlie through narrow eyes for several seconds without responding. Then he smiled briefly, his white handlebar mustache rising up at the sides and then falling quickly. He rose out of his chair again slowly, moved to the edge of the porch and leaned against the supporting post. He gestured out toward the mountains to the west. "Charlie, under all of this land out here, far as we can see from this porch, is the Pocahontas Coal Field, the richest, thickest, finest seam of pure, low-sulfur coal the world has ever known. Miners have been pulling coal out of the ground in West Virginia for a hundred and seventy years – to fuel the industrial revolution, to fight two world wars, power the railroads and the great steel mills of the Ohio Valley, and to heat the homes and factories of the northeast for most of this century."

Hank turned and leaned his back against the post and faced Charlie with his hands in his pockets. Charlie could see the veteran teacher in Hank coming out and sat back in his chair to listen.

"D'you know that it was coal from the southern counties here that powered the U.S. Navy in World War I? Navy had to have the "smokeless" coal so the German U-boats couldn't see the smoke plumes of the ships through their periscopes. So the miners down here broke their backs digging out enough coal to supply the Navy and the rest of the war effort." Hank pointed up toward Main Street. "That's when the Red Bone mine first opened, 1917, to supply the coal for the Navy.

Hank turned and spit tobacco juice over the side. "It was the railroads that changed everything. The railroads started it all, back in the 1880's and '90's, when they finally laid tracks through the mountains here, the Norfolk & Western, and opened up the coal field, and just as important, brought in the thousands of workers needed by the coal mining industry . . . all the *throw-away* people that the mines needed because it was so labor intensive back then, and dangerous. So the railroad brought in the people who didn't have any other options, the poor southern blacks and the Europeans, right off the boat from Ellis Island – the Italians, Slavs, Irish, Hungarians – they came by the thousands. The mining companies would pay the fare for immigrant families to come to West Virginia and as soon as they got off the train they were in debt to the company – a debt they'd never get out of."

Hank lumbered back to his chair at the table and then continued in a more somber voice. "In 1907 Charlie, there was an accident, up in Monongah, in Marion County, an explosion. Official count was 361 fatalities – still the worst mine disaster in U.S. History. But unofficial accounts at the time say the death toll was a lot higher because of all the immigrants who couldn't speak English and had names too hard to write, so they'd just send them down the hole to work without worrying about accounting for them." Hank shook his head. "That's the way it was back then. The mines needed people that nobody cared about so they could make their profits in a dangerous business. In just the first two decades of the century, more than 20,000 U.S. coal miners were killed. But it didn't matter because they were replaceable and it was the only way to get the coal out of the ground. You know, there was a study done that showed that the life expectancy of a West Virginia coal miner during World War I was less than that of an infantryman on the battlefields of Europe.

"Even before the railroads came, the mining companies and the speculators had come in and bought up all the land and the mineral rights to whatever land they couldn't buy. Farmers were forced off their land, one way or the other, and West Virginia became owned by the mining companies. Even today, most of the state – over three quarters of the land area – is owned by out-of-state companies." Hank looked up at Charlie to make sure he had his eye. "Companies like Ackerly, and Continental Electric Systems, and CanAmex."

"Yeah, but Hank, a lot of people have made a very good living as miners . . ."

Hank slammed his hand down on the table making the cribbage board jump and startling Charlie. The old man's black eyes glistened with anger. "*Goddammit* Charlie! You ain't been listening to me at all. A *good living. A good living!* What's a *good living* Charlie? A hundred years of pulling coal out of the ground, the best coal there is, to help this country fight two great wars, fuel the steel industry, power the most prosperous economy the world has ever known, and what do we have to show for it? Look around you Charlie. You see any great wealth in evidence from all those years of production? See any *old money* around this town, or anywhere in McDowell County? All those years of death and misery and heartache and men working like slaves . . . "

Hank closed his eyes and took a deep breath to calm himself. His voice was softer when he spoke again but the anger was still in his eyes. "What do we have to show for it Charlie? What's our legacy from the coal industry?" Hank turned and looked out at what was now complete darkness, the silhouettes of the mountains just barely visible against the night sky. "What we got is the second poorest state in the union and the highest child poverty rate. We got a state population that's dropping like a rock 'cause there's no jobs, no future for the young people, leaving us with too many old people to take care of – people too old and too poor to go anywhere else. We got fifty thousand retired miners with the black lung, suffocating in their own fluids, getting' ready to die before their time, and the rest of 'em losing their retirements and their health insurance 'cause all the old coal companies been picked clean of any assets worth anything and now gone bankrupt." Hank was getting louder now. He leaned closer to Charlie over the table and spit flew from his lips with every word. "We got abandoned buildings and abandoned towns. And we got monuments – in Monongah, Bartley, Havaco, Eccles, Farmington – all *over* West Virginia we got monuments – to the men who gave up their lives to this heartless industry. And we got old coalmines and gob piles leaking acid waste turning our streams orange and polluting our water supplies. We got abandoned mines caving in, swallowing peoples' homes, and we got companies still coming here, now to openly rape the land with their *mountaintop disasters,* to get what's left of the coal 'cause *what the fuck!"* Hank slammed his palm down hard on the table again, "this is just *West Virginia* and that's the way it's always been down here so it don't matter none!" He grimaced and shut his eyes for several seconds.

Hank took some deep breaths and paused for a few moments, then he nodded his head in thought. "You know, that's the worst of it Charlie. Our legacy from the coal industry is that West Virginia's now a *joke* to the rest of the country. Poor, ignorant hillbillies, too dumb to raise themselves out of poverty. So it don't really matter what the big companies do down there 'cause it's just *Appalachia* and them hillbillies don't care so why should anyone. That's the worst of it Charlie," he repeated softly.

Hank leaned onto the table toward Charlie. "Let me ask you something Burden. If you wanted to blow the top third off of Angel Mountain and push it all over the side – ten square miles of overburden – destroying the streams and wildlife habitat and hundreds of years of forest growth, but instead of West Virginia, Angel Mountain was in California, or Oregon, or Vermont, or in the Catskills . . . how successful you think you'd be? Could mining companies get away with that anywhere else in the country but West Virginia or Kentucky Charlie?"

Charlie could only smile weakly, conceding Hank's point.

"You bet they couldn't, and they wouldn't even try. But down here, this is just *Appalachia*, so who gives a shit." Hank's voice grew weaker and he turned away from Charlie as if he was now talking to himself. "People here are still poor and desperate with no options. Like we just arrived from Ellis Island," he said softly. "So don't tell me how good coal mining is for the people and for the state or for McDowell County. Always been a deal with the devil and the devil's been winning for a hundred years."

They sat in silence in the dark for a few minutes. Finally Hank stirred, arising achingly from his chair. "Time for an old man to get to bed."

"Yeah, me too. Goodnight Hank," Charlie said getting up from his chair.

At his screen door, Hank stopped and looked back toward Charlie. "Burden, that's a good thing you're doing with the kids' library and the ball fields. Nobody ever done something like that for this town before. Nobody ever given this town anything. That's a good thing you're doing."

Charlie nodded in the darkness. "Yeah, thanks Hank. Thanks. I appreciate your saying that."

*   *   *

The moment he drove out of the woods and felt the smooth pavement of the new road that encircled the power plant, Charlie knew something was wrong. The main gate into the site had been wheeled open and several vehicles, including a white police car, were lined up on the short section of road that led over the drainage ditch and through the gate. The company's black Navigator was in the lead position followed by the police car, a Toyota Land Cruiser, and then, a Chevy Suburban with dark tinted windows and some kind of official looking insignia on the door.

As Charlie turned the Lexus to go through the gate, he noticed another strange car off to his right sitting at the side of the access road. It was a dark blue Crown Victoria with several long antennas and a spotlight mounted in front of the mirror on the driver's door. Two men wearing sunglasses sat unmoving in the car. Charlie glanced at his watch while he considered why the men would be wearing sunglasses so early in the morning. The scene would have looked suspicious at any time, let alone 6:15AM.

Standing just outside of the small guard house, Chief Security Officer Krebs, stared Charlie through the gate without acknowledgment. Krebs being on duty at the gate this early in the morning was also strange. As he drove past the line of vehicles, Charlie saw that the insignia on the doors of the Suburban was for the U.S. Drug Enforcement Agency.

In the parking lot outside the administration building Charlie noticed Terry Summers' white Corvette. As he got out of his car, he saw the ominous looking black CanAmex helicopter sitting out in the middle of the field. *This was it then,* Charlie knew, *the infamous Plan-B that Yarbrough had been keeping up his sleeve.*

Before Charlie could start toward the administration building, the double doors to the building burst open and a collection of serious-looking men streamed out into the parking lot. Charlie recognized Vernon Yarbrough and Terry Summers, and then Leonard, the lawyer, wearing his customary three-piece suit and carrying a briefcase, but all of the others were strangers to him. Two of the men wore what looked like dark blue battle fatigues and hard vests with "DEA" in large white letters on the back. Forty-five caliber pistols were holstered at the side of their belts. They headed for the Suburban.

A tall, overweight policeman with a toothpick in his mouth walked over and stood by his cruiser as if awaiting further instructions. Four other men, two wearing business suits, and two in rugged looking casual wear, climbed into the Land Cruiser. A few of the men eyed Charlie quickly with thin, professional squints and then turned away without expression.

Upon seeing Charlie, Yarbrough and Terry Summers exchanged glances. The lawyer motioned Summers toward the Navigator and then detoured from his path to approach Charlie. Yarbrough was wearing sharply pressed blue jeans, a soft leather bomber jacket and black boots, obviously dressed for some kind of action that he was unaccustomed to. The lawyer flashed a quick smile but the campaign handshake was missing.

"Burden," said Yarbrough with a quick nod.

"What's up?" said Charlie motioning toward the motorcade.

"Going up to see our pig farmer one last time," said Yarbrough with hardly a hint of a drawl. "Want to come?" he asked without enthusiasm.

It was obvious to Charlie, that he wasn't intended to be part of this operation. "No, no thanks," he answered. "Let me know how it turns out."

Yarbrough eyed Charlie warily for a few seconds. "Thought it best to keep this option under wraps as much as possible. Less people involved the better . . . . for security."

Charlie watched the other men getting into their vehicles. "Why all the firepower?" he asked. "Expecting farmer DeWitt to come out shooting?"

Yarbrough smiled and glanced quickly over at the entourage and then back at Charlie. "Well, it appears that farmer DeWitt's been growing some contraband up there that our law enforcement friends here may have a problem with. I'm going along 'cause I just might be able to help DeWitt through this situation, but you never know what a man will do when he's up against the wall. Just taking precautions." The lawyer turned abruptly on his heels and strode quickly away toward the Navigator. Terry Summers was at the door of the big vehicle, watching Charlie. Yarbrough spoke into a walkie-talkie as he climbed into the Navigator.

The caravan pulled out aggressively onto the access road in close formation. Charlie stood in the parking lot and watched as the powerful vehicles quickly disappeared into the woods sending up a cloud of dust from the old road. Then he noticed the Crown Victoria still parked on the access road, the man in the passenger seat staring straight at him from behind the black sunglasses. Charlie stared back for a few seconds, then turned away and walked at a normal step toward the administration building. When he reached the corner of the building, he heard the car start up and pull away. Taking a few steps back toward the end of the building, Charlie watched the big Ford drive down the new road and turn into the woods, moving at a much more normal speed than the rest of the caravan.

"*Fuck!*" said Charlie moving quickly to the double door of the administration building. He fumbled with the keys, and then with the alarm code inside.

He moved quickly through the main room, passing by the big center table that was used for spreading out blueprints. Several empty doughnut boxes along with numerous paper coffee cups, a pile of creamers and sugar bags, and some half-eaten muffins, littered the table. Charlie gritted his teeth at the sight and felt the muscles in his neck tighten.

"Goddamn mother fuckers!" he said as he reached out and swept a box off the table as he passed by. Several half-full coffee cups splashed their contents among the nearby desks and computers.

In his office he dropped into his chair and yanked open the bottom drawer of his desk to find the small McDowell County phone book that he'd never before had occasion to use. He put the phone book on the middle of the desk in front of him, slammed the drawer shut, and then stopped. He looked out the window at the powerful black Bell 430 with the CanAmex lightning bolts on the side. *Stop and think for a moment! This was serious business now and it was time to declare once and for all, which side he was on.* He knew there was no going back and there were serious consequences if it were discovered that he interfered with their raid on the DeWitt farm. *But what was he going to do? What could he do?* Charlie chewed on the end of the fingernail of his right thumb as he contemplated the situation. *God, what kind of juice did CanAmex and their Charleston law firm have to be able to muster the DEA and the County Sheriff's Department, and who knows who the other guys were – probably from the U.S. Attorney's office – to take part in this game of showdown with Bud DeWitt? Money buys power all right.*

Charlie shook his head and slumped back in his chair. *Could he even stop what had already been put in motion?* He looked at his watch – 6:25. *He could very well be unable to do anything to help the DeWitts, and still give himself away. He could cut his own throat and bring down Dietrich Delahunt & Mackey along with him, all for nothing.* He thought quickly about Lucien Mackey, and then Ellen and her new house. *Damn! It was a bad risk to try to stop it.* Of that, he was certain.

He thought about Bud DeWitt and his wife Alice up on Angel Mountain. Probably having breakfast, unaware that the power of the Federal, State and County governments would be descending on them within the hour and their lives would never be the same again. Suddenly, Yarbrough's words came back to Charlie. *'Never know what a man will do when he's up against the wall.'* A cold shiver went through Charlie as he thought about Bud DeWitt, the proud farmer who vowed to be buried on Angel Mountain, and then the DEA agents with their black forty-fives and more weapons for sure in the back of the Land Cruiser and the patrol car. *Was this another Ruby Ridge in the making? "Back woods drug bust in West Virginia hills erupts in gun battle between federal agents and drug-crazed family at remote mountain hideout."* Not very likely, with Yarbrough in charge, Charlie concluded. The CES merger with its attendant PUC hearings didn't need headlines like that, but *Plan-B* certainly had the potential for tragedy.

Charlie remembered Sarah DeWitt – Natty's mother – and his promise to her. *'I'm going to do whatever I can to prevent it. I don't know if I can stop it, but I'll try'* he had said to her. And he'd told Natty the same thing, on the porch in front of *Barney's* that night. Then, to his surprise, Cecil Thomas, his boyhood pal flashed through his mind. Cecil, his best friend in the world for so long, who he'd left behind when he was anointed *prince of the city* by Duncan McCord. Charlie chuckled and shook his head. "Cecil, you *prick!*" he whispered.

Charlie tore open the thin phone book to the D's. He went up and down the column several times, *Dewire, Dewolfe . . .* no DeWitt. *Shit!* Now what? Charlie grabbed the phone and dialed information. *No listing for any DeWitt. Natty would have the number.* He started to look up Oakes. *Damn, he couldn't call her at home. What if her husband answered? How would he explain the call? Plus, he couldn't leave a trail, and Yarbrough's investigators were certain to check phone records afterward if Option B went into the toilet.* Charlie looked at his watch. *She'd be out running now anyway... 6:30 . . . where would she be? On the mountainside trail if she'd started at her usual time.* Charlie grabbed the keys out of his pocket as he ran through the center room. *Why hadn't he seen her on the road when he was driving in? Maybe she was a little late today and he'd turned off just before she'd reached the access road.* He felt the outside of his jacket pocket to make sure his cell phone was there.

Charlie locked the outside door but didn't bother with the alarm on his way out. At the end of the building, he slowed his pace when he remembered Krebs on duty at the front gate. His presence meant that he had long been part of Yarbrough's team. Charlie leisurely climbed into the Lexus and drove slowly to the gate house. He lowered the window after he'd come to a stop next to Krebs.

"Forgot my lap-top," said Charlie with a smile. "Gotta go back into town. May have breakfast while I'm there," he added buying some extra time. "See you later on."

Krebs just leaned against the guard shack with his arms crossed and nodded vaguely.

Charlie pulled slowly out onto the access road. He made a mental note to fire Chief Security Officer Krebs the first opportunity he got.

When he reached the woods, out of view from the guard house, Charlie gunned the accelerator making the Lexus fishtail briefly on the sandy pavement. The car bucked and bumped through the holes and ruts that were hardly noticeable at the slow speed he normally used on the road that had been broken up years ago by over-loaded coal trucks.

Coming out of the woods to South County Road, Charlie stopped in the middle of the road. He cupped his eyes and looked as far up toward Red Bone as he could, trying to see any little speck of movement that might be Natty. If she'd started later than usual, she might still be on this first leg of her run. Seeing nothing, Charlie turned right and floored it. The Lexus *wooshed* off powerfully down South County Road.

He glanced at the clock on the dash trying to calculate when Yarbrough's caravan would reach the farm. *A normal fifty-minute trip, they'd probably do it forty today at the attack speed they would be using. The road up Angel Mountain, thankfully, with all the s-curves and steep grades would be slow going for the big SUVs no matter what kind of a hurry they were in.* At any rate, he knew he had to find Natty within the next ten to fifteen minutes for her to call Bud DeWitt in time for them to be able to do *anything* to foil Yarbrough.

Christ, what the hell would they be able to do in just twenty or thirty minutes anyway? How much pot would they have growing up there – a small plot?

Several acres? What the fuck were they thinking about anyway – growing marijuana on a pig farm? Charlie slammed on the brakes as he flew past the wooden plank bridge over the stream that was the turn-off to the road that led up past Oakes Hollow and then up to the old logging road.

The road seemed steeper driving up it than it had the many times he'd run down it. The bumps and the ruts also had more impact on a car than on a pedestrian. Charlie accelerated as safely as he could through several sharp turns and severe grades, until about a half mile from the bridge, he saw the narrow stone-covered road on the left that he had been watching for. A small hand-painted sign that he'd never noticed jogging down the hill from the other direction, said "Oakes Hollow." The weather-beaten sign was wedged into the boulders at the side of the road. The crude lettering on the sign made it look more like a warning than a greeting.

Charlie stopped the car and looked up the precipitous section of road that went up to Oakes Hollow. *Maybe Natty was at home. Maybe she hadn't gone out running at all that morning.* Charlie thought about driving up and trying to find her. *No, it wasn't likely. She ran every morning.* He'd try the trail first. Then, if he didn't find her, he'd go into Oakes Hollow. The gray stones of the road reminded him briefly of the driveway at the Quail Hollow Lane house in Mamaroneck.

He stamped down on the accelerator. The Lexus edged sideways as the rocks and dust flew into the air, and then straightened out abruptly as it hit a brief patch of ancient pavement. In another minute he was up to the spot where the old logging road had been cut into the forest. He turned off the car, leaving the keys in the ignition, and got out. At the side of the road he climbed over the familiar barrier log and started off at a trot through the dark woods toward the mountain trail.

The boulder felt cool and damp on Natty's bare legs as she sat on the edge with her feet dangling over the side. She glanced at her watch. Another few minutes, then she'd have to hustle. She didn't want to be late for school, but it was her first visit to the rock since she brought Charlie Burden up there, and she wanted to finish reliving that special morning in her mind. Right up to where she threw up on him anyway. She chuckled. *God, didn't she grow a pair of balls, coming right out and asking him if there was "something" going on between them! What if he'd just laughed at her and said, 'c'mon little girl, don't be silly. You're just a nothing, little hillbilly. But he didn't say nothin' like that did he? He didn't laugh at her.* She closed her eyes and thought about the words that Charlie did say that morning and even though they scared her to death, she couldn't help replaying the sound of his voice in her head.

Then she thought about the phone call on Monday. Jack Garvey calling to hire Buck for the wood cutting project. The job that Charlie Burden had arranged. Finally, a call that wasn't all bad news or a bill collector. It was the first time in weeks she'd seen Buck smile as he bounded out of the trailer to share his news with Big Frank and his brothers.

Natty put her hands on the rock behind her and pushed away from the edge. As she rolled to the right to stand up, she immediately noticed the movement – something out of place in the scene that had no moving parts – far down the trail, a long way off, but something definitely moving. She focused on the movement and saw that it was a person, too far off to identify or to see if they were running or walking, but a person coming toward her, which was cause for concern. It was pretty rare to see anyone on the trail.

Natty went quickly through the grotto, climbed down the path back to the trail and resumed her run. Whether there was someone up ahead on the trail or not, she was still going to be late for work if she didn't make a good pace all the way to the top of Oakes Hollow.

After just a few minutes of hard running the person Natty had seen from up on the boulder came into view. It was a man wearing khaki pants and a jacket and work boots and he was jogging toward her. Her apprehension level grew until at about a hundred yards she saw that it was Charlie. She smiled and felt relief, and then, suddenly alarm again. *This wasn't good. This was trouble – Charlie Burden, in his work clothes, coming down the trail at her from the wrong direction.* She slowed down, then came to a walk about twenty yards from him. As they came together, Charlie pulled a cell phone from his jacket pocket and opened it up.

"Natty, call your grandfather," said Charlie, handing her the phone.

She took the phone without comment and slowly pushed the small buttons. Charlie had to reach over and push the green *send* button for her. She flashed a quick nervous smile.

"They got something growing up there they shouldn't have?" Charlie asked.

"Oh *shit!*" Natty exclaimed rolling her eyeballs.

"Tell him the marines are on their way."

They walked together along the trail at a leisurely pace. There didn't seem much point now in worrying about being late for work. The school would survive without her for a few minutes. It had been a quick conversation. Her mother answered the phone. 'The police are on the way up. They know about the cornfield. They'll be there in about twenty minutes,' was all Natty had said.

Charlie described to Natty the makeup of Yarbrough's strike force, including the DEA agents and the other SUV carrying what were probably state police. "There was also a cop in a county sheriff's cruiser. Seemed like more of a local guy. Big guy, overweight, with a thin mustache."

Natty pursed her lips and nodded her head knowingly. "Yeah, that'd be Wayne Lester, a deputy sheriff. Went to high school with him. He was an asshole then and he's still an asshole."

"They going to be able to do anything?" Charlie asked.

Natty shrugged her shoulders. "I don't know. Never asked about it. Never talked much about *Petey's garden*. Known about it since I was a kid he's been growing it. Right in the middle of the cornfield. Seemed to get a little bigger every year."

Natty squinted off to the southwest, in the general direction of Angel Mountain. "I remember the first time I ever smelled it. I was eight years old," she said. *During that terrible summer after Annie died, when everyone was miserable and she wandered around the farm and up and down Angel Mountain, like she'd done the previous year exploring everything with her little sister, but now all alone.* "I went walking by myself down to the chicken house which is way down at the low end of the farm and I heard a voice from down behind the house so I sneaked down and peeked around the corner and I smelled this sweet smoke that was floatin' by, and sittin' there on the rocks next to the stream is my mama and Uncle Petey both smokin' these corn cob pipes with a plastic bag full of weed on the rock between them. 'Course, I didn't know what it was at the time." Natty went silent for a few seconds as they continued walking. "Pretty sure that was before they started sleeping together." She laughed. "Hey, *welcome to West Virginia*, huh Charlie? Bet you don't hear stories like this back in Marmana – what is it?"

"Mamaroneck," said Charlie, smiling down at her.

Natty nodded briefly and then walked along quietly, her mind clearly occupied by Angel Mountain. "Mama always told me that Petey just grew it for them – for him and mama – and didn't sell any of it." She looked off toward Angel Mountain. "But I *know* that ain't true. Petey grows way too much for just the two of them. Done it before, you know. Sold the stuff. Went away for a year in jail when I was in sixth grade. I think when he and Bud go up to Huntington few times a year to sell their scrap iron, Petey sells some of his pot too. Just part of making a living on a little dirt-patch farm in West Virginia. But now instead of Petey going to jail, Bud and Alice are going to lose their farm." Natty glanced up at Charlie. "*That* don't seem fair does it?"

Charlie didn't answer her. He thought about Hank and his history lesson about coal mining. '*Nothing fair about what the coal companies done to the people of West Virginia. And nothin's changed in a hundred years.*' Maybe he was up against a force that was just too big to do anything about.

"No, it's *not* fair Natty, but let's wait and see what happens," Charlie said, trying to sound optimistic.

Natty furrowed her brow as the thought hit her. "Charlie, if Bud and Petey *are* able to do something, to get rid of the pot before they get up there, they're going to blame *you*, aren't they? They're going to know it was *you* that tipped Bud off, and then you're going to be in some deep shit aren't you?" She stopped walking and turned toward him with a concerned look on her face.

Charlie stopped and just shrugged. He smiled at her to alleviate her fears. "Eventually they might be able to trace the cell phone call, but I'll deal with it. In the mean time, I'll just play dumb. There were other people involved in this. Leak could have come from a lot of places."

"*Damn* Charlie." Natty started walking again at a quicker pace. "You shouldn't have done this. The agreement was that you'd do what you could without hurting yourself, without hurting your company. You remember? That night in front of the store?"

"I remember," said Charlie. "Don't worry about it. I'll be okay," sounding more confident than he was. "I just hope nothing, uh, foolish happens up there."

They walked along in silence, both engrossed in their own thoughts, until they entered the dense woods at the end of the trail. As Natty's jumping off point drew near, they both slowed their pace.

"Buck got the call, on Monday," Natty said smiling up at Charlie. "About the timber job."

"Yeah, okay, that's good," said Charlie. Reminded of Buck, he looked down at her searching for the scar over her eye and then over her mouth

"Charlie, you have no idea *how* good that is," she said, her face lighting up with excitement. "That was the best call we've had in the past twelve years." She reached a hand out and touched Charlie's forearm lightly. "Thanks for doing that Charlie. Buck really needed that."

Charlie smiled thinly. "Yeah, I hope it works out for him," he said, trying to sound sincere.

They came to a stop at the spot where Natty would go through the bushes to the top of Oakes Hollow. She turned to face Charlie. "Should I try to call you later? If I find out what happened up there?" Natty asked.

Charlie heard her words but as he looked at her face he couldn't help thinking about the scars and Buck, and the beating she must have endured. He took two steps closer to her, reached out his right hand and with his index finger, gently moved back the shock of hair falling across her eyebrow. The tip of his finger grazed her skin across the scar.

"Why didn't you tell me about this?" he asked softly but firmly. "When you were telling me about Buck."

Natty was taken by surprise. And she was nervous being this close to Charlie and feeling him touch her. She wanted to be mad, to be indignant at the question, but the look of concern on Charlie's face wouldn't let her. No man had ever shown her the kind of affection that Charlie Burden had just shown with one little gesture, one little question. She took a deep breath.

"Ain't nothing to tell about," she whispered. "People make mistakes is all. Buck made a little mistake and – "

"That's not a *mistake*," said Charlie, his voice rising with anger. He shook his head and looked away, mad at himself. She didn't deserve to be scolded by him. He looked back down into her eyes and spoke more softly. "Why'd you stay with him after that?" he asked. "You shouldn't have stayed with him."

Natty flashed a quick nervous smile then looked away. She shrugged her shoulders and took a few steps backwards then turned and walked toward the opening in the bushes.

Charlie thought that she must be angry and was going to just leave without saying anything more.

"Natty, I'm sorry if you think this is none of my business, but ..."

Natty stopped with her back to Charlie and turned her head to the side to listen. When Charlie hesitated, she turned around and faced him again. "But *what* Charlie?"

He shrugged his shoulders. "I'm worried about you Natty. I'm worried about you and the kids."

Natty threw her arms together across her chest and hunched her shoulders in an effort to fight her emotions. She looked away, across the trail into the dark woods until the feeling passed. She didn't want to talk about Buck and the beating he gave her, *ever*, with anybody, but she couldn't be mad at Charlie for being the first man that ever really seemed to care about her.

She turned back to face Charlie who hadn't moved from the spot where he had touched her. She smiled briefly. "It was a hard day for Buck, that day he, uh …hit me. It was a strange, queer kind of day for everyone in Red Bone. After every day being mostly like the one before it, and then all of a sudden all these strange, rich, beautiful, powerful people come flying in on helicopters with all their exciting news and giving out free food and all that free booze – all afternoon they drank – well, *shit*, wasn't all Buck's fault *that* day."

Natty looked over at Charlie and saw the quizzical look on his face. She smiled at him and took a couple of leisurely steps away from the bushes. "That was the day you and your friend Duncan McCord came to Red Bone. Came with all them politicians and everybody and that beautiful TV woman from Charleston." She gazed off into the forest as she spoke, avoiding the look of puzzlement that she knew would be on Charlie's face. "You had on a real nice tan suit and a beautiful white shirt that practically shined in the sunlight and a maroon tie." She smiled to herself at the image. "Christ, you looked like you just stepped out of one of those ads in *Vanity Fair*. And you wore suspenders."

"Natty, when was …?"

She continued without hearing him. "You and Mr. McCord came walking down along side the tent, right past where Buck and all his boys were drinking themselves silly, and you stopped at one table and you both got cigars." Natty looked over at Charlie and flashed a brief smile. "See, I always knew you smoked cigars."

Charlie shrugged. "I don't remember anything about that day. I remember vaguely, coming down for the announcement but …"

"Course you don't remember it Charlie. Why would you? Wasn't a big deal for you. Wasn't *nothin'* for *you*. But for *us* . . . ." Natty looked down at the ground and moved a small stone around with the toe of her running shoe as she recalled the memory of looking up and seeing Duncan McCord standing in front of her.

"Your friend Duncan said some nice things to me . . . course I made a jerk out of myself, and then he gave me this beautiful CanAmex jacket. And then, well that night, Buck come home drunk and wanted to know how I got the jacket, and I was a little looped myself, and," she hesitated and shrugged, "and maybe feeling a little, um, proud or somethin' and sayin' some stuff I shouldn't have and then, well …" Natty turned away and stared into the dark woods. "Buck just lost control of himself," she whispered. "It was dark and I know he couldn't see what he was doing to me and …" She scrunched up her cheeks and closed her eyes briefly as if to put and end to the thought.

"Natty, I don't understand what the connection is with that day and Buck …"

She turned toward him quickly. "Well that's just *it* Charlie," Natty said. "You don't understand how things *are* down here. This ain't Westchester County. Ain't no million-dollar houses down here. This is a hard place to live. Hard place for a man to make a living and have a family. I *told* you that once." She paused to calm herself. She wasn't mad at Charlie. "Buck sees men like you and Duncan McCord come down here for a couple hours, walking around looking so smug and successful and rich, smokin' your cigars and doling out free beer and food and a billion dollar project like it's nothin', and flying around in shiny black helicopters with gorgeous TV girls . . . well *course* he's going to be envious and feel small, feel like more of a failure then he already is." Natty paused in thought and then glanced back towards Oakes Hollow. "Just wasn't fair to Buck, that day, Charlie" she said softly. "Wasn't fair to him."

Charlie watched her and remained silent. He was thinking about the irony of Buck being envious of him. *Should he tell her how much he ached to trade places with Buck that very moment? To be her husband and care for her, protect her and make love to her, and be a father to Pie and Cat and live down here in the purity and solitude of the mountains.* The idea sent a warm glow through him. Then Natty spoke again.

"Ain't an easy place for a woman either Charlie, to try to answer your original question." She'd turned to face him and took a couple of steps closer. "Especially a woman with kids, and one retarded to boot. Ain't a lot of prospects for a woman down here, so you don't tend to pack up and head for the door every time there's a little . . . *excitement* in your marriage. Got enough welfare families in McDowell County without me takin' Pie and Cat off to live in some dirt-floor shanty with no heat and nothin' to look forward to 'cept a jar of corn liquor and that glassy fix your eyeballs get when you quit trying."

Natty took a step closer to Charlie and looked up into his eyes and smiled, the broad light-up-a-room smile that told him she wasn't angry about his questions. "Charlie, down here, if you're lucky enough to even *find* someone to love, well, you got to hold on to that tight as you can, like staying on a buckin' horse, you know? So that's what I'm doing, holding on, trying to make it come out right, and enjoying my daydreams in the mean time." She raised her eyebrows. "Okay?"

Charlie smiled with resignation and nodded. "Okay," he said. It was time to move on. He reached out a hand and playfully tugged down on the bill of her spider-man hat, like he always did with Pie. "Gotta go," he said.

Natty laughed. "Yeah me too," she said, taking off her hat and tucking it in the waistband of her shorts. Her hair fell wildly down around her face causing her to shake her head back. "So should I call you if I hear anything?" She gestured off to the south toward Angel Mountain.

Charlie thought for a moment. "No, probably not. Safer if you didn't. I'll find out soon enough anyway."

Natty nodded. "Okay. Yeah, you're right." She started toward the gap in the bushes. "Hey, you coming to our soccer game tomorrow? Home game. We're four and oh now, tearing up the league!"

"No, I wish I could. Going up to New York tonight for a while. Closing on the house on Monday," Charlie answered.

"The old house?"

"The new one."

Natty just nodded without saying anything. Then, she squinted her eyes and looked up at Charlie. "You coming back?" she asked softly.

Charlie chuckled. "Yeah, I'll be back," he said starting down the path. After a few steps, he turned and looked back, but Natty had disappeared into the bushes.

From back up on the boulder, the sun rising over the Alleghenies to the east was clearly visible, orange and warm in the cool air, igniting the tops of the mountains of the westernmost part of Virginia to the south. And closer, to the southwest, rising out of the hills still gray with shadow, a well-defined plume of dark smoke reached up to a cloud of wispy haze suspended over Angel Mountain.

Chapter 21

The store was on Lexington Avenue somewhere in the high forties, Charlie was certain. It had been years since he'd been there but there was a time when he was a fairly frequent visitor – when the kids were younger – shopping for baseball gloves, balls of all types, bats, lacrosse sticks, and cleats – *every year it seemed* – new soccer and baseball shoes. It was hard to find because it was on the second floor over a luggage store and a camera shop, the kind of team sporting goods store that Charlie thought must be unique to Manhattan. The store was more like a warehouse than a retail store, a labyrinth of high-ceilinged rooms connected by inclined ramps, each piled high with brown boxes.

Even at eleven o'clock in the morning on a Wednesday, the store was busy. The clerks – hunch-backed old men who all acted like owners – were busy shepherding customers up and down the ramps to the various sections of the store for each sport. Charlie found his way to a huge room stacked high with soccer equipment and got the attention of a salesman.

"Need uniforms for a soccer team," Charlie said.

"Little late in the season aren'tcha?"

"We're starting over," said Charlie with a smile. "Red shirts, black shorts and red socks. Under-14 team, fifteen players."

"Eighteen players," said the clerk, motioning for Charlie to follow him toward a back aisle. "That's the package."

"Okay, eighteen," said Charlie. "And some black warm-up jackets."

"How about some matching pants? Look real sharp," said the salesman warming up to the opportunity.

"Why not," said Charlie.

The clerk pulled down several large boxes and showed Charlie two shirt styles they had in stock. Charlie chose the more expensive of the two, a solid, blood - red silk from Nike, with a black collar and black stripes running down the sides from the armpits to the waist. The light–weight black nylon shorts had the Nike swoosh in red. They were the latest style the salesman said, the hottest thing on the market. Comes with numbers on the back and for just five dollars per shirt you could put the team name and logo on the left breast.

"*The Bones*," said Charlie.

The salesman smiled and nodded. "Got just the thing for you," he said leading Charlie over to a large book of team insignias, clip-art pictures and old logos. He went deep into the heavy book and then found the page he was looking for, and there it was, a ferocious looking, glowing silver skull and cross bones with red fire in the eyes. Charlie laughed when he saw it. It was perfect! He imagined the look on Pie's face when he saw his new shirt.

"Put it on the back of the jackets too," said Charlie.

The salesman raised an eyebrow. "Getting a little pricey now but I'll see what I can do for you." He led Charlie back to another aisle and after a short search found what he was looking for. He pulled down a large box and expertly opened it with his pocket razor. The shiny jet-black warm-up jackets were individually wrapped in plastic. "Top of the line Nike jackets. Seventy-two bucks a copy but I'll throw in the team name and the skull on the back for nothing. How's that?"

Charlie smiled. "How about the pants?"

"Team must have rich parents," said the clerk making more notes on his clipboard.

"Yeah," said Charlie smiling. "They're all in the energy business. Money's no object with these parents."

The order came to $3,500. "Take about two to three weeks . . ."

"I need it all in Red Bone, West Virginia by next week," said Charlie pulling out a corporate American Express Platinum Card. "Make it an even four grand if you can get it all down there by Monday."

The clerk smiled as he took Charlie's credit card. "Red Bone. Must be a real ritzy town."

"Yeah, it's quite a place," said Charlie

The mid-town, noon rush hour was in full flurry when Charlie came back out onto the sidewalk. The revolving doors of the office buildings and the banks were spinning out the clerks and managers and CEO's headed for lunch, shopping, or simply to enjoy the crisp fall air and a brisk mid-day walk in the world's greatest city.

Charlie went up to 48th Street and headed west. He felt good about the soccer uniforms. It was something that the kids would really appreciate, and there was no reason why Natty's team had to *look* like the poorest team in the league. He couldn't wait to see Pie's face when he saw the skull and cross bones on the warm-up jackets. Charlie was confident that the uniforms would indeed arrive in Red Bone on Monday. While some people were leery about doing business with merchants in New York, Charlie knew from experience that you may pay the highest prices – as he was sure he had for the soccer outfits – but once the deal was made, city merchants would always live up to their end of the bargain. It was a kind of high-priced, professional integrity that was part of the commercial culture of New York.

Charlie looked at his watch and saw that he had plenty of time until his two o'clock meeting with the CanAmex and Kerns & Yarbrough people back at the DD&M boardroom. He'd take a walk through Rockefeller Center, over to Broadway and back down through Times Square before heading back to the office on Park Ave. Lunch at Nathan's for a dog with everything on it and a root beer would complete the quick dose of New York that he badly needed before heading back to Red Bone that night.

Standing at the front window bar in Nathan's eating his hot dog, Charlie was hypnotized by the ceaseless parade of traffic in the street and on the sidewalk, pushing its way along Broadway. Then, across the street, between the buses and the trucks and the never ending sea of yellow cabs, an image caught his eye and made him refocus so he could look through the moving traffic and see the posters lining the wooden wall of the temporary pedestrian shelter. Charlie smiled. If he hadn't been away from the city, if he hadn't seen the image on the bulletin board in the alcove between *Barney's General Store* and *Eve's Restaurant* his first night in Red Bone, he would never have noticed the trademark icon of *Les Miserables*, the haunting bereted image of the waif Cosette that had decorated New York for so long it had become invisible to the locals. It reminded him of the trip sponsored by the Red Bone Baptist Church, scheduled for November. He immediately thought of Natty and wondered if she would be making the trip. *God, wouldn't she love to see New York! But, no, it didn't seem likely that she would want to take the time, or spend the money even if she could afford it. No, it was a little too extravagant for the mountain girl who never spent a dime on herself.* A glimmer of a plan began to form in the back of Charlie's mind.

His thoughts of Natty and the New York trip were dispelled as soon as he began the walk back to Park Avenue, replaced by anxiety over the impending meeting with Jack Torkelson, Larry Tuthill and who knows who else from CanAmex (probably a lawyer or two), along with Vernon Yarbrough who had been summoned from Charleston, plus Lucien Mackey.

Lucien had sounded worried when he reached Charlie at the old house in Mamaroneck on Sunday. Charlie had spent the weekend packing boxes for the move, which would happen after he'd gone back to West Virginia. The move that Ellen would orchestrate, when she was ready, after the renovation and redecorating – *amazing, that a million-plus dollar house could need so much work!* And after all their old furniture was sold – *how crazy it was of Charlie to think that their old furniture would fit with the décor of the hacienda.* Ellen was in fact the next morning leaving for a week-long shopping trip to Santa Fe and then Phoenix - *for the larger pieces* - accompanied by her new best friend, an interior decorator from Darien, who would be having a fine year at Charlie's expense.

"Torkelson and Tuthill are coming to town on Wednesday and they want you to stick around for a meeting," said Lucien. "Larry said Torkelson was bullshit mad over that Angel Mountain fiasco and they were bringing that lawyer up from Charleston and they were going to find out what went wrong. You have anything to do with that Charlie?"

Charlie considered the question for a moment before he replied. Obviously Tuthill must have expressed his suspicion of him to Lucien who was now caught in the middle. "No Lucien," he lied, to keep his friend above the fray. "It wasn't me who messed up their plans."

And that would be his story, Charlie mused as he crossed Fifth Avenue at 44th Street. *Screw 'em.* If they wanted to act like gangsters, then he didn't know anything about the plan and he had no idea what had happened until he got in touch with Terry Summers from the plane on Friday night. Charlie smiled inwardly as he recalled his brief conversation with Summers who was having a cocktail on the deck at his apartment in Bluefield. Even though it was obvious to Charlie that Summers had some vested interest in the CanAmex side of the Angel Mountain issue, the junior engineer was in good humor over the debacle of that morning.

"Charlie, you had to be there to appreciate it," Summers reflected laconically. "Yarbrough's sitting there at the picnic table out in front of the house, sitting across from farmer DeWitt, and looking real smug, ready to close the deal. And the feds and that county cop are all standing around relaxing, drinking lemonade that the farmer's wife brought out and letting Yarbrough do his thing, you know." Summers paused to take a sip of his drink.

"So Yarbrough says to the farmer, 'now we know you got something illegal growing in that corn field up there,' and he points up toward the corn, which is about eight feet tall now. And farmer DeWitt looks up toward the field and just keeps staring at it for what seemed like at least a minute, and then all of sudden, *whump,* the damn field is totally engulfed in flames. The whole thing, all at once, flames are shooting up twenty feet. We could feel the heat down there a hundred yards away. And DeWitt looks back at Yarbrough and he winks at him and says, 'what corn field?'" Summers laughed. "Oh Christ, Charlie, it was funny. Course Yarbrough didn't get much of kick out it.

"We all went up there then, staying clear of the field because the heat was intense, and round back of the field there's a barn with this thousand gallon gasoline tank and a two hundred foot hose. And Petey, the son, he's standing there smelling like a gasoline station, watching it burn and when we all get up to him he says, stuttering real bad, 't-time to c-clear the field.'

"Well it was real obvious to everyone that Petey had sprayed down the field with gasoline, probably really soaking the pot plants, and then tossed a torch in there and ..." Summers voice fell away and was softer and more serious when he resumed. "So they had to get tipped off Charlie – twenty, thirty minutes at least – to give the corn a good soaking and, well, Yarbrough's not happy."

Charlie glanced at his reflection in the polished copper panel of the elevator rising to the sixth floor of the Dietrich Delahunt & Mackey building. He noted the difference in his appearance from the thousands of times he'd ridden this elevator during his years at the firm. His hair was longer, curling over the top of his ears slightly and at the back of his neck, and his face was darker from so many hours in the sun at the construction site. He was also tie-less, forgoing the normal DD&M corporate look for khaki chinos, a white cotton dress shirt, a black blazer and his topsiders without socks. If he was going to take a pummeling from Torkelson, Tuthill and Yarbrough, and maybe even lose his job today, he was going to be comfortable doing it.

The conference room was more crowded than Charlie had expected when he walked in five minutes late. The table was covered with plastic food containers, napkins, plastic utensils and a variety of beverage containers. Charlie was a little relieved to see that a meeting and working lunch had preceded his appearance and that he wasn't the lead item on the agenda today. But there were too many people in the room, and the make up of the group bothered him. He immediately got the feeling that there was more at stake here than an inquiry about the Angel Mountain incident. There was another agenda in play that he was unaware of and it made him uncomfortable.

At the far end of the long table, in his usual isolated position, was Jack Torkelson with only a bottle of mineral water and a glass of ice in front of him. Larry Tuthill who would be directing the meeting sat near the middle of the table. To his left were two men who Charlie knew vaguely as CanAmex lawyers. Directly across from Tuthill was Vernon Yarbrough with Leonard at his side. The Charleston lawyers had no lunch containers in front of them and by the way they were looking into their briefcases it appeared that they had just preceded Charlie into the conference room.

As Charlie stood, acknowledging the people he knew around the table – there were too many to bother with the customary hand shakes – he couldn't help focusing immediately on the individuals who seemed out of place. Seated by himself between the Charleston lawyers and Torkelson, was Warren Brand, the ultra-ambitious Vice Chair of the DD&M Executive Committee. Directly across the table from him were two other younger members of the executive committee, shills of Brand, Charlie had no doubt, and accomplices in whatever scheme Brand was working on. And he was working on *something*, it was obvious by his attendance at this meeting with Dietrich Delahunt & Mackey's largest and most powerful client. Brand's position at the table, not next to, but closest to Jack Torkelson, also had meaning to Charlie. He recalled his last contact with Warren Brand, in his office just before leaving for West Virginia, Brand trying to schmooze his Giants tickets out of him.

At the near end of the table closest to the door, Lucien Mackey stood to offer Charlie his hand, as always. Charlie smiled at his old friend as he accepted Lucien's huge bone-crushing shake. "Nice to see you again Charlie," said Lucien, always a paragon of cordiality under all circumstances. "Take a seat, have something to drink. Hungry?"

"No, no thanks," said Charlie grinning. "Just had a Nathan's." Charlie took a chair a space away from Lucien, trying to spare his old friend the appearance of being too closely aligned with him.

After a few moments of fussing with a napkin and cleaning up the remnants of a turkey sandwich in front of him, Larry Tuthill re-started the meeting.

"Okay, now that Charlie and the Kerns & Yarbrough folks are here, we can get to these West Virginia items here." Tuthill looked down at some notes in front of him. He looked over at Charlie with a quick, forced smile. "Now Charlie, first of all let me say that the Red Bone project is going along extremely well. *Extremely well*. Under budget and ahead of schedule." He chuckled. "Just the way we like it." Tuthill looked at Charlie as if to invite comment.

Charlie smiled briefly. "I know."

"Yeah, that's right. 'Course you do." Tuthill looked around the table with a wide grin.

Charlie took the opportunity to take a glance around the table himself. First at Jack Torkelson at the far end whose face was noncommittal as he took a sip of water. Then at Vernon Yarbrough. The lawyer's eyes were glued to his notes in front of him, the stern set of his jaw muscles revealed the smoldering anger within.

"Now Charlie," Tuthill continued. "We've got a couple of issues here we need to discuss today having to do with the Red Bone situation. First off is the issue of the Planning Board meeting down there, couple of weeks ago, and how we went from putting a new roof on some little library to building a brand new structure along with some kind of *athletic field megaplex* that we never discussed, or for that matter, approved." Tuthill stopped talking and looked over at Charlie, along with everyone else at the table except for Yarbrough.

"You said you had two issues, Larry," said Charlie. "What's the second one?"

Vernon Yarbrough slapped the table hard with his open hand. "You know *goddamn well* what the second issue is!" he exploded, startling the others at the table, particularly Warren Brand and the other DD&M Executive Committee members who weren't familiar with the Charleston lawyer's style or demeanor. He glared at Charlie and jabbed his right forefinger through the air for emphasis. "I used up a lot of valuable capital last week, with a lot of important people down there Burden. Called in some big markers from some powerful people ... the DEA, state cops, States Attorney's Office." The lawyer looked away from Charlie and shook his head with exasperation. "Sittin' there ready to close the deal with that old pig farmer, and *whoosh,* the damn field goes up like a fucking napalm strike in the Mekong Delta. And *Goddamit* Burden, you're the only one who could have tipped them off. And I want to know why," he added sitting back in his chair.

All eyes were on Charlie and Larry Tuttle didn't say anything, indicating that he was content with moving the Angel Mountain incident to the front of the discussion. As Charlie moved his chair closer to the table to address the meeting, his eyes met those of Warren Brand. He was staring at Charlie with furrowed brow and a hard set to his mouth, looking outwardly more serious about the issue than he was entitled to be. Charlie was stumped as to what Brand's interest was here, and it was the only thing about the meeting that worried him. He could take care of CanAmex because in the end, all they cared about was results and he was building their power plant much faster and cheaper than they had expected, and that was worth a lot more than the pride and reputation of some hillbilly law firm. And the Angel Mountain coal, they'd just get through eminent domain which is how it should have been done in the first place. But Brand was a puzzle.

"Alright Vernon," Charlie said calmly, putting his arms on the conference table, "first of all, I didn't call the farmer, so stop accusing me of ..."

"My man Krebs at the gate saw you leave a few minutes after we set out for the mountain!" Yarbrough said loudly.

'*My man Krebs.*' *A slip by Yarbrough.* Charlie made another mental note to get rid of Security Chief Krebs. "I was going back to town to get my laptop, and I told Krebs that." Yarbrough sat back and glowered in his seat with his arms crossed.

After a pause, Charlie continued. "Now Vernon, let me tell you a couple of things about your raid on Angel Mountain. First of all you had too many people involved, too many possibilities of a leak. Which is what happened." Charlie looked down at the table and paused for effect. "Vernon, did you know that that local cop you had along – Wayne Lester is his name – he was a high school sweetheart of Natty DeWitt, the farmer's granddaughter? And that he's still got the hots for her?"

Yarbrough looked as if an electrical charge had passed through him. He turned quickly to Leonard at his side, who just shook his head and raised his shoulders.

"*Wha What?* How do you know that Burden? Who *told* you that?" Yarbrough was clearly flustered.

Charlie stayed on the offensive. "Cause everybody in *town* knows it. My landlady told me. My neighbor, Hankinson, the Planning Board Chairman, told me he taught them in school and you couldn't pry them apart. *Christ* Yarbrough, what were you thinking? Didn't you do any background checks on those people?" Yarbrough again turned to Leonard to try to throw off some of the blame.

Before Yarbrough could compose himself, Charlie pressed the attack. "Now Vernon, let me tell you something else about your plan that you may not have realized." Charlie paused to make sure he had the lawyer's attention and then rose to his feet and leaned out with his hands flat on the table towards Yarbrough. "It was the *stupidest*, most *fucked up*, most *ill-advised* scheme I ever heard of and you're the luckiest man in this room it blew up in your face." Charlie stood up straight with his hands in his pockets and looked directly at Larry Tuthill.

"Larry, I don't know what you guys were thinking about, okaying a harebrained scheme like that," Charlie said while pointing at Vernon Yarbrough. Larry Tuthill winced a little and looked over at Yarbrough, as he realized that Charlie Burden was probably right and was soon to make him look like a complete ass.

"You go up there with an army, like the *fucking Gestapo* . . ." Charlie shook his head in wonderment. "What a *disaster* you guys almost caused." Charlie moved around the open area at the end of the table and took his time knowing he had the group's complete attention. "Cause let me tell you what would have happened," he continued like a history professor lecturing a class. "The farmer and his son . . . *they would have gone to jail*," he said loudly. "There is *no way* they're going to sell you the farm under those conditions, no way at all, and you should have *known* that Vernon," he said looking directly at the chagrined lawyer. "They're too proud," he said more softly. "They're too proud, and it's all they've got in the world to show for a lifetime of sweat and hard work . . . and for all the heartache they've suffered." The sound of Alice DeWitt's voice flashed through Charlie's mind. "Their whole family's buried up there on that mountain." He shook his head slowly. "No, they don't sell. Not that family, and it was lunacy to think they would.

"So now you've got the DEA, and the State Police and a field full of marijuana, and you're all done Vern, you've shot your wad, so now the cops do their part and arrest the farmer and his son, right?" Yarbrough had no rebuttal.

"And then what happens Vern?" Charlie had moved around the end of the table to have a more direct view of Yarbrough, who offered no response. "Well you should know Vern. Two men in jail. Next thing that happens is they get a lawyer. Maybe a sharp criminal lawyer from Charleston. And the lawyer listens to the pig farmer's story, and the first thing he says is, *'what the hell was a corporate lawyer from Charleston representing both the CanAmex Corporation and the Ackerly Coal Company, doing on a drug raid with the DEA and the State Police?'"*

Larry Tuthill winced at the mention of CanAmex and stole a quick look down the table at Jack Torkelson who sat motionless, concentrating on Charlie's words.

"And then farmer DeWitt tells him the whole story," Charlie continued, "about the Angel Mountain coal and how this same Charleston lawyer had been up several times trying to buy the farm. So our criminal lawyer drops a dime and all of a sudden Vern, because of you, we've got a nice story for the front page of the Charleston Gazette and every other paper in West Virginia about how the CanAmex Corporation was trying to extort a local family out of their farm like it was the late eighteen hundreds all over again.

"But worst of all Vern, as we all know we've got a pretty important PUC hearing coming up in the spring concerning *the merger with Continental Electric Systems.*" Charlie purposely emphasized the magic words that made even Jack Torkelson at the end of the table shift his weight slightly in his chair. "But now, instead of worrying about a dirt - poor farmer or his hillbilly granddaughter, now you've got a big time criminal attorney – one of your own, Vern – with his fist around your client's balls and a multi-billion dollar merger at stake."

Charlie looked quickly at Larry Tuthill. "How's that feel Larry?" Then standing taller, Charlie stared down at the far end of the table. "Jack?" Jack Torkelson took a sip of his water without replying.

Charlie walked back to his chair, shaking his head. "It was an asinine plan Yarbrough, and you're lucky that cop ratted you out," he said as he took his seat again.

Vernon Yarbrough leaned forward onto the table. It was his turn but he didn't seem too anxious to debate Charlie's synopsis. Charlie knew that the CES merger was the wild card in this game and his prognostication was too sound and too ominous for the lawyer to refute. "Well, a course, we didn't see it coming out that way," Yarbrough offered, unaccustomed to meekness, "but you never know what might of happened. Maybe it would have . . ."

"Yeah, okay Vern," Charlie cut him off. "Now about the Planning Board and the library roof thing." Vernon Yarbrough sat back, relieved that they were moving on from the Angel Mountain fiasco.

"We got lucky there too. Hankinson, the Chairman, has become a close friend of mine. He lives next door to me in the apartment building in Red Bone." Charlie sat back in his chair in a more relaxed position for the easy part of the meeting. "We play cribbage almost every evening," Charlie said with a smile. "So at the beginning of the meeting he pulls me aside . . . you saw him Vern, right? . . . and tells me we've got some trouble with the other two Planning Board members. They're going to okay the pond relocation because Hank got their commitment, but they don't think much of CanAmex or the roof project so they're going to sock it to us down the road by making us jump through hoops and apply for permits for everything we want to do."

"Like *what*?" Vernon Yarbrough asked, trying to regain a leadership position with his client.

"Like making us get a permit for bringing in the turbines over the town roads, three different permits," Charlie shot back quickly. "Like a permit for cutting the right-of-way through the forest ..."

"They can't ..." Yarbrough tried.

"Or for flying helicopters over the town, or for taking water from the Heavenly River, or, or for having *port-a-potties on the site!*" Charlie said loudly. "They can do anything they want Vern, and they're a couple of miserable pricks according to Hank. So if they're not happy, they can just shut us down anytime they want."

"C'mon Burden, there's laws and statutes that . . ."

"Oh Vern, don't tell me about statutes!" Charlie raised his voice to keep his momentum. "You know the way those backwoods boards operate Vern. They can destroy you with red tape and delays in spite of the statutes and by the time you get 'em into court you're *two years* behind schedule."

Larry Tuthill visibly flinched at the mention of a two-year delay. Torkelson took a quick sip of his mineral water. Yarbrough sat back in resignation.

"So I had to improvise," Charlie continued. "We build them a new building and some athletic fields and we get the permanent cooperation of the planning board. Now we own them," Charlie added, knowing the kind of words CanAmex liked to hear. "Plus," he leaned forward onto the table to play another trump card, "when the PUC hearings come around in the spring, we've got a show-piece of community involvement to put on display for the state wide media. And we get it all for under a million bucks."

"Less than a million?" Larry Tuthill asked.

"Right around a million probably, to do it right," Charlie answered.

"And we've got the board on our side now? They reacted positively to your *revised* plan?"

Charlie grinned widely. "Larry, the crowd stood and cheered, along with the Planning Board guys."

"They cheered?" asked Tuthill, looking over at Yarbrough. "Vern, that what happened?"

Yarbrough nodded grudgingly. "Yeah," he said softly. "They loved it."

"When's the last time CanAmex got a standing ovation at a town meeting Larry?" Charlie asked, pressing his advantage.

Larry Tuthill sat back in his chair with a broad smile. "That's good Charlie. That's pretty good."

At the end of the table, Jack Torkelson stirred, drawing the group's attention. He turned in his chair to square up with the table indicating that he was about to speak.

"Okay," he said in his customary whisper. "Let's put this all behind us. Charlie, you go back down there and keep the plant ahead of schedule and build the town its library and baseball field. Take care of the planning board, and keep an eye on the DeWitt granddaughter. Neutralize her with this new library. Make it a first class project, spare no expense, but make it clear to the girl that it all stops if she causes trouble. You're right, it could help with the PUC hearings."

Torkelson turned toward the Charleston lawyers. "Yarbrough, you get started on the eminent domain proceedings, like we discussed. Get the judge and everyone else on the same page, same timing. Spend whatever you have to to keep it quiet but *get the job done*."

"Already in the works, Jack," Yarbrough replied confidently. "All set for mid – November. Going to be a county initiative and we'll have the hearing down there in Red Bone. Be a real quiet, boring little proceeding."

"Then we're done here," Torkelson announced.

Charlie closed the door to his office and blew out a deep breath. He'd lied and bluffed his way through the inquiry and played on his client's weak points and come away in a stronger position than when he'd started. But he had no illusions about what had just taken place or about his position on the CanAmex account or within the hierarchy of Dietrich Delahunt & Mackey. His days were numbered, it was clear from the inquest that he'd just left. He survived just long enough to finish the job in Red Bone because they needed him there, particularly because of his relationship with Hank, and with the *DeWitt granddaughter*, but after they had taken the farm and after the turbines were in ahead of schedule, Torkelson and Tuthill were going to put a bullet in his head and he'd be done with CanAmex and done at Dietrich Delahunt & Mackey.

His thoughts were interrupted by a soft rap on the door. Lucien Mackey shut the door behind him and stood close to Charlie. He spoke softly. "Nice job Charlie," he said with thin smile. "You handled that beautifully. We live to fight another day," he added cryptically.

Charlie leaned close and looked his friend directly in the eye. "What's going on Lucien? What's up with Brand?"

Lucien walked over and dropped his huge frame into one of the low leather chairs next to the window looking out on Park Avenue. He looked tired and drawn as he pointed to the other chair indicating that Charlie should take a seat also.

Mackey gazed out the window and shook his head slowly. "My time is about up here Charlie. They're going to squeeze me out, Brand and the rest of the committee."

"That's impossible Lucien." Charlie was shocked by his friend's statement. "There's no way they can . . ."

"Times have changed Charlie," Lucien interrupted. "The young guys, led by Brand, are gaining on us and eventually they'll have the votes. They'll move the company out of New York and sell this building, and all the *remaining* partners will reap the financial windfall."

"C'mon Lucien. That's an old issue. It's been brought up and put down every year since I've been here. You've made it clear that you'd never move the company or sell the building and you've always had more than enough votes . . ."

Lucien smiled and held up his hand to silence Charlie. "Brand has CanAmex now and they're too big, too powerful now for me to stand up to."

"How the hell did that happen?" asked Charlie, still stunned by Lucien's revelation. "How did Brand get . . ."

"It's not Brand, Charlie," Lucien interrupted. "He's not capable of managing something like this – we both know that. It's Torkelson. It's Torkelson, Charlie. He's behind it all."

Charlie just sat back in his seat ready to listen.

"Torkelson's star is rising fast Charlie. He *is* CanAmex now that Duncan and Red Landon are so far removed from operational matters. He's been a huge part of their growth strategy and their success, and this Red Bone plant will be the crown jewel on his resume. He brings this one in – the biggest, most efficient, most profitable non-nuclear plant ever built in North America – brings it in ahead of schedule and a hundred million dollars under budget, then there's no stopping him. He'll have the power to do whatever he wants at CanAmex."

"Maybe I should dump some ball bearings into the electrical conduits," Charlie offered without conviction.

Lucien smiled thinly. "Not the way we do things, heh Charlie?"

"So Torkelson and Brand have a deal, is that it Lucien?"

Lucien smiled thinly. "My spies tell me that sometime before the next full board meeting in the spring, Torkelson's going to use his leverage to pressure enough votes to back Brand for managing partner, *and* pass a resolution to move out of New York and sell the building. I'll be voted out and handed a golden parachute, and, I'm afraid, so will you my good friend, along with several other partners."

"And he'll have plenty of leverage," Charlie responded. "Christ, next year we stand to make what – thirty million in fees from all the CanAmex business?"

"Probably more with a couple of new projects they're talking about now," said Mackey. "And Torkelson will have the power by then to take it all away if he wants to. He's practically running the company now."

Charlie gazed out the window for a moment watching the traffic on Park Avenue, thinking about their situation. He looked back at Lucien. "So what does Torkelson get? What's his deal with Brand?" Charlie's voice had dropped into the lower tone that men use to discuss the darker issues of business transactions.

Lucien Mackey leaned forward with his hands locked, arms on his knees and looked down at his highly polished black shoes. Shifting his eyes up to engage Charlie's, Mackey spoke in a deep-throated whisper. "My guy tells me that Brand had a couple of belts with him one night and let it slip, that Torkelson gets five mil out of the deal and something a little short of that for Tuthill too, all on the quiet, after Brand takes over and the building gets sold."

Charlie shook his head. "So he's a crook. A cheap fucking extortionist," Charlie said bitterly.

"Yeah, but you'd never be able to prove it." Lucien leaned back in his chair and looked out the window. "That's the way it is now Charlie. The world's changing. It's all about money now. *Everything's* about money. Money and the power to make more money. And having it all *today*."

Charlie suddenly thought about the China project, Lucien's dream and his passion, that he would be cut off from if he were forced out of the company. Lucien may never see the China project completed . . . and Charlie would probably never see it at all. *Damn, this was turning into a swamp that there was no way out of. Why bother with any of it any more? Why not just pack it in and leave the company now and forget about China, forget about West Virginia? Let some one else build their plant, and just get free of these people.* Then he thought about Ellen and her new house, the *hacienda* that she was so thrilled with and proud of, that would be a severe financial problem if he were to leave the company abruptly. Out of the corner of his eye, Charlie noticed on his desk, the stack of plans and architectural drawings of small libraries and athletic fields that Nina Matlin, DD&M's librarian had compiled from sources that only she could draw on. *Yes, he still had things left to do in West Virginia, some responsibilities beyond the CanAmex plant.*

Then he thought about Natty Oakes and his heart skipped a beat when he pictured in his mind how she looked that brief moment when she took off her hat and shook out her hair the last time he saw her, on the trail the morning of the raid. He recalled her last words to him ... *you coming back?* And then he thought about Pie and how good it felt to pick him up and spin him around, and hug him, and watch him make that grotesque, comical, contortion of laughter on his face that was the expression of pure joy. *Yes, he'd be going back. God, he couldn't wait to get back to West Virginia! That's where his life was now.*

"Well I've got a company to run," Lucien's words jarred Charlie from his thoughts, "and you've got a power plant to build Charlie." Lucien was up out of his chair with his hand extended. Charlie rose up to see his friend off.

"The barbarians are at the gate Charlie," Lucien said with a grin.

"Well, we'll find a way to fight them off Lucien. We always do," said Charlie gripping his friend's hand.

Lucien nodded aggressively. "Yeah, we'll find a way," he said loudly, putting on his customary self-confident smile, but Charlie could see that his eyes didn't agree.

Chapter 22

The yellow school bus lurched and swayed along the winding road as the gray-haired woman, leaning as far forward as she could to see the road through thick bifocals, struggled with the over-sized steering wheel. Sitting sideways in the front seat across the aisle, shoulders resting against the side window, Natty kept a wary eye on the driver and on the road approaching through the split windshield, her left hand squeezing the top of the seat as they went into each turn. Although Geneva Gunnells had been the elementary school bus driver for nearly forty years, Natty forced herself to be vigilant for the moment when the seventy-year-old's clock might stop ticking and she'd have to leap across the aisle and grab the wheel before the bus and her soccer team plunged through a guard rail and off into oblivion.

"How you doin' 'Neva?" Natty called out over the noise of the whining engine.

The driver half turned her head. "Aye? What's that?" she yelled back.

Natty just smiled and shook her head briefly. It wasn't worth trying to carry on a conversation with Geneva while she was driving the noisy bus. The old woman's hearing was at about the same stage as her eyesight.

Natty decided to try to relax and forget about the twisting road. Geneva Gunnells had driven the road up to Welch probably a thousand times in her life and she'd make it again this trip.

Two seats behind the driver, Emma Lowe sat by herself trying to read a thick textbook. The bumping and jostling of the bus didn't help her concentration on the page that she stared at blankly as the book moved around in her lap. Behind Emma, there were two empty seats on each side of the bus, the *Bones* preferring to congregate in the rear seats.

In the back seat of the bus, Zack Willard was holding court as he always did, talking loudly and laughing with his huge, white grin, while Jimmy Hopson and George Jarrell, twisted around in the seat in front of him, were laughing and yelling to be heard as they contributed to the story. As best Natty could tell, they were imitating some teacher from the middle school. Sitting next to Zack in the rear seat was Paul, who Zack had adopted as his "main man" and was engaged in a season-long project to get him to use some English swear words. Paul grinned along with the others although Natty knew he probably had no idea what they were laughing about. Standing in the aisle with his long arms holding on to the overhead safety railings, Sammy Willard would alternately throw his head back and stomp his foot on the floor of the bus as the joke continued. Next to him, with his head only coming up to around Sammy's armpit, the Pie Man, holding on to the edge of a seat, was pushing his way into the middle of the action. His back was to Natty but she could tell from the hunch of his shoulders that he had on one of his severe *happy faces.*

There seemed to be some extra enthusiasm in her team today, and while none of them would admit it, Natty knew that it was because this was the first game they would be playing with their new uniforms. That the game was against Welch, the *Bones'* biggest rival, with their expensive blue uniforms, only added to their excitement. Natty herself had to admit that she didn't want to miss the look on the faces of the Welch coach and the smug parents on the Welch side of the field when her team filed off the bus.

Natty looked over at Emma, still scowling into her book. She had her left leg wedged between the side of the bus and the seat in front of her as she usually did, and her right leg stretched out straight under the seat. Her shiny black warm-up jacket was zippered all the way up forming a snug turtleneck collar. As she read, Emma chewed on the short length of cord attached to the jacket's zipper. The matching black pants had a red stripe running down the outside seam that Natty had to concede looked very sharp, although she would have preferred for the team to wear red warm-ups rather than the ominous-looking black. But the kids were ecstatic about the whole outfit and were still having trouble believing that they were really wearing soccer uniforms that would be the envy of every player in the league.

Natty had a tough time believing it herself when she discovered the six boxes piled just inside the door of the children's library. She'd gone in to get the balls and her folding blackboard before Wednesday's practice and there they were. A note taped to the top box said only, "Mrs. Oakes – A gift from the CanAmex Corp." It wasn't signed, but he didn't have to sign it. The boxes all had white shipping labels from a sporting goods store in New York City, addressed to Charlie Burden c/o *Barney's General Store. He must have noticed her reaching up over the door for the key that day they walked down the hill together, Charlie's first weekend in Red Bone, when he went up and inspected the roof.*

After finding an old screw driver to score the tough packing tape, she was finally able to get a box open but still couldn't figure out what the contents were until she pulled out one of the red shirts and saw *The Bones* inscription and the silver skull and cross bones on the breast. Natty's mouth fell open and she lost her breath for a second when she realized the boxes contained soccer uniforms for her kids, expensive Nike uniforms that you probably couldn't even find in West Virginia. Her amazement grew as she discovered the black shorts and red socks, and then the incredible warm-up suits. Then she found an envelope with a form-letter thank-you to Charlie from the salesman along with a packing slip and a pink copy of the invoice. Natty gasped and nearly doubled over when she saw the total at the bottom of the long invoice. *Four thousand dollars! For soccer uniforms. My God, what a different world he comes from!* She'd gotten this year's red, numbered T-shirts for less than a hundred dollars for the whole team, and if you needed black shorts, they were $3.49 at the Wal-Mart in Bluefield. *And why would he do this? Why did he care?*

Natty looked back toward the rear of the bus, toward her *four thousand dollar team.* They had quieted down a little as they got closer to Welch. *Maybe they were nervous about showing off their new uniforms.* No, that didn't seem right to Natty. The whole team was so proud of their uniforms they couldn't wait for this game to come. Then Sammy Willard moved to the side and she could see

Zack, again at the center of the group, but now the smiles and the laughter were gone and Zack was talking in earnest tones and gesturing and pointing at different boys and Natty knew he was talking about today's game and the Welch team and he was getting *The Bones* ready. That was good, Natty thought to herself, because she knew this was going to be a tougher game than when they took Welch by surprise in the first game of the season in Red Bone. Welch was always a strong team and their coach hated to lose, especially to Natty's team. Plus, Natty knew that Welch had been missing a few of its better players for that first game when they took *The Bones* too lightly.

Natty glanced at her watch and looked outside to see where they were. It was quarter of five and they were still ten miles or so from Welch. It was going to be close to make the five o'clock game in time. Geneva Gunnells was hunched intently over the steering wheel, wrestling the bus away from the soft shoulder of the curving road. Natty knew it was hopeless to try to get her to speed up. And probably dangerous too. She just hoped they wouldn't arrive more than the allowable ten minutes late, or that prick coach of the Welch team would demand a forfeit.

*   *   *

Charlie Burden skipped down the last flight of stairs that led to the vestibule between the store and the restaurant. He was in a good mood, anticipating an enjoyable afternoon and evening with Pullman Hankinson. He'd spent the morning with the surveying crew down at the soccer field plotting out the new drainage system, and then some time with the demolition contractor that was going to take down the old library. He called it a day around one o'clock and walked up the hill to take a shower and get ready for the trip over to Welch to watch *The Bones'* soccer game with Hank.

Hank had knocked on his door a few minutes earlier to tell him that he was going out to gas up the Chrysler at Gus Lowe's garage and he'd meet Charlie out in front of the store in fifteen minutes.

Having some time to spare, Charlie wandered into the restaurant to say hi to Eve if she was around. It still bothered him that she had obviously cooled to him after being so friendly his first two months in Red Bone and at some point he needed to find out why.

In the first booth immediately inside the door, against the front windows, he recognized the unmistakable form of Mabel Willard filling most of one side of the booth. Across from her sat Ada Lowe and a white woman that he didn't recognize.

Mabel Willard's huge smile and a loud "well haloo mister Burden!" along with a summoning wave, brought Charlie to the side of the booth. Taped to the side of the table was a hand-lettered poster stating "New York City Trip! Sign up today!"

Mabel slid over toward the window, squeezing tight to the wall to leave just enough room on the bench for Charlie. "Come sit down with us here mister

Burden, for a second. Need to talk to you 'bout somthin' you might take an interest in."

"Well, I've only got a few minutes," Charlie said as he settled into the booth. He nodded to Ada Lowe. "Going over to Welch with Hank to watch the Willard brothers and Emma play soccer." Charlie didn't want to keep Hank waiting but the sign about the Red Bone Baptist Church's New York trip to see *Les Miserables*, reminded him of a thought he'd had in New York.

Ada Lowe smiled. "Oh, that's nice mister Burden. I'm too old to be traveling to all them games, but that's nice that you boys are going over."

Mabel introduced Charlie to the third woman, a travel agent from Bluefield who was handling the details of the church trip to New York.

"Now then Mister Burden," Mabel started in not to waste time, "I'm thinking that you might be interested in going on our little trip once you see how reasonable an offer we're promotin', and maybe your friend Pullman Hankinson too, although knowin' how close that old coot is with his wallet, I wouldn't count on his companionship. But we surely do need a few more sign-ups as we only got fifteen out of the twenty bodies we need to get these special group rates." Mabel looked over at the travel agent who smiled and nodded her agreement.

Charlie listened politely, wondering why *anyone* had signed up for the trip, as Mabel rattled off the details of the New York *adventure* . . . a ten-hour bus trip each way with a stop for lunch at a *Bob Evans* in Pennsylvania, two nights at the Milford Plaza, and of course, the trip's salvation – a Saturday matinee ticket to *Les Miserables*. And all for just $321, which, Charlie had to agree, in spite of the bus trip, was probably a pretty good value. "Plus you ain't never had as much fun as you're going to have singin' Negro spirituals for ten hours with a bus load of crazy black women!" Mabel whooped, making Charlie laugh along with the other women.

"So what do you say Mister Burden," Mabel got back to business, slapping the fingers of her right hand on the table for emphasis, "can we sign you up and get a small deposit today?"

Charlie was still smiling from Mabel's presentation, but now they wanted an answer. He knew he wasn't going to be taking a ten-hour bus ride to New York, or staying at the Milford Plaza, but he did want to make sure that the trip came off, and of course, that Natty Oakes was on it. He wasn't sure why that was important to him but he knew that if anybody in Red Bone deserved to go, and would enjoy seeing New York it was Natty. Also, the prospect of somehow meeting up with her in New York and showing her some of the city was irresistible.

Charlie smiled at Mabel Willard and shook his head. "No ladies, I'm sorry, but I won't be able to make your trip, as much as I'd love to see *Les Miserables* again, I can't go."

Mabel sighed and patted Charlie on the arm. "That's alright mister Burden, we'll find some others somewheres to fill up the trip."

"How about Natty?" Charlie asked. "Is she going?"

Ada Lowe pursed her lips and shook her head. "No, no, Natty ain't goin', that poor girl. She'd just *love* to go – always wanted to go to New York City she says – but she's feeling real bad 'bout owing Gus money for repairing her little car there, so she really don't have the money to spend."

Charlie nodded, pulling out his wallet and platinum American Express card. "Okay," he said, "here's what I'll do. Put the last five trips on this." He handed the card to the travel agent. Then find five more people who want to go but can't afford it." He smiled at Mabel. "Just make sure Natty is one of them."

When she finally realized what Charlie was doing for them, Mabel grinned from ear to ear. "That girl goin' to have a *wonderful time* in New York City!"

The Chrysler New Yorker was actually a very comfortable ride when it hit a rare stretch of road without any bumps, ruts or potholes to challenge the ancient car's suspension. Charlie leaned back into the once - soft leather seat and stretched his legs out in front of him, taking advantage of the big car's roominess.

"They don't build cars like this anymore Hank," said Charlie, looking over at the old man hunched over the chrome and wood-trimmed steering wheel.

"And a good thing, too," Hank replied. "An environmental disaster is what it is, burning oil and too much gas, and fouling the air." Hank looked over at Charlie with a glint in his eye. "If I didn't love it so much, I'd feel guilty."

Charlie laughed and rolled down the window to enjoy the still warm October afternoon air. He was enjoying himself, riding along with his friend on a beautiful fall day, the workweek over and things going well at the plant. The pond problem was behind him and he wouldn't have to worry about Angel Mountain for a while, and now he had an exciting new project in the library and athletic fields that was finally getting under way. And to top it off, he was on his way to watch his new favorite team, *The Bones*, in action. Plus, he had to admit, the anticipation of seeing Natty Oakes again added to the warmth of the moment. Charlie hadn't seen her since returning from New York, resisting the temptation to go out early to run the mountain trail with her. He told himself that he wasn't avoiding her, just being prudent.

But he did get her note. Pushed under his apartment door that morning – a quick detour from her run – *Mr. Burden: Please thank the CanAmex Company for the new uniforms. The kids love them! Game tonight in Welch, five o'clock, if you want to see how they look. Sally and me will be at the Roadhouse later. Buy you a beer. Nat.*

It was a hard invitation to pass up, and Hank was happy for the suggestion to attend the game and for the opportunity to let Charlie buy him dinner afterward at *Moody's Roadhouse*, although he warned Charlie that the place could, on occasion, get a little raucous on a Friday night. "Well Hank, I'm about due for another fistfight," Charlie laughed. "It's been a couple of months."

Hank had insisted on driving, as the big Chrysler needed some exercise, plus he thought if they had some extra time, he wanted to show Charlie a spot he might find interesting. They left Old Red Bone an hour earlier than necessary. As was any time with Pullman Hankinson, Charlie knew it would be an hour very well spent.

They drove out South County Road and took the shortcut through the woods and onto the new road around the power plant to Cold Springs Road. A hundred yards past the plant, they had to slow down to a stop as a huge Mack diesel tractor, belching black smoke from the two tall exhausts behind the cab, strained mightily to pull its way out of the dense woods and up onto Cold Springs Road. Behind the cab was a long flatbed with tall, rust - colored iron pylons along the sides to contain the massive pile of several dozen freshly cut tree trunks, some up to two feet in diameter. The entire load was wrapped in thick chains and topped-off with a huge claw- arm lifter folded down on top of the timber from the front of the trailer.

"These are the ones they can get to the road," Charlie pointed out to Hank. "Little farther in the terrain gets so rugged, trees'll have to be pulled out by the helicopters."

Hank edged the Chrysler forward a few yards to where they could see down the newly carved dirt road that wound its way several hundred yards into the dense woods. At the beginning of the road, at what was the base camp for the timbering operation, a long white trailer sat up on blocks as if it would be there a long time. A sign on the side of the trailer near the door said "Garvey Lumber." Down the road Charlie could see a flurry of activity and hear the *putt, putt* idle of the big chain saws, followed by a high pitched whine of a chain blade ripping through live wood. The sound of men's voices calling out to each other carried back to them, followed by a crescendo of crackling and snapping that presaged the majestic, slow-motion fall of a towering pine, bouncing once before coming to rest. Charlie breathed in the heady mixture of sawdust, pine scent and exhaust from the gasoline engines and he envied the men working down the road.

"That's a good day's work they're putting in down there, eh Charlie?"

Charlie turned back to Hank and nodded. "Yeah, Hank. You earn your money when you're cutting trees." He looked back out toward the activity down the dirt road. "Kind of work that let's you know you've accomplished something," he added almost to himself.

Hank put the Chrysler in gear again and pulled out after the logging truck. Along both sides of Cold Springs Road, several dozen cars and pickups were parked at haphazard angles in the tall grass between the road and the woods. A white pickup truck caught Charlie's eye. It was the same white truck he'd seen pulled over on this same road back near the power plant, the day he and Pie rode the bulldozer around the perimeter of the site. The same truck that Natty had reluctantly climbed into when they were walking up the hill from the library.

Charlie glanced back through the trees toward the sound of the chainsaws and while he wouldn't wish any harm to befall Buck, he couldn't prevent the flicker of fantasy that rushed over him now of how things might be if Buck Oakes were to draw his last breath of life from beneath a ten-ton trunk of a white oak.

A rush of acceleration as the Chrysler pulled out to pass the logging truck, jerked Charlie's attention away from the work site, away from thoughts of Buck, and away from Natty. They were on their way again and Charlie stretched out in the big bench seat to enjoy the scenery and the company of his good friend. It was too nice of a day, too pleasant of an occasion, to brood over childish fantasies.

They rode along enjoying each other's silence, making good time in the heavy car as Hank showed his prowess at maneuvering through the tight turns that he'd mastered in his sixty years of driving the narrow roads of McDowell County. Occasionally, Hank would point out something of interest along the road – mostly of things that *used* to be – two closed elementary schools; a derelict factory once involved in the production of mining equipment; a drive-in movie theater with its dozens of now rusted speaker pipes pushing through the high weeds at haphazard angles; an old Dairy Queen, the sign long since removed, but its identity betrayed by the distinctive architecture of the roof. Hank's commentaries were brief.

As they got closer to Welch, Hank again broke the silence. "Wanted to come over early to show you a spot you might be interested in seein' while you're down here. Place that's got some history behind it having to do with what I was trying to tell you about coal mining in the southern counties." Hank looked over to see Charlie looking back at him with rapt attention written on his face. Hank smiled under his white bush of whiskers and turned back to the road. It felt good, once again, to have a willing student.

"First thing you need to understand is that if there was ever an industry that cried out for a labor union, it was coal mining. Back in 1890, when the United Mine Workers of America was formed over in Ohio, and then for a good part of the first half of the 1900's, coal mining was about as close to chattel slavery as anything we had in this country since the Civil War. Especially in southern West Virginia. We had lots of coal that the rest of the country needed and we had lots of cheap labor – the blacks from the south and immigrants from Europe – just pouring in for the chance to earn *any* kind of a living for their families.

"The coal companies owned the towns, owned the houses, owned the store, and paid the miners slave wages in scrip that could only be used at the company store at inflated prices. The miners were systematically cheated by the clerkweighmen on the amount of coal they were credited with, and the working conditions in the mines were lethal. Between 1890 and 1920, West Virginia had twice the mine death rate of any other state. I told you about Monongah in 1907, but there were others – Switchback, Eccles, Jed, Layland – mines blowin' up 'cause of shoddy safety procedures. But these were all the *throwaway people*, so nobody cared too much 'cause business was good and America needed its coal.

"So you can see that the opportunity for organized labor was ripe, but it wasn't that easy back then. Didn't have the labor laws we got now . . . National Labor Relations Act didn't happen until 1935. It was a lot rougher game then. When the Union finally started to send organizers down here – including Mary Harris Jones, who you probably know better as *Mother Jones* – the coal companies got together and formed the Kanawha County Coal Operators Association. Then, they hired the infamous Baldwin-Felts Detective Agency in Bluefield to provide *mine security*." Hank glanced over at Charlie to see if he showed any recognition of the name. Charlie just shrugged his ignorance as they passed a sign that said 1-mile to Welch.

"Baldwin-Felts was for years just an army-for-hire of thugs and gunmen, leg breakers used to intimidate miners and union organizers. And they were effective. Baldwin-Felts made these southern counties, McDowell, Logan, and Mingo – "bloody Mingo" it came to be known as – hazardous duty for organizers and union men. Just the name "Baldwin-Felts" filled the miner and his family with terror. Baldwin-Felts was so powerful, they operated like some kind of law enforcement agency 'cause the coal companies owned the politicians and most of the sheriffs down here. One of the owners, Albert Felts, used to wear a sheriff's badge from Harlan County, Kentucky, and he called his henchmen *deputies*."

Hank reached into his jacket pocket and brought out a leather pouch of chewing tobacco, which he laid on the seat next to him. His fingers expertly squeezed out a generous chaw. Facetiously, as always, he offered the bag to Charlie who held up a hand to decline his friend's offering.

"Well the result of all this oppression," Hank continued, "as you can imagine, was violence, in the form of the famous West Virginia Mine Wars." Hank looked over at Charlie again for a sign of confirmation.

Charlie raised his eyebrows. "Sorry Hank. Not familiar with them," he pleaded.

"*Christ!* If it had been in New York or Connecticut, you would've studied 'em in grade school." Hank shook his head slightly with exasperation. "*Important damned events in the history of the American labor movement,*" he added, hitting the steering wheel with the palm of his hand for emphasis.

"All started in April, 1912," Hank began, obviously having told the story before, "with a strike by miners up at Paint Creek and Cabin Creek in Kanawha County, and wouldn't end until September, 1921, at the battle of Blair Mountain, over near Logan, when the miners gave up rather than fight federal troops that President Harding had sent down here to stop the *insurrection.*" Hank shook his head ruefully. "That was the end of the Union down here for many years," he said softly. "And the miners of southern West Virginia paid the price for a long, long time."

They passed a sign that read *Welch, County Seat, Population: 1,434.* "Been a while since they updated that sign I'd guess," Hank noted.

As Hank continued with his story, Charlie looked around him at the town. He had been into Welch once before, for the dinner meeting with the Kerns & Yarbrough lawyers before the Planning Board meeting, but he hadn't been able to see much of the town. It reminded him of Red Bone, but bigger. The main streets were lined with the same style of old three and four story stone buildings as the *Barney's* building in Red Bone and many of the first floor retail spaces were vacant. But where Red Bone was situated up high, on the side of the mountain, Welch was down low, in a valley, surrounded by hills that gave way to more hills and then mountains behind them. Hank paused in his story to point out the Tug Fork that ran along the western boundary of the town. "Lot of history in that river, Charlie. Lot of history," he repeated wistfully. "But that's a lesson for another day," he said with a smile.

Hank turned right onto Court Street. "Mine wars were interrupted by the First World War when everyone more or less put their own problems behind them for the sake of the war effort. Country needed the low-sulfur, *smokeless* coal from down here, wages improved a little, and there was plenty of work for everyone, so the union organizing activities went away for a while."

Hank pulled the big car into a U-turn and then into a small parking area in front of a very old gray stone building that sat atop a hill that rose precipitously from the street. Tall narrow windows, arched at the top, gave the building an ominous, gothic appearance. A tall clock tower at the center of the building looked as if it would provide an excellent view of the town. From the parking area, a long straight cement stairway with a railing in the middle climbed the steep face of the hill to a series of wide marble steps in front of the main entrance to the building. A small sign at the bottom of the stairs said only, "Welch County Courthouse."

Hank turned off the car and got out, pausing for a moment to lean back and look up at the imposing structure. He started toward the stairway motioning for Charlie to follow. "When the war ended," Hank began again, "country went into a recession, miners got laid off and had their wages cut, and the violence started brewing again, all leading up to the mine war of 1921 and Blair Mountain. Couple of incidents though, leading up to that tragedy worth knowing about.

"First thing was, in 1919, to help keep the union organizers out, the Logan County Operators Association put the Logan County Sheriff – scoundrel named Don Chafin – on the payroll along with his army of deputies who harassed and beat and arrested anyone participating in union organizing." Hank paused to catch his breath halfway up the stairway and looked over at Charlie. "Like I said, times were different then. It was legalized oppression and it must have been *hell* to live with." Hank shook his head at the thought.

Charlie studied Hank closely, amazed again at the depth of his friend's empathy for his fellow West Virginians, even to miners who lived eighty years earlier.

"Thing was is, that it wasn't that unusual," Hank said as he started up the stairs again. "Coal companies bought up a lot of law officers and politicians. Whatever they needed to keep the union out.

"Chafin went a little too far in his brutality though and in the summer of 1919, five thousand miners gathered together up in Marmet, south of Charleston, for a march on Logan County. March was stopped by another worthless son-of-a-bitch Governor in the pockets of the coal operators, who promised a government investigation into the activities of Chafin's thugs." Hank stopped to spit a brown mouthful of tobacco juice onto the brown grass lawn next to the stairway. "Nothin' ever came of it a course. Another damn whitewash as always."

They'd reached the top of the stairs and Charlie examined the building for activity. There were a few lights on inside but no sign of anyone coming or going from the building. *Late on a Friday afternoon, they were probably getting ready to close up for the week.* Charlie was curious as to what Hank wanted to show him in the old building.

But instead of walking toward the front door, Hank turned and eased himself down slowly to a seat on the top step of the stairway. He pointed to a spot across from him on the same stair. "Here, Charlie," he said. "Sit down right here."

"What all that led to Charlie, was the story I wanted to tell you about today." Hank paused and looked around them slowly seeming to studying the cracked and worn cement slabs that went from the stairs to the steps in front of the building. Then he looked back out toward the town spread out below them. "I'll skip some of the background, but in the spring of 1920, the non-union miners over in Mingo County went on strike, which as you can imagine got the coal companies pretty agitated along with the Baldwin-Felts company whose job it was to prevent that sort of thing. Then, to stoke the fire even more, in May of that year, couple of tough and courageous Union men, Fred Mooney and Bill Blizzard came down and spoke to an assembly of 3,000 miners in a little town down on the Kentucky border called Matewan." Hank looked over at Charlie, again for a sign of recognition.

"I've heard of Matewan," said Charlie.

Hank just nodded absent mindedly, still thinking about the history.

"Well the result of that rally was 1,500 miners joining the United Mine Workers of America, and that was bad news for the coal operators. So, Baldwin-Felts was called in to take care of the situation, and on May 19th, 1920, twelve Baldwin-Felts "detectives" got off the train in Matewan, all of 'em wearing pistol belts and a few carrying satchels containing Thompson sub-machine guns. Situation was so serious that the gang was led by Albert and Lee Felts themselves, two of the three Felts brothers, owners of the company.

"Now what was different about Matewan then, was that while the coal company owned the housing, Matewan was an independent town with its own government. It had its own mayor, fellow named Cable Testerman, and its own Sheriff, a young man – 31 years old at the time – named Sid Hatfield. No relation to the Hatfields you're thinking about." Hank paused for a moment in thought, then he looked over at Charlie, squinting his eyes as if he was looking back in time. "Can you *imagine* the *guts* it took for a young fellow like that to stand up to a gang of seasoned, professional thugs like the Baldwin-Felts men." Hank shook his head in wonderment.

"Well that's what happened. Sid Hatfield, along with Testerman, confronted the Baldwin-Felts men at the train station and told them he wouldn't stand for any miners being put out of their homes in his jurisdiction and that there'd be trouble if they did. Course Albert Felts ignored him and took his gang out to the Stone Mountain coal camp just outside Matewan and evicted six families of miners who'd joined the Union. Threw all their belongings – clothes, furniture, utensils – outside in a cold, drizzling rain. Made an example of them and said they'd be back for more.

"By the time the Baldwin-Felts men got back to Matewan, word had spread about the evictions and also that Sheriff Sid Hatfield was standing up for the miners and was going to arrest Albert Felts. So dozens of miners armed themselves and headed into town.

"What happened next was probably what you've heard about, or maybe saw in the movies – the battle of Matewan, sometimes called the "Matewan massacre" – the deadliest shootout in American history."

Hank shifted his weight on the hard step, spit some tobacco juice onto the grass and wiped his mouth and whiskers with the sleeve of his old suit jacket. He leaned back with his arms stretched out behind him, palms on the cement and gazed off in the distance as if he was picturing the fight in his mind. "Young Hatfield, along with the mayor and a few deputies and miners, marched right up to the Baldwin-Felts men on the covered wooden boardwalk in front of Chambers Hardware Store. Told them he was arresting the lot of them. 'Course that wasn't something any Baldwin-Felts man would ever put up with. So it being a rainy day, Albert Felts was wearing a long raincoat and underneath his coat he drew out his pistol and at point blank range, through his coat, he shot and killed Mayor Cabel Testerman and the battle was on."

Hank looked over at Charlie with a gleam in his eye and the sound of pride rising in his voice. "But that was a bad day for Baldwin-Felts 'cause they didn't know who they were dealing with when they went up against Sid Hatfield. Sid drew his guns and killed Albert Felts and a few of the other detectives in the first few seconds of the fight. Hundreds of shots were fired according to witnesses and when it was all over, the street was littered with bodies. Seven Baldwin-Felts men were dead, including Albert and Lee Felts. Two miners had been killed plus four others wounded."

Hank nodded his head as he thought about the famous incident. "That was an important day for the Union and for the miners – the battle of Matewan, May 19th, 1920 – not just because some Baldwin-Felts men were killed, but because the miners *finally had a hero*, a lawman who was fearless and tough enough to stand up to the mine operators and their hired thugs and to *beat them, Goddammit!*" Hank slapped his hand down hard on the worn surface of the step.

Charlie looked over at Hank and could see that his friend's eyes were glistening. He remained silent while Hank took a few moments before continuing.

"Yeah, Sid Hatfield became a hero all right," Hank said softly. "A hero to the miners and to the labor movement. 'Cause no lawman had ever done something like that before – standing up toe-to-toe with Baldwin-Felts to protect miners – that wasn't the way sheriffs down here kept their jobs. But young Hatfield did what was right 'cause the miners were *his* people." Hank went silent for a moment and then shook his head slowly. "Tough time to be a hero though," he exhaled with a sound of sadness in his voice.

Hank drew in a deep breath and turned to Charlie. He regained his normal story teller's voice. "Tom Felts, the last brother who now owned Baldwin-Felts, swore that he'd avenge the deaths of Albert and Lee. First he used his contacts to have Sid, along with 22 other townspeople, indicted for murder in the Matewan killings. Case went to trial in January, 1921, at the Williamson courthouse in Mingo County, where charges were dismissed against most of the accused, and the rest including Hatfield, were acquitted.

"But Felts wouldn't give up so he hatched a new plan. He had Sid and his good friend and deputy, Ed Chambers who was also a union supporter in Matewan, indicted on a totally unrelated, trumped up charge of shooting up a town over here in McDowell County. The sheriff of McDowell County told Sid that nothing would come of it and that he and Chambers needed to come over here for a quick hearing and that would be the end of it. Said he'd guarantee their safety."

Hank took out his pocket watch and saw that it was almost five o'clock. He started to push himself up stiffly from the hard step. "Don't want to be late for the start of the game," he said. Charlie stood up quickly and reached over to help Hank up. They both stood on the cement landing at the top of the stairs. "Way Natty's team's going this year, we could miss a couple of goals being a few minutes late," Hank added with a chuckle.

Charlie didn't say anything. He knew there was more to the story but he'd let Hank tell it in his own time. Hank just stood looking down the long stairway, lost in his thoughts while Charlie waited. His voice was soft again when he resumed.

"It was August 1st, 1921, a hot, sunny day. Too hot to be wearing wool suits and starched collars, but that's what Sid and Ed Chambers were wearing for their court appearance when they walked up these stairs here that we just come up." Hank gestured with his chin toward the stairway, his hands in his pockets. After a pause, he turned and looked over at the front door of the building. "But the Sheriff of McDowell County wasn't around that day, nor any of his deputies. They weren't anywhere near this town, when Hatfield and Chambers – both of 'em unarmed – walked up these stairs with their wives that beautiful summer morning. And when they got to the top of the stairs right here where we're standing," Hank looked over toward the front door of the courthouse, "out of that door come a fellow named C.E. Lively, a Baldwin-Felts assassin, along with two other gunmen. They walked right up to Sid Hatfield and Ed Chambers and murdered them, in front of their wives, right here where we're standing." Charlie looked around him at the cracked cement at his feet. "Hatfield fell right about where you are," Hank pointed over at a spot on the walk, "and then to finish the job, Lively walked over and put one more bullet in Sid's head while his wife watched in horror. Then the murderers just walked down these stairs and drove off. They were never brought to trial. Never brought to justice."

Hank looked down the stairway and then back at the doorway of the courthouse. He shuffled his feet a little and then stood still with his hands in his pockets, staring down at the cement landing where they were standing. Charlie got the impression that Hank was saying a silent prayer for Sid Hatfield and Ed Chambers.

Finally Hank looked up at Charlie. He smiled, his white whiskers rising at the sides of his mouth while he studied Charlie with soft, friendly eyes. "Sid Hatfield was a handsome young man Charlie … only a few pictures ever taken of him … tall, and lean with a strong jaw and clear eyes and the look of a good man about him." Hank nodded his head a few times. "Reminds me a lot of you Charlie."

Charlie laughed. "Yeah, okay Hank. Don't try to make me into a modern day Sid Hatfield. I'm not doing anything to warrant that kind of comparison." Then he added, "and nobody's going to be shooting me down in the street. Times have changed Hank." Charlie looked at his watch. "We'd better get going," he said starting for the stairway.

But Hank stood fast. "Charlie, *dammit,* I keep tellin' you," he said in a low voice. "*Nothing's* changed here in a hundred years. The coal operators are just big companies now, like Ackerly and CanAmex, and Baldwin-Felts is a law firm in Charleston or Washington, but it's all still the same and when it comes to takin' coal out of the ground, you'd better stay out of their way."

Hank paused for a moment to catch his breath, then leaned in a little closer to his friend. "I know what you *did* Charlie," he said, "on the Angel Mountain thing ... sending up a warning to Bud DeWitt."

Charlie couldn't hide his surprise. "How did you know about ..."

Hank interrupted him. "Not much happens around here I *don't* find out about, sooner or later Charlie. But the point is, Bud DeWitt would have lost his farm for sure, and he and Petey both'd probably have gone to jail anyway, and that would have been a goddamn crime, a *goddamn tragedy,* weren't for you standin' up for 'em."

Charlie just stared at Hank for a moment, wondering if he should say anything to confirm what the old man seemed to already know. Finally, he gave in. "Hank, it's not that big a deal. C'mon, let's go," he said moving toward the stairway.

Hank reached out and held his arm. "Charlie, if *I* know what you did, *they* know what you did, and that's not good," he said quietly. "You need to be careful now."

Charlie's instinct was to laugh it off, but when he looked into Hank's eyes he saw the look of concern, the same sad, angry expression of empathy that came over his friend when he talked about his fellow West Virginians, old miners, the victims of Buffalo Creek, or Sid Hatfield and Ed Chambers. And he respected Hank too much to ignore his words. He nodded and put his hand on his friend's shoulder. "Okay Hank," he said softly. "Okay. I'll be careful."

Chapter 23

The Welch team was using the whole field for their warm-ups when the yellow bus from Red Bone finally pulled into the parking lot at the end of the field. Natty got off the bus first, caught the eye of the opposing coach and made a show of looking at her watch and holding up seven fingers to show that they had arrived in time. The coach just stood with his feet spread apart, arms crossed, scowling across the field at Natty. He was standing between two other taller men who were talking as they also watched *The Bones* get off the bus. Natty recognized one of the men right away from his light sport coat and tie as Kyle Loftus, the commissioner of the league. It took her a moment to see that the other man was the coach's good friend, Deputy Sheriff Wayne Lester. He wasn't wearing his uniform and looked, to Natty's eye, a little seedier than normal in blue jeans, flannel shirt and a hunting vest.

The blue clad Welch team stopped their warm-up activities to watch *The Bones* trot toward their side of the field in their startling new warm-up suits. Normally a team showing up with new unis would receive a fair amount of ribbing and catcalls from the opposing team, but the presence of the intimidating Zack and Sammy Willard, Paul, the new star of the league, and the fear-inspiring Emma Lowe, the league's unchallenged scoring leader, dampened the blue team's bravado. Plus, the shiny black warm-ups made the undefeated *Bones* look even more imposing.

Up the field a ways from the visitor's bench area, Charlie and Hank sat just off the sideline on ancient aluminum folding chairs that Hank had stored in the trunk of the Chrysler. There were only a handful of people on the *Bones* side of the field in contrast to the home side where the small bleachers was nearly filled and spectators in folding chairs lined the sideline.

Hank tapped Charlie's leg to draw his attention to *The Bones* coming off the bus at the far end of the field. "Take a look at this," Hank said with a chuckle, surprised by the team's new look.

Charlie felt a rush of satisfaction in seeing the obvious pride the team had in their new uniforms. He quickly picked out the Pie Man, the shortest of *The Bones*, whose warm-up jacket reached down well below his waist. The boy had his Yankees hat on backwards with the brim tipped up in the back at a jaunty angle, and an *all business* expression on his small face that made Charlie grin. The Pie Man, he could easily see, was exploding with pride over his team's new uniforms.

Watching the team strip off their warm-ups, revealing the new blood-red shirts, shiny black shorts and red stockings, it didn't take Hank long to speculate on the source of the expensive new outfits. "Now where do you suppose Natty got them flashy new suits? Looks a little rich for a team from Red Bone." He eyed Charlie with suspicion. "More like what teams from New York might wear, don't you think?"

Charlie winked at his friend. "Maybe they had a bake sale."

The Bones quickly took the field without benefit of a warm-up but when Natty noticed that the umpire hadn't yet arrived, she called out to Zack Willard to lead the team in a jog around the field. On the sideline, Kyle Loftus was busy on his cell phone, no doubt trying to locate the missing official.

Charlie watched the activities on the field with a sense of déjà vous. How many of his kids' games, first in East Windsor and then in Mamaroneck, had he attended where they had to wait for a tardy official, or have a parent fill in? He'd done it himself several times in soccer, baseball and basketball. The missing official would always be a part of kids' sports everywhere he concluded.

Natty trotted across the field to confer with the opposing coach. She was wearing her customary blue jeans, running shoes and her baggy blue sweater. Charlie smiled to himself. *No, the sharp new uniforms would be great for the kids, but it wasn't Natty's style to wear anything that might draw attention to herself.*

Kyle Loftus folded up his phone and strode toward the two coaches on the field. "Wife says he must have forgotten about the game. Took his kids to the mall in Bluefield."

The Welch coach shook his head. "Asshole." He spit tobacco juice on the field in front of Natty. "Well let's find somebody to ref," he said, looking back toward the bleachers. Natty scanned the few faces on her side of the field.

"Should be somebody ain't got a kid playing in the game," Natty offered.

"Yeah, well good luck on that."

Then Natty spied Hank and Charlie sitting by themselves far up the field. She'd been wondering all the way up from Red Bone, if Charlie was going to take her up on her invitation, and now her heart skipped a beat when she saw him staring back at her with a grin on his face. "I got somebody," Natty said, starting off toward the sideline.

She stopped about ten yards from where the two men were sitting. "Say Hank ... Charlie," she said with a nod toward the men.

"Natty," said Hank. Charlie just smiled and remained silent, knowing what was coming.

"Got no umpire for the game. So, I uh, was wondering if either of you boys think you might be fit enough to run up and down the field with these kids, that is if you know something about the rules of soccer, of course." Neither man moved. Natty fidgeted. "Cause they'll find somebody on their side of the field and that won't be ..."

Charlie saved her, pushing himself up out of his chair. He pulled his sweater off, tossed it on the chair and started walking toward the center of the field. "For this you'll have to buy me a *pitcher* of beer," he said with a grin as he passed Natty.

"You're going to need it," she laughed, turning to jog back towards her bench.

Seeing the Pie Man standing along the sideline watching his approach with wide-eyed wonderment, Charlie walked over to his little pal.

"Chowly. Chowly will be the umpiwa?" The boy's shoulders were hunched and the beginning of a *happy face* was puffing up his cheeks.

"Hey Pie Man. You ready to play?" Charlie grinned at the boy and held up a palm for their high five. He took off his watch and pulled out his keys and wallet and handed them to Pie. "Here, throw these in your bag. And let me borrow this," he said taking Pie's Yankees hat from his head. The boy beamed as Charlie put his Yankees hat on backwards and started toward the center of the field.

"Here you go ump," said Natty, tossing Charlie a whistle on a cord of rawhide.

"Thanks coach," he said walking backwards toward the center of the field. "Love the new uniforms," he added.

Natty wrinkled her nose at him. "Yeah, Santa Claus brought 'em."

Charlie was met at the center of the field by the opposing coach who wasn't interested in any amenities. "Now you done any of this before fellah?" He didn't wait for an answer. He got up close to Charlie. "What you need to watch for with this team is the offsides," he said out of the side of his mouth. "Team's famous for being offsides, 'specially that girl, so you got to watch her."

Charlie had already concluded that the Welch coach was a repulsive moron and while he'd try to call an impartial game, he hoped that Natty's team would bury them again as they had in Red Bone. He bent over and rolled each leg of his khaki chinos up a few inches over his running shoes, ignoring the coach who was still talking.

"And they can get rough too." He lowered his voice. "Got to watch them black boys. Like to throw their elbows and hips around, know what I'm sayin'?"

Charlie stood back up straight, pulled the bottom of his long-sleeved white polo shirt out of his pants, pushed his sleeves up and reached in his pocket for his sunglasses. He put the whistle in his mouth and blew a loud, sharp tweet, startling the Welch coach only a few feet away from him. He dropped the whistle from his mouth and smiled.

"Let's go coach. Get your team out here. Keep the time on your side. Let me know when there's two minutes left in the half." Then he turned abruptly and walked toward Natty's side of the field. He blew the whistle again. "Let's get going coach," he yelled to Natty. "I got somewhere to be tonight."

Natty who was huddled up giving *The Bones* their last instructions, turned and saw Charlie with his pant legs rolled up, shirt out, wearing sunglasses and Pie's Yankees hat, and couldn't stifle a yelp of laughter. She put her hand over her mouth to hide her grin. Charlie grinned back, and then blew the whistle loudly once again.

The Bones had first possession. Gilbert Steele pushed the ball sideways to Emma who flicked it back to Paul, then wheeled around and raced down the field as Paul lofted a long ball toward the corner, and the game was on.

Being on the field was a different view from sitting on the sideline, and Charlie was surprised at first at how fast the kids moved and how hard they kicked the ball, but then he'd always reffed younger kids' games, and these players were almost all just a year away from high school. He also quickly realized that a few of these players were exceptional for their age. Emma Lowe and Paul, Natty's midfielder from Poland, were obvious superstars who could take over a game.

And the Willard brothers with their superior foot speed, which would always be the single most important factor in kids' soccer, dominated whatever sector of the field they were in.

But the blue team also had a player that Charlie could see was an exceptional soccer player. It was the tall, blond haired boy named Gabe that Charlie had followed down the hill from the store before the first game in Red Bone. Gabe was playing mid-field opposite Paul and was proving to be every bit his equal. The boy was a pleasure to watch, always in control, always in the right position, with a powerful kick from either foot, and an excellent passer. Charlie also appreciated the fact that the blond boy, while strong and aggressive, was also a fine sportsman – several times after inadvertent rough contact, he had reached down to help one of the *Bones'* players to his feet.

After a few frenetic trips up and down the field, Charlie was feeling winded and wondering if he was in over his head trying to ref a game at this level. Fortunately, both teams started a little conservatively, sending a lot of long balls up and down the field and few whistles were needed. Soon, it all started coming back to him and he was able to relax as he got accustomed to the pace of play and remembered that the umpire's chief responsibilities were to keep the game from getting too rough, and stay out of the way. After a few minutes, Charlie was having more fun than he'd had in a long time, trotting up and down the field on a beautiful fall afternoon, surrounded by good kids playing a great game. He suddenly felt like he was back in East Windsor, fifteen years earlier, when life was never better.

As in their first game in Red Bone, the Welch team was getting the better of the early play. Playing only two forwards and four midfielders, their obvious strategy was to keep the ball in the *Bones'* end of the field by just dumping it downfield at every opportunity and loading up the pressure in the mid-field. While it was a strategy that didn't yield many good scoring opportunities, it was very effective in bottling up the other team.

Charlie had seen this style of defensive play before, many times. It made for a boring but easy-to-ref game, which was fine with him, and it was an accepted strategy for a team that couldn't match up offensively. And, so far, it was effective. *The Bones* were back on their heels and were getting a little frustrated. Charlie also noticed that the Welch team had six substitutes on the sideline versus only the Pie Man for Natty's team. It also appeared to Charlie that the Welch team had several players on the field that hadn't played in the first game in Red Bone, including a couple of bigger boys on defense. This was beginning to look like a tough game for the undefeated *Bones.*

The second part of the blue team's strategy was revealed the first time the *Bones* were able to get the ball up to Emma Lowe. One of the Welch fullbacks, a short but wide and rugged looking boy they called Rudy, quickly jumped roughly in front of Emma with minimal effort at going after the ball. It was obvious that his job was to shadow Emma and do whatever he had to to keep her away from the ball. It was probably a foul that Charlie should have called, but he let it go because it was marginal and he didn't want to show any favoritism to Natty's team, or appear to show any to Emma because she was a girl.

As the ball headed back up field, Charlie jogged up Natty's side of the field.

"Gotta call that one ref," Natty said calmly, strolling slowly along the sideline, her arms folded across her chest. It was the first thing he'd heard her say in the game.

In contrast, on the Welch side of the field the demonstrative coach was lumbering up and down the field with the flow of the action, his foghorn voice calling out instructions to his players (and to the umpire) without letup. It seemed to Charlie after a while, that his players for the most part just tuned him out, and Charlie tried to do the same.

Natty heard the coach yelling, and she heard Charlie's whistles and the usual shouts of encouragement and criticism from the spectators along the sideline. But as the game settled in to an evenly-matched defensive struggle she began to lose her concentration, and gradually the sights and sounds of the game dimmed to background noise as she gazed out at the field – her *Spiderman* cap pulled down low to hide her eyes – and indulged herself by focusing completely on Charlie Burden. She watched him glide across the field, light on his feet yet powerful and confident, as though he'd reffed hundreds of games before, and having fun. He looked like a teenager with Pie's hat on backwards, the sunglasses, and the goofy effect of the rolled up pant legs, but so obviously a man, surely the most attractive man she'd ever met in person. A few of the women along the Welch side of the field had raised an eye when Charlie took the field and then leaned together for intimate comments about the unknown visitor. But these women from West Virginia, Natty knew, had no chance at all with the handsome stranger. They weren't in the same league, culturally, economically, or educationally, with Charlie Burden. Although, they would never know that by talking to him.

But there he was, right in front of her. This rich, successful, beautiful man from New York, running up and down a shabby soccer field in McDowell County, West Virginia, volunteering to be a fill-in ref – a job that nobody ever wanted – in a little league game in which he didn't even have a kid playing. And he was there because of her – sure, because of Pie too, but mostly because she was there – and that suddenly amazed her. And it frightened her. She thought about what he had said to her, up on the boulder, the words she'd never forget '. . . ' I've been thinking about you every minute of every day.' That's what he had said.

The ball scooted across the sideline rolling directly toward Hank and the empty chair next to him. He reached an arm down too late to stop the ball from running past him. One of the little kids patrolling the sidelines ran after it.

"Hey there, you in the chair," the umpire called out. "You gotta be a little quicker going after those balls." Charlie was grinning widely at his friend. Hank laughed, shrugged his shoulders and waved at the ref.

Christ, just look at the joy he's brought into that old man's life, just by being his friend. Hank, who had been wallowing in loneliness since Alva Paine died, sitting there now at a kids' soccer game enjoying the low sun and the smell of wood smoke in the fall air. Hank never came to an away game before. Weren't for Charlie, he'd be back up in his apartment by himself, reading his books and rotting away too quickly, like so many of the old people she had cared for over the years..

Then she noticed Pie, moving up and down the sideline, following the action. But it wasn't the ball he was watching. It was his pal Charlie he was riveted on, a proud *happy face* revealing his excitement at having his adult buddy, wearing *his* special Yankees hat, on display for everyone to see. Natty watched her son, bouncing along the sideline, clapping his hands, animated, barely able to contain his joy in having Charlie on the field.

Look at how much Pie had changed in the few months he'd known Charlie! The little boy she so desperately loved was finally developing some self-esteem and confidence that he could do things, be something, and that he wasn't so different from the other kids. Now he was enthusiastic about school and computers, and actually liked math and someday he was going to be an 'engineewa just like Chowly.' The kind of personal development she'd been unable to nurture in her son by herself all these years, achieved through just a few weeks of affection, encouragement and friendship with Charlie Burden. All he's needed his whole short life was an adult male to treat him like a regular kid . . . and show him some love.

"Subs!" Natty looked up to see Charlie with his hand up waving the Welch substitutes onto the field, all six at one time. He was looking over at her.

"Yeah, okay, Pie Man, go in for Gilbert at forward."

The boy leaped onto the field, his short legs churning as fast as they could go. He pointed at Gilbert Steele but he took an indirect path that allowed him to run past Charlie on his way to the forward position. Charlie smiled and gave his pal a wink as he scooted by. Then he brought down his hand with a sharp toot from the whistle to restart play with a Welch throw-in.

Natty watched him dance neatly out of the way of a skirmish of players, always staying in good position to watch the action. *Christ, is there anything he isn't good at?* Here he was, a fill-in, and everyone around the field would agree that he was the best umpire in the league. Suddenly the ball was sent soaring down the field and Charlie went into a semi-sprint to stay with the action. He was partially lost to her view behind the herd of players headed in the same direction.

And soon he would be gone from West Virginia. Because he was a duck out of water in McDowell County – too special, too New York, too successful to be stuck in a place like this for very long – and soon he would be leaving. 'China,' that's what he'd said. As soon as the turbines are in. When would that be? Natty thrust her hands into the pockets of her jeans as she moved up the sideline, straining to see Charlie through the swirl of players. She swallowed hard to fight the empty feeling that rose from inside her as she thought for the first time about Charlie suddenly disappearing from their lives for good. She forced herself to take a deep breath. *So why? Why did she persist in this lie to herself? Why couldn't she accept the fact that Charlie Burden was the man she had been waiting for most of her life, since she was twelve years old and all alone on Angel Mountain when she*

*started the daydream, the big one, the one she'd grown up with and had been
working on and enjoying and refusing to give up on for nearly twenty years. The
dream that she'd lose herself in while running, or in her quiet times of solitude up
on the boulder. Why couldn't she accept the fact that she'd been in love with
Charlie from the exact moment she heard him say her name for the first time that
night on the boardwalk in front of the store?*

The ball bounced off Natty's knee, startling her. She picked it up and tossed
it to Sammy Willard for a throw in and then glanced quickly out at Charlie to see
if he had noticed that she wasn't paying attention to the game, but he was headed
back up the field.

*And why did she persist in this fairy tale about Buck? The story she'd been
telling herself for years and to Charlie Burden that day on the trail after she'd
thrown up on his shoe. About 'not being ready to give up on Buck yet,' that
'there's a good man inside him,' and all that 'it wasn't his fault' bullshit. She
knew the truth. The truth was that she wasn't ready to give up on Buck because
she didn't have any other options, and she'd seen too many single, lonely welfare
mothers trying to raise kids in a place that wasn't easy on single mothers. That's
what she wasn't ready for. That, and admitting to the world that she was unloved
by a man. Christ, when would she ever be ready to give up on Buck? Did he have
to grind her up and run her through a fucking wood chipper before she'd finally
give up on him? This stupid, romantic lie would be one that she'd regret for the
rest of her life. Of that she was certain.*

A roar from the opposite side of the field shocked Natty out of her thoughts.
She looked up to see the blue team high-fiving each other as they headed back
towards the middle of the field. A disgusted Brenda Giles flung the ball angrily
out of the *Bones'* goal.

After twenty minutes of scoreless play, the blue team's strategy had paid
off. The *Bones'* goalie, Brenda Giles, had come fifteen yards out of the goal to
play an innocent clear-in. But instead of catching the ball, she inexplicably chose
to punch it away from an oncoming blue forward. The ball went straight out
toward the center of the field to the onrushing midfielder Gabe, who took the ball
cleanly off a high bounce and expertly lofted a long lob over the frantically
retreating goalie. The ball bounced once and crossed the goal line a moment
before the diving Brenda could swat it away.

Natty was embarrassed. Her team had given up a goal and she hadn't even
seen it. She clapped her hands together hard to snap herself out of her stupid *little
girl* thoughts. "C'mon Bones. We'll get it back. Let's go Bones. You can do it,"
she called out a little more loudly than normal.

It was the first time *The Bones* had been behind all season and it was
obvious that it was a situation they wanted to correct as quickly as possible. When
play started again, *The Bones*, led by Zack Willard, were playing in a higher gear.
But the Welch team, encouraged by their lead, also picked up their intensity, and
very quickly the game began to get rough. The chippy play actually worked in the
Bones' favor as some of the Welch players started running around too

aggressively and were beginning to get caught out of position for their defensive set-up.

After a few minutes of heavy banging in mid-field, Zack Willard gained control of the ball with some room to move up field. He raced it over the mid-field line and sent a perfect feed through to Emma cutting on a diagonal from the center of the field. The ball was past the fullbacks and too far from the Welch sweeper to reach before Emma, with her blazing speed, would gather it in for a dangerous shot on goal. But just before Emma reached the ball, from her blind right side, Rudy hurtled himself into her with a low shoulder sending Emma tumbling out of control, crashing into another Welch player, her mouth smashing into the second player's knee as she fell to the ground.

It was as vicious a tackle as Charlie had ever seen in kids' soccer and he blew his whistle loudly as he raced over towards Emma who was lying on the field with blood flowing from her lower lip. His anger rose as he watched the grinning Rudy exchange high fives with the blue sweeper. Then he heard the Welch coach from the sideline.

"Atta boy Rudy. Way to watch her. Good clean tackle. Way to be tough!"

Charlie felt his jaw muscles tighten. A rough play on the field was one thing but an irresponsible comment from a coach was another. He took a deep breath to try to calm himself as he watched Natty help Emma regain her feet, still dazed, the small towel pressed to her mouth red with blood. He whirled and headed for the far sideline and the Welch coach who had a sarcastic smirk on his face as he awaited Charlie.

"That's a yellow card for that kid," said Charlie. "And a yellow card for you too," he said closing in on the short but powerfully built coach.

The coach's eyebrows rose and he scowled at Charlie incredulously. "Hey don't get carried away buddy. You're just a sub here. Yellow card for *what?* That was a clean play," he said loudly for everyone to hear. He pointed out toward the field. "And if that *little girl* out there can't take it, maybe she shouldn't be playing in a boy's game."

Charlie took a step closer to him and spoke in a low voice. "It was a dirty hit, and one more like that and he's out."

The coach shook his head and waved the back of his hand at Charlie as he turned and started towards his bench area. "I don't know where you're from buddy but that's how we play soccer around here," he said out of the side of his mouth, his back towards Charlie. He clapped his hands loudly. "Let's get going. C'mon Blue, keep it up," he called out to his team.

Charlie pursued him. When the coach stopped walking and turned toward the field, Charlie was right in front of him. He leaned in close. The coach's face was unshaven and Charlie could detect the faint odor of some kind of alcohol he couldn't identify. "One more irresponsible comment out of you and you're gone too," said Charlie. "Now grow up and start acting like a coach. These are kids out here."

The coach crossed his arms and stared up at Charlie. "Screw you asshole."

The veins in Charlie's neck stood out as he remained silent, trying to prevent himself from kicking the shit out of the Welch coach right there on the field.

The coach seized on Charlie's hesitation. "C'mon, get out there and get the game going, or we'll find someone else to ref."

Charlie gained control of himself. This guy wasn't worth the effort. He nodded at the coach. "You've been warned coach," he said taking a step backward. It was then that Charlie happened to notice, directly in back of the coach a few yards beyond the sideline, two men who were staring intently back at him. One was the insurance man – the President of the league, Hank had told him – who he'd watched giving Natty a hard time at the game in Red Bone. But it was the other man who got Charlie's attention. He was tall and heavy with a pencil thin mustache, and a toothpick bouncing around between his puffy lips. He wore a hunting vest and blue jeans and although Charlie didn't know him, he was certain that he'd seen the man before some place. The man's angry scowl and penetrating stare directed at Charlie convinced him.

Gilbert Steele was back in the game, replacing Emma who was on the bench trying to stop the blood flowing from her cut lip. Natty called out for Sammy Willard and Jimmy Hopson to move up to forward with Gilbert and the Pie Man to play mid-field.

Without Emma to watch, the Welch defenders became more aggressive, moving up the field to press the attack. A minute before halftime, thanks in part to a misplay by Zack Willard in front of the goal, the blue team scored again. Angered by the incident with Emma, Zack had been trying to do too much, too quickly, and instead of just redirecting a long lead-in safely to the sideline, he tried to control the ball and dribble straight back through the Welch forward line. Losing the ball to a good tackle, the ball ended up in a mad scramble in front of the goal. As so often happens, the ball came squirting out to an unattended blue forward playing the far post and he drove it quickly into the back of the net. *The Bones* trailed 2-0 at the half.

Charlie walked over and sat down next to Hank.

"Rough game," said Hank.

"Yeah, that's my fault," said Charlie tossing his sunglasses on the ground under his chair and pulling his sweater on. The sun had dropped behind the nearby hills and the air had become cooler. The field lights had come on automatically sometime during the first half.

"I should have given that kid a yellow card the first time he got rough. I let it go, and that's what happens."

Natty walked over and tossed Charlie a plastic water bottle. Her team was still wandering slowly out to the spot in front of the goal where they would sit on the grass and rest for the second half.

"How's Emma?" Charlie asked, unscrewing the cap of the bottle.

Natty shrugged and looked out toward her team. "She's got some bruises and her lip is swollen, but she's okay. Emma's a pretty tough kid, physically."

Natty waited while Charlie took a long drink from the bottle. "Hey Charlie, I'm sorry 'bout the coach, and all that. Wouldn't have asked you to ref if I'd known ..."

"It's okay." Charlie smiled at her. "I can handle him."

Natty frowned and exchanged a look with Hank, then she flashed Charlie a quick smile and started out toward her team.

Charlie sat down in the chair next to Hank. "So what's with the Welch coach?"

Hank shifted his chaw to the cheek away from Charlie, and squinted across the field. "He's a tough customer that one. Used to be a cop but got a little too rough one time too many. Forced to resign after a few years." Hank turned and spit his tobacco juice in the dirt next to his chair. "Drives a truck now, for the Teamsters." Hank looked sideways at Charlie. "Got a temper too," he said softly.

Charlie nodded to his friend. "Okay, I got you. But I don't think we'll have any trouble next half." He looked across the field to where the Welch coach was remonstrating to his team, pounding his fist into his hand to make a point.

Charlie passed the halftime talking to Hank and telling him about his plans for the athletic fields in Red Bone. After about ten minutes Charlie again noticed the two men he'd seen staring at him from the sideline. They were in the parking area in back of the bleachers standing next to a late model Cadillac with the front door open. The two men were drinking something from red plastic cups.

"Back to work," he said rising out of his chair.

The second half started much like the first had, with the Welch team concentrating on defense. With a two goal lead, the strategy made even more sense. The midfielders were content to just loft the ball down to the *Bones'* end of the field every chance they got. On defense, Rudy stuck close to Emma wherever she went.

Emma's lower lip had swollen to double its normal size, made even more noticeable by the butterfly bandage Natty had applied to the cut. She had some dried blood, which showed up as dark blotches, on the front of her new red jersey. There was also a smear of dried blood on her right leg just above the knee. She also appeared to be limping slightly when she walked.

From the beginning of the half, Rudy took every opportunity, no doubt following his coach's instructions, to bump Emma and to cut her off roughly when she attempted to get into the play. Charlie called several fouls on him but most of Rudy's roughness on Emma was away from the ball when Charlie wasn't watching.

As the second half settled down into a well-executed defensive effort by the blue team and time ran off the clock, Rudy became more emboldened by the *Bones'* frustration and began to taunt Emma, quietly at first, and then as his confidence grew, more loudly to entertain his teammates.

"Hey whatcha got on your leg there Emma? That blood from your period? Hey, Emma's having her period! Watch out she'll get some on you." Rudy was enjoying himself now and kept up a steady barrage of insults whenever the ball was in other end of the field. "How long you been havin' your period Emma? Think you'd have bigger tits by now. That is if you're really a girl."

Emma tried her best to ignore Rudy and moved continually away from him but he shadowed her relentlessly and kept up a non-stop patter of taunts. She also couldn't help noticing the grins and snickers of the other Welch defensive players as Rudy kept up his attack.

On the sideline, Natty could hear what was going on and she could see that the taunting was getting to Emma. The girl's shoulders began to sag and she was losing her concentration on the game. Several times Emma looked over at her and Natty could see her blinking rapidly to fight back the tears. Natty shook her head and tried to smile some encouragement to her, but she knew that Emma's shyness was now paralyzing her on the field.

Rudy soon found a new sensitive spot. "Hey Emma, nice lip you got there. You got big lips anyways Emma. So what color *are* you girl? You kinda like half and half ain't you Emma? How come your momma don't have them big lips?"

Charlie could hear snatches of what was being said in the Welch end of the field and he could see the smiles on the some of the blue defenders, but he was too busy to know who was saying what to whom. He also didn't notice that Emma Lowe was moving very slowly and was in tears. As he blew the whistle for a blue throw - in directly in front of the Welch bench, Charlie was surprised to hear someone on the field calling out to him.

"Ref, hey ref. Time out. Time out."

Charlie looked up to see Gabe, the blond-headed Welch midfielder looking over at him making a T with his hands as he walked purposefully up the middle of the field. Uncertain about the rules, Charlie nudged George Jarrell standing next to him. "You get timeouts?" he asked softly.

"Yeah, one each half."

Charlie blew the whistle loudly. "Time out, blue," he called out, pointing to the bench.

"What the fuck?" The bewildered Welch coach started walking out onto the field to find out what was going on. Gabe ignored his coach and continued walking up the field under the eyes of both teams. He had an angry look on his face and he was headed directly at the still smirking Rudy. The stocky fullback was taken by surprise when Gabe fired two hands into his chest knocking him backward off his feet.

"You cut the shit right now Rudy. You play soccer and you shut the fuck up!" Gabe said, as Rudy scrambled to his feet. "You hear me?" The boys came chest to chest but it was evident that Rudy wanted no part of a fight with the taller, stronger Gabe who pushed him backwards again and pointed a finger in his face. "And you leave her alone. You stop talking to her, you stop talking shit, and you stop fouling her! You got that Rudy? Just play soccer!"

The Welch coach got to the boys just ahead of Charlie. He clamped a huge hand around Gabe's elbow and yanked him roughly toward the sideline. The coach twisted his body to put his head close to the boy's face as he dragged him off the field. "How about you mindin' your own *god damn* business kid, and keepin' your *damn* mouth shut!" The coach was spitting with anger. "I'm the coach of this team, not you." He pulled the boy all the way to the bench area where he finally released his grip and pushed him roughly. "And you can rest your mouth on the bench for the rest of this game. You're all done."

Gabe picked up his sweatshirt from the bench area and kept on walking as the coach sent one of the subs onto the field.

When the blue team called time-out Natty had started out onto the field to try to console Emma and get her mind back into the game. With a 2-0 deficit she needed Emma to get it going. But when Gabe reached Rudy and shocked her by shoving him roughly to the ground, Natty stopped to watch and then listen as Gabe admonished his teammate. Natty stood still and eyed Emma, just a few yards away from where Gabe was yelling at Rudy. As the Welch team's best player gave himself up for Emma, Natty just backed quietly off the field. This was a situation that she would let Emma deal with on her own.

"C'mon ref! Let's get this game going!" the Welch coach bellowed from the sideline, clapping his hands loudly. With a 2-0 lead on the best team in the league, he was understandably anxious to get the clock started for the last ten minutes of the game.

When the game started again, the blue team appeared to be a little shaken by the defection of their star midfielder. Rudy also had lost some of his bravado and now played in silence, but the anger showed on his face. Sensing a let down, *The Bones* with their undefeated record on the line and time running out, picked up their intensity and began moving around the field a step faster. And Emma now played with a determination that was motivated by a combination of emotions that she'd never before experienced on a soccer field: *elation* at the gallantry of Gabe, a boy she only knew very slightly from the many soccer games in which they had competed over the years – both of them too shy to ever say anything to each other; and *anger,* at Rudy for his taunts and his dirty play, and at the Welch coach for his treatment of her defender.

The *Bones* now controlled the action with speed and sharp passing and a tempo of play that the blue team was no match for. After keeping the ball in the Welch end of the field for several minutes, Sammy Willard corralled the ball with some open space near the left sideline. He took his time and sent a blistering cross into the center of the field where the streaking Emma Lowe knifed through several Welch defenders at the eighteen yard line and leaping high in the air, took the ball on her chest. The ball went softly into the air in slow motion as the Welch fullbacks converged, but Emma never let it hit the ground as she left her feet and went sideways in the air for a vicious sidewinder kick with her left foot that took the ball three feet off the ground and sent a rocket past the startled goalie into the back of the net. Emma was suddenly again, a world-class athlete playing with kids. She quickly bounced to her feet and ran into the Welch goal to retrieve the ball. With the angry look of determination still on her face, she threw the ball hard back toward the center circle and ran up the field. Her teammates could see there would be no high-fives to celebrate this goal.

The Welch coach was incensed. As his team walked back up field for the restart of play, he was ten yards onto the field screaming at his fullbacks and Rudy in particular.

"She's your responsibility Rudy! Don't you let her run free like that, boy. You know what to do. Now stop playing like a pussy and do your job, or you'll be on the bench too!"

Charlie glared at the coach as he listened to him admonish his players, and was an instant away from blowing the whistle and tossing the coach out of the game, but there had been enough anger on the field already without a another confrontation. He hoped that the rest of the game would just play out without incident.

The *Bones'* relentless attack continued as soon as the ball was put in play. And the Welch team, fired up by their coach's tirade and determined to protect their one goal lead, responded with a higher level of intensity. The game got instantly more physical – on both sides. With both teams playing equally rough, Charlie let everything but the most flagrant fouls go in an effort to conclude the game.

Emma also showed that she could get rough when the game called for it. Streaking back into the center of the field to catch a blue midfielder dribbling just a second too long, she curled around low into the ball carrier from the side with a hard tackle that normally would have been called a foul, but at this stage of this game, she knew it was the play to make. The ball went directly to Paul who had watched Emma coming back and had perfectly anticipated her tackle. With Gabe out of the game, Paul had more room to maneuver and he dribbled past two Welch defenders in the center of the field. Emma had bounced up from the ground, headed back up field and turned on the jets showing her incredible speed to get into an offensive position.

"Two minutes!" The gray haired woman who was keeping the time on the home side of the field called out in a weak voice. Charlie turned to her and nodded with a quick smile as he trotted toward the Welch end of the field.

As he had done many times before, Paul brought the ball over the center line and waited as long as he could, until a Welch defender was almost on him, before lofting the ball high toward the right corner in front of the streaking Emma. The long pass was measured perfectly to keep Emma on-side and to a spot she would easily reach before the blue fullbacks. As Emma approached the bouncing ball, calculating her angle to the goal, she could sense an ominous movement to her blind side. Flashing back to earlier in the game, she turned just in time to see Rudy coming straight at her at full speed. Emma refused the natural instinct to slow up and lose the race to the ball, choosing instead to fire her right arm out in a rigid stiff-arm, the hard base of her palm smashing into the bridge of Rudy's nose, knocking the unsuspecting boy cleanly off his feet as she hurtled past him to the ball.

The blue sweeper was positioned between Emma and the goal, his feet dancing nervously and a look of abject fear on his face as the league's best player bore down on him. Emma had the ball glued to her right foot as she danced quickly around him, juking left, then right, and back to the left again as the sweeper's feet went out from under him. Welch players were sliding through the grass trying to poke the ball away while the goalie moved out to cut down the angle, but Emma could do whatever she wanted with a ball on her foot fifteen yards from the goal in the center of the field. At the left post, Sammy Willard was wide open and waiting for the pass that Emma normally would have made. But this time she drove the ball home with a blistering shot too hard for the goalie to even react to, placed tauntingly inches over his left shoulder. Again she ran into the goal and grabbed the ball to get the game restarted quickly.

The home side of the field was screaming in protest. The Welch coach was out on the field running down Charlie. "That was a foul. A foul, *Goddammit*! What are you looking at buddy?" he screamed a few feet away from Charlie. "That's no goal. You can't count that. She hit my guy in the face!"

Charlie pointed to the center of the field as he turned toward the incensed coach. "Tie game," he called out loudly. Then softly to the coach he added "That was a good clean stiff arm."

"One minute," called out the timekeeper.

"Emma you *fucking whore*! I'm going to get you for that." Rudy was trudging back up field like a bull, oblivious to the blood that was flowing freely from his nose, which appeared to be a little crooked.

Charlie stopped and turned to the boy, "Hey, watch your language ..."

He was distracted by the voice of Kyle Loftus who was also out on the field just a few yards behind him, his tie loosened and half of his shirttail pulled out. "That was no goal fellah!" he screamed at Charlie "That was a flagrant foul on that girl!" His arms were waving and he was pointing at Charlie. "You will *never* ref in this league again my friend!"

Charlie had to turn toward the league president to see if he was serious. Charlie grinned at him as he trotted away shaking his head.

Players were still trotting back into position when Charlie blew the whistle for the restart. Several of the *Bones* were on the wrong side of the fifty yard line and the Welch coach and the league commissioner were still on the field screaming at him but he didn't care. With only about a minute left in the game, he wanted to give the *Bones* one more chance to score and win the game.

The ball caromed around in mid-field for a few seconds before Zack Willard came across the center line like a freight train through the mass of players and knocked a blue mid-fielder off the ball. He dribbled through a pair of defenders, forcing the ball past them with brute strength and raced toward the goal. With time slipping away and all the players from both teams converging on the goal, Zack let loose a powerful low shot from twenty-five yards out that the Welch sweeper dove for and made a fabulous head save just a few yards in front of the goal. The momentum of the ball carried it spinning across the end line.

"Corner," Charlie called out quickly running across the field pointing to the right corner.

"*There's no time left you asshole!*" the Welch coach screamed at him from well out onto the field. Charlie looked over at the old woman who was keeping the time. She just shrugged at him, not knowing what to do.

"Ten seconds left," Charlie yelled. "Corner kick."

"Paul," Natty yelled, pointing to the ball. Then she waved everyone up into the penalty area. She wanted Paul to take the kick because next to Emma, he had the best left-footed shot to curl it in towards the goal, and she wanted Emma on the field.

Paul raced to the corner and readied himself for the kick. Just before he took his long stride to the ball, he looked up to find Emma. She was dancing around lightly just outside the box to evade the blocking efforts of one of the blue defenders. The instant they made eye contact Emma nodded to Paul, made a quick feint and a spin that freed her from her defender and sprinted toward the mass of players in front of the goal on an angle to the back post. As soon as Emma moved, Paul stepped into the ball and sent it soaring toward the goal. The ball was high and long and flew over the heads of most of the players and looked like it would sail across the field untouched, until Emma, still knifing toward the goal, sprang into the air, her head three feet over the scrum, and pounded the ball with her forehead past the flailing goalie and into the net.

As Emma was coming down, Rudy was going up, in the other direction directly into his unsuspecting victim. Rudy led with the top of his forehead and caught Emma just above the right eye with a sickening smack, sending her backwards in mid-air. She landed on her back with her head snapping heavily against the ground, the blood already flowing from the gash in her eyebrow.

Charlie was still pointing into the goal when Emma got hit. He blew his whistle two quick bursts to signal the end of the game and let it drop from his mouth as he sprinted toward Emma and Rudy who was standing over her.

"How'd that feel, you cunt?" Rudy yelled down at her, the blood still flowing from his misshapen nose. "That's what you get for . . ." Rudy never got another word out before Zack Willard, with a five yard running start, drove his shoulder into Rudy's stomach and carried him through the air and into the goal. Rolling and tangled in the goal's netting, Zack was still able to get off several hard punches to Rudy's face before Charlie, on his knees in the goal, could wrap his arms around the powerful boy. As he struggled to pull Zack away from the cowering Rudy, Charlie could see Natty on the ground hunched over Emma. Then, next to him, the legs of the Welch coach.

"I want that nigger suspended for the season! He attacked my guy!" The coach's red face was inches from Charlie's ear as he struggled to restrain the now frenzied Zack Willard.

"Who you callin' a nigger?" Zack spit out angrily trying to kick his way out of Charlie's arms.

Rolling on the ground with Zack, Charlie could see that several other skirmishes had started out on the field. He saw Sammy Willard swinging away at somebody and Matt Hatfield wrestling someone on the ground close to the still prone Emma being shielded by Natty. The Welch coach was trying to extricate the bloodied Rudy from the goal netting and he saw Kyle Loftus trying to separate two other combatants wrestling just in front of the goal. Several adults from both sides were now running onto the field to quell what was now an all out brawl.

Then there was the sound of a loud, commanding voice that cut through all of the chaos on the field. "All *right! That's enough!*" it announced to everyone. It was the voice of authority that Hank had developed in his fifty-year career as a school teacher and principal. "*That's enough,*" he repeated. "It's all over." Hank was pulling kids apart roughly and giving them his angry eye, and in a few seconds all the fighting had stopped and the teams had started drifting away from each other.

Charlie had pulled Zack to his feet and dragged him out of the goal and several yards beyond the end line. "Okay, it's all over Zack. No more," Charlie said softly. "You did what you had to do. And now it's over." Looking back over the field to see where the Welch coach was, Charlie was relieved to see Emma on her feet, walking slowly toward the sideline next to Natty, with a towel pressed to her eyebrow. "Now you go see how Emma is. I'll take care of the coach. Okay?"

The boy's muscles relaxed and he seemed to slump in Charlie's arms. "Yeah, okay," he whispered. "Okay. I'm okay." he said nodding.

But Charlie could feel the boy's tears dropping onto his forearm. He released his grip from behind but kept his arm around Zack's shoulders, which developed more into a hug as he came around to look into the boy's face. "Hey Zack," Charlie said to make eye contact. "He shouldn't have said that," Charlie said firmly. "He shouldn't have said what he said. But all I can tell you is there are a lot of ignorant, stupid people in the world, and he's one of them. So don't worry about what somebody like that says. Okay?" The boy grunted and then wiped his eyes with the bottom of his new shirt, which was torn in the middle.

Charlie started walking Zack up the sideline to where the *Bones* were packing up their gear, but his eyes were trained across the field on the Welch coach who was involved in what looked like an argument with two other men on his way to the parking lot behind the bleachers.

As they neared the *Bones'* bench area, Charlie gave Zack a firm pat on the back, and left him to start across the field. Natty saw him and started toward him. When Charlie saw her he slowed down. "How's Emma?" he asked, still walking toward the center of the field.

"She's okay. She'll be okay," Natty said. "Going to have another bruise. Probably going to need a couple of stitches, but she'll be okay." Charlie nodded without saying anything. He glanced quickly toward the parking lot to find the coach and then stopped and faced Natty so she wouldn't have to follow him all the way across the field.

"Going to take her to the clinic when we get back, for the stitches," Natty said. "Then I'm going to stay with her for a while. Make sure she doesn't have a concussion."

"Yeah, that's a good idea," said Charlie.

"So, gotta cancel on the *Roadhouse* tonight." Natty smiled briefly. "Owe you a pitcher."

"That's okay." Charlie said, as he started walking away from her. "Going to have a word with the coach here,"

"Charlie, don't do anything crazy," Natty called after him. "Just a soccer game."

"Going to talk to him, that's all," he said, turning his back to her.

The two men that the coach had been arguing with were still standing near the sideline as Charlie approached. They both came toward him so Charlie stopped to see what they had to say.

"Hey buddy, just wanted you to know, you did a nice job out there, and the coach, well he's gone. Should have gotten rid of him a long time ago. But this was it. This was his last game."

Charlie just nodded to them both and continued walking as he eyed the coach in the parking lot behind the bleachers, tossing a bag into the trunk of his car. The coach saw Charlie approaching and put on the wry smile he'd used when Charlie first confronted him during the game. He crossed his arms defiantly across his chest, awaiting Charlie's complaint.

Charlie hadn't decided what he was going to do, until he saw the smirk on the coach's face and thought about the tears in Zack's eyes. Charlie's neck and jaw muscles bulged with anger. He walked straight up to the coach and drove his right fist as hard as he could fire it, straight into the coach's stomach. The shorter man gasped and doubled over and vomited violently into the gray cinders of the parking lot. While he was still gasping for air, Charlie yanked his hair with his left hand pulling the coach's head up and pinning it against the top of the car. Charlie stepped forward with his left foot and drove his right knee up between the other man's legs. The coach's whole body shuddered with pain. Tears came to his eyes and he heaved again down the front of his shirt as Charlie kept his head against the car.

"Remember this feeling," Charlie forced out between his clenched teeth. "This is how a young black kid feels when an adult calls him a nigger. Now you're going to apologize to Zack Willard but I don't want a good kid like that anywhere near a piece of scum like you, so you'll apologize to me and I'll pass it on to him." Charlie took a menacing step backwards with his right leg. "Now let's hear it or you're going to need a fucking colostomy bag before you get out of this parking lot."

The coach, his eyes closed and tears and vomit running down his face, held up his hands as he struggled for air. "No, no," he managed weakly. "Sorry. Sorry Zack," he whispered hoarsely.

"Don't ever let me see you near a kids' soccer game again," said Charlie. He released his grasp of the coach's hair and let him slide down the side of the car to the ground.

As Charlie walked back across the field, he noticed out of the corner of his eye, a Cadillac pulling up quickly in back of the coach's car. Kyle Loftus and the man with the thin mustache got out and hurried over to the still-gasping coach.

Natty had given Hank, Charlie's wallet and keys, and started toward the bus with the slow-moving Emma. The bruise to her thigh had stiffened up making her limp noticeably. She held an ice bag to her eye and still had the butterfly bandage on her swollen lip.

Natty looked at her star player and smiled. "Looks like you had fun today Em," she said trying to cheer her up. Emma grimaced as she tried to smile.

"Did we win the game?" she asked softly.

Natty shrugged and pursed her lips. "I'm not sure. You got the goal, but I'm not sure what the league is going to do after all this. Doesn't matter," she said putting her arm around Emma's shoulders. "That was one hell of a game you played kid."

The rest of *The Bones* were already on the bus and Geneva Gunnells was standing in the doorway signifying that she was getting impatient to get going. As they walked past the goal at the end of the field, Natty noticed someone still sitting on the grass over on the home side of the field at about the five yard line. Emma noticed him too. It was Gabe, the banished Welch midfielder who was sitting with his arms on his knees watching them.

A few yards from the bus, Emma stopped. She looked over at Gabe, who just stared back at her, and then at Natty. Natty smiled at her and nodded. "Go ahead Em. We'll wait for you."

Emma blinked her eyes rapidly and took in a deep breath to overcome her shyness and started walking toward Gabe. She still held the ice bag to her right eye and moved slowly with her stiff-legged limp, causing the boy to jump up quickly and start walking toward her.

Natty was headed for the door of the bus to give Emma some privacy when a white Lincoln Town Car pulled up in back of the bus and a trim, well-dressed man of about fifty got out and came quickly around the big car. Natty saw that there were two women with him who remained in the car. He smiled at Natty as he approached to put her at ease. "Hello Mrs. Oakes," he said, still five yards away. He had a business card in his left hand and his right hand extended. He introduced himself and they shook hands.

Natty glanced over at Emma and Gabe who were talking at a safe distance from each other. She looked back down at the card in her hand and smiled as she read the title written in italics under the man's name. *Director, United States Junior Soccer Development Team.*

"We're going to invite Emma to join the team next summer," the man said. "We play all over the world. Best competition there is. Four years from now she'll be on the Olympic Team."

Natty laughed. "Wow. You seem pretty confident. You sure she'll be able to make your team?"

The man chuckled and looked over at Emma. "*Make* the team?" He shook his head. "We're going to build the team around her."

Emma and Gabe had stopped about ten feet from each other, unsure of how close they should get and then unsure of what to say. Finally Gabe spoke first. "Emma, I, uh, wanted to apologize for my team. They, uh, shouldn't a treated you like that and said that stuff to you." He looked down at the ground and scowled at the thought. "That ain't right. That ain't the way to play soccer." He glanced briefly down the field. "Most a the team ain't like that, you know. Mostly good guys, 'cept Rudy's a jerk, and the coach too. He's a ..." Gabe just shrugged and left the sentence unfinished. He thrust his hands into the pockets of his hooded sweatshirt, and fidgeted nervously. "So anyways, that's all I wanted to say. Good game you played. *Real* good game." His voice and his eyebrows rose with enthusiasm and he grinned broadly. "*Damn!* Three best goals I ever saw!" Then he went silent, afraid he was talking too much.

So it was Emma's turn to say something. She wasn't sure if her voice would work. "Thanks," she squeaked out softly. And then a little more loudly, "thanks for, um, helping me there. That, you know, really helped me. Hope you didn't get in trouble."

"Naw, that don't matter. Think the coach is in deep shit, way some a the parents were talking, so, well it don't matter anyway."

Emma glanced back at the bus and saw Natty in her front, right seat and Geneva Gunnells at the wheel. "Well I got to go," she said, taking a step backward.

The boy took his hands out of his pockets and took a step toward her. "Say Emma listen. I, uh, was wondering something."

Emma stopped and took a step closer to him. They were now close enough to touch each other.

"I was wondering, uh, if you were going to play for Red Bone High next year. You and the Willards and that Polish kid ... you think you'll all be playing for Red Bone?"

Emma shrugged. "Yeah, I guess. I think Zack and Sammy goin' to play soccer now 'stead of football but I ain't sure. Paul goin' to play soccer for sure."

Gabe nodded as he digested the information. "Cause I was thinking," his eyebrows went up again, "I got an aunt lives in Red Bone, and I could, you know, live over there and transfer to Red Bone High to play soccer." Gabe couldn't hide the excitement in his voice. "So we could play on the same team, me and you and the Willard boys and that new kid."

Emma smiled broadly through the pain of her lip and her rapidly swelling eyebrow.

"*That'd* be a pretty good team," she said excitedly, "with you playing with us."

"*Hell,* state champions four years in a row is what *that* team'd be!" said Gabe proudly. "Go up there and kick the *crap* out of them teams from Charleston and Morgantown!" They both laughed, as they enjoyed the idea of playing together on what would assuredly be a powerhouse high school soccer team.

The loud blare of the school bus horn startled them both back into silence. Then they just looked at each other for a moment without speaking. This time Emma spoke first. "Got to go," she said. "Thanks Gabe, for helping me today."

"Yeah, that's okay," he said. He held out his fist to her.

Emma smiled nervously as she brought her left fist up slowly and pressed her knuckles into Gabe's. The feel of the boy's cool skin against her own sent a shiver up her arm.

"I'll see you Emma." Gabe said, taking a step back. "Can't wait for next year."

On the bus, Emma surprised Natty by squeezing in next to her in the front seat, unable to contain her excitement from whatever it was she and Gabe had discussed. Natty had never seen Emma so giddy with happiness, even with all the bruises she had absorbed that day. "So what gives Em?" Natty smiled coyly and leaned close to her star player. "What did Price Valiant have to say that's got you bubblin' over?"

Emma told her how Gabe had apologized for his team and then what Gabe had said, about transferring to Red Bone and how excited he was about playing on the same team. "Says we'd be state champions four years in a row! Then he said he couldn't *wait* for next year," Emma said in an excited whisper. As the bus pulled out of the parking lot, Emma leaned back to look out the window to watch Gabe jogging down the street by himself in the opposite direction. Natty smiled and patted Emma's leg on the seat next to her.

"Yeah, that'll be quite a soccer team Em. Quite a team." Natty took the business card she was holding to her right hand and pushed it into the back pocket of her jeans.

Walking back across the soccer field, Charlie watched the yellow bus lumber out of the parking lot and then spied Hank leaning against the front fender of the Chrysler waiting for him. He walked slowly, drained by the afternoon's calamity and disgusted with himself for letting the game get out of control, disgusted with the coach for what he'd done to Zack Willard, and still shaking from the moment of pure hatred he'd experienced behind the bleachers. Hank's hard, black eyes bore into him as he got close to the car. Hank turned his head to spit onto the dusty shoulder of the road.

"Feel better?" Hank asked, knowing that Charlie had had some kind of confrontation with the coach.

Charlie avoided Hank's eyes. "Feel like shit." He gestured toward the car. "C'mon, I need a drink."

Chapter 24

*M*oody's *Roadhouse* sat a few feet off the dusty shoulder of South County Road, a hundred yards east of the intersection known as *The Crossroads*. Bigger than it looked from the outside, the *Roadhouse* was actually three buildings that came together in a L shape: a very old two-story clapboard covered house at the corner; a long shed-like structure along the main road that housed the restaurant and bar; and around the corner on the unpaved side street, a smaller flat-roofed house topped by a garish neon sign that announced *Fat Cats*, underlined with smaller letters promising *Adult Entertainment*. Every window of the *Roadhouse* was illuminated by neon beer signs, surrounding the complex with a warm holiday-like hue of color in the early evening dusk.

The hard-packed dirt and gravel parking lot that wrapped around the rear of the *Roadhouse* was already half-filled, mostly with pick-up trucks, when Hank pulled the Chrysler into a spot behind the restaurant.

Charlie recognized a few faces in the nearly full restaurant. Hank knew everyone. At a small table in the back of the room, Hank spied his two fellow Planning Board members, Earl Fitch and Jimmy Haggerman, who waved them over. Still in a sour mood over the events at the soccer game, Charlie was in no hurry for dinner and was grateful for the invitation to join Hank's friends who were both nursing bourbons and a nearly empty pitcher of beer. Charlie ordered another pitcher and four more Jim Beams.

"Probably a law against meeting like this, aye Hank?" said Jimmy Haggerman. He was a tall, thin man who Charlie knew was in his late sixties but looked older. He wore an ancient green baseball cap adorned with a barely legible Norfolk & Western logo. The cap was pushed back on his head revealing straight, soft white hair. His strong face had a permanent wrinkled tan and with his clear blue eyes, in another setting, he could have passed for a retired banker or Fortune 100 chief executive, instead of the forty-year railroad man he was.

"It's an open meeting," said Earl Fitch, the barber. "Anybody can partake, long as they buy the beer." He grinned at Charlie. "Appears you could use a little trim there Mr. Burden," he said eying the hair curling over Charlie's ears.

"Yeah, I'll have to go up and see you pretty soon," said Charlie.

"Lookin' a little glum there tonight Charlie. Everything okay with you?"

The waitress arrived with the drinks, allowing Charlie to sidestep the question as he reached for his wallet. Without thinking he pulled out a hundred dollar bill and immediately regretted the unintentional ostentatiousness of the display.

Hank stepped in for Charlie. "Had a little problem over at the kids soccer game, got a little unpleasant. One of their boys gave our Emma a good knock to the head." He went on to summarize the game for Earl and Jimmy. When Hank mentioned the name of the Welch coach, both men nodded knowingly.

"That boy's always been trouble. Shouldn'ta ever been coaching a kids' team," said Earl Fitch. Jimmy Haggerman nodded in agreement as he casually turned to look over his shoulder to inspect the bar at the end of the room that was filling up with young men in blue jeans and vests along with a few business types in polyester jackets and loosened ties. The noise in the room was picking up with the growing crowd and action at the two pool tables.

"Charlie went over and had a talk with him after the game," Hank said, glancing sideways at Charlie. "He have anything to say Charlie?"

Charlie smiled thinly and shrugged. "No, he wasn't very talkative." Charlie was anxious to get off the subject of the Welch coach. He still felt sick inside at what had happened behind the bleachers. He had beaten a man up, again, just like Nardi at the hockey game in July. He'd lost his temper and lashed out viciously like a punk thug bully, and while both Nardi and the coach deserved a good beating, Charlie knew that this was a new side of him that had bubbled to the surface recently and it said more about himself than about the two men he had fought.

The other men could see that Charlie was troubled by his run-in with the coach and took the conversation in other directions. Over a couple of pitchers of beer and another round of bourbons, Earl told some funny stories about misadventures at his barber shop and Jimmy Haggerman recalled some of the strange occurrences from his years on the train – stories the three old friends had shared many times over the years, retold for Charlie's benefit.

Charlie accepted a short, fat cigar from Earl Fitch and with a couple of shots of bourbon under his belt soon began to relax and put the calamitous soccer game out of his mind.

After a while Earl and Jimmy excused themselves – they'd already stayed later than they had intended – and Hank and Charlie ordered sandwiches before the kitchen closed. In the large room off the bar, in the main house, they could hear a blue grass band warming up, while the restaurant was beginning to absorb more patrons from the bar-side.

Watching the people passing through the bar while they ate, Charlie recognized Natty's sister-in-law, Sally Oakes, the vivacious red head who appeared to be well-known around the crowded bar. She was with Yancy Oakes and his large wife and as they squeezed through the crowd, Charlie also thought he saw Eve Brewster pass by. Their appearance quickened Charlie's pulse in anticipation of the chance that maybe Natty had changed her mind and come out after all. He kept an eye out for her while he and Hank talked and ate. When they were done eating Charlie talked Hank into having one more bourbon, and relit his cigar.

"Gonna go drain the monster," said Hank rising painfully on his old knees. There were two choices for the men's room, he told Charlie – a small one upstairs in the main house, or a larger one out behind *Fat Cats,* accessible by the long wood-plank deck out the back door of the bar. He, like most of the men, would use the john at *Fat Cats.* "Easier than climbin' the stairs. Might sneak a little peek at the main stage while I'm over there," Hank said with a wink.

Charlie nodded to his friend and pulled on his cigar. *Fat Cats . . . where Hugo Paxton had his fatal heart attack. He'd have to go over later and check out the talent, out of respect for Hugo.* Charlie smiled to himself. He could see why the *Roadhouse* was a favorite spot of Hugo's. A steady stream of women with tight jeans, bare midriffs and too much makeup – some who looked too young to be in a bar, some too old – were making their way to the crowded room where the band was in full swing.

The bar area had thinned out a little after the band had started, allowing Charlie a clearer look through the crowd, still hopeful that Natty might appear. *She'd look pretty plain among this group of girls all dolled up and dressed to show everything they had or didn't have,* Charlie mused. *But still, even with no makeup or jewelry, she'd be the most attractive woman in the place.*

Then he saw the face. Across the room, on the other side of the bar – hidden now by the bartender at the cash register, but still standing there. When the bartender moved away, there he was, glaring straight at Charlie, the pencil thin mustache pushed up by the menacing scowl, a toothpick dancing nervously between puffy lips. The man from the soccer game that Charlie knew from somewhere else. *But where?*

The bartender returned with three long-neck Budweisers he placed on the bar in front of the man with the toothpick. Charlie turned away but kept the visage of the stranger's face in his head trying to recall where he'd seen him before today. When he looked back toward the cash register the man was gone. Charlie craned his neck to the side trying to peer through the young men in their vests and baseball caps hunched over the bar, when his vision was suddenly blocked by someone standing next to the table. It was Eve Brewster.

"Hey Charlie. Looking for someone?" Eve said playfully as she eased herself into Hank's chair. She was seated before Charlie could stand politely to welcome her.

"Hi Eve. How *are* you?" Charlie smiled.

Eve put her glass on the table. It was a clear drink with some ice and piece of lime. In her left hand, she held a pack of Merit 100s and a Bic lighter. "I'm okay Charlie," she said with a weary smile. She looked around the inside of the *Roadhouse.* "Don't come here much anymore. Used to come a lot, in the old days." She smiled. "In my younger days."

"Interesting place," said Charlie looking back toward the bar.

"Only reason I came tonight was that Natty said she and Sal were comin' out."

"Yeah me too." Charlie watched Eve closely for a reaction.

Eve just stared back at Charlie for a few moments with her tired eyes and then reached for a cigarette. Charlie noticed Hank sitting at another table, engaged in conversation with an older couple. He leaned forward with his elbows on the table, determined to find out why his relationship with Eve had changed. "You know Eve, up until about a month ago, I thought we were pretty good friends, and then you, um, well I think you got the wrong idea about something and started to, ah, treat me differently."

Eve lit a cigarette and turned her head to blow a long white cloud of smoke away from Charlie. She looked back at him and smiled briefly and shrugged her

shoulders. "Yeah, I'm sorry 'bout that Charlie. Don't want to be mad at you, but
... well, I've been worrying about my brothers for so long, sharing their pain, you
know, I just naturally come down on their side of things, sometimes without
thinking too hard about it. You know what I mean Charlie?"

"Well I guess I do, but, Eve you have to believe me when I tell you there's
nothing going on with me and Natty. We're just friends. That's all it is and that's
all it's going to be." Charlie sat back in his chair and drew on his cigar, awaiting
Eve's response.

Eve sat still, staring at Charlie with one eye closed in a questioning look.
Then a smile grew slowly across her broad face. "*You and Natty.* That's what you
think this is about?"

Charlie was at a loss. "Well, yeah. I mean, I know you've seen us running
together a couple of times and . . ."

"And you've been going to her soccer games, and become the best friend
her son's ever had, and of course, you let her drive your car around for a week
there when hers was tore up." Eve shook her head and laughed. "Shit Charlie,
everyone in Red Bone's seen the sparks flyin' between you two since you landed
here. Then you get up there at the Planning Board meeting and Natty's at the
podium, and you're telling everyone how you're going to build us a brand new
athletic field and a new library, but you're lookin' right at Natty and your eyes are
locked like two kids at the junior prom. *Christ*, all we needed was some violin
music."

Charlie was taken by surprise by Eve's revelation of the public nature of his
relationship with Natty. "But Eve, there's nothing going on," Charlie replied
quickly. "That's what I'm telling you. We're just --"

"Charlie," Eve cut him off shaking her head and leaning closer onto the
table. She turned her head to the side as she took a few moments to compose her
thoughts. When she looked back at him, she smiled and her eyes were soft as was
her voice. "Charlie, let me tell you something. There isn't a woman living in
McDowell County, including myself, who ain't hoping and praying that you'll fall
mad in love with that girl and take her and her two wonderful children away from
here and give her the kind of life she deserves." Eve rapped her knuckles on the
table for emphasis and raised her eyebrows as if to ask Charlie if he understood
what she was saying.

It took Charlie several seconds to grasp what Eve was telling him. Now he
was totally perplexed. "But what about your brother?" Charlie finally asked softly.

Eve fell back into her seat. "Buck's an asshole. He's my brother and I love
him and I'll always be concerned for him, but he ain't never deserved one second
of that girl's companionship, let alone the mindless adoration she's been holdin'
out for him for the last twenty years now since she was just a kid in grade school."

Eve took a long drag on her cigarette and shook her head sideways. "Don't
worry 'bout Buck. He's too dumb to know how lucky he is. Natty goes, he just
finds some big-titted hillbilly girl with no brain and he's happy as a clam." Eve sat
back in her chair and looked at her watch. "Never given them kids any fathering
anyway," she added bitterly.

Charlie finished his bourbon and looked over at Hank who was now at a different table with three older men who looked like they were enjoying his company. Charlie was starting to feel the effects of too many Jim Beams and a long day. He needed to use the men's room but he still hadn't gotten things straight with Eve.

"Okay then, Eve," he said, a little slurred. "If it's not about Natty, then what is it? What's our problem?"

Eve shrugged innocently. "It's the coal Charlie. The surface mine on Angel Mountain. We need that mine. My brothers need that mine." She leaned forward again in earnestness. "Don't you see Charlie? Yancy and Ransom, and Buck too, along with most of the other men in McDowell County, been having too many years of tough times trying to make a living around here. Going from one meaningless, low pay job to the next, or more likely no job at all for long stretches. Never having a real occupation or career. After a while it beats you down, you know, and you start to lose everything . . . your self respect, your sense of humor, any ambition you ever had." She took a long drag on her cigarette, turned her head and blew a cloud of smoke toward the ceiling before looking back at Charlie. "There's a sadness comes over a place. You see it here Charlie, I know you do. Hell, all you got to do is look around at the men in this room here." Eve nodded her head behind her.

Charlie glanced briefly toward the bar looking for the man with the toothpick. He didn't have to examine the crowd to know what Eve was talking about. He'd felt it since he first came to McDowell County – the quiet resignation and learned sense of inferiority, along with the latent anger that the men seemed to share. The inability to hold your eye for very long.

"So that mine is *important* Charlie," Eve interrupted his thought. "God, it's like a miracle -- huge power plant and a big mine like that coming here to McDowell County, with local men getting preference for the jobs. That mine'll put these men to working for the next twenty years, at good paying jobs, in a real career. Being a *union miner*, Christ, that's about all any of these fellahs *ever* wanted out of life. And now they got a chance."

Eve looked down at the table and made a job out of snuffing out her cigarette in a gray cardboard ash tray while Charlie waited for her to continue. She finally looked up with an accusatory look, one eyebrow raised in question. "And you're trying to stop the mine on Angel Mountain, Charlie," she said quietly. "Don't ask me how I know that, but I know it's true." She paused to allow Charlie a response, which didn't come, so she continued. "Don't understand it, seeing as how it's your company and all that wants the mine, but, well I was figuring *that* was about you and Natty, but if you say ..."

"No, it's not about Natty." Charlie looked around him at the people in the bar as he wondered if there was any way he could explain it to Eve. *She wouldn't understand anything about the deck being stacked in favor of the large corporations versus the little guy, including the sham of deregulation – of banking, airlines, communications, and so many other industries and now utilities. Or how the state and federal government bureaucracies were now all in the pockets of the multinationals and their lobbyists and lawyers and the fix was in for the rich to keep getting richer while the poor would keep getting poorer, and how sick he was of being on the wrong side for so many years. And no, she wouldn't understand how it felt to be a professional lackey who had become successful far beyond his talents and been promoted to a social class that he never belonged in simply because he had the right roommate in college. Nor would she understand his empathy for Bud and Alice DeWitt and their little mountainside farm, symbols in the struggle that he knew would be his last chance at redemption.*

Charlie looked back at Eve and smiled. "It's complicated Eve, but the DeWitts don't deserve to lose their farm, and the environment doesn't deserve to be wounded by another mountaintop-removal mine. That's about as simple as I can make it."

Eve just stared at him blankly for a few seconds before flashing a quick smile. "Well okay Charlie," she said looking at her watch. "I *don't* understand it, but you're a good man. And I hear it's all a done deal anyway. Going to court in a few weeks and they'll be taking the farm by eminent domain and it's all settled." She gathered up her cigarettes and lighter. "Union's already taking names of McDowell County men want to work on the mine." She held out a hand to Charlie. "So, still friends?"

Charlie took her hand in his. "Friends Eve, whatever happens."

Eve left and Charlie finally rose slowly out of the hard wooden chair. His body ached, his bladder was ready to burst and his eyes were having a little trouble focusing. It would be good to settle into the big, cushy seat of the Chrysler for the ride back to Red Bone. He stopped next to the booth where Hank was sitting with three other men, all at least as old as Hank. Charlie noticed they were all drinking coffee from old brown ceramic mugs. He shook hands with each of the men as Hank introduced them.

"I'm just going to go out back here for a second Hank, then I'll be ready to go."

"Yeah, late enough for us," said Hank.

Charlie made his way slowly through the bar to a windowless wood plank door that was held closed by long springs and an antique thumb-latch handle. The heavy door slammed behind him with a familiar crack that he had been listening to all evening.

The night air was cooler than he'd expected. It was probably hotter inside the *Roadhouse* than he'd realized, but either way, the air felt good, with the scent of autumn that reminded him of Halloween. The rear of the *Roadhouse* was in almost pitch darkness save for a strong spotlight on the back wall of *Fat Cats*. Pointed directly toward him, the spotlight served less to illuminate the wooden decking, than to blind Charlie as he tried to pick his way through the darkness.

A door opened immediately under the spotlight and Charlie could see two figures emerge, one who it was clear even in the silhouetted darkness was pulling up his zipper. Charlie watched as the two men made their way around the near corner of *Fat Cats* and pulled open what was obviously the rear door of the bar. Loud voices and shrill catcalls escaped through the opening along with the familiar strains of *"The Hustle,"* the anthem of strip bars everywhere. The door closed shutting off the sound and leaving the building in darkness behind the blinding rays of the spotlight, but now Charlie had his bearings and while he couldn't see the wooden walkway even a few feet in front of him, he knew the direction he had to go in. His left hand found a wooden railing. To his right was a wall with small, screened windows up near the roof overhang. The sound of dishes rattling and the distinct metallic snap of a walk-in cooler door being opened, announced that his was the restaurant's kitchen.

Charlie inched his way along the dark boardwalk and then almost stumbled as the walk suddenly angled downward. Holding his right hand up to shield his eyes from the spotlight, Charlie suddenly realized with a chuckle that he was on a ramp and that *The Roadhouse* and *Fat Cats* were in fact, *wheelchair accessible.*

He passed the corner of the kitchen and then felt the cinders of the parking lot under his feet. A few yards further on, he could vaguely make out in the darkness another ramp that led up to the rear of *Fat Cats.*

Suddenly there was a flash directly in front of him. It was a lighter held by a man sitting on the railing about twenty feet ahead. The man's head was down as he lit his cigarette. In the pitch darkness the lighter's flame was strong, casting a wide circle of illumination that Charlie was grateful for as it showed the path to the other ramp. He took a few more steps across the cinders, when the man, still lighting his cigarette, brought his head up and turned toward Charlie. The Zippo was extinguished with a sharp clank of the top closing, but the instant of illumination was enough for Charlie to recognize the thin mustache and the puffy lips and the permanent scowl of the man from the soccer game.

Charlie stopped in his tracks. This didn't feel right. He tried to squint through the blinding rays of the spotlight to find the man but could only catch a sporadic glimpse of the red end of his cigarette. Then it came to him – along with an instant flash of realization of the trouble he was in – the picture suddenly clear in his mind, of the morning of the raid on Angel Mountain and the man with the mustache in his police uniform standing next to the white Sheriff's Department cruiser up at the front of Yarbrough's caravan. *Deputy Sheriff Wayne Lester,* Natty had told him, whom he had pushed the blame off onto for the raid's failure. No, this wasn't a good situation, Charlie told himself as he tightened up both fists.

Then the spotlight disappeared and Charlie's face felt like it had exploded. He saw a hundred spotlights as the world spun around him, on his hands and knees at first, and then knees and one shoulder as he listed uncontrollably trying to determine which way was up. He could taste the blood flowing warm into his mouth and then into his left eye as he fought for balance with the top of his head pushing at the ground. Then he felt a powerful jolt across the middle of his back that sounded like someone beating a rug with a broom handle. And then the pain came, in waves, and the lights grew dimmer as they circled away from him in a vortex he was being sucked into.

Charlie fought for consciousness. He forced himself to draw in some air in spite of the blood filling his mouth and nostrils. Finding the ground with his hands, he pushed himself up to all fours and spit out a mouthful of blood and then grimaced from the excruciating pain in his nose and his back.

"Remember this feeling boy." The familiar voice was just inches from Charlie's ear but he wasn't sure which ear. "This's what it feels like when a big shot New Yorker comes down here and fucks with wrong guy." The voice took a step backward on the cinders. "And here's one for your little nigger pal." The coach's foot came silently through the darkness, up into Charlie's stomach. The air left his lungs and a crippling wave of nausea squeezed at his guts forcing Charlie to gasp for air and swallow repeatedly to keep from vomiting. But in spite of the pain or perhaps because of it, Charlie had regained his consciousness and his head was clear enough for him to understand the seriousness of his situation. He needed to do something.

A few feet away from his head, Charlie could see the coach's familiar black soccer cleats, but when he reached out to grab a foot, his arm wouldn't work right and he just pawed the air harmlessly with his hand.

"Alright boys, get him on his feet. I'm going to mess up his face a little."

Two new sets of shoes shuffled through the cinders to come up on each side of Charlie. The boots with the blue jeans would be Wayne Lester. On the other side, Charlie recognized the brown loafers and tan slacks of Kyle Loftus. Rough hands grabbed hold of his arms and reached under his armpits to pull him up. Charlie knew he needed to stay down. If they pulled him to his feet he would be defenseless. But when he tried to fight off the hands, he had no power and when he squirmed, his back lit up with fire. Unable to resist, he went dead-weight against the arms that were pulling him up for the real beating to come.

Then he heard the sickening smack. It was a sound he knew well, of fist against flesh and bone. And then again, and once again in rapid succession along with the sound of feet shuffling quickly around in the cinders, and then the hands released him. Charlie turned his head to the side in time to see the coach land heavily on the ground a few feet away from him, his black soccer shoes now scraping slowly against the dirt. Then he heard Deputy Sheriff Wayne Lester speak for the first time.

"Ain't your fight Buck." His voice sounded surprisingly timid. "This boy's got this comin' to him."

"Three on one ain't much of a fight Wayne." The deep, gravelly voice was confident and strong. Charlie was immediately glad that the voice was on his side. "Plus a two-by- four." Charlie heard the hollow sound of a piece of wood hitting the ground. "What's matter Wayne, you forget your nightstick?"

"That wasn't me Buck," Wayne Lester pleaded. "I didn't know he was going to use a board on him."

"Yeah, bullshit. Just your style, you and these little girls you're hanging out with."

Kyle Loftus took a tentative step forward. "Wayne's right Buck. He had it coming ..."

"Beat it Kyle, less you want to be next after Deputy Lester and I settle an old score here." Buck's leg brushed Charlie's shoulder as he took a stride forward.

"Hold on Buck," said Wayne Lester, buying time. "We was doin' you a favor here. This guy's been red hot after your wife since he got here. Been thick with Natty all over town, runnin' with her in the morning, and pallin' around with the kid."

"Fuck you Lester," Buck spit out as he cocked his right arm and reached out his left in the darkness to find his target.

"It's true Buck," said Kyle Loftus taking a hesitant step toward the two men. "How do you think you got that loggin' job with Garvey?"

Buck stopped his assault on Wayne Lester. "That's all bullshit. What's this guy want with Natty?"

"Pat told me himself," said Loftus. "Says Burden called him up and told him to put you on."

"Why else you think Garvey'd give a loser like you a job," Lester added, feeling a little bolder. "And he's trying to kill the Angel Mountain mine 'cause Natty's been whispering' in his ear about the DeWitts and her mama."

"That ain't true . . ." Buck sounded less sure of himself.

"I was *there* Buck. When they torched the field. Burden tipped 'em off. The lawyers in Charleston got his cell phone record for that morning. Show's Burden called up to the farm right after we started up there."

Charlie groaned as he pushed himself to a sitting position. His back felt like it was on fire when he tried to get a deep breath. He attempted to talk but his mouth was full of blood, which he spit on the ground next to him.

"Wake up Buck, and see what's going on," said Kyle Loftus as he bent over to pull the groggy coach to his feet. "Come on, let's get out of here."

Two headlights on high-beam roared at the men from across the parking lot. As the big Chrysler slid through the gravel, stopping just short of the scene of the fight, Hank leaned on the horn. Buck took off up the ramp toward *Fat Cats,* while Wayne Lester went back into the bar, passing a dozen men headed the other way in response to the blaring horn. Kyle Loftus pulled the still groggy coach through the dark parking lot to the brown Cadillac.

* * *

The ceiling fan was turning in the wrong direction. Charlie was certain. All the times he had opened his eyes in the morning in the big bedroom to see the fan turning slowly, it was always spinning clockwise. Then he moved, not much more than a twitch, and the shooting pain in his back, neck and head reminded him cruelly that he wasn't in his apartment. Without moving his head, he could see the light green curtains hanging from an aluminum halo around the bed, and then the shiny steel railings on either side of him that confirmed he was in a hospital bed. The noises of the small ward came through and under the curtains: low voices of visitors; the brisk swish of a nurse moving efficiently through her duties; and then the unmistakable sounds of a baseball game on a television with the volume just barely audible.

Baseball! Christ, what time was it? Charlie labored to lift his left arm off the bed to look at his watch, but it wasn't on his wrist.

"Almost two-thirty. Bout time you woke up. I was about to pull the sheet up over your head and call a priest."

Charlie turned his head to the left to see Natty rising out of a metal folding chair and next to her, the Pie Man jumping up to follow her to the side of the bed. Pie had his Yankees hat on backwards, and a wide-eyed look of fear on his face. Charlie couldn't prevent a painful chuckle.

"Hey Pie Man. How's my best bud?" Charlie held up his palm for a more gentle than usual high-five from the boy. He held onto Pie's hand as the boy stood up on the bottom frame of the bed to get a better view. Pie pointed a short finger towards Charlie's face.

"Chowly look like a waccoon."

Charlie grimaced as he laughed. "Oh yeah. That's what a broken nose does to you." He reached over with his hand to feel the gauze bandage that covered the gash on the bridge of his nose and then the thick bandage over his left eyebrow. "Fourth time for me, or maybe the fifth. I can't remember."

"Whewa you in a fight Chowly?"

"Well, it wasn't much of a fight. Don't remember much of it," said Charlie trying to be vague for the boy's sake.

"So, how do you feel Charlie?" Natty asked, to change the subject.

"I don't know. How do I look?"

"Doctor says you'll be all right. Took x-rays of your back. Just a deep bruise."

Charlie recalled the excruciating pain of the two-by-four digging into the flesh of his back as he felt for the tight bandage around his torso.

"Course, you won't be getting any modeling jobs with that nose rearranged like that."

Charlie smiled. "Did he say when I could leave?"

"Tomorrow. Just wants to check on concussion. Hank said he'll come and pick you up. He just left a little while ago, been here all night and all morning."

The word *concussion* reminded Charlie of the incident at the soccer game. "How's Emma?"

"Fine. A lot better than you are. No problems. Just some stitches."

After a pause, Charlie said, "that was quite a game, huh?" Pie just stared at Charlie examining the battered face as if he was unsure who it was laying in the bed. Charlie poked him in the belly eliciting a brief smile. "C'mon Pie Man, it's not that bad. I'll be okay in a couple of days."

After a few moments of uneasy silence, Natty reached into the front pocket of her blue jeans. "Pie, why don't you go out in the hall and get a soda from the machine and let me talk to Charlie for a few minutes." She pulled a crumpled dollar bill out and squeezed it into Pie's hand.

"Okay mama. I will wait fowa you outside. Goodbye Chowly. I will see you tomawwo." He dropped to the floor and slapped Charlie a high five before going out through the split in the drawn curtains.

Charlie reached for the bed control lying next to his right hand. He winced with pain as he raised up the head of the bed to where he could look directly at Natty. He let out a deep breath as the movement and the pain subsided. "I must look like hell to scare him like that."

Natty smiled. "Yeah, you look pretty ugly." She leaned in closer to examine the bandages and the gauze rolls in his nose, the professional care-giver unable to resist her natural instincts. She squinted with concern as she put her right hand against his forehead, and then feeling normal temperature, pushed a few matted strands of hair up and away from the bandage over his eye.

Her hand felt soft and cool and soothing on his warm flesh and he longed to reach up and touch her fingers and put his palm against hers and explore her hand with the tips of his fingers.

Sensing that her touch had crossed the line from concern to intimacy, Natty took her hand away and crossed her arms in front of her. She smiled briefly at Charlie and looked around her at the small enclosure made by the curtains. "I was in this same bed couple of years ago." She motioned briefly with a hand toward her left eyebrow. "For this."

Charlie just watched her without comment. He knew it wasn't a subject that Natty wanted to talk about. He waited while Natty looked down at her boots then stuck her hands in the front pockets of her blue jeans as she rubbed her thigh against the side of the bed. Finally she looked up at him with a troubled look on her face.

"Hank says he thought he saw Buck there last night," she said quietly. "When he drove the car up to where you was . . . says he might a seen Buck running off, along with . . . sure he seen Kyle Loftus and maybe Wayne Lester – ain't sure – but . . . ." Her voice trailed off. She took a breath. "Charlie, did Buck do this to you?" she whispered. Her eyes were glistening. "Cause if he *did*, that would . . . ."

"No, Natty no." Charlie tried to shake his head. "Buck saved my life, or at least my pretty face anyway, what's left of it. I don't know where he came from, but those other three were getting ready to pound me pretty good. Guess they didn't like losing a soccer game in the last ten seconds."

Natty smiled but she had a worried look on her face. "Buck didn't come home 'til real late last night – 'bout three in the morning. And he was pretty drunk, I can tell. Slept in the living room." She rocked nervously on the balls of her feet and squinted in thought. "Ain't the first time for that a course, but, well he's been pretty good since he started working. Buck really loves that job, cuttin' trees, and he's been a lot better and, well I'm glad it wasn't Buck that –"

"Natty, some things were said last night – after Buck helped me – some stuff that may be a problem for you. Wayne Lester, well Buck was about to go after him –"

"*Damn*, Lester's nothin' but trouble. Buck's had it in for him for a couple of years now, but I was hopin' he'd just let it go. It's probably why he helped you in the first place, just to have a go at Lester."

"Probably. But Lester didn't want to fight Buck so he started talking his way out of it, and he was saying things . . . saying things about us."

"*Us?*"

"Well more about *me* than you, but stuff about *us.*"

"Oh shit."

"Told Buck that I've been after you since I came here, and how we've gone running and been together a lot and that now I'm trying to stop the Angel Mountain project because of, you know, how I feel about you, that kind of thing." Charlie sounded embarrassed.

Natty rolled her eyeballs. "*Damn,* how does he come up with shit like that?"

"And Loftus told him about me calling Pat Garvey about the job."

"*Aw geeze,* that ain't good." Natty shook her head dejectedly. "Crap," she said softly. "Things were going okay. Still don't pay no attention to the kids, but least he was coming home."

"Natty, I'm sorry about all this." Charlie reached out and touched her forearm softly with the tips of his fingers. "But if he does anything to you, you've got to get out of there, and you've got to call me right away."

Natty looked down at his fingers on her arm and suddenly recalled the same empty feeling she'd had at the soccer game when she was watching Charlie on the field and thought about him leaving them for good very soon. She looked up at him and smiled briefly. "No, I'll be okay. He ain't like that any more." Natty scowled and shook her head. "Damn that weasel Wayne Lester. What's he got to go shootin' his mouth off for?"

Charlie took his hand away from Natty's arm. "Well, that may be my fault," he said. He tried to push himself up a little taller in the bed. "When I was in New York last week, we had a meeting about the Angel Mountain raid, and well, I had to do a little tap dancing around the truth about what happened."

"Yeah, I guess you were in a tough spot, huh. So what'd you tell 'em?"

Charlie smiled and shrugged his shoulders. "Blamed it all on Wayne Lester. Said that you and he went to high school together, like you told me, except that you two were, you know, very close."

Natty scrunched up her face. "Ugly thought."

"It gets worse," Charlie said wincing as he tried to change his position. He smiled sheepishly. "I kind of implied that you two might still be, uh, seeing each other a little, and that's why Lester tipped you off about the raid."

"Aw *geeze* Charlie!" Natty rolled her eyeballs. She stared at Charlie with an exasperated look. Then she grinned. "You really told 'em that?"

"Yeah, I couldn't think of anything else."

Natty giggled. "*Christ,* Lester must be rip-shit."

"Yeah, I'm sure he is. But, they know about the call on my cell phone that morning, so he's probably off the hook."

Natty scowled with worry. "That means they know it was you. CanAmex knows. Is that going to be trouble for you Charlie?"

Charlie shrugged. "No, I don't think so. I think they figure there's nothing more I can do, and they want me to keep the plant on schedule and to build the library and the fields. They're going to take the farm by eminent domain anyway. Do you know what that means?"

"Yeah, sort of. Grandpa Bud explained it to me. Says he got some legal papers from the Sheriff last week about a hearing or something in November at the High School. Says he talked to a lawyer but most likely he's going to lose the farm," she said softly.

"Looks that way," said Charlie with a sigh, suddenly feeling the combined weight of the CanAmex Corporation, Ackerly Coal, and Kerns & Yarbrough, like a suffocating pressure on his chest. He looked up at Natty's face and stared into the her ice blue eyes, for the first time not trying to mask his affection for her. He reached out and took her hand in his, knowing that he'd crossed a line, and not caring any longer. "I'm sorry Natty, but I don't know if there's anything anyone can do to stop it now."

Natty was looking down at their hands. Charlie's thumb was gently rubbing the back of her hand while she squeezed his fingers just a little harder. "Yeah, okay Charlie," she whispered. "You did what you could." For a few nervous seconds they just held hands.

Finally she pulled her hand slowly from his and straightened up as if to leave. She glanced around at the curtain behind her to see if there was any sign of Pie. Turning back to Charlie, she shrugged. "Got to go," she said taking a step backward. Then she stopped. "Thanks for the uniforms Charlie. I didn't get a chance before, you know, to buy you a beer, but . . . *wow,* the kids really love them."

"You're welcome," said Charlie softly, not taking his eyes away from her face. For several moments they stood frozen in silence. Natty felt like she had stopped breathing and her heart was pounding in her chest. Then she came forward quickly and leaned over and kissed Charlie on the lips, softly, but a telling moment longer than appropriate for just a "thank you" or "old friends" kiss. She straightened up slowly, no longer nervous. She ran her palm across his forehead pushing his hair away from the bandage.

"Thanks Charlie, for everything," she whispered softly and then turned and went out through the curtain.

Chapter 25

Charlie looked up from the drawings spread out on the rear deck of the Navigator to watch the truck dump its load of stones at around what would be the middle of the new soccer field. A small green bulldozer stood by, ready to spread the load. Charlie caught the eye of his foreman of the athletic field project standing out on the field and grinned as the foreman rolled his eyes and shook his head. The foreman thought the stone foundation and the extensive drainage system beneath, were a needless extravagance for little league soccer and baseball fields, as were the sprinkler system and light towers. But Charlie had decided that there would be no skimping, no lessening of expectations on the project because it was in McDowell County, West Virginia. They were going to build a first-class library and athletic complex that the people of Mamaroneck, or Darien, or Greenwich would be proud of. This was also *his* project. Probably the last project that he would have full control over for some time. Now that he knew that CanAmex was aware of the call on his cell phone to the DeWitts on Angel Mountain that morning, he was certain that as soon as his work on the power plant was done he would be finished with CanAmex, and his career at Dietrich Delahunt & Mackey would also soon be over. The intelligence about the cell phone call was at least one good thing to come out of the beating he took at *Moody's Roadhouse.* Now he knew where he stood.

Charlie reached up and gently pinched the bridge of his nose. It had been a week since the fight and the swelling and the black eyes had mostly disappeared, although he could still move the loose cartilage in his nose. The doctor recommended reconstructive surgery, which Charlie declined. After having an S-shaped nose for most of his adult life, he'd feel conspicuous without it. Plus, when he got back to New York, he'd want to play some hockey again, and nothing said *"player not to screw with"* like a mangled nose.

Of course there was another good thing that came out of the fight – Natty's visit to the hospital, and then the kiss that Charlie could still feel on his lips. *Or was it a good thing?* The kiss that Charlie was *almost* certain was more than a friendship kiss. *It felt like more, but . . . was that just the way Natty is – affectionate and tender, and appreciative? Maybe it was nothing. Maybe it had nothing to do with her feelings about him, which he had to admit, would probably be just as well.*

He'd only seen Natty once since the day at the hospital, when she stuck her head and shoulders out the window of the yellow school bus as it strained to make it up the hill to Main Street on its way to the soccer game in Bluefield, and gave him a shrill whistle, a wave, and her trademark smile. The Pie Man had come into the office after school to use his computer the day after the game and spent the first ten minutes excitedly trying to replay the details of the game for Charlie. The *Bones* had won again, 5 - 2, the first time they had ever beaten the team from Bluefield.

Charlie pulled his shoulders forward, stretching his still sore back in an effort to put Natty out of his mind and get back to work. Up the hill, a power shovel was piling the rubble from the collapsed library into one of the huge dump trucks from the power plant. A couple of loads and it would all be gone, leveled and scraped down to the bare earth, ready to start over.

Looking up the hill and envisioning the new library reminded him again of Ellen, and the books that they would need to acquire to complete the project. A library wasn't a library without books. And it reminded him of the phone call to Ellen he'd made earlier in the week, the call that still bothered him. The first phone call to Ellen he could remember in which he had substantially distorted the truth if not out and out lied.

It was about the coming weekend, Columbus Day Weekend, an occasion they spent every year at the house in Vermont – with the children when they were younger, but in recent years more often just the two of them – to enjoy the incredible foliage display and one last round of golf at Sugarbush. Even after he had quit the country club and replaced golf nearly entirely with running, Charlie could still get excited about the two or three times a year he played at the unpretentious Sugarbush GC, a rugged mountain course with spectacular scenery and no flat lies.

This year, Ellen had invited Dave and Linda Marchetti to go to Vermont with them, which was fine with Charlie when he read Ellen's e-mail about it a month ago. Dave and Linda were both golfers and also good company if the weather was bad. Just two weeks earlier, in their weekly phone call, Charlie had reconfirmed to Ellen his plans to fly up to New York on Thursday night so they could be on the road early Friday morning.

But when the time came to actually commit to the trip, to make the arrangements, Charlie knew he didn't want to go. His heart wasn't in it. Once, he looked forward to a weekend of luxury leisure, spectacular scenery and gourmet dining in the Green Mountains, but now it all seemed trite to him. Plus, his life was now centered in Red Bone, West Virginia, and he didn't want to leave. What he really wanted to do this weekend was go to the *Bones* soccer game Saturday morning in Princeton. And he wanted to spend some time with the Pie Man, and of course Natty was never out of his mind now. She was, if he had to admit it, the biggest reason he wanted to stay. Their paths hadn't crossed since the hospital and going out to run with her in the morning, which he ached to do, was probably too risky now after everything that was said to Buck that night behind the *Roadhouse.* But he missed her and he wanted to see her.

He told Ellen a poor version of the truth. *He had been involved in an altercation in a bar and inadvertently had his nose broken by a wild elbow intended for someone else. He had to go back into the hospital this week for a quick resetting of the bones – in and out in an hour, nothing serious – but it would be very uncomfortable flying, and he really wasn't up for a five hour drive to Vermont. Plus he had turf for the athletic fields coming, possibly this weekend, and he should be here for that, and he was busy with other things.* All of it was at least distantly related to the truth, even if none of it was the real reason. The silence on her end of the phone was palpable. Ellen pleaded briefly but didn't have time for a protracted debate. She half-heartedly proposed putting off the trip to the following weekend, which Charlie quickly dispelled with a fabricated schedule of meetings instead of the real reason – the Michigan-Ohio State game on that Saturday and his promised *lobster and beer* party with Pie. Ellen signed off with a curt, *"fine Charlie. Take care of yourself. Call me next week."*

Walking up the hill, Charlie looked back and saw his "field of dreams" becoming a reality. He visualized the final landscaping and the gardens and shrubbery in the area between the athletic fields, surrounding the fountain and gazebo, with park benches and green expanses for picnicking or lying out in the sun, and could see that it would indeed be a place of tranquil beauty. They were building more than just athletic fields. It would be a community park that all of McDowell County would take pride in.

He glanced over at the tree cutters in the outfield as a good size maple fell right where it was supposed to. It reminded him of his tennis court project at the old house and he suffered a nostalgic pang for the wonderful, therapeutic days he'd enjoyed cutting trees and pulling up the stumps. Charlie almost laughed as the idea came into his head. He made a mental note to call Pat Garvey as soon as his schedule allowed.

Charlie pulled the hood of his windbreaker up over his head as it started to rain, and looked at his watch. Six o'clock, time to call it a day. Unlike the previous week, this would be a nice quiet, uneventful Friday night. He'd see if Hank wanted to have a beer and some cribbage on the porch and a late dinner down at *Eve's*.

The Honda's old windshield wipers chattered madly against the sudden downpour as Natty drove slowly along Cold Spring Road looking for the turnoff onto the new road around the power plant. She had to come to almost a complete stop to make the sharp turn that also went steeply up a short grade. Turning the corner, she noticed water bubbling up against the left edge of the older section of the road just before it joined the new pavement, and a steady stream washing across the road. To the right, the land dropped off precipitously down to a stream bed that ran along Cold Spring Road. A culvert under the road gushed water onto a series of rugged boulders that sent a spray up into the evening air. It seemed to Natty that there was something odd about the way the water ran across the road here. She concluded that it must have been caused by the location of the power plant and the construction of the new road. In the mountains, building anything always rerouted some running water. It was probably nothing, although looking down at the fall-off to the streambed, it seemed that a guardrail on that side of the road would be a good idea.

The rain had turned to a sprinkle by the time she reached South County Road. Natty hesitated at the turn with thoughts of just going home to spend some time with the kids before falling into bed early. It had been a hard week and a hard day and she was ready to just come to a complete stop. But she knew that Woody and Mr. Jacks were expecting her and that Woody really needed his legs rewrapped, and she needed to check Mr. Jacks' meds and make sure he'd been eating enough this week. And they both needed their Friday night glass of *Jack Daniels*. Natty chuckled and shook her head as she took a left and headed toward Old Red Bone. *Maybe it was better to have such a simple life that a can of beer and a shot of Jack Daniels was the high point of your week.* She laughed again as she realized that it would be the high point of her week too.

Starting up the steep hill to Main Street, Natty looked up at the fourth floor porch, as she always did now, and caught a quick glimpse of Charlie and Hank – only their heads visible above the porch railing – sitting at their cribbage table. She offered a quick little toot of the horn just as the angle of the hill obscured them from her vision.

The store was closed so Natty tracked down Eve in the back of the restaurant and got the key. She would just leave the money on the counter and put the key on the inside stairway when she was done. Eve told her that Woody and Mr. Jacks had been over for lunch and she had given them a good meal of meatloaf and mashed potatoes.

From the cooler she got a six-pack of 16-oz Budweisers, a pint of Jack Daniels from the liquor shelf behind the counter and a carton of Marlboros from a low cupboard. Then she took a tin of Red Man chewing tobacco from a box next to the cash register. After counting out the bills from her wallet, Natty sighed, put the carton of cigarettes back and reached up and took down five packs from the overhead rack and tossed them in the bag. Coming out from behind the counter, she pulled a large bag of pork rinds from the wire rack and stuffed it into the bag.

"Want some company?"

The voice a few feet away from her almost made her drop the bag. Natty turned quickly to see Charlie Burden smiling at her, leaning against the doorframe, his hands in the pockets of his blue jeans. He was wearing an old brown flannel shirt and his running shoes.

"*Christ* Charlie, you scared the *shit* out of me."

Charlie grinned. "Sorry." He straightened up and gestured toward the *Pocahontas Hotel*. "Heard you beep. Figured you were on your way over to see your friends across the street. Mind if I tag along? You invited me once."

Natty took a deep breath and smiled as she regained her composure from being startled and from seeing Charlie Burden again. "Sure," she said softly. "Woody and Mr. Jacks'll get a big kick out of that." She moved forward and held out the bag to Charlie. "Here, you can carry this then."

Charlie took the bag and they moved out into the vestibule. Natty flipped the light switch on her way out. Just as she was about to lock the door she stopped. "Forgot something," she said. "Wait a second." She went back into the dark store. Finding her way in the dark, Natty went behind the counter again and slid open the glass door to the small selection of cigars that Eve kept on hand. She pulled out two Macanudos in short white sleeves that she knew, at seven dollars apiece, were the most expensive cigars Eve carried. She pushed the tubes into the front pocket of her jeans and closed the cabinet. She'd pay Eve for the cigars next week.

Natty picked up her equipment bag from the boardwalk and hung it on her shoulder. There was no sign of life anywhere on Main Street as they went down the wooden steps and started across the street toward the *Pocahontas Hotel*. Wet leaves clung to the street and floated in the large brown puddles they had to make their way around. The rain had made the air thick with moisture and every sound they made seemed to echo all the way down to Earl Fitch's barber shop.

"How's your nose?" Natty asked, to break the silence.

"Prettier than ever," Charlie chuckled, "but it still wiggles a little."

Charlie carried the bag of beer up against his chest with one arm. He felt like he was in high school again carrying a book bag for a girl he had a crush on. It was a good feeling. The feeling he always had when he was with Natty.

"*Oh*! I almost forgot," Natty said, stopping in her tracks and facing Charlie with an excited look on her face. "Mabel told me about the New York trip. *Geeze Charlie,* you shouldn't a done that. That's way too generous of you."

"Not my money. It's CanAmex's and they can afford it. You going to be able to make the trip?"

Natty started walking again. "How can I *not* go? Free trip to New York. *God,* I been wanting to go to New York since I was a kid." She looked up at Charlie. "You going to be there?"

"I don't know, maybe, if I can I will. I'd love to show you *my* favorite running trail – up Fifth Avenue, over to Rockefeller Center, back down Broadway to Times Square – it's wonderful, early in the morning on the weekend. It's deserted and peaceful, really a very beautiful place. It's a side of Manhattan most people never see. Little bit like the trail along the mountain . . . always something interesting to look it."

"Sounds great," said Natty. "Probably going to be the most exciting thing *I'll* ever do . . . and seeing a real show, and stayin' in a hotel and everything, well . . . be nice if you could be there."

"Yeah, well we'll see. How's the team doing?"

Natty smiled. "*God,* what a season. Doin' great! Only a few games left and I don't think anyone's going to beat us this year. And Emma's really drawing a crowd. Word's out about her now and we got people comin' from all over to watch her play."

"You weren't wrong about her. She's the best I've ever seen," said Charlie.

"Think we're probably going to get invited to the tournament in Charleston. It's every year right after Thanksgiving. Usually the best team in our league gets invited if they got a really good record. Always been Bluefield or Princeton, sometimes Welch. But never the *Bones.*" Natty laughed. "That would be a treat for the kids."

They reached the covered alcove at the front of what was once the *Pocahontas Hotel* and Charlie stopped. He needed to ask Natty a question before they went in. Natty sensed his hesitation and turned to face him.

"Natty, did uh, Buck say anything? About the fight. Did he do anything?" Charlie asked. He was looking her face over for any signs.

Natty shrugged. "Yeah, he asked me about the woodcutting job. Just told him that I'd mentioned it to you that he needed work, is all. He's okay with that. He knows that's how the world works."

"How about Angel Mountain?"

"Yeah, he asked how come you were against that, and I just said, 'well I wasn't sure you *were*, but *if* you were trying to stop it, it had nothing to do with me. Must be all about business.'" Natty turned toward the door. "He's okay with all that. Ain't a problem."

Charlie didn't move. "Did he ask you about *us*?" Charlie still wasn't convinced that Natty was safe around Buck.

Natty smiled and wrinkled her nose. "Nah, didn't say a thing about that. Asked about the job and Angel Mountain but . . ." She smiled and shrugged her shoulders. "Never been worried too much about me." She pulled open the heavy ancient door to the *Pocahontas Hotel* and led Charlie inside.

The dark lobby was lit only by a bare light bulb hanging where once, it was apparent from the heavy white chain falling from the ceiling, a grand chandelier must have hung. To the left of the lobby, what was once the main dining room or great room, appeared to be filled with old furniture and various building materials. To the right, a still elegant marble counter was covered with dust and littered with paper coffee cups and old paint cans connected by cobwebs. The silence of the lobby was broken only by a soft, scurrying sound somewhere off behind the counter.

"Rat or a cat," said Natty. "Plenty of both living here."

Natty led them straight through the lobby down a wide hallway toward the back of the building. They went past the cage of an ancient elevator and into almost complete darkness before Natty took a left onto what Charlie could now see was an open staircase dimly illuminated by another bare light bulb on one of the upper floors.

As they trudged quietly up the stairs, Natty thought about what she had just told Charlie in answer to his last question. It was true, Buck hadn't asked her anything about her and Charlie – he never seemed to ever care enough to have a jealous thought – but, there was *the look*. She wouldn't tell Charlie about it because it would be too hard to explain, like she was imagining something, and she'd sound stupid trying. But *she* knew it was something. The first time she'd ever seen Buck *watching* her. *Looking at her like men look at women.* During the *Monday Night Football* game, sta[ ]at the sink washing the dishes. Standing there in just her underpants and a ta[ ]p – maybe that had something to do with it – and out of the corner of her eye, seeing that Buck was looking at her from the couch. Not watching the game, but studying her, with his elbow up on the arm of the sofa and chewing pensively on a thumbnail. She didn't look at him, but turned to the small refrigerator and opened the door halfway to see his reflection in the shiny steel strip along the top of the door, and there was no mistake – he was watching her, watching her move, and . . . *what? Maybe admiring her thin legs and her small butt.* Then she looked at him and smiled, but he turned quickly back to the game and took a long swig from an *Iron City* beer can. *But he had been watching her, and that was something different.*

They reached the third floor and walked down a hallway past several silent doorways. The wood flooring sagged in the middle and creaked with every step. Since they'd entered the building, Charlie could only think about how quickly a fire would rip through the ancient structure. He looked around for signs of a sprinkler system and found none.

At room 310, Natty rapped on the door, winked at Charlie, and pushed it open. "Hey boys," said Natty loudly, "nurse Ratched here for your weekly lobotomies."

Charlie followed Natty into a large, high-ceiling room that was filled with the unmistakable odor of men's bodies and stale tobacco smoke. The room was dimly lighted by a small reading lamp on a table next to an iron framed bed just inside the door, and by the television set on a stand that had been rolled away from the wall toward the center of the room for better viewing. "Wheel of Fortune" was playing loudly on the TV.

"Well *wheehee*, lookee here Mr. Jacks, we got us some company." From behind Natty, through the darkness of the room, Charlie could just make out the shape of a large black man as he pushed himself laboriously up out of an oversized recliner that took up a good amount of space in front of the TV. Beyond him, against the outside wall, a small, wiry black man with patches of gray fuzz on his head and thick bifocals was sitting in a hard-back chair at a wooden table in front of a slightly opened window. The smaller man ground a cigarette into a large round ashtray and using the corner of the table and the back of the chair for support, pushed himself up to greet their visitors.

Natty turned to let Charlie come forward. "Boys, this is Charlie Burden. Charlie's the *big mule* down at the new power plant. In charge of the *whole* project. Some reason he was interested in meeting a coupla beat up old Negro coal miners."

The larger man lumbered forward and held out a massive hand to Charlie. Natty introduced him. "Charlie, this is my friend Mr. Woodrow Givens."

"*Wheehee* Charlie," the man chuckled, taking Charlie's hand. He had a high-pitched, breathless voice that reminded Charlie of an old prize fighter. "You must be somethin' *real* special, 'cause Miz Natty knows, we only allows the *best* kinda people to come up and visit us here in the palace."

"And this is my friend Mr. Kerm▮▮▮ks," Natty said as the smaller man turned off the TV set and slowly squeez▮▮▮st his roommate to reach a bony hand out to Charlie.

"I's very pleased to meet you Mr. Burden," said Mr. Jacks, holding Charlie's hand in both of his for an extra moment. He had the deep, raspy voice of a long-time smoker. It took him a moment to compose the words in his head before speaking again. "It is truly an honor . . . for us to welcome you to our home."

"Thank you Mr. Jacks," said Charlie. "I'm glad I finally had the chance to meet you fellows. Natty's mentioned you a lot."

"*Wheehee*, probably telling you all about what a great lover I is," said the large man with a chuckle as he shuffled back to his recliner.

"Keep dreaming Woody, it's good for you," said Natty taking the bag from Charlie and putting it on an old, steel-framed kitchen table around the corner from the TV. She took the beer out and put it in the ancient Amana refrigerator. "Only had enough for five," she said bringing the cigarettes over to Mr. Jacks' table.

The old man nodded several times before he responded. "Thas okay Natty, thas fine, I got enough." He handed Natty a tattered envelope. She counted out the bills that she needed and put the envelope into a drawer in the table. She went back to the bag and tossed the can of Red Man to Woody.

"Well thank you Natty, but don't you think in honor of our guest, we should have a little visit with *Mr. Daniels?*"

"Later, Woody. You know the rules. Business first, now take off them pants."

"*Wheehee*," Woody grinned at Charlie. "If she don't sound like a workin' girl from Cinder Bottom."

Natty pulled a wooden chair from the kitchen area and put it next to the television. "C'mon Charlie, sit down and tell these fellows about your power plant."

Charlie moved over and sat down. "Well, what you might be interested in is that when it's up and running at full capacity, the plant will be using about eight thousand tons of coal a day."

"*Damn!*" said Woody Givens. "That's more coal than we brought out of a mine in a month in th'old days." Woody tossed his pants on the bed, pulled the lever on the recliner and leaned back bringing his legs up to waist level. Charlie could see that both legs were completely wrapped in brown gauze bandages from the ankles to mid-thigh.

While Charlie continued his description of the generating plant to the attentive ex-coal miners, Natty went about her work. She opened her case on the bed and took out a plastic bottle of some kind of lotion and two new rolled up bandages. Then she carefully unwrapped the bandages from Woody's legs, starting at the ankles and working her way up. When the loose bandage became too cumbersome, she took a scissors out of her bag and expertly snipped it off and began again. Woody's bare legs looked like they were cast in gray concrete, with painfully thick ankles.

Charlie told them about the three massive boilers and the coal crushing complex that would turn the coal into a fine, explosive dust, and then about the scrubber units that would cleanse the smoke of nearly all impurities. The men were impressed by the $300 million price tag for the scrubber. They were impressed by all of the big numbers associated with the project.

Natty smiled at their wide-eyed incredulity as she rubbed lotion into her hands and began massaging Woody's massive legs starting with his feet. Her hands were small but strong and she squeezed the hardened flesh vigorously enough to make Woody wince with the pleasure of the pain. After a few minutes of hard work, she stopped and pulled her sweater off over her head and tossed it on the bed.

Charlie continued his story about the power plant to his entranced audience, telling them about the turbines under construction in Ohio and the control room being built in California. As he spoke, he looked back and fourth between Mr. Jacks to his left, and Woody in his recliner, but didn't miss an opportunity to watch Natty as she worked.

Under her sweater she had on a plain gray T-shirt that, like everything else she wore, was a size too big for her. The short sleeves revealed her thin arms that were moist now with sweat and bulging with sinew along with her neck muscles as she strained to knead some life into the large man's cold flesh. Breathing deep from exertion, she ignored her hair that had gradually come loose from her tie-back and now hung down over most of her face. When Charlie stopped talking, she looked over at him suddenly and flashed him a dazzling smile that lit up the dark room and made his heart race. He thought she looked like the most beautiful woman he'd ever seen.

As Natty turned back to her work on Woody's right leg, Charlie watched her for a moment in silence. He watched her squeeze and knead the old black man's legs, and he thought about her coming to do this each week, to care for these old men and visit with them and bring them a little comfort and cheer in their last days, not as part of her job any more, but just as a friend because it was something she wanted, needed to do.

"Why don't you boys tell Charlie a little about coal mining?" Natty said, with a quick smile at Charlie, as if she was trying to interrupt his thoughts.

There was silence in the room. After a few moments, Woody Givens murmured softly, almost to himself, "coal minin'. . . yeah . . . now that's a life." The old man looked down at his hands in his lap and chuckled. He held his hands up to Charlie and smiled. "Thiz what a life a coal minin' gets ya." All of the fingers on his massive hands were crooked and gnarled. One pinky was bent outward at the knuckle, and the thumb of his left hand was missing. He dropped his hands to his lap with a sigh. "Weren't a bad life though, later on. Early times was hard, before the union got some changes." He scowled with an ancient thought. "Then, when things got better and the pay got better 'cause a the union, the *Negro* miners became *nigger* miners again and could only work in the dog holes where they was still bustin' stone by hand and skimpin' on the shorin' and cheatin' on the count."

Natty was rewrapping the old miner's left leg. "Don't get all worked up Woody," she said. "Look at the life of luxury you're living now in retirement 'cause of all them years as a miner."

Woody burst into a huge white smile and laughed. "*Wheehee*, you're right about that child. Got the good life now, livin' with my friend Mr. Jacks over here and gettin' visited and looked after by the nicest folks." He slapped his thigh and chuckled again. "Yeah, got the good life now," he said softly. He looked up at Natty. "Did I tell you Mabel Willard brought us up a hot turkey pot pie t'other day?"

Natty just smiled at him as she finished wrapping his right leg. "Tell Charlie about the Red Bone mine Woody. He'd be interested in that."

"Best mine I ever worked in. Last eight years as a miner was right here. Course by that time I wasn't a nigger any more. I was *Mister Givens*, shift foreman." The old man laughed. "That's what forty-four years a workin' underground gets ya. A little bit a respect after all. Yep, forty-four years," he repeated quietly, almost to himself. "Yeah, this was a good mine here, good work," he said, looking up at Charlie, the smile back on his face. "Slope mine safer and easier than the deep mines."

"A slope mine?" Charlie wasn't familiar with the term.

Mr. Jacks was eager to join the conversation. "Slope mine is how you mine a seam a coal thas *up* in a mountain 'stead a way down in the ground," he said. Mr. Jacks stopped to cough and then went into a short, wet hacking fit. He pulled up and old coffee can from the floor and spit a mouthful of black liquid into it.

Woody took over the story. "See, not all the coal is underground in the Pocahontas field," he said. " Lot of it's up in the hills."

Charlie was curious. "So how do you get the coal out?" he asked.

"Why it's the oldest way there is to mine coal. You just get up to where the coal is, and you push a tunnel right into it. Entrance called a drift mouth. Sometimes you do two or three drift mouths if need be. Then you just go in and bring out the coal."

"Do they still do slope mines?"

Woody shrugged and shook his head. "Naw, hardly ever see a slope mine anymore, lest it's a real small operation. Now they just blast away the mountain and bring in the big shovels and push it all over the side."

"Mountaintop - removal mining," said Charlie.

Woody scowled derisively. "Ain't even minin', what they do now. Usin' dynamite to destroy a whole mountain. No skill, no engineerin' at all in that."

"So instead of mountaintop - removal, you could still get the coal out by doing a slope mine?"

Natty looked back at Charlie as she moved past him to take Mr. Jacks' blood pressure. She could see by the look on his face and the question in his voice that this was a new idea to him.

"Well a course, you *could*," said Woody pulling his pants back on over his rewrapped legs. "Problem is it cost more – 'bout twelve dollars a ton, number I always heard. That's a lot a money on a big mine. Course, some a that money goes into miners' pockets, which ain't all bad. Put more miners to work in a slope mine, but a man's labor cost more than dynamite."

Natty recorded Mr. Jacks' blood pressure in her notebook, and then began counting the pills left in several small bottles on the table, all the while paying attention to the conversation between Charlie and Woody Givens. *Was there still some hope of saving Angel Mountain?*

"Twelve dollars a ton," Charlie said. He sat back in his chair and nodded affirmatively. "Yeah, that's a of a lot of money," he said softly as he did the quick math in his head, trying to determine if it really *was* a lot of money. *Thirteen million a year. More than 250 million over the life of the mine. A significant amount, even to CanAmex. Hard case to make. But he needed to learn more about the feasibility of a slope mine for Angel Mountain and he needed the information quickly.* Charlie was angry with himself for being so ignorant of coal mining methods and for assuming that there was no alternative to mountaintop - removal mining.

The sound of a flip-top being snapped behind him jarred Charlie from his thoughts. Natty handed him a Budweiser and then brought one over to Woody. She went back into the refrigerator and came out with one for herself and for Mr. Jacks, which she placed on the table at his side.

"Okay boys, workday's over," she said sounding tired. She took a long pull on the cold beer and put it on the kitchen table. Natty got four juice glasses down from a cupboard, pulled the bottle of Jack Daniels from the bag and filled each glass. Charlie got up to help her, taking the glasses to Mr. Jacks and Woody.

"Why thank you Mr. Burden," said Woody, holding his glass up. "I say we have a toast to the successful completion of Charlie's power plant."

Natty held up her glass and smiled at Charlie. "To Charlie's power plant," she said, and took a good size sip of the whiskey. The liquor warmed her but couldn't dispel the momentary feeling of emptiness that always came with the realization that Charlie's time in West Virginia was very temporary. She went over and sat on the bed next to Woody's chair.

"Now that's about the best sippin' whiskey there is," said Woody, savoring his *Jack Daniels.* Then the room went silent for a few moments as if everyone had drifted off to private thoughts fueled by the warmth of the liquor.

Natty broke the silence. "Hey, almost forgot," she said leaning back and reaching into a front pocket of her jeans for the two cigars in the white tubes. She handed one to Charlie as she got up to go over to the table next to Mr. Jacks.

"You think of everything," said Charlie, sliding the Macanudo from its tube.

Natty cut the tip of her cigar with a small pen knife and handed the knife to Charlie. She returned to her seat on the bed with a pack of matches and an old glass ashtray that she put on the floor between them. Charlie clipped off the tip of his cigar and watched Natty light up. She moved the match slowly around the edge of the end of the cigar while she puffed to get a good head going. He could see that this was not the first cigar Natty had ever smoked. Charlie lit his cigar and puffed with obvious pleasure.

"How 'bout this boys," said Natty blowing out a cloud of gray smoke into the dimly lit room. "Cold Bud, a shot of *old number 7,* a good cigar, and great company." She smiled and winked at Woody Givens. He grinned with pleasure.

"You said it all there child," said Woody taking another sip of his whiskey.

Charlie leaned back in his chair and smiled at Natty. "This is probably pretty much what heaven is like," he said, taking another pull on his cigar. Woody grinned with pleasure at their visitor and then at Natty.

For another hour Charlie listened and basked in the company of Natty and the two old coal miners as they talked and joked and reminisced about Old Red Bone, the *Pocahontas Hotel* and its former residents. They finished the *Jack*

Daniels and shared the last two Budweisers. Sitting in the dark, musty old room of the ancient hotel, in a hidden-away corner of Appalachia, Charlie felt as warm and contented and at peace with life as he had in a very long time.

The cold, damp air of the street was refreshing after the closeness of the smoky room. They walked down the middle of Main Street toward the *Barney's Building* making a long, slow detour around a huge puddle. Natty's voice was amplified by the thick air. "Thanks Charlie, for doing that." She nodded back toward the *Pocahontas Hotel.* "You got no idea how much that means to them. Boys don't get many visitors, " she said softly.

Charlie looked down at Natty walking next to him. "I enjoyed it a lot, the whole evening. Meeting Woody and Mr. Jacks, and . . . well, hey, you're quite a nurse."

Natty laughed. "'Cause, I treat my patients with Marlboros and Jack Daniels?"

"No, no," Charlie protested. "I mean it. You're wonderful to – "

Natty shook her head and cut him off. "Those boys, they ain't got much time left. Kermel ain't got long at all way he's goin', and Woody," she sighed sadly, "pretty soon they'll start cuttin' his legs off little by little, and he'll have to live in one of them old residence hospitals in Charleston or Beckley." Natty exhaled a deep breath. "God, I'm going to miss them," she said softly.

"Hey," she said, touching Charlie's arm. "That was real nice, inviting them to your lobster and football party with the Pie Man next week. They'll really enjoy that."

"Yeah, that's good. I'm glad they want to come. It'll be fun." Charlie looked down at Natty. "You know you're invited too."

"Yeah? Lobsters huh. Where you getting lobsters around here?"

"Having my son ship them down here from Boston. They pack them in ice and send them anywhere you want. Be in Charleston Friday night and the CanAmex helicopter will bring them down Saturday morning."

Natty nodded. "Yeah, that shouldn't cost too much."

Charlie laughed. "So you'll come?"

"Never had a lobster. Suppose I shouldn't miss the chance."

They walked in silence the last few yards toward where Natty's car was parked in front of *Barney's General Store.* A nervous tension surrounded them, made more acute by the absolute stillness of the street. The only sound to be heard was their light footfalls on the wet pavement and the sounds of their breathing. Natty's heart beat fast with anticipation of what may be about to happen just a few steps away. She wondered what time it was but didn't want to look at her watch and have Charlie think that she was in hurry.

Charlie adjusted the strap of Natty's equipment bag on his shoulder. He took a deep breath and swallowed back the nervousness in his throat as they walked through the darkness toward the circle of dim light in front of the store. The street was illuminated solely by a lonely bulb in the old fashioned street lamp on the far side of Main Street. It reminded Charlie of the New Haven street lamps of his youth that his gang used to regularly throw stones at to see who could be the first to pop the little bulb and send a shower of sparks toward the pavement. He looked up at it and wondered how many shots it would take him to take out the bulb tonight. Probably a lot more than he needed when he was thirteen.

Then they were at Natty's car. She opened the back door of the Honda. Charlie put her case in the back seat of the car and shut the door softly but still loud enough to cause a dog to bark somewhere far down Main Street. He looked up at the Barney's building and saw no lights on anywhere. "Thanks Natty, for letting me come along," Charlie said, breaking the silence. "Lot of history in those two."

Natty turned away from the car and gazed back up Main Street toward the *Pocahontas Hotel,* crossing her arms in front of her to fight the chill of the evening. "Yeah, lot of the history of West Virginia livin' up in that room."

"They really appreciate what you do for them," said Charlie.

Natty shrugged and smiled nervously. She put her hands in her pockets, leaned back against the door of the Honda, seemingly lost in thought about something, probably the two elderly gentlemen they'd just left, Charlie guessed. He stood a few feet away from her with his hands in the front pockets of his jeans and used the opportunity to study her small delicate face in the dim light. She hadn't bothered to pull back her hair and it continued to hang down limply around her face with the usual shock draped across the scar over her left eye. He thought about Natty venturing alone each week into the old rooming house to massage the legs of a destitute old black man and share a glass of whiskey with them afterward. He saw her lighting up her cigar, and he couldn't help smiling at her, and wondering if there was another woman anywhere, like Natty. He knew there wasn't.

Then Natty looked down at her feet and spoke without looking at him. "Charlie, I been thinking a lot lately about you leaving here, you know, about your project being mostly done and you moving away, going to China, like you said." She turned her head and looked into the darkness across the street, as if she needed to avoid Charlie's eyes. "Gives me a real empty feeling," she said softly.

"I've got some time left here Natty. Won't be before . . ."

"Charlie," she said, turning back to look up into his face, "what I'm saying here is . . . well, if you were to ask me to go upstairs, for a beer or something, well, I'd probably go with you." Then she pursed her lips and shrugged nervously as if to say '*there, I got it out, and I'm glad I did.*'

Charlie swallowed hard and managed a quick smile before turning away. He squinted at the glowing bulb in the street lamp across Main Street as he composed his thoughts. He needed to get this right because he knew that Natty had made a decision that was probably as difficult as any choice she'd ever made, the decision that he had been subtly, subliminally, coaxing her towards since the revelation of their feelings for each other up on the boulder. But now he needed to say *no* to her, and also deny himself what he had been aching for all evening and thinking about since his first night in Red Bone four months earlier when he first saw Natty in the store behind them. He took in a deep breath and exhaled slowly, stalling for time.

"Nat, we can't do that," he said finally. "Not tonight." He looked down and shuffled his feet while he searched for the words, still trying to make sense of it all to himself.

Natty pressed a little harder against the side of the car and blew out a deep breath. "Well that's a relief," she said. "I ain't too sure I got clean underwear on anyway."

They both laughed. The laugh they seemed to share a lot, thought Charlie as he smiled down into Natty's eyes. He reached out a hand and gently pushed back the tress of hair falling across her left eye, then put his hand back in his pocket.

"Earlier this week Nat," he continued, "I had to lie to my wife. I had to lie about *you,* and I didn't like how that felt."

Natty squinted up at him. "Why'd you have to lie about *me,* Charlie?"

"Well, not about you directly. It was about why I couldn't go up to Vermont with her this weekend. I made up some stuff about my broken nose and too much work and other stuff, but it was about you. It was *all* about you. You're the reason I didn't want to go. I wanted to stay here and see you, and do what we did tonight, and go to the soccer game tomorrow and see the kids and Pie, and watch you on the sideline."

Natty dug her hands deeper into her pockets, turned away from the light and looked down at her feet to hide her face in the shadows of her hair. Charlie knew he was embarrassing her but he had to go on. "And I wanted to be alone with you," he said softly, "and hear you say the words you just said."

Natty sniffed in the darkness and her voice was small. "So, *what* Charlie?"

Charlie drew in a deep breath to calm himself. "Nat, last winter my wife was having an affair . . . tennis pro at her country club . . . and I found out about it from someone else. I can still remember how that felt . . . when I found out."

"I know what that feels like Charlie," she said softly.

Charlie nodded and then grimaced briefly with the painful memory. "I don't know which felt worse, my wife having an affair, or having someone else tell me about it."

Natty wiped her eyes with the sleeve of her sweater. Charlie looked down at her and resisted the powerful urge to reach out and pull her to him and wrap his arms around her. He knew what that would lead to.

"So I can't do that to her," he continued. "I want this, whatever happens with us, to be different from that. It *is* different. I need to talk to Ellen, in person. I need to tell her about this, about how I feel . . . before anything happens."

Natty folded her arms across her chest and turned back into the light. A wet track of a tear was visible down one cheek. She wiped her nose with the sleeve of her sweater and smiled thinly. "Geeze Charlie, you goin' for like *husband of the year* or something?"

Charlie laughed. "No, not hardly," he said looking away. "I'm nothing like that."

Natty bounced on her feet lightly to keep warm. Then she went still. "So, what are you going to *tell* her Charlie?"

Charlie shrugged. "I don't know. I haven't gotten that far." They both chuckled. He looked out across the street, up towards where he knew the remains of the ancient coal tipple still loomed in the darkness. "First, I'm going to tell her that I still love her." He paused in thought for a few seconds. "We've been married for twenty-seven years, and for twenty-six of those years, Ellen was as good a wife and companion and mother, as a woman can be, and one mistake, one . . . experiment, doesn't wipe all that out, no matter what you see on TV and in the movies." He shuffled on his feet slightly and squinted into the street light. "Plus, it wasn't all her fault, what happened. You remember how you told me it wasn't all Buck's fault that day he hit you?" He looked down into Natty's face. She just nodded briefly. "Well, Ellen's thing, that wasn't all her fault either. I have to share the blame in that."

"What'd you *do* Charlie?"

He looked down to see the curious look on Natty's face. Charlie shrugged. "I guess mainly, I *changed*," he said softly. "We had a nice life together, *the good life*, some people would say. Then, after the kids were gone, and my job changed a lot and I was making more money, then, I changed. We were living the life that Ellen always wanted, and then I found out I didn't really care for that life. So I made some decisions, mostly about myself, without thinking enough about her. I abandoned her, not physically, but socially, spiritually, and then I pretended that it shouldn't matter." He smiled at Natty. "It's hard to explain."

Natty smiled and nodded in silence.

Charlie looked down at the ground and spoke softly. "Then, I have to tell her that I . . . I met this woman in West Virginia. A remarkable woman. The nicest, kindest . . . funniest," they both chuckled, "most selfless woman I ever met." He looked up from his feet and met Natty's eyes. "A woman who has no idea of how beautiful she is or how special she is."

Natty turned away from the light again to hide her face.

"I probably *won't* tell Ellen about how my palms get sweaty and my heart beats like a bass drum and I lose my breath every time I see this woman – that wouldn't be fair – but, I will have to tell her that I can't get this woman out of my head and I'm not sure I ever will. And that I love her kids like my own kids . . . and when the time comes, to leave West Virginia, to leave her . . . I'm not sure I'll be able to do that."

In the darkness, Natty tried to blink away the tears as best she could. After several moments of silence, she gave in and brought her sleeve up and pressed her eyes into it. She sniffed and then sighed as she turned back into the light. She managed a quick smile.

"You okay?" asked Charlie. "You're not going to throw up on me are you?"

Natty laughed. "I'm okay," she said softly, "just never been called *remarkable* before." They both chuckled lightly. "Got to go," she nearly whispered, turning to find the door handle with her left hand while she ran the sleeve of her right arm across her eyes.

Charlie watched her until the Honda, sending up white clouds of exhaust vapor into the cool night air, disappeared around the corner headed down South County Road.

Chapter 26

The soccer field in Princeton was hidden behind a middle school that appeared to Charlie to be of more recent vintage than most of the buildings in McDowell County. The parking lot, though not filled, had more cars than Charlie would have expected for a little league soccer game. He knew he was in the right place when he saw the familiar yellow school bus from Red Bone parked at one end of the lot, the elderly woman driver still in her seat concentrating on a book propped up on the steering wheel.

Walking up a short hill to the field, Charlie zipped up his windbreaker against the morning chill. The sky was slate gray threatening more rain, and a slight breeze watered the eyes with a slap of cold that reminded him of Vermont.

The umpire was carrying a ball to the center of the field and on the far sideline Charlie could see *The Bones* huddled up for Natty's last minute pep talk. He began to feel the gnawing deep in his gut that he always experienced now when he saw her, made more acute by the shared intimacies of the previous evening. Then the Princeton team ran onto the field with great enthusiasm amid a smattering of applause from the bleachers. The umpire blew his whistle and *The Bones* took the field. As the umpire checked with each team's goaltender, Charlie stole a glance over at the *Bones'* bench area. Natty was wearing her customary blue jeans and high boots, but today she had on a *Bones'* black warm-up jacket that was a size too large for her. With her blue *Spiderman* hat pulled down tightly against the wind, she could have easily been mistaken for a boy.

Charlie stood at the end line with a small group of spectators and turned his attention to the game. The action had moved down to the *Bones'* end of the field as the Princeton team, outfitted in very sharp purple shirts, carried the early play.

Charlie looked out and found Emma walking slowly backwards toward them, and then turning and jogging lazily, almost unconcerned, directly toward the defender assigned to shadow her. Charlie had seen this act before and he almost laughed out loud as the defender stopped to stand his ground, refusing to retreat any farther – dead meat, his goose already cooked because you can't get that close to Emma that far out without help behind you. And then the ball was in the air from Paul headed for the right corner of the field and Emma was off, blazing past the startled defender.

Charlie had watched Emma play several times, but now up close to the field, concentrating only on her, he marveled at her athleticism as she effortlessly controlled the bouncing ball and advanced toward the goal. With the ball at her feet, she seemed to move at a quicker pace than everyone else on the field, a bundle of kinetic energy ready to explode in any direction, her feet always dancing like magic wands passing over and around the ball, waiting for the opportunity to slash past a terrified opponent.

Emma let the ball roll freely a few feet ahead of her as she calmly looked over the field seeming to ignore the insignificant defender racing down on her. She faked a start along the end line and pulled the ball back to her left as the fullback sped hopelessly past her, then deftly side-stepped another defender and left him behind with a magical spin move, the ball stuck to her lightning fast feet as she glided along the end line toward the goal.

Ten yards from the near goal post, with the sweeper and another defender almost on her, Emma stopped, moved the ball smartly to her left to gain the little space she needed, and with her left foot, chipped a high floater toward the far end of the goal where Paul, at the end of a perfectly timed run, simply took the ball on his chest and walked it into the goal. She had made it look too easy, and the home crowd and the spectators along the end line knew right away that everything they had heard about this spectacular girl playing on a boys' team was true.

It didn't take long for the *Bones* to settle down to their game and for the Princeton team to lose most of their confidence and begin playing back on their heels. A few minutes later Emma corralled a bouncing ball in the center of the field at the eighteen yard line with a split second of space. Without an instant of hesitation, she unleashed a bullet into the top corner of the net that the goalie didn't even have time to flinch at.

Charlie watched the *Bones'* star as she jogged back up the field and took a wide detour toward the visitor's sideline for an enthusiastic high-five from a taller boy with blond hair who was clapping and grinning widely. Charlie recognized the Welch midfielder named Gabe and chuckled to himself as he realized why the great Emma Lowe seemed to be playing with an even brighter flare and intensity today.

After a valiant defensive stand by the Princeton team, keeping the ball out of their end of the field for nearly ten minutes, Emma scored again on a spectacular solo run through the defense and an easy blast past the helpless goalie. When Sammy Willard scored off a corner kick a few minutes later, Natty called a time-out. She put Emma and Sammy back on defense, and put the Pie Man in the game to play forward with Billy Staten and Gilbert Steele. It was readily apparent that the Princeton team was overmatched today and there was no need to let the score get out of hand.

Charlie stood by himself on the *Bones'* side of the field at about the twenty-yard line and watched the Pie Man lunging around the middle of the field, always a few steps too late to the free balls, usually ending up stretched out on the grass, but always bouncing up quickly to get back into the play. He seemed to Charlie to also be playing with a little extra determination today. With Emma and Sammy Willard now back on defense booming balls up the field, Pie and the other *Bones* forwards had plenty of chances but were overmatched by the relieved Princeton defenders. Pie though, as always, put on a good show, especially on the rare occasions when he was able to gain control of the ball for a few entertaining seconds and dribble a few yards forward in his inimitable, head-down, frenetic style.

Finally a long ball went past the purple defenders and rolled up the field toward Charlie with Pie and the other forwards in hot pursuit. Charlie wanted to get Pie's attention so the boy would know he was there and had been watching his heroic efforts.

The ball went over the end line and Pie stopped, bent over with his hands on his knees to catch his breath about fifteen yards from Charlie.

"Hey there, you Pie Man, good job!" Charlie called out with a wide grin.

Pie straightened up right away with a smile on his face and took a few steps toward Charlie. He raised a hand for their usual "high-five" wave. "Hello Chowly," he said, still short of breath and flushed from exertion. The boy looked like he was about to say something else, but he stopped and for just a fleeting moment averted his eyes to somewhere up on the hill beyond Charlie and then back again.

Charlie grinned and pointed to the goalie just as he sent a long goal kick back up field. Pie whirled and raced off to join the action. Charlie chuckled at Pie's "penguin" style of sprinting. He was glad he'd been able to make contact with his little buddy, but there was something off in Pie's greeting that made him wonder if everything was okay with the boy. He realized that Pie was winded and in the middle of a soccer game, but by this time he knew his friend well enough to sense a subtle uneasiness in him. His wave lacked the usual enthusiasm and although Pie had grinned, it wasn't the *happy face* that he always greeted Charlie with, and that was different.

When the play was down in the *Bones* end of the field, Charlie would steal a glance along the side line to watch Natty – and think about last night and what they had come so close to. He watched her moving calmly along the side line, still coaching her team even though it was a mismatch and she'd instructed her best players not to cross the mid-field line.

She turned to follow the ball up the field and saw Charlie. Natty had her hands in the pockets of the black warm-up jacket and the bill of the *Spider-Man* cap pulled down low over her eyes, but her smile from forty yards away made Charlie's heart thump and forced him to draw in a cold breath. It was a quick smile though, *more of a friendly hello kind of a smile, wasn't it?* And then she quickly turned her attention back to the game.

Charlie watched her come to a stop and rock back and forth on the heels of her tan construction boots, her thin legs and small waist superbly camouflaged in the baggy jeans. He thought about running behind her on the mountain trail in the summer and he could see her pull up her shirt to wipe her brow revealing the smooth skin of her lower back and her tiny waist and hips. He envisioned her up on the boulder, lying back on her elbows next to him, gazing out at the mountains telling him her stories, giggling, smiling, laughing at herself, her T-shirt pulled tightly around her breasts, her smooth legs splayed out lazily on the curved rock, having no conception of how alluring she was. Then he saw her kneading the cold flesh of the old black man's legs, the muscles in her arms and hands shining with moisture in the dim light of the dark, smoky room, and then sitting on the bed, laughing and sipping *Jack Daniels* with the three men, and enjoying her cigar.

When she turned abruptly to move back up the field, there was something in the moment that made Charlie shudder, a wave of cold emptiness suddenly engulfing him as he knew, at that moment, that the previous night he had made a horrible mistake. He knew that if he had taken her upstairs and they had made love, their fate would have been sealed and today would have been the first day of an edgy, nervous, giddy, mine-field of a future that they would be gloriously, rapturously exploring together. Charlie ached for that feeling – to be sharing that with Natty – but he knew, somehow, that the opportunity was lost. He bounced on the balls of his feet to keep the circulation going in his legs and tried to concentrate on the game.

Charlie stared out at the field for the rest of the half without really seeing the game. He stood by himself on the sideline feeling suddenly alone and vulnerable. Then two sharp tweets from the umpire's whistle signaling halftime brought him out of his reverie. He took a deep breath, pulled his shoulders to the front to stretch out his sore back and told himself to knock off this irrational spell of self-pity or whatever it was he was experiencing. *He'd come to watch The Bones and Pie play soccer, which they were doing magnificently, so enjoy the rest of the game and stop imagining things.*

The Bones, now in their black warm-up jackets, were all carrying their water bottles slowly out to the spot in front of the goal where they would sit on the grass and listen to Natty's halftime instructions. Charlie looked for Pie and saw him in the middle of the pack, eyes forward as he headed for the goal. Then he turned to find Natty, hoping they would have a few words before she joined her team. He watched her as she hoisted the strap of her athletic bag onto her right shoulder and started out for the goal.

Charlie took a few steps onto the field to catch her eye and then stopped as two men approached her from the home side of the field. They appeared to be in their early forties with a professional look about them. One wore a hounds tooth blazer, the other a short suede jacket. Natty stopped and shook hands with the men as they introduced themselves. They seemed to be having a light-hearted discussion, smiling and nodding a lot, probably about the play of *The Bones,* before one of the men got a little more serious and began to occupy the conversation. Natty listened intently, nodding several times with a few words in return, and then smiled broadly as she shook hands again with both of the men. They turned to go back across the field and Natty started out again to join her team in front of the goal.

When she saw Charlie, Natty stopped and then seemed to hesitate, looking back toward her team once before turning and ambling slowly toward him. Charlie stood still, his hands pushed down into the pockets of his windbreaker, watching Natty approach. When she was still twenty feet away from him, he nodded toward the two men still walking across the field. "Good news?" he asked.

Natty stopped and glanced toward the men and then back at Charlie. She flashed a quick smile and raised her eyebrows. "Yeah, I guess it *is* good news," she said. "Invited us to the Thanksgiving tournament in Charleston. First time ever for a team from Red Bone." She looked over at her team assembled on the grass in front of the goal. "Kids are going to be thrilled," she said still watching them.

Charlie remained silent watching her. He could see that there was something distant about her, about the way she spoke, the way she seemed to want to avoid his eyes, and the same feeling of emptiness that he'd experienced earlier, swept over him once again.

Then she turned toward him and squinted with a wrinkled up nose as he'd seen her do before when she had something on her mind and was searching for the words. She adjusted the strap of the athletic bag on her shoulder and let out a sigh. "Charlie," she breathed out softly. "Buck's here."

It took Charlie by surprise. He tried a quick smile, then nodded. "Where – " he started, but Natty cut him off.

"Up on the hill, in back of you. With Sally and his brother Ransom."

Charlie could feel the eyes on the hill trained upon them. He bounced on the balls of his feet and then shrugged. "Well, that's good. That's good that he came to watch Pie play," he said, trying to sound sincere.

"Yeah. First time. First time ever, Buck's come to one of our games." Natty glanced over at her team for a few moments before looking back at him. "Seven years, and he finally comes to a game . . ." she said, almost to herself.

Charlie looked over at the *Bones* sitting on the grass in front of the goal. "Natty, uh, *thanks* for last night," he said, needing to change the subject. "For taking me over to meet Woody and Mr. Jacks, and for . . . well, it was a real nice evening. I enjoyed that a lot."

Natty nodded, and then crossed her arms across her chest and looked down at the ground between them as if to hide her words from prying eyes. "Charlie, last night . . ." She hesitated. "Last night, that was like the best date I ever *had.*" She let out a sigh and looked up. "I gotta go Charlie." Her eyes darted almost imperceptibly up the hill behind him and then back again. "Okay?" she said very softly.

"Yeah, I understand Nat." Charlie pulled his left hand out and made a show of looking at his watch. "I've got to get going anyway," he said, starting to back away from her toward the sideline.

Natty rejoined her team and gave them the good news about the tournament. Charlie heard the *Bones'* excited response as he walked slowly, inconspicuously along the now deserted end line making his way back toward the parking lot. He'd skip the second half of today's game. The game was well in hand, and he had work to do.

*   *   *

The words of Woody Givens bounced around in Charlie's head as he waited for his office computer to warm up. *'Slope mine, easiest way there is to mine coal . . . twelve dollars a ton . . . put more miners to work in a slope mine.'*

Charlie glanced out his office window toward the massive outline of the power plant and behind it the quickly rising structure of the coal crushing complex. There were quite a few cars in the parking lot for a Saturday afternoon, although Charlie realized that while some of the sub-contractors were now working six-day weeks to make year-end performance bonuses, many of the cars belonged to workers who had taken the CanAmex chopper up to Charleston to get away for the Columbus Day weekend.

The project was now well ahead of schedule with no major problems looming on the horizon, which also meant it was beating budget too – all of which helped Charlie to survive his now prickly relationship with CanAmex. In addition to keeping the project ahead of schedule and under budget, he'd also solved the cooling pond problem and established a good relationship with the Red Bone Planning Board chairman – very important issues to his client – earning him a temporary stay of execution.

But Angel Mountain was a disaster, for him personally and for Dietrich, Delahunt & Mackey. He not only hadn't secured the purchase of the DeWitt farm, he had declared his allegiance to the enemy and worse than that, he had been exposed. That was a mortal sin, and when the timing best suited CanAmex, Jack Torkelson was going to administer an ignominious end to Charlie Burden's career, of that Charlie had no doubt. Dietrich, Delahunt & Mackey would survive in some form, without Charlie and Lucien Mackey – purged along with a dozen or so allies – replaced by Warren Brand and his lieutenants, including Terry Summers, with an Executive Committee handpicked by Jack Torkelson. Within a year they would move the company to some class–B space in Fort Lee, sell the building in Manhattan, divide up the assets, pick over the bones like a pack of vultures and sell what was left at an inflated price to one of the mid-size engineering firms blinded by the prospect of acquiring some big time CanAmex contracts.

All of it seemed preordained now to Charlie. And maybe it was – with or without Angel Mountain – just a sign of the times, the way the business world operated these days. To the victor goes the spoils, and Jack Torkelson was piling up the wins and accumulating power, the same kind of power that Duncan McCord had once used to install Charlie Burden at Dietrich, Delahunt & Mackey, and anoint him as the "CanAmex" guy. And now it would be somebody else. Terry Summers probably.

Charlie gazed through the office window, past the building and the line of yellow and green construction vehicles, up toward the hills that rose quickly around the perimeter of the site and his jaw and neck muscles tightened with anger. His anger wasn't for himself or for Lucien Mackey or any of his doomed compatriots at DD&M. They were all educated, successful people with resources who could, in the end, withstand a little professional upheaval in their careers. For some, it would probably be a blessing. He and Lucien and the others would be fine. Their professional reputations and their balance sheets would take a hit but they'd survive the Angel Mountain fiasco and move on. But Bud and Alice DeWitt would not. Nor would their son Petey or Natty's mother, Sarah. They were going to lose their farm and their livelihood, and more important, they were going to lose their heritage – the familial bond to the land that came from four generations of DeWitts born and buried on Angel Mountain. And then Angel Mountain was going to disappear. *Hard to feel close to a piece of land that has been pulverized by a thousand tons of AMFO and turned into valley fill.*

Charlie shook his head slowly with disgust as he thought also about the financial abyss the DeWitts would be tossed into with the loss of their farm, the value of their property set at the minimum by Vernon Yarbrough and his puppet judge as retribution for all of Yarbrough's futile efforts to talk them off the mountain. Now it would be their turn to crawl.

The computer tinkled out its familiar musical welcome and pulled Charlie's attention from the window. He rolled his chair closer and let out a sigh as he began what he knew would be a long and pointless effort to learn more about the methods and economics of pulling coal out of the ground. His search for an alternative to the destruction of Angel Mountain would be fruitless, he was certain. The economic advantage of mountaintop-removal had been proven at scores of mines throughout West Virginia and Kentucky over three decades and nothing in his research of slope mines was going to change that. Yet, in the back of his mind was the nagging question of the *qualitative, non-measurable* costs of mountaintop-removal that Charlie just couldn't dismiss from the equation. Hank's angry accusation that evening out on the porch continued to reverberate in Charlie's head. *"If Angel Mountain was in California . . .or Vermont . . . in the Catskills . . ." Of course Hank was right. You could never obliterate a mountain, covering over streams and wildlife habitat, anywhere outside of Appalachia. So what was it that made the cost of mountaintop-removal too high to be feasible anywhere outside of the most economically depressed region of the country?*

Charlie shook his head and chuckled at the absurdity of his thesis as he logged on and began his search. He started with a query to Nina Matlin, the DD&M librarian who was the single best source of information about anything. He requested everything she could find on the economics of coal mining, specifically *mountaintop-removal* versus *traditional* methods of mining. She would search the DD&M database as well as the many professional research services subscribed to by engineering firms, plus some sources that she alone would know about. He added that he needed the information ASAP, which he knew would mean that on Monday he would be downloading volumes of information from Nina.

Then Charlie launched his own search for sites about *coal mining, coal mining methods,* and *mountaintop-removal-mining.* The mountaintop-removal search yielded dozens of sites and hundreds of articles and files devoted to the horrors of mountaintop-removal, most of them emanating from Logan, Mingo and McDowell Counties of West Virginia. He downloaded a variety of files, including a lengthy series by the Charleston Gazette, and sent them to the printer. He'd read them in the evening back at the apartment.

Charlie spent the rest of the afternoon reading about coal mining at Web sites sponsored by several industry and trade associations. He read the fairly simplistic but informative descriptions of *deep mines, drift* and *slope mines, surface mines,* and the various techniques for extracting coal from the ground, from *hand-loading* in the early days to *room and pillar mining,* and *long-wall* and *short-wall* technology imported from Europe. He read about the introduction of the *continuous mining machine* that brought a new level of efficiency to the mining industry along with the microscopic coal dust that created *black lung disease* that crippled and cut short the lives of a generation of miners. It was all mildly interesting, but lacking solid economic data, it wouldn't help his quixotic struggle to save Angel Mountain.

He read with more interest about the history of coal mining in West Virginia . . . from just after the Civil War, the impact of the railroads, industrial revolution, the immigrants, the hardships, disasters, union struggles, the Mine Wars – even a brief recount of the Matewan Massacre and Sid Hatfield. Then the war years when West Virginia's mines operated twenty-four hours a day to fuel the great steel mills of the Ohio Valley to provide the raw materials for the greatest industrial production effort in the history of the world. And then the modern era and the collapse of the coal mining industry, the loss of great numbers of mining and supporting industry jobs and the long-term recession that settled over Appalachia . . . all concurrent with the increase in the number of huge surface mines and the environmental catastrophe of *mountaintop-removal.*

Charlie saved a few articles, sent a few to the printer, logged off and put his computer to sleep. He quickly changed into a sweat suit and put on his running shoes, anxious to punish his body and numb his mind with a hard five – miler before it got too dark. Whatever it took to avoid thinking about Natty Oakes.

After four laps on the smooth new road encircling the power plant, Charlie decided to just leave his car locked up at the site and push himself to the edge with another mile and a half sprint back to the apartment. He took the access road through the woods, turned left on South County Road and headed for Old Red Bone.

Charlie ran past the windowless hulk of the old elementary school, and then an abandoned trailer being swallowed by the ubiquitous kudzu vines. Farther up the road was the leaf-covered, concrete rubble of the parking lot of a long disappeared motel and another deserted building with boarded windows and a loading dock partially hidden by overgrown scrub bushes. He remembered how he'd noticed the derelict structures on his first trip into Old Red Bone, but hardly ever after that. Now with the painful history of West Virginia's coal mining industry fresh on his mind he couldn't help *seeing* the visual evidence. And Hank's words echoed in his mind once again . . . *'You see any great wealth around here? See any old money in this town?'* How right Hank was. After more than a *hundred years* of production of one of the country's most valuable resources – an *indispensable* resource in the economic history of the nation – what did West Virginia and McDowell County and the town of Red Bone have to show for it? *Crumbling roads and derelict buildings . . . Monongah and Farmington and Buffalo Creek . . .homes and towns sinking into abandoned mines . . . streambeds stained orange with ferrous oxide. . . drinking water that ran brown. . . too many old people. . . children living in poverty. . . a town that couldn't afford to patch the roof of its library . . . Woody and Mr. Jacks squatting in an abandoned firetrap waiting to die . . . Bud and Alice DeWitt, who hadn't suffered enough with the deaths of their sons, now soon to lose everything . . . and, Natty Oakes and her retarded son . . . and her husband, Buck, 'the luckiest man in*

McDowell County.' Charlie stumbled to a ragged stop in the middle of the dark, deserted road. He'd had enough. He bent over, hands on knees, gasping for breath, his lungs burning from the cold air, the sweat running off his forehead to a puddle on the sandy pavement at his feet. He thought he might throw up.

Natty walked slowly across the field under the weight of her athletic bag. She would be the last one on the bus as always. Far up ahead of her she saw Emma and Gabe walking together. They would take a seat together a little further back in the bus from where Emma normally sat. Natty smiled to herself. That was alright. She had never seen Emma happier.

"Yeah, hold on there miz Oakes." The voice came from behind Natty.

She knew who it was before she reluctantly stopped and turned to face Kyle Loftus. He was wearing a brown corduroy sport jacket with elbow patches, and a tie. In his left hand he carried the ever-present cell phone, not currently in use. He slowed up his pace when he saw that Natty had come to a stop.

"Well, well, that was a severe beating you laid on these folks," said the league president as he approached Natty. "Six - nothing, that's quite a team you got there."

"What do you want Kyle? The bus is waiting. I got to get these kids home."

Kyle Loftus grinned and pointed toward the bus with his cell phone. "Yeah, that's quite a team . . . the *Boners*." Natty stared at him blankly. "Understand you got the invite to the Thanksgiving tournament, up in Charleston," Loftus said, getting to the point.

"You *know* we did Kyle. So what?"

"Yeah, well, we had a league meeting other night, 'cause of that ugly incident at the game in Welch, and well, I got to inform you that you got two players who is suspended from any sort a post-season play."

"*What!* What kind a shit are you trying to pull Loftus?" The veins in Natty's neck were standing out as she took a step closer to him.

"You heard me," Loftus replied firmly.

"What players? Why?" Natty glanced up the hill to see if Buck was still there but there was no sign of him or Sally or Ransom.

"You lose that . . . the Willard boy, Zack Willard. Suspended for starting a fight. And the girl too, Emma . . . flagrant foul. Broke that kid's nose. Dirtiest play I ever ..."

"You go *fuck* yourself Loftus. You can't do this!" Natty whirled around almost hitting the league president with her duffle bag as she started out again for the bus.

"Can do it and did do it," Loftus called after her. "You go up to that tournament, those two are out. That's the ruling."

Natty spun around briefly. "You put it in writing," she yelled not knowing what else to say.

"Already in the mail."

"I can appeal it," Natty yelled back over her shoulder.

Loftus grinned widely. "Be my guest."

*　*　*

The blinking red light on the Hewlett-Packard DeskJet printer was calling for another black ink cartridge. Charlie looked over the stacks of printed pages on his kitchen table, many marked up with red circles and underlines, and at the crinkled yellow legal pad in front of him, a dozen pages black with notes. He tossed the pad and his pen onto the table sending another dozen sheets over the side to the floor where a small pile already resided. He reached over to his laptop, clicked on "abort print," and grabbed the bottle of Heineken on the corner of the table. He didn't have another ink cartridge and he didn't need the document anyway. It wouldn't help. None of it would help.

Charlie looked at his watch. Tuesday night had stretched into Wednesday morning and now it was 3:00 a.m. For nearly eight hours straight he'd been reading downloads from Nina Matlin, printing out and rereading reports and economic analyses, studying charts, and going back on-line to various links to find additional studies and charts to print out, and all the while making notes on a yellow legal pad. And now he was done. He stood up to stretch his legs and took the bottle of Heineken out onto the back porch. The air was cold but the lack of any hint of a breeze made it very tolerable after a long night inside the apartment. He wished he had a cigar.

Charlie flipped the light switch on the brick wall next to the door. The dim light from the tired old brass fixture up on the wall cast a yellowish hue over the wooden card table and chairs directly beneath it. Charlie sat down at the table in his high-back chair and slouched back to let his legs stretch out lazily in front of him. He was tired physically and mentally. He was tired of the fruitless project that he'd just wasted the last eight hours on. He wasn't going to save Angel Mountain based on any economic analysis of the cost differential between mountaintop-removal and a slope mine. It wasn't going to happen. Mountaintop-removal was a no-brainer when it came to making money in the coal mining business. The best he could possibly do was to reduce the differential to around $10 a ton, and even that required a great many vague assumptions and liberal cost estimates associated with the construction of the huge dragline, the monstrous piece of machinery required for large-scale strip mining, plus the cost of disassembling the dragline ten or fifteen years later when the mine was exhausted. *Too many assumptions. Too many estimates. Too much bullshit.* Companies like CanAmex don't make economic decisions based on bullshit.

Even the best case – *$10 a ton* – was a death sentence for Angel Mountain. CanAmex wasn't going to pay $10 million dollars a year – more than *$150 million* over the life of the mine – to preserve a decrepit old pig farm, and the beautiful view from the top of Angel Mountain.

Charlie took a swig of his beer and chuckled over the thought, choking momentarily, before laughing again out loud and setting his beer bottle down hard on the table. He wiped his mouth with a shirt sleeve and looked over at the cigar box at the edge of the table next to the wall. Hank had put a piece of hard plastic over the box with a rock on it for the wind. Charlie moved the rock and the plastic and opened the ancient brown box. From under the two decks of dog-eared playing cards, he extracted the annual appointment book that Hank used to record their cribbage winnings and losses. He took off the rubber bands that held it closed and leafed through the first two thirds of the book, which recorded the many years of games between Hank and Alva Paine. Then he reached mid-September, where the last page-and-a-half of scores were his. Charlie shook his head in amazement as he compared his measly part of the book – after what seemed like hundreds of games he'd played with Hank since coming to Red Bone – to the book's eight and a half months worth of scores for Hank and Alva Paine. *Nineteen years worth of cribbage games . . . now that was a friendship!* Charlie looked at the last page. He was down $407 to Hank. He shook his head and chuckled. *How the fuck does he do that?* Charlie could see that he'd won about an equal number of games, but Hank always seemed to win a little more money in his wins and lose a little less in his losses, than Charlie. *It's all in the pegging,* thought Charlie, resolving to improve a few points in every game.

He looked down at the last page of scores again and did a quick calculation of the number of games needed to reach the bottom of the page. If he stayed in West Virginia through April, which was the original schedule, they *may* finish the page. And that would be it for Charlie in the cribbage book – eight months for Alva Paine, and two days in September for Charlie – hardly even a factor in Hank's scorebook. *Hardly a factor at all in West Virginia.*

Charlie closed the book, wrapped it again with the rubber bands and placed it back in the cigar box. He reached up on the wall in back of him and flipped the light switch plunging the porch into darkness again. The western ridge of Red Bone Mountain was barely discernable in the dim light of a quarter moon further reduced by overcast clouds. Gazing off into the blackness, Charlie had a sudden pang of longing for the lights and the noise and aromas of Times Square, the traffic on Park Avenue, and the mid-day crush of pedestrians on the sidewalks of Manhattan. He was tired of the isolation and the silence of West Virginia, and the loneliness. Before the soccer game in Princeton, he hadn't felt lonely at all, but then that changed – he recalled the look in Natty's eyes when she said *'Buck's here'* – and now he didn't know where his relationship stood with both her and Pie. He shook his head in wonderment. *Christ, how could the guy going to one lousy soccer game affect them so much?* Charlie finished his beer and reached over and put the rock back on top of the cigar box. *That's okay,* thought Charlie. *We'll finish up here in a few more months, build the library and the fields and get the turbines in – maybe as early as March – and then it's off to China, or somewhere else, anywhere else, and everything will be about the same as it always was in Red Bone, West Virginia.*

Charlie pushed himself up from the hard chair and went back inside to the kitchen table. *One more thing to do though. One last try, for Budd and Alice DeWitt who, in a few weeks are going to lose their farm in a totally rehearsed, bought- and- paid- for eminent domain hearing.* He sat down in front of his laptop and searched through his address book for Duncan McCord's home e-mail address, the private listing reserved for a very few personal friends and old teammates privileged to possess the listing because they understood that it was never to be used for any business related correspondence. Charlie knew he was about to break the rule as he started typing.

Duncan – In a few weeks, through an eminent domain proceeding, the Ackerly Coal Company and CanAmex are going to destroy a family living on a small farm on Angel Mountain, West Virginia. Within weeks of the displacement of the DeWitt family from Angel Mountain, the destruction of the mountain will commence with the beginning of a mountaintop-removal surface coal mine. Mountaintop-removal mining is an environmental catastrophe that would be inconceivable anywhere outside of the economically depressed region of Appalachia, where the population is thin, the people voiceless, and the politicians are owned by the coal mining industry.

Charlie chuckled as he reread the last sentence. *'So what's the problem?'* Duncan would say. *That's just how we like things!* Charlie inserted several hot links here to sites about mountaintop-removal that he knew Duncan wouldn't bother with.

It's clear to me now that the surface mine for Angel Mountain was planned long ago and is the main reason that the plant was sited in McDowell County. I learned recently that Jack Torkelson and Larry Tuthill, along with the President of Ackerly Coal, visited Angel Mountain two years before the final selection process began. And it makes sense. The economic advantage of a mountaintop-removal mine on Angel Mountain, will make the Red Bone plant the lowest- cost, most efficient fossil fuel generating plant in North America for the next twenty years. But of course, you knew that. Very soon, you'll own the plant and the coal company with the mineral rights to Angel Mountain along with the contract to supply the coal to the Red Bone generating facility. Maybe there is room in all this integration for doing the right thing for the environment, and doing the right thing for an elderly couple who don't deserve one minute of the harassment they've taken from your lawyers and the coal people down here.

Charlie pursed his lips and shook his head. This was going nowhere. Duncan would probably just hit the delete key at this point and conclude that Charlie's mind had gone fuzzy in the isolation of the mountains of West Virginia. *Perhaps he'd be right. Maybe that's exactly what had happened,* thought Charlie sitting with his arms folded, rereading the letter. He looked at his watch and decided to press on, even if it was pointless. He'd state his case, just for the record if nothing else.

There are alternatives to mountaintop-removal, other methods of extracting the coal without the ecological annihilation of all plant and animal forms on Angel Mountain, and without the grossly unfair persecution of the DeWitt family. They are admittedly more costly, but in the overall impact of the decision, an alternative should be considered. A slope mine on the mountain could harvest the coal at a premium of $8 to $10 per ton over a surface mine.

Charlie grimaced at the *$8 lie. So what, it wouldn't matter anyway. If Duncan even made it this far, it was now case closed. A few taps on a calculator and Duncan would be certain that Charlie had flipped his lid.* He inserted a few more links here to some vague, inconclusive studies of the cost differential, more for effect than anything else, and decided to wrap it up. Charlie thought for a moment about including a reference to the merger with Continental Electric and the cryptic briefing he'd received from Vernon Yarbrough in New York about the possible *bribing of a federal judge* to secure the mountaintop-removal variance. He blew out a sigh as he quickly discarded that potential mine-field. It was all a moot point now. The merger was sailing through the approvals processes in adjoining states. The new Bush administration, in lock step with the mining industry, had already called for relaxing the restrictions on surface mines, ensuring nearly universal support for, and very little opposition to a mountaintop-removal variance for Angel Mountain – whether the judge was paid for or not. He'd stick to what was relevant and not burden Duncan with any potentially incriminating information.

In conclusion, Duncan, this isn't how we should be acting down here. West Virginia, one of the most resource-rich states in the history of the Country is now our second poorest because this is how corporate interests have been treating Appalachia for a hundred years – taking the coal, exporting the wealth and crippling the workers, and leaving behind only impoverishment, heartache, hopelessness, and ecological ruin. Maybe it's time for us to cut it out.

Looking forward to an old fashioned Big Ten ass kicking of OSU this weekend. Go Blue!

Charlie

Charlie did a spell-check and read over the letter one last time. He briefly considered deleting the whole thing and starting over when he was less tired and his head clearer and could write a much longer, more detailed, better thought out case. *No, Duncan would easily see through the economic bullshit no matter how he dressed it up. Better to be brief. He'd wasted enough time on the whole thing already.* Charlie hit the *send* button. *Sorry Bud, Alice. It's the best I can do.*

A few seconds later, Charlie received an e-mail, Out-of-Office Auto Reply from Duncan. *I will be out of the Country until the 10th of November, attending conferences in Switzerland and Belgium followed by a vacation week in the Canary Islands. Will respond to your e-mail when I return. Duncan McCord.*

Charlie sat and stared at the message on the screen of the laptop, and then smiled, followed by a hearty laugh. *Switzerland, Belgium and the Canary Islands -- long way from the topless bars in Detroit you used to love Dunc.* He turned off the computer and went to bed, leaving the hundreds of pages of *mountaintop-removal* data scattered across and under the kitchen table.

Chapter 27

As soon as they pried off the lid of the first packing crate, Charlie was glad he'd invited Eve Brewster to the party. The lobsters were three and four pounders, much too big to cook in any pot in Charlie's small kitchen. Sending the oversize lobsters was typical of his son Scott, Charlie knew. *First class, top-shelf, only the best! That was Scott these days.*

Pie's eyes went wide with amazement and he took a tentative half step backward when he saw the six lobsters lying in the plastic bag of ice. Eve Brewster laughed at his reaction as she reached in and pulled out one of the little monsters and placed it on the restaurant kitchen's floor. Immediately it started waving its banded claws and futilely scraping its legs and tail for traction on the smooth tile floor.

"Chowly, the lobstwa is vewy ugly. Do you weally eat it?" Pie was edging forward for a better look at the foreign creature.

"Pie Man, you're going to *love* lobster. All kids love lobster," said Charlie taking two more out of the ice and thrusting them toward Pie, who retreated with laughter. Charlie put them on the floor. He looked at Eve. "And we're going to have plenty of lobster to eat." With a dozen huge lobsters, they were going to have far more than enough to go around. Charlie broke out two Stroh's beers from the case he'd also had the helicopter bring in and handed one to Eve.

"Little early for this isn't it Charlie?" said Eve taking the beer and flipping it open.

Charlie grinned and held up his beer for a toast. "It's the *Michigan-Ohio State* game Eve. Gotta get tuned up."

Charlie helped Eve get a huge, dust covered pot down from a hook high up on a wall, and put the lobsters in the walk-in cooler, then he and Pie went upstairs to get the apartment ready for their guests. Charlie stopped into the store first for a fifth of *Jack Daniels* and a large bag of pork rinds.

They rearranged the living room, moving the overstuffed sofa and love seat around the big, round coffee table facing the television set with the armchair between them. It would be a little crowded eating off the table while they watched the game but they'd manage.

"Okay Chowly, I am weady fowa a beewa now," said Pie when they finished with the furniture.

"You got it Pie Man," said Charlie, heading to the refrigerator. He came out with a can of *Muggs* Root Beer he'd gotten for the occasion. Pie lit up with a *happy face.* Charlie opened another *Stroh's* and they toasted. "To the University of Michigan, Pie Man."

"The Univoosity of *Mishgan!*" Pie repeated, as they touched cans.

Charlie sat down on one of the kitchen chairs to bring him down to the boy's level.

"You know Pie, some day *you* may be going to the University of Michigan." Pie looked at him blankly for a few moments, then scrunched up his face as he often did when trying to figure out an arithmetic problem at his computer.

"Chowly," he said softly, "what do you *do* at Univoosity of Mishgan?"

Charlie chuckled at his own ignorance. "Well Pie, it's a *college*, where you go to learn things and read lots of books and become *educated.* So you can become an engineer or a teacher or a doctor, or whatever you want to be when you get older. But first you have to go to a college and read and study and work hard, like you do on your computer, like you do in school."

Pie nodded thoughtfully and then his face began to contort into another *happy face.* "And you go to footbawel games and dwink loth of *beewa!*"

Charlie laughed and poked him in the stomach. "Naw, you'd want to go to Michigan State for that. C'mon, let's go over and get Mr. Jacks and Woody."

Hank was coming in as they left, carrying an armload of snacks and a clear bottle of something that looked to Charlie menacingly like moonshine. Hank winked at Charlie. On the stairway they met Eve on her way up with a huge bowl of salad, a basket of bread and rolls, and two large bottles of wine. *Jesus*, thought Charlie, *we'll be lucky if anybody's still awake by halftime.*

With Charlie helping Woody, and the Pie Man holding on to Mr. Jacks, they slowly made their way down the stairs of the *Pocahontas Hotel* and across the street. As they came up the steps to the boardwalk, Earl Fitch, wearing his white barbering shirt, was coming out of *Brewster's General Store* with a handful of cigars. Charlie told him about the game and all the extra lobster they were going to have and invited him to the party. He said he'd be up around game time, when he closed the barber shop.

Hiking up the four flights of stairs to Charlie's apartment proved to be a challenge, especially for Woody, who needed to rest at each landing. Mr. Jacks was just slow, and confused about where they were going, but had less trouble climbing the stairs. After about ten minutes, they finally made it to the fourth floor. Charlie settled the two black men comfortably onto the soft couch, put out a large bowl of *Stroh's* beer on ice in front of them on the coffee table, and turned on the television.

Eve and Hank had been busy during their absence. The kitchen table was crowded with plates, additional silverware, a pile of napkins, and bowls for the butter, which Eve had brought up from the restaurant. She even had small lobster forks and a few shell crushers, which Charlie never would have thought of until it came time to eat. They'd put out large bowls of chips, cheese curls that Pie hovered over, and then the pork rinds on the table in front of Woody Givens who smiled appreciatively.

Hank took a seat on the love seat adjacent to the couch to visit with Woody and Mr. Jacks, and with Pie who was busy trying all the snacks. Hank had a beer as well as a small glass of the home-made corn liquor he'd brought. Eve poured herself a glass of Chablis and after getting two loaves of garlic bread ready for the oven, she went out the back door to the porch to take in the view.

Charlie pulled a *Stroh's* out of the bowl of ice and followed her to the porch. She was leaning on the railing, gazing off to the southwest. "Forgot what a great view you get from up here. I should charge you guys more for rent."

"No question about that,' said Charlie. He told her about inviting Earl Fitch up.

"That's good," said Eve, "Earl will enjoy this and we're going to have plenty of lobster left over. I'd invite Mabel Willard up but she'd never make it up the stairs. So maybe I'll take some lobster over to her and the boys later on, if that's okay?"

"Sure, that'd be great," said Charlie. He leaned onto the railing next to Eve. "Thanks for all your help with this Eve, you've been great."

Eve lit a Merit 100 and shrugged it off. "C'mon Charlie," she said with a sideways glance, gesturing down to the torn up soccer field below them. "You make new libraries and ball fields for us. I make garlic bread." They both laughed.

Charlie took a swig of beer, glanced at his watch and then looked out toward the far end of South County Road. It was getting close to game time.

"Don't worry, she'll be here," said Eve with a smile.

Charlie looked over toward the far off mountains to the south. "Yeah, well maybe. Maybe not." He thought about the last time he'd seen Natty, a week ago at the soccer game in Princeton.

"Heard that Buck was at the soccer game. That he saw you there talkin' to Nat." It was like Eve Brewster was reading his mind.

"Yeah, that was a surprise," said Charlie.

Eve took a sip of her wine and squinted into the low sun. "Don't mean *nothin'*," she said softly.

"What? What do you mean?"

"Mean it don't mean a *goddamn* thing now, after all this time, Buck finally showing some interest in them kids, in his wife." Eve shook her head angrily. "Imagine, beatin' that sweet girl way he done and still thinkin' you're forever gonna be the love a her life."

"Well . . . means something to her I think," Charlie said softly. He could hear the ABC pre-game show and the familiar marching band music coming from the television inside.

Eve turned toward Charlie and grabbed his faded Michigan T-shirt to pull him closer. She looked angry. "Charlie, it's too late for Buck now, that's what I'm telling you. That girl's so dippy over you that Buck got nothing to do with it any more. It's *all* up to you."

"C'mon Eve, how do you know if – "

"Cause I *know* Charlie," Eve said. "Cause women know 'bout these things." She let go of Charlie's shirt and squinted down the road. "Important thing now Charlie is how *you* feel, about Natty." She leaned sideways against the railing with her weight on her left elbow and eyed Charlie warily. "So how *do* you feel about her, Charlie? Where you at in all this? And don't give me any of that *bullshit* about '*nothin' happenin' tween you two*' like you were peddlin' that night you got beat up at the *Roadhouse*. I *know* there's nothin' happenin'. . . *that's* the damn problem." She turned to look down the hill. "I want to know what's in your heart Charlie," she said softly.

Charlie put his beer on the railing and leaned against the vertical post next to him with his arms crossed against his chest. *There it was . . . the question . . . the question he'd been dodging in his own mind for four months. How did he really feel about Natty?* He thought about their conversation in the dark street a week earlier. He'd tried to tell Natty how he felt about her then, but what *had* he said? *Did he really tell her anything?* He told her that *she made his palms sweat* and his *heart beat faster*, and that she was *remarkable*. And, that he still loved his wife. *God, what a coward. What an asshole.*

He looked down at Eve who was studying his face intently. He grimaced nervously and then released a long sigh, giving up the fight. "God Eve," he whispered, "I've never been in love with any woman like I love Natty." He shrugged helplessly. "I've never felt like this before."

Eve smiled broadly, giddy at finally hearing Charlie say what she had hoped he'd say. "Well Charlie, I *knew* that, but tellin' *me* ain't doin' anyone any good. You gotta tell it to *Natty*. And you got to tell her *soon*, 'cause timing's everything in love and war . . . it's *true* . . . and you two could end up makin' a mistake'll haunt you the rest of your lives, you keep waitin' for destiny to take its course and for life to be perfect where nobody ever gets hurt."

Charlie recalled the sick feeling that came over him at the soccer game when he sensed that Natty had slipped away from him. "Yeah Eve, I know," he said softly. "I just haven't had the balls to . . . haven't had the balls to admit it to myself I guess."

"So *tell* her Charlie," Eve said emphatically. "Tell her tonight. Will you?"

"*Christ* Eve," Charlie chuckled. "Give me a break here . . ."

"I'll have Pie come down and sleep over at my place tonight. And you do what you have to do." Eve took a sip of wine. She turned close to Charlie and lowered her voice for emphasis. "You *tell* that girl how you feel, and then you make love to her like she ain't *never* been made love to before . . . which won't be too goddamn difficult." Eve's jaw line tightened with anger. "Next time a man makes *love* to that girl be the *first time* to my mind," she hissed lowly.

Charlie heard the crowd noise from the television signifying the opening kickoff. He looked down the hill just as the faded red Accord came speeding into view. "We'll see Eve. We'll see what happens."

Eve frowned and looked down at the approaching car. "Charlie, you may never get the chance again," she said softly

At the bottom of the hill, Natty put her arm out of the window and waved as she leaned loudly on the horn. Charlie and Eve laughed and waved back. Charlie could see Natty grinning as she leaned close to the windshield to look up at them and his stomach suddenly felt empty and his heart began to pound in his chest.

Natty breezed into the apartment arm-in-arm with Earl Fitch who was carrying another twelve-pack of beer and a bottle of wine. "Well look at this handsome devil I found on the way up here," she said, making Earl Fitch grin with embarrassment. "*Woo woo*, go *Michigan*," she called out, flashing a smile to Charlie in the kitchen. "Game start yet?"

Earl shook hands around the room and shared a few words with Woody and Mr. Jacks, while Natty hugged Eve and Hank, and then went to the back of the couch and leaned over to put an arm around the shoulders of the old black men. "How you boys doin'? Okay?" she said softly, looking them over, like a nurse. She cuffed Pie playfully, put an arm around his neck and pulled him to her. The boy grinned an aborted *happy face* with his mouth half-stuffed with cheese curls.

"Mama, Chowly and me ouwa dwinking bewas!" he said proudly, holding up the can of root beer.

"Yeah that's good, never too young to start," she said turning a suspicious eye to Charlie who was bringing two more chairs in from the kitchen. He put the chairs in place behind the couch and then they were facing each other just a couple of feet apart. It would have been natural for Natty to hug him, like a friend, as she had the others. But when their eyes met they both hesitated, and the moment passed. The crowd noise from the television grabbed Charlie's attention as a Michigan runner broke free for a long gain.

"*Yeah!*," Charlie shouted instinctively. "Go Blue." He laughed and offered up a high-five to Natty. She smiled broadly and slapped his open palm hard.

"Okay, let's get this party going," she said, climbing over the back of the couch, wedging herself in between Woody and Mr. Jacks. She reached into the bowl of ice on the table and pulled out a Stroh's. "*Go Michigan*," she said loudly, punching the air as the Wolverines got another first down.

It took a while for the group assembled in front of the small television to embrace the Michigan cause, but led by Charlie's enthusiasm, supported loudly by Natty and Pie – when he didn't have his face in the cheese curls – they gradually got caught up in the spirit of the game, cheering raucously at every positive play for Michigan and applauding each Ohio State miscue. This was, after all, Charlie's party and it was his team, so they would do their part. Hank and Earl Fitch, aided no doubt, by the occasional sip of Hank's moonshine, quickly became demonstrative Michigan fans, with Hank – to Pie's hysterical amusement – firing cheese curls at the television screen whenever Michigan was penalized.

The level of enthusiasm was raised noticeably when Charlie brought out the bottle of *Jack Daniels* and a shot glass for each of the adults to toast each Wolverine score. Natty took control of the bottle and won a brief argument with Charlie that the extra point after a Michigan touchdown early in the second quarter, was a separate score, requiring another toast. Charlie didn't protest too strenuously. After an Ohio State turnover and quick field goal by Michigan, followed by a toast – glasses clinking and high-fives all around – even Woody and Mr. Jacks opened up and began rooting loudly for the striped helmets.

It was a good half for Michigan, and a good party. Everyone was having a good time, especially Charlie. From his chair behind the couch, Charlie looked around the room and suddenly realized what a diverse group of friends they were . . . Hank, the teacher, a man of integrity and intellect; Earl Fitch, happy and proud to be the barber of Red Bone, West Virginia; Woody and Mr. Jacks, simple men who never had a choice but to labor their way through a hard life in the mines; Eve Brewster, a one-person aid society and everyone's friend; and a twelve-year-old boy with Down Syndrome and a name from a nursery rhyme who had become Charlie's best friend. And then there was Natty. *What was she? How do you describe her?* Charlie watched her as Natty suddenly stood up in the warm room to pull off her bulky blue sweater revealing a white, sleeveless jersey that clung tightly to her breasts and her small waist. She turned to toss the sweater onto the floor behind the couch and smiled briefly at Charlie just as a completed Michigan pass and a cheer from the room pulled her attention back to the TV. *Natty? She could be anything she wanted to be . . . a backwoods hillbilly living in a trailer in Appalachia . . . or a model on the cover of Cosmopolitan.*

It was definitely a strange group. *But was there a nicer, more agreeable, or more enjoyable bunch of people anywhere, to sit around with on a Saturday afternoon to watch the Michigan-Ohio State game?* Charlie felt a rush of satisfaction as he thought about his buddies from Michigan, old classmates and teammates, who would be watching the game on wide-screens in sumptuous family rooms and mahogany-lined, members-only lounges at exclusive country clubs, and none having nearly as good a time as he was.

At the end of the first quarter, Eve slipped away to go down to the kitchen to turn on the stove to get the water boiling in the huge pot. A little while later, after another Michigan touchdown (and another shot of *Jack Daniels*), Charlie and Pie went down to put the lobsters in while Natty and Eve cleared the big coffee table, set out the plates and prepared the salad, garlic bread and melted butter.

Just before the second half got under way, Charlie and Pie made their triumphant entrance into the apartment carrying platters of steaming, red lobsters. Charlie's large platter was piled high with nine of the huge lobsters, while Pie, beaming with pride, held a tray out before him carrying the champion of the bunch, a five-pound behemoth that Charlie had selected for Pie's dinner.

Charlie held the platter around for everyone to select a lobster – a little timidly by Mr. Jacks, Natty and Woody sitting on the couch, who plainly would be eating their first lobster ever – and then took a seat on the floor next to Pie with Eve to his right, sitting with her back to the television. No one had touched their lobster and there was a moment of silence before Eve spoke.

"Hank, you want to do the grace here?"

Hank inched forward in the big chair and cleared his throat. "I'd be honored to Eve," he said, reaching out his left hand to Earl Fitch next to him and his right to Woody Givens. Everyone then joined hands – Charlie with Eve and Pie who giggled as he locked hands with Charlie and held onto Mr. Jacks' fingers, which felt hard and smooth. On the couch Natty squeezed the hands of Woody and Mr. Jacks and pulled them together affectionately in front of her under her breast.

"Lord," Hank started, bowing his head, "we need to thank you for these gifts that you've bestowed on us this day, but, *Christ* Lord, I think you gone a little overboard in the bounty department with this feast we got in front of us here." They all chuckled. "We'd all be real fortunate to have a slice of Eve's meatloaf tonight, never mind this incredible meal we got here." Hank nodded his head affirmatively several times. "But we *are* thankful Lord, and we want you to know that, for this and all your blessings you've brought to us this day." He looked up at Woody next to him and then around the circle. "We're thankful to have another day with our old friends Woody Givens and Mr. Kermel Jacks, and *all* our friends." He shook his left hand holding Earl's hand, and looked at Eve and then Natty and winked at the Pie Man. Hank lowered his head again. "And Lord, we also got to offer up here, some additional thanks for visitin' upon us a few months ago, a *special* friend, someone who's done a lot for us all, done a lot for this town, and . . . someone we know's going to have to be leavin' us sometime soon, 'cause he left his home and his family to come down here for a while and do good things, and well . . ." Charlie looked up with a perturbed smirk on his face to get Hank to wrap it up and met Natty's eyes. She blinked twice quickly and then looked down again. ". . . we're all gonna miss him when that day comes, particularly those of us winning considerable amounts of money at cribbage." Everyone laughed. "So, we all thank you for sending us Charlie Burden for a little while," Hank looked up and winked at Charlie, "and we all thank Charlie for this wonderful dinner. Amen."

"Amen," everyone said.

"*Thank God*," Eve exhaled. "Drag that out any longer Hank, damn football season'd be over.

"Let's eat," said Earl, ripping the tail off a steaming lobster.

And the feast was on. Charlie helped Pie with his, while Natty and the two black men watched Earl and Charlie and the others and learned how to eat lobster as they went along. Cracking one of the huge claws first, Charlie dunked the succulent meat in Pie's butter dish, and then everyone watched as Pie tried his first bite of lobster. Charlie grinned and then had to laugh with pleasure as the boy's face lit up with wonderment.

"Oh *Chowly*, lobstwa is *vewy* delicious!" Everyone laughed with enjoyment at Pie's reaction. Charlie laughed and reached into a cooler on the floor behind him for beers for Earl, Eve and himself.

They had to turn the volume up on the TV to hear it over the noise of cracking shells and the eating and gabbing of the now gregarious diners. Pie was especially animated in his enjoyment of this new-found delicacy. Charlie showed him and Natty how to break the claw arms at the knuckles and push out the choice meat with one of the tiny forks. With all the easy meat available, it was hardly worth going after the smaller legs, but Pie was having a wonderful time exploring all facets of this mysterious new creature.

Michigan got a touchdown and they finished off the *Jack Daniels* after having to search through the rubble of lobster shells, butter bowls, beer cans and used napkins littering the table to find all the shot glasses. Hank brought up his bottle of clear corn liquor from under the table with which to toast subsequent scores, which was met with unanimous approval.

Glancing at the television screen at the moment of a close-up of a Michigan cheerleader, Charlie suddenly jumped to his feet. "Oh *geeze*, Pie Man, I completely forgot! I've got something for you," he said, starting out toward the bedroom with a slight waver to his step. He came back into the room with a white plastic bag, which he tossed to the grinning Pie Man. "Been holding on to this for you just for today's game."

Pie reached into the bag and slowly brought out the dark blue shirt that Charlie had purchased at the Newark airport. His shoulders hunched with glee and his eyes grew wide as he stood and unfolded the shirt to reveal the yellow "Michigan" lettering. He held the shirt out in front of him. "Look Mama, Univoosity of *Mishgan!*"

Natty stood up and reached over for the shirt. "Hey, let me see it Pie," she said grabbing hold of the shirt. She quickly pulled it over her head and down over her jersey.

"*Mama!*" Pie protested.

"How's that look?" said Natty, grinning at Charlie. "Look like a cheerleader?"

"Maybe the mother of a cheerleader," Eve squawked with a grin, clearly feeling the afternoon's liquor.

By the time the game ended with Michigan winning 31-17, everyone was stuffed, Hank's moonshine was gone, and Mr. Jacks was sound asleep, snoring loudly with his head on his chest next to Natty. They sat around the table for another hour, sipping wine and coffee, and talking in the low-key, relaxed way that good friends can make conversation and laughter about any subject after a long day. They talked about food and sports and growing old and nothing serious.

Eventually the conversation came around to Natty's soccer team and the incredible season *The Bones* were having and their invitation to the Thanksgiving weekend tournament in Charleston. Immediately, a troubled look came over Natty. "Don't know if we'll be going to the tournament after all," she said reluctantly. She told the story of her run-in with Kyle Loftus after the game in Princeton. "Ain't going up there without Emma and Zack. Wouldn't be fair to them or the rest of the kids. Those are all good teams get invited to that tournament. *Real good teams!* Probably better than us anyway, even *with* Emma and Zack. So, we ain't going up there to get the snot beat out of us, which is just what Kyle Loftus wants to happen." Charlie listened in silence, sucking on a thin lobster leg, while the others voiced their anger at the league's decision. Hank, having been at the game in Welch and witnessed the incidents and the fight, was particularly incensed.

"Going to get an appeal hearing," said Natty offhandedly, "but that ain't going to do any good. Be at Loftus' office in Welch, with him and his two buddies that run the league, so I'll probably just skip that."

Charlie dropped the hollow lobster leg onto his plate. "Keep the appeal hearing Nat," he said. "I'll go with you. May be some way to get him to change his mind."

Natty shrugged, and then grinned at Charlie. "Going to beat him up for me Charlie?" Everyone laughed.

Charlie grinned back at her. "Not a bad idea."

The table and a good part of the floor around it was a trash heap of bowls of red lobster parts, unfinished salads, bread crusts, many beer cans and spent napkins. But nobody cared. It had been a wonderful feast, a great football game and a very enjoyable afternoon for all, and now as darkness came through the tall windows, everyone was moving considerably slower.

Eve got up and busied herself in the kitchen packing up some salad and rolls to go with two of the leftover lobsters she was going to bring to Mabel Willard's. "I'll come back and help clean up after I take this down to Mabel and the boys," she said heading for the door. "And Pie Man, you'll be sleeping down at my place tonight, special treat," she said grinning at Pie, and then winking at Natty as she turned and left the apartment.

Hank excused himself to visit the bathroom to rinse out his shirt that he'd dripped butter on, and Natty forced herself to get up from the couch to start clearing the mess from the coffee table. She brought some plates into the kitchen.

Earl Fitch reached into his breast pocket and brought out two fat cigars, holding them up to Charlie. "What do you say Charlie. Cigar on the porch?"

"Earl, you're reading my mind." Charlie slowly climbed to his feet and followed Earl toward the door to the porch.

Passing through the kitchen, Earl Fitch squeezed by Natty standing at the sink scraping off plates under the running water. Natty felt Charlie behind her and then his hands holding her biceps and shaking her playfully. "We'll do that stuff later," he said as she turned to smile up at him. "Come out and have a cigar with us."

Natty laughed. "No, one cigar a year is about enough for me," she said watching him go through the screen door and disappear in the darkness of the porch. She stood still for a moment at the sink, savoring the still tingling feeling she had in her arms where Charlie had briefly held her. She closed her eyes and felt a stirring deep inside and thought about when everyone would be leaving, and knew that very soon she would be alone in the apartment with Charlie. And she sensed that Charlie was thinking about it too.

Pie was sitting on the couch, his eyes half closed, leaning his head against Woody's huge arm, staring a golf tournament on the television. The boy's face was still covered with butter grease, bread crumbs and other residue from the meal as was his Tee-shirt and the lap of his pants. In one hand he held on to several cheese curls as if he'd forgotten they were there. Natty smiled down at him. It had been a big day for the Pie Man, one he'd be talking about for a long time. *The day we had the lobstwas at Chowly's!*

Natty leaned over to pick up another load from the coffee table when she thought she heard a light rapping at the door. She listened again, trying to tune out the sound of the television, and there it was, a polite three soft taps on the door, so low that no one else could hear it.

She pulled open the door and stood staring at an apparition, a vision from another world, she was sure, because the last thing she expected to see was a *stranger* standing in the hallway on the fourth floor of the *Barney's Building.* Natty stood in silence, mute from her surprise, staring at what had to be the most beautiful woman she had ever seen up close. The woman was taller than she was, with shining, lustrous black hair that fell not quite to her shoulders from under a fashionable black fur hat. She stood with her hands in the front slash pockets of an elegant long black leather coat with a high collar. The obviously expensive coat was shiny and supple and looked glove-soft as it hugged her trim frame. Just visible below the ankle-length coat were the high-heeled black boots required by such a coat. The woman's dark eye makeup perfectly accentuated her hazel eyes, which seemed to glow with inner light in the dim hallway, and her lips were painted a deep red. She wore delicate diamond earrings that sparkled with the slightest movement.

The stranger smiled pleasantly at Natty's surprise. Her eyes fluttered down briefly to the yellow *Michigan* lettering across Natty's chest, and back up. Then came a real smile with a full set of beautiful white teeth, and a slight up-tilt of the head as she pulled a gloved hand from her right pocket and held her arm out straight to Natty. "Hello," she said, "I'm Ellen Burden."

Natty reached out and clasped the hand. She held on while she cleared her throat and tried to think. "Oh, Charlie's wife," she managed softly. *Holy shit! Charlie's wife's standing here in the fucking hallway!* She attempted a smile not knowing if her facial muscles were working properly. "Natty ..." she whispered hoarsely. She cleared her throat. "Natty Oakes," she said louder. *Oh geeze, this isn't going to look good for Charlie.*

Ellen Burden chuckled as she looked at their still clasped hands. "Well it's a pleasure to meet you Natty. This *is* Charlie's apartment, isn't it?"

Natty finally let go of her hand. Ellen Burden's pleasant nature had put Natty at ease allowing her to recover her wits. She smiled broadly at Charlie's wife. "Why yes ma'am, it sure is," she said adding a little extra drawl. "C'mon in here ma'am, and *welcome to West Virginia!*"

Ellen came into the room and found herself standing next to the coffee table. She took a quick glance at the couch where an old, wiry black man with white hair was asleep with his head on his chest, and another huge black man was sitting with his arm around the shoulders of a little mongoloid boy who looked to be asleep with some kind of curious concoction smeared across his face and a hand full of orange mush. She turned to flash a quick smile at Natty who had shut the door behind her, and then she looked down at the lobster shell littered table. "Oh yes," she said almost to herself. "The Ohio State game. I'd almost forgotten."

"Yes ma'am, and it was a beauty . . . thirty-one, seventeen, Michigan," said Natty.

Ellen smiled at Natty and her eyes went down again briefly to the blue Tee-shirt. "How nice," she said, and then looked away to scan the inside of the apartment.

Woody Givens finally noticing the newcomer, had pushed himself up slowly from the couch. "Miz Burden, this here's Woody Givens, lives across the street," said Natty, at the same time pointing to the end of the couch where Mr. Jacks had awakened with his face up if he was sniffing the air for a new scent.

"And over there is Kermel Jacks, his roommate. "Boys, like you to meet Miz Ellen Burden, come all the way down here from New York to visit Charlie."

Woody held out a big paw, which Ellen squeezed strongly. "Well *weehee,* sure is a pleasure to meet you ma'am," said Woody. Ellen nodded and smiled.

On the couch, Mr. Jacks squinted through his thick bifocals trying to see what was going on. "What? What's that?" said the old man. "Charlie's mother's here?"

Ellen smiled pleasantly while Natty grabbed a used napkin from the table and holding Pie's head with her left hand, rubbed the napkin over her sleeping son's greasy face. "And this little pecker here," she said, standing up straight and tossing the napkin back on the table, "is my son, the *Pie Man.*"

Ellen Burden looked down at the boy pensively for a few moments and then at Natty. "He's about . . . what, twelve or thirteen?"

"Yeah, 'bout twelve, close as we can figure," said Natty with a grin. Out of the corner of her eye she saw Hank coming out of the bedroom. "And just look who's comin' now," she said, redirecting Ellen's attention to the approaching figure.

Hank had taken his shirt off and pulled his suspenders up over his naked torso. His white goatee and the long ends of the handlebar mustache hung low and were matted with yellow butter stains. The pale folds of liver- spotted flesh jiggled as he lumbered on tired legs into the living room.

Natty scooted around the coffee table to intercept him. She put an arm around Hank's back and pulled him close to her, driving a breast into his bony ribs. "And this old show dog here's my boyfriend Pullman Hankinson," she said with a proud grin. Before Hank could react she said, "Hank, this beautiful lady's Charlie's wife, Miz Ellen Burden."

The afternoon's liquor may have slowed Hank's reaction time but it hadn't dulled his wits. He reached out his right hand to Charlie's wife while he reached his left arm around Natty and pulled her closer with his hand on her waist. "Why Miz *Burdan* it sure is a pleasure to meet any wife of Charlie's. Had one myself once," he said with a deep laugh. He turned and nuzzled Natty's ear. "Could be I'll be getting' me another 'fore too long."

Natty put her arms around Hank's neck and kissed him on his whiskered-covered cheek, while he, obviously enjoying his new roll, held her close to him with his hand on Natty's back. "Aw Hank, you need to stop teasin' me now," she purred.

Natty turned her head back toward Ellen Burden and was startled to see Charlie standing in back of his wife, enjoying the show with a wide grin on his face.

"Hello Ellen," he said.

Charlie's wife turned her head first and then her body followed. She tilted her head slightly and smiled at her husband as she examined his face. "Darling," she said warmly, "and how *is* your nose?"

"Much better," he said, moving forward and hugging his wife. "*This* is a surprise." Over Ellen's shoulder he grinned at Hank and Natty, still holding onto each other.

"Duncan made all the arrangements . . . the helicopter from Charleston, and then a very nice man, Mr. Krebs, the security guard, drove me up here."

Charlie just nodded as they separated. He held out a hand toward Hank and Natty. "And you've met everyone?"

"Yes," said Ellen spinning around once more. "I've met all of your friends." Hank and Natty nodded and smiled and cuddled together, while Woody Givens continued to stare wide-eyed at both of them trying to figure out what had come over them.

The screen door banged shut as Earl Fitch came toward them through the kitchen.

"Oh, and here's one more," Ellen said with a chuckle.

Charlie introduced her to Earl Fitch, and then there was a gap of silence in the room.

Finally Natty said, "Charlie, Eve and me'll come up and clean up this mess tomorrow, so, we'll all be getting' out a here now." She leaned over the couch and shook Pie awake. "C'mon Pie Man, time to go. Let's go Mr. Jacks, time to go home."

Earl and Hank thanked Charlie for dinner and fled quickly out the door followed by a perplexed Woody Givens and Natty, herding Mr. Jacks and Pie – still half asleep – along with her. "Thanks Charlie," Natty called out loudly over her shoulder on the way out, "Hank and me had a great time."

Hank slipped quietly into his apartment while Natty and Earl helped Woody and Mr. Jacks down the stairs. Pie was asleep on his feet so Natty deposited him on the couch in Eve's apartment. In the vestibule at the bottom of the stairs stood a green paisley patterned suitcase with brown leather trim. Natty stopped for a moment and gazed at the expensive looking bag. *Geeze, even her suitcase is beautiful.* She and Earl each holding on to a black man, made their way out onto the boardwalk and down to the street.

After getting Woody and Mr. Jacks safely home, Natty and Earl Fitch came out of the *Pocahontas Hotel* and walked together slowly in the dark down the middle of Main Street. Earl lit up a cigar for the walk home to his apartment over the barber shop. "Charlie's wife's a pretty handsome woman," he said, between puffs to get his cigar going.

Natty chuckled softly. "She's beautiful."

"And how 'bout that coat? Never seen a coat like that before on a woman. Must have cost Charlie a pretty penny I'll bet."

"Yeah, I guess,' said Natty, not very interested in discussing Mrs. Charlie Burden. She suddenly felt the chill of the night and remembered that she was still wearing Pie's new Michigan shirt and that she'd left her sweater on the floor behind the couch at Charlie's

Eve was stepping up to the boardwalk, just back from Mabel Willard's when she saw Natty and Earl enter the dim circle of light in the street in front of the store. Earl waved and continued on as Natty made her way slowly toward Eve. She stopped next to the red Accord, parked at an angle in front of *Barney's General Store.*

Eve held her palms up. "What happened to the party?"

Natty shrugged. "Charlie had company." She paused to let Eve suffer a bit, then smiled. "His wife dropped in."

Eve's jaw fell open. *"No shit?"*

Natty nodded. "Flew down from New York today."

"Aw geeze Nat," Eve said shaking her head. She started to say something else but Natty cut her off with a wave as she pulled open the door of the Accord.

"You got Pie on your couch Eve. See you tomorrow." Natty got in the car and pulled the door closed, not wanting any more conversation for this day. She'd go home and go to sleep, and tomorrow morning she'd get out early and go for a long, hard run. Maybe seven or eight miles.

*   *   *

Charlie and Ellen seated themselves in a booth at a front window of *Eve's Restaurant.* The restaurant was fairly busy, as it usually was on a Sunday morning, with half a dozen customers sitting at the counter and a like amount at the tables and booths. After they'd ordered the blueberry pancakes, Charlie went over to the store to get a paper. Most of the restaurant patrons used the opportunity of Charlie's absence to steal another peek at the stunning, raven – haired wife of the power plant boss, down on a visit from New York. She was clearly in a different league from any woman in Red Bone – her eyes beautifully made up, wearing a gorgeous lavender turtle-neck sweater and tightly pressed designer blue jeans. Red Bone women just didn't look like this on a Sunday morning

Charlie returned to the booth with the Charleston Sunday Gazette-Mail. Ellen looked askance at the paper. "No *Times*?"

Charlie laughed, pulling out the sports section. "No *Imus In The Morning* either."

Ellen rolled her eyes. "How do you *stand* it?" she asked sarcastically.

"It's pure hell," Charlie answered as he searched for the pro football news to see who the Giants were playing.

They were drinking their coffee and reading the paper when Hank came in and took a stool at the counter behind Charlie. Ellen smiled brightly and gave him the friendly *finger-wiggle* wave used for new acquaintances whose name you can't remember. Charlie turned to see who it was. "Hey Hank, how you doing?"

"Morning Charlie, miz Burden," said Hank with a nod.

Charlie turned back to Ellen for a second and then twisted around again to face Hank, his arm up on the back of the booth for support. "Natty sleeping in this morning Hank?" Charlie had a mischievous grin that was hidden from his wife.

Hank coughed, and his eyes darted around the restaurant to see if anyone had heard. He dabbed his mouth with a napkin even though he hadn't yet eaten anything. "Yeah, that's right," he said quietly. "She, ah, got a little tired out last night. Gonna sleep in for a while."

Charlie was still grinning at him. "Yeah well, she's quite a girl you got there, real live wire. Say hi to her for us, will you?"

Hank's whiskers were bouncing up and down nervously while his eyes circled the room again. "Yeah, she's somethin' all right," he half mumbled. The young waitress arrived in front of Hank with a coffee pot, sparing him any further torture from Charlie who struggled to wipe the smile off his face as he turned back to his wife. Ellen just eyed Hank for a moment before turning to look through the front window.

"Oh look, there are your friends, Mr. Woody and Jack," she said. Charlie turned to see the two elderly black men helping each other shuffle across Main Street.

"This really is a small place," said Ellen. "Everyone probably knows everyone else in town," she added, still gazing through the window.

"Yeah pretty much," said Charlie as their pancakes arrived.

When they were just about done with breakfast, Ellen looked up and smiled at somebody approaching behind Charlie.

"*Hello*, mith Chowly, I am the Pie Man," the boy said, coming to a stop next to the booth. He held up his hand to Ellen for a high-five.

"Well good morning, um, *Pie Man*," she said, smiling and touching his hand lightly with her palm. "Nice to see you wide awake."

Pie just stared at her for a moment and then turned to Charlie. "Hello Chowly." They exchanged a high-five and Charlie pulled the front of Pie's Yankees hat down over his eyes making him laugh. Pie straightened his hat and looked back at Ellen. "Someday I will go to Univoosity of Mishgan and I will become a engineewa like Chowly," he said proudly.

Ellen smiled broadly and reached out a hand and touched the boy's shoulder. "Well Pie Man, that's *wonderful.* I think you'll make a terrific engineer, just like Charlie."

Eve Brewster's voice came to them from the doorway to the kitchen. "C'mon Pie, your pancakes are ready." She waved briefly to Charlie as Pie ran off, and then added a quick smile for Charlie's wife.

"He's delightful," said Ellen, eying Charlie who was looking out toward the street.

"Yeah, he's a good kid."

Ellen and Charlie's eyes met for a few seconds but neither said anything. Finally Ellen smiled and looked out through the big window. "C'mon, lets take a walk Charlie. Show me your baseball field."

They walked slowly down the hill toward the rubble of the athletic fields under construction. The site lay motionless before them with no activity taking place on Sunday.

"You really have to go back to New York tonight?"

Ellen nodded. "Yeah, I have a luncheon meeting tomorrow. I'm being brought onto the Board of Directors of the Westchester Fine Arts Council."

Charlie smiled at her. "Hey, that's great. Congratulations." Ellen's new position as President of Hickory Hills Country Club was already paying dividends. Her new address on Quail Hollow Lane probably didn't hurt either. "How's the house?"

"It's coming along," she said with a tone that told Charlie it was going to cost them another fifty thousand before she was done. "Planning a Christmas party, for the Club people, and the neighborhood," she looked up at Charlie, "and of course any of your friends you want to invite."

"Sounds great," said Charlie, pushing the idea quickly out of his thoughts.

They stopped at the site of the children's library and Charlie walked Ellen around the footprint of where the structure would be as he described the new building. She could see his excitement for the project as he went into detail about the activity rooms with their skylights, the computer room, and cozy reading nooks.

"Maybe we can get some books from the Westchester Library Association," Ellen offered.

"I was going to ask you about that," said Charlie.

"I'll bring it up at the next Board meeting. Could be a nice charitable project."

They walked down the hill and crossed the stone and sand base of the new soccer field as Charlie pointed out the features of the athletic complex. Between the soccer and baseball fields, they went up the wooden steps of the nearly completed gazebo and walked around the circular floor with Charlie describing the landscaping and the fountain and gardens that would eventually complete the park-like setting.

Ellen sat down on the bench ringing the inside of the gazebo and gazed out at the piles of gravel and sand, the pyramid of irrigation pipes, and the idle construction machinery. "You've been busy here Charlie. This is quite an undertaking. Is this normal? Doing a project like this for a small town?"

Charlie sat down on the bench about ten feet away from Ellen. "No, I guess this is a little unusual, a project this extensive. But we owed this town something, and we also needed some good PR to fall back on, so . . . it'll be a nice park when we're done, another month or so."

Ellen smiled at him. "Well, that's nice, that you're doing something nice for these people," Ellen said, her voice falling away as her eyes drifted out toward the hills surrounding them.

They sat for a while in silence, enjoying the morning sun as it warmed up the southern section of the gazebo. Charlie was thinking about drainage and turf and winter frost. Ellen's voice brought him back to the present.

"*So*, Charlie . . . have you slept with her yet?

Charlie just continued staring out at the soccer field. One of the things he loved about Ellen was her intellect and her perceptiveness. While she loved to talk, Ellen was one of the world's great observers and listeners. She could sit quietly in a room full of people for a few minutes and tell you everything that was going on between them. There was no sense in trying to dissuade her of what they both knew to be true. Charlie squinted briefly, a twinge of emotional pain, and then looked over at his wife.

"No." He managed a weak smile then looked at the floor at his feet. "No, not yet."

"But you plan to?"

Charlie shrugged. "I don't know. It's a little complicated."

"Because she's *married*?"

Charlie chuckled. "Because *I* am." He looked over at her, but she was looking away, up toward the old red stone buildings of Red Bone at the top of the hill. Charlie wondered if she was thinking about the prospect of losing him, or about *opportunity*. He had no doubt that in the circles she now traveled, Ellen, with her looks, intelligence and sophistication, could easily bag one of Westchester's upper-tier, old-money scions and move effortlessly into a life of wealth and leisure that would make the Quail Hollow Lane house look like servants' quarters. That was another thing he loved about Ellen – she could always take care of herself.

Finally Ellen looked back at Charlie. Her face showed no anger. "She's a lovely girl Charlie."

"Well, she's very, uh, *different* all right."

"May want to rethink the hairdo though," Ellen deadpanned. Then she looked at Charlie out of the corner of her eye and they both smiled.

Charlie stood up and put his hands in his pockets, facing Ellen. "So you didn't buy that act she and Hank were putting on."

Ellen laughed as she got up from the bench. "Not for a second." Then her eyes narrowed and the smile drained from her face as she took a step closer to Charlie. She crossed her arms and looked out at the field for a moment and then back at Charlie. She exhaled a sigh and spoke softly. "I knew the moment she opened the door . . . that I'd be losing you to her."

"Ellen," Charlie protested softly, "That's not . . . I don't know what's going to happen. We haven't even . . ."

"Charlie, Charlie," she interrupted, coming close to him. She put a hand on his chest and paused to compose her thoughts. "Listen Charlie. You've been a wonderful husband and the perfect father, but just because our children have grown up and don't need us anymore and that part of our lives is over, doesn't mean we have to shrivel up and stop living and let our emotions die." Her eyes were slightly moist. "I love you Charlie, and I always will, no matter what happens, whether we stay together or . . . if we go in different directions. But you need to find out . . . what you want, what you want to do, and what you need in your life. And *God knows* . . . after the last couple of years . . . you need *something* different Charlie." She touched his arm briefly. "So, you need to explore this thing with, um . . ."

"Natty," said Charlie.

Ellen smiled briefly and stepped back. She pushed her hands into the slash pockets of her leather coat and shrugged with her elbows. "Because if you don't, you'll always be wondering, and it 'll never be exactly right with us again." She looked up into Charlie's eyes and smiled. "Believe me about this Charlie. I know."

After an early dinner in Welch, at which Ellen told him about the house, the country club, and their neighbors, whom she'd had already gotten the complete low down on, they drove back to the plant. The CanAmex helicopter was waiting for her, the turbo whining lowly at idle, the running lights blinking, ready for take-off. Charlie went on board and stowed Ellen's Luis Vuitton bag in the luggage locker while she buckled in. She'd taken her cell phone and a copy of *Town & Country* from her shoulder bag and put them on the seat next to her. As the large blades began to turn in earnest, Charlie leaned over and kissed his wife goodbye. She smiled at him. "Good luck Charlie," she said. "See you at Thanksgiving." Charlie just nodded and then squeezed her hand before leaving her alone in the helicopter. He stood next to his car and watched the helicopter lift a few feet into the air and then spin around to the north. Through the window, Ellen smiled with a wave, the cell phone already up to her ear.

Chapter 28

The ground fog clung to the low spots like thick smoke, hiding the pavement in front of the Lexus as Charlie crept along Cold Spring Road. Peering out the passenger's window for signs of the turnoff to the lumber camp, he finally started seeing the cars and pickups parked at untidy angles in the weeds between the shoulder of the road and the woods. He found a spot, took his athletic bag from the trunk, and locked up the Lexus, which looked out of place among the vehicles of the lumber men.

He was fifteen minutes early, but already, through the swirling mist at the bottom of the hill, Charlie could see a dozen men loitering around the equipment shed. They were waiting in small groups of two and three, talking quietly, smoking, and sipping coffee from Styrofoam cups. He could feel their eyes on him as he made his way carefully down the steep dirt and stone road, the canvas bag over his shoulder, wondering how the big, heavily-loaded lumber trucks ever made it up the incline to Cold Spring Road.

The professional wood cutters would easily recognize that he wasn't one of them. Charlie had his hard hat, goggles, earplugs and gloves in his bag, but he was without the OSHA-required canvas chaps or leggings that the other men wore. Plus, word would have spread by now about the *big mule* of the power plant coming out for a day of *recreational woodcutting,* and even stranger – *doing it for no pay.*

That's okay. They could stare and wonder all they want. Charlie had longed for a day of physical exertion out in the fresh air for quite a while. And now that he was finally able to work it into his schedule, it came at just the right time – a day for him to work his body to exhaustion and clear his mind of the frustration of the past week and a half since the lobster party and Ellen's untimely appearance in Red Bone.

First Ellen had unnerved him with her seeming indifference to the potential crumbling of their marriage, and Charlie also hadn't seen Natty for a week and half, and what was more telling, the Pie Man hadn't come into the office to use his computer since the lobster party. Ellen's presence had affected Natty – that was certain – and Charlie felt again the emptiness that accompanied the realization that his relationship with Natty was more fantasy than real.

So a day at hard labor in the deep woods would be cathartic. It would also give him a close-up view of the progress of the wood-clearing project. Pat Garvey told him to report in to the foreman at seven o'clock, bring a hardhat, goggles, ear plugs, steel-toed boots, gloves, and a big lunch because he'd be out there all day. The foreman would give him some leg protectors to wear and assign him to a crew.

Charlie went into the equipment shed and introduced himself to the foreman, a big, red-faced Irishman named Devine. "Oh yeah, all ready for ya mister Burden. Got ya teamed up with some of our best boys, good crew," he said looking down at the roster on his clipboard. "Mister Garvey said, 'just make sure you don't get hurt out there' so we got ya with some real good woodcutters." He handed Charlie a plastic-wrapped package of new chaps that was sitting on the desk, and twisted around to peer out the side window of the shed. He straightened up and started for the door. "C'mon I'll introduce you to the boys."

They walked around to the side of the shed where several battered and scratched utility vans were being loaded with equipment. Devine had a pronounced limp as he led Charlie to the first van in line. Two men were carrying large chainsaws to the van as Charlie and the foreman approached. The lumberjacks deposited the saws roughly on the floor of the truck and turned toward Devine. "G'mornin' dere boss," one of the men said in a heavy French Canadian accent that Charlie had become very familiar with during his college hockey days.

"Frenchy, Dogface," Devine gestured to Charlie coming up behind him. "This is mister Charlie Burden, fellah I was telling you about. Charlie's going to go up and cut some wood with you, just for today. So your job is to make sure he don't get hurt."

Charlie winced a little at Devine's warning as he reached out and shook hands with the two men. Frenchy, who was around thirty years old, was at least six-foot-six and had the physique of a world-class weight lifter. His neck, shoulders and arms rippled with muscles and his huge hand felt like it was made of iron. He had jet black hair pulled back into a short pony tail under a red bandanna. Dogface was a foot shorter and probably a little older, but with a similar physique on a smaller scale. He had a long, bony face with a long nose, a protruding forehead, and sunken cheeks bulging out on one side with a large chaw of tobacco. His massive forearms were covered with tattoos. Both men glanced at the brand new chaps Charlie carried under his arm, and then back to Devine.

The foreman looked down at his clipboard as he spoke, as if to avoid the eyes of the lumber men. "You boys'll be limbin' and buckin' today out at pole eight."

The displeasure of the men at the day's assignment was evident. "Aw, c'mon dere boss," said Frenchy, "don't be wastin' us on dat baby stuff. We got a lot a da big trees to bring down out dere." Dogface just shook his head derisively and went back to loading two large gasoline cans, and a dispenser of bar oil into the truck.

"Well we got a mess a logs down at pole eight to get ready for the helicopters comin' tomorrow. Been down a coupla days now, ready for limbin', so that's where we need ya." Devine looked up defiantly with his chin out and rapped his pencil point into the clipboard several times indicating that the discussion was over.

Frenchy broke into a broad grin and put a huge hand on the foreman's shoulder. "Okay boss man, you are de boss," he said winking at Charlie. "We have a good time anyway, prunin' da bushes today. And mister Charlie, we take good care of him, Dogface and me and Bucky. We bring him back tonight, good as a shiny new penny dere, aye?" Frenchy dropped an old canvas duffle bag from his shoulder, tossed it into the truck and headed for the driver's door.

Charlie wasn't sure if he heard Frenchy correctly, but Devine confirmed his fear.

"Yeah, where the hell *is* Buck anyway?" said the foreman wheeling around looking for the missing member of the crew.

"He's bringing the water there boss," said Dogface thumbing back towards the large water tank behind the equipment shed.

Even before he turned his head to look, it all clicked into place in Charlie's mind. *Of course Pat Garvey would have told Devine to put him with Buck. He'd made the call for Buck to get him his job, so Garvey naturally would think there was some sort of relationship there and that Charlie would be comfortable working with Buck.*

And then Buck Oakes was next to Devine. He put the heavy yellow, plastic water bucket down at his feet and stared coolly at Charlie.

"Buck, guess you already know Charlie Burden here. Charlie's gonna do some limbin' with us today. Says he knows how to use a chainsaw." Devine looked over at Charlie. "That right Burden?"

"Yeah, I've used a chainsaw," said Charlie, holding out his hand to Buck. "Nice to see you again Buck."

Buck took his hand briefly. "Yeah, how ya doin'?" he mumbled lowly.

Charlie recognized the deep, gravely voice he'd last heard on his knees in the *Roadhouse* parking lot. He smiled and raised his eyebrows. "Better than the last time we met." Buck just nodded briefly and looked away toward the equipment.

Up close, Buck looked bigger and more powerful than he'd appeared the two times Charlie had seen him sitting in his truck. He certainly had the neck and shoulders of a football player, and the black mustache and goatee and the small dark eyes, projected an ominous aura. Standing this close to Buck, Charlie could feel the anger and violence lurking just below the surface. He'd have to bury, at least for the day, the image he had in his mind of Natty taking a beating from the powerful man in front of him. Today, he'd just try to avoid any confrontation and get along with Buck . . . *the luckiest man in McDowell County.*

The loud horn of the van ended any further conversation. Frenchy's head was out the driver's window looking back at them. "C'mon dere, lets go, aye Bucky?" He grinned and banged the outside of the door with a huge hand. "Got us some wood t'cut."

Dogface took a seat up in the cab with Frenchy while Charlie and Buck climbed into the open back of the van. Buck pulled up and secured the short gate at the back, and they maneuvered their way through the equipment and gas cans to take seats facing each other on benches that ran along both sides of the truck. Under the benches was jammed tight with chains and pulleys, chocks, coils of heavy rope, boxes of various tools and a large first-aid kit. Behind the benches, on the side walls hung a selection of handsaws, heavy iron pry bars of various lengths, an extension pole with a curved saw blade at the end, and behind all the other equipment, flush against each wall of the truck were two, very old, six-foot-long, two-man crosscut saws.

Looking around the interior of the crowded van, Charlie noticed the two-man saw in back of Buck. It looked like an antique. He gestured at it with his chin. "You still use those?"

Buck turned to see the old saw. "Naw, not really." He gestured to the front of the truck. "Frenchy and Dog like to take down a tree with it once in a while. For the *art a lumberjackin'* and at kinda shit. They're both fuckin' nuts anyway. They *love* cuttin' wood." Buck busied himself with adjusting the tension on one of the saws, making it clear that he wasn't in the mood for any more idle chatter.

After a rough ten-minute ride along what must have been a new trail through the woods, they came upon a large clearing where several pieces of yellow logging machinery with lobster-like pinching claws on one end and bulldozer blades on the rear, sat idle. The clearing was covered with sawdust and woodchips, and piles of long, thin logs awaiting the trucks that would take them out of the woods and down to Pat Garvey's mill. They went across the clearing and continued down the logging road, gradually descending into a long gulley populated on both sides of the road by large tree stumps surrounded by aprons of matted down sawdust. Looking out the back of the van up the hill behind them, Charlie could see hundreds of stumps over the quarter of a mile path, and tried to imagine the labor needed to remove that many trees on this kind of terrain. This was clearly work for rugged men who knew their trade, and Charlie started to feel guilty for thinking that he could belong out here, even for one day.

The truck lurched to a stop and Frenchy and Dogface were at the back of the truck before Charlie could even untangle himself from the rubble of equipment at his feet. They unloaded all of the equipment onto the ground and only then did Charlie look up and survey the job ahead of them. Up the slope from them about twenty-five yards, on the high side of the gully, a sea of brown, gold and green foliage covered an area that looked to Charlie to be about the size of a football field. It was impossible to tell how many trees were down among the tangled pile of limbs and branches. It seemed to Charlie like a job that would take weeks.

Buck went back into the truck and brought out some extra chains, a tool box and a small crow bar, and put them in his pine-sap covered duffle bag. Frenchy and Dogface were strapping on plastic leg protectors that looked like they'd been through the first World War, which reminded Charlie to get his chaps from the truck. He tossed the package in his bag instead of looking like a complete rookie trying to figure out how to put them on in front of the loggers.

"Okay Bucky, why don't you and Charlie go down the end dere, and me and Dog'll start up here," said Frenchy looking up the slope. "We'll meetcha in the middle," he added with a big grin to Charlie. The incline was steeper and the trees a little bigger where Frenchy and Dogface would be working, so it looked like a good offer to Charlie.

Buck just shouldered his bag, grabbed a saw and one of the gas cans, and started out toward the far end of the field of fallen trees, leaving Charlie the other saw and the smaller oil can to carry. By the time Charlie reached the top of the slope where Buck was filling the oil bladder of his saw, they could hear the high-pitched whine of the chain saws at work at the far distant end of the trees.

Buck took Charlie up to the top of the slope and then down between the first two trees and showed him how to cut a limb lock. Then it was Charlie's turn. Charlie had to pull the starter rope a few times to get his saw running.

"Good," said Buck. "How's that feel?"

Charlie nodded. "Feels a little lighter than I thought it would be."

"We'll see how light it feels about four o'clock," Buck said, turning to move down the trunk a few feet. He pointed out a twisted limb for Charlie to cut. After a couple of tentative incisions, Charlie managed to sheer off the limb cleanly without any pitch back. Buck nodded, put his ear protectors in place and moved ten yards over to another, larger tree and went to work.

Charlie watched him for a few seconds as he quickly and methodically went through some large limbs, working steadily along one side of the fallen tree. While Buck didn't have much going for him in terms of people skills, Charlie could see that he was a true craftsman when it came to cutting trees, moving the powerful saw deftly like an extension of his arm, with no wasted motion. Down at the other end of the field of downed trees, Charlie could see Frenchy and Dogface moving through their work at a similar steady, efficient pace.

Charlie went to work on his tree, clumsily at first, but then quickly gaining confidence as he became accustomed to the power of the saw, the long bar, and the chain that got sharpened every night. Soon he was ripping methodically through the limbs even some that were a foot wide at the trunk.

After an hour, the sun had risen high enough in the cloudless sky for a clear shot at the slope of the gulley and Charlie was soon sweating profusely. He stopped to take off his sweatshirt and then saw Buck coming down the hill to him carrying his own two – liter water bottle and Charlie's little bottle of Dasani. He tossed the small bottle to Charlie. "You're gonna need more water."

"Yeah, you're right," said Charlie after taking a generous swig. One more drink and Charlie had emptied the bottle.

Buck took the small bottle from him and filled it from his nearly full bottle. "That'll last you to the break," said Buck handing it back to Charlie.

"Thanks," said Charlie, but Buck had already started off down the hill toward his saw.

They each limbed two more trees before the ten-thirty break – "Union rules, no exceptions," Buck said tersely, as they walked down the hill toward the van and the orange water bucket that Charlie was eager to visit. Frenchy and Dogface were already at the truck eating apples. Frenchy reached into a bag in the truck, tossed Charlie an apple, and held up a huge palm for a high-five. The Canadian grinned. "Hey hey dere Charlie, you cut da wood like an old time logger up dere. I watch you some time and you do some good work. First day and you keepin' up okay dere wid Bucky, aye?" He looked over toward Buck with a wide grin. "Course Bucky ain't a real logger though. More of a painter or a sheet-rocker maybe, when he gets da work, aye Bucky?" Dogface was also grinning in Buck's direction.

Buck just ignored the Canadians as he went to the back of the truck. He reached into the bag, took out two apples and went and sat down on an old stump.

Charlie slumped onto the back bumper of the truck, eating his apple, drinking water from his refilled Dasani bottle and wondering if he was going to last all day. Frenchy laughed at Charlie's exhaustion. "You be okay dere Charlie. We cut seven, eight more trees before lunch and den afternoon be much easier, buckin' the trunks. We get done early and den just relax for a while. Maybe have some fun," he said, with a wink to Dogface.

Frenchy and Dogface sat down on a wide, gray boulder next to the road, eating their apples. "Hey Bucky," said Frenchy, "how's dat soccer team of your wife's dere you was tellin' us about, aye? Still winnin' everyting?"

Buck glanced over at Charlie at the mention of his wife. Their eyes met. Charlie smiled. "Yeah, how *are* the *Bones* doing lately?" he asked, surprised that Buck had even mentioned the team to the other loggers.

Buck shrugged to hide any real enthusiasm for the team, but his voice gave him away. "Won again last night. Eight - nothin' ass kickin'. Schmuck team up in Keystone. Not even a game."

"So when do they go to dat tournament dere in Charleston?" asked Frenchy.

Buck squinted painfully into the sun and shook his head. "Nat don't think they're goin' now 'cause a the two best players they got getting suspended for the tournament. Says she got a meetin' next Tuesday to try to appeal but it ain't gonna do no good, so she ain't takin' the team up there without their two best players."

"Where's the appeal hearing going to be?" asked Charlie, trying to sound just mildly curious.

Buck eyed Charlie warily for a few seconds and shrugged his shoulders as he looked away. "Gonna be at Kyle Loftus' office in Welch. Prick scheduled it for two o'clock just to make it tougher on Nat to be there, her workin' and everything."

Two o'clock on Tuesday. Not much time. Charlie wondered if Natty was even going to go to the hearing now, but for what he had in mind, it almost didn't matter. He stood up slowly from the bumper of the truck and tossed away his apple core into the weeds. He filled his Dasani bottle at the water cooler under the amused eyes of the loggers. "I need to check in with the plant," said Charlie, starting out toward the hill. "See you up top," he said to Buck.

Charlie unzipped the pocket on the side of his bag and took out his cell phone. He clicked through the electronic directory until he came to several numbers for Vernon Yarbrough. He chose the lawyer's cell phone – he didn't have time to be leaving voice-mail messages.

"Yarbrough," the lawyer growled after four rings.

"Hello Vern . . . Charlie Burden." Charlie smiled as he visualized the look on the face of the lawyer whom he had lambasted at the Angel Mountain raid inquest in the Dietrich Delahunt & Mackey boardroom. That was the last time they had spoken.

"Yeah Burden, what can I do for you?"

"Well Vern, I need a favor."

"Uh huh, a favor." Charlie could hear a door close as Yarbrough paused, probably to get comfortable in a big leather chair behind a big mahogany desk.

"Now Burden, why don't you remind me again just why it is that I should give a *flying fuck* about *anything* you might want."

Charlie chuckled at the predictable response. "Hey, c'mon Vern, you're more of a team-player than that, I know you are. Plus you're forgetting how I saved your ass on the Angel Mountain thing."

"Saved my *what?*" Yarbrough said, loudly. He was getting peeved.

It was time for Charlie to get serious, plus Buck was starting back up the hill. Charlie got up and started moving into the woods to stay out of Buck's earshot. "Okay Vern, listen. You're still on retainer to CanAmex, and when I'm here, I speak for my client. Plus, this concern's DeWitt's granddaughter and it could help in the eminent domain hearing." He knew he had the lawyer's attention now.

After a few seconds of silence, Yarbrough gave in. "Okay Burden, what's it about? Charlie went quickly through the story of Natty's team, *The Bones,* the soccer game in Welch and the fight, the Charleston tournament, and the suspensions of Emma and Zack. Yarbrough remained silent through it all, but Charlie could tell he was taking notes – the professional lawyer under all circumstances.

"The hearing's Tuesday, in Welch, at this guy Loftus' office."

"Not much time to get ready," said Yarbrough.

"Yeah, I know. I just found out about it."

"So what do you want *me* to do?" asked Yarbrough

Charlie smiled. "Do what you do best Vern. Show up at the hearing and plead Mrs. Oakes' case and get Loftus to lift the suspensions."

"And all this has *what* to do with the eminent domain hearing?"

Charlie took in a deep breath. "Vern, you do this and I'll see that Natty Oakes doesn't testify at the hearing."

Yarbrough let out a deep laugh. "Burden, that girl can get up and dance naked on the judge's bench for all I care. She can testify 'til she's blue in the face . . . come December we'll still be makin' footballs out a them pigs and havin' a nice chicken barbecue up on that farm while we blow the top off of Angel Mountain."

"Well Vern, you're probably right," Charlie said softly, "but you may not like some of the things she could be testifying about. Some things the PUC may not like hearing about either."

The threat sat there between them like a lit firecracker for a few seconds while Yarbrough quickly went over in his mind everything that Charlie Burden could know about the taking of Angel Mountain. They both already knew which side Charlie was on, so the propriety of him passing information on to Natty Oakes to make public was a moot point. Finally, in the face of uncertainty, which all lawyers detest, he chose the path of least risk, as Charlie knew he would. Showing up in Welch to stare down a small-town insurance man wasn't heavy lifting for Vernon Yarbrough, plus it would be a day's worth of billable hours toward the retainer plus some inflated travel expenses.

"Okay Burden, okay, "he said softly. "I don't need anything you're sellin' today, but I'll help you out. I'll do what I can, but I can't promise anything because we don't have a lot of time."

Charlie smiled through the phone. "Vern, I'm just sorry we never got that round of golf in at your club. That would have been fun."

"Yeah, maybe next year Burden," the lawyer said without conviction.

"Yeah, next year we'll do it Vern. See you Tuesday in Welch." Charlie put the phone away and went back to work.

Like Buck on the next tree over, and Frenchy and Dogface who were gradually getting closer to them, Charlie fell into an unhurried but productive rhythm, moving steadily down the tree trunk, the rest of the world blocked out by the noise of the saw and the earplugs and goggles, alone with his thoughts and the work in front of him. Maybe it was this one-on-one-with-nature feeling of isolation that appealed to loggers and made them love this job in the woods to the point that all other work was unsuitable. Even though it was a job for younger men, Charlie could understand the siren song of the forest for woodcutters.

He spent the next two hours locked in this vacuum of physical exertion, noise and extreme contentment, working on a fantasy of being a lumberjack and having a house in the woods on a lake, and in his daydream, Natty was his wife and Pie and Cat their children. It was a warm, wonderful daydream.

A tap on the shoulder and Charlie turned to see Buck's small, dark eyes boring into him. A flash of fear went through him as he wondered for a moment if Buck was looking into his mind and could somehow read his thoughts and see that he was thinking about Natty. "Lunch," said Buck gesturing down toward the truck and then turning abruptly to go up the hill toward his duffle bag.

Frenchy and Dogface laughed when Charlie opened up his lone, tiny peanut butter sandwich. Buck just shook his head. Frenchy insisted that Charlie take a half of his second roast beef sandwich and Dogface tossed him a large orange. They all drank water from the cooler. Charlie and Dogface sat eating on the boulder, Buck back on his seat on the stump, and Frenchy sat on the ground in the shade of the truck leaning back against a rear wheel. The cloudless sky had turned a dark blue and the sun cut through the cool autumn air and felt warm on their thighs and shoulders. Charlie lifted his face to the sun, the sweet smell of fresh sawdust and tree sap in his nostrils, and wondered if this wasn't the best occupation in the world.

While they were having lunch, Charlie noticed that Frenchy would occasionally turn and look off down the gulley, past the downed trees they were working on and up towards the dark forest that continued along the ridge line. From the boulder where he sat, Charlie could see a stand of massive fir trees about fifty yards beyond where they were working. He could make out the spray-painted red X marking most of the trees. Frenchy, he surmised, was probably evaluating his work for the rest of the week.

Finishing his sandwich, Frenchy sprang to his feet, picked up his water bottle and started out down the gulley. "I take a little walk," he said over his shoulder, "den I come back and we cut up dese logs for da helicopter, and be done for today, aye boys?" He didn't wait for a response.

Charlie and Buck went back up the hill and started working on the last of the trees to be limbed. Dogface had gone all the way back to the beginning of the downed trees and had started cutting the big trunks in half to accommodate the weight the helicopters could lift. In the other direction, Charlie saw Frenchy climbing up the long slope, leaning back occasionally to survey the towering fir trees at the top of the ridge. A few minutes later, when he glanced down toward where Dogface was working, there was Frenchy, back on his saw, powering through the center of a large yellow Oak, sawdust flying around him, the big saw screaming at the hard wood.

It was three o'clock by the time Buck and Charlie had finished with the limbs and went back to where they had started to begin bucking the logs in half. This felt more like lumberjacking now to Charlie, slicing through the thick trunks with long, sustained cuts, the saw whining at its loudest, his legs and boots covered with sawdust, and the smell of fresh sap and bar oil filling the air. Even as his arms began to shake with fatigue from the long day's work, he was reveling in the satisfaction of what they had accomplished that day. It was a feeling he hadn't experienced in a long time. Just after four o'clock, they met Frenchy and Dogface in the middle.

"Hokay Charlie," said Frenchy, turning off his saw. "Das a good job you do today." He held up his hand for a high five.

"We all done for the day?" asked Charlie, his arms and back aching for rest.

Frenchy hefted his bag over his shoulder and picked up his saw. He looked down towards Buck who was already halfway down to the truck and then up towards the tall pine forest farther down the ridge. "Yeah, well maybe we still got some fun ahead of us before we go back." He turned and grinned at Dogface. "Aye, Dog man?" Dogface just rolled his eyes and shook his head.

When they reached the truck with the equipment, Buck was sitting on the stump eating an apple. "Bucky you do some good woodcutting today," said Frenchy grinning. "You are for sure now a real lumberjack."

Buck tossed the apple away and got to his feet. "Yeah great. Now let's get the fuck outta here. I got a beer waitin' for me down the *Roadhouse*."

Frenchy dropped his saw and duffle in the sand and reached into the truck for an apple. "Hey what's the hurry dere Bucky, huh? Is still early, and maybe Dog and me, we got a little proposition for you and Charlie, aye?"

"I don't want to hear it Frenchy. Let's go."

Frenchy started walking down the road in front of the truck eating his apple. "C'mon Bucky, I want to show you something you don't see so very often."

Buck sighed with disinterest but his curiosity was piqued. He slowly followed Frenchy down the gulley. Charlie and Dogface followed Buck. Frenchy walked about fifty yards down the road and then started up the slope to his right toward the ridgeline, stopping halfway up.

"Yeah, so what's the deal?" said Buck coming up next to him.

Frenchy was looking up the hill. "See dem two big firs, side by each up dere Bucky?" Buck, and Charlie and Dogface, looked up toward the top of the hill where two magnificent fir trees, each over 100 feet tall, dominated the ridgeline. They looked to be at least three feet across. Both wore red spray-painted X's, marking them for removal.

"Yeah, we'll cut 'em down tomorrow, next week, so what?" said Buck, turning to go back.

Frenchy grabbed his arm. "Bucky, dem two trees is like identical twins. Same size each one, same wood. And look how *big* dey are," he said pointing up toward the trees. "Bucky," he implored, "we may never get da chance again to take down such a tree by hand." He clapped a big hand on Buck's shoulder. "Like dey did in da old days, aye?"

"Nah, I ain't in the mood Frenchy." Buck shook his arm free and started walking. "Plus Burden ain't a woodcutter."

Frenchy spit some of his apple onto the ground. "I tink Charlie already must be more woodcutter den you for walking away from a tree cuttin' contest." Buck stopped in his tracks and spun around to glare at Frenchy. Frenchy grinned and held up a fifty dollar bill. "Fifty bucks for da first tree down, me and Dog, you and Charlie, wid the two-man saws. You pick your tree."

Charlie could see Buck's jaw muscles twitch and his eyes narrow with anger. He obviously wasn't used to backing down from a challenge. His eyes flickered for a moment back up toward the big trees, and then back to Frenchy. "No, that's stupid," he spit out quietly. "Burden ain't a woodcutter." He turned again and started walking down the hill.

"We'll do it," said Charlie loudly. Buck stopped and looked at Charlie. "You got a bet," said Charlie looking up at Frenchy.

Frenchy laughed and clapped his hands together loudly. "Well hokay Charlie. Atta a boy!" He looked at Buck and pointed at Charlie. "You see dere Bucky? Charlie, he's a *real* woodcutter he is."

Buck strode quickly over to Charlie and pulled him far enough away from the other two men, not to be overheard. He leaned in close and whispered angrily. "Burden, you don't know what the fuck you're getting' into here. You ever take a big tree down with a crosscut saw that's dull as a butter knife? Halfway through, you'll think your back is on fire and your arms are gonna fall off, but you can't stop. You ever feel *anything* like that?" Buck didn't wait for an answer. He lowered his voice again. "Listen Burden, these guys, they're fuckin' pros at this shit. This is what they do, Frenchy and Dog, they enter lumberjack contests *man*. *Christ* they been on *ESPN*," he pleaded.

Charlie took a deep breath and squinted up toward the big trees for a moment and then glanced over at Frenchy and Dogface who were both grinning back at him. He looked back at Buck and shrugged his shoulders. "So *what. Fuck 'em.*" he said softly. "We can beat these guys." He whirled away from Buck and went back toward Frenchy and Dogface. "You're on Frenchy," said Charlie, reaching for his wallet. "But it's *two hundred* – a hundred bucks a man," he said pulling out two hundred dollar bills.

Frenchy clapped his hands together again and broke into a huge grin. "Well das why you da *big mule* Charlie!"

Buck pushed by Charlie and went up the slope a few steps, eyeing the two big trees. "One condition," he said, turning to Frenchy, "gotta hit the water bucket with the trunk."

Frenchy laughed again and threw away his apple core. "Whatever you want Bucky," he said starting off purposefully down the hill toward the truck. He and Dogface exchanged a high-five. "We land dat tree smack on Charlie's little bitty water bottle if dat make it better for you," he called back. He and Dogface laughed their way down the slope.

At the truck Buck and Frenchy both threw several iron wedges, a mallet and an axe in their bags, and then pulled out the long two-man crosscut saws. They sprayed them down with lubricating oil and examined the teeth and handles, finally agreeing that there was no advantage to either saw. At the yellow water cooler, Buck filled his plastic bottle and then Frenchy and Dogface did the same. Buck put the two liter bottle to his mouth, drained half of it without stopping and then handed it to Charlie. "Drink it all," said Buck. "You're going to need it."

While Charlie was still drinking, Buck kicked over the plastic water cooler sending the remaining water into the sand. He tossed his bag to Charlie, hefted the long crosscut saw over his left shoulder, picked up the empty water bucket in his right hand and started off down the logging road after Frenchy and Dogface who were already headed up the toward the ridgeline.

The two fir trees were twenty yards apart and to Charlie, they were even bigger – nearly three feet wide – than they looked from the bottom of the hill. Buck took his time examining both trees before he chose the tree on the right as they looked down the slope.

"Whoa dere Bucky! I tink you might a taken da wrong tree dere," said Frenchy moving his equipment to the base of the other tree. "Dis tree look a little more tired den at one." Frenchy and Dogface shared a laugh over Frenchy's gamesmanship.

"Trees both the same," Buck said to Charlie as he spread out the wedges, axe and mallet at the base of their tree. "But this one'll fall straighter I think."

Buck and Frenchy went down the slope to position the water cooler. They maneuvered a loose two-foot tall stump to a spot fifty feet down the slope where the falling trunk of either tree would hit it without interference from the high branches. They negotiated a position equidistant between the two trees and placed the yellow plastic barrel on top. It was an inviting target.

Buck jogged back up the slope. "Let me see your hands," he said, rummaging in his duffle bag. Charlie took off his gloves and displayed his palms. Buck pulled open a jar of Vaseline and smeared Charlie's hands with it. "You'll be bleedin' through your gloves in ten minutes without this." Buck brought Charlie around to the front of the tree and showed him how they were going to cut a notch centered on the line to the water cooler. He kept his voice low. "Frenchy won't bother with a notch. He'll figure he can hit it without one, but this's real stringy wood, tough shot."

They went back behind the tree and Buck explained how they were going to cut on a slightly downward angle about a foot into the tree, and then hammer the wedges in to keep the saw from binding. "Tree settles down on the saw, your done." Buck picked up a handle of the saw to show Charlie how to grip it. "Lean into the tree and pull hard, don't push, and don't stop. Use your legs and your back and arms, all together."

"I'll learn as we go," said Charlie with a grin.

Buck leaned in a little closer. "Listen Burden, I got to tell you . . ." He lowered his voice even more. "I ain't got a hundred bucks on me, so . . ."

"We're not going to lose," said Charlie with a grin. "I guarantee it." Buck rolled his eyes nervously and shook his head as he stood up, pulling his gloves on.

Frenchy and Dogface had taken their shirts off even though the air was cooling rapidly as the late afternoon sun dropped behind the hills to the west. Tying a new bandana across his forehead, his orange gloves tucked into the front of his pants, Frenchy walked over toward Charlie and Buck. The muscle definition of his chest and shoulders under his suspenders was indeed intimidating. Charlie was reminded of a professional wrestler. The lumberjack had a serious look on his face. "Okay Charlie,' he said, pointing to a spot ten yards behind and off to the side of tree, "when she starts to go, you move quickly to way back here." He picked up a few loose branches on the ground and tossed them aside. "Don't go directly behind the stump, and don't wait. When you hear it crackin', you go quick, aye Charlie? And you watch up overhead. Dese trees be bringing down some limbs wit dem."

Charlie looked over his escape route and nodded.

"Okay den Bucky," said Frenchy with a big grin as he backtracked to his tree. "You say when."

Charlie and Buck started in front of the tree with a horizontal cut for the notch. With their first few stokes, Charlie suddenly realized how difficult a task it was going to be to bring down the huge tree. Even after they got the timing of their stroke coordinated, it felt like the old saw would take hours to go all the way through the massive tree between them. Compared to the chain saws they had used all day, the crosscut saw was – as Buck had described it – like using a butter knife.

When they finally completed the notch and moved to the rear of the tree, it seemed to Charlie that they were already too far behind in the race to catch up. With his back to the other tree, he could hear that Frenchy and Dogface were stroking their saw at a faster and more powerful tempo than he and Buck. *He must have lost his mind, betting two hundred dollars on a tree cutting contest with two professional lumberjacks!* "C'mon Buck," Charlie exhaled, "a little faster."

Buck glanced past Charlie towards the other tree. "We're okay Burden. Just lean into the cut. We're okay."

Gradually they settled into a strong, powerful rhythm, with Charlie simply trying to mimic Buck's technique. Charlie was impressed with Buck's strength as his shoulder and neck muscles bulged with each stroke. He was also impressed with Buck's focus and drive, as his small, dark eyes burned brightly with the flame of competitiveness. As Buck's face gradually lit up with determination, it occurred to Charlie that Buck was having his first enjoyable moment of the day, and also, that he was a man who didn't like to lose. Buck, he could see was a match for either of the lumberjacks at the next tree. Now, if only Charlie could hold up his end. And it was getting tougher with every stroke.

After ten minutes, Charlie's hands and arms were burning and they weren't even a third of the way through the tree. He tried to use more leg and back, but he could feel the fresh scar tissue across his back protesting the abuse. He was having trouble catching his breath and the sweat had started to pour freely from his forehead, into his eyes, stinging and salty, but he couldn't let go of the saw to wipe them so he just shook his head violently.

"Doin' okay Burden," Buck exhaled. "Stay strong. Long, strong pulls. You got it."

Buck's words helped. Charlie breathed deeply and set his jaw and got mad at the tree. He ignored the pain in his hands and back and focused on each individual pull, leaning hard into the tree for the maximum cut on each stroke.

Charlie and Buck were about a foot into the tree when they heard Frenchy and Dogface stop and start hammering the iron wedges into the cut behind their saw. It only took them a few seconds before they were back on the saw, again ripping through the big tree at an aggressive pace. It wasn't a good sign. Charlie looked over at Buck who shook his head. "Another six inches," he grunted, which meant they were that far behind Frenchy.

They cut hard for another few minutes before Buck suddenly stopped. "Wedges," he said breathlessly, scrambling behind the tree picking up the axe and the big wedge for the center of the cut. Charlie welcomed the moment of relief from the saw but found that he had trouble making his arms work as he reached for his wedge and the mallet. He felt like he was moving in slow motion. Finally he got the wedge into the cut and managed a feeble hit with the mallet, just as Buck landed a massive blow to the big wedge with the back of the axe. "Watch out," said Buck, taking a step toward Charlie while bringing the axe back for another long left-handed swing. Charlie had hardly moved when Buck brought the axe through the air with a powerful swing, landing a loud, metallic blow dead on Charlie's wedge, sending it well into the cut. Buck stood up and looked down the slope at the yellow water bucket to see if they were on target. "Okay," he said, tossing the axe to the front of the tree. "Let's go."

For the next ten minutes, Charlie and Buck leaned into the saw with long, powerful strokes. Charlie's hands and arms and back were beyond hurting, and his light gray, long-sleeved tee shirt was now completely dark with sweat as were the front of his blue jeans down to the thighs. The wound on his back was burning and he thought he could feel skin tearing apart with each pull of the saw. He could feel the liquid seeping down his back but he couldn't tell if it was just sweat until he looked down and noticed the creeping ooze of dark maroon coming around the left side of his shirt at the ribs. Inside his right glove, Charlie could also feel the burn of torn away blisters and the slippery combination of blood and loose skin.

He looked over at Buck and saw the look of determination still set on his face, the dark eyes dancing back and forth between their saw, and Frenchy's tree.

"Doin' great Burden. Doin' great," Buck spit out between breaths, the sweat flying from his brow. "We're gonna beat these assholes Burden." Charlie thought Buck almost smiled. Inside the bloody glove Charlie squeezed his right hand tighter around the ancient wooden handle and gritted his teeth as he leaned into the stroke as hard as he could.

They were just beyond the halfway point through the trunk when a cold wind started blowing through the trees. The sun had disappeared behind the dark forest and the temperature was dropping quickly. Twigs and small branches started raining down on them as the tops of the trees swayed menacingly in the darkening sky far above them. Numb with pain, Charlie started to feel the chills and nausea of hypothermia as the cold wind blew against his sweat-soaked clothing and hair. He thought he might pass out.

"Dogface is crampin'" Buck said in an excited whisper. "Dog's crampin' up."

Behind them, Charlie could hear that the other saw had slowed its pace noticeably. He turned his head for a quick glance over at the other tree and saw that Dogface had a look of excruciating pain on his face and that Frenchy was talking to him in a low voice, coaching him through it. As he turned back to his own tree, Charlie vomited on his right arm, a watery milky liquid sprinkled with what looked like small pieces of red apple skin. He spit repeatedly to try to break the long strings of saliva that hung down from his mouth to the front of his shirt, before deciding to just ignore them.

The wind swirled harder sending the tops of the trees swaying back and forth, knocking loose some larger, old dead limbs. The men could hear the hollow sound of the fragile branches falling through the tree and instinctively hugged the trunk a little closer. As the big tree moved in the wind, Charlie could hear the trunk groaning and felt the big roots heaving beneath his feet. A large limb crashed through the branches above them, splintering into a shower of dead wood that hit the ground around them, and Charlie suddenly realized the danger of the situation they were in with two massive trees ready to crash to the forest floor after occupying the space above them for a hundred and fifty years. These trees weren't going to go meekly.

Buck sensed his partner's anxiety. "C'mon Burden, don't let up,' he yelled. "Pull hard, we're almost there."

Charlie closed his eyes to shut out the pain and the fear and continued to pull the saw through the stubborn old tree as best he could but his stroke was slowing with every pull as all feeling in his arms and hands were gone. "Buck," he rasped softly with no saliva left in his mouth, "this is the last tree I ever cut down."

Then the wood popped like a firecracker next to Charlie's ear, jarring his eyes open. The cut had widened several inches and when he looked up, he could see that both trees were leaning slightly downhill. Then the wind picked up again sending the tops of the trees swaying sideways. Buck was in front of the tree now, driving the axe violently into the notch to adjust the fall angle, yelling to be heard over the wind. "She's goin' Burden, move back!" he shouted.

"Charlie, get back!" yelled Frenchy, still responsible for Charlie's safety.

Charlie pried his hands off the saw handle and tried to run back to the spot that Frenchy had pointed out to him earlier. But his legs were too weak and they gave out at the knees, dropping him to all fours. He scrambled slowly like a wounded dog over the bare ground that was littered with twigs, branches and pine needles, feeling the earth under him heave in protest as the big roots strained to keep the old trees upright. Then an ungodly explosion of cracking wood made Charlie spin around onto his seat to watch the violent ending. He was amazed to see Buck standing next to the tree with the axe in one hand, watching as both trees simultaneously began their long, final trip to earth. Frenchy, also impervious to the danger, had moved over to a position between the two trees and stood with his hands on hips to watch the trees fall.

Then the trees disappeared from Charlie's view, crashing thunderously to earth down the slope, sending a cloud of dust high into the air and eerily illuminating the area around the stumps with daylight as if the shades of the forest had suddenly been thrown open..

Charlie watched the two men for their reaction. They both stood motionless for several seconds. Then Buck bent at the knees and sprang into the air while letting out a mighty whoop. With one long stride and an athletic jump, he was on top of the fallen tree trunk, arms raised into the air with one hand wielding the big axe like it was a toy. "*Yeah baby!* That's what I'm talkin' about boys and girls!" Buck was strutting down the log, bouncing on bent knees, arms overhead, and bobbing his head forward and back like a turkey. "*Direct fucking hit* is what I'm lookin' at here woodcutters." Buck was grinning ear to ear as he came back up the log. "Hey, c'mon Burden," he yelled, noticing Charlie still sitting on the ground back in the safety zone. He waved a hand motioning Charlie forward. "C'mon, you gotta see this, man!" he called out.

Charlie struggled to his feet and limped toward the fallen tree. He was beginning to feel his arms and hands again and managed a smile toward his partner. Buck disappeared again, dancing down the trunk of the tree. Frenchy had come over and met Charlie at the top of the slope with his hand extended and his usual grin back on his face. "So when was da last time you have dat much fun, aye Charlie?"

Charlie laughed. "Yeah, been a while." He looked down the slope and saw Buck, grinning up at him, standing on top of the wide log directly over the spot where beneath it, shards of torn yellow plastic were sticking out from the flattened water cooler. Charlie grinned at Buck, and chuckled, and then had to laugh as Buck strut crazily up the log toward him. Buck was laughing too, and it seemed to Charlie like it was the first time Buck had laughed in a long time.

Frenchy was also enjoying Buck's performance. He stood to the side of the stump grinning, watching Buck, and then clapped his hands together several times. "Hokay boys, good job, Buck and Charlie. Good job," he repeated. Buck took Frenchy's hand. "Das some good woodcutting dere Bucky," he said softly as they shook hands. Frenchy handed Buck two, hundred-dollar bills and winked at him. "Next time we don't give you Charlie for a partner."

Charlie sat down on the stump, exhausted, watching Frenchy and Dogface walk down the hill toward the truck with their equipment. *Just another day at the office for the lumberjacks, capped off by a delightful 'happy hour' on the two-man crosscut saw taking down the biggest tree in the forest.* He poured the little bit of water remaining in the *Dasani* bottle over his bloody right palm. The flesh had been rearranged in ugly white folds and he couldn't close his hand, but he knew from past experience that it would be okay in about a week.

Behind him Charlie heard Buck gather up the equipment and drop his bag on the ground a few yards away. Charlie turned his head just in time to see Buck pull a long hunting knife out of a hard leather sheath as he came up behind him. The blade glistened in the dim light, but Charlie's tired body was incapable of any evasive movement. He glanced down the hill quickly for the other men but they were nowhere in sight. He instinctively tightened his back muscles.

"Hold still," said Buck, gingerly peeling up the bottom of Charlie's bloody tee shirt. The razor – sharp knife sliced easily through the middle of the wet shirt up to the neckline. "Christ Burden, little grunt work and you city guys just fall apart," Buck said with a chuckle. He pulled the shirt carefully away from Charlie's bloody back, then over each shoulder and tossed it to the ground.

"It's an old wound," said Charlie. Buck handed him a clean long-sleeved tee shirt from his bag, and a bandana to wrap his hand in. The shirt felt warm and dry. Charlie put it on and just slumped down on the stump where he sat, too tired to move.

Buck jumped up and sat on the end of the fallen trunk next to the stump. "Say Burden," Buck said, furrowing his brow, "how'd you know we could beat those guys?"

Charlie looked down the hill to where Frenchy and Dogface were putting their equipment in the truck. "Cause they were too cocky Buck." Charlie smiled up at him. "And we weren't."

"Yeah, that's for sure," said Buck, reaching into his front pocket and pulling out the bills that Frenchy had given him. "Here's your hundred." Charlie took it and stuffed it into his back pocket. "Buy you a drink down the *Roadhouse*, if you're goin'" said Buck.

Charlie smiled at the mention of the *Roadhouse*. "No," he said, "I think I'll get my hand wrapped and go soak in the tub."

Buck jumped up from his seat on the trunk, looked down the hill at the flattened water cooler and laughed again at the result. "Well I got three days off and a paycheck, plus a hundred a Frenchy's dollars in my pocket so I'll be goin' on a little toot myself."

Charlie squinted up at Buck from his seat on the stump. He tried to sound friendly. "Maybe you should just go *home* Buck."

Buck turned to Charlie slowly and the angry scowl he'd worn for most of the day, returned to his face. He glared at Charlie for a few seconds as if he was trying to decipher in his mind the implications of Charlie's words. "What do *you* know about my home Burden?" Buck spit out angrily.

Charlie shrugged and let out a sigh. He didn't want to get into it with Buck and he shouldn't have said anything, but now he had no choice. "What I *know* Buck," he said calmly, looking off down the hill, "is that one of these days, you're going to wake up and you'll be my age, and your kids will all of a sudden be grown up, and you'll have missed out on the most enjoyable thing there is in life." He looked up into Buck's dark eyes. "Being a father. Being a father to young kids who need you . . . a father to great kids, like you've got." Charlie frowned with disgust because he knew that Buck didn't get it. "You're going to miss it all Buck and you'll never get those years back." Charlie pushed himself up from the stump to try to end the conversation and get going. Buck had an angry, confused look on his face and he stood his ground in front of Charlie..

"So maybe *you'd* like to be goin' home in place a me, huh, that it? Like those boys was sayin' at the *Roadhouse* that night. All that stuff about runnin' with Nat and pallin' around with the kid, and . . ." Buck's voice was getting louder and he was inching closer to Charlie as he spoke . . . "and, I don't know what else you been doin'.""

Charlie wanted to turn away and just let it go, but he wasn't going to back down from Buck. "Nobody's been doin' anything Buck. The Pie Man was the first person I met down here and he's a *great* kid and I like him a real lot. And Natty showed me her running trail along the mountain and I ran with her a couple of mornings, and that's all. That's *it* Buck. That's what's going on." Charlie could feel his neck muscles tightening as the anger rose inside him. He forced himself to turn and stride away from Buck. He went around to the other side of the stump and reached down for the crosscut saw.

Buck went over and snatched up his equipment bag but wasn't ready to let the conversation end there. "Yeah, well maybe you ought a just stay the fuck away from my family," he said, sounding a little less combative as if he'd suddenly realized who he was talking to. "And just keep the fuck out of my business."

Charlie threw the saw down and moved back in front of Buck and put his face up close to the younger man. Charlie's jaw muscles bulged with anger as he put his left index finger up close to Buck's face. "Buck, I'll stay out of your business," he hissed through clenched teeth. "And you can go on being a shitty father and your kids'll do all right anyway. And you can keep being a shitty husband and someday soon you're going to lose Natty, whether I got anything to do with it or not." He pushed the end of his finger into Buck's chest. "But Buck," he lowered his voice, "you *ever* hit that girl again, I'm comin' after you." There was fire in Charlie's eyes. "You understand me Buck?"

Buck swallowed hard and glared back at Charlie with anger, but he didn't move or say anything for several seconds. Finally, the loud horn of the truck blared at the base of the hill. They both looked down to see that Frenchy had turned the truck around to head back and had his head out of the window, grinning up at them. "C'mon dere girls," he yelled up at them. "You can fuck echudder up de ass all daway back now. Let's *go*, aye?"

They rode back in silence in the back of the van, avoiding eye contact. Charlie opened up the first-aid kit and took out a small tube of antiseptic cream and a wide, gauze bandage package and put them into his canvas bag. Then he put his gloves back on, wincing as he pushed his swollen and skinned right hand into the stiff glove. He noticed Buck eyeing him curiously. Charlie smiled briefly. "Don't want you guys getting in trouble with Devine." Buck just looked away.

They were nearing the foreman's shed. Charlie reached down and zipped up his bag. "Listen Buck," he said softly, "thanks for all your help and everything today. I enjoyed it a lot, even pukin' all over myself." Buck couldn't keep a smile off his face. Charlie held out his gloved right hand. "You're a great woodcutter Buck. I'd cut down a tree with you any time." Buck took his hand briefly and nodded almost imperceptibly .

The truck stopped at the shed and Buck started to rise off the bench. Charlie spoke again. "Do me a favor Buck, will you?" Buck stopped to listen. "When you *do* get home, tell Pie about how we beat those two lumberjacks and cut that tree down and landed it right on top of that water bucket. Will you do that? Pie will get a real kick out of that."

Buck hesitated for a second, then shrugged as he started up out of the truck. "Yeah, sure," he grumbled lowly. "I'll tell him about it."

Chapter 29

The road into Welch was nearly deserted as were most of the downtown streets when Natty reached the town just before two o'clock. It wasn't always like this, she recalled. When she was a kid, it seemed like the huge coal trucks were always coming and going along the roads of McDowell County – straining and belching black smoke in one direction, banging and rattling along noisily with their empty bins on the return trips. And there were more logging trucks and pick-ups and cars . . . more of everything, once. McDowell County had changed a lot in the last twenty-three years.

Natty thought she knew where the Loftus Insurance Agency was, but now she was having doubts as she drove down Main Street and began to get anxious about being late. *It was just like Kyle to cancel the hearing if she was a minute late.* Then she chuckled to herself and sighed as she remembered the futility of the whole thing. *It was all a waste of time anyway, so what difference did it make if she was late? She wouldn't have even scheduled the hearing if it wasn't for Charlie, and now Charlie . . . she hadn't seen him for two weeks, and well, that was probably it for him.* Natty drew in a deep breath to fill the hole in her chest that came with thoughts of Charlie Burden.

She passed the Olander Legal Clinic just as Ted Olander, the lawyer she had gone to see a few months earlier, came out the front door. He glanced briefly at the red Accord and its driver, but showed no sign of recognition. Natty thought back about their meeting. *Boy, did he have those utility guys pegged right! 'Not like regular business people . . . cutthroats in fine suits . . . in the end, they aren't going to play fair.'* She should have listened to him. He was telling her about Charlie Burden.

The meeting was going to be a waste of time, and an enormous inconvenience – screwing up her day for a trip into Welch, and now she wouldn't get home until eight o'clock – but she owed it to Emma and Zack, and the rest of the team, to at least show up and try to get their suspensions for the tournament rescinded. Even if she just ended up telling off Kyle Loftus in front of the other two lackeys on the committee, she'd get some satisfaction out of it.

Then she saw the blue Lexus, and over it a sign for the Loftus Insurance Agency, and her heart raced and her palms became moist. She hadn't expected Charlie to show up after his wife had come to town, but there was no mistaking the car that was parked, angled-in, in front of the renovated modern brick and wood façade of the insurance agency that took up a large corner of one of Welch's many ancient stone buildings. She pulled in leaving a few spaces between her car and Charlie's, hurriedly twisted the rear-view mirror lower and scowled with disgust. Out of habit, she quickly pulled the shock of hair falling across her forehead a little lower over her left eyebrow. She put her hand on the mirror to push it back into place, but hesitated as she focused on her image in the small frame. She leaned forward and looked at her eyes, then raised up to see her mouth before slumping back in her seat. Natty gazed into the mirror but her mind was seeing Ellen Burden standing in the hallway outside Charlie's apartment, looking – *perfect* – *perfectly beautiful,* and so *confident,* her silky black hair shining, eyes made-up like a magazine model, and her lips painted an elegant dark maroon – a shade only beautiful women could wear. Natty wondered if she should start wearing a little eye makeup, and maybe even some lipstick once in a while – like she did for a time in high school, before Buck came back. Before she got too busy with a lot of other things to worry about makeup. *Never made much difference to anyone what I look like,* she said to herself as she pushed the mirror away and reached for the door handle.

Inside the vestibule of the agency, through a window to her right, Natty saw Charlie sitting in a small waiting area surrounded by tall green plants. He was wearing a black blazer, white shirt and silver tie. The professional outfit seemed strange to her, like he was different person than the one she knew. *But he* was *a different person than the one she knew, wasn't he?* Charlie sat with his legs crossed reading a Time Magazine.

To Natty's left as she entered the office, behind a counter, several women were busy on phones and at their computers. A man stood waiting at the counter with a handful of papers and a license plate. To her right sat a receptionist and behind her, a set of executive offices behind dark, smoked-glass, floor-to-ceiling windows. Several men were working at large desks in the comfortable looking offices. Natty was starting to feel intimidated by the professional look and sounds of McDowell County's largest insurance agency. She was also nervous about seeing Charlie for the first time since she'd come face-to-face with his incredible wife and realized what a charade this fantasy of hers was, and how Charlie had just been using her and Pie to help his company take Angel Mountain. She took a deep breath.

Straight ahead, an open door revealed a dark-paneled conference room from which Natty could make out the low murmur of men's voices. Just as she was about to step toward the receptionist's desk, Kyle Loftus appeared in the doorway of the conference room. He wore an expensive looking gray suit. "Mrs. Oakes, we'll be with you in just a minute," he said, flashing a quick smile and holding up an index finger. Then he saw Charlie sitting in the waiting area and the smile left his face. "He with you?"

Natty turned and saw that Charlie was on his feet and coming toward her. Charlie spoke before she did. "Yes, I'm with Mrs. Oakes," he said, with a quick smile to Natty, moving past her towards Loftus. "I reffed the game in question . . . remember? So I thought I should be here to make sure the facts are straight," he said as he brushed past Loftus and went into the conference room without bothering to offer his hand. Loftus hesitated and then followed, as did Natty.

Charlie introduced himself to the other two men and handed out business cards. "I'm in charge of the construction of the new power plant over in Red Bone," he said, to explain the New York City address on his card, but more to make sure they knew who they were dealing with. Kyle Loftus took a chair on the far side of the table and cursorily introduced the other members of the committee as *Frank* and *Dave.* Natty recognized one as a coach of one of the Welch little league baseball teams. The other, she knew was Loftus' brother-in-law and an employee of the Loftus Insurance Agency.

Charlie moved to the middle of the table and sat down, leaving two chairs open to his left. Natty sat down next to him. She smiled briefly at the other two men across the table, and waited for Loftus, who was sitting with his arms crossed and a bored look on his face. Finally he leaned forward and put his arms on the table.

"What we got here is a real simple issue, 'cause, as you may recall, I was *at* the game and saw everything that happened." Loftus glanced briefly at Frank and Dave, and gestured toward them with his left hand. "We discussed it all a couple of weeks ago and agreed, unanimously, that suspension of the two players from any post-season play was *completely* warranted under the rules and the bi-laws of this association." The other two men nodded in agreement. "So there it is," he said slapping the table lightly with the palms of both hands. He flashed a toothy smile at Natty and then at Charlie and raised his palms to invite a response. Charlie looked at Natty and remained silent.

"Well, um," Natty said softly, clearing her throat. "It ain't fair, 'cause, you know it was all that other team's fault," she said, her voice rising. "That coach, and that kid Rudy, they started all the trouble and you *know* it Kyle and, well it ain't fair that my kids . . ."

Kyle Loftus was shaking his head impatiently. "Don't matter about the other team. The coach has been dealt with, and their season's over anyway so it don't matter about that kid. He ain't going to any tournament." Loftus looked at his watch.

Charlie leaned forward onto the table. "Well, it *does* matter," he said firmly, anger in his voice. "You've got two kids who are going to be harmed unfairly and a whole team that's going to be punished because," he looked directly at Kyle Loftus, "you and your buddy, the coach, got your egos bruised that day."

Loftus sat back in his chair with a wry grin. "Seems like somebody else took a little bruisin' that day." The two men next to him smirked knowingly.

Charlie banged the table with his fist. "This isn't *about* me or anything that happened after that game," he said angrily. "Now I want you guys to do the right thing, right now, and let those kids play in the tournament."

Kyle Loftus sniffed and shook his head. "That ain't gonna happen my friend," he said, pushing his chair away from the table. He pointed an index finger at Natty. "Natty, you take that girl and that black boy up to Charleston, they ain't gonna let your team on the field." He slapped the table and smiled. "And *that's* the name a that tune."

Loftus was startled as Vernon Yarbrough filled the doorway of the conference room. Loftus scowled with irritation. "Help you with something there fella'?" Loftus said, as Yarbrough entered the room followed by the bespectacled Leonard in a three-piece suit carrying a large aluminum briefcase.

Vernon Yarbrough just smiled pleasantly as he came to the edge of the table. He tossed a business card down softly in front of Kyle Loftus and then to each of the men next to him. As they examined his card, the lawyer turned to

Natty and held out his hand. "Mrs. Oakes, how nice to see you again." Natty remembered him from the pond hearing as they shook hands briefly. "Charlie," he said, reaching past Natty. "How's everything at the Red Bone project?"

"Everything's great Vern. It's going good," said Charlie, relieved that the lawyer had finally appeared. The presence of Leonard was also a nice touch.

"Well that's fine Charlie, that's fine," said Yarbrough remaining standing. "The Governor's real pleased with the way the whole project is going. Real interested in that new athletic complex you're building over there too. Matter of fact he'd like to come down and . . ."

Kyle Loftus cleared his throat loudly causing Yarbrough to glance at him sharply. He started to speak but Yarbrough cut him off. "Why certainly, Mr. Loftus, you'd like to get down to business here. I can understand that." With his eyes still fixed on Kyle Loftus, Yarbrough held out a hand to Leonard who had taken the seat to Charlie's right. As Leonard opened the shiny briefcase, Yarbrough continued. "I'm here representing Mrs. Oakes, and the two juvenile victims in this matter, Emma Lowe and Zachary Willard." Leonard had pulled out three packets of documents, each about twenty pages stapled together, and reached over to hand them to his boss. Charlie could recognize from a quick glance at the cover pages that they were some sort of legal notice.

Yarbrough looked at the cover page of one packet and then tossed it down in front of Loftus's brother-in-law, smacking the table with its weight. Each of the other men then got their copies, which they picked up tentatively and began scanning the front page. Yarbrough sat down in the seat next to Natty. Leonard snapped his briefcase shut. After a few moments of allowing the men to glance briefly at the documents in front of them, Yarbrough leaned forward and put his arms on the table. "What you're looking at here gentlemen, is a million dollar civil suit against each of you for the irreparable harm you'll be causing my clients with this pernicious, discriminatory, and I might add, racially motivated decision of yours. I'm sorry, I should have asked earlier – are you men represented by counsel today?"

Frank and Dave looked at each other nervously. Kyle Loftus forced a thin smile and tossed the packet to the middle of the table. "This is bullshit. It's all bullshit," he said glancing at his brother-in-law. "It's *bullshit*. It's nothing," he said with a shrug, then sat back in his chair, crossing his arms defiantly.

Vernon Yarbrough put his elbows on the table and rubbed his palms together slowly in front of his face. "Hmm, *bullshit*," he said softly. "That's an interesting word . . . *bullshit*," he repeated, nodding pensively. Two seats away, Charlie cringed inwardly and had to suppress a smile as he awaited the eruption he knew was coming.

"So Mr. Loftus," the lawyer continued softly, "it's your contention that this morning I left my *very* comfortable office in Charleston, along with my associate Leonard here, to board a noisy and dangerous helicopter at the *Chuck Yeager Airport*," Yarbrough's voice was rising in volume and his words quickening, "for a ninety-minute flight down here to *godforsaken* McDowell County, to present to you gentlemen a carefully and professionally prepared legal document which is in fact -" He slammed the table top as he shouted. "*Just bullshit?*"

Yarbrough put one hand back on the arm of his chair and leaned forward across the table. His face was now flushed with anger and his jaw set tight. His voice was deep and loud, uncaring if he was overheard in the outer office. "Well gentlemen, let me tell you about that little pile of bullshit sitting in front of you! What you have there is a *minimum* of two years of litigation and a hundred thousand dollars in legal fees for each of you – I *shit you not gentlemen* – and in the end, we may not get the million, but we'll get six *goddamn good figures*, and I'll be going after your houses and your cars and your wives' little *pinky* rings just to cover *my* fee, and when you're done with my personally guided tour through the West Virginia tort system, you hillbillies' be riding *fucking* mules around these mountains sellin' long-term care insurance to dyin' coal miners!"

Yarbrough sprang to his feet slamming his chair hard against the wall. He held out his hand to Leonard while still staring angrily at the three men across the table. Leonard quickly snapped open the large briefcase and pulled out a manila folder, which he handed to his boss.

Natty sat in stunned silence, trying to grasp the idea that this monster of a lawyer could actually be on *her* side and feeling a little sorry for Loftus and the other men. Charlie crossed his hands over his mouth and nose to keep from chuckling.

"Now Mr. Loftus," said Yarbrough, with slightly less volume, "in your best interest sir, you and I need to caucus in private for a moment." He moved toward the door holding the file folder at his side.

Loftus, his face now locked in a nervous scowl, hesitated then got up and followed Yarbrough from the room. They went into Loftus' corner office behind the smoked-glass wall. Yarbrough noticed a floor-to-ceiling curtain along the wall and pulled it closed.

The insurance man took refuge in the tall leather chair behind his desk and motioned for Yarbrough to take a seat in front of it. The lawyer ignored him and came around behind the desk and stood menacingly at Loftus' side. He tossed the file down on the desk and spoke softly. "Now Mr. Loftus, what you got to do right now is to pick out which one of those pictures in there you'd like us to send to your wife."

Loftus opened the file and groaned. The first picture was an eight-by-ten, black and white shot of an overweight but very buxom woman in her mid – twenties with long, stringy blond hair, coming down an outside stairway from a second floor apartment. The next picture showed Kyle Loftus descending the same stairway. The third picture showed Loftus and the girl locked in an embrace on the top landing of the stairway.

"*Jesus Christ,*" Loftus moaned with pain, "this was just two days ago. How the hell? You put an investigator on me over this little league *crap*?"

Vernon Yarbrough reached down, closed the file and leaned in close to Loftus' ear. "My friend, you need to very quickly – within the next ten or fifteen seconds or so – fully embrace the idea that this issue is a lot more important to some very powerful people than it is to *you*. Then you need to go back into that conference room and make it right with that woman in there or believe me brother Loftus, I will make *fucking you over* my number one hobby well into my retirement years."

Natty got up and left quickly, as soon as Kyle Loftus came back into the room and announced, to the obvious relief of Frank and Dave, that the appeal was accepted and the suspensions were lifted. She shook hands and thanked Vernon Yarbrough for his help on her way out, but avoided looking at Charlie.

Out in the street, Natty walked quickly to her car. As she reached for the door handle, she heard Charlie behind her, standing on the other side of his car. "Good luck Nat," he said.

Natty froze for a few seconds, not wanting to turn and see the man who had been such a huge part of her life for the past four months, even if he had been using her and Pie. But, she knew she still owed Charlie a lot, especially for Vernon Yarbrough's appearance today. Finally, she turned with her arms crossed at her chest, and looked at Charlie. He smiled back. "Well that's a start," he said.

A dark blue Ford Crown Victoria slid to a stop in the sandy street in front of the insurance agency. The two men in the front seat both wore dark sunglasses. Natty and Charlie turned to see Vernon Yarbrough and Leonard clamber into the back seat. The big car accelerated noisily up the street.

Natty watched the Ford drive away as she ambled slowly over to the side of the Lexus, then looked down through the glass roof. "I used to have a car like this," she said. She looked up and smiled briefly at Charlie across the top of the car. "For a week." Charlie smiled and waited.

"Thanks Charlie, for today, for doin' this." She nodded back toward the insurance agency.

"Yeah well, I had to make a little deal with the lawyers for that," said Charlie. He leaned onto the top of the car with his hands clasped in front of him. "Had to promise that you wouldn't be testifying at the eminent domain hearing on Angel Mountain."

Natty squinted with curiosity and tilted her head. "So, what do they think I might be testifying *about?*"

Charlie shrugged. "Nothing you could know about unless I told it to you."

Natty stared at Charlie for a few moments pondering what he had said. "And that wouldn't be good for you," she said, half as a question.

"Just stuff that wouldn't save Angel Mountain but might cause some problems with a merger that CanAmex is involved in."

Natty rolled her eyeballs in confusion. "Well, I ain't much for testifying anyway." After a few moments she looked off toward the hills surrounding Welch. "So Angel Mountain, that's a hopeless case now, right?"

Charlie sighed. "Yeah, it is I'm afraid. There's no stopping it now. The hearing's just going to be a formality."

"Yeah, that's what Bud says. That's what his lawyer told him." Natty chuckled. "Got a lawyer who's about eighty years old, an old friend from

Mullens." She nodded back toward the street where the Crown Victoria had stopped. "Nothing like the lawyers your side's got."

Charlie clenched his teeth and shook his head. "I'm sorry about Angel Mountain Nat. I tried to stop it, but . . . it was too big."

"Yeah, well anyway, the kids'll be real happy when I tell 'em they can play." Natty squinted into the low sun as a cloud moved out of the way. "Felt kind a good," she said with a brief smile, "for a change, bein' on the same side as the big boys, side with the expensive lawyers."

"Sometimes it helps," said Charlie.

Natty looked down the street where dust still hung in the air from the big car that took Yarbrough away. She thought about the meeting with Loftus and the file that Yarbrough had in his hand, and how abruptly it ended. And then she thought about Ellen Burden standing in the hallway and then hugging Charlie.

"How's Pie?" asked Charlie, cutting into her thoughts. "Haven't seen him in a while." Natty just shrugged her shoulders. "Haven't seen you around either," he continued. Natty didn't say anything. Charlie spread his fingers out on the moon roof in front of him. "So what happened Nat?"

Natty crossed her arms across her chest. She didn't want to have this conversation but now she had to. She shrugged with resignation. "Moment I saw. . . your wife standing in the door, I knew what a jerk I'd been . . . for thinkin' stuff about us, and for trusting you."

"Natty," Charlie protested.

She shook her head not to be interrupted. "Woman like that don't come all the way down to Red Bone lest she's really . . ."

"Nat, you've got that all wrong," said Charlie firmly.

Natty moved forward and put her arms on top of the Lexus, her fingers only a few inches away from Charlie's. She looked down through the tinted glass roof as she spoke, almost in a whisper. "Geeze Charlie, what are you doin', sayin' all that stuff to me when you got a wife like that at home?" She looked up at Charlie. "She's like a . . . movie star, or, like the President or something. She's . . ."

"I fell in love with someone else Nat." Charlie inched his left hand forward and their fingertips touched. Natty swallowed hard and looked down at their hands. "And I've never lied to you Nat, about anything. I told you how I felt, that night we went over to see Woody and Mr. Jacks. That was the truth."

After a few seconds she looked up at Charlie. "Did you tell her about . . ." she hesitated, afraid to say the word, "you know, what you said you were going to tell her?"

"I didn't have to. She knew. Said she knew, the moment you opened the door that night . . . she knew that I was . . . in love with you," Charlie said softly.

Natty looked down at her feet, stalling for time as she took deep breaths to slow her heart. She wasn't prepared to hear Charlie say the words. She said softly, "that night, standin' there lookin' at her in the hallway, all she had to do was say *boo* and I woulda peed in my pants."

Charlie laughed and watched her for a few moments before speaking again. "I met Buck last week. We cut down some trees together. Had a good day."

"Yeah, I heard," said Natty looking up, grateful for a change of subject. "Heard Buck tellin' Pie all about it. It was *real* nice, Buck tellin' Pie a story . . . first time in a long time Buck's said much of anything to Pie. All about cutting wood with Pie's pal *Charlie*. 'Bout how you two beat some real good loggers, cuttin' down a big tree and won a hundred bucks each. Pie was *so* proud. Had his *happy face* on for about an hour."

Charlie laughed. "Yeah, we had a good day."

Natty made a face. "Damn Charlie," she said softly, "couldn't you and Buck of just had a fistfight or something, like in the movies? You know, *fightin' over the girl* kind of thing?" Natty smiled. "Instead of becoming pals? Christ, now Buck's in love with you too." She looked up quickly when she realized what she had said.

Charlie looked away from her with a scowl on his face. "Well, Buck and I didn't exactly part company as best friends that day," he said.

"Why, what happened?"

He shrugged off the question. "Nothing. Just little stuff. How's Pie?" Charlie asked.

Natty wrinkled up her nose briefly. "Confused, I guess. Misses you, but mostly misses his computer." They both grinned. She shook her head ruefully. "My fault," she whispered. "My fault. I'll have him go see you."

"Yeah, I'd like to see him before I leave. Have to go up to New York for a while." Then he remembered the Red Bone Baptist Church trip to New York that coming weekend. "Are you still going on the New York trip?"

Natty smiled and shrugged her shoulders. "Well, I guess I'll have to now. No reason not to."

"Good. We'll go for a run. I'll meet you in front of your hotel, Saturday morning, six-thirty."

Natty smiled and nodded without saying anything. Finally she looked at her watch and straightened up off the car. "Got some old people I still need to see today. Gotta go. I'll see you in New York." She smiled inwardly at the way that sounded.

Charlie watched her get into the Honda and drive off, already thinking about seeing Natty in New York.

* * *

At the same time that Charlie and Natty walked out of the Loftus Insurance Agency in Welch, a gray Nissan Sentra – the cheapest car available at the Avis desk at the *Yeager Airport* in Charleston – labored slowly up Angel Mountain Road. The car went a short ways past the DeWitt farm before backing up and pulling in under the huge oak tree that had covered the driveway and Sarah's small flower garden with a thick layer of large, leathery, brown leaves.

The driver made a note in a small, tattered spiral notebook before getting out of the car. He was a tall, gaunt man in his late sixties or early seventies with a protruding adam's apple, a face full of deep lines, and permanently squinting eyes.

He wore an old gray suit, white shirt and tie, a rumpled khaki rain coat and a gray
fedora that had obviously served its owner for many years. The man glanced at his
watch and shook his head, perturbed with himself for being late. He should have
started out earlier.

As he lumbered slowly up the wooden stairs onto the porch, an observer
would wager that the man was a long-time insurance agent or encyclopedia
salesman, or maybe a process server, but not the owner and chief operative of the
largest private investigations firm in Toronto.

At the front door he took off his hat and shook hands with Bud and Alice
DeWitt. They knew who he was. The man had called on the phone a week earlier
and he and Bud chatted for a while and for some reason Bud trusted the man –
maybe it was his reference to growing up on a wheat farm in Manitoba – and
answered his questions about the farm and about attempts to buy the farm. And
now he was there, an hour later than he'd said he would be there, but he was there
at the farm wanting to know everything Bud and Alice could tell him about the
men who had come to see them, trying to buy the farm, in detail – names, dates,
the time they came, the time they left, what they'd said, how much they'd offered.
The man was particularly interested in everything Bud and Alice could remember
about the day the corn field burned – who was there, what was said, what was the
offer, how many vehicles, how many *police cars,* what kind of uniforms the men
were wearing. He didn't ask them anything about what was growing in the field or
how it burned, only about the men who came that day. Later the man would go up
and walk around the still charred ground of the field, and then around the
perimeter of the farm, and in the failing light of early evening he'd drive up to the
top of Angel Mountain, stopping first at the cemetery and the high pond, and then
up to where the green-boxed seismograph machines were still set up on the high
plateau, making frequent notations in the spiral notebook. He'd stay for dinner
with the DeWitts, listening attentively to Bud and Alice as he encouraged them to
talk about the family's history on Angel Mountain, offering little about himself or
his mission.

After refusing repeated offers to stay the night, the man made the four-hour
drive back to Charleston, took a room at a Quality Inn near the airport, and arose
early the next morning for a seven-thirty flight to Toronto.

*   *   *

A full crew was at work on the library – two men on the roof finishing up
the shingling, and several up on the outside scaffolding installing windows on the
second floor – trying to get the outside of the building buttoned up against the
approaching cold weather. As he pulled into the parking area just up the hill from
the library, Charlie could hear the familiar staccato *bang* of several carpenters'
hammers echoing around the empty interior, the sound of real work being done on
a project.

Charlie glanced up toward Old Red Bone, to the porch on the fourth floor to
see if Hank might be out enjoying the warmth of the setting sun, but the chairs

were empty. The backs of the buildings up on Main Street glowed a particularly warm shade of orange from the nearly horizontal rays of the late-afternoon November sun. It was a sight that Charlie knew he would miss dearly when the time came for him to leave Red Bone.

And that time, Charlie knew, could be much closer than originally planned. He thought again about the meeting in New York tomorrow afternoon that he had been summoned to. The message had come from Larry Tuthill, to meet with a committee of CanAmex, and Dietrich Delahunt & Mackey people, to review CanAmex projects that Charlie had previously been working on. Once, it would have seemed like a fairly benign meeting, scheduled for a Friday afternoon as they often were, so the CanAmex people would have an excuse for being in New York for the weekend. And the agenda was entirely plausible. But the fact that Terry Summers and Warren Brand were to be part of the meeting along with some other young DD&M employees that Charlie didn't know very well, was a warning signal. Friday afternoon was also the time when high level management coups were normally launched, to give the company two days to clean up the mess and manage the spin. With his recent history with CanAmex, the construction of the generating plant far ahead of schedule, and the *eminent domain* taking of Angel Mountain assured in another two weeks, Charlie knew he was now very expendable. There was a good chance that tomorrow he would have no job and no reason to return to Red Bone next week.

Charlie walked through the bottom floor of the library, inspecting the locker rooms and shower facilities, the storage areas, and the control room for the sprinkler systems and lights for the soccer and baseball fields. He chuckled as he looked over the complexity of all the controls and timers. Hank would have to find someone who could learn how to work it all.

He went up the stairs to the second floor where the powerful aroma of new wood construction flooded his senses with a wave of *déjà vu* – as it always did – of so many projects he had worked on in the good years of his career, before he ended up staring into a computer and going from one meeting to another. Sawdust, trimmings, tape, twine, nails, and all the other detritus of construction littered the floor. That was the way carpenters worked and eventually it would all come together in a beautifully finished project with little evidence of the many, many hours of skilled craftsmanship that produced it. Over the years, walking through many projects, Charlie had often lamented the fact that he had chosen engineering over finish-carpentry as a career. More often than not, carpentry seemed to him to be a much more rewarding and satisfying occupation and he never passed up the opportunity to grab a hammer and do some framing, or miter a corner of molding for one of the carpenters patient enough to let Charlie intrude on his work.

Walking up the wide center stairway to the upper floor, Charlie smiled at how beautifully the light from the skylights illuminated and filled the floor with warmth. The several small, partitioned reading nooks would be wonderfully cozy and welcoming spots for the children and (Charlie had no doubt), many of the adults of Red Bone.

There were no workmen on the floor, although just overhead Charlie could hear the crackling footsteps and muffled voices of the roofers. He sat down on one of the low, child-size semi-circular benches that would eventually have padded seats, and looked around him imagining the final result. The thick wood of the building insulated out most of the noise from below giving the upper floor an isolated, serene quality. He thought about the children of Red Bone cuddled up with their books on the wide, cushioned benches, and as he let his mind rest, eyes half-closed against the haze of sunlight gathered by the big windows overlooking the soccer field, he thought about Natty's daughter, Cat, the tiny girl with the long, silky blond hair, who rarely spoke or even smiled, who was always staring into the big picture book whenever Charlie saw her sitting in the bleachers, or laying on the grass next to a soccer field. *Cat will love this spot, up on the top floor of the library, alone and safe. Her special place . . . like Natty's boulder.* Charlie closed his eyes and ached to hold the little girl in his lap and read *Charlie And The Chocolate Factory*, and *The Indian In The Cupboard*, and *The Dragons of Blueland* to her, and a wave of sweet warmth swept over him as he surrendered to the blissful daydream.

A creaking sound from the stairway brought Charlie's attention back to the present. From his bench he watched the opening in the floor while slowly, tentatively, the backwards *New York Yankees* hat crept into view. Charlie remained silent until the boy slowly started turning his head to inspect the floor and saw Charlie grinning at him a few feet away. Pie stopped and his eyes widened in a combination of shock and joy, and the *happy face* came over him in a rush, causing his shoulders to hunch up, paralyzing him for a moment on the stairway as he looked away and strained to catch his breath. Finally, he was able to climb the last step to the floor, jumped in front of Charlie and gyrated slowly while trying to control his *happy face,* unsure of what he should do next.

Charlie laughed as he raised up both palms to the boy. Pie leaned forward and pressed his small hands into Charlie's, their fingers interlocking. Charlie squeezed Pie's hands for a few moments before speaking. "Hello Pie Man," he said softly. "I've missed you."

Pie bounced on his knees, still holding Charlie's hands as he stopped grinning enough to speak. "I went to yowa office but they say Chowly not wowking. Say Chowly gone to New Yowk."

Charlie let go of the boy's hands and knocked his cap down over his eyes. "Yeah, I'm going to New York tonight." He knocked Pie playfully on the chin.

"Momma tell me I can go to see you now," he said, shuffling his feet, pushing his hands down into the pockets of his denim overalls. "I wide my bicycle up da hill and I see Chowly's cowa pawked hewa."

Charlie laughed at the boy's excitement. "C'mon, Pie Man, sit down here," he said, "tell me about school, and the soccer team. I understand *The Bones* are going to a tournament in Charleston."

Once he got started, Pie rattled on, non-stop for ten minutes about school and their last two soccer games, which *The Bones* won easily, and about the *big townament* they were going to in *Chowlyston* on Thanksgiving weekend. Finally, he ran out of talk and he and Charlie just sat together for a few moments in silence while dark shadows crept over the floor as the sun dropped away from the skylights.

Charlie was just about to suggest that they go up to *Eve's Restaurant* for a soda when the boy spoke again.

"Chowly?" he asked in a small voice.

"What Pie?"

"Will you tell me the stowy about you and my papa cutting down the big twee?"

Charlie smiled and nodded, then turned halfway on the bench toward Pie as the boy, wide-eyed with anticipation, folded his legs underneath himself.

"Well, your papa and I were out in the deep woods, way down where it's so hard to get to that some of the trees there are over two hundred years old. We were cutting trees with two professional lumberjacks named Frenchy and Dogface, two of the best loggers you'll ever run into," said Charlie, beginning the story that he knew Pie would cherish for the rest of his life.

Chapter 30

The bus was unlike anything Natty had ever ridden on before. It was purple and silver with dark tinted windows, towering over the road as it pulled out of the Red Bone Baptist Church parking lot. A five hour trip to the motel in Pennsylvania and then another four hours on Friday morning into New York. Natty had been dreading the trip for the last few days, but a free trip to New York with two nights in a hotel, a ticket to *Les Miserables*, and a dinner at *Tavern On The Green* courtesy of Charlie Burden, was too much to pass up.

She felt uncomfortable about leaving the kids, and Buck too – she'd never been away from them overnight before except when she was in the hospital, and she was uneasy about not seeing some of her patients on Friday, but the main source of the gnawing sensation deep in her stomach, she knew, was Charlie Burden. He was going to be in New York definitely now, and they even had kind of a date set up – *'we'll go for a run on Saturday morning'* – didn't they? And she knew if anything was ever going to happen between them, it needed to happen this weekend.

Mabel Willard put a huge soft hand over Natty's on the armrest between the seats. "You okay girl?" she said, obviously sensing Natty's unrest.

Natty, her head still pressed back against the seat, turned halfway toward Mabel. "Ain't even out of Red Bone and I'm already homesick," she said with a chuckle. "Ain't been out of West Virginia since high school when we went to Washington on a field trip.

Mabel Willard patted Natty's hand comfortingly and twisted her huge bulk to bring her head over closer. "Been a long time for me too," she said softly. "Twelve years. Since Lorena . . . when she was havin' her troubles, and I had to go up there to Detroit and then bring the boys home."

Natty turned her hand over and squeezed Mabel's. "Yeah, I remember that. I was pregnant with Pie when Lorena died." Natty brought up the picture in her mind of Mabel's beautiful, smart, talented daughter Lorena, two years ahead of her in school and so self - confident and ready for the world, who couldn't wait to leave McDowell County to seek her fortune in the big city, and wound up a year later in a Detroit tenement, the mother of twins, and a year after that dead from an overdose of heroin.

"Went up there and took them babies away from that man, carryin' 'em one in each arm and took the bus back down here."

They remained silent for a few moments, each woman lost in her own thoughts. Then Natty rolled to her left toward Mabel and brought her right hand over and placed it affectionately on the black woman's large forearm. She noted again how soft and warm black skin always seemed to feel. Natty had the side of her head against the leather seat. "Mabel?" she almost whispered. "Do you still miss her . . . after all these years? I mean, do you still think about her a lot?"

Mabel sighed and put her left hand over Natty's. "Well, Zack and Sammy are a handful, you know that." Natty smiled knowingly. "But, yeah," Mabel's voice cracked, "I think about Lorena every day, first thing when I get up in the morning, last thing at night. Mother never stops missin' her child."

After a few moments of thought, Natty said, "how about a father? Think they miss their kids like that?"

Mabel sniffed and straightened up a little. "Well, you know, men are *scum* a course, so they don't miss nothin' for too long but their drinks and their pussy and their TV sets." Natty burst out laughing as did Mabel. They quieted down after a few moments and remained silent, their hands still clasped together. Then Mabel squirmed a little and slid down a bit in her seat to bring her face over closer to Natty. She lowered her voice to make sure no one could overhear them. "But child, if you're asking me what I *think* you're asking me, well then, I'm going to give you my say one time and then zip up my fat mouth forever on the subject, and whatever you end up doin',' ain't *no one* in McDowell County, including myself'll ever say you shouldn't a done whatever you chose to do. 'Cause child, you *earned* that right, after everything come down on you in your lifetime – losin' your daddy and then little Annie there, bless her soul, and raisin' them kids most by yourself, and then helpin' so many old people and so many sick people all these years all over McDowell County – *my God child,"* Mabel was whispering louder and faster, *"you earned* the right to finally*, one time in your life, do somethin' just for yourself and for them children!"* Mabel looked up and around her to see if anyone had overheard. Satisfied, she continued in a lower voice. "Now you know Buck Oakes was never one of my favorites. Had him in grade-school and early on had him pegged for . . . well, never could warm up to the boy or his daddy. Sorry to have to say that, but that's way it is. And then he went and took advantage of you there and made you have to quit high school like that . . ."

Natty laughed and shook Mabel's arm. "Wasn't quite the way it was Mabel. That was all as much *my* doin' as it was Buck's."

"Yeah, yeah, I know child. You was in *love*," Mabel said, shaking her head with an angry scowl, "and you was still in love that night he beat you like . . . like he beat up all them boys in school, and put you in the hospital for two weeks when you couldn't eat solid food for a month." Mabel stopped abruptly and drew in a deep breath to calm her anger.

Natty rubbed the black woman's forearm tenderly. "That was just one time Mabel. A mistake is all, 'cause of his drinking and the way things came out that day."

"There been others. I know. I can tell. That kind a thing ain't a one-time mistake. Seen enough glassy-eyed, bruised women around McDowell County in my time to know," said Mabel. Natty didn't say anything. She already knew Mabel's opinion of Buck and there wasn't any point to arguing with her because deep inside, she knew that Mabel had most of it right.

After a long pause, Natty stretched her eyebrows up to look into Mabel's huge brown eyes. "So what should I *do* Mabel?" Natty asked softly.

The angry grimace drained away from Mabel's face and her voice was softer too. "Natty, child, you got to do what your heart tells you to do, without – *for one time in your life* – caring *most* about what *Buck* thinks of it all, 'cause he

don't deserve one more *second* of you feeling guilty about what happens to him."
Mabel brought her left hand over and squeezed Natty's hand in both of hers as she
looked past Natty out the big window and spoke softly again. "Charlie's a good
man Nat, better than any you're going to find around McDowell County, that's
sure. Seen that first time I met him, on the porch in front of the store, that day
Sammy told you he wanted to play soccer. And I could see then – only his second
day in Red Bone – Charlie was already moonin' helpless over you like you was a
couple of high school kids, way he was watchin' you over, and the *look* in his eye.
Whether he knew it or not that day don't matter. He was a goner!"

Natty and Mabel both giggled. Natty pushed the black woman's arm
playfully. "Go on Mabel you didn't know nothin' of the sort."

Mabel fell back into her seat and let go of Natty's hand. She tilted her head
for one last comment. "Well, I knows what I knows," she said softly, "and that
man loves you and them children like no man's ever done before, so . . . it's now
all up to you child to make something out of it or don't." She waved a flat hand
through the air signaling finality. "And that's all I'll be sayin' 'bout that subject."

"Well . . . think you're bein' a little too romantic about things Mabel." Natty
sat back in her seat and glanced out the window. "Little no-account hillbilly girl
with two kids – one retarded, other we're not too sure about – ain't much of a
catch when you take a close look at things," she said half to Mabel, half to herself.
She turned again toward the window. Mabel crossed her arms and rolled her head
away as if to try to nap. "More like just daydream stuff," Natty whispered.
*Successful, handsome man like Charlie Burden, from New York, even thinking two
thoughts about such a girl from Red Bone, West Virginia is just crazy. How could
she be imagining such thoughts?*

Natty gazed out the window, dull-eyed and unaware of the scenery passing
by as the large bus struggled with the narrow road and the endless curves it had to
endure all the way up to the highway. She was watching Charlie Burden standing
next to the Lexus as she put her arms on top of the car and then, looking down
through the glass roof hearing him say it again – *the L word. He said it! Said it
twice in fact. 'Fell in love with someone else' he said, and then talking about his
wife, 'she knew I was in love with you.' Not exactly comin' right out with the three
little words, but goddamn close enough!* Natty smiled and let the warmth of that
moment, the sound of Charlie's voice, engulf her once again. *The first time in her
life any man had said he loved her . . . least one not pantin' and humpin' up a hot
sweat in the back of Big Frank's Chevy Blazer.* She almost giggled to herself.

Natty noticed for the first time that they were now on the highway and the
bus was speeding along, headed for Pennsylvania and the motel, and then
tomorrow morning, New York City. *And then what?* She wouldn't see him
tomorrow she didn't think. After they checked into the hotel, they were going on a
bus tour and to the Empire State Building, and then to dinner at the fancy
restaurant in Central Park. But, Charlie was going to meet her for a run on
Saturday morning, *'six-thirty, in front of the hotel.'* Natty thought about the new
dark blue warm-up suit with the white stripes down the pants and down the
sleeves, she had bought at the mall in Bluefield. She didn't want to embarrass

Charlie by looking like a rag picker when they went running in New York. Then she would get her hair done, before the two-o'clock matinee show. She instinctively felt her right front pants pocket where she had tucked her small wad of money – including the fifty dollars she'd budgeted to get her hair trimmed a little bit. *Even in New York, fifty bucks would be enough to get her hair done!*

They had an extra ticket to *Les Miserables*, which they all agreed she would offer to Charlie. Then, after the play, it was free-time for everyone the travel agent had said. *So that would be their time. Saturday night, after the show. Maybe they'd have dinner. A real date! And in New York City no less.* Natty smiled as she thought about the short, black dress with the matching jacket she'd bought for the occasion – she'd bring it back to the store on Monday – and the silver high-heels she borrowed from Sally. *Christ, I hope I can walk in them!* Natty tried unsuccessfully to remember the last time she wore high-heels. She swallowed hard. So tomorrow night something would finally happen between them. Charlie had already told her how *he* felt, so now it was up to her and she knew, she could feel it in her bones, that this might be her last chance . . . to make the dream come true. Because Charlie wouldn't be in West Virginia much longer. She wasn't sure why, but she sensed that he could be gone right after the Angel Mountain hearing – another ten days – and then Charlie might be gone, with nothing happening between them, nothing resolved, the opportunity gone, after all the affection and obvious feelings between them over all these months. *Not even a kiss, unless you count that cheap little peck when Charlie was in the hospital and she was afraid Pie would come in the room, and even then, that was more, what?. . . medicinal, than sexual.* But this weekend would be different. This weekend would be special.

Natty put her head against the cold window and looked down at the black pavement racing past as the bus seemed to be trying to make up for lost time spent on the slow, winding roads of McDowell County. She took a deep breath to slow her nervous heart and blinked her eyes to rid them of the moisture that grew as she lost the battle to avoid thinking about Buck. *'Don't feel guilty about Buck. Don't worry what Buck thinks'* everyone was telling her. *Mabel, Eve – Buck's own sister – even Sally, 'You don't owe Buck dick,'* Sally had said to her once. Natty's mother had always disliked Buck and that had turned to hatred after the beating, the day the helicopters came. *Everyone's against Buck.* Natty pushed the tip of her index finger across her left eye and then the right. *And now, she was too.*

She closed her eyes and couldn't help smiling to herself as she recalled Buck's voice and the look on Pie's face as his father told him the story about cutting down the big tree with Charlie and winning the bet from the two lumberjacks. And then Buck picking up Cat and actually talking to her and saying her name, which he hadn't done since she was a baby, and the girl even smiling a quick little scared smile, watching her mother carefully for a clue as to how she should respond. Then Natty remembered how she caught Buck checking her out when she was at the refrigerator in her underwear, looking her over like he hadn't realized that she looked like that. They were clumsy, awkward displays, because Buck still didn't know how to be a father or a husband, but they were the kind of clues Natty had been looking for and waiting for, for twelve years. She knew for certain that Buck had been acting different lately, since he'd gotten the logging job and after what was said at the fight at *The Roadhouse,* and then after the day cutting trees with Charlie. *Something* had made Buck think about things a little bit and act a little different at home, she was sure of that. He wouldn't be getting any *father of the year award* anytime soon, and he'd still come home drunk on the nights before his off-days, but not as late and maybe not as drunk as before. And at least he came home now.

Natty opened her eyes and took the thin travel brochure from the seat pocket in front of her. She looked at the picture of the Milford Plaza Hotel, dramatically lighted against the night sky. Natty sighed deeply and nodded her head to herself. *Like everyone says, I don't owe you nothing Buck, least not this weekend.*

The final leg of the trip, through the Holland Tunnel and up Manhattan to the hotel, was all a blur to Natty. She tried to watch everything through the large bus window – the soaring buildings as well as the close-up view next to the bus of the neighborhoods, apartment buildings, stores, the people and the cars and trucks that constantly encircled them but there was too much to look at.

As the bus moved up 8th Avenue, the buildings got taller, the traffic thicker, and the noise heavier. Soon they were surrounded by a sea of yellow taxis, all moving too fast for the crowded conditions Natty thought, and all seemingly blowing their horns constantly.

Natty had to giggle out loud at the raucous, overcrowded circus that was Manhattan at mid-day on a Friday. Mabel and most of the other women of the Red Bone Baptist Church Social Club just stared wide-eyed through the windows at the bewildering sights around them.

They turned onto West 45th Street and came to a stop in front of the Milford Plaza Hotel. After claiming their luggage on the sidewalk, the travel agent led them into the hotel lobby jammed with groups milling about, where they waited for thirty minutes for the travel agent to check them in and hand out their room keys.

Natty and Mabel both laughed when they opened the door to their room and saw how tiny it was. Then they laughed again when they saw the room rates posted on the door of the closet – and this was supposed to be one of the *cheaper* hotels in New York! They unpacked and, with an hour before their bus tour departed, they went to the room next door and talked Ada and Janice Lowe into going out to find Times Square with them.

Natty and the three women got lost immediately, going the wrong direction outside of the 45th Street entrance and then heading north on 8th Avenue. After a couple of blocks they dug out the little map the travel agent had distributed and after turning completely around several times on the sidewalk while looking up at the street signs, figured out the direction they needed to go. Finally they found Broadway and headed south, slowly amongst the pedestrian traffic, wide-eyed with wonderment at the enormity of everything in New York City. They stopped, tentatively, to watch the street shows – a juggler, a two-woman rock 'n roll band, and then three black teenagers putting on an incredible break-dancing show accompanied by two energetic bongo drummers. The electric music and the hollow knocks of the bongos combined with the constant din of traffic horns and the roar of buses and trucks accelerating away from stop lights, produced a sound unlike anything the women from West Virginia had heard before.

The aroma of sausage, onions, and fresh coffee, drifting through the air made the women hungry. At several small restaurants they passed, Mabel and Janice Lowe leaned in close to check out the posted menus and came away rolling their eyeballs at the prices. "Well we ain't eatin' *there!*" Mabel would announce. Ada Lowe just laughed. She'd been to New York before, several times, although not in the last twenty years, but she knew what to expect of big city prices.

They went into the *Disney Store* where Natty swallowed hard at the twenty-four-dollar prices but bought a *Mickey Mouse* "I Love New York" tee-shirt for Cat, and a *New York Yankees* shirt for Pie. Stuffing her small wad of bills back in her front pocket, she started to wonder if she could afford to get her hair done in the morning.

Heading back to the hotel, Natty pulled the three black women into *Starbucks* where they got stuck in line with no way to escape the six-dollar cost of a *tall* – the smallest coffee they had. Mabel just shook her head, eyes bulging with incredulity at the prices. Ada and Natty just laughed, and split the cost of four corn muffins for the group. They found a table at the window, ate and watched the never-ending parade of pedestrians passing by them on the sidewalk, and enjoyed a stream of jokes and laughter about what everything cost in New York City. Then realizing the time, and uncertain of whether or not they could ever find the *Milford Plaza* again, they quick-walked back to the hotel so they wouldn't miss the tour bus and the trip to the Empire State Building. Later they would have some sorely needed nap time, before departing for dinner at *Tavern On The Green*, a very special treat, the travel agent said, courtesy of their friend, Mr. Charlie Burden.

The old elevator in the Dietrich Delahunt & Mackey building moved slowly. Charlie figured he could have almost run up the stairs to the sixth floor from the second floor guest apartments in the same time it took the elevator. But he was in no hurry today. This was one more meeting he wasn't looking forward to.

His fears were confirmed when he glanced into the boardroom on the way to his office. He couldn't identify everyone, but there were too many people in the room for a projects meeting. He did see Terry Summers and Larry Tuthill, and most notably, a couple of other DD&M Executive Committee members that he knew to be lieutenants in Warren Brand's cabal. They had no real reason to be at a meeting about CanAmex business. So the meeting would be about something else.

"Hey Charlie," he heard someone call out from the room as he went passed. It was two o'clock and the men in the boardroom were no doubt anxious to get the meeting over with to get an early start to their weekends. Charlie ignored the call. *Fuck 'em, they can wait,* he said to himself as he strode purposefully down the hallway. He was going to see Lucien Mackey before he stepped into the wolves den. Lucien had called him a few minutes earlier with a cryptically brief message to stop into his office before going to the boardroom.

Lucien Mackey looked old and tired sitting in one of the black leather chairs at the huge glass coffee table at the front of his office. "Hello Charlie," he said without rising, motioning him to the couch at his left. Charlie walked over to shake hands with his old friend. He was surprised to see someone else in the office, standing at the dry bar against the inside wall. It was his old golfing pal, Mal Berman, Counsel to DD&M and Lucien's personal lawyer. He was pouring himself a drink.

"Hello Charlie," Mal Berman said warmly, coming over to join them at the coffee table. "Like something?"

"Hi Mal, no, I'm fine," said Charlie shaking hands with the lawyer. "I've got a big meeting in a few minutes," he said with a wide grin. "Important for my career advancement." Charlie sat on the couch, Mal Berman took the armchair opposite Lucien.

Charlie's joke made Lucien smile briefly. He breathed out heavily. "Well it's over Charlie. Brand's got the votes, more than enough, and they just voted. We just came from there."

Charlie sat forward in surprise. "How could they take a vote? *I'm* on the Executive Committee!"

"Didn't need you Charlie," responded Mal Berman. "Had a solid majority. Called an *emergency session* – which could be arguable – on the grounds that an important client needed to address the Committee on short notice."

"That's horseshit, they can't do that!"

Lucien smiled benignly and leaned forward in his chair. "They can Charlie. And they did."

"They've got the votes Charlie, that's the important thing," said Berman. "You want to challenge them in court on procedural grounds?" The lawyer took a sip of his Manhattan and placed the glass down lightly on the table. "Never happen. Be moot before you ever got before a judge."

Charlie remained silent for a few moments, thinking. He was surprised things were moving this quickly. "How did it happen so fast?"

Lucien reached out and opened the rosewood humidor on the table. He offered Charlie a cigar, which he declined, before taking one out for himself. "Torkelson made it happen Charlie. He and Tuthill, accompanied by Brand, visited a few Board members in person, called the others by phone. Reviewed for them the size of the revenue stream that all the current CanAmex projects provided for DD&M and gave them a preview of all the new CanAmex business they would be directing DD&M's way over the next fifteen years – hydroelectrics in Canada, half a dozen gas and coal plants in the U.S., rebuilding the system in Mexico – you know what the numbers are Charlie."

"Billions if he can deliver them all," said Charlie.

Lucien lit his cigar and puffed on it for a few moments before continuing. "And the immediate payoff – huge bonuses next year from the sale of the building."

"Yeah, minus Torkelson and Tuthill's take," said Charlie.

"Never be able to prove that part though. They're too clever by far," said Lucien.

Mal Berman leaned over the table towards Charlie. "Some of these guys on the Board are going to double their net worth in six months," he said, "plus, the promise of an extremely profitable company for the rest of their careers."

"Pretty hard to pass up," said Charlie, "if you're stupid enough to trust Torkelson to deliver or Warren Brand to manage it all."

"Well Torkelson did a pretty good selling job," said Lucien somberly. "His star is rising fast with CanAmex, so he gets to call the shots, because he's delivering the goods." Lucien waved his cigar at Charlie and chuckled. "You're half responsible for this Charlie, with that great job you're doing in West Virginia. Plant's way under budget and ahead of schedule, and with that Angel Mountain coal, CanAmex will soon be operating the most efficient large-scale generator in North America, and that's *very* significant – to CanAmex, Wall Street, the politicians."

"Which all helps the stock price," Mal Berman interjected, "and makes the merger with Continental Electric a better deal all around for everyone."

"When you're flying as high as Torkelson is, you get a lot of leverage," said Lucien, "and he's using it to take control of Dietrich Delahunt & Mackey. Sure, Warren Brand will be in this office, but Torkelson will be calling the shots." Lucien Mackey looked across the room to the picture of his father on the wall. "And that's not healthy," he said softly, "not a good situation."

After a few moments of silence, Charlie asked, "so, what about you Lucien?"

Lucien Mackey breathed out a long cloud of smoke, then shrugged his shoulders. "Well, it won't be finalized until the full Board meeting in December, but, I'm out. Oh I can hang around until then – can't do any company business, can't sign any contracts or hire and fire, but I can use the office if I want." Lucien smiled at Charlie and chuckled. "I can come in and pretend I still have a job here, but, after the Board meeting in December I'm out. They buy me out. Time to retire."

Charlie shook his head and looked at his watch.

"Don't know what they have planned for you Charlie," said Lucien. "Brand knows you're too smart for him, but he also knows you're close with Duncan McCord, so that's a problem for him."

Charlie laughed as he arose to leave for the boardroom. "Well that's a problem I'm not going to solve for him." He shook hands with his two old friends. "I'll let you know what happens."

Some of the men in the Boardroom were having cocktails and had loosened their ties when Charlie finally made his appearance, thirty minutes late. He shook hands with Larry Tuthill and a few of the DD&M people, but didn't bother to go around to the other side of the table to greet Warren Brand. Charlie nodded to Terry Summers and took a vacant seat not far from the door. In the corner of the room, a secretary was taking the minutes on a shorthand pad.

When everyone else was seated, Warren Brand moved to his chair at the middle of the table. He studied some notes in front of him for a few seconds before looking up and then over at Charlie as if he'd just discovered him in the room. He smiled briefly and leaned back in the high-backed chair, his forearms along each armrest. Charlie thought he looked even a little more cocky than usual.

"Yes, Charlie. Thanks for coming in," said Brand. "This won't take long." Charlie remained silent, watching Brand at work. He had an annoying technique of always smiling while he spoke. "Well, I know you met with Lucien," Brand continued, "so you know what's happening here. The Executive Committee met in emergency session this afternoon, at the behest of Mr. Tuthill and our client, CanAmex Energy, and, as of December, *I* will be managing partner, with a new Executive Committee, and Lucien will be leaving the company . . . with an excellent package, I should add."

Charlie's blood was boiling but he sat calmly, listening to Brand, because he knew short of diving across the table and taking out a good selection of Brand's cosmetically perfected front teeth with a straight right hand, there was nothing to be gained from this meeting. Any grievance he had would have to become a legal issue.

"Now as for your own status Charlie," Brand leaned forward onto the table and smiled, "you'll of course be off the Exec, but we do have some *great* news for you."

Brand looked around the table for support and then gestured with an open hand toward Larry Tuthill. "Because of the personal recommendation of Larry for the great job you're doing down in West Virginia, along with the high regard you're held in here at DD&M, we'd like you to wrap things up down there over the next few weeks, hand the project off to Summers here, and then," he paused and let a wide grin sweep over his face, "we're going to give you what you wanted back in the spring. We want you to take over the second dam project in China."

Charlie stared blankly at Brand for a few moments while he digested this new twist. He had to admit, he was surprised. Finally, he smiled thinly, forcing himself not to burst out laughing. *Torkelson and Tuthill had the power, but they were still scared shitless of Duncan McCord, so they'd have to spare Charlie Burden. China! That was perfect. Brand gets him off the Board and out of the country, and Torkelson gets him a world away from any CanAmex business and away from Duncan McCord. It was the perfect solution!*

Charlie chuckled and then shrugged resignedly. "Okay Warren," he said, looking at his watch. "I've got some things to finish up in Red Bone . . . I don't know how long it will take me. Then I'll think about China." Charlie stood up from his seat but didn't move away from the side of the table. "But before I leave, I've gotta tell you guys what you've done here today." He looked around the table at the other Executive Committee members. "Not Warren," he pointed at Brand, "he knows what he's doing, and this isn't new for him. He's always been a back-biting little scum-sucking slug whose only talent in this business was to find the right asshole to crawl up." Warren Brand closed his notebook abruptly and stood up. Charlie ignored him. "And now he's Torkelson's butt boy and you guys are turning this company over to them, and it's the beginning of the end." Charlie put his hands in his pockets and looked down at the table in thought. He said softly, "you've insulted and shamed and embarrassed Dietrich Delahunt & Mackey's greatest asset, the man who built this company, and you'll *never* get past that." Charlie shook his head disgustedly. He gritted his teeth to keep the emotion out of his eyes. "What were you guys thinking about?" he said, almost to himself as he started for the door.

*   *   *

The November air was wintry at six o'clock in the morning. The forecast was for warming into the fifties that afternoon and rain in the evening, but it felt like snow when Charlie started out for the *Milford Plaza*. His breath, like every other current of warm air escaping into the deserted streets, turned to gray fog for a brief moment before rising away. He wore calfskin gloves and his New York Giants hat against the cold. In the pouch at the front of his sweatshirt, he had stuffed some cotton mittens and a wool "CanAmex" toque that he had found in the apartment. Natty, he was certain, wouldn't have thought about how cold it might be early in the morning, running in New York, and wouldn't have thought to bring gloves or a hat.

Charlie crossed the wide expanse of Park Avenue, enjoying the rare opportunity to saunter leisurely across the deserted street. Early morning on the weekends in mid-town was a magical time, when Charlie felt like he had the magnificent city all to himself to explore and appreciate. An empty bus went past on the opposite side of the street heading south. A few cabs with their headlights still lit trundled home the casualties of a Friday night gone on too long. The only noise breaking the morning stillness was a street sweeper down around 3737th Street moving toward him slowly like some sort of wounded animal. There wasn't another pedestrian in sight. It was a wonderful time and place for a run. *Almost as good as the trail along the south side of Red Bone Mountain.*

Crossing Fifth Avenue at the library, Charlie went over 42nd Street and then up Broadway through Times Square. He went in the front entrance of the *Milford Plaza* on 45th Street and looked around the lobby. Natty was nowhere in sight. He went out the 8th Avenue entrance and walked the short distance to the corner to see if she'd gone out the other door. He glanced at his watch and saw that it was only twenty-five past six, then he was startled by the voice behind him.

"Hey soldier. Looking for a good time?"

Charlie laughed and turned to see Natty grinning at him a few feet away. She was wearing a dark blue warm-up suit with the short top zipped all the way up and the collar raised. The new trim outfit made her look even smaller than she usually did in her baggy shorts and oversized shirts. Her hands were in her pockets. Charlie saw that he was right – she hadn't brought gloves, or even the *Spiderman* cap. He just looked at her for a moment smiling, then took a step toward her. He resisted the overpowering urge he had to wrap his arms around her and hold her tightly against him. "Hi Nat," he said, pulling the mittens out of his pouch.

"Hey Charlie."

Charlie handed her the mittens. "Thanks. Cold morning," she said, putting on the mittens while Charlie took out the wool toque. He moved closer and stretched the hat over her head and straightened it with the palms of his hands, moving them down each side of her head and over her ears. His finger tips touched her neck lightly.

Natty's heart surged at the feeling of Charlie's hands on her. She thought he might kiss her, but he just smiled and stepped back.

"Ready?" he said.

"Gotta do at least five miles to work off that dinner from last night."

Charlie started out. "C'mon," he said. "I'll show you what heaven is like for a runner in New York."

They went north on 8th Avenue, running on the vacant sidewalk at a very slow pace to warm up and to be able to talk without breathing hard. Natty told him all about their trip from Red Bone. At Columbus Circle, they turned and headed back down Broadway. Several joggers were heading into Central Park but Charlie knew that wouldn't be as exciting for Natty as seeing the famous streets and sights of Manhattan. And he was right.

"Wow, this is pretty neat," said Natty, "running on Broadway, just like the stars!"

As they went through Times Square, she told him all about yesterday's excursion there with Mabel Willard and Ada and Janice Lowe, making Charlie laugh over the familiar story of the out-of-towners' reaction to New York prices. He could see the look on the faces of the black women over the price of a cup of coffee at Starbucks, after being accustomed to Eve's Restaurant prices.

They went east on 39th Street and ran on the sidewalk of the narrower street, which was dark and cold with no direct exposure yet to the morning light. Natty told him all about their bus tour and their trip up the Empire State Building. She was effusive in her praise for their fabulous dinner at *Tavern On The Green*. The Red Bone Baptist Church Social Club was unanimously impressed with every detail of the restaurant and the elegant dinner. It was an experience the women would remember and talk about for the rest of their lives. Most of them, Natty added, would never again eat at such a fine restaurant.

"That's good," said Charlie, "I knew they'd enjoy that." He was glad he'd added the Central Park restaurant to their itinerary. Most New Yorkers eschewed the eatery as a *déclassé* tourist trap, but Charlie knew that no restaurant in New York could make a group of poor black women from West Virginia feel for a little while like they were part of high society, like *Tavern On The Green* would.

They ran a straight shot along 39th Street, crossing the wide Avenues with scant concern for any traffic. Occasionally they would slow for a moment to let a cab or limousine pass, but for the most part their run was unimpeded, and they made good time on the old, flat street, watching out only for cracks in the sidewalk and heating grates.

Crossing Park Avenue, Natty was startled to feel a rumble under their feet, making Charlie chuckle. "Subway" he assured her. Pointing to the right, Charlie showed Natty the Dietrich Delahunt & Mackey building on the next block south. He was staying there this weekend in one of the guest apartments he told her.

Natty looked over at him. "How come not in Manara – Mamano – Ma . . ."

"Mamaroneck," Charlie prompted. "No sense to going up there. Ellen's in Boca Raton, working on her tan and playing tennis. Plus I had a meeting here yesterday afternoon," said Charlie.

"Good meeting?" she asked.

Charlie hesitated to answer, not wanting to get into it. "No, not really," he said.

"Anything to do with Angel Mountain?"

"Yeah, a little bit, but not entirely. It was about a lot of stuff. Things are changing in the company. Things are changing with CanAmex." He shrugged. "That's the way business is." Natty could tell that it wasn't a good meeting for Charlie, which, she knew instinctively, meant that his time in Red Bone had grown shorter.

They ran up First Avenue so Charlie could show her the United Nations Building, always an impressive sight to first-time visitors. Natty beamed at being so close to the famous landmark she had seen so many times in pictures and on television. Even early in the morning on a Saturday, there were many lights on in the large building.

Charlie led her onto 48th Street, headed back west. "C'mon," he said, surging ahead of her, "let's work up a sweat." Natty responded easily, as he knew she would, settling comfortably into Charlie's aggressive pace. They turned right onto Lexington and ran in the street. The wide boulevard gave Natty the opportunity to clearly see the height of the sky scrapers, which made her giggle and roll her eyeballs at their enormity. "How can they *build* things that tall?" she asked more than once.

They were both breathing deeply by the time they reached 57th Street, where they went left and ran on the sidewalk because of a little more street traffic. They now had to dodge some morning dog-walkers and a few slow-moving joggers wearing headphones and the latest in colorful lycra running wear and expensive shoes.

They went down Fifth Avenue, slowing to a more leisurely pace so Natty could enjoy the stores and the opulence of the famous street. Charlie pointed out Tiffany's and Trump Tower and Natty peered into several parked limousines they passed to see if anyone famous could be seen behind the dark glass, making Charlie laugh.

Suddenly Natty left Charlie on the sidewalk and dashed across Fifth Avenue, dodging several cabs, and went a short way down a side street. Charlie stopped and watched her slow to a walk in front of some sort of basement shop and go a few steps down the stairs. Walking across the wide avenue, Charlie could see that it was a chic looking women's' salon with a French name. He waited for her on the corner.

"I just wanted to see when they opened," Natty said as she walked back toward Charlie. "But they got a little sign that says "by appointment only." Charlie just nodded, not wanting to tell her that a beauty salon just off Fifth Avenue was probably a little out of her price range. They started walking, which was fine with Charlie. They'd gone more than five miles he figured, and it would be nice to just walk with Natty for a while.

"I was planning on getting something done with my hair while I was in New York," Natty said, pulling off the toque and shaking out her crinkled locks.

"Your hair looks fine," said Charlie, and he meant it.

Natty laughed. "Yeah, like a mop somebody just washed the gym floor with." She pulled the hat on again over her damp forehead, leaving it high on her head, the top of the toque flopping to the side. "Course, I ain't too sure I can still afford it after buying two T-shirts and a couple of corn muffins in this town."

Charlie laughed as he reached into a zippered pocket for a small cell-phone. "Maybe you can," he said still chuckling. He flipped open the phone and pushed a few buttons. He stopped walking and put the phone to his ear, smiling at Natty. She strolled over to the window of a women's clothing store, instinctively wanting to give Charlie his privacy. "Hello Carlos," she heard him say. "I need a little favor." He turned his back to her as he spoke into the phone. "Okay Carlos, thanks. Nine thirty. Take care of Lucien." he said, moving toward Natty. He folded up the phone and put it away. "C'mon," he said to Natty. "I'll show you Rockefeller Center."

They walked down Fifth Avenue at a leisurely pace now that the run was over. "You've got a nine-thirty appointment at the *Carlos Marche Salon* on Park Avenue. He's a good friend of mine. The salon is on the first floor of our building, the one I showed you. A car will pick you up in front of your hotel."

Natty wrinkled up her nose. "A *car*?"

"They have their own limo for customers."

Natty slowed down a bit. "I don't know Charlie. A *salon* on *Park Avenue* . . . sounds a little ritzy. Maybe I'll just skip it."

"Can't skip it. The appointment's already been made. You know how hard it is to get an appointment at the *Carlos Marche Salon* on a Saturday morning?" Charlie asked playfully.

Natty shook her head. "But Charlie, I only got fifty dollars to get my hair done, and after that, I'll be walkin' around Times Square with a tin cup if I want another coffee at Starbucks."

"Don't worry about it," said Charlie. "You won't be paying. Carlos owes me. I gave him my New York Giants season tickets when I left for West Virginia," he said, knowing that the Giants tickets had nothing to do with the favor Carlos was doing him. He wouldn't bother to tell Natty that *fifty dollars* was about the minimum *tip* for a stylist at the *Carlos Marche Salon.*

"Oh, ticket!" said Natty, reaching into a pocket of her sweat pants. "I forgot. This is for you." She handed Charlie the ticket to *Les Miserables*. "We had an extra."

Charlie looked at the matinee ticket to the *Imperial Theatre* on West 45th. He'd planned on working in the office most of the day and then meeting Natty for dinner after the show. But it had been a couple of years since he'd last seen the magnificent musical and the thought of being there to watch Natty's reaction to her first Broadway show and it being the incomparable *Les Miz,* was too exciting to pass up. "Wow, that's great," he said. "Can't wait to see it again."

"Again?" Natty looked up at him curiously. "How many times you seen this show?"

"This will be the fourth."

She blinked slowly and shook her head. "It's *that* good?"

Charlie smiled with pride, glad now that he'd forced Natty to come on the trip. "It's *better,"* he said softly.

They walked leisurely through Rockefeller Center, stopping at one of the restaurants for two coffees and bagels to go, that Charlie wouldn't reveal the price of. While they ate their bagels and sipped coffee, Charlie gave Natty a brief history of Rockefeller Center and pointed out the different buildings and some of the famous artwork included in the facades. Then they stood at the railing of the ice rink watching a lone maintenance man skate around the ice pushing a wide shovel. The skater looked up and waved to the only spectators and then did a graceful spin behind his shovel. Natty and Charlie clapped their gloved hands together. As they moved away from the railing, Natty waved to the skater who raised his cap to her.

Charlie showed her *Radio City Music Hall,* and then they walked down the Avenue of The Americas and then over 45th Street. From the corner of Broadway, Natty could see the *Milford Plaza* awning at the end of the block. She pulled off the mittens and toque and handed them to Charlie. "Here, save these for next time, okay?"

Charlie nodded and tucked them into his pouch. "How about tomorrow? Same time. We'll go downtown. I'll show you the Brooklyn Bridge, the most beautiful bridge in the world."

"Yeah, sounds great," said Natty, bouncing on the balls of her feet. "We're just going to a couple of museums tomorrow and then leaving for home around three." Natty looked up at Charlie, thinking that maybe she'd be spending the whole day tomorrow with him instead of going to the museums.

Charlie smiled down at her and reached out his right hand to brush aside the lock of hair that fell instinctively across her left eyebrow. He shrugged his shoulders and put his hands in his pouch. "So, I'll see you later, at the show."

"Yeah, okay. Thanks for everything, the run, you know. Everything."

Charlie looked up the street. "And tonight, we'll have dinner, after the show?"

Natty wrinkled up her nose and grinned. "Sure, why not," she said playfully. "Course you'll have to pay 'cause another few hours in this town and I'll be selling my shoes to get a grilled cheese sandwich."

"It's a deal," said Charlie, laughing. "I'll wait for you across the street after the show gets out."

Natty looked at her watch. "Oh, oh. Gotta go and get my shower done so I don't miss my *limousine*," she said, starting to back away.

"See you later," said Charlie, turning to walk back to Park Avenue.

Natty walked a few steps toward the *Milford Plaza* and then turned to watch Charlie trotting across Broadway. She wondered if he had any idea of how special the morning had been for her . . . how easy it had been for Charlie to give her the best date she'd ever had in her whole life! *Running the streets of Manhattan with this wonderful, handsome man who said he was in love with her, and sharing coffee and bagels, talking, and walking through Rockefeller Center on a Saturday morning . . . a morning she would remember vividly until she grew old and couldn't remember any more.* She wrinkled her nose and shook her head as she spun around and started walking toward the hotel. *Nah, Charlie wouldn't know anything about stuff like that.*

Chapter 31

Natty stood on the sidewalk as the white limousine pulled away from the curb. She wished she had a camera to take a picture of the incredible car she had just ridden through Manhattan in, with its own phone and a television and dark tinted windows, just like the limousines the movie stars rode in to the Academy Awards show that she and Sally loved to watch together on TV.

She wasn't sure she was in the right place until she saw the elegant silver lettering on the side of the building just to the right of the main entrance. In small script, easy to overlook – as if no one cared if anyone noticed – it said *Carlos Marche Salon*, and under it, *New York*, and then, *Paris*. "Wow, *Paris*," Natty said out loud. *Well I prefer the New York location myself* she said to herself, walking toward the entrance. The large glass doors were emblazoned with black lettering . . . *Dietrich Delahunt & Mackey, Engineers, New York, San Francisco, Washington, D.C., Beijing.* She looked at the sign and felt that familiar shudder of insecurity she often experienced when she thought about the life that Charlie Burden led.

From the small lobby she went tentatively through an elegant, carved wooden door that held a small polished metal plate signifying the *Carlos Marche Salon.* Inside, Natty thought she'd entered a museum or an art gallery. Colorful paintings adorned the fabric covered walls, and expensive looking tables held expensive looking wood carvings, statuary and crystal. To her right there was a small waiting area with thick white carpeting and black furniture. A thin credenza against one wall held an assortment of wine bottles and other beverages.

One of the two very uncomfortable looking black enameled chairs in the waiting area was occupied by a woman with long black hair wearing large sunglasses, a suede jacket and blue jeans tucked inside tall leather boots. Talking very softly into a cell phone, the woman looked up briefly at Natty and then back toward the floor again. Natty was sure it was the actress Demi Moore who had starred in her all-time favorite movie *Ghost,* but then again, maybe it wasn't. *New York was filled with beautiful women that looked like movie stars.*

To Natty's left, a very thin black woman, her long hair cascading around her shoulders in tight braids adorned with colorful beads, sat behind a wide mahogany table desk. Only a telephone and a leather-bound appointment book sat on the desk. The woman wore a small headset with an attached microphone that she was speaking into softly. She looked up and smiled at Natty as she pressed a button on the phone. *'Carlos Marche Salon'* Natty heard her say. Then the woman began speaking French. Apparently the telephone made no sound when it rang . . . nothing interrupted the elegant silence of the salon except for the very faint sound of classical music.

Natty stood inside the door wondering what she should do next. Her first instinct was to turn around and go out and find her way back to the hotel. *What the hell did you get me into here Charlie? Standing in a fancy beauty parlor on Park*

Avenue in New York City with the receptionist speaking French and maybe Demi Moore sitting in the waiting room!

Then a woman appeared without a sound from around a corner and stood in front of Natty smiling warmly. She was a very attractive woman in her late forties with shoulder-length brown hair with gold highlights set in tight curls . . . *serious hair, Sally would call it.* The beauty of her face was accentuated by the dark outline of her eyes and dark red lipstick, making Natty feel suddenly very plain next to her. The woman wore tight black leather pants, a white blouse and tan vest, and had an air of authority about her. Her eyes never left Natty's face and hair, totally ignoring *maybe Demi Moore* a few feet away.

"Hello Mrs. Oakes," she said softly, "I'm Tina. I'll take you back to Mr. Marche's studio now." *Maybe Demi Moore* stopped talking into her cell phone and looked up again at Natty, this time with more interest.

They went down a hallway past several closed arched wooden doors. From behind one door, Natty could hear the sound of a hair dryer. At the end of the hallway, they went down three stairs and Tina pulled open the heavy door for Natty and they entered what appeared to be another art gallery. The floor of the room was covered in thick white carpeting except for a small tiled area surrounding a styling chair. To their right, in a dimly lit office area, a man was sitting at an antique dark wood pedestal desk, talking on a cordless phone. When the two women entered he put down the phone immediately and came out from behind the desk.

The man was probably in his early fifties, Natty judged, with closely cropped naturally curly hair that had begun to cross over from brown to grey. Just a few inches taller than Natty, he had the physique of a gymnast and moved with grace and confidence. He wore a beige cashmere sweater that contrasted perfectly with the most beautiful light brown skin Natty had ever seen. As he approached her, his dazzling white smile held no pretensions. She suddenly felt completely at ease and in the right place.

"Hello Natty," he said warmly with a trace of a Caribbean accent as he extended his hand. "I am Carlos Marche."

He brought Natty onto the tile next to the chair where the lighting was better. Carlos Marche stood a few feet in front of her, his eyes going from her face to her hair and back. Tina stood off to the side studying Natty also. Carlos reached out both hands to the sides of Natty's face and held her hair out away from her neck. "So," he said, letting her hair down again, "you're going to the theater this afternoon." He winked at Tina. "And then dinner with our friend Charlie Burden."

"Yeah, first time I ever been to a show," Natty said softly. "First time in New York. So, I thought I'd get something done with my hair while I was here." Natty shrugged, a little embarrassed over the condition of her hair. "Maybe just a little trim, you know, don't need anything fancy."

Carlos Marche took a half step backward, studying Natty's hair for a few moments more, a serious look on his face. "How much time have we got?" he asked softly, glancing at Tina.

Natty tried to help them. "Well the show starts at . . ."

Carlos grinned and came forward a step, shaking his head to interrupt Natty. He took both her hands in his and looked into her eyes. "Natty, do you trust me?" he asked.

Natty shrugged. "Sure I do," she laughed. "You know this stuff a lot better than I do."

"Okay good, that's good," he said, motioning her to the styling chair. He turned to Tina who was already poking at her PDA with a metal stylus. "I'll need Javier for color, then Monica for nails," he said to her, then he smiled, "and you'll do makeup." Tina smiled and raised her eyebrows to Natty. It was immediately apparent to Natty that she was getting the *A-Team* of the *Carlos Marche Salon*.

She sat down in the soft, leather padded chair and looked around the interior of Carlos Marche's private studio where New York's rich and famous, movie stars and celebrities came to become beautiful at the hands of Carlos Marche and Tina. *And today was Natty Oakes' turn.*

Charlie made dinner reservations at a restaurant on 43rd Street near Fifth Avenue that he knew Natty would like. It was within walking distance from the theater, classy enough without being stuffy and served a mixed American Grille and Italian menu she would be comfortable with. The reservations were for eight o'clock, which would give them time to go up to the *Atrium* at the *Marriott Marquis* for a drink first. She would enjoy the view looking down at *Times Square* from the bar.

At one o'clock, he pulled on a grey hounds tooth jacket over a black wool jersey and started out for the *Imperial Theatre*. It would be good to get some fresh air and a little more exercise before settling in for the almost four-hour play. He had plenty of time and he didn't want to be late. Plus, like most Broadway shows, *Les Miz* had a strict policy of not seating late-comers until the first scene-break. It didn't matter. Charlie considered being late for a live stage show the height of rudeness and disrespect for the actors and musicians. For *Les Miz,* he'd be in his seat twenty minutes early.

Charlie took 40th Street, and then turned up Madison Avenue. He jogged across 42nd Street dodging the usual mid-day Saturday traffic jam and resumed his brisk walking pace. His cell phone vibrated in his jacket pocket.

"Hi Charlie. Is this a good time?" It was Ellen.

Charlie had to laugh out loud. "Yes Ellen, your timing's perfect."

"I'm on the beach at the *Boca Raton Club,* in a cabana actually. Linda's gone back to the room. It's hot here. How is everything in New York?"

Charlie slowed his walk and told her about the meetings with Lucien and Mal Berman. She listened intently as he broke the news of the management coup taking place at Dietrich Delahunt & Mackey. Then he told her about the meeting with Warren Brand and the Executive Committee and his imminent posting to China. "They're afraid of Duncan so they want me as far away as possible."

"*My God* Charlie. Are you okay?"

"Yes Ellen, nothing to worry about," said Charlie, crossing Broadway. "In fact, we'll probably be in for very large bonus next year if I stay with the company."

"*If you stay?* Charlie, China was what we wanted all along, wasn't it?"

Charlie had to smile at Ellen's use of the word *we*. "Yeah, China. That'll be good," said Charlie absently, "that'll be a nice change."

There was a long pause between them and then Ellen spoke again. "So, is your friend in New York this weekend?" she asked softly.

Charlie hesitated as he looked out for the traffic as he crossed 44th Street. "Um, yeah, they're going to see *Les Miz* this afternoon, and then to dinner at *Tavern On The Green*," he lied.

"Oh, so you won't be seeing her?"

Charlie stopped on the sidewalk. He was almost to the corner of 45th Street. "No, I don't know," he said vaguely. "Maybe for a run tomorrow morning."

"Oh, she's a runner too."

"Yeah, sort of."

Ellen waited a few seconds to see if Charlie had any more to add. "Well okay Charlie, I'm going to go. Don't forget about Thanksgiving. We're all set for Vermont. Scottie is going up and Jennifer is flying into Burlington."

"Yeah, wouldn't miss it," said Charlie softly. "

"Good, okay. Love you Charlie," said Ellen. She clicked off without waiting for a reply.

Damn, Charlie said to himself as he closed the phone and jammed it in his pocket. *Lying to his wife was becoming a regular thing, and he still hated the feeling.*

Getting to the theater early and listening to the orchestra warming up was part of the excitement of a Broadway show. Charlie liked to walk down and peek into the orchestra pit and listen to the musicians running softly through the scales, adjusting valves and reeds and strings, producing a babble of sounds that in a few minutes would be transformed into a beautiful, thrilling score.

The theater was filling and Charlie turned to walk back up the center aisle to find his seat. The travel agent had secured for The Red Bone Baptist Church Social Club a section of very good seats, orchestra center – right, starting with the tenth row back. From the arrangement of colorfully dressed black women already in their seats, along with the travel agent who waved excitedly to him from her seat, Charlie deduced that their seats were spread over three different rows. His seat was in the row farthest back, between the travel agent and Mabel Willard's cousin from Keystone.

Charlie watched the rest of the group gradually fill in the empty seats in the two rows in front of him. The women seemed to be smiling and enjoying themselves. Most of them waved to the travel agent and to him, grinning broadly as they found their seats. Charlie wondered if they didn't seem to be having too much fun. Then Mabel Willard and Ada and Janice Lowe appeared at the end of the aisle two rows in front of Charlie. They shuffled through to their seats, also giggling, as if they were all in on some secret joke. Mabel looked at Charlie and grinned even wider. Before dropping her huge bulk down into the seat, she took a quick glance up toward the back of the theater, and then smiled at Charlie again. There was an empty seat between Mabel and Ada Lowe.

The lights blinked. Charlie looked at his watch. The orchestra had been silent for a while and would soon begin playing in earnest. Most of the seats in the theater were filled, but Natty was nowhere in sight. Charlie looked down at his PlayBill to see if he recognized any of the names in the cast. He might have seen *Javer*, and *Fantine* before. The house lights dimmed and the orchestra began playing. Charlie looked up to see an usher in the aisle, two rows down, and then a slight figure sidling quickly through the row to the one empty seat. But it wasn't Natty, he was sure, even though it was dark now with the curtain open and the spotlights trained on the stage. It was a woman – a small woman – or a girl, he was fairly certain, but a little taller than Natty and her hair was very short, cut like a man's as best he could see in her silhouette from the dark stage lighting of the first act as *Jean Valjean* labored on the chain gang. And when the lights would flicker brighter through the theater, Charlie could see that her hair was very light, a golden – almost white – shade of blonde. The woman settled quickly into the seat next to Mabel Willard and sat perfectly still.

Charlie had a clear view of her two rows down and a few seats to his left and while his head faced the stage, his eyes kept darting back to the mysterious figure. She had Natty's long thin neck and wide shoulders, but he still wasn't convinced, until just as the stage lights came up dramatically, she happened to turn to Ada Lowe and Charlie could see the profile of her delicate chin and small nose and the outline of her cheeks when she smiled and he knew it was her. Although it wasn't really her. This was a beautiful, sophisticated New Yorker for sure, maybe a model or an actress anyone observing her would think. He had to smile to himself in the darkness. *He should have known. An artist and perfectionist like Carlos Marche wouldn't temporize or play it safe on an opportunity like Natty Oakes. He'd reach deep inside her and bring up her spirit and every ounce of her incredible beauty and put it out there on display for the world and challenge weaker men to deal with it. That's what he did for a living.* Charlie turned his eyes back to the stage, took in a deep breath and tried hard to concentrate on the greatest play in the history of the musical theater.

Finally the familiar strains of *Do You Hear The People Sing?* announced the approach of intermission. Charlie watched Natty and all of the women of the Red Bone Baptist Church Social Club applaud vigorously as the house lights came up. Then Charlie rose to let Mabel's cousin and a few other women pass through to the aisle along with the travel agent. "Scuse me Mister *Burdan*," Mabel's cousin breathed out hurriedly, "my bladder's about to burst all over me and nat wouldn't be a pretty sight." All of the women laughed, sharing the same sentiment Charlie surmised from their urgency to reach the aisle. He sat down again and perused his PlayBill as most of the seats slowly emptied.

Charlie shifted his eyes up to see that in their section only Natty's seat was still occupied. All of the women of the Red Bone Baptist Church Social Club had quickly deserted the rows as if by design, leaving just he and Natty. He watched her as she looked to her left where there was nothing particular to look at and then down to her lap. Then her shoulders heaved with a deep sigh and she stood up. She hesitated for a second before turning around to face Charlie.

Charlie rose out of his seat slowly, his eyes transfixed on the woman before him, obviously Natty, but so incredibly transformed that for an instant he thought it must be someone else. Her hair was shorn like a man's long ragged crew-cut, in a child's shade of light blond that seemed to glow on its own in the dim light of the theater. But it was Natty's face – the first time he'd ever seen her with makeup – that made Charlie's heart pound with insecurity. The thin dark outline of her eyes and gentle sweep of her eyelashes made her blue eyes sparkle, and a light pink lip gloss shined with moisture. She had on a short black dress with a high neckline and a matching long-sleeved jacket that seemed a little too dressy for a matinee but looked perfectly natural on such an obviously sophisticated woman. Then Charlie notice she was wearing earrings – small, dangling silver chains – as well as a thin silver choker at her neck. Charlie tried to clear his throat, nervously, and take in a breath of air as the realization hit him full force. *Yes, of course it was Natty. And she was absolutely stunning.*

Natty flashed a quick nervous smile. "*Hey* Charlie," she said with a small wave of her hand. She wrinkled her nose and shrugged her shoulders. "So, what do you think?"

Charlie smiled at her and then furrowed his brow inquisitively. "You do something to your hair?" he said. They both laughed.

Charlie motioned Natty toward the aisle and then led her down to the low wall overlooking the empty orchestra pit. Standing next to her Charlie detected an alluring scent, also new for Natty. "Um, perfume too?"

Natty smiled shyly. "It's Tina's, you know, Carlos' assistant." Natty touched one of her earrings. "Her jewelry too. I have to give it to you tonight so you can give it back to her." Natty laughed. "At midnight I turn into a hillbilly again."

Charlie stared at her while trying to look like he wasn't staring. Up close, she looked even more beautiful. Gone was the broad shock of hair across her forehead and the tousled locks that fell along the side of her face that Natty had always hidden behind. Her short hair now revealed the exquisite lines of her face and neck and focused attention on Natty's crystal blue eyes and wide sensuous mouth. The light blond coloring and short, almost haphazard cut of her hair would have made for a severe, daring look on most women, but on Natty it looked easy and natural, the hairstyle she was born to.

Charlie couldn't help grinning as he looked at her. "You look . . . *incredible*," he said softly.

Natty smiled, embarrassed. "Thanks," she nearly whispered. "It's just the make-up and the jewelry." She giggled. "It's still me."

Charlie looked down and noticed that she was wearing high heels, and for the first time since he'd known her, nylons, which made her thin legs look like a dancer's. "You're taller, too," he said with a chuckle.

Natty bounced on her knees. "God, these shoes are killing me. Think I'm going to break a leg walking in them." She looked up at Charlie and laughed. "Not easy, trying to be a woman."

Charlie looked up the aisle to see that some of the women from their group were headed back to their seats. "How do you like the show?" he asked.

Natty turned to look at the stage and clasped her hands together. "Oh Charlie, it's wonderful! I can't believe these people can do this, the music and the singing and everything. It's so much better than I thought it could be. I can't believe they're going to do the whole show again tonight."

Charlie nodded. "Yeah, it's hard work. But these are the best stage actors and singers and dancers in the world. This is *Broadway.*"

Natty saw that the seats were filling up again, but she had something she needed to say before they went back. "Charlie, um," she looked down at her feet before looking up into Charlie's face, "thanks. Thank you for everything, you know, for this whole trip and for this morning and for Carlos and Tina, and well for everything. This has been like the *best* day of my whole life."

Charlie gazed down into Natty's face and felt his heart race. He flashed a half smile. "It's not over yet," he said softly as the house lights blinked. They started up the aisle.

As they got to Natty's row, Charlie pulled a folded handkerchief from his jacket pocket and handed it to her. She looked at him quizzically. He smiled. "You're going to need it," he said, leaving her to take his own seat.

Charlie watched the second half of *Les Miserables*, if not immune to, at least prepared for, the heart-wrenching scenes and songs that took first-time viewers by surprise and invariably left them with red, swollen eyes and a lap-full of spent tissues by the time the final curtain fell. He would glance occasionally over at Natty to watch her reaction to the unfolding sadness and she, along with the rest of the Red Bone Baptist Church Social Club, didn't disappoint him. Starting with the defeat at the barricade and the death of the boy, Gavroche, and the other rebels, through Eponine's death and heart breaking lament with Marius, "*A Little Fall Of Rain,*" Valjean's soulful prayer, "*Bring Him Home,*" and then the ultimate tear-jerker, "*Take My Hand,*" as the dying Valjean, along with Cosette, are reunited with Fantine, Natty's shoulders were heaving continuously with silent sobs as she pressed Charlie's handkerchief to her face. And in spite of the sadness of the play, Charlie had to chuckle to himself quietly as the women of the Red Bone Baptist Church Social Club began to moan in unison with an occasional soft wail thrown in at the sadder moments. It was probably how the women mourned together in the church, Charlie guessed, and while it was a little disconcerting, he was sure it wasn't a completely new sound from a *Le Miz* audience. He was glad the women had gotten so emotionally involved. They would remember *Les Miserables* for the rest of their lives.

From across the narrow street, Charlie watched the orderly crowd flow slowly out of the *Imperial Theatre.* The lights from the several other theaters on the cozy street made it feel like daytime even though the November sky was dark at six o'clock. A few limousines and black cars for hire were parked on both sides of the street that was now clogged with pedestrians heading towards Times Square and its subway stops, restaurants, bars and stores. They would join the thousands of other matinee patrons leaving *The John Golden, The Lyceum, Majestic, Schubert, Martin Beck, The Winter Garden* and a dozen other historic theaters in the neighborhood at the same time. A little way up the street, two green Peter Pan busses waited for their tour passengers with motors running. Charlie wondered if they'd be making a stop at the old bus station in New Haven not far from his boyhood home.

Leaning back against a smooth marble wall at the edge of the sidewalk, Charlie watched the crowd drift slowly out of the theater. He wondered if it took longer for *Les Miserables* to empty out after a performance, with most of the women in the audience needing to visit the ladies' room to repair the damage done by tears and tissues.

Mabel Willard with Ada and Janice Lowe finally appeared, followed shortly by the rest of the group. The travel agent and a few of the other women headed down 45th Street toward Times Square, while Mabel, Ada and Janice went up the sidewalk in the other direction. *Probably heading back to the hotel for a nap before dinner,* Charlie guessed. The exiting crowd had dissipated to a trickle when Natty finally appeared on the sidewalk.

Still clutching Charlie's handkerchief Natty started across the street. She had the sophisticated stylish look, but the slow, eyes-down walk in the obviously unfamiliar high heels gave her away. As she got to the curb, Natty looked up and Charlie could see that *Les Miz* had definitely taken its toll on Tina's make-up job. Natty averted her eyes in embarrassment as she came up to Charlie. "Well," she said, with a sniffle, "I didn't think *that* was so funny." They both chuckled. She handed Charlie his mascara-streaked handkerchief. "You could have warned me."

Charlie smiled and held Natty's chin up and dabbed a black speck that she had missed on one cheek. Even with her make-up seriously depleted, she still looked incredibly beautiful. "That would have spoiled all the fun," he said softly.

Her eyes welled up again. "They didn't have to kill the little boy," she said, and then giggled at her own sensitivity.

Charlie smiled and dabbed her eyes with the handkerchief. "C'mon, let's go have a drink."

They walked over 45th Street and down Broadway in no hurry, enjoying the sights and sounds of Times Square and the feeling of shared closeness that came from being surrounded by and completely invisible to thousands of other pedestrians. It was a familiar sensation to Charlie but a new experience for Natty, and it felt good to her, to be finally all alone with Charlie.

Charlie told her about his plan to go up to the classy *Atrium* in the *Marriott Marquis* for a drink but as they passed a crowded Irish-themed restaurant and bar, Natty stopped, took Charlie's hand in hers and pulled him toward the saloon entrance. "C'mon, let's go in here."

She pulled him through the crowded bar until they finally found two vacant stools. Charlie was disappointed when she let go of his hand to jump up onto her seat. It had felt cool and moist and sensual having her fingers wrapped tightly around his and he wanted the feeling to go on.

The bartender was in front of them immediately, smiling at Natty and tossing down two *Amstel Lite* coasters on the bar. Charlie had to chuckle to himself as he watched the attentiveness and level of service generated by an attractive woman. And it wasn't just the bartender. Already he could see men standing around the bar continuing their conversations and sipping their drinks while moving subtly for a better angle to get a look at the small blond with the short hair. Natty ordered two *Jack Daniels* straight up and two *Harp's* pints, and put a twenty dollar bill on the bar. She looked up quizzically at Charlie. "That enough?" she asked meekly.

Charlie put another twenty on top of hers. "Just in case," he said.

Natty rolled her eyeballs. "Be a tough town for an alcoholic."

Their drinks came and Natty kicked off her shoes as she picked up her *Jack Daniels*. "Okay, who should we toast to?"

Charlie held his glass up to hers. "To Woody and Mr. Jacks, our friends," he said.

Natty smiled and nodded her head in agreement. "To Woody and Mr. Jacks," she said softly, "sittin' up in their room in the *Pocahontas Hotel*. Our friends." Natty looked out towards the street, her eyes unfocussed. "Boy, that seems like a long way away from here, doesn't it?"

"Yeah, it is a long way," said Charlie.

They sat close together and drank slowly and talked for a long time and ordered another round and forgot about the *Marriott Marquis*. They talked about their children, about *The Bones* and the upcoming soccer tournament, about Angel Mountain and the DeWitts and Natty's mother and Uncle Petey and where they would go after the *eminent domain* hearing and lost their farm. Another *Jack Daniels* and *Harp's* came and they talked about the library and the soccer field, the power plant and the changes at DD&M, and then Charlie told her about China.

Natty gazed at a spot on Charlie's jacket and nodded absently, mellowed by the liquor and the large beers. Her eyes rejoined his. "You going to go?"

Charlie drained the rest of his beer and looked at his watch. He stood up from his stool, his thighs tight against Natty's knees and shrugged. "I don't know," he said. "It depends."

"On what?"

He shrugged again. "On how some things go in West Virginia." He smiled down at her. "Now it's time to get to the restaurant. *You* need to eat."

Natty grinned up at him. "I need to *pee*," she said, standing up, forced tightly against Charlie by the crush of the crowded bar. For a moment, they looked into each other's eyes and Natty was an instant away from reaching up and putting both hands behind Charlie's neck and pulling him down to her and kissing him on the mouth, but she hesitated, and then dropped her eyes from his. *No, their first real kiss shouldn't be here in this crowded barroom.* Then Charlie backed into the aisle and Natty looked down to find her shoes.

They walked a little more briskly to the restaurant, talking and enjoying the cool night air and the excitement of the theater district on a Saturday night. It would take them about ten minutes Charlie thought, and they would be a few minutes late for their reservation, but it didn't matter. With Natty by his side, it seemed like nothing mattered. It was turning into a magical day, a day to cherish every minute.

The restaurant was perfect, a place that Natty would really enjoy, thought Charlie. Romantically subdued lighting, not too crowded, and a candlelit table with a starched white tablecloth, near the window overlooking the busy sidewalk. She smiled her approval.

Charlie ordered a bottle of wine in lieu of cocktails, which was fine with Natty after the *Jack Daniels* and beer. He approved the wine and told the waiter they were in no hurry and would take a while looking at the menu. Natty felt like she was in the middle of a movie.

"Another toast," said Charlie, holding up his glass. "To *The Bones* and winning the tournament in Charleston."

Natty held up her glass. "To *The Bones*, the best dressed soccer team in West Virginia."

They touched glasses and started to sip the wine when something on the sidewalk outside the large window caught Natty's eye. She turned and laughed. "Oh *God,* Charlie, *look.*" She put down her glass and sat back in her chair to watch.

Charlie had to lean toward Natty while twisting his head around to see what she could see, and there on the sidewalk, examining the restaurant's menu box, were the unmistakable figures of Mabel Willard, and Ada and Janice Lowe. Mabel and Janice were standing behind Ada who had the job of reading the menu through her thick bifocals to no doubt check out the dollar amounts following the entrée descriptions. Mabel and Janice looked tired and cold and not very optimistic. Ada was leaning in close to the menu and squinting severely to see the small type.

Charlie chuckled and grinned at Natty as he put his napkin on the table. "I'll go get them," he said, rising from his chair. He reached into his pocket for his money clip, peeling off a twenty, which he pressed into the waiter's hand as he moved toward the front door. "We're going to need a bigger table," he said.

"Is not a problem sir," said the waiter.

After several minutes on the sidewalk, cajoling, begging, and finally threatening the three ladies, Charlie was able to coax the women into the restaurant. Like the hostess of the table, Natty hugged each of the women and tried her best to make them relax and feel welcome. Charlie hung up their coats and came back to find himself sitting across the round table from Natty.

Mabel put her hand over Natty's on the table and had a huge grin on as she looked back and forth between Natty and Charlie. "So what about our little girl here Charlie? Cleans up pretty good when she wants to, huh?" The other women giggled.

"C'mon Mabel," Natty protested softly.

Charlie just smiled at Natty. "So what have you ladies been up to?" he asked, to change the subject.

Mabel, Ada and Janice had gone back to the hotel for a nap before venturing out to look for a *nice* restaurant for dinner, and had been wandering around for an hour and a half trying to find someplace *reasonable* that they could get into without reservations. Charlie felt sorry for the ladies and was glad they'd stumbled by the restaurant. *New York isn't an easy place for first-time tourists of limited means.* And he felt somewhat responsible for them.

Charlie finally convinced the ladies (with Natty's help), that CanAmex would be footing the bill for dinner, which they were a little more comfortable with than they would be with the truth. Then, after more cajoling, they relented to having before-dinner cocktails – *Southern Comfort Manhattans* for Mabel and Ada, and white wine for Janice – but with the understanding as Mabel put forth strongly, that 'none of the ladies would be ordering that *fifty-two dollar steak* they saw on the menu!'

With the drinks and Natty and Charlie's hospitality, the women gradually relaxed and warmed up to the occasion. Soon, Mabel Willard was occupying center stage with her accustomed non-stop monolog about whatever subject popped into her head and had everyone at the table (and a few neighboring tables) in stitches with her observations about New York and New Yorkers and New York prices. They had another round of drinks and Charlie ordered two bottles of wine for the table. The women were enjoying themselves now and there was no more talk about how they were imposing. And in spite of the change of plans, Charlie and Natty were enjoying themselves too. It was a nice table to be having dinner at. Occasionally, Charlie would catch Natty's eye and she would smile at him and he could see that she was also enjoying the moment and didn't feel imposed upon. *No, that wasn't an emotion that Natty would be too familiar with.*

When the ladies refused to order appetizers, Charlie ordered a selection for the table to share, and then Natty confiscated the menus to keep them from focusing on the prices. She knew the women well enough, she said, to order for them. Their waiter stood by with his pad and pencil.

"Now Mabel, I know you love veal, so how about the *Veal Marsala?*"

"How much is it?" said Mabel sternly.

Natty and Charlie laughed. "It's very reasonable," said Natty.

"What's the cheapest thing on the menu?" asked Mabel.

"The *Veal Marsala.*"

"Okay, I'll have *that* then."

"Good, " said Natty, turning to Janice Lowe next to her. "Jan, *Chicken Parmesan* for you, right?"

"Does it cost more than what Mabel's having?"

"No, it's the same price. Cheapest thing on the menu," Natty said.

"Okay then, I'll have the *Chicken Parmesan,* thank you," said Janice.

Natty looked over to Ada and then down at the menu. "Now Ada, how about . . ."

Ada Lowe held her glass in the air. "I'm going to have another *Manhattan* and that fifty-two dollar *steak!*" said the old black woman, breaking up the table along with a couple of nearby eavesdroppers.

For the next two hours they talked and ate, drank two more bottles of wine and enjoyed a wonderful meal, one of the best they'd ever had, the women from West Virginia agreed. Mabel, as always, had occupied most of the conversation but later gave way to Ada who fascinated them with her stories of growing up in the coal fields of Appalachia in the thirties and forties. Even Janice Lowe, as shy as her daughter Emma, joined the conversation when it got around to *The Bones* and their star player. "All that girl talks about now is that boy Gabe from Welch, and how they're going to play together on the high school team next year," said Janice in her timid voice. "And he comes over and they go to kickin' soccer balls to each other for *hours*, they do!"

Natty laughed. "I think our little Emma's in *love*, is what I think!"

"Well, she sure is happy about *somethin'*," said Janice.

They had coffee while sharing some decadently rich desserts, and before they knew it, it was past eleven o'clock.

On her way out of the restaurant Natty waited until the rest of the group went out, then she spent her last fifteen dollars on a long cigar for Charlie. He just smiled at her and nodded when she gave it to him. He lighted it on the sidewalk as the group started up 48th Street for the walk back to the *Milford Plaza*. They walked the slow, contented walk of late night diners who had stayed too long and eaten too much. It was a pleasant, warm feeling, even with a damp mist developing in the cool night air.

"Now you kids don't have to worry 'bout us," said Mabel over her shoulder to Charlie and Natty following behind the other three women. "We can find our ways to the hotel just fine."

"We'll take you there Mabel," said Charlie. He laughed. "Want to make sure you ladies don't sneak off and go out night-clubbing." The women shrieked at the suggestion.

Natty, walking slowly in her high heels and Charlie enjoying his cigar, gradually fell a little ways behind the other women and were out of earshot. "Was a nice dinner Charlie, huh? It was okay, *right*?" said Natty.

Charlie blew out a mouthful of smoke. "Yeah," he said softly, "it was a *real* nice dinner. I'm glad we found them. I think they really enjoyed themselves. I did too." Charlie thought about Natty next to him and the three ladies in front of them – poor women from Appalachia, from McDowell County, West Virginia, one of the poorest counties in America – and tried to remember when he'd enjoyed a dinner out with people more than he had tonight. Certainly not the regular dinners with Ellen and their country club friends at one of New York or Westchester's finer restaurants, with the conversation devoted *ad nauseam* to the art of living well. *Natty and Mabel, and Ada and Janice Lowe were people without egos or jealousies, without greed or pretensions, with no agendas or ambitions beyond being decent people living a decent life. God, it's nice to be around them.*

Natty interrupted Charlie's thoughts. "Been a nice day, huh Charlie?" She bumped Charlie's side with hers and smiled.

Charlie nodded. "Yeah, been a great day." He grinned down at her. "And a *long* day too. . . since six-thirty this morning."

Natty nodded in agreement and laughed. "Maybe that's why my eyes are closing."

It was quarter of twelve when they got back to the main entrance of the Milford Plaza. Mabel, Ada, and Janice thanked Charlie profusely and each gave him a long hug. Then they hugged Natty and quickly filed through the revolving door to the hotel lobby, leaving her and Charlie on the sidewalk. There was a steady stream of pedestrian traffic entering and exiting the hotel and along the 45th Street sidewalk, even nearing midnight.

Charlie stood in front of Natty and looked down into her face, her make-up job totally depleted and her eyelids heavy. He chuckled at her condition. "Time for you to get to bed little girl."

Natty blinked sleepily and nodded. "Yeah, I guess that's it for me."

Charlie came forward, kissed her lightly on the forehead, and then backed away. "Goodnight Nat. See you in the morning. It'll be a nice morning for a run."

Natty folded her arms across her chest to ward off the cold. She squinted up at Charlie and wrinkled her nose. "You know, I get tired of thankin' you for everything all the time Charlie, so I'm going to just stop doin' that. But, the ladies had a good time tonight . . . a *great* time . . . one of those occasions they'll be talking about for a long time, and me too." She nodded her head in affirmation. "That was real nice."

Charlie just watched her for a few seconds, not saying anything, not wanting to leave her. Finally he smiled at her and shrugged. "Go to sleep Nat. I'll see you in the morning," he said, backing away from her.

"Why don't you take a cab, Charlie?" she said.

"No, I'm just going to walk and enjoy my cigar. It's not far," he said moving backwards a few steps. "Night Nat." She waved to him and tried to smile.

A group of German schoolgirls were crowded into the elevator foyer when Natty got there. She had to pass up three elevators before finally squeezing into one that seemed to stop at every floor on the way up to twelve. Natty pulled out her key card as she padded down the carpeted hallway. Mabel would probably be fast asleep already, she thought, so she'd try not to wake her.

Standing in front of her door Natty reached out to put the key in the lighted slot, but stopped. She looked down at the card suspended in air inches away from the slot and then up at the door in front of her, the door to safety and security and a warm bed. *The door to her same old life. The door back to Red Bone and Buck and being happy if he came home before the sun rose, and hoping to make it through another night without a beating or another day without an old, sick, poor person dying on her. The door back to the same crummy little room in the same crummy little trailer for her children – hillbilly kids with no future and no way out of the mountains. Because if she went through the door the night was over, and when would she ever get another chance to be with Charlie? Shit, Charlie! What happened?* She squeezed her cheeks up tight to her eyes to stop the tears but they came anyway. Then, she turned and ran down the hallway.

A man in the elevator asked her if she was all right and she nodded and smiled and wiped away the tears. It took forever to reach the lobby. *Which door had she come in? And why were there so many goddamned people hanging around the lobby at midnight?* She maneuvered through the crowd and out onto 8th Avenue, and knew right away it wasn't where she'd left Charlie. There were several empty cabs at the curb but she didn't have any money and didn't know the address anyway. She ran to the corner, slowly in the painful high heels. 46th Street. *Shit! What direction was it to Times Square and then to Park Avenue?*

Natty ran clumsily back down to the corner of 45th Street and recognized where she was. She went past the hotel entrance and then the theaters, and was relieved to find Broadway, but she couldn't believe the amount of traffic and the number of pedestrians still crowding the sidewalks after midnight, the entire area lit up like daylight by the big signs high overhead. The cabs were bumper-to-bumper, and the sidewalk crowd was heavier with men, moving more slowly, a little blacker and hipper and threatening than it was in the afternoon. Everyone seemed like a giant to her now as she dodged her way through the crowd, the flashing, flowing, colored lights from the stores and the billboards confusing her and making everything look different from how it looked in the daytime. She heard a few calls from behind her – '*hey baby, hey mama where you goin' in such a hurry?*'- as she struggled to find the route she and Charlie had taken on their run in the morning, which seemed like days ago. She should have paid attention to how the white limousine drove her to the *Carlos Marche Salon*, but all she looked at was the inside of the car.

She knew she had to cross Broadway and then go south for a few blocks – *how many? she had no idea* – and then left again and across a few more of the big north - and - south Avenues she remembered from studying the little map. *But how would she recognize Charlie's building if she could even find Park Avenue?*

She edged along next to a huge herd of people traversing Times Square at a light. Then they were on a traffic island waiting interminably for the sea of racing cabs to come to a brief stop. When the light changed, Natty moved diagonally across the wide expanse cutting dangerously through the traffic coming to a stop in the other direction. And then it started to rain.

The sidewalk was still crowded with slow moving walkers and people milling about in front of restaurants, movie theaters and xxx clubs. *God, how can all these people still be out here so late at night?* The pace was too slow. She'd never catch up to Charlie before he got to his building. It had taken her too long to go up and down the elevator at the hotel.

At the corner of 43rd Street, she saw that there was less traffic on the cross street and she would be able move faster. She stopped and kicked off her shoes, scooped them up by the straps in her left hand, her small purse in her right hand, and sprinted down the sidewalk. Her short dress was easy to run in and she ran as fast as her vision of the sidewalk would allow on the dark street.

It was a steady rain now and Natty was thoroughly soaked by the time she darted across the Avenue of The Americas just in front of the traffic racing away from the light. She ran in the street where the sidewalk was dark but the traffic forced her back to the irregular sidewalk where the cracks in the cement and the heating grates tore at the soles of her nylons.

At Madison Avenue, she turned right and ran on the nearly empty wide sidewalk. She remembered that in the morning, they had run along a *Thirty-something Street* most of the way, but she wasn't sure which one. The traffic was racing at high speed along 42nd Street, so she crossed Madison first, and took a brief rest at the corner while waiting for the light to change. There was a large wrought iron basket overflowing with trash at the crosswalk. Natty tossed her wet high heels onto the pile; she was tired of carrying them and she hated the shoes anyway. She looked at her watch. *Christ, Charlie probably got a taxi as soon as it started raining and he's already in his building and she'd have no way to contact him.* She wondered if big office buildings on Park Avenue had doorbells. She edged anxiously out onto 42nd Street wondering if the light would ever stop the endless flow of traffic.

She ran fast now and her lungs and legs were starting to feel the early burn that felt so good to her on South County Road just before hitting the steep climb up to Old Red Bone. The soles of her pantyhose had torn away completely and the foot parts were now flopping around her ankles.

39th Street didn't look familiar so she ran on to 38th. At the corner she stopped and ran back a short way to the recessed doorway of a foreign airline sales office and pulled off her pantyhose and rolled them in a ball. She deposited them in the trash container at the corner with a chuckle. *They must find some weird stuff in the public trash in New York City!*

Natty jogged down 38th Street and was relieved to see she was finally at Park Avenue. It was wider than she'd recalled it from earlier in the day, and the street was heavy with fast moving traffic. She scanned the sidewalk on the opposite side of the street as far as she could see in each direction without seeing anyone who looked like Charlie. She had no idea of what the building looked like from afar.

She jogged across Park Avenue in less of a hurry now. The futility of the situation was starting to set in and Natty was resolved to the fact that Charlie was already in his apartment, probably fast asleep. Tomorrow, he'd be outside her hotel in the morning and they'd go for a run and they'd talk and maybe walk a little and get cup of coffee somewhere and that would be fun, and then she'd go on the museum tour and then back to Red Bone and maybe she'd see Charlie again, maybe not, the way things were going with his company. Maybe he'd just go to China now without even going back to West Virginia, and forget all about her.

Natty looked up at the buildings and sighed. She decided to go a block in each direction looking for the *Carlos Marche* sign and then give it up and walk back to the *Milford Plaza* and hope she didn't get mugged. She went south at a fast walk and found nothing. Then she retraced her steps and headed north. There was very little pedestrian traffic on the sidewalk, and the buildings and few store fronts on Park Avenue were dark. Natty was starting to shiver from the cold now. The rain had abated but the temperature seemed to be dropping, and her short dress and jacket were soaked. She could feel the sideways glances of the few late-night walkers taking note of the barefoot woman, soaked and searching for something – like a lost dog – and suddenly felt foolish and very alone.

Passing a small shop, Natty noticed a full length mirror facing the sidewalk at the end of its front window. She glanced at her reflection as she went passed and then stopped and went back and walked up close to the mirror. She'd forgotten about her haircut, and it looked strange to her, like she was looking at someone else. The rain had matted down her hair, making it look even shorter. She ran her fingers through it to rough it up and then backed away from the mirror a few feet to get a full view. She had to admit to herself that even after running halfway across Manhattan barefoot in the pouring rain at midnight, she didn't look bad. She stared into the mirror and wondered what Buck was going to say about her new look.

She turned away from the window and then saw the silver lettering for the *Carlos Marche Salon* a few yards away from her at the same time she heard Charlie's voice.

"Natty?" His voice came from the shadows under the overhang in front of the large glass front doors. Then he stepped out into the light. "Nat?" he repeated.

Natty had stopped in her tracks when she heard him. Now they were twenty feet apart.

"Hey Charlie." She saw that he was without his sport jacket. He must have gone inside and come back out. She moved slowly toward him. "How'd you know I'd come?" She stopped a few yards away from him.

"I didn't. I was just hoping. Thought I'd come out and take a look." He smiled. "I'm glad you came Nat. I'm surprised you could find it."

Natty smiled. "Wasn't easy." She crossed her arms in front of her. "Lost my shoes, and then my stockings," she said with a chuckle.

"I can see. You must be freezing."

"Nah, I'm okay. Little wet, but . . ." She looked around her nervously.

Charlie watched her for few moments before speaking. "You want to come up?" he asked softly.

Natty smiled at him. Then her eyes went up and her head followed, looking toward the lights visible on the second floor. She stared at the second floor windows for a few seconds and then took in a deep breath and let it out slowly. She looked down toward the sidewalk at her feet and squeezed her eyes shut. "*God dammit*," she whispered to herself. "God *dammit*," she repeated angrily, stamping her bare foot against the wet sidewalk. She looked up and Charlie saw tears in her eyes.

He took a long step toward her and put his hands on her upper arms. "Nat, what is it?"

She shook her head and had to take another deep breath. Tears ran down her cheeks. She shrugged her shoulders. "I can't do this," she said softly. She looked up into Charlie's eyes. "I love you Charlie," her voice squeaked, "but I can't *do* this."

"Natty . . ."

She dropped her arms, twisting away from him and took several quick steps across the sidewalk. Then she stopped abruptly with her back to Charlie. He watched her shake her head in frustration and then ball her fists in anger and swing them through the air. "What the *fuck* is wrong with me Charlie?" she said loudly, turning halfway toward him. An older couple slowly walking a small white poodle was approaching them. She opened her fists and shook her palms in the air. "People have affairs and jump into bed with each other all the time! Why is it so *goddamned hard for us?*" she pleaded. The older couple and the poodle were between them. They smiled amusedly at Natty. She smiled with embarrassment. "Sorry," she said softly. The man chuckled and tipped his hat. Natty watched them move away down the sidewalk out of earshot. She sniffed and rubbed the tears from her eyes with both hands as she moved back closer to Charlie. She crossed her arms over her chest and smiled at him. "I'm sorry Charlie."

"Don't be," he said. "It's okay Nat, I . . ."

She shook her head. "I came all the way to New York just to spend the night with you Charlie, to make us . . . you know, to make something happen with us, 'cause, well, I love you Charlie," the tears flowed again, "'cause you're the most wonderful man I'll ever meet in *my* life – *Christ* Charlie, you're like the top ten all rolled into *one* – and I think you love me too, but . . ." Natty blinked her eyes rapidly. "Now we're here, and," she scrunched up her cheeks against the tears and shrugged, "and I can't do it. I can't *do* it Charlie." She squinted up at him pleadingly. "I can't do that to Buck."

"Natty, it's okay. I understand." Charlie moved forward and put his palms on Natty's cheeks and wiped the tears gently from her eyes with his thumbs. "Remember that night we visited Woody and Mr. Jacks the first time?"

"Yeah, I remember," she said softly, covering Charlie's hands with her own. "*Course* I remember . . . the night you said I was *remarkable*." They both chuckled. They stood close together for a few seconds, and then Charlie kissed her lightly on the forehead and took his hands from her face. Natty held onto his hands as they dropped between them and wrinkled up her nose. "So how come this is so hard for us Charlie? What's the matter with us?"

Charlie squeezed her hands. "There's *nothing* the matter with us Nat," he said firmly. "I think we're just two moral people who find it hard to cheat on their spouses. And I think you're wrong . . . a lot of people do it, but I think *most* people are like *us*. Most people find it very hard to do."

"Yeah well, *most people* ain't married to *Buck*," Natty said, letting go of Charlie's hands. She turned away from him and walked a few steps away. She put her arms across her chest and her feet together and gazed off down Park Avenue at the tall buildings. She turned back to Charlie. "So, what should I do Charlie?"

Charlie put his hands in his pockets and looked out at the traffic on Park Avenue while he thought. After a few seconds he nodded, as if to himself, and smiled at Natty. "How about you go back to Red Bone and tell Buck that you're leaving him and that you and I are in love?"

Natty smiled and wrinkled up her nose. "How about *you* tell him." Charlie laughed. They were both silent for a few seconds and then the rain started again.

"Sure you don't want to come inside and warm up? said Charlie.

Natty smiled at him and looked up at the second floor again. "Charlie, if I was to go in there with you, I'd probably never go back to Red Bone again."

"What about your kids?"

Natty squinted. "*What* kids?" They laughed and then stood in silence for several moments. Natty took off her earrings and the silver choker. She looked at the jewelry in her palm for a few seconds as the rain splattered around the silver chains. She handed them to Charlie. "Tell Tina thanks, okay?" Charlie nodded. "Can you get me a cab, Charlie? I gotta go."

Charlie moved to the curb with a hand in the air. It was probably the easiest time of day to get a cab on Park Avenue. One pulled over much quicker than Charlie had wanted. He reached a twenty-dollar bill through the window and told the driver, "Milford Plaza."

As she got into the cab, Natty stopped with an open door between them. "Charlie, think we should probably skip the run tomorrow, okay? I gotta figure this out."

Charlie put his hands on top of Natty's at the top of the door and squeezed them gently. "Yeah, okay Nat. You let me know what you want to do. I'll see you down in Red Bone. See you in about a week."

She smiled tightly. "Yeah, see you Charlie." The cab pulled away from the curb quickly, turned left and rumbled toward 8th Avenue. Natty let her head fall back against the top of the seat and closed her eyes and thought about taking a long hard run up South County Road and along the side of Red Bone Mountain and sitting for a while in the morning sun up on the boulder and enjoying her daydreams.

Chapter 32

E ve Brewster was standing in the Red Bone Baptist Church parking lot when the bus pulled in on Sunday night. She wore a long winter coat, buttoned up against the evening cold and a sad, tired face. At her feet were a half dozen Merit 100 cigarette butts flattened against the sandy pavement.

Natty knew it was trouble as soon as she saw her. Through the window, their eyes met with no smile or wave or even a glimmer of welcome from Eve, and Natty knew that something bad had happened to someone. It wouldn't be Buck or the kids – Sally or Rose or maybe even Big Frank would have been there – so most likely it was one of her clients, someone that Eve was also close to. With their eyes still locked as the bus rolled slowly to a stop, Natty winced with the pain of realization.

With her hands jammed into the jacket pockets of her new blue warm-up suit, Natty already had tears in her eyes as she walked slowly from the bus. Eve laughed and cried at the same time when she saw Natty's new hair style. She moved toward Natty and enveloped her in her arms and held her close. "Oh God Natty, you look sooo beautiful!" she said, squeezing her tight. Then she sobbed. "I'm so sorry Nat."

Eve released her grip and they separated a few inches but still held onto each other. Natty looked up into Eve's bloodshot eyes. "It's Mr. Jacks, huh Eve?"

Eve's lips quivered as she took in a deep breath. She grimaced with pain and shook her head. "No honey, it's Woody."

Woody Givens died in his chair in his room in the *Pocahontas Hotel* on Saturday night, about the same time that Natty, Charlie and the ladies were having dinner in New York. Natty squeezed her eyes tightly for several seconds to shut out the pain then leaned against Eve and sobbed once. "Aw geeze Evie, not Woody. He wasn't supposed to . . ." She looked up at Eve suddenly and winced again. "Oh *God*, what about Mr. Jacks?"

"We put him in Charlie's place. Hank and I brought him over and got his things and put him up at Charlie's so we could watch him," said Eve. "Didn't think Charlie would mind."

"No, he won't mind," Natty said softly, wiping the tears from her eyes. She pulled away from Eve and started back toward the bus. "Gotta get my bag and go see Mr. Jacks."

"They're going to move him to a home up in Beckley next week," Eve called after her. "Hank talked to someone."

Natty stopped and shrugged. "Geeze Eve, you'd think we could do better than that."

Natty left her car in front of the store and walked over to the *Pocahontas Hotel*. She found her way through the darkness of the first floor to the stairway, which was still lighted by the single bulb from high up on the fourth floor. She wanted to get anything else that Mr. Jacks might need, but also she wanted to, in her own way, say goodbye to her friend Woody Givens. For over twenty years – since she was a little girl – she'd known Woody, the huge, gentle black man who would call her over in the restaurant and always give her a shiny quarter, no matter how poor he was. Sometimes he'd walk down the hill and push Natty on the swing when she was watching Buck and the other boys play baseball. He was one of her first true friends in Red Bone, someone she knew she could count on to always be her friend and not leave her.

The room smelled the same – it always would – of tobacco smoke and men's bodies. Natty loved the smell of the room. She turned on the floor lamp standing next to Woody's chair and looked around. Mr. Jacks' table and his drawer had been cleaned out and there was nothing left in his dresser. Eve and Hank must have taken it all across the street. The refrigerator was empty and unplugged with a dishtowel hanging over the door to keep it open a crack.

Natty went over and sat down on Woody's bed, sliding toward the middle where the springs and the thin mattress had long ago given up the fight to support the weight of the large man. She looked at his empty chair in front of the small TV and beyond it, Mr. Jacks' straight chair against the wall next to the window, still cracked an inch to let the smoke out. She thought about all the times over the years that she had come up here, and how the two old black men would smile and perk up and always be so glad to see her, and they'd tell her stories and rib each other mercilessly in good fun, and so enjoy their beer and a small glass of *Jack Daniels* and never complain about anything, even after their bodies started to fail and their minds began to dim. Never a bitter word about the hard lives they were born into or the unfairness of working forty years in the mines to end their days in a dark, dingy room in Red Bone, West Virginia – the last residents of the *Pocahontas Hotel.* Natty always felt safe and warm in this room. She was going to miss it.

Natty reached down under the bed for Woody's secret cigar box where he kept his valuables. She was surprised there was so little in it – an old set of keys to locks long forgotten; a small wad of bills in a paper clip that totaled thirty-eight dollars; a brittle, folded copy of his Army discharge form; several old UMWA membership cards; and a plastic ID card with a small picture of Woody next to a line in bold letters that read: *Woodrow Givens,* SHIFT FOREMAN, and under it *Poca Coal Company # 7, Red Bone, WV.* Natty put the ID card in her pocket. She'd add it to her own little box she kept at the back of the bottom drawer of her dresser. The box with Birdie Merkely's *Pensacola* picture. With the cigar box under her arm, she took a long look around the room and turned off the light.

Going down the stairs for the last time, Natty couldn't hold back the tears any longer. She stepped slowly, holding on to the banister, and sobbed for Woody and also for Mr. Jacks who, she knew, wouldn't last long in a strange home in Beckley without his friend. Outside the front door she stopped and wiped her eyes and took in several deep breaths of the cold night air and started back toward the *Barney's Building.* She walked slowly down the middle of Main Street, suddenly tired from the adventuresome weekend, tired of crying, tired of feeling so alone. *God, how do people live in small towns filled with old people getting ready to die?*

Charlie's apartment already reeked of tobacco smoke. Natty opened the door quietly and saw Mr. Jacks sitting next to the kitchen table with his back against the wall smoking a cigarette and talking to Hank, sitting at the table with his back to her.

"Hey Mr. Jacks," she said, leaning over and kissing him on the forehead. She smiled at Hank whose eyes were as bloodshot as she imagined hers were, and put a hand on his shoulder. "I'm going to try to call Charlie," she said to Hank who nodded his agreement and looked back to Mr. Jacks.

Natty went to the roll top desk where she'd seen one of Charlie's business cards. In the kitchen, she took the phone off the hook and saw that it was cordless. She studied it and pressed some buttons until it lit up. She went out on the porch and held the small card under the yellow light up on the brick wall over the card table. First, she tried the Dietrich Delahunt & Mackey number and got a recorded message. Then she dialed his cell phone number.

Charlie answered after two rings. "Hank?"

"No, it's me, Charlie. Natty," she said.

"What'd you do, break into my apartment?" Charlie said with a chuckle.

Natty walked toward the dark end of the porch away from the open kitchen door. "Charlie . . . *Woody* died . . . Saturday night."

"*Aw no*. Geeze Nat. I'm sorry," Charlie said softly. "That's lousy, *Jesus*. Poor Woody. What was it?"

"His heart they figure."

"What about Mr. Jacks?"

"We got him up here in your apartment. Hank and Eve brought him over."

"Good, that's good. Can't leave him in his room."

Natty squeezed her eyes shut for a second and drew in a deep breath. "Yeah, he'll be going to a nursing home up in Beckley they got for old coal miners, Eve says. 'Bout a week or so."

Charlie remained silent. He could feel Natty's sorrow over the phone and didn't know what to say. He could hear her sniffing away her tears. "I'll be down there in a few days," he said finally. "I'll be down for the Angel Mountain hearing on Friday. It's going to be at the High School."

"Yeah, I knew that," said Natty weakly. Neither of them spoke for several seconds. Natty leaned on the porch railing and looked out at the black night to the west. There wasn't a flicker of light anywhere. She swallowed hard. "Charlie?" she said to make sure the cordless phone was still working.

"Yeah I'm here Nat." he answered.

"Charlie, I've been thinking. Thinking about a lot a things since yesterday." He remained silent. "Thinking about *us* and everything, you know . . ." Natty paused and heard only Charlie's breathing. "And . . . *shit Charlie,* you ain't goin' to help me out at all here are you?"

Charlie smiled. "Go on Nat."

Natty breathed deeply for a few seconds and then backed away from the railing and leaned back against the wall. The bricks felt warm against her back. "Charlie, will you take me away from here?" she said very softly. "Me and my kids? Will you take us away from Red Bone to . . . somewhere else, somewhere we can be, you know. . . like a family?" Tears rolled down her cheeks again. "That's what I want to do Charlie." She wiped her cheek with her fingers and stopped talking. She winced at Charlie's silence, wondering once again if she was making a fool of herself.

Charlie cleared his throat. "Natty, are you sure that's what you want?"

"Yeah, Charlie, I'm sure," she said sobbing softly. "I'm sure. I love you Charlie and I don't want to lose you," she sobbed louder and the tears ran onto the phone, "and I can't *do* this any more *Charlie* . . ."

"Nat, Nat, it's okay," he said, trying to calm her. "Nat, of course I will."

"You *will* Charlie?"

"You *know* that's what I want. I love you Nat. I love you, and I love the kids."

Natty closed her eyes and drew in a deep breath of air to stop sobbing. She wiped her eyes with her sleeve, sniffed her tears back, and smiled, and then she giggled. "*Jesus Charlie*, been waitin' my whole life to hear someone say that to me and now you're a thousand miles away and I can't even hug you or kiss you or anything."

Charlie chuckled. "Don't worry, you'll get your chance."

There was a long silent pause between them. Natty cleared her throat. "Charlie, I'll tell Buck. When it's right, I'll tell Buck."

"Yeah, you have to do that. Listen Nat, I don't know what's going to happen after the hearing. I may not be working down there so . . ."

"Charlie, I'd have to leave real soon, you know, after I tell Buck. I can't tell him and then stay around here for too long."

"Yeah, I know that. When do you want to leave?" asked Charlie.

Natty swallowed the nervousness rising up from her stomach and tried to think. "Um, can't leave before the soccer tournament. Gotta stay for that, for the kids."

"Okay," said Charlie firmly. "Right after the tournament. When you get back from Charleston, have your stuff and the kids' things ready to go, and we'll leave then."

"Yeah, okay Charlie, right after the tournament. We'll leave then. We'll find somewhere to go and . . ."

Charlie cut in. "I'll figure that out Nat. I'll take care of it."

Natty smiled into the phone. "Okay Charlie. I'm going to go now. I'm going to go see Mr. Jacks."

"Give him a hug for me Nat. See you Friday."

*   *   *

A white super-stretch limo pulled into the Red Bone High School parking lot right behind Charlie. He watched it in his rearview mirror as it veered away toward the door that opened to the long hallway leading to the gymnasium. Charlie backed the Lexus into a spot next to the rusted chain link fence and turned off the car. He watched the limo driver open one of the rear doors and then trot around to open the other door. The first to exit was Leonard, the Kerns & Yarbrough lawyer, carrying two briefcases. He was followed by two other young lawyer types, wearing dark suits and also carrying expensive looking briefcases. From the door facing Charlie, the huge form of Kevin Mulrooney slowly emerged followed by two other men Charlie didn't recognize but who seemed to be with the man from Ackerly Coal. Mulrooney took a last swig from a clear plastic cup and tossed it to the pavement. Finally, the silver mane of Vernon Yarbrough arose on the far side of the limo. The lawyer surveyed the area around him, buttoned the jacket of his dark blue suit and took his briefcase from Leonard. Satisfied that his team was accounted for, Yarbrough started for the side door of the High School.

Charlie got out of the Lexus and walked across the parking lot. He had to shield his eyes from the brown leaves and dust that circled through the air on the cold wind of the gray day. *A lousy day, for a lousy event,* thought Charlie. In a few minutes, he knew, Bud and Alice DeWitt were going to have their farm taken from them by the system . . . a corrupt system of big business, influential lobbyists, and powerful law firms trampling on the rights of the poor and the disenfranchised. And the system was also going to trample on him a little bit after the hearing, when Torkelson and Tuthill, and Warren Brand consolidated their power. Charlie had to smile when he thought of how little it mattered to him now that he and Natty were going to be together. But that would be no comfort to Bud and Alice DeWitt.

There were a dozen cars in the parking lot but Charlie didn't see Natty's Accord as he made his way to the door. He noticed a gray van with government plates, an old brown pick-up truck that he'd seen parked next to the barn on Angel Mountain, and the company's black Navigator that Terry Summers must be driving.

Charlie walked down the long, dark hallway and stood in the doorway of the gymnasium to survey the scene. The rows of folding chairs were set up facing him, and to his right, just inside the door, several uniformed men were busy setting up what appeared to be a temporary judge's bench, a witness box with a microphone, and a voice-activated stenography machine on a small folding table in front of the judge's bench. Charlie surmised that the judge probably wanted to be close to the door to make a quick getaway after the hearing.

Two long wooden tables were set up at the front of the makeshift courtroom. At the table directly in front of Charlie, Budd and Alice DeWitt sat pulled in close to the edge, motionless with stoic looks on their faces. Bud was wearing his farming overalls and the same *Peterbilt* hat he'd been wearing the last time Charlie had seen him. In the first row of folding chairs behind the DeWitts, Natty's mother Sarah sat next to Petey DeWitt. Sitting at one end of the table, a small, elderly white-haired man was fondling a sheaf of notes in his hands while he leaned forward and spoke to the DeWitts in a low voice. Dandruff sparkled on the shoulders of the lawyer's blue blazer. On the floor at his feet was a very old leather briefcase.

At the other table, Leonard was in earnest discussion with the two other young lawyers. The table was covered with files and note pads. Under the table were two plastic file boxes filled with multicolored tabbed folders. Beyond the table, standing under the folded up basketball backboard, a group of smiling men surrounded a red-faced Kevin Mulrooney enjoying a light-hearted conversation. In Mulrooney's group, Charlie recognized the representative from the Governor's Office and the State Senator who had appeared at the *cooling pond* hearing before the Planning Board two months earlier.

A few yards away from the coal men, Terry Summers and two other men Charlie didn't know, stood listening closely as Warren Brand held forth on some topic while he coolly eyed Charlie across the room. Charlie was surprised to see Brand. He hadn't expected that. His career with Dietrich Delahunt & Mackey may be over sooner than he'd expected. Then Charlie was surprised again as he looked to the far corner of the gym and saw Vernon Yarbrough with his back to him, in close conversation with Larry Tuthill to his right, and staring at Charlie over Yarbrough's shoulder, the imposing figure of Jack Torkelson. Charlie couldn't imagine why Torkelson was present, and immediately wondered if all this time, he had somehow underestimated the importance to CanAmex of the taking of the Angel Mountain farm.

As he walked over to the DeWitt table, Charlie scanned the dozen or so spectators seated in the rows of folding chairs of the "public" section of the courtroom. There were two groups of men who were obviously miners and had a personal interest in the hearing, an elderly couple, and few individuals that Charlie had seen before in Eve's restaurant. In the center of the back row Charlie noticed an older man with short gray hair who didn't seem like a local to him. The man wore a rumpled khaki trench coat over a brown suit, a white shirt with a loose collar and a thin black tie. In his lap he held an old gray fedora. Even seated, you could tell that the man was tall. He had a thin, weathered face with slits for eyes and a protruding Adam's apple visible above his wilted collar.

Bud DeWitt stood as Charlie approached the front of the table. He took Charlie's hand. "Hello Mr. Burden," he said quietly.

Charlie smiled grimly. "Sorry it had to come to this Bud." He looked down at Alice who raised her eyes to his briefly with a only a flicker of a smile. Bud DeWitt nodded and sat down in his chair. Charlie could see that the DeWitt's weren't in a very talkative mood. He nodded at Sarah DeWitt sitting behind Alice as he moved around the table. She smiled at him while her sky-blue eyes seemed to look right through him.

Charlie walked back to where he saw there were a few single folding chairs beyond the last row of seats. He wanted to be out of the way, just a fly on the wall, to observe the proceedings. If it weren't for Natty – to in some way support her and her family – he would have just skipped the hearing. But now he was there and he'd just have to suffer through the well-rehearsed performance of the insufferable Vernon Yarbrough and his troupe of actors, and afterward, the open condescension of the victorious Torkelson and Tuthill, and the sniffing superiority of Warren Brand. *It was the price you paid for being on the losing side.*

At least he'd get to see Natty today and that would almost make it worth it – if she showed up. He hadn't seen her since New York, since Park Avenue in the rain . . . since before her phone call from the porch. Charlie's heart beat faster in anticipation of seeing her again, especially now that they had declared their love and made their plans – like a couple of high school kids running away together after the senior prom. Charlie chuckled to himself at the thought. It was a pretty harebrained scheme, but in their situations, it was probably the only way it was going to happen with him and Natty, and now that they'd committed to it, it was like a huge weight had been lifted from his chest. He was sure that this is what he wanted . . . in truth he knew it that morning in the store when he was trying on the boots and Natty came around the corner of the aisle following Pie. He knew the moment he saw her. It just took a while to sink in. Charlie smiled to himself as he pictured her standing there in her Spiderman hat, baggy jeans and construction boots. And then he wondered again as he had so often over the past few days, how two people could be so in love with each other without having had sex or even any of the physical contact that leads couples to *believing* they're in love. But Charlie had no doubts about any of it, and he knew that the happiness he now felt in anticipation of once again *sharing* a life with a woman he loved and with children who needed him, was what he had been so desperately missing over the last few years. And now he'd have it all again. He looked at his watch and wondered where she was. It was only a few minutes before the three o'clock start of the hearing.

Charlie stretched his legs out in front of him and slid down a little in his seat to relax and observe the hearing. A few more spectators came through the door – a couple of miners and their wives; a few older couples who stopped to talk briefly with the DeWitts; and then Hank who looked around the gym and furrowed his brow with disgust as he walked over to speak with Bud and Alice. He nodded briefly to Charlie and then took a seat behind the DeWitts next to Petey. The door clicked open again and a pair of young professional looking men in business suits came in, stopped just inside the door to look around and study the crowd. Then they walked to the last row of chairs and took the two end seats just in front of Charlie. His guess was that they were lawyers or maybe entrepreneurs involved in some way with the coal mining industry, and like every other suit in the room, looking for opportunity in the taking of Angel Mountain.

The sound of loud footsteps in the hallway gained Charlie's attention. He looked up to see a distinguished looking man with gray hair, wearing a gray pin-striped suit and carrying a black robe over his arm, breeze into the gym followed closely by two men carrying large briefcases, and a woman who went straight to the stenograph table.

Tall and tan and smiling like a movie star, the judge shook hands with Leonard and the two other lawyers before moving on to Mulrooney's group to shake hands with the coal man and the two politicians. Then he strode purposefully toward the back of the room where a grinning Vernon Yarbrough was advancing with his hand extended. They moved in close to share some levity and then walked back to where Larry Tuthill and Jack Torkelson were standing.

The CanAmex men shook hands with the judge and chatted amiably. Charlie could see that this wasn't the first time the men had met. He shook his head with disgust. *These guys were so emboldened with power and contemptuous of the locals, they wouldn't even bother to hide their collusion.*

Yarbrough and the judge walked back to the front of the room to get things started. The lawyer took his seat at the middle of the table next to Leonard, while one of the judge's assistants helped the judge into his robe. The second assistant was at the judge's bench emptying the contents of one of the briefcases – a brown accordion file, a small desk lamp, a large bottle of spring water, a glass, and a gavel.

One of the uniformed court officers suddenly banged a heavy staff on the gym floor three times announcing, "here ye, here ye, here ye. The fourth circuit court of the state of West Virginia, now in session. The Honorable Winthrop Goodman presiding." And the hearing was on.

The judge briefly described for the public what the purpose of the hearing was and explained that it was a *hearing* and not a trial and that the rules were different, and that at the end of the day, after listening to arguments by both side, *he* would render a binding decision. Then the judge began to read a lengthy summary of the *Eminent Domain* statute under which the hearing was taking place. In a barely audible voice, reading the obviously required notice as quickly as he could, the judge droned on for several minutes reciting the legalese-filled description of the statute with numerous references to *the legal authority of the state . . .* for the *public good . . . in the public interest . . .for fair market value . . .* Charlie wondered if he was trying to put the room to sleep so no one would be aware of what was going on.

The judge finally put down the statute and took off his reading glasses. "And as you can see," he said, "we have moved the venue of this hearing down here to lovely Red Bone for the convenience of the DeWitts and any witnesses they may wish to call." *And to get away from any press scrutiny . . . and late on a Friday afternoon just to make sure,* Charlie said to himself as he watched the judge smile benevolently toward Bud and Alice DeWitt. They stared back at him without expression.

The judge turned quickly to Vernon Yarbrough and the other lawyers and smiled as he held his hands out, palms up. "Mr. Callahan, representing the State, and Mr. Yarbrough for the petitioners, the Ackerly Coal Company and the CanAmex Energy Company, gentlemen, you *have* the floor. Make your case please."

One of the young lawyers at the table rose and reading from a notepad, introduced into evidence a dozen briefs of precedent-setting cases of past uses of *eminent domain* by the State of West Virginia to seize private property to be used by the coal mining industry. In a dry, businesslike manner, the lawyer achieved his goal of establishing for the court that this was a very routine and commonplace occurrence in West Virginia. Charlie wasn't surprised. *'Been like that for a hundred years and it's still the same today,'* Hank's words echoed through his head. He had to admit though that the lawyer and the precedents cited were very effective in making it seem that it was almost the State's *duty* to take the Angel Mountain farm. The DeWitt's lawyer offered no objection to the introduction of the precedents.

Just as the lawyer finished up, handing the sheaf of briefs to the bench, the gym door opened and Natty came into the room followed by the Pie Man. They both seemed surprised by the transformation of the gymnasium and a little intimidated by the number of strange men in the room wearing suits. She smiled meekly toward the judge and quickly took the seat next to her mother with Pie taking the seat on the end of the row. Charlie watched her, as did many of the other men in the room, he noticed. She'd returned to the *no make-up, no jewelry* look, but with her daring new hair style and platinum blond coloring, she couldn't hide any more.

Vernon Yarbrough stood for his turn. Using the area in front of the bench as his stage, he launched into his opening statement without the use of any notes. "This is a *textbook* case for the proper use of the *eminent domain* statute," he began. Smiling and turning lightly on his feet and using his hands for emphasis while his deep voice filled the gymnasium, he quickly had the attention of the entire room. "A huge, untapped asset, a major seam of low-sulfur coal needed for the *environmentally positive* operation of our magnificent new, billion dollar power plant, putting hundreds of McDowell County miners to work." Several of the miners in the audience voiced their approval of this point with '*here, heres*' and a few '*right-ons*' earning a smiling rebuke and a soft gavel tap from the judge. "Bringing home paychecks . . . bountiful *union-wage paychecks*," Yarbrough was interrupted again by the miners' affirmations, "to benefit the families and wives and children of McDowell County. Paychecks that will pump new life into the economy of one our State's most depressed areas and provide for better schools and a modern new hospital, prosperous stores and a robust economy." There wasn't a card in the deck that Yarbrough wasn't playing in his assault on the DeWitt farm.

Charlie saw Natty turn around in her seat. He caught her eye and winked. She smiled at him for several seconds, concealing nothing, and then continued to look around at the other people in the room. He could see any feeling of hope drain from her face as she saw all the CanAmex and Ackerly men in attendance, as if it finally came home to her that it was all too big, too important to these powerful companies for the DeWitts to stand up to. She chewed on her bottom lip as she glanced quickly back at Charlie for a moment before turning forward again. She leaned over to Pie and said something. The boy turned around in his seat, his eyes nearly closed and the tip of his tongue sticking through his tight lips as the *happy face* came over him. He found Charlie and trotted softly back to him. Yarbrough continued his speech.

"Hello Chowly," Pie said softly as they exchanged a quiet high-five. Pie was wearing his Yankees hat backwards, and had on his Michigan tee shirt over a long-sleeved, white jersey.

"C'mon, sit down," said Charlie, dragging another single chair next to his. Charlie squeezed the sides of Pie's knee with his fingers forcing Pie to let out a soft squeal as he wrestled with Charlie's hand, earning them a stern look from one of the court officers. Charlie sat back and listened again to Vernon Yarbrough as he made the DeWitt farm sound like the most worthless piece of real estate in West Virginia.

"Tax returns going back twenty years will show that the DeWitt farm is *not* a viable agricultural business," said Yarbrough, delivering another packet of documents to the bench, "and the assessed value of the property is in fact *substantially* less than the considerable sum my clients have very generously offered in compensation."

Charlie leaned in close to Pie. "Do you know what's going on here Pie?"

The boy slumped in his seat and shrugged. The happy face was gone. "Mama say gwampa and mawmaw will have to move away fwom the fowm. Mama was mad." Charlie put his arm around the back of Pie's seat and squeezed his shoulder lightly, then looked over at Natty sitting next to her mother in back of Bud and Alice DeWitt. They were all listening to Vernon Yarbrough doing what he does best, earning his five figure monthly retainer fee by leaving nothing to chance, and it all had to be excruciatingly painful to the DeWitts. The muscles on Charlie's neck and jaw began to tighten with anger and frustration over the charade being played out in front of the corrupt judge. If it weren't for Natty, he would have gotten up and left.

Yarbrough finished his statement and called to the witness stand, the representative from the Governor's office who described the two-year old agreement between the State and CanAmex that all of the coal for the new power plant would come from McDowell County mines. The miners in the audience again voiced their approval and received a quick smile and a raised palm from Yarbrough. Next up was an engineer from Ackerly Coal who testified that an Angel Mountain surface mine was the only economically feasible method of supplying the new plant with McDowell County coal. He was followed by another engineer from CanAmex, Charlie had never seen before, who used a lot of technical jargon to explain how the plant couldn't operate at peak capacity without the Angel Mountain coal, resulting in many fewer jobs at the plant and a much lower level of profitability. Charlie knew that most of it was gibberish but there would be no way for the DeWitt's lawyer to refute any of it. It was all for show anyway he reminded himself.

Early on, the DeWitt's lawyer, in a barely audible voice tried to object to a witness' statement only to earn a loud rebuttal and an angry scowl from Yarbrough. The lawyer remained silent for the rest of the State's case.

Yarbrough finished with his last witness and then introduced to the court a document stating that his client, the Ackerly Coal Company, was willing to assume the State's liability for *just compensation* for the property taken, and would pay the DeWitts *one hundred thousand dollars* for the farm, "well beyond the assessed value of the property, as your honor can see from the certified appraisal," Yarbrough added. The lawyer turned and smiled thinly at Bud DeWitt, "And as a gesture of goodwill, we offer to include in the compensation, any attorney's fees incurred by the DeWitts in regard to this hearing as well."

Yarbrough glared for a few moments at the farmer before turning back to the judge to indicate that his side was through.

Just as the DeWitt's lawyer struggled to his feet to make his statement, Charlie felt a hand on his shoulder. He turned to find Larry Tuthill squatting next to his chair. "Charlie," he said softly with a nod. "We're about done here so I wanted to give you this before we left." Tuthill was reaching inside his suit jacket. He pulled out a plain white envelope. Charlie could see that his name was scrawled on the front of the envelope as Tuthill thrust it into his hand. The CanAmex man's eyes danced around the gym as he spoke. "I know this didn't work out the way we'd planned but it's all ending up at the same place, and a deal is a deal." He looked at Charlie and smiled. "Right my friend?" He gave Charlie's leg a soft pat as he stood up. "See you around Charlie." Larry Tuthill strode off to rejoin Jack Torkelson standing against the wall.

Charlie studied the envelope he held before him in his lap. He noticed Pie next to him looking at the envelope too with a curious look on his face. Charlie winked at him and smiled. He quietly unsealed the flap of the envelope and spread it open. It was a check drawn on a bank in Huntington, with the account name *ACC Holdings Inc.* and made out to Charlie, in hand-written blue ink. The amount was for *$317,841*. In the bottom left corner was the notation *"consulting fee."* Charlie squinted in concentration. He'd forgotten all about the curious offer that Tuthill had made in New York so many months earlier at the meeting with Yarbrough and Terry Summers – the authorization to pay up to a million dollars to the DeWitts, and split whatever they had left over after buying the farm. Charlie gazed down at the envelope trying to figure it out. *The whole thing still makes no sense, especially now.* He pushed the envelope into his inside pocket and looked up to find the man in the back row with the protruding Adam's apple staring at him from a few yards away. The man turned back to the front of the gym without changing his expression. Charlie watched him for a few seconds trying to recall if he had ever seen him before. The man obviously had *some* interest in the proceedings beyond mere curiosity. The thought flashed through Charlie's mind that *maybe he was a hit-man hired by Torkelson and Tuthill to get rid of any Charlie Burden problem they thought they might have.* He chuckled to himself but at the same time, he glanced back over his shoulder at Torkelson and Larry Tuthill who stood close together talking softly, ignoring anything the DeWitt's lawyer might have to say. Charlie looked over at Kevin Mulrooney, the crude, unscrupulous coal man, standing with his back to the front of the room, conversing with the State Senator. Then Charlie looked at Vernon Yarbrough, the scheming power broker and influence peddler who was no doubt the architect of all the machinations at play in the room. The lawyer was sitting with his arms crossed, a smug half-smile on his face as he *allowed* Bud DeWitt and his lawyer their last at-bats. And then, it finally came to Charlie . . . he fingered the check in his pocket again . . . *three hundred thousand dollars. It was just a payoff! A simple backroom piece of grimy corruption, to buy his silence.* He almost laughed out loud at his own ignorance. *They'd told him about the payoff to the judge – a felony that if it became public would scuttle the merger with Continental Electric*

Systems – so that he'd protect his friend Duncan McCord by keeping him out of the whole Angel Mountain affair and now that the deal was done, they were buying his permanent silence by making him a partner to the scheme. There was no million dollar split between himself and Yarbrough and Terry Summers. He was the only one who would be getting paid off and if the scheme blew up afterward, he would be the one holding the bag in the form of a three hundred thousand dollar payoff. Charlie looked down at his lap, smiled to himself and shook his head. *God, how fucking stupid can a person be?* Now he had to figure out what he was going to do with the check.

At the front of the room the DeWitt's lawyer was stumbling badly. His statement was disorganized and rambling and in places, incoherent. He tried to cite some precedent in the DeWitt's favor but couldn't find the notes he was looking for. He mentioned *mountaintop-removal* mining, getting a forceful objection from Vernon Yarbrough. "*No one* had mentioned anything about *mountaintop-removal*," the lawyer admonished. It was not part of this case. Charlie smiled to himself. *No, that would be a separate closed-door hearing between the judge and Yarbrough over cocktails at their club.* Charlie caught the judge looking at his watch and then glancing at one of his assistants. It was already *five o'clock* and the buzz level of the room was beginning to rise. It was almost over now.

Then Bud DeWitt took the stand, painfully settling into the witness chair for his futile statement. His lawyer slumped down in his seat studying his notes. This wasn't going to be pretty, Charlie could see. There was no sense to it and Bud's lawyer should see that. As Bud started to speak, Natty got up and moved quickly toward the gymnasium door. Charlie could see from the slump of her shoulders that she couldn't take any more. There would be tears in her eyes. Next to him, Pie was leaning against his arm with heavy eyelids, ready to fall asleep.

Bud started with the story of his great grandfather, an officer in the Army of the West who settled on Angel Mountain after the Civil War. But Bud was nervous and not a great speaker and spoke in a halting, often unintelligible manner causing the judge to interrupt him to ask if could "get on with it a little quicker," making Bud even more nervous. No one in the room except his family, Charlie could see, was paying any attention to Bud's story . . . *the only story at the hearing worth telling and the only testimony worth listening to.* His jaw and neck muscles again tightened with anger.

Charlie started to get up to go out and find Natty when one of the young businessmen sitting in front of him turned and said something to his companion, and then to Charlie's surprise, the first man looked over at the older man with the Adam's apple. The younger man tapped his watch as his companion rose out of his chair and pulled out a black cell phone and hit several buttons. He walked directly toward a back corner of the gym. The older man in the center of the row just turned his head and looked over to where most of the CanAmex and Ackerly men were standing next to the big wire-protected windows. The November sky was dark with no lights to be seen. Charlie turned to watch the man with the cell

phone, curious as to what it might have been that set him into action. There was
something going on in the room that Charlie wasn't privy to and he was curious.

Pie heard it first. The boy opened his eyes and picked his head up off of
Charlie's arm and turned, his nose in the air, like a dog listening for his masters
footsteps. Then he sat up straight and looked wide-eyed at Charlie. "Chowly," he
whispered. "The helicoptwa is coming!"

Charlie furrowed his brow at Pie, not hearing anything. He turned his head
to the side, looking at the floor, straining to hear over the hum of voices in the
gym. Then he heard it too, clearly and louder by the second, the deep *thwump* of a
fast approaching helicopter – one of the CanAmex Bell 430s Charlie was certain
after hearing it land so many times over the last few months. He looked out the
tall windows of the gymnasium, as were many others in the court room including
the judge, to see a beam of flashing light reflecting off a row of green dumpsters
in the alley next to the gym. Pie was on his feet with excitement, looking out the
window and then straight up as the thunderous noise of the twin turbines seemed
to be hovering directly over them. Bud DeWitt had stopped talking and all
attention in the room was on the incredible noise outside. All attention, Charlie
noticed, but the man on the cell phone at the back of the gym. He continued
talking calmly into the phone, his eyes trained on the proceedings at the front of
the room as the noise gradually abated, the helicopter seeming to move off toward
the athletic field on the other side of the school. Then the sound of the helicopter
disappeared completely, except to a trained ear like Charlie's, who could still
make out the high-pitched whine of the turbines shutting down. Charlie turned
back to the front of the room and settled down in his seat again. The helicopter, he
concluded, was there to pick up Torkelson and Tuthill and whoever else would be
joining their entourage that evening.

"Your honor, if we could continue?" Vernon Yarbrough was standing at the
table, looking around the room trying to regain control of the proceedings. The
judge nodded in agreement and looked over at Bud DeWitt's lawyer.

"Is your witness about finished councilor? It's getting late in the day and
I'm sure . . ." He was interrupted by the loud click of the gymnasium door being
aggressively pulled open, and the entrance of a tall, powerful looking man with a
large round head well on its way to complete baldness. The man had a short neck
and hunched shoulders of an offensive lineman and was wearing an ill-fitting suit
and rumpled black raincoat that looked like he'd slept in it. He stood with his
hands on his hips and a disagreeable look on his face as he peered around the
room as if to figure out just what was going on. The newcomer paid no attention
to the judge or the other court officers who were glaring at him inquisitively.

Charlie sat still in his seat with his hands in his pockets, his legs stretched
out in front of him, unable to keep a smile off his face. He didn't know what was
going on but he knew it was going to be something very entertaining now with
this dramatic entrance of his old friend, Red Landon, the Chief Operations Officer
of CanAmex Energy Ltd, one of the most powerful men in the utility industry,
Duncan McCord's second in command, and Jack Torkelson's boss. Despite his
always rough and rumpled appearance, Red Landon, Charlie knew, was probably

the sharpest and toughest utility executive on the planet, and from the look on his face, Charlie could see that he hadn't come to Red Bone, West Virginia, on a social call.

Charlie glanced over his shoulder and saw Jack Torkelson moving forward slowly with Larry Tuthill a few steps behind. Both men looked like they'd seen a ghost. Then the gymnasium seemed to come alive with movement. The young man in front of Charlie got up and had a brief conversation with Red Landon who then started toward the back of the gym. The man with the protruding Adam's apple arose quickly and turned to find Torkelson and Tuthill. At the same moment came the sound of a stampede of loud footsteps coming quickly down the hallway. Charlie turned back to the front of the room and sat up in astonishment as Lucien Mackey and Charlie's old golfing companion, Mal Berman the lawyer, came through the door. They were followed into the gym by a tall, distinguished looking man in his sixties and two other young men carrying briefcases who appeared to be with him. Charlie recognized the tall man to be the CEO of Continental Electric Systems, CanAmex's merger partner. He and his two assistants headed straight for a red-faced Kevin Mulrooney against the outside wall of the gym.

The judge banged his gavel three times. "Order in the courtroom please!" He raised his eyebrows to Vernon Yarbrough. "Could somebody tell me what's going on here?" he cried. None of the newcomers paid him any attention.

Red Landon passed by Charlie without taking his eyes off of Jack Torkelson, but he placed a heavy hand on Charlie's shoulder as he went by. Lucien Mackey made straight for Warren Brand and Terry Summers, and Mal Berman went to the front of the bench and leaned in for a private conversation with the judge. The two young men who had been sitting in front of Charlie were now wearing rectangular, plastic credentials hanging from silver chains around their necks. As one of the men passed by Charlie, he could read on the badge, in large bold letters: SEC, and beneath it, *Investigations Division.*

Next to Charlie, the Pie Man was swiveling around in wonderment, watching all the important looking men in action. His face showed his apprehension. "Chowly," he said, still watching the movement around them, "whas going on?"

Charlie smiled as he took another look around the room. "I'm not sure Pie, but I've got a feeling that our team is making a big comeback in the fourth quarter."

In a dark section of the hallway just outside the gymnasium door, Natty sat on the shallow bench at the base of the folded-up section of portable bleachers. She didn't want to hear and watch Bud DeWitt and his lawyer make a pathetic plea for some kind of leniency from the judge and all the lawyers and the big corporation men. None of them cared. All they wanted was their coal and they weren't interested in family history or the sweat and blood and heartache that five generations of DeWitts had poured into the Angel Mountain farm. They didn't want to hear about all the DeWitt men who had put down their plows to go off to fight America's two world wars and Korea and Viet Nam, or about the ones who never made it back to West Virginia. And they didn't want to hear about any DeWitt children and grandchildren buried up on the side of Angel Mountain. They didn't want to hear any of it. Natty replayed in her mind the words of the lawyer in Welch . . . *'in the end Mrs. Oakes, you'll lose . . . in the end, they'll carve up Angel Mountain and take their coal.'* Natty clenched her teeth in anger. Better for Bud to just stand up and give the judge and the rest of them his middle finger and walk out, than grovel through his pathetic, heroic, sad, wonderful story of the DeWitt family. But no, Bud would never do that. Bud would be a gentleman to the end. Natty wiped the tears from her cheeks and wished she had a cigarette.

She heard the roar of the helicopter overhead coming in to take the CanAmex men or maybe the judge back to Charleston, and knew the hearing would soon be over. Then the outside door at the end of the hallway was pulled open and she watched the silhouette of the large man with the hunched shoulders come quickly down the hall. The man didn't even look at Natty as he went by her and yanked open the door to the gym. He looked to Natty like he must be a coal company man who was late for the hearing. Then came the group of men noisily down the hall, not in as much of a hurry as the first man but walking faster than normal. In the dark hallway it was difficult to see their faces, but Natty could see that they were all well dressed in expensive suits and appeared to be lawyers or businessmen. They definitely weren't from McDowell County, or even West Virginia. One of the men, a large solid looking older man with beautifully coiffed gray hair smiled at Natty as they went by. She didn't know what was going on now with all these newcomers, but from the look of them it could only mean bad news. *More utility and coal men and lawyers here to celebrate another victory over the evil farmers.* Natty leaned back against the inclined surface of the wooden bleachers and closed her eyes to rest them and maybe even get a quick nap in while she waited for the hearing to end.

She heard the distant click of the outside door opening once more but ignored it, choosing to keep her eyes and her mind shut to the rest of the day's proceedings. *Just another late-comer to the lawyers' party*, she could tell from the sound of the hard, expensive shoes hitting the old wooden flooring of the hallway. *Forceful, confident, but walking more slowly than the others. Close to her now.* And then the footsteps stopped. Natty waited to hear the gymnasium door being pulled open, but instead heard a voice, right in front of her. A voice that – even after two and half years – she knew immediately. "Are you all right miss?"

Natty opened her eyes and saw Duncan McCord standing a foot away from her, his arms hanging down in front of him with his fingers interlocked, leaning forward with a concerned look on his face. He was wearing the same black, tailored suit he'd worn to the picnic, *the day the helicopters came.* Natty smiled. "You gotta stop using that same line on me all the time. I'm sick of it," she said softly, looking up at the CanAmex president.

Duncan McCord didn't move or change expression. He just stared at Natty for a few seconds and then gradually a smile came over his face. He nodded with the memory. "You've changed your hair Natty, but you still have beautiful eyes," said McCord straightening up.

"Thank you," Natty almost whispered, shocked that the CanAmex man remembered her. She took in a deep breath and sat up on the bench.

McCord turned his head toward the gymnasium door. "So, what's going on here today Natty?"

Natty shrugged. "Oh, they're taking my grandpa's farm away from him, the lawyers and the coal men."

McCord looked from Natty toward the gym and back again. He put his hands in his pants pockets and turned and looked toward the gym for several seconds shaking his head slowly. "Those *fucking* lawyers!" he said loudly, turning back to Natty with an angry look on his face. She burst out laughing and then covered her mouth quickly, afraid that they may have heard her in the gym. It was the first time she'd laughed that week and it felt good for a change.

McCord grinned at her and then started off in no particular hurry towards the gym door. "Well, let's see if we can't do something about your grandpa's farm," he said without looking back.

It only took a few seconds for the tumultuous buzz of the many furtive conversations in the gym to come to a complete halt. Duncan McCord stood inside the gym door, hands in his pockets, feet spread wide as he coolly scanned the room, one time, slowly with black, penetrating eyes that missed nothing. The silence of the room didn't hurry him, and even those in the gym who didn't know who he was, knew better than to interrupt him.

Finally, McCord looked over at the judge and nodded. He took his hands out of his pockets and walked over to the witness box where Bud DeWitt still sat, dumbfounded, his *Peterbilt* hat in his lap. "You Bud DeWitt?" McCord asked in a voice just loud enough to be heard throughout the gym.

"Yeah, ah, yessir," Bud answered.

McCord smiled and held out his hand just as Natty quietly came back into the gym. "Mr. DeWitt, I'm Duncan McCord," they shook hands, "president of the CanAmex Energy Company, and I personally apologize for the troubles you've been put through over this. You can sit down now sir. This is all over."

McCord smiled at Bud and patted him lightly on the shoulder as the farmer passed in front of him going back to his seat. Then he walked past the judge's bench to the front of the other table and stood in front of Vernon Yarbrough. "You our lawyer?" said McCord.

Yarbrough rose quickly with the practiced grin coming on like an involuntary spasm, his right hand pushing forward toward McCord. "Why yes sir. Vernon Yarb . . ."

"You're fired," said McCord with no hint of a smile on his face, his hands at his sides. With his left hand he made a fist with thumb extended and jerked it toward the door. "Get out!" he said angrily. "*Now*, before I kick your ass all over this room." Yarbrough went white and then, he and Leonard, fumbling with briefcases, clumsily tried to find an escape route through the folding chairs to the door. The two politicians chose this time to make their exit as well.

McCord turned to the room. "And that goes for the rest of you bums." He found Torkelson and Tuthill and pointed two fingers at them and then made the thumb gesture once again. Red Landon with anger written across his face, was between Torkelson and Tuthill, with a firm hold on each man's arm, ushering them forcefully toward the door accompanied by several other men and one of the SEC men.

Then McCord found Kevin Mulrooney, already on his way to the door between two Continental Electric Systems people and the second SEC man. McCord gave him an angry *thumbing* for good measure. Following close behind them were Warren Brand and Terry Summers accompanied by Lucien Mackey.

Charlie sat still in his chair wondering if he was actually imagining the whole scene taking place around him. Next to him, the Pie Man was spinning around, wide-eyed so as not to miss any of the spectacle, which he didn't understand but knew instinctively was good for his grandpa and grandma. Charlie was still stunned by the sudden appearance of Duncan McCord, who, he knew was not in Red Bone, West Virginia, just to stop the taking of one little mountainside farm. He didn't understand it, but for now he'd just sit back and enjoy the show and feel good for Bud and Alice DeWitt.

At the front of the room, Duncan McCord didn't have to ask for the attention of the room. As soon as he started speaking the room went quiet again except for the judge and his assistants packing up their things. McCord ignored them. "This hearing never should have happened. This is not the way the CanAmex Energy Company or its subsidiaries operates, and I apologize to the DeWitt family for the way some of our representatives have treated them." McCord looked over to where the DeWitts were all standing and nodded with a thin smile. He turned back to the room "We have no intention of using our financial or political power to circumvent the laws or regulations of any State or government agency to be a party to the environmental catastrophe of mountaintop – removal coal mining. It's not going to happen . . . in West Virginia, or anywhere else."

McCord looked directly at the group of miners who sat stone still, all with the same tired look of futility on their faces. "The miners in the room should know that our subsidiary, the Ackerly Coal Company, will still be opening a coal mine on Angel Mountain and hiring plenty of union miners, all they can find, to operate a slope mine that will fuel the Red Bone power plant for the next twenty years." McCord smiled as some of the miners stirred and looked at each other, some with raised eyebrows – about as enthusiastic as they were going to get right now. "You'll be mining Angel Mountain the old way, the way it should be done, without destroying what God put down here to make West Virginia a special place." He looked back toward the DeWitts who were all standing close together now. "Without destroying the history and tradition of one of your State's great families."

Charlie looked over at the DeWitts and noticed Hank standing with his arm around Alice's shoulders. He thought he saw a tear running down the side of Hank's face. Natty was hugging Bud DeWitt's arm and smiling broadly, her eyes riveted on McCord.

"It'll cost us more," McCord continued, "and make it more expensive to run our power plant." McCord shrugged. "It's a good cost though, more miners put to work, more families making a living, and better for the environment . . . it's a price we'll pay." He crossed his arms and looked down at the floor for a few seconds before continuing. The room returned to absolute silence. "You know, for a long time," he began softly, "for most of the last century, big companies – coal companies and steel companies and utilities – have been taking unfair advantage of coal miners and the coal mining areas of this country, with West Virginia right at the top of the list I'd guess. So," McCord narrowed his eyes in thought as he gazed out over the room, "now that the CanAmex Energy Company is getting into the coal mining business, well, as an old friend of mine so eloquently put it not long ago, *maybe it's time for us to just cut it out.*" McCord put his hands in his pockets, looked out and winked at Charlie sitting in the middle of the room.

When it was clear that the CanAmex President was through, Pullman Hankinson clapped his wrinkled old hands together loudly and then again, and then the miners joined in, and soon the entire room, which by this time was made up nearly entirely of McDowell County residents, was again applauding this outsider as many of them had done two and a half years earlier at a picnic on a beautiful day in June.

As if what had happened had just finally sunk in, the DeWitt clan was jubilant in the front of the gym. Natty hugged her mother and Petey, and Hank was hugging both Bud and Alice, and well wishers were trying to get at them as well.

Charlie sat in his chair content to watch the celebration with the Pie Man standing at his side. Then something kicked his ankle hard and he looked up to see Duncan McCord staring down at him with an angry look on his face. "You screwed up a good vacation in the Canary Islands, Burden."

Charlie smiled up at his old friend. "That's tough."

McCord turned his menacing stare at Pie and then at his Michigan T-shirt. He grinned and held out a fist. "Go Blue."

Pie's face scrunched up into an instant *happy face* as he touched knuckles with the CanAmex president. McCord studied the boy for a few seconds, his brow furrowed in concentration and then looked back at Charlie. His thoughts were interrupted by the sound of Natty's voice. "C'mon Pie Man, we gotta go." Natty was standing about ten feet away from them.

"Yeth mama," he said, going over to Natty and leaning against her side.

Charlie came to his feet. "Dunc, this is . . ."

"We've met," said McCord, smiling at Natty. "A couple of times now."

Natty's *light up a room smile* returned as she watched Charlie's eyebrows rise with curiosity. She'd let him wonder. "Going' out to the *Roadhouse* for a beer to celebrate," said Natty. "Love to have you boys join us."

McCord shrugged. "Nothing in the world I'd rather do right now, but I've got to get back to Toronto tonight."

"And I need to spend a few minutes with Duncan before he leaves. Maybe I'll see you there later," said Charlie.

Natty smiled at the two men and then squinted in thought for a second. She nodded toward Charlie. "I don't say *thank you* to Charlie any more 'cause I got sick of doing that." She turned to McCord. "But I'll say *thank you* to you Mr. McCord." Natty glanced at the front of the room where the DeWitts and Hank were still gathered, and back at McCord. "Probably no way for you to ever know how much good you did here today," she said softly.

McCord studied Natty and Pie at her side for a moment and then smiled. "You're welcome," he said.

McCord handed Charlie one of the short dark cigars he'd bummed from a miner in the parking lot. They stopped and turned away from the wind to light them before starting out on the perimeter of the high school's athletic field. In the center of the field, the black CanAmex helicopter hissed and whined as it began its warm-up sequence. They walked slowly, to enjoy their short time together.

"It was all about money," said McCord. "Plain old greed and corruption, and arrogance that down here, nobody would care about what they did." McCord spit a piece of tobacco and shook his head angrily. "It was all Torkelson. Lining his pockets, using his position and the opportunity down here to get rich quick. That's the trouble with hiring these fucking government bureaucrats. They work at shit jobs for years then the first chance they get in the private sector they get blinded by the big numbers and figure the system owes them a fat bonus and a retirement home on Jupiter Island."

They walked along the cinder track that had weeds growing out of it. "Three years ago, Torkelson went to Ackerly and found a willing player in Mulrooney. He wanted five million to site the new plant in southern West Virginia, right in the heart of Ackerly's operations. Well Mulrooney knows he's got a jackpot full of coal in Angel Mountain, and that mountaintop-removal is just about finished because of the environmentalists, so he offers Torkelson *ten million* for the coal contract for Ackerly plus CanAmex using its political muscle to get a mountaintop variance for Angel Mountain. By the way, your numbers were a little off. It's about forty percent cheaper now to do a surface mine."

"Expensive difference," said Charlie.

"Yeah, about *a half a billion* over twenty years. Makes ten million a pretty good investment up-front."

"So how'd you get on to him?"

"Red figured it out," said McCord. "After your e-mail we started looking into the whole situation and he figured out that Torkelson and Tuthill were just spending too much time down here. Too much on this Angel Mountain thing. He smelled a rat.

"We put our investigator on it – the tall guy with the fedora – and he did some phone taps, broke into their e-mails, cell phones. It was all illegal but we got what we needed. Mulrooney's got a big mouth and he's a drunk so we knew that's where the money was coming from. Then our guy got lucky and stumbled across Mulrooney's girl friend who was also his secretary, and she spilled everything.

Torkelson was getting the big dough, but he had to include Tuthill – two million he was getting – plus a million for that cocksucker lawyer. What's his name?"

"Yarbrough," said Charlie.

McCord stopped and turned to face Charlie. "Yeah, Yarbrough. That was his scheme, that raid with the cops and the DEA." McCord grimaced angrily. "Asshole. He's lucky nobody got killed that day."

"Yeah, it could have turned out tragic," said Charlie.

McCord eyed his friend warily as he puffed on the cigar. "Understand someone tipped off farmer DeWitt they were coming."

Charlie flicked the ash from his cigar. "Yeah, that's what I heard too."

"Someone using your cell phone."

Charlie shrugged. "Gotta stop leaving it lying around."

"Lucien told me you did a nice tap dance all over that lawyer in New York. Told me about it when he called to tell me about your guy Brand and *his* deal with Torkelson and the Executive Committee and all that."

Charlie looked over and saw Lucien Mackey and Mal Berman at the edge of the field. They were talking with the two SEC men and the tall investigator from Toronto. "So where does all that stand now?" said Charlie. "What's Lucien's situation?"

"He was never out. That was never going to happen. Red went ballistic when he heard what Torkelson was trying to pull, taking control of DD&M plus a million dollar payoff from Brand." McCord looked back toward the parking lot. "Red might be beating the shit out of Torkelson right now. I better find him."

"What about Brand?"

"He's all done. Red's going to New York on Monday. Lucien will call another Executive Committee meeting and Red will lay it all out for them. The other kid too, the pretty boy . . ."

"Summers."

"Yeah, he's gone too. He was in for a half a million. They brought him in after we announced the merger with CES and Hugo Paxton died and they sucked you into the scheme to keep me out of it. They wanted him in to keep an eye on you. They also didn't think a big shot like you would be getting too involved in things down here, and Summers could represent DD&M for them."

Charlie chuckled at the irony. "What about the judge? How much was he in for?"

McCord shook his head. "Judge was clean. He was ready to do his country club pals a favor and get a variance for the surface mine. He was on the team but not on the take."

"So that was just for my benefit, to get me to want the farm as much as they did, to protect you and the merger."

McCord laughed. "Yeah, nice job," he said sarcastically, "first chance you get, you screw me and go over to the farmer's team."

"They paid me more," said Charlie with a grin. He took out the check from his jacket pocket. "Tuthill gave me this during the hearing. My payoff I guess. It's a check for three hundred thousand plus."

McCord looked down at the envelope in Charlie's hands. He thought for a few seconds, turning over the ramifications in his mind. He blew out a mouthful of smoke and resumed walking, Charlie at his side. "Well it's not my money, and the SEC is okay with everything 'cause we blew the whistle on ourselves and came down here and made it all public – that's why I'm here, part of the deal – so why don't you do something good with it down here. Just don't put it in your bank account."

Charlie slid the envelope back into his inside pocket. "Yeah, I think I have a real good use for it. They need a lot down here."

"Good," said McCord stopping once again. He threw his cigar into the weeds and faced Charlie once more. "You're doing okay Burden aren't you? Ellen told me all about your big new house, she was real excited."

"Yeah Dunc, I'm doing fine. I don't need the money."

"That's not what I meant Charlie." McCord studied Charlie's face in the shadowy light of the athletic field. "You break your nose again?" He squinted to see better. "Christ you get uglier every time I see you. What happened?"

Charlie laughed and felt the still lose cartilage in the bridge of his nose. "Nothing, took a high stick in a bar one night." He shrugged. "It's a rough town."

McCord went serious. "So, what's up with you and Ellen?"

Charlie could see that McCord probably received some information about him and Natty during the investigation. He took a last puff on his cigar and tossed it away. "Ellen and I are going to split up," he said softly. "We're . . . moving in different directions. Have been for a long time."

McCord nodded. "That's a good break for Ellen. You've been holding her back for years." Charlie grinned and nodded in agreement.

"This have anything to do with the girl," McCord nodded back toward the school, "and the kid?"

Charlie gazed over toward the parking lot. "Yeah," said Charlie, "it's got a lot to do with them."

McCord nodded in thought and looked off into the darkness behind Charlie. "Can't turn back the clock Charlie. Can't make up for past mistakes," he said softly, looking back at his friend.

"Yeah, I know that Dunc. Not trying to. It's not about me."

McCord studied Charlie's face for a moment before he was satisfied. "So what are you going to do?"

Charlie laughed. "I'm not sure yet. Think we might find some small town somewhere. Maybe Vermont, or Wyoming. I was thinking about becoming a carpenter."

McCord just stared pensively at Charlie for a few seconds, then looked at his watch and glanced toward the helicopter. "Well, I got to get going." He smiled at Charlie. "You're a fucking asshole Burden," he said shaking his head, "but . . . *Jesus Charlie,*" he said softly, "I envy you to death."

The two friends shook hands and McCord turned and darted toward the helicopter which immediately went into a higher pitch, lighting up the field with its flood lights. A minute later, it disappeared into the black sky heading north.

Chapter 33

The new field was already firm and if the weather stayed warm through the rest of November, it would need mowing soon. Natty couldn't keep from smiling as she walked around the new green turf and recalled the hard, uneven dirt and weed patch that was the old soccer field. *Wait 'til Kyle Loftus and the rest of the teams in the league see this field next year!*

There weren't any lines on the field and the new goals wouldn't arrive until sometime next spring but *The Bones* didn't need any lines or goals for this practice. What they needed was just some running time and wind sprints so they wouldn't be too out of shape for their opening game of the tournament on Friday. That was the game Natty was worried about. The team's last game was two weeks ago and they'd only been able to have one practice at the high school field since then because it got dark so early now. She was afraid her team may not be in shape to run for the first game. After that, with a game under their belts, they'd be okay, but now they needed a hard practice. *Of course, if she hadn't gone off to New York for a weekend the kids could have gotten another practice in!* Natty closed her eyes and took in a deep breath of the cool, Sunday afternoon air and allowed herself a momentary flashback to her early morning walk through Rockefeller Center with Charlie. *It didn't turn out quite as planned . . . but still a weekend she'd remember for ever.*

Natty watched her players spread out in a line across the field, dribbling balls from one end of the field to the other and back. Out in front of the pack was Emma, and next to her, *The Bones'* new assistant coach, Gabe, the midfielder from Welch and Emma's new best friend. They seemed to always be sharing a laugh and having fun when they were together, which Natty was thrilled to see because it was a wonderful, new experience for Emma. Behind them and closing fast were the Willard brothers and Paul, followed by Matt Hatfield, Jimmy Hopson and George Jarrell. Bringing up the rear as always were Jason Bailey and the Steele brothers, with the Pie Man a few yards behind. Brenda Giles was bouncing down the field using the goaltender's long side-step while holding a ball.

Natty turned to look up the hill toward Main Street to see if there was any sign of Billy Staten. The small black boy had missed the previous practice as well and none of the kids had seen him in school the last few days. Billy was a capable enough defender and she couldn't afford to lose him. Her team would be short-handed enough compared to the other teams in the tournament that would all show up with seventeen or eighteen players.

At the top of the hill, a car turned from Main Street onto South County Road, but Natty knew right away it wasn't Billy's father's old utility van. It was Charlie Burden's blue Lexus. She wandered over to the side of the road as Charlie came down the hill. He slowed to a stop next to her. Natty leaned onto the top of the car and looked down through the moon roof. In the small backseat she could see a canvas tennis bag that looked full and Charlie's briefcase.

Charlie closed the door and faced her over the car. "Looks like this is getting to be our regular way of meeting," he said.

Natty smiled. "Probably a good idea to keep a car between us at all times." She looked down into the car again. "Taking a trip?" she asked.

"Yeah, I have to go up to New York for a few days – some meetings to sort out all the fallout from the hearing. Then we're going up to Vermont, Wednesday night, for Thanksgiving."

"You coming back?" Natty deadpanned before flashing a grin.

"Sunday night," said Charlie watching her closely. "Planning on Sunday night."

"Gonna miss the tournament."

"Yeah, I know," said Charlie wistfully, "wish I could go." Charlie looked over at *The Bones* running up the field. "But we made plans. My daughter's flying in from Illinois, and my son's even going up, so . . ." Charlie shrugged. "And, I need to have some time with Ellen," he said softly.

Natty drummed her fingers on the top of the car and looked off at the pine forest that climbed up the long flank of Red Bone Mountain behind Charlie. "Charlie, you know, that phone call, when I called you after Woody died, well maybe that wasn't real fair to you, and you know, if you want to think it all over some more . . ."

Charlie smiled and shook his head. "No Nat, I don't need to think it over at all. I don't have any doubts." He tilted his head slightly to better see Natty's eyes. "How about you?"

Natty looked at him and smiled and then looked down into the car, embarrassed. "God, no Charlie," she almost whispered. "Best thing ever happened to me. Best thing ever happened to my kids too. Hell, I've been dreamin' about this my whole life, and now it's about to happen . . ." She looked away and the excitement drained from her face, and her nose wrinkled up in thought. "Just that, well, I ain't said anything to Buck yet. Hasn't been a good time for that yet."

"How's Buck been lately?" asked Charlie.

Natty squinted her eyes and shrugged. "He's been, you know . . . *okay*. Different. Since he started working, and the fight at the *Roadhouse*, and that day he spent with you cuttin' the trees . . . he's been . . . better." Her eyebrows went up and she shook her head. "Don't *mean* nothin'. Don't change a thing." Natty chewed on her bottom lip for a second. "Just makes it, you know, a little harder, that's all," she said softly. She stood up straight and bounced on her toes for a second. "I'm going to tell him Charlie," she said forcefully. "This week, before we go to Charleston on Friday. I'll tell him."

Charlie smiled and nodded toward Natty. "How'd he like your hair?"

Natty laughed. "Said I look like a dyke." She crossed her arms in front of her and smiled with embarrassment. "He likes it. I can tell."

Charlie just watched her for a few seconds. Then he reached into the pocket of his sports jacket. He brought out a key ring with a key and a small yellow plastic replica of a lantern on it and handed it across the car to Natty. "Here, this is an apartment in Bluefield we keep. Nobody's in it." Natty took the key ring and looked at the label. "Take the kids there when you get back from Charleston, Sunday night. I'll meet you there later, whenever I get back. Do you know where it is?"

"Yeah," said Natty. "I know it. High class place."

Charlie grinned. "Nothing but the best for you. Oh, and take this too." He reached into his other pocket and brought out a thick, black cell phone. "Turn it on when you're in Charleston, in case I have to reach you." He chuckled as Natty studied the phone anxiously. "Just push the green button when you want to do something."

"Okay Charlie," Natty said, taking a step back from the car. "Better get back to practice. See you Sunday night."

"Yeah, I'll see you then Nat. Good luck at the tournament."

Natty just smiled, taking a few slow steps backwards.

"Chowly! Chowly!" The Pie Man yelled running past his mother with a soccer ball under his arm. He came around the car with his hand up for their high-five. Charlie grinned and slapped his hand hard. "Chowly, will you come to owa touwnament in Chowlyston?"

"No Pie, I can't. I have to go up to New York."

Natty had started back toward the soccer field. She turned halfway around. "C'mon Pie, Charlie's got to go," she called. "Let's play some soccer."

Charlie knocked Pie's hat down over his eyes. "But I got a feeling the Pie Man's going to get a *goal* this weekend."

The boy turned and ran after his mother. "I will get a gowal just fowa you Chowly," he yelled spinning around. "I will get a gowal fowa Chowly in Chowlyston!" The boy's shoulders shuddered with laughter at his joke and Charlie could tell that the Pie Man had on a huge *happy face* as he ran back to the field.

*   *   *

The parking lots were filled so Natty finally had Geneva Gunnells just stop the bus as close as they could get to the soccer complex where *The Bones* grabbed up their equipment bags and started out on the long walk up to the soccer fields. Natty looked at her watch and scowled when she saw that it was ten-thirty. They were supposed to report in at least an hour before their eleven o'clock game time. *That's all they needed, to be disqualified from the tournament after a four hour bus ride!* Some of her players looked like they were still asleep as they got off the old yellow school bus.

"C'mon you guys, let's look alive here!" Natty called out, clapping her hands. "We're late. We gotta get up to the fields quick now." When everyone was off the bus, Geneva Gunnells got her book out from under her seat and pulled the door shut abruptly. She wasn't happy about having to come up to Charleston and stay overnight at a *Red Roof Inn* – maybe *two nights* if *The Bones* made the final on Sunday.

Natty trotted after her team that was now jogging through the parking lot with Zack Willard at the head of the line. Carrying her heavy equipment bag, Natty was having a tough time keeping up. Finally she just slowed to a walk and took in the sights of what she now realized was a big-time kids soccer tournament. The parking lots were full and there were cars and vans and RVs parked on wide expanses of grass as well. People were streaming up the hill towards the fields carrying folding chairs and coolers. She watched *The Bones* run through a boulevard of tents and concession stands lined up outside the main gate, attracting the attention of all the spectators with their flashy black warm-up suits with the skull and crossbones on the back. *How proud the kids were of those uniforms! And how much better the team had become since trading in the plain tee-shirts and Wal-Mart shorts for the red jerseys and black Nike shorts! All thanks to Charlie Burden. It seemed like all the good things that had happened in Red Bone the last few months were because of Charlie . . . the man she and her children would be living with on Monday.*

Natty swallowed back the feeling of anxiousness that came with thinking about what she and Charlie were planning, made worse – her own fault, she knew – because she still hadn't been able to tell Buck. *There was just never the right time! And then . . . Buck, asking all about the tournament and wishing her luck and then even giving Pie a firm pat on the back and telling him to 'play hard kid, give it everything you got, 'cause you only get one shot,' and then they had to leave so early. Shit! She'd call him from the motel that night.*

At the top of the hill Natty's anxiousness was replaced by cold fear. It looked like there were soccer fields everywhere, as far as she could see, and there were already some games going on and teams warming up on other fields and crowds were cheering and soccer balls were flying through the air and she had no idea where *The Bones* were. She felt a little better when she saw that the games in progress were between younger kids and she remembered that there were several different age categories for the tournament. *The Bones* were in the oldest division. Then she saw Gabe waving to her from in front of a tent about fifty yards away.

As she got close to the tent, Gabe, grinning as he always seemed to be doing, trotted over to her and took the equipment bag from her shoulder. "You register in here coach," he said, starting off toward the fields. "We're on field three."

In the tent Natty registered and got the schedule and rosters of the other teams and listened to a quick summary of the format. There were eight teams in their division, four from West Virginia, two from Ohio, one from Kentucky, and one from Pittsburgh. You played one game on Friday, two on Saturday and if you got that far, the championship game on Sunday. The Friday losers also played on Saturday morning and the winners with the highest goal totals were back in the Saturday afternoon games. All Natty could think about was playing four games in three days with only one substitute, and that being Pie. *Maybe she had bitten off a little more than she could chew in accepting an invitation to a real tournament.*

"Don't worry too much about the format Mrs. Oakes," said the tournament director, "we're pretty sure it'll be two of the top four seeds playing on Sunday," he said with a big grin. Natty looked down at the pairings and saw that *The Bones* were seeded fourth, with the team from Morgantown third, Charleston second, and seeded first was the team from Pittsburgh with a record of 18 - 0. She looked down at *The Bones* and saw their record listed as 14 -1, which was the first time she knew that the league had taken the *brawl game* with Welch away from them. Natty smiled to herself. *Kyle, you worthless asshole!* "Better get a hustle on there, coach," said the tournament director looking at his watch, "gettin' close to game time now."

At Field #3, Natty had to walk across the field to get to the bench area. Both teams were on the same side. *The Bones* still in their warm-up suits were going through their standard pre-game warm-up calisthenics under the direction of Zack Willard who was so determined, he hadn't cracked a smile or made a joke since he got on the bus that morning. At the end of the field, Gabe was kicking balls at Brenda Giles in the goal.

Natty looked over the opposition as she crossed the field. They wore dark green shirts, black shorts and green stockings, and looked to Natty like an average team in their league – a few tall players, some short players, a few older looking, some young looking – all boys. On the field adjacent to theirs, two more teams from their division were also warming up. These teams looked more formidable to her – bigger and stronger and maybe a little more organized in their warm-up drills than the team from Ohio. *One game at a time,* she told herself turning back to her own field, *and try not to get embarrassed in the first game!*

The Bones had stripped off their warm-up suits and were now getting ready in earnest, in a fast-paced, two passes and a shot drill. In a corner of the field, as was her usual routine, Emma Lowe was laying flat with her chest and face pressed against the grass, unmoving with her legs straight out at what looked like excruciating right angles from her body, her arms stretched straight out over her head.

Natty noticed that the side and end lines were beginning to fill in with spectators, standing and in folding chairs. She didn't know who they were or why they'd be interested in this game, just that they weren't from Red Bone. *Wouldn't be any parents or friends of her kids could afford to come all the way up to Charleston just to watch a soccer game. Must be just local people or maybe they're all from Ohio.*

An older man in a sharp black referee outfit came striding across the field followed by a younger man and a woman in similar outfits carrying flags, and behind them, two boys each carrying a mesh bag of silver balls. At a table on the sideline at mid-field, a man and a woman seated themselves and set out some notebooks and a time clock. Natty had to chuckle to herself at all the officials. *This was real soccer!*

When Natty saw the umpire look at his watch, pick up a ball and start walking to the center of the field, she went out onto the field and clapped her hands. "Okay *Bones,* bring it in," she called.

Several of the Ohio team's players lingered around mid-field on the way to their bench, taking their first look at Emma Lowe whom they had obviously heard about. Emma had finally arisen from her position and was trotting up the field toward the *Bones'* bench area. Behind her coming from the goal carrying three soccer balls, Gabe called out to her. "Hey Em," he said rolling a ball along the ground toward her, "take one." Emma turned and saw the rolling ball and took a short shuffle step and one long stride with her right leg and snapped her left foot through the ball with a sharp crack that sounded like a firecracker going off. From thirty yards out, the ball rocketed a foot over the center of the crossbar and over a retaining fence beyond the goal and onto an adjacent field where some younger kids were playing. Gabe laughed and grinned broadly at the dumbfounded players in green before running off to fetch the ball. Emma just looked toward the ground, gathering her long black hair into her game-time pony tail as she walked to the bench.

Just as the game was about to start, a photographer with cameras and equipment bags hanging off of him came trotting across the field. *The Bones* quickly formed up for their tournament picture at midfield. Some players sat on the grass, while the second row knelt. Natty stood between Emma and Brenda in the middle of the back row with her arms around the shoulders of her two girls. The entire team beamed with pride in their shiny red and black uniforms. It would be a picture Natty knew she and all the players would treasure.

A few minutes into the game, Natty's nervousness disappeared. She could tell from a few trips up and down the field that the team from Ohio was going to be no match for *The Bones.* Their forwards weren't fast enough to force the game past Zack Willard or the other defenders, and their full-backs and sweeper were never going to be able keep up with Emma and Sammy Willard. Their best players were in the mid-field but they still couldn't deal with Paul who was just too fast and too skillful. Natty started thinking about ways to hold down the score. She didn't want to embarrass these kids who had traveled a long way and were obviously very excited about playing in the tournament.

Natty could see the first goal coming as Paul raced the ball across mid-field with open field ahead of him. She almost wanted to call out to the green defenders to back up because they were giving up too much room behind them and they weren't going to put Emma offside because she didn't need to be offside to beat them.

Paul placed a perfect long pass out to the left flank to Sammy Willard who faked a run up the sideline, cut it off abruptly and lofted a long high ball toward the far right corner. Emma, who had put the green defenders to sleep by playing possum for the first several minutes of the game, suddenly streaked past the stunned fullback, tipped the ball to herself and headed toward the goal. She easily dribbled past one defender and then magically spun through two others with an electrifying move that had the spectators applauding even before she brought the ball calmly into the goal box and stared the helpless goalie in the eye before pushing a slow roller into the left corner of the goal.

"She makes it look too easy." The voice right next to Natty startled her. She turned and saw a handsome young man in a shiny maroon warm-up suit and baseball cap. Natty smiled and turned back to the field.

"Yeah, been watching her play since she was seven years old and she still amazes me," said Natty.

The man introduced himself to Natty. He was the coach of the team from Charleston, which was playing the next game on Field 3.

"So how's your team?" asked Natty, recalling that the Charleston team was seeded second.

"Oh, we're good," he said with a smile, "we're pretty good. Like your team."

"Gonna win the tournament?" said Natty moving up the sideline a little.

The man laughed. "No, not us. Not you either. No one's going to beat the team from Pittsburgh. They're loaded. It's an all-star team, put together at the beginning of the year just to win this tournament." The coach followed Natty along the sideline. "They're fast and they're big, and strong, and they got a great coach. They could beat most any high school team in the state."

Natty turned and moved back toward him. "Thanks for the encouragement," she said with a laugh. Out on the field, Paul ripped a shot that hit the cross bar and caromed twenty yards straight out to the middle of the field where Emma took it in mid-air and sent a sizzling low skidder into the left corner of the goal before the goalie even knew where the ball was.

"Wow," said the Charleston coach shaking his head, "she's incredible."

"Yeah," said Natty, turning to find the Pie Man, the lone figure on their bench behind her. "Pie, go in for Emma," she called to him. Pie jumped up off the bench and pulled off his Yankees hat before running over to the scorer's table.

"Where are your extras?" said the coach looking at *The Bones'* empty bench.

Natty laughed and nodded to Pie. "That's him," she said. "Had another sub but he moved away last week."

The coach looked perplexed. "You know you can take up to three kids from other teams in your league if you're short of fifteen players. Didn't your league president tell you that?"

Natty turned and looked up at the man. "You're kidding. I didn't know anything about that. *Damn.* That would have really helped. These kids're gonna be dead after two more games tomorrow."

"That's why they do it," said the coach. "Four games in three days is a lot for these kids. You gotta have subs." Almost on cue, the referee blew his whistle and waved Pie and four new players in green onto the field.

"Well, too late now," said Natty, just as she turned to see Gabe on the sideline giving Emma a high-five as she ran off the field. "Hey," she said, grabbing the coach's arm. "I got one right here," she said pointing to Gabe. "He played on another team, so how do I get him on the roster?"

The coach squinted in thought and shrugged. "Well maybe they'd allow it, if you could get written permission from your league president. Maybe get it faxed up here. They'd probably let you put him on the team. Course, I'd protest it when you played us." The coach touched Natty's elbow and laughed. "Just kidding coach," he said, "be fine with us."

Natty looked up at the handsome young man next to her and smiled. She liked the coach of the Charleston team. "Thanks," she said. "Thanks a lot. I'll look into it." She looked over at Gabe who was back on the sideline, calling out encouragement to *The Bones* and some instruction to the Pie Man, and thought about having him in the *Bones* mid-field next to Paul.

A sudden cheer from the spectators turned Natty's attention back to the game. *The Bones* had scored again. From the high-fiving on the field, it looked like it must have been Paul who scored.

"That kid can play too," said the Charleston coach. Natty just smiled and clapped her hands. She was beginning to wonder if he was going to stand next to her for the whole game. She walked up the sideline a little to watch the restart, and when she stopped, she heard his voice again next to her, a little softer. "So I was wondering if maybe tonight you'd like to have dinner with me, you know, after you get your team settled in at the motel."

Natty just stared out at the field for a few seconds absorbing the surprising words. She turned to the man next to her who was smiling down at her with his arms crossed at his chest. He was probably in his late twenties, just a few years younger than she was. She looked up at his face again and saw that he was indeed very handsome, with gleaming white teeth and a nice, wholesome, honest look to him. The kind of man that was born to be a husband and a father. She put her hands in the pockets of her warm-up jacket and smiled at him. "Sorry," she said. "Thanks. Thanks for the invitation, but . . . I'm married"

"Oh no, gee, I'm sorry," the coach stammered, losing his smile and dropping his hands to his side. "I didn't mean to . . . I just didn't see a ring, that's all."

"It's okay," said Natty chuckling at his discomfort. She pulled her left hand from her pocket and looked at it. "I just don't wear a ring. I never . . . well, I never liked wearing one."

The coach hunched his shoulders and had on a chagrinned smile. "Well, no harm done, I hope. Just didn't know."

"No harm done," said Natty.

"Okay, listen, I'm going to go over to the tent and check on getting your other player on the team. See what I can do."

"Geeze, thanks," said Natty. They shook hands and the coach disappeared into the milling crowd that was much heavier around their end of the field where *The Bones* were shooting towards. Natty stole a peak toward the end of the field as the coach reappeared, walking the end line behind the goal. He stopped to talk to a few people and waved to some others, always with a friendly smile as he made his way across the field. Natty could see that he must be well-known in the Charleston soccer world. He must like kids a lot too, being the coach of a team.

With the score 5 – 0 in the second half, Natty put Emma and Sammy back on defense and had Pie and the Steele brothers play the forward line. She couldn't tell the kids to stop playing but she knew if she left Emma and Sammy up front and the Ohio team got any more demoralized, the score would be in double figures very quickly. With Emma back on defense, some of the spectators folded up their chairs and went off to find another game to watch.

With a few minutes left in the game, Paul scored the *Bones'* sixth goal on a thirty yard floater that went in just over the goalie's outstretched hands. He looked over at Natty and shrugged because he knew she didn't want them to score any more but it wasn't the kind of shot you'd expect to score on. Natty just smiled at him and clapped for his goal.

"That's a mistake, trying to hold down the score," said the familiar voice next to her. She looked around to see the coach of the Charleston team holding a piece of paper in his hand. "Goal differential is used to break ties for teams that lose one of their first two games."

Natty smiled up at him. "I'll remember that when we play your team." They both laughed.

"Here," he said, handing Natty the paper. "Have your league president write this out with your player's information, sign it and fax it to the number there at the top and they'll let your kid play. Get it done tonight and they'll let him play tomorrow's games."

Natty could hardly believe what he was telling her as she studied the handwritten instructions. She looked up just as he started backing away. "Hey, thanks, this is . . ."

"Gotta go find my team coach," he said with a grin. "Good luck tomorrow."

"Yeah, you too," she called after him.

After dinner at McDonald's they went back to the motel and Natty collected all the shirts and socks in a laundry bag. The shorts wouldn't need washing until Saturday night, if they weren't on their way home.

Natty sat on the edge of the bed with her equipment bag at her feet, counting out the bills left in the envelope marked "breakfast – Saturday." She already used some of it at McDonald's, and now she needed a few more dollars for the coin operated laundry they'd passed on the way in. She tucked the bills in the front pocket of her jeans and then reached into a zippered pocket of the big bag and took out Charlie's cell phone and put it in the pocket of her warm-up jacket. "Be back in about an hour," she said to Geneva Gunnells who was reading a book on the bed and to Emma and Brenda Giles who were sitting on the floor watching television.

She checked the two boys' rooms to make sure nobody was killing anyone, hefted the laundry bag over her shoulder and walked around to the side of the motel where they'd had to park the bus. It was dark and cold and had started to drizzle – the onset of the rain that was supposed to be moving in for the rest of the weekend. The wipers on the bus clattered across the cold glass making the going slow as Natty strained to see through the windows to find the Laundromat.

Natty stuffed everything into two washers, emptied a small box of Tide from the vending machine and shoved four quarters into each coin box. She took out the cell phone and sat down on a bench near the dryers, but it was too noisy with all the machines going, plus there were several women sitting nearby reading magazines. Natty needed some privacy for this phone call.

Outside it was still drizzling and the traffic from the street made it still too noisy for a normal conversation and Natty didn't want to have to yell into the phone when she told Buck that she and the kids were leaving him. Her heart was already racing as she shut the folding door of the dark school bus behind her. From the pocket behind the driver's seat, she pulled out Geneva's long silver flashlight and walked back and took a seat at the middle of the bus in the darkness. She took a deep breath and watched the rain splatter against the window distorting the flaring headlights of the traffic in the street. Finally, she sighed and looked down at Charlie's cell phone in her hand. It halfway startled her when it lit up and beeped to life when she hit a button. It sounded louder in the quiet of the school bus. Then she pulled out the paper that the Charleston coach had given her with the instructions and the tournament director's fax number, and put it on the seat next to the flashlight. After she talked to Buck, she'd call Sally and see if she could go into Welch and find Kyle Loftus and have him fax the information to the tournament.

She hadn't really expected Buck to be home at nine o'clock on a Friday night after cutting trees all day. *Make more sense to call down to Moody's Roadhouse, if she had the number.*

"Yeah?" Buck's growl took her by surprise. "Who'sis?" he barked impatiently when there was no reply.

Natty cleared her throat. "Buck," she whispered, and cleared her throat again. "Buck, it's me, Nat," she said louder.

"Oh. Hey. Hey Nat," he said more softly. "So, what's happenin' up there? How's the tournament?"

"Yeah, it's good. We won our first game. Six nothin'. Wasn't too good a team."

"Hey, you'll be kickin' ass all weekend," Buck said enthusiastically. "Ain't no one gonna beat *The Bones*. Hey? Right?"

Natty smiled. "I don't know, there's couple a great teams and the team from Pittsburgh is supposed to be unbeatable."

"Hey *fuck that* huh Nat? Them iron heads from Pittsburgh ain't never played against Emma Lowe and the Willard boys," he chuckled, "and sure enough they ain't never played against the *Pie Man* before."

Natty laughed and took a deep breath and tried to blink away the moisture that was welling up in her eyes. "Yeah Buck," she whispered. "That's right. They ain't never played *The Bones* before."

"There you go," said Buck. "Can't beat em less you *know* you can beat em."

"Yeah, so how come you're home on a Friday night? Roadhouse burn down?"

"Nah, just, uh tired from workin' all day, and Sally and Charlotte went into Bluefield for the movies."

"Yeah?"

"So I got Cat here. Me and Cat are watchin' a tape."

"You and Cat." Natty said softly.

"Yeah. Watchin' *Home Alone*. Stupid movie but the kid knows every *word* of it," he said loudly with a chuckle. "It's *unbelievable*."

"Yeah it's her favorite movie," Natty said weakly. "She's seen it a hundred times." Natty bit her lower lip and squeezed her eyes tightly closed for several seconds.

"Nat? You there?"

"Yeah Buck, I'm here," she said loudly, drawing in a deep breath. She turned and gazed at the flaring headlights in the rain splattered window for a few seconds. Then she looked down and saw the white piece of paper on the seat next to her. "Hey Buck, listen, I need you to do something real important." She explained the situation with Gabe and then turned on Geneva's flashlight and dictated the permission information for Kyle Loftus to sign and gave Buck the fax number it had to go to.

"I'll go into Welch tonight and drag that asshole out of bed. Don't worry, I'll get your kid on the team."

Natty sniffed and looked at her watch in the glow from the headlights in the street. "Naw Buck, why don't you just stay with Cat," she said softly. "Watch your movie. Be better you go over in the morning anyway."

"Yeah okay. Probably right. I'll go find Loftus first thing in the morning."

"Thanks Buck. That will really help a lot, we get Gabe on the team."

Buck laughed. "See? I told you. That Pittsburgh team'll be eatin' your shit and lovin' it by the time you get done with 'em."

"Yeah Buck," Natty laughed. "Okay." There was a long pause between them. "Okay Buck," Natty said finally, "I gotta go now. Say g'night to Cat for me."

"Yeah, I will Nat. Good luck up there."

Natty hit the red button and Charlie's phone went dark. She turned off the flashlight on the seat next to her and sat in the darkness without moving for several minutes. She stared at the rain running down the window and then chuckled and then laughed out loud, wiping the tears from her eyes as she pictured Buck sitting on the couch next to Cat watching *Home Alone.*

In the Saturday morning game, *The Bones* beat the team from Kentucky 5 – 0 with only slightly more effort than they'd had to use in their first game. The Kentucky team had lost to Pittsburgh on Friday by a 12 – 0 score.

On the way back to the field in the afternoon, Natty checked in the tent to see if the fax from Kyle Loftus had shown up but nobody knew anything about it or had seen any fax. She wouldn't say anything to Gabe until she got permission to use him so he wouldn't be too disappointed if it never came, which, dealing with Kyle Loftus, was a distinct possibility. Gabe, she knew, would be beyond ecstatic over the chance to play with Emma and *The Bones* in a tournament game.

They hadn't needed him in the morning game but now, Natty knew, the party was over when she saw the match-ups for the afternoon semifinals. The Pittsburgh team would be playing Morgantown and *The Bones* were playing the team from Charleston. She'd watched the first half of their game on Friday and could see that the friendly Charleston coach was being a little modest when he said his team was "pretty good." They were a powerhouse, solid on offense, defense and in the mid-field, and Natty knew it would be a tough game.

The rain had stopped for the morning games, but now it was sprinkling steadily as Natty made her way toward Field #1 through the milling spectators, many of whom were now holding umbrellas. *The Bones* were already on the field warming up for their second game of the day. Fortunately the morning game, like Friday's, wasn't overly competitive, but *The Bones* still had to run the field and play the game with only one sub. They were going to be a tired bunch by the end of the day. She pulled her *Spiderman* hat down tightly against the breeze and started to jog. Then she heard a voice behind her.

"Hey there Miz Oakes, that you? Hold up there coach."

Natty stopped and turned to see the tournament director, outfitted in a brown rain poncho and wide brimmed hat, coming up behind her. He pulled a piece of paper from under the shelter of the poncho. "Got your permit here to use the Miller kid, Gabe Miller, on your team. We added him to your roster."

Natty took the paper, unfolding it quickly trying not to let it get wet, and saw Kyle Loftus' signature at the bottom. Her face lit up with excitement but the director had already turned to head back to the shelter of the tent. "Thank you," she called after him. "Thank you," she repeated even after she had turned and started sprinting toward the field. Natty smiled as she pictured in her mind what would have been a very short and direct negotiation between Buck and Kyle Loftus.

Natty dug through her equipment bag and found the extra red shirt and black shorts, still in their plastic packaging. Then she started rooting through the kids' bags looking for socks and some extra shin guards, which she finally found in Paul's bag. In another bag she found a mouth-guard that looked fairly clean. She poured some water over it and then looked out to the field to find Gabe. He was rolling balls out of the goal to a semi-circle of shooters just outside the box. Natty waved and called him over.

Gabe's mouth dropped open and his eyes nearly popped out of his head when he read the soggy fax. He turned and gaped at Natty and she just laughed and handed him the uniform. "Welcome to *The Bones,*" she said. "Better get suited up, game's about to start."

She gathered the team around her and told them about the rule the tournament had about bringing three players from other teams in their league. "Well we only got one," she said, grinning at Emma who went agape at the realization that she was talking about Gabe.

"You mean Gabe's gonna play for us?" Emma squealed. It was the loudest thing Natty had ever heard her say. The rest of *The Bones* were laughing excitedly too, knowing that Gabe was one of the best and toughest players in the league.

"Make a circle now so Gabe can get dressed," Natty instructed them, as she saw the referee crew walking across the field. "Hurry up, game's going to be starting. Emma, you and Brenda turn your backs now." Gabe would have to play in his sneakers but Natty knew it wouldn't bother him a bit.

"Hear you got a new player."

Natty turned and saw the handsome young Charleston coach walking toward her. "Yeah, thanks to you," she said as they shook hands.

The coach shrugged. "It's just a game." He smiled down at her. "Good luck Mrs. Oakes."

"Yeah, you too, coach." Natty looked back out onto the field and noticed how many spectators were at the game. Field #1 was the featured field of the complex, the only field with bleachers and they looked to be totally filled. The sideline across the field, as well as the end lines, were also packed tightly with people standing and in folding chairs holding umbrellas. Natty was amazed that so many people wanted to watch this game even in a steady rain.

As soon as the game started it was evident that the *Charleston Chargers* were a great team, easily the best team they'd faced all year. Their positioning and spacing was perfect and they always knew where to play the ball. They had excellent speed, some very strong legs and they worked beautifully together, always communicating and helping each other out. The *Chargers* were a machine and they dominated play for the first ten minutes of the game and just missed scoring on three separate occasions.

But then *The Bones* gradually raised the level of their game as Natty had seen them do several times during the season when they were severely challenged. It had also taken a little while for the team to get used to Gabe playing the midfield to the right of Paul.

Gabe was indeed a force on the field and Natty could see right away that *The Bones* would have little chance of beating the *Chargers* without their new player. Charleston tended to be a little bigger and stronger on the ball than a lot of the *Bones'* players, with the exception of Gabe. Paul and Emma and Sammy were faster, but Gabe soon showed that in addition to his all around skills, he was as strong on the ball as anyone on the field. No one dribbled through or around Gabe or took the ball away from him in a fifty-fifty situation. On one occasion, when Gabe smartly stopped an advancing *Charger* and then dribbled the ball powerfully through two players to start a good rush up the field, Natty happened to glance over and see the Charleston coach looking back at her with a sarcastic smirk on his face and his index "finger gun" pointed at his temple, making her laugh. He smiled at her and shook his head ruefully.

The Chargers had started the game with only two forwards and an extra defender assigned to help double-team Emma and the strategy was working beautifully especially on the slow, wet field. *The Bones* star had few chances, the best coming on a twenty-five yard bullet that banged off the cross bar, after which, the *Chargers* defense tightened up on her even more. The teams slogged to a scoreless first half, but not before Hardy Steele severely sprained an ankle, again leaving *The Bones* with just The Pie Man as their lone substitute.

Fifteen minutes into the second half, *The Bones* began to wear down. The Charleston team used six replacements, running two or three subs at a time into the game at nearly every whistle. Natty put Pie into the game for a few minutes in the second half but he was too much of a defensive liability and she couldn't afford to keep him on the field for very long. The fresher *Chargers,* playing tighter man-to-man defense were beginning to pen *The Bones* in their own end of the field for long stretches, and were getting more and better opportunities to score as the half wound on. Natty could see that her players were just a step slower now, and she didn't have an answer for the *Charger's* pressure.

With ten minutes left in the game, the rain finally stopped and it became windy and cold. It felt like the temperature had dropped twenty degrees in just a few minutes. The dead-tired *Bones,* with their uniforms soaked were now feeling the mind-numbing cold and the frustration of seeing the game starting to slip away from them. When Brenda Giles made a miraculous diving save causing a loud chorus of both groans and cheers from the crowd, Natty called a time-out. There were five minutes left in the game.

She and Pie gathered up water bottles and trotted out to the center of the field where she could talk to her team in private. They gathered closely around her, bundling together against the wind and the cold, eager for some plan, a ray of hope as to how they could survive this game. Natty knelt in the middle of the tight circle looking up at her mud-covered, bruised and exhausted *Bones.* "Okay, we got five minutes left," she said confidently, "and we're going to beat these guys because we're the better team. But we don't want to go to overtime, so we need to win it right now. Okay, from now on, Zack, Georgie, Jimmie, everyone on defense, you get a shot at the ball, you just kick it as far down field as you can, no more passing it out, don't worry about possession. Same with the midfielders. Paul, Gabe, Matt, you get an opening you hit it down the field toward a corner. Okay?" She looked around at the tired but attentive faces for confirmation. She grinned. "Okay, here's the hard part. We get a good clear going, I want everyone rushing up the field. Defense, you get it out, you head up the field as fast as you can go. Same with the midfield, boot it long and go. Forget about defending. I want three players on the ball and everyone else goes to the goal. We'll probably only get one good chance so when it comes, everybody moves up fast."

Play restarted with a goal kick from Brenda that got up in the swirling wind and didn't go anywhere, and the *Chargers* resumed their attack. Natty could see that the other coach had put in a similar strategy as the *Chargers* defenders were all up past midfield to apply the lethal pressure that would win the game. She wondered if maybe that wasn't a mistake with Emma Lowe on the field. *The Bones* fought off their fatigue and battled valiantly, especially Zack Willard who seemed to be everywhere, but they struggled in vain for the next few minutes to get the ball out of their own end.

Just as the scorekeeper announced that there were two minutes left, the crowd gasped as a Charleston player took an open shot from fifteen yards that Brenda Giles leaped for and punched almost straight up in the air. The ball hung over the field for an eternity, dropping toward a spot ten yards directly in front of the goal where both teams converged on it. Natty held her breath because it could so easily result in a goal with so many *Chargers* in the box waiting to end the game. But it was Zack Willard rising out of the pack, three feet off the ground with opposing players bouncing off him, who caught the ball with a perfectly timed header sending it on a long high arc toward the middle of the field. Paul had taken off as soon as he saw Zack lining up his header and beat two *Charger* midfielders to the ball, and the stampede was on. Ten yards short of midfield, Paul played the ball sideways to a dry patch of grass to his right and hit it as hard as he'd ever kicked a soccer ball – in America *or* Poland. Gabe raced past him in pursuit of Emma and a half dozen *Chargers* who were all racing up the field. The ball landed twenty yards beyond Emma who was in an even foot race with a *Charger*. But ten yards from the ball Emma shifted to another gear and cleanly beat him to the ball. Just as she controlled it a *Charger* slid into her from the side cutting her feet out from under her on a bad tackle and sent her sliding through the mud, helplessly just a few yards from the ball, which another *Chargers'* defender was running down. The ref let the play go. It was apparent he wasn't giving out any free kicks to either team for the rest of the game.

Lying in a pool of mud, out of the play, Emma turned her head just in time to see Gabe hurdling over her on a direct path to the ball. Gabe and the *Charger* fullback kicked the ball at the same time but Gabe wouldn't relent. He powered the ball through the defender as he knocked him off stride with his shoulder, and then chased the rolling ball toward the end line, twelve yards to the right of the goal. Two *Chargers* were bearing down on him. He looked back for Emma but she was still on the ground with a defender standing over her. Sammy Willard was in the box at the near end of the goal but he was effectively fronted by the *Chargers'* big sweeper. Gabe corralled the ball and played it a little deeper, gaining another second of time. Then he looked back and saw Zack Willard flying down the middle of the field like a runaway locomotive, knees pumping high and arms firing like pistons, being pursued by a pack of *Chargers* as if he was again running for an open field touchdown. Gabe put his head down and calculated in his mind, the spot where he would put the ball, and didn't look up again. Just before the first *Charger* reached him, he sent his right foot through and under the ball sending a high chip shot floating toward the penalty kick spot out in front of the goal. Just as the ball took off, two defenders crashed into him sending him tumbling beyond the end line into a patch of mud and cinders where he could only lift up his head and watch as Zack Willard flashed through his vision coming straight for the goal at high speed and made the silver ball disappear with a leaping, vicious header and an ungodly scream. Then Gabe saw the ball in the back of the goal, just before Zack's momentum sent him sliding on his stomach past the goalie and into the netting.

From his mud puddle, Gabe looked over and saw Emma still laying on the ground grinning back at him. He laughed and held a victorious fist up in the air. Zack Willard holding the ball out in front of him, raced to midfield and did a fifteen-yard belly-flop slide through the deepest puddle on the field. When he got up, you couldn't tell what color his shirt was.

The Bones easily killed off the last few seconds of the game with Emma putting on a dazzling display of open field ball control, capped by a vicious left-footed bullet just over the cross bar in the final seconds. The crowd gave both teams a sustained ovation for what was truly an incredible soccer game. Natty watched her mud-covered, battered team coming slowly off the field, too exhausted to even celebrate, and couldn't believe they actually had to play another game tomorrow.

Natty called Buck again from the parking lot at the Laundromat. She left Emma and Gabe inside to watch the several loads they had going. Tonight they were washing everything – shirts, shorts, socks, even a pile of underwear the kids would just have to sort out somehow to find the rightful owners. They would at least *look* like a real team when they played Pittsburgh the following afternoon. Pittsburgh had beaten Morgantown, 5 – 0 in the other semifinal. It looked like the Charleston coach was right in his handicapping of the tournament.

From the dark school bus Natty watched Emma and Gabe through the big window of the Laundromat. They were sitting next to each other on a bench talking, first one, then the other, always attentive, smiling, polite to each other, with an occasional laugh, and never running out of conversation. What fast friends they had become. Natty loved watching them be together.

Natty pressed the final button on Charlie's phone and swallowed hard. She wasn't sure what she would tell Buck or how she would say it, but this was it for her, time was up. Charlie would be coming back tomorrow night and she would be picking up her car at the high school with their clothes in the trunk and only have to go up and get Cat, and then drive to the apartment in Bluefield. And it would be over. Her breathing relaxed as the phone continued to ring with no answer. Finally she pushed the red button.

Sally picked up on the second ring. Natty told her about the tournament and that they were in Sunday's Championship game, and that she'd tried to call Buck.

"Yeah, Cat's over here," said Sally. "Staying with us for the night 'cause Buck went out. Don't know where."

"Oh, okay," said Natty softly. "That's good, you got Cat."

Sally could feel her disappointment. "He spent the whole day with her Nat."

"Yeah?"

"Took her up to Welch first thing in the morning and then they had lunch up there and went to the video store. Come back and watched some movie together, just the two of 'em. Cat had a special day."

Natty was silent for a few moments, then she smiled to herself. "Yeah, okay thanks Sal. Just tell Buck we won and we're playing Pittsburgh tomorrow." She clicked off and sat still in the darkness and thought about Charlie up in Vermont with his family, and tomorrow he was going to tell his wife – the beautiful, sophisticated Ellen Burden – that he was leaving her for a mousy little hillbilly girl with a retarded son named *Pie Man* and a daughter who's entire vocabulary consisted of dialog from *Home Alone* . . . Natty chuckled . . . and *she* was the one who couldn't tell Buck!

Natty slept an hour later than usual, went for a three mile run in the rain and then drove the bus to a Krogers and spent their last thirty dollars on five boxes of cereal, three gallons of milk, two large cartons of orange juice and three bunches of bananas. That was all they'd have to eat until they got back to Red Bone that night. Natty kicked herself for not managing their funds better because she knew that win or lose today, *The Bones* were going to be starving after the game, and it was going to be a long ride home. Too many meals at McDonald's – which was more expensive than Natty had thought – was the problem, but McDonald's was a rare treat for her kids so, *what the hell, they'd get by on cereal and bananas today.*

Natty let herself into the room and dropped the groceries on the bed and then noticed that Emma and Brenda Giles weren't in the room. Geneva Gunnells was in a chair pulled close to the window for light, reading her book.

"Where's Em and Brenda?" Natty asked.

Geneva didn't look up from her book. "Gone next door to the boys' room I'd guess."

Natty rolled her eyeballs. "Nice chaperoning 'Neva," she said sarcastically.

"They be okay, good kids," Geneva said, still reading.

"Got some cereal here," said Natty taking a box of *Rice Chex* and four bananas out of one of the bags. She put a gallon of milk on the dresser next to their bowls and plastic spoons, and grabbed up the other bags to bring to the boys.

She knocked on the first door and stood in the rain waiting while nobody answered. Walking down to the second boys' room, she thought she saw the curtain move as she went past, then she heard from inside the room the unmistakable giggling and jumping around sounds of kids at mischief.

Natty knocked three times before the door finally swung open slowly. She stood in the rain, dumbfounded, her mouth open in shock as she stared at the sight in front of her, of Jimmie Hopson, George Jerrell, Matt Hatfield and Sammy Willard standing just inside the door, all grinning from ear to ear, all with their heads completely shaved, each one bald as a soccer ball.

"Oh my God!" she finally managed. She stepped into the room, now grinning at the spectacle as she saw Paul and Gabe jumping on one of the beds, also bald, and the chubby Steele brothers who now resembled snowmen with their shining domes. Then Pie squeezed through the other boys, his face locked into an ultimate *happy face*, his head shaved as smooth as a billiard ball. Natty put the bags on the floor and yelped with laughter as she hugged her son who was bouncing with excitement. The kids were having so much fun that Natty couldn't help but enjoy it with them. She rubbed everyone's head and laughed and rolled her eyeballs in fun, and then she stopped, suddenly . . . the smile left her face as she remembered that Emma and Brenda weren't in their room. And then they came out of the bathroom, Brenda first, followed by Emma, grinning nervously, their hair gone, scalps shaved clean, followed by a bald Zack Willard still holding a disposable plastic razor. His white grin lit up the little motel room.

Natty covered her mouth and stared at Brenda and Emma in shock. Finally she laughed and shook her head. "Your mothers are going to *kill* me," she said with a shriek. Then she moved forward quickly and hugged the two girls and kissed the tops of their heads.

"Now this's what I calls a *team!*" roared Zack Willard, who was answered by a loud chorus of *"Bones, Bones, Bones"* from the jumping, laughing and high-fiving, bald soccer team. Natty couldn't disagree with him at all as she joined the demonstration. She stopped worrying about whether *The Bones* would be up for the Championship game.

The Pittsburgh *Golden Knights* were big and fast and strong, just like the coach of the Charleston team had told her, but they were cocky too, maybe a little *too* cocky, Natty thought as the game got under way. Unlike the Charleston team, Pittsburgh played three forwards and four midfielders, and didn't bother to assign an extra defender to Emma Lowe. They were all about *offense* . . . everyone moving up to press the attack and keep the ball in the offensive zone – like they played every game – and they weren't about to change tactics because of some *girl.* Natty had seen the attitude before, from teams in their own league, and knew that inevitably, Emma always made them pay for not respecting her.

Natty also wondered if maybe the *Knights* hadn't had it a little too easy in the tournament so far. They hadn't been in a tough game like *The Bones* had against Charleston, and now, when they saw that they were playing a *real* team, it looked like the *Knights* might have tightened up a bit. While Pittsburgh enjoyed an early territorial advantage, they'd had few good chances on goal as Zack Willard skillfully directed the defense and personally dominated the defensive zone. *The Bones* played them even through the first twenty minutes. The constant rain had also helped to slow down both offenses. The field was becoming soggier and muddier by the minute, with puddles that would stop a rolling ball dead. It became quickly apparent that this would be a low scoring game.

Just when it seemed like the half would play out to a scoreless tie Paul stole a careless pass in the midfield, dribbled easily around a *Knights* defender and quickly advanced another ten yards. Emma just jogged lazily ahead of the play as Paul waited for her move. As she closed in on the fullback in front of her, Emma suddenly faked her usual run to the outside and then spun back toward the middle of the field, cutting between the fullback and the sweeper just as Paul threaded her a perfect through-ball putting her in alone, one-on-one with the goal tender twenty yards out. While everyone on the field thought that she would dribble in closer for a better shot, Emma knew that there was standing water and slippery mud in front of the goal and defenders closing on her from behind, and she didn't need to get any closer. She tipped the ball with her right foot to slow it up and then instantly pulled the trigger with her deadly left leg, blasting through it as she had a thousand times before kicking at the rusted iron pipe in the small hollow on the north side of Red Bone Mountain, hooking the ball on a blazing path into the top left corner of the net. The goal tender never even moved. *The Bones* gathered around Emma and Paul and spontaneously created a new goal celebration with everyone in turn rubbing the tops of their bald heads. The crowd cheered them on with a long ovation in appreciation of the great goal.

It was only then that Natty finally notice how large the crowd encircling the field had become. The bleachers were filled and covered by umbrellas, and the opposite sideline and end lines were three-deep with spectators in rain-gear, trying to find space for their umbrellas. Then she noticed for the first time, that there were a significant number of little girls in soccer outfits along the sidelines at their end of the field, and they were all now cheering happily for Emma's goal. Natty also thought she caught a glimpse along the end line of the two women from North Carolina, the scouts who had come to *The Bones'* first game to watch Emma, but in the driving rain it was hard to be sure.

At halftime, Natty told her team to be patient and continue to play good solid defense and wait for their openings on offense. A cocky, proud team like the *Knights* that was used to winning and scoring a lot of goals would become more and more frustrated and then careless as the second half went on, and one more goal would win the game.

Ten minutes into the second half, the strategy was working perfectly. Paul and Gabe were hanging back a little and clogging up the middle of the field, forcing the *Knights* to try to go over them with long balls. But Zack Willard was too fast and too strong and he cleaned up everything that came into the defensive zone. Natty's primary worry became the fatigue level of her team. Pittsburgh had six solid subs they sent in and out of the game regularly. With Hardy Steele unable to play with his sprained ankle, she had only the Pie Man on the bench. Still, with the downpour and the slow field, the game so far hadn't been anywhere near the total war they'd had with Charleston, so she thought her players could hold up for another twenty minutes.

Then, Zack Willard broke his leg. He simply slipped in the mud while planting his foot to kick the ball and he went down awkwardly with his leg twisted under him and didn't get up. The game was stopped for twenty minutes while the medics applied an inflatable cast and then loaded him into an ambulance that drove out onto the field leaving deep tire ruts in the mud that quickly filled up with water. Kneeling in the mud next to Zack, holding an umbrella over him and holding his hand as the medics worked, all Natty could think about was whether Zack would be able to play football again.

Natty walked back to her team, gathered in front of their bench, with tears in her eyes. Gabe came toward her. His uniform was soaked, his legs, socks and high-top sneakers were caked with mud, and he had a nasty red welt over one eye from an errant elbow. Natty couldn't help chuckling at the sight.

"I'll play sweeper now coach," he offered. "I can play there."

Natty nodded her agreement. "Good. Thanks Gabe," she said leading him back to the team. She huddled *The Bones* up as the ref blew his whistle impatiently, anxious to get the game going again as the rain started to increase in intensity. "Okay," she said, trying to sound positive. "Gabe's sweeper, Pie you're in at forward and Sammy you take Gabe's spot." She stopped and took in a deep breath as she turned and watched the ambulance pull away with its red light flashing.

Before she could say anything else, Paul stepped forward and clapped his hands loudly. "Okay now my bones," he said loudly. It was the first time some of them had ever heard the Polish boy speak. "For friend of mine Sack, we play now like crazy mother fuckers to kick this ass of team we play, for Sack would want." He looked intensely around the circle of faces. "Okay my bones?" Then he grinned and reached up and rubbed the tops of the two bald heads next to him. Natty and the rest of the team burst into laughter and they all started rubbing the tops of as many heads as they could get to on their way back out onto the field. Natty was thankful. It was a far better pep talk than she could have given.

Gabe was an able replacement at sweeper and Sammy was a solid midfielder, but there was no way to make up for the dominating presence of Zack Willard on the field. Natty could feel the tide shifting as Pittsburgh picked up their intensity in an effort to get the tying goal. *The Bones* were also starting to hit the wall. Four games in three days with virtually no subs and the pressure of a one goal lead on an exhausting muddy field, was all catching up with them. Players were starting to walk and to slip more and take their eye off the ball when they were kicking, and now the *Bones* were a step slower to the free balls.

At left forward, Pie was running as hard as he could, but he was barely a factor, usually ending up sliding through the mud out of the play as the *Knights* moved the ball up field. He, along with Emma and George Jerrell were now mostly playing in the middle of the field frantically trying to slow down the relentless attack of the *Knights*. Natty prayed for the clock to keep moving and for *The Bones* to just send it up the field a few more times.

But the desperate and talented team from Pittsburgh showed why they had been undefeated all season. They ran hard and pressed without letup and kept the ball in the *Bones'* end of the field. Gabe and Paul and Emma were all over the field now battling valiantly to keep the ball away from the front of the goal. Brenda Giles was also doing some heroic goaltending, coming far off the line to leap on everything she could get to, and then taking as long as she could before putting the ball in play again.

Natty forced herself to walk up to the scorer's table to check the time – 'just under five minutes' the timekeeper told her just as Gabe made a miraculous diving save on a ball rolling into the open corner of the goal with Brenda laying flat on her stomach ten yards away. The ball went over the end line for a corner kick.

It looked to Natty as if the *Golden Knights* had twenty players in the box as the corner kick floated up in the wind and the rain and finally disappeared into the frantic group of jumping, pushing and kicking players in front of the goal. The crowd around the field screamed in agony along with Natty as the ball pin-balled around the box with no one getting a solid foot to it. There were a half dozen players laying in the mud, including Brenda Giles, when the ball just slipped away from her grasp and squirted free to a *Knight* with finally a clear path to the goal. He emphatically buried it into the netting causing the entire Pittsburgh bench to race onto the field in wild celebration of the tying goal.

Just as the umpire placed the ball down in the center circle for the restart, the dark sky opened up and the rain became a torrential downpour. Natty thought she could hear the sound of thunder off to the south. She knew there couldn't be much time left on the clock and was glad to see Emma take the back-pass from Paul and just blast the ball long downfield toward the far left corner. Emma always knew the correct play on a soccer field. The ball bounced once and then just stuck in the mud short of the end line. Then came two sharp toots from the ref's whistle ending regulation play, probably a minute early because of the weather.

The early whistle was okay with Natty as was the ten-minute overtime they would play. She was certain that her team, playing full defense for ten minutes could kill off the overtime. Then, they'd go into a five-man shootout, which she knew, with Emma, Paul, Gabe, Sammy, and Matt Hatfield as shooters and Brenda in goal, would favor *The Bones*. They'd kill off the overtime and take their chances in the shootout. Natty felt confident. She huddled up her team and started to give them the strategy when she heard her name being called out.

"Say there miz Oakes." Natty looked up to see the umpire standing at the scorer's table with the other officials, the Pittsburgh coach and the tournament director, waving her over.

"Listen, miz Oakes, what we're gonna do here, 'cause a the weather," the umpire said as she closed in on the group, "is just play the overtime and that'll be it. Not gonna go into a shootout."

Natty pushed up the Spiderman cap and raised her eyebrows. "What if it's still tied?"

The tournament director spoke up from under his poncho and wide brim hat. "Well, we'll just go by goal differential for the tournament is all we can do."

"You can't do that!" Natty shouted. "They can play for a tie. That's like giving them the tournament," she pleaded, holding her hands out wide.

"Well that's what it's gonna be," the director said with finality, turning away from the group. The umpire blew his whistle and turned and started jogging out to the center of the field.

The thunder boomed closer and the wind blew the rain sideways in gusts as Natty trotted back to her team. She didn't like it but knew it was probably a good decision the way the weather was. *Be lucky if we all don't get killed out here. And shit, it's just a game.*

Natty huddled her team again, ignoring the umpire's repeated whistles to get the overtime started. She explained the ruling to *The Bones*. "Okay, we're getting screwed but that's the way it is. The only way we can win is to score in the overtime, so they got the advantage of being able to play for a tie and they win the tournament." She shook her head angrily, still mad at the officials.

"Naw, you're wrong coach," Gabe stood with his hands on his hips, covered with dirt and red scrapes, a wide buck-toothed grin across his face. Everyone looked at him. "We got the advantage coach, 'cause we don't have to play any more defense. But *they do.*"

Natty smiled at him and then laughed, nodding her head in agreement. "You know Gabe, you're right. *We* got the advantage." She clapped her hands together. "Okay *Bones,* we got ten minutes to win this thing. Let's go!"

Her team ran enthusiastically back out onto the field, everyone but Pie who stood just on the field waiting for his mother's attention. Then she turned and saw him looking at her, a pained expression on his face. Natty was surprised. He needed to be out at his position at left forward. The overtime was about to start. "Pie Man, what is it? What's the matter?" she said moving toward him quickly.

"Mama," he said softly. "Papa's here." He half turned and pointed across the field.

"Wha . . .? When?" Natty said, squinting into the rain to see the spectators still lining the field.

"Fowa the second half he come. He was yelling to me."

"Yeah, okay, go head Pie," she said pushing him toward the field still scanning the sideline. The ball was already in play. Then she saw Buck, because of his height, staring back at her, the black mustache and goatee looking ever ominous even from across a soccer field. She smiled and waved, but the crowd cheering grabbed away her attention as the *Knights* moved the ball toward the *Bones'* goal.

The rain was pelting down and it was hard to pick out the ball all the way down the field. She kept her eye on Brenda Giles just as the goal tender made a wonderful save on a hard rolling shot. Brenda punted the ball against the strong wind and Natty took in a deep breath as the ball seemed to stop in mid-air. Then, Natty heard a shrill beeping sound from just behind her. After ignoring it for eight or nine beeps, Natty finally looked behind her and saw that the noise was coming from her equipment bag sitting in the mud a few feet away. Reaching into the bag quickly while trying to still watch the action on the field, Natty finally located Charlie's cell phone. She looked down and pressed the green button as the rain splattered across the illuminated display panel. "Hey Charlie," she said, her eyes on the field. "Where are you?"

"On the plane, coming into Charleston," he said. The noise of the rain made it difficult to hear him. "What's happening? Are you still playing?"

Natty laughed and half yelled into the phone. "We're in overtime in the Championship game. It's pouring and your phone's getting all wet."

"Don't worry about it." Charlie spoke louder. "Tell me what's happening."

George Jerrell had made a nice play to steal the ball and hit it up the left side line to mid-field. Natty tried to give Charlie a short-hand version of the play-by-play. The Pie Man was scrambling frantically for the ball amid a circle of players, and then she saw Buck moving along the sideline impervious to the spectators behind him, staying even with Pie and calling out instructions, amplified every few seconds with a hand clap when Pie got his foot on the ball. And then Paul got some room and kicked it farther up the sideline and Pie took off after it with Buck moving up the sideline with him step-for-step, calling out to him and clapping his hands as Pie ran as hard as he ever had, encouraged by his father cheering him on for the first time in his life, and Natty sobbed suddenly into the phone and the tears flowed down her cheeks, washed away instantly by the driving rain.

Thunder boomed almost right over them as a *Knights* defender cleared the ball to mid-field with a powerful kick that sent everyone racing in the other direction. Natty saw the timekeeper hold up two fingers to her and the other coach. "Two minutes left Charlie. Ball's down in our end. Think we're probably out of time." The ball went out of bounds for a *Knight's* throw in. Pittsburgh used the time to put some subs in the game.

"How was Vermont?" Natty yelled, trying to shield the phone with the brim of her hat.

"It was nice," said Charlie. "It was good seeing the kids, and everything, you know, but . . ." A thunder clap drowned out his words.

"What Charlie?" Natty yelled trying to block her other ear. Then she saw Buck directly across the field staring at her, watching her have her conversation on a cell phone, and they both knew it was obvious who she was talking to. And then she heard the crowd roar and saw the ball in the air coming out of the *Bones'* end of the field, a low liner, helped along now by the swirling wind, headed straight at the Pittsburgh sweeper. He played it perfectly bending slightly for a solid, low header that sent the ball in the other direction. But then flashing across the ball's path Emma Lowe took it straight in the chest at full speed and never broke stride as she pushed it ahead and raced straight toward the stunned sweeper who moved too quickly to his left just as Emma magically moved in the same instant to *her* left and then she was alone in the center of the field thirty yards from only the goal tender in front of her. There couldn't be more than a few seconds left in the game. Natty gasped and shouted into the phone. *"Emma's in alone Charlie! She's all alone!"*

Just five yards behind Emma, four *Golden Knights* were racing after her as fast as they could run, but Natty knew no one was going to catch Emma Lowe from behind before she could get her shot off. The goalie was moving out. Without realizing it, Natty was pressing the phone against the side of her face harder and harder as she watched. The crowd was roaring over the deafening noise of the torrential rain. An umbrella flew across the field. *"Hit it Emma!"* she cried out. *"Hit it now!"* It was an easy goal for Emma, with either foot, either side, *she couldn't miss* . . . from twenty yards, and then fifteen, but Emma still didn't shoot. *"Pull the trigger now, Em! Don't wait!"* Natty yelled into the phone as she jumped up and down moving out ten yards onto the field. And then the goalie was making his move, smartly, the correct play, with the ball maybe just a foot too far out in front of Emma, rushing out at her and going down lengthwise in front of her sliding toward her. But the ball wasn't too far in front of her. It was right where she wanted it, waiting for the instant the goalie started out, committed irrevocably to his slide. She took the long stride she'd been saving and tipped the ball directly to her right as the goalie slid under her jump, regained possession and looked at the wide open net eight yards away.

Natty raised two arms in triumph, the black phone held high up in the rain, and then watched in agony as Emma still didn't shoot, and the squad of pursuing *Knights* overtook her, sliding, tumbling and diving through the mud to take Emma down and block the goal line in front of her, but not before she planted her left foot and without even looking, swept the ball smoothly with the instep of her right foot on a path directly along the goal line toward the left post. Natty writhed in agony. *"Emma! Emma, what are you doing!"* she screamed.

But Emma always knew what she was doing on a soccer field, and Natty gasped as she followed the path of the rolling ball and there at the left end of the goal, all alone, was the Pie Man. And then she saw Buck, on the end line beyond the goalie, bent over with his hands cupped at his mouth yelling out to Pie. And then she saw her son, ready himself and shuffle his feet for position as the rolling, bouncing ball came toward him in the torn-up, grassless dirt and she covered her mouth with fear that he'd slip or miss the ball entirely as he often did, and she held her breath. But he didn't miss it. He stepped into it perfectly, like he'd seen Emma and Paul and Zack do all season and he powered it into the back of the netting with authority.

Natty pulled the phone back down and screamed. "Oh my *God* Charlie! *Pie got a goal! We won the tournament!"*

She ran out onto the field and then stopped to watch when she saw Buck, holding Pie up high, hugging him against his chest with one powerful arm, the other held up in triumph, spinning them both around in a circle. The Pie Man held his arms aloft, and had on the most severe *happy face* of his life. The joy on her husband's face reminded Natty of the Buck of their youth, so long ago. She knew she was crying but it was raining so hard she wasn't sure. Then Buck put Pie down to let him run off and celebrate with his teammates. He turned to find Natty and walked toward her. Buck stopped a few feet away and looked down at the phone in her hand and then back at her face. She rubbed her eyes with her right sleeve and smiled at him.

"Thanks for coming Buck," she said softly.

He shrugged his shoulders. "I'm tryin' Nat."

She nodded. "Yeah, I know you are Buck. I know that."

Chapter 34

When the heat finally came up, the bus started to smell like a wet dog. Some of the kids had changed out of their uniforms into dry clothes, adding their mud-caked shirts, shorts and socks to the mélange of wet bags, towels and warm-up suits stuffed under the seats and piled in the aisle. Natty just sat in her wet warm-ups deciding it was too much trouble to try to change into anything. Everything she had was damp anyway. Everything on the bus was wet. It was going to be a long, uncomfortable ride back to Red Bone in the old yellow school bus.

It would have been worse if Buck hadn't had the sixty dollars on him that Natty borrowed to make one more stop at McDonald's. At least the kids weren't starving. She thought about Buck driving all the way up to Charleston in his truck – four hours minimum in the lousy weather – just to watch their soccer game. Good thing he came too – to give her the money to feed the team, and to volunteer to go to the hospital and bring Zack home after they put a cast on his leg. No telling what time they'd be getting home if they had to wait for Zack.

Natty glanced over at Geneva Gunnells leaning over the steering wheel trying to see through the rain flooding over the windshield wipers. "Let me know if you need a break Neva," said Natty. The old woman just grunted sarcastically as if she was the only person who could drive the bus. Natty chuckled. Geneva was too old to still be driving a bus but she'd driven these roads in plenty of bad weather for over forty years and she'd get them home again tonight.

Natty twisted around to look at her team. She saw the two-foot tall tournament trophy in its own seat across the aisle. It was mostly plastic – a silver soccer player with a ball at the end of his foot, standing on a round platform held up by four, foot-tall, round columns – with a small engraved plaque screwed into the heavy wooden base . . . *"12th Annual Charleston Youth Soccer League Thanksgiving Tournament, First Place, The Bones, Red Bone, West Virginia."* Natty thought that maybe there would be a good spot for it in the new library. *How proud the kids were going to be of that trophy!*

In the seat just behind the trophy sat Gabe and Emma, their bald heads almost touching as they hunched together, still talking, quietly, smiling at each other. Natty wondered how they could have so much to continuously chat about. *They'd said more to each other this weekend than she and Buck had said to each other all year.* Behind them, the rest of *The Bones* were spread out trying to find a comfortable position on the hard small seats to go to sleep. Her team was exhausted and wet and now, with their bellies filled with Quarter Pounders and French fries, most of them would sleep all the way back to the High School. And so would she.

Natty crossed her arms for warmth and sunk down in her seat with her shoulder pressed against the window. If she remained perfectly still, she found that she couldn't feel the wetness of the clothing against her skin. She closed her eyes and couldn't any longer avoid thinking about the problem that lay ahead, when they got back to Red Bone. The *problem* that she had been daydreaming about since she was barely a teenager, and now that it was here, only a few hours away from coming true, she didn't know if she could go through with it. She was supposed to take the kids and meet Charlie at the apartment in Bluefield. *But how could she do that now, without having had the backbone to tell Buck? And now Buck would be bringing Zack home and she had to go up and see Mabel and tell her what happened and be there when Buck got there and how could she tell him then? After he'd gone all the way up to Charleston to watch their game, and run up and down the sideline in the pouring rain yelling out encouragement to Pie – words her son had never heard before from his father – and after he'd picked up Pie and hugged him finally, for like the first time in his whole life and spun him around and made their son the proudest kid in America.* Natty chewed on her lip and let the tears slip down her cheeks and fall onto her wet jacket. In the dark of the school bus, sitting alone, no one in the world could see the tears of happiness for her son. Before she could resolve her dilemma, Natty's mind and body surrendered to the exhaustion of the long, incredible weekend.

Charlie pressed the phone into its cradle in the back of the seat in front of him and looked out the small window at his left shoulder. Far ahead a line of orange from the setting sun spread out in front of the plane. Beneath them a blanket of dark clouds hid the rugged landscape of West Virginia. Somewhere down there ahead of them, Natty Oakes and *The Bones* were celebrating their victory – *tournament champions* – and the winning goal scored by *The Pie Man!*

The flight attendant arrived with a large cup of ice and two small bottles of Canadian Club. Charlie put down the tray in front of him and poured both of the shots over the ice. He stared out the dark window and thought about the wonderful weekend he'd had in Vermont, a special weekend with the kids, like they'd enjoyed so many times in the years gone by when they'd pile the kids and the dog and all their baggage into the Dodge Caravan and head off to the mountains. Now it was different, with Jennifer flying in from Evanston and Scott driving up from Boston, but close enough. Close enough to raise up some vivid memories of their best years. An old-time turkey dinner with plenty of wine and a fire in the fireplace, several hours of Detroit Lions football on TV, and later a game of Yahtzee pulled from the worn-out pile of games on top of the tall bookcase. There hadn't been enough snow for skiing on Friday so they took a long walk – the four of them – around the golf course, all eighteen holes, following the cart path where there was one, or walking down the middle of the fairways, breathing in the spectacular Sugarbush views and the clean, cold November air of the Green Mountains that always held the promise of snow.

And then Saturday night, alone on the deck with Ellen while the kids went into Montpelier to the splendid old Capitol Theater for a movie. They bundled up and sat with their brandies and talked – mostly Charlie this time for a change, because he had all the news, news he had been saving until Scott wasn't around – about the hearing in Red Bone and the shocking news about Torkelson, Tuthill, Warren Brand and the others, and the surprising appearance of Duncan McCord and Red Landon. It was an entertaining story and Ellen was enthralled. Then the meetings in New York earlier in the week with Lucien and the rest of the Executive Committee and how they wanted him to take over the China project, not as just an on-site Senior Engineer, but the *whole* project – six months as *Deputy Superintendent* and then *complete responsibility* for the second dam. Three years in China with a walled-estate in Beijing including a full-time housekeeping staff, gardener, and his personal driver/translator, plus a cottage at the project site, helicopter and Lear jet at his disposal and a million-dollar salary. They sat in silence for a while before Charlie told her that he hadn't decided on what he was going to do, that he needed to think about China, although, he had to concede, it was a *pretty spectacular* opportunity. He left it at that. And Ellen didn't press him. After a while she smiled at him in the dim yellow light that filtered onto the deck from the family room and reached over and took his hand and said, very quietly, "Okay, Charlie. You decide what you want to do." And then, when all the talk about the company and China had all been said, and there was silence on the deck, and it was the perfect opportunity to say the words – to tell Ellen about Natty and her children, and the apartment in Bluefield where Charlie would be staying with them on Sunday night – Charlie sighed and took a sip of brandy, and squeezed Ellen's hand and they sat in silence watching the stars in the black sky over Lincoln Peak.

Was it just *cowardice,* or was it *indecision*, Charlie asked himself gazing out at the darkness of the thick clouds covering West Virginia. He had the chance to tell Ellen and he let it pass. He even had the feeling all weekend in Vermont that Ellen was *waiting* for him to deliver some *news about the woman in West Virginia.* But he couldn't do it. Or *wouldn't* do it? *Did it make a difference?* Did it matter *why* he didn't tell her?

Charlie took large sip of Canadian Club and closed his eyes and leaned back in his seat as the liquor warmed the back of his throat, and he saw Natty standing just inches away from him in front of the orchestra pit at the *Imperial Theatre* and he could smell her perfume and see her glistening lips and her beautiful, embarrassed smile and he ached for her as he had been aching for her since his first weekend in Red Bone. He knew that he'd never before met a woman like Natty, and that he wanted to spend every waking moment with her. He hadn't changed his mind, but just delayed the decision for a while. He'd meet her tonight in Bluefield and they'd just go from there. Charlie tried in his mind to make it all sound simple, but he knew it wasn't.

The seat belt sign chimed on just before the plane bucked violently as they descended into the clouds on their approach to Yeager Airport. Charlie finished his drink and watched the curling snakes of water move across the small window at his shoulder. There was nothing but blackness below them, down where Natty and *The Bones* in their yellow school bus were headed back to Red Bone.

The bus lurched with a noisy downshift of the gears and Natty's head slid along the cold glass of the window, sending a tremor of pain through her stiff neck. She struggled to go back to sleep but after a few seconds, a strange, foreign sound made her open her eyes and straighten up in her seat, slowly, scowling with the discomfort of rearranging her aching neck and shoulders. She twisted around painfully to survey the interior of the dark bus. There was no movement anywhere. Across the aisle, Gabe was asleep with his head on Emma's shoulder, while she was tucked into the darkness close to the window.

Natty felt the bus swerve slightly and shot a glance over at Geneva Gunnells, leaning a little farther than normal over the big steering wheel. Then she noticed the sound again – of water rushing down the streambed running alongside the road. She could see the white spray of foam where the water crashed into a boulder or a tree or a sign, and in the dull yellow beams of the headlights through the front window she could see the water sweeping toward them across the pavement in diagonal ripples.

Natty pulled herself up from her seat and went and squatted next to Geneva. "Pretty bad Neva, huh?" There wasn't another light to be seen on the road and the clouds eliminated any moonlight there might have been.

"Not so bad," said the elderly driver. "Road's okay. Gettin' a little higher up soon. We be okay." She flashed a quick, nervous smile at Natty.

Natty stood up and put a hand on Geneva's shoulder. "Okay Neva. Let me know if you need a break. I can drive for a while." But she knew Geneva wouldn't let her. She never did.

Natty turned and walked toward the back of the bus to inspect her sleeping, wet, dirty, championship soccer team, and as she now realized again with a start, her *bald* soccer team. She rolled her eyes and shook her head when she thought of the reaction some of the parents were going to have to her bringing all the kids home with shaved heads – including the two girls! *For sure, the last time they let her take a team to an overnight tournament!*

She had to step gingerly over the piles of wet clothing, gym bags, McDonald's bags and empty soda containers, and turn sideways to avoid the feet, knees, elbows and bald heads sticking out into the aisle. Everyone was fast asleep, which was good, thought Natty, because the stink in the back of the bus was *wretched.* In the second to the last seat she found Pie, stretched out across the seat with his head and shoulders on Sammy Willard's lap. Sammy was asleep against the window with his arm across Pie's chest. Pie had both hands resting on his stomach on top of his Yankees hat. Natty stood still looking down at her son – the *soccer star* – even though everyone knew it was Emma's goal, Pie could still enjoy his moment and nobody on the team, least of all Emma, would ever take it away from him. Natty couldn't help smiling with pride. Pie had grown so much during the season and really *had* become a *normal* little boy and no longer the *little retarded kid.* And now he had some real friends and real teammates and a championship season to talk about for years to come that he had played a real part in, *thanks to Emma.*

Natty went back to the front of the bus and slumped sideways into her seat. With her back against the window she looked over again at the tournament trophy. A wave of exhaustion swept over her, not from the weekend or the bus trip home, but the entire season. *And what a season it was!* Going from worrying about whether she'd have enough players for a team, to the addition of the super-athletic Willard brothers, the marvelous Paul who made everyone on the team a better player, and then Gabe for the two most important games – two games they wouldn't have won without him. And then the tournament and the championship – the *best* under-fourteen team in the state! Natty glanced over at Gabe and Emma and couldn't help smiling. Certainly *they'd* grown over the season. The whole team had grown and become better people than they were before – Natty was certain of that – and that made it a pretty good season.

Natty crossed her arms and looked at the mud-caked sneakers on her feet sticking out into the aisle and thought about how much *she* had changed too. She'd met Charlie Burden and gone to New York, had her hair styled and made into a *real* woman for a short time anyway, and had felt for the first time what it was like to be loved by a man. *But she knew there was someone else who had changed over the season too, probably more than anyone.* Natty looked to the rear of the bus, through the back window to see if she could see any headlights, to see if Buck's truck might be coming up behind them. But there was only darkness.

She noticed then that they were on Cold Springs Road not far from the cut-through around the power plant. Natty swallowed hard and let out a deep sigh with the frightening realization that they were just a few minutes from the high school and her car with the hastily packed bags with their clothes in the trunk, and the key to the apartment in Bluefield over the visor.

Geneva Gunnells slowed the bus almost to a stop so as not to miss the turn-off onto the power plant road in the dark. The bus made the sharp right hand turn, whining in first gear to climb the short incline over the culvert. Out the side window, through the darkness Natty could see the foamy white spray of the fast moving water hitting the boulders down on the streambed below them. Then the bus shuddered and the engine raced at a higher pitch as Geneva tried to accelerate, but they weren't moving. Natty instinctively gripped the pole in front of her as the rear of the bus slid noticeably to the right. Geneva gunned the engine to no avail. She applied the break and the bus stood still, angled up the incline with a slight cant to the right. Geneva shifted into reverse and immediately the rear of the bus began to sink and slide farther toward the chasm. She tried to put it into first gear again but it was too late. The roadway over the stream, weakened by the torrent of water forced around and under the cast iron culvert was collapsing under the rear wheels of the bus.

Natty turned around and watched in horror as the bus slowly slid down the hill toward the stream and started to twist onto its left side. She leaped up screaming as loud as she could, *"Wake up! Everyone, wake up. Wake up!"* she yelled desperately, stumbling toward the rear of the bus trying to hold on to the steel handles on top of the seats. Natty got halfway to the back of the bus when it rolled hard onto its left side and she lost her grip. She hit the edge of a seat, spun around and landed hard on the side of the bus hitting her head just above the window. In the absolute darkness, she couldn't tell if her eyes were open or closed or in what direction the bus was sliding. Pressed against the cold metal skin of the bus Natty wedged her forearms under her face for protection and held still, waiting – praying – for the bus to stop moving. She could feel a liquid on her hands and knew that the water must be coming in, but it wasn't cold, it was warm – and slippery. She tried to raise her head, to try to get up, but excruciating pain shot through her neck and forehead and the bus started spinning beneath her, around and around like they were in a whirlpool. Natty put her face back on her arms to wait for the bus to stop spinning and watched the stars twinkling in the black sky beneath her as she spun down into the darkness.

The bus careened down the stream bed, crashing noisily on the boulders that ripped at the sheet metal and cracked the windows on the left side as it bounced and slid and floated through the rushing water until it finally came to rest on its side in the middle of the stream, thirty feet below Cold Springs Road. The headlights of the bus remained on, the left one still visible a foot beneath the surface of the rushing water. Steam gushed out from under the hood like the last hot breaths of a dying dragon.

The icy water shocked Natty awake and then covered her mouth and nose causing her to choke and pull her head up abruptly. Immediately she felt the searing pain in her head and then another sharp pain in her rib cage that was wedged tightly against the front edge of a seat. She heard voices and someone was groaning, and then she remembered what had happened and where she was. "*Oh my God! Oh Jesus!*" she moaned, twisting her body and pushing as hard as she could with her arms against the frame of the window under her. She reached up to find the handlebar on the top of the seat and finally pulled herself erect, standing on the side of the bus just above the window. The interior of the bus was pitch black but she could hear voices and movement from the rear where most of the kids had been sitting.

She heard Matt Hatfield's voice. "Gilbert, you fat fuck! You're standin' on top of me."

"I lost my glasses," said Gilbert Steele.

"Hey, that was pretty cool," said George Jarrell.

"Man, it stinks in here," Natty heard someone say, making her chuckle and relieving her anxiety a little. She started to move and immediately felt a stabbing pain in her side as well as the blood dripping down into her left eye. Cold water was swirling over her ankles.

"Okay, everyone listen to me," Natty called out in the darkness. "When I call your name, say 'here' and let me know if you're hurt. We'll start with the defense . . .Brenda? Jason, Jimmy Hopson?" They were all okay. "Georgie?" *Okay.* "Midfielders . . . Paul, Matt, Sammy?" *Okay, okay.*

"Think my arm's broken coach," Matt Hatfield groaned painfully, "but I'm okay."

"Hardy Steele? Pie?"

"Okay," said Hardy. *Silence.*

"*Pie Man!*" Natty said louder. "Pie, where are you?" she said instinctively trying to move toward the rear of the bus. Then she heard his voice.

"I'm okay mama," said Pie in a muffled voice from somewhere down low. "But I can't find my New Yowk Yankeeth hat!" he called out angrily.

A loud clank came from the rear of the bus and a wave of cold air swept in along with the noise of the water rushing down the streambed behind them. "Hey, I got the back door open," said Sammy Willard. "C'mon, let's get out of here."

"Sammy, be careful of the . . ." Natty was distracted by a loud groan from the front of the bus. "*Oh Jesus,* Neva? Neva are you hurt? I'm coming." Natty moved forward, edging along the side wall just under the roof line. She heard Gabe's voice from up front.

"I'm up here Miz Oakes. Think Miz Gunnells could be having a heart attack or somethin'."

Natty came upon somebody moving in one of the seats. "That you Emma? You okay?"

Emma's voice was soft, as always. "I'm okay Natty," she seemed to grunt. "Just twisted around a little. I'll be okay. Go help Miz Gunnells."

Natty had to clamber through some duffle bags and climb over one of the seats to reach the driver's compartment. She leaned in close to Geneva and felt her breath and heard her moan lowly with pain. Natty stood back to figure out how to get the old woman out of the bus and noticed a tiny speck of silver from behind the seat. It was Geneva's long flashlight. She pulled it from the pocket and turned it on. The intensity of the light blinded her for a second. She shined it toward the rear of the bus just in time to see the last bald head disappear through the emergency door. She couldn't tell who it was but guessed that it must have been Emma. Sammy Willard was standing outside helping the others get out.

Natty turned the light around and saw that Gabe had pulled the old woman up out of her driver's seat and was holding her from the rear with his arms under her shoulders. She was conscious but dazed. Natty looked closely into her face which was contorted with pain.

"Think maybe my hip's broken," Geneva whispered, sucking in a quick painful breath of air.

Natty shined the light through the front windshield and saw that the torrent of water seemed to be increasing in volume. The floor of the sideways bus was now almost a foot under water. "Well we can't keep her here 'til help comes," Natty said to Gabe next to her. "Bus might get washed further down the stream."

She shined the light toward the rear and shook her head. "Never be able to carry her through all that." Natty turned and pulled the lever for the folding door and was almost surprised when it opened directly over their heads. She looked up, perplexed as to how they were going to get the old woman – even though she only weighed about ninety pounds – up and through the door. But Gabe had it figured out. He instructed Natty to get up into the stairway of the bus where she now stood with her shoulders outside the top of the bus. She briefly shined the powerful light up onto the steep embankment where she saw her team picking their way up the slope, single file, and pulling themselves up over the guardrail onto the pavement. She let out a long breath of relief, knowing how lucky they had been. *Now if we can just get Geneva out!*

Natty laid the flashlight on the top of the bus next to her and reached down to grab Geneva under the armpits as Gabe held the injured woman up to her. Natty had no idea what was coming next until Gabe balanced himself on the edge of the driver's seat and then sprang up through the door, suspending himself in the opening like a gymnast on the parallel bars. He rocked forward slightly, pulling his legs up through the door and shooting them out behind him. In an instant he was standing over Natty, bending down through the door to take hold of Geneva and pull her up out of the bus. Natty scrambled up onto the top side of the bus, tucked the flashlight into her waistband and she and Gabe lowered Geneva down, first to the side of the engine compartment and then into Gabe's arms standing in the stream. Then Natty jumped down. The cold water was up to her waist and moving swiftly. She held on to Gabe's arm to help him fight the current as he carried Geneva to shore.

Sammy and Paul came bounding down the slope when they saw Natty's flashlight coming up out of the bus, and together, the three boys carried Geneva Gunnells up to the road with Natty illuminating the way. It was a long, precarious hike up the muddy, rock-strewn slope and when they finally reached the top, Natty suddenly felt a rush of relief and exhaustion, and could now feel all the dull pains in her side and head and neck that she had been able to ignore during the emergency. She sat down on the ground next to Geneva and gingerly felt the wound over her left eye and could tell that it was still bleeding. She touched the spot where it stung and knew that it was cut in the same place, right on the old scar. Gabe had taken off his wet sweatshirt and was tucking it under Geneva Gunnells' head.

Sammy's voice interrupted her thoughts. "Hey Miz Oakes, how 'bout I run up to the power plant and get some help? Only 'bout a mile from here. They always got a security guard. Get up there in a couple minutes."

Natty looked up and down the dark road. "Yeah, okay Sammy. We could be here all night waiting for someone to come along this road, and we need to get Neva to the hospital." She handed him the flashlight. "Here, take this so you can see where you're going, and Gabe, why don't you go with him, just in case."

"Sure Miz Oakes," said Gabe, glad to have a mission.

"And be careful going over the culvert. Road's all broken up there," she called after them as the two boys jogged off. A trace of moonlight had broken through the roiling clouds providing enough light to discern shapes in the dark.

Natty took off her blue warm-up jacket and wedged it underneath Geneva's back to try to make her more comfortable. "Help will be here in a little while Neva,' Natty said squeezing the old woman's bony hand. You did a great job Neva. Nothing you could do about the road givin' out." Geneva just scowled, angry at herself.

Natty stood up and turned around to look down at their mortally wounded bus, laying dark in the cold stream, and felt sad. The old bus had taken them to a lot of soccer games over the years. The water had risen a little more and was churning violently against the front grill, splashing up onto the windshield. The headlights had finally gone out.

Natty crossed her arms and walked a little ways up the road for warmth. All she had on now was a long-sleeved white undershirt that was wet like everything else. She looked up toward the corner where the road had crumbled over the culvert and thought about Sammy and Gabe. She knew they'd be all right. They were tough, athletic kids. They'd probably be at the power plant now, the way they could run. *The way they could run.* Natty grimaced and squeezed her eyes shut. *The way* they *could run!* She felt her heart skip and was instantly paralyzed by a shock wave of fear that wracked her entire body. *Oh God, no! This isn't right.* She struggled for a breath of air and bolted forward toward the shadowy figures of her team sitting and standing, cold and tired along the cracked shoulder of the road a few yards away. She didn't have to count them. She knew before she reached them, but still she held out hope. *"Oh dear God, how could I do this?"* she whimpered, looking frantically into the face of each of the children – with their bald heads, nearly indistinguishable in the dark. *"How could I let this happen again?"* She cried, wiping the blood from her eye with her left sleeve. *"Oh my God!"* she gasped leaping to the top of the guardrail looking down at the dark bus. Then she screamed, as loud as she could, in anguish and despair . . . *"Em-ma!"* . . . and jumped out as far as she could, sliding and bouncing and tumbling down the embankment, tearing her clothing and her skin on rocks and roots. Half way down, on the steepest section, she went head-over-heels and landed on her face and chest, sliding over rocks and dead branches. She crawled over fallen trees and stumbled and clambered her way over the large boulders at the edge of the stream. *"Emma, I'm coming!"* she yelled jumping into the icy water. But the current was much swifter now and she immediately was thrown sideways against some boulders she couldn't see in the dark, smashing her left knee. She couldn't move her leg for a few seconds and floated with the current toward the back of the bus, which was just as well because she knew she'd never be able to get back on top of the bus to go through the folding door.

Natty banged on the top of the bus as she floated toward the rear, to let Emma know she was there. At the end of the bus, more rocks in the water scraped at her knees and ankles and slowed her movement, allowing Natty to grab hold of the emergency door that was folded out to the surface of the water. She ignored the pain in her left knee and pulled herself up onto the door and scrambled into the bus. *"Emma? Emma,* where are you?" she yelled over the noise of the water. She heard a small voice from up front.

"Here, *please.* I'm stuck. I'm up here," Emma managed weakly.

Natty pulled her way frantically through the refuse that had built up in the rear of the bus and made her way forward along the windows, holding on to the top edges of the right-side seats that were now eye-level with her. "Hold on Em, I'm coming," she said trying to sound confident. The water in the bus was up to her knees now.

A few seats before where she knew Emma was, Natty's left foot went through a window. She could feel the glass slashing through her warm-up pants and cutting into her leg and thought she might black out from the pain. She fell to her right knee to support her weight without moving her left leg, which the glass was tearing at. The boulders must have punched a hole and made cracks in the glass, and now Natty's left knee was stuck, surrounded by razor edges of the shards of glass. "*Fuck. Shit. Goddamn it!*" Natty had her head down taking in deep breaths to manage the incredible pain that worsened with every twitch.

"Natty?" she heard Emma say softly. Then she heard the girl coughing and spitting out water.

Oh Jesus! Natty pushed up with her arms and got her right foot under her. She stuffed the bottom of her shirt into her mouth, closed her eyes, and pulled her left leg violently up through the broken glass, clenching down on the wet shirt with her teeth as hard as she could, and she was free.

She took one tenuous step with her left leg and knew right away it was useless, so she hopped forward on her right foot, pulling herself along by the seat handles overhead. Then she saw Emma's hand holding on to the top edge of the seat in front of her, pulling her twisted body up to keep her head out of the water. "Okay Em, okay, I'm here," said Natty squeezing down into the seat to support Emma's back. She thought about how long Emma had been down here, holding on for her life. Her arms and her stomach and neck muscles must be exhausted. Natty pushed forward, wrapping her right arm around the girl and put her left hand at the back of Emma's head, holding it above the water so Emma could finally rest. Emma started sobbing softly. Natty squeezed her tightly and kissed the top of her bald head.

"My leg's stuck," said Emma between sobs, "and it hurts a lot. I thought I could get it out."

They sat huddled together in silence for a full minute while Emma just breathed deeply and relaxed her muscles. Then a strange, familiar noise broke the silence. It was a beeping noise, directly over Natty's head. She and Emma both looked up. The sound was coming from Natty athletic bag, stuck on the top edge of the seat, in the middle aisle of the bus. Stretching her arm out as far as she could, Natty was just able to reach an edge of the canvas bag and pull it down to them in the water. She recognized the beeping noise now as she struggled to unzip the long bag. Charlie's phone was glowing with a soft green light inside the dark bag. Natty pulled it out. "You expecting a call?" she said softly. Emma giggled. Natty pressed the green button.

"Charlie?"

"Hey, how's the championship coach?"

"Charlie, listen to me. The bus crashed, on Cold Springs Road and went down into the stream . . . "

"*What? How did . . .*"

"*Charlie!*" Natty yelled. "*We need help!* I'm on the bus with Emma. Her foot's stuck and the bus is filling up with water. *Get help Charlie, right away!* We're right near the turn-off to the power plant."

"Okay, the pilot's calling the plant now and we'll call the State Police. I'm on the helicopter. We're almost to Red Bone."

"Charlie, I gotta go. Hurry." Natty hit the red button and put the phone back into the bag and tossed it up over the seat. She could feel the cold water swirling around them and knew that it was rising and she needed to get busy.

"Okay, hold on again for a minute Em. I'm going to go down and see if I can get your leg free." Emma reached up and grasped the seat handle once again. Natty squeezed out from behind her and she immediately knew that her knee was seriously injured. It felt like her lower leg was just wobbling around and she could tell it was bleeding badly. With her hands she managed to pull her left leg behind her, and crawled along the sidewall to the seat in front of Emma. She took a deep breath and went down into the water running her hands along Emma's leg up to where the sidewall was pushed in. Natty couldn't see anything in the dark water but she could tell with her fingers that it was hopeless. There was no give at all in the hard steel of the bus wall or in the seat stanchions and it felt like Emma's entire lower leg was crushed in the small space. Natty came up for a gasp of air and then moved forward to where she could go down and reach Emma's foot to see if there was any way she could just force it free. When she applied just a small amount of pressure, she could feel Emma writhe with the pain. There was no room to force her leg out.

Natty came up and crawled on her hands and right knee back to Emma and squeezed in behind her again. Emma released her grip and fell back exhausted against Natty. The water was now up to Emma's neck. Natty held her tightly and put her face against Emma's head. "Alright Em, your leg's locked in there pretty good but help should be coming real soon. Sammy and Gabe ran up to the power plant so help should be on the way. We just gotta sit tight and wait, okay?" Emma nodded her head in silence. Natty could feel the girl's entire body shivering. She pressed her cheek against Emma's head and exhaled warm breaths onto her skin. "We'll be okay Em. Help is on the way," Natty whispered.

Jesus Christ, where the fuck are they? They should be here by now. Then Natty remembered the impassable road at the corner and realized that they probably had to come the long way around, out through the crossroads.

Natty closed her eyes for a few moments, holding tightly to Emma. It was the only thing to do, Natty told herself. Just be calm. Then she suddenly felt the water on her chin just as Emma coughed and struggled to pull herself up a little higher. The water was rising faster now.

Natty pushed forward and raised Emma's mouth another inch above the water, but she could see that it would be only a matter of minutes, the way the stream was rising, before Emma would be under. *"Emma, pull yourself up, hard. Hold on! I gotta find something for you to breath through!"* Emma reached for the bar again, now just barely able to keep her mouth out of the water.

Natty pulled out from behind her as quickly as she could, trying not to scream from the excruciating pain in her knee. She stood up on her right leg and tried to remember in the darkness where she might find something for Emma to breath through. She saw her athletic bag and pulled it down and struggled with the zipper. She went through everything inside it with her hands, finding nothing. She stuffed the bag down in back of Emma to help support her. Natty hopped frantically toward the back of the bus. She found a duffle bag and a backpack and rifled through them with her hands and found nothing. *Jesus, give me a ballpoint pen or a straw or something! A McDonald's straw! Shit, they were all over the place.* Natty plunged down under the water and swept her hands along the sidewall and the windows searching for one of the large soda containers that so many of the kids had. All she felt was the mess of clothing and shoes and shin guards and duffle bags. She came up for air gasping and pushed herself through the water back toward Emma.

Emma's right arm was still locked on the seat railing but her left hand was waving and splashing frantically and her face was under water. Natty lunged toward her and put her left hand under Emma's head, took in as deep a breath as she could hold and squeezed Emma's nose shut with her right hand. She plunged her face into the water and covered Emma's mouth with her lips and exhaled while the girl desperately sucked in Natty's air. Natty came up for another lung-full of air and then again pressed her open lips tightly against Emma's. She repeated it three more times as quickly as she could.

Natty came up and had to stop and take some deep breaths herself and cough out some water she'd taken in. She breathed in as deeply as she could but couldn't seem to catch her breath. She felt Emma's hand pulling at her. Just as she took in a final deep breath, a powerful beam of light came into the bus through the windows over Natty's head, and then she heard the roar of a helicopter hovering somewhere above. The beam of light illuminated Emma's face under the water . . . she looked as white as a ghost. Natty gave her all of her air and came up gasping herself. She struggled for her breath, coughing again, and then, out of the corner of her eye she saw it, to her left, shining in the light of the helicopter's spotlight, the little silver soccer player with the ball on his foot. The rest of the tournament trophy was underwater, but Natty knew right away it was the answer to her prayers. She gave Emma one last lung-full and then dove for the trophy.

Natty pushed herself erect on her right leg and pulled the trophy from the water holding on to one of the long plastic tubes that connected the base of the trophy with the platform holding the soccer player. She smashed the top platform of the trophy as hard as she could against the steel edge of a seat, sending the little soccer player flying off into the water. One of the plastic tubes she was after cracked open and revealed a metal rod running between the platforms. She felt the underside of the base with her fingers and felt the tightly bolted nut and washer. *Oh my God! Don't do this to me!* She tried to turn the small nut with her wet fingers but it wouldn't move. Frantic, she smashed the trophy again against the seat rail and felt a little give in the plastic supports. Then she heard Emma's hand splashing the water.

Emma's face was now several inches underwater. Natty dropped the trophy and lunged back to Emma. She gave her air three times and had to stop to try to catch her own breath, inhaling as deeply as she could but it didn't seem to be doing anything and she knew Emma wasn't getting enough air from her. Natty could now tell from the rapidity of the rising bubbles from Emma's mouth when she was about out of air. She gave her another lung-full and then reached down for the trophy. The light from the helicopter had moved toward the back of the bus forcing Natty to again work in darkness.

Grasping opposing tubes of the trophy and wrenching them back and forth, Natty discovered, would loosen the bolts, but still not enough to be able to turn one of the nuts. Natty pulled and twisted the trophy as violently as she could and then felt Emma's hand grabbing her leg. But Natty was out of breath from her exertion. She went back down to Emma but had nearly no air in her lungs and had to pull away abruptly when Emma sucked everything out of her, causing the girl to cough violently under the water. Natty desperately tried to fill her lungs and transfer the air to Emma who continued to cough and gasp and frantically suck from Natty's mouth but she wasn't getting any air. Natty went up and down again into the bubbling water again and again as fast as she could trying get a breath into Emma to stop her coughing but she knew Emma wasn't getting enough air and it would only be a matter of seconds before her lungs filled with water.

Natty exploded out of the water gasping for air and sobbing in despair. Over and over she smashed the trophy as hard as she could against the seat rail and finally she felt it crack and then shatter and then pieces were flying off and she had one of the foot-long plastic tubes in her hand. She lunged back to Emma and pushed the tube between her lips and squeezed her nose shut. Emma coughed up through the tube, again and again, gagging, unable to get her breath. Natty could hear the gurgling in the tube and could do nothing. She cradled Emma's head in her arm for support while squeezing the girl's mouth firmly around the tube. *"C'mon Em,"* she pleaded, tears filling her eyes, *"You can do it Em. Breathe Emma, breathe!"*

Finally the coughing became less severe and Natty thought she could feel Emma swallowing small gulps of the water in the tube, and then Natty felt Emma's lungs expand with air against her stomach and she could hear Emma's deep breathing through the end of the inch-wide tube. Suddenly, with a deafening roar, another light from above moved over them and illuminated the entire bus as if it was daylight. Natty looked up and could see another helicopter- bigger and louder than the first one – with two huge floodlights on its underside. Natty squeezed her friend under the water and smiled down at her. Emma was six inches under the water now, but the end of the tube was far above the surface, and help was just minutes away.

Natty pulled herself up a little ways and leaned toward the middle of the bus to where she could see out the windows above them, up to the roadway above the stream. The road, which was in complete darkness a few minutes earlier, was now awash in red lights and flashing blue lights, and more lights arriving, and a powerful spotlight panned along the bus, which Natty had to look away from when it shined on her. Then she saw flashlights bouncing down the embankment.

Natty tickled the back of Emma's head with her fingertips to try to convey her happiness, to let her know it was almost over. She moved back toward Emma, to slide down behind her again. But out of the corner of her eye, there was something moving, outside, making her turn to look out through the right half of the windshield that was still above the water. Natty stared at the mirage in front of her, a bad joke her oxygen- deprived mind was surely playing on her. She smiled and slowly looked down at Emma, and then back up through the windshield at the streambed lit up like daylight by the rescue lights, and blinked her eyes when it was still there – a hundred yards up the gulley . . . now fifty yards – higher than the top of the bus, stretching across the streambed half-way up the embankment, a wall of black angry water, rolling and rumbling toward them with a roar that was now drowning out the helicopters overhead. *Oh Jesus Emma! I'm sorry.* Natty sunk down behind the seat and wrapped her arms around her friend. She closed her eyes and put her face under the water with her cheek on Emma's forehead, squeezing her tightly while she braced for the hit.

The wave with its deadly cargo of stones and sand and tree limbs smashed through the windshield filling the bus with muddy, broiling water. The water picked up the bus and sent it screeching and banging and twisting its way over the rocks and then careening down a ten-foot waterfall to deeper, slower water where it rocked once then rolled onto its top and moved downstream another fifty yards until it hit the submerged trunk of a white oak and came to a stop with its four tires just breaking the surface of the water like the paws of a drowned possum. The current slowly turned the bus sideways against the stream. And then it was still. The rushing water flowed smoothly over the underside of the bus and then down the streambed.

The bus was in total darkness again. Natty opened her eyes but couldn't see anything and didn't know which way was up. She floated slowly through the water, desperate for air, her lungs ready to explode. Then there was light, from outside, dim at first, coming in the windows below and in front of her, and she could now see her bubbles rising to her left. She pushed off with her right leg and followed a bubble up, up toward the floor of the bus overhead. Natty reached out and grabbed the edge of something hard and pulled herself up and pressed her face, her nose and mouth against the hard rubber matting of the floor of the bus and tasted the grit and the dirt, but there was no air there. Holding on to the seat stanchions, she pulled herself along searching for air, swiftly at first and then more slowly. There was no air.

Natty floated down through the murky water that was now shimmering with light from the low windows and felt warm again as she flowed effortlessly through the clouds, and then she smiled and even had to giggle, letting out small bubbles, when she saw her, finally, after so many years, reaching down to her, backwards with her arms out straight, palms up, her small fingers curved and still. Her chin was up and her mouth open slightly, looking so relaxed and contented and happy as she should be, her dark eyes open wide and unmoving, watching Natty come close, lightly touching her hands and then kissing her softly on the forehead. Natty closed her eyes and rubbed her cheek softly against the smooth scalp and smiled. *Oh Annie, I've missed you so much.* And then Natty was falling away from her sister, quickly, down and down through the dark water, unable to stop herself.

Buck pulled Natty through the door, reached up for the hard edge of the overturned bus and with his right hand on Natty's stomach and thrust her lifeless body up to the waiting hands of the two paramedics on top of the bus. They used Buck as an operating table, down on all-fours in the foot of water flowing over the bus, pushing hard on Natty's back and stretching out her shoulders, and then pumping her chest while they forced the oxygen through a tube into her lungs, until finally, she coughed slightly, and coughed again and then gagged and coughed harder and harder and then vomited a stomach-full of brown water onto the back of Buck's neck.

Two volunteer firemen wearing diving masks and scuba tanks came out of the bus and fought their way slowly through the current to shore. They checked with the paramedics on top of the bus and one of the firemen dropped his tank and mask and flippers on the rocks and went up the road and brought back a blanket they wrapped around Natty as Buck carried her up from the stream.

Two hours later, after all the children had been taken away and the police cars and the TV truck had left and the helicopters had gone and only one ambulance and a fire truck remained, the two firemen returned to the bus with an acetylene torch and cut away the iron stanchions of the seat, and brought out Emma Lowe's body.

Chapter 35

Hank was sitting on the bench in front of the store waiting for him when Charlie came out. The old man was dressed in his brown suit and faded white shirt, the only suit Charlie had ever seen him wear. They presented quite a contrast with Charlie in a twelve hundred dollar *Joseph Aboud* charcoal suit, but Charlie didn't care and neither would Hank. They both had dressed as finely as they could, to express as much respect as clothes could show on a day when words would be difficult to come by.

They walked slowly up Main Street without talking. A cold autumn wind blew against them standing Charlie's hair up and making their eyes water. Hank's white locks were pulled back into a tight pony tail tied with a black ribbon that fluttered in the breeze. They walked past *The Spur* – the gin mill still dark at ten in the morning – and the vacant United Mineworkers of America storefront that was rumored to be reopening soon, and next to it, Earl Fitch's barbershop – closed for the day, a handwritten sign in the window said.

They went past Depot Street, its pavement cracked and crumbling, still laced with the brown weeds of summer, now waiting for the frost to finish them off. Charlie stopped and looked up the hill toward the rusting hulk of the old coal tipple sitting at the base of the looming face of Red Bone Mountain. He thought again about the thousands of faceless immigrants who had trudged up the hill for so many years to work in the mine, and also the poor, black men, like Woody and Mr. Jacks, who worked their whole lives in the mines and ended with nothing but broken bodies and tired minds. Hank stopped and looked back at him. "Whatcha thinkin' Burden?"

Charlie looked at his friend and squinted and then shrugged. "Thinking that Alice DeWitt was right . . . there *is* a lot of heartache in these mountains."

Hank thought about that for a second, then turned and resumed walking up Main Street. "Had our share," he said almost to himself.

Past Depot Street the *old homes* section of Main Street started – the once-grand three-story homes built in the thirties for the mining company managers, merchants and professionals of the day. Now they were run-down relics, most in need of paint and new roofs, some needing quite a bit more. The oaks and sugar maples in the front yards were bigger now than when the children of the mine managers played under them, their old roots pushing up through the weeds and dirt-covered yards too shady now for fine lawns.

At the next corner, across Main Street, Sammy Willard was sitting on the front steps of one of the better kept homes on the street. He was wearing a tie and a white shirt and a suit jacket several sizes too small for him. Hank stopped and looked over at him. "Want to walk up with us?" he called over to Sammy.

"Naw, gotta wait for grandma and Zack. She makin' some pants for Zack to fit over his cast," he said without moving. Hank just nodded without comment and turned to his right and started up Cornelia Street with Charlie at his side.

The street went steeply uphill as did all the side streets on the mountain side of Main Street, and Charlie and Hank walked slowly. Hank wanted to be there when the door opened, but they were still a little early. Up ahead, a station wagon was parked in front of an austere looking white block of a house, and a man was carrying two floral displays up the short walk. Only a small sign on the wall next to the door identified the building as a funeral home. Charlie was surprised there wasn't a long line of people waiting at the door, and no traffic on the street with only a few cars in the small lot next to the building. He thought about the traffic jam and the crowds of mourners that would be produced by the wake of a popular young athlete in Mamaroneck. But Red Bone was a small town in a sparsely populated county of Appalachia, so there was no waiting line for Emma Lowe.

Janice and Gus Lowe remained seated in the front row of folding chairs throughout the wake. Gus held his arm around his wife who remained hunched over, unmoving, in silent anguish. Ada Lowe stood to the right of the casket greeting the mourners. Hank stood with her for a while and then Eve Brewster took his place, joined by Mabel Willard when she arrived with the boys.

Zack stood on his crutches next to Sammy who kneeled in front of their teammate's coffin until Mabel nodded that they could move away. Neither boy cried; they just looked scared. The black wig and Emma's sunken cheeks made her look much older than the girl they knew.

Hank went and sat next to Janice Lowe, taking her hand and leaning close for soft words with her and Gus while Charlie took a seat by himself in a middle row. For two hours he sat and watched a steady stream of mourners file past the simple coffin. Most of the people he recognized – people from the restaurant, members of the Red Bone Baptist Church Social Club, a few teammates with a parent. Earl Fitch and Jimmy Haggerman paid their respects and then sat in Charlie's row for a while. Kyle Loftus with Deputy Sheriff Wayne Lester came through without making eye contact with Charlie. Gabe the soccer player from Welch, looking miserable, sat with a woman who must have been his grandmother. Some of the tradesmen from the power plant stopped in and then Charlie was surprised to see the loggers, Frenchy and Dogface, who stopped briefly to shake hands with Charlie on their way out.

Big Frank and Rose Oakes came in with Ransom and Sally, along with Yancy and Charlotte. A few minutes later, Bud and Alice DeWitt walked up the aisle, followed by Sarah DeWitt and Petey.

Sarah DeWitt noticed Charlie and surprised him by coming over and sitting next to him. She put her hand on his and spoke very softly. "Natty's been taken to the hospital in Charleston, for an operation on her leg. It's very serious – severed tendons and ligaments – and she has broken ribs, and bruises and . . ." Her eyes filled with moisture as she stopped to take in a breath of air. Charlie squeezed her hand. Sarah looked down at her lap. "She hasn't hardly said anything since the accident. She can't remember it . . . the accident . . . and she hasn't cried." Sarah flashed a brief smile and then seemed to drift off for several seconds before catching her place. "Doctor says it's a . . . *fugue* state, or something . . . temporary thing most likely, so . . ." She shrugged and patted Charlie's hand as she stood up.

Charlie attempted to smile. "Thank you," he said, even though he'd already gotten a more extensive report by phone from the hospital in Charleston.

The funeral was in the afternoon – Janice Lowe insisted on getting it all done in one day and the cemetery was just up in back of the funeral parlor – followed by a reception at *Eve's Restaurant*. Only about twenty people went back to the restaurant where there was enough food set out for twice that many. At one end of the counter, Eve had set up a bar, which was where most of the party had congregated. Charlie had a *Canadian Club* and tried his best to have a conversation with Janice and Gus Lowe who sat by themselves in a booth, but like the rest of the day, there was just too much pain in everyone's eyes for the usual well meaning small talk.

Charlie saw the glow of Eve's cigarette on the porch and went outside. They stood in silence against the porch railing looking out at the dimly lit street, ignoring the cold wind that blew up Main Street. Charlie broke the silence. "I'd like to pay for this Eve," he gestured back toward the restaurant, "for the reception. The Lowes don't need, you know . . ."

Eve flicked a half-smoked Merit 100 into the street and turned to Charlie. She put her palms on his chest and smoothed out his jacket. "Charlie," she said softly, "put your checkbook away. You can't buy away your grief anymore. You're one of us now." She looked up into his eyes and attempted a smile. Charlie pulled her close and wrapped his arms around her, burying her face in his jacket, and they both sobbed softly and held each other and cried their final tears for Emma.

Charlie waited three days and then drove to Charleston. The hospital was an ancient brownstone building in an old section of downtown with narrow streets and nowhere to park. After circling through the only public lot for twenty minutes, he finally found a parking spot, and then the main lobby. Natty had been transferred to a far wing. After walking what seemed like miles of twisting, ramped, crowded corridors, Charlie finally found the psychiatric ward.

Natty's doctor was a gray-haired woman in her sixties who studied Natty's file carefully through steel-rimmed glasses before looking up again at Charlie. She smiled pleasantly as she sat back and let the spectacles fall to her chest. "Natty can't remember anything from the last, oh, month or so, as best we can pin it down. *Traumatic amnesia.* She couldn't deal with what happened, so the brain blocks it all out and takes a little extra just for good measure. Actually a pretty common occurrence, in varying degrees, in traumatic situations. She doesn't remember anything about the accident. She also doesn't seem to remember anything about her soccer team." The woman stood up and closed the file. "A temporary condition, in most cases," she said coming around the desk. "When she gets home, in familiar surroundings, she'll remember more and more. Come on, I'll take you to her. Try not to bring up recent events. We need to let her heal at her own pace."

The doctor walked Charlie down the hall toward Natty's room. "The hardest part will be the accident, and the events of that day. May take a long time for her to deal with that. The brain will try to block that out as long as it can. Rest of it will come back gradually." They stopped outside a room. The doctor looked up at Charlie and spoke in a low voice. "Tell me, do you know the husband, Buck?"

Charlie shrugged. "Yes, I've met him. Know him a little. Why?"

"Oh, I was just wondering why he hasn't been in to see her."

Charlie raised his eyebrows. "He hasn't visited her yet?"

She shook her head slowly. "Not since the first day. He came up with her, first day, for the operation on her knee. But not since then. Seems strange.'

"Well, he's got some of his own issues," said Charlie.

"He could help her a lot." The doctor shrugged and nodded toward the room. "On the right next to the window."

The room was cool and silent and dark, illuminated only by the late afternoon light from the gray sky coming through two large windows. Three beds were vacant and a plastic curtain was pulled to the end of the fourth.

Charlie stood at the end of the bed unnoticed. Natty was sitting up with her head against the pillow staring out the window. Her left leg was in a full cast from mid-thigh, elevated from the bed by wires and a brace suspended from a frame over the bed. A bandage covered her left eyebrow. Charlie watched her stare out the window, entranced, rarely even blinking, lost in thought . . . *about what,* Charlie wondered. He cleared his throat and she slowly turned toward him. She looked surprised.

"*Hey,* Mr. Burden," she said weakly, instinctively feeling for the top of her robe. She smiled at him. "This's a surprise. You shouldn't a come all the way up here just to visit me." Her words came more slowly than normal.

Charlie smiled and moved around to a straight back metal chair sitting between the bed and the window. From here, with the full light from the window on her, Charlie could see numerous bruises and abrasions on her face and hands. Her left cheek was swollen and the skin under her eye was purple. Natty looked like she'd been in a fight for her life. "How are you feeling?" Charlie asked, sitting down in the chair.

Natty smiled without answering for a second, as if it took a little more time to process the words now. "Well, I won't be goin' runnin' for a while," she said knocking the cast with her knuckle, "if ever. Depends on how the operation comes out, doctor says. Knee was pretty messed up." She squirmed uncomfortably. "Worst is the broken ribs though, every time I move, you know." She grimaced with pain, took a deep breath and seemed to relax. Then she smiled and pointed toward several flower arrangements on a table next to the curtain. "Thanks for the flowers. Yours is the biggest one."

Charlie glanced at the flowers without seeing them. "You're welcome."

After a few moments, Natty turned back toward Charlie. "So how's your power plant coming along?"

"Good, very good. Ahead of schedule and under budget." Charlie said, the standard answer.

"Well that's great. That's great," she said softly. "So now you'll be going to China pretty soon, like you wanted all along, right?"

"China?"

"Yeah, like you told me when we walked down the hill to the library. Said you'd be going to China soon."

Charlie watched Natty's eyes carefully. "Yeah, that's right. I'll be leaving for China in another month or so."

She smiled briefly and glanced back out the window for a few seconds, as if she was resting, and then a troubled look came over her face as she turned back to Charlie. "Think you'll be able to do anything about Angel Mountain before you leave? Mama was in, and she didn't say nothin' but I could tell she's worried about Angel Mountain and Grandpa losin' the farm."

Charlie studied her face, still so incapable of concealment or duplicity, and even under the cuts and bruises and thick bandage, the most beautiful face he'd ever seen.

"Mr. Burden?"

He smiled at her. "Oh, no, you don't have to worry about the farm. It's all taken care of. Your grandpa won't be losing his farm."

Natty looked surprised, and elated. "Wow, that's real good news. That's great! Thank you Mr. Burden."

"Thought we'd gotten over that *Mr. Burden* stuff."

Natty smiled and looked out the window again. After a few moments in thought she turned back to Charlie. "Sorry I threw up on your sneaker that day, up on the boulder," she said softly.

"You remember that?"

"Yeah, course I do." She grinned and averted her eyes embarrassedly. "That was a real nice morning, 'cept for pukin' on you."

"Yeah, it was," said Charlie.

"Probably said some stuff we shouldn't of, huh Charlie?"

"Yeah, maybe," he said softly, trying to make it easier for her.

"And then the night we went over and saw Woody and Mr. Jacks," Natty said, "that was a good time too." She was nodding her head, and added softly, almost to herself, "always remember that night."

"That *was* a nice night," Charlie agreed.

Natty chuckled. "Yeah, *geeze*, I can't wait to see Woody and Mr. Jacks again. I miss those old boys. Sometimes I'm pretty sure they're the two best friends I got in the world." She raised her eyebrows to Charlie. "They okay Charlie? You seen 'em around in the restaurant?"

Charlie swallowed hard and his heart thumped in his chest. "Uhm, well, I haven't seen them in a while Natty, so . . ." He looked up and saw that Natty had her hand up to her face trying to hide a grin.

"What?" said Charlie.

Natty shrugged and her eyes went down to her lap. "Aw, it's nothin'. Just sounds funny to me when I hear you say my name, is all. For a while there, I wasn't too sure you even *knew* my name."

"I *always* knew your name, Natty."

Natty seemed to study his face for a few seconds, then looked out the window again. Charlie just waited for her. Finally she turned back and her eyes found his. "Charlie, you know I'm having trouble remembering stuff, you know, mind's kind a fuzzy, from an accident they said." Charlie just nodded to her. "And well, Eve and Mabel come up the other day, and I was wondering what happened to my hair, you know." She reached up and twisted a short lock of platinum hair in her fingers. "So Mabel told me all about the trip to New York, and staying in the hotel, and getting' my hair done at your friend's place and going to the show and everything." Natty rolled her eyeballs. "God, what was I thinkin' about, goin' off to *New York City* for a weekend, leavin' the kids and Buck."

"It was a real nice weekend," said Charlie smiling. "We went for a run in the morning through Times Square and across Manhattan, up to 57th Street and down Fifth Avenue. We took a walk through Rockefeller Center. About the nicest run I ever had," he said softly.

"And you and I went out for dinner, Mabel said, and then ran into her and Ada and Janice Lowe and made them have dinner with us." Natty chuckled at the thought.

Charlie grinned at the memory. "Yeah, it was okay though. It was nice. *Real* nice. The ladies enjoyed it. We all had a great time."

Natty's smile disappeared and she was quiet for a few seconds, squinting her eyes in concentration as she composed her thoughts.

"What is it Natty?"

"Well Charlie, since I can't remember nothin', I need you to tell me." She looked out the window while her face scrunched up nervously. Then she shrugged with resignation and looked directly into Charlie's eyes. "I need to know if, you know, if anything happened between us in New York. If we . . ."

"Nothing happened Nat. Nothing at all. We just had a nice dinner with the ladies, then I walked you back to your hotel and we said goodnight on the sidewalk. And that was it. Nothing happened between us." Charlie's heart beat faster as he recalled their meeting later, in the rain on the sidewalk on Park Avenue, when he ached for her so desperately and wanted her to come inside and stay with him forever, and then watched her leave in the taxi. It wouldn't do her any good to hear that part of the story. "It was a nice weekend, but nothing happened between us Nat."

Natty nodded her acceptance and looked down at her hands in her lap. "Well that sucks, huh Charlie?" she said, looking up at him with a sparkle in her eye. They both laughed. "No, that's good Charlie," she said softly. "That's . . . good."

"Yeah," he agreed.

They talked about Pie for a while and his work on the computer and how well he was doing in school. Natty didn't say anything about soccer or *The Bones* and Charlie didn't either. They talked about Hank a little. "That's real good, you movin' in up there next to Mr. Hankinson." She nodded in affirmation. "Hank ain't been the same since Alva Paine died, so, that's good," she said softly.

There was a long silence, then their eyes met and there was nothing left to talk about. Charlie looked at his watch and smiled tightly. "Well, I need to get back down to Red Bone." He stood up next to the bed. Natty held her hand out to him.

"Thanks for everything. For helping Pie, and for Angel Mountain, and, well for everything you done for us."

Charlie held her hand and squeezed it gently and ran his thumb over the back of it before letting go. "Take care of yourself Mrs. Oakes." He didn't know what else to say. "Take care of your family."

Natty smiled up at him. "I will," she said. "We'll be okay. Goodbye Mr. Burden."

After an hour on the road back to Red Bone, the radio off, alone with his thoughts, Charlie took out his cell phone and speed-dialed Lucien Mackey's office. It was only six o'clock, still much too early for Lucien to have called it a day.

"Hello Charlie," Lucien answered softly as if he could read Charlie's mind from a thousand miles away. "How is everything down there?"

"Been a hard week, Lucien." Charlie sighed audibly. "Hard thing to deal with."

"I can imagine," said Mackey, closing his eyes and shaking his head, "*goddamn* tragedy."

Neither man spoke for several seconds. "Lucien, I've decided . . . I've decided to take the China job. I need to . . . I think I should do that."

"You're *sure* Charlie?"

"Yeah, I'm sure Lucien. It's time to go."

"Okay Charlie. That's good. I think that's best for everyone. I'm glad you made that decision."

"Need to do it quickly Lucien."

"I understand Charlie. I've got someone in mind for the Red Bone project. I'll send him down next week and you can get him started. Then I'll make the China arrangements."

"Yeah, thanks Lucien. Like to be out of here in a few weeks."

"I can understand that Charlie. I'll take care of it. I'll take care of everything."

"We'll be in Aspen for Christmas, with Ellen and the kids."

"That'll be good for you Charlie. Just what you need."

"Then, mid-January, I'll be ready to go to China."

"Sounds perfect Charlie. I'll take care of everything"

"Thanks Lucien. See you soon my friend."

* * *

The yellow school bus looked tiny sitting next to the giant road grader in the heavy equipment lot. Charlie had agreed to store it there temporarily after the state police and the insurance investigators had completed their work on it three days after the accident. Yellow police evidence tape made an X over the folding door and across the gaping hole where the rear door had once been.

Charlie pulled the tape off, pushed in the folding door and stepped up into the bus. It was cold and damp and dirty inside. The windshield was gone and most of the windows were smashed or missing completely. The key was still in the ignition in the *on* position.

Charlie started slowly toward the back of the bus, taking in everything, trying to imagine what took place there, when the bus was upside down, underwater in the raging stream. He wasn't looking for anything, but just needed to see the inside of the bus before the salvage company came to tow it away the next day.

All of the kids' athletic bags and anything else of any discernable value had been removed but the interior of the bus still looked like the inside of a dumpster. A thin layer of dirt coated the ceiling, walls and seats, and two inches of mud, sand and stones covered the floor of the bus, mixed in with a good amount of trash, dirty towels, and some unidentifiable pieces of clothing. One of the seats was tossed on top of another seat to Charlie's left, the jagged, scorched edges of the ends of its legs sticking up in the air. Across the aisle, an open space, where the stumps of the legs still glowed silver where the acetylene torches had burned away the gray paint.

Charlie stepped on something under the mud and reached down to dig it out. It was a round, wooden disc about two inches thick weighing several pounds. It still had a few bolts and some broken shards of plastic columns hanging off it. Charlie rubbed the dirt from the outside edge and saw the engraved brass plate – *12th Annual Charleston Youth Soccer League Thanksgiving Tournament, First Place, The Bones, Red Bone, West Virginia.* He unscrewed the remaining bolts and rubbed off more of the dirt. Charlie ran his thumb over the inscription again and wondered if it wouldn't be better for everyone if he just left the remains of the trophy on the bus to get towed away in the morning. He shook his head. *No, it was an accomplishment for all the kids, and some day the heartache would be over and they'd want a memorial to their friend.* Charlie clutched the heavy disc against his side and continued toward the back of the bus.

Under one of the rear seats, amid a pile of dirt, McDonald's bags, soda cups, and rags, something caught Charlie's eye, a speck of something familiar. He bent down and peered under the seat into the trash until he spied it, covered with mud, just a small but unmistakable swatch of a once silver, embroidered logo, now gray with dirt. Charlie dug his fingers into the hardened mud and pulled out the hat. The brim was creased and folded up at a strange angle and the hat was brown with embedded mud, but it was definitely Pie's *"New Yowk Yankeeth"* hat. Charlie smiled when he thought about how thrilled his little pal was going to be to get it back, and then let out a deep sigh as he thought about how soon he would be leaving West Virginia for good. He quickly left the bus without bothering to close the folding door on his way back to the office. There was a lot of work to do to get the power plant ready for the next *big mule.*

At four o'clock Charlie called it quits and drove back up to the apartment. He'd missed his run for several days and now he needed a good, long hard workout – for his body, but more for his mind, to help him forget for a while – and he wanted to run the mountain trail while there was still enough light to see by. He went out to the porch as he pulled on a gray sweatshirt. The sun was disappearing fast in the steel gray sky to the west but he calculated that he'd have just enough daylight to make it to the end of the mountain trail, which was good enough. He could run the logging road and then South County Road back up to Old Red Bone in the dark without a problem.

Charlie pounded down the trail at a very fast pace, to beat the failing light, but also to fight the cold wind that buffeted the side of the mountain. The trail was still exhilarating and the view spectacular, but with the leaves and vegetation off the trees and bushes, it was now more exposed to the wind. In spite of the cold, he was working up a good sweat under his warm-ups.

At the halfway point along the mountain, Charlie looked up to where Natty's boulder sat at the edge of the high stand of tall evergreens and had a momentary urge to leave the trail and climb up to it. But it was getting dark, and *what was the point to it now?* He wondered if Natty would ever make it up to her *special place* again. Charlie took in a deep breath and ran even harder, and forced himself to think about something else. He was glad now that he only had a short time left in Red Bone. *The sooner he left West Virginia, the sooner he could start forgetting her.*

Charlie was winded and wind-blown by the time he reached the protection of the dense pine forest near the top of Oakes' Hollow. He slowed to a jog and then to a walk over the soft covering of pine needles. The only sound in the woods was his rapid, deep breathing. He came to a stop at the spot where he and Natty had their talk after they came down from the boulder. He gazed down at the old stumps where they had sat, and stood still, enjoying for a moment the warmth and stillness of the woods as he caught his breath. It was dark now – only a faint shadow of light made it through the trees – but he was close enough to the logging road. He'd stay for another minute – maybe his last time in these woods. He closed his eyes and breathed deeply and pictured Natty sitting on the stump with her bony shoulders and thin arms, the mop of hair hanging down over much of her face, and heard her voice and saw her beautiful white smile and the glint in her eyes, and he ached for her to be there.

Then Charlie's heart froze as he heard the metallic click, menacing and deadly, unmistakably not of the woods or of nature, but man-made and only a few yards away. Charlie swallowed hard and breathed in to calm his racing pulse, and then opened his eyes to the black and gray shadows of the trees in front of him, where the sound came from. He blinked his eyes to see, trying not to move, to show any awareness, but there was nothing. Then a movement, a white speck appeared and disappeared just a few yards away, giving him something to focus on and then slowly the darkness retreated and a shape emerged – the eye, a head, hand and forearm, then the dull metallic glint of the crossbow, and the silver tip of an arrow aimed at the middle of his face.

"Been waitin' for you Burden." Buck's voice was coarse and angry, just above a whisper. He moved slowly out of the trees, the deadly arrow tip still trained on Charlie's face. "Shame how much you look like a doe hoppin' through the woods in the dark in that sweat suit." He stopped moving and Charlie could see his darkened face pressed against the bow's stock. "This distance, put one right through your left eye, arrow'd go halfway out the back a your head."

Charlie backed away slowly. "Buck, there's no need for this. This is stupid Buck."

Buck moved after him. "Thought I told you to stay away from my family. Stay away from my wife."

"I haven't done anything with your wife Buck," Charlie said, still taking small steps backwards toward the trail. Buck stopped moving and Charlie thought he was getting ready to pull the trigger. "Buck," he breathed, "don't do this. This is a mistake you'll . . ."

"Yeah, this a mistake too?" Buck snarled, tossing something shiny into the pine needles at Charlie's feet.

Charlie looked down and recognized the yellow plastic lantern at the end of the small chain and ring of keys to the condo in Bluefield. Buck must have found them in Natty's car parked at the high school, along with her clothes.

"You know what them keys are, don't you Burden?"

Charlie stared at the keys without answering, thinking of what he could say to prevent the deadly arrow from ripping through his eye socket and into his brain.

Buck moved a step closer. "You was stealin' my wife Burden. Stealin' my family."

Charlie looked down at the key chain and thought about Pie, and Cat, and about Natty driving out to the condo in Bluefield, and about how close they'd come to a new life together. And now it was over – because of a tragic accident and the death of a young girl – and now Natty was left with *Buck*. The muscles on Charlie's neck and jaw tightened with anger, and he looked up. He took a step closer to the deadly arrow point. "Buck you don't *have* a family 'cause you've never been a *father*. And you don't *have* a wife 'cause you've never been a *husband*. All you've ever been is a drunken, fucking bully who beats his wife and ignores his kids, and Natty was sick of it. Nobody was *stealing* her," Charlie said angrily. "Natty was leaving you because she'd had enough." Charlie turned his head back up the trail toward the boulder but it was too dark to see. He lowered his voice. "Natty'd been in love with you since the fourth grade. Twelve years of marriage, she tried, but then she'd had enough. She was tired of the meanness and the infidelity, and seeing her kids grow up with no father, and she was tired of seeing her friends dying and having no one to help her, no one to put their arms around her and comfort her." Charlie shook his head. "She was tired of being alone Buck. Tired of not being loved."

Charlie reached down and picked up the key chain and dusted it off. "You're not going to shoot me Buck, 'cause you're a coward, you always have been. You've been afraid to be a husband, afraid to be a father. You've been afraid to finally admit to yourself that you're not a high school football star anymore and become a *man* and do the things that *men* do." Charlie turned his back to Buck and started walking back towards the trail. Ten yards away from Buck, Charlie heard the bow-gun clatter to the ground.

"Burden, help me." Buck sounded like he was crying. Charlie stopped. "I don't want to lose my wife Burden. I don't want to lose my kids."

Charlie turned around. It was pitch dark now and he couldn't see Buck but he knew where he was. "Buck, don't you get it?" Charlie nearly shouted. "Natty can't remember anything. She can't remember that she finally got up the courage to leave you, so now you get a second chance you don't deserve."

"But I been *tryin'* Burden, since before the accident, since I started workin', I been tryin'" Buck pleaded.

There were a few seconds of silence before Charlie responded. "Yeah I know you have Buck," he said softly. "I know you have."

"I ain't a bum Burden. I'm ain't some wife-beatin' drunk. I'm just . . . well, things never turned out like I thought they would, and I never wanted to get married and have the kid . . . and then, ah *fuck,* everything just kept getting' worse all the time . . ."

"Buck, time to be a man. You want your family? Then be a *father.* You want your wife?" Charlie hesitated. "Then be a *husband,*" he said softly. There was a long silence between them.

"What do I need to do Burden? What should I do?"

Charlie took a few steps closer to Buck. "Tomorrow morning Buck, you take Pie and Cat up to Charleston, to the hospital, and you walk into Natty's room holding their hands, being their father, and you make sure she sees you holding their hands. And then you go up close to her and you tell Natty you love her and that you've always loved her, since that day you came back from Morgantown, and then you put that big Red Bone High football ring on her finger 'til you find something better, and you tell her that marrying her was the *best day of your life!* Then you tell her how someday you're going to buy her a little house with a white picket fence on a nice little street, and then . . ." In the darkness Charlie reached up with the sleeve of his sweatshirt and wiped tears from both cheeks. "And then, well, then you'll be okay for a while, and you'll get your chance, to keep your family. Then it'll be all up to you what happens after that."

Buck stayed silent for several seconds, as if to make sure Charlie was done. Then he cleared his throat. "Okay, Burden. I'll do all that. Tomorrow, first thing. I'll take the kids up there."

"Yeah, good Buck," Charlie said wearily. "Do it just like I said."

"Yeah, I will." Buck reached down and picked up the bow-gun. "Sorry if I scared you. Had the safety on all the time."

"No, wasn't scared a bit," Charlie said with a chuckle, turning to leave. After a few steps he stopped and turned back. "Hey Buck?"

"Yeah?"

"The tree-cutting's about all done out there."

"Yeah, I'm already laid off."

Charlie hesitated for a few seconds. "Well I got a job for you at the power plant. Permanent job if you want it."

"Yeah, course I do," said Buck coming closer. "That's all I need."

"One thing though, you can't drink any more. I don't mean getting drunk. I mean you got to give it all up, booze, beer, everything. Completely on the wagon."

"I can do that, " said Buck firmly. "I ain't an alcoholic. I just drink 'cause . . . 'cause there's nothin' else."

"Well, now you got something else, right Buck?"

"Yeah Burden," he said quietly. "I got somethin' else now."

Charlie was silent for a few seconds, thinking. "Okay," he said finally, "come and see me next week at the plant." He turned and started walking along the trail.

"Yeah, I will, next week," said Buck. "Hey Burden, thanks," he called into the darkness, but Charlie was gone.

Chapter 36

Charlie wedged his lap-top case into the over-stuffed trunk of the Lexus, then tossed his overcoat on top of the luggage. He unzipped a pocket of his briefcase and withdrew a large brown envelope before carefully pushing down on the trunk lid. Hank stood waiting for him at the corner. The two men crossed South County Road and walked down the hill toward the library. After a few moments of silence, Hank looked up at the gray sky. "Supposed to get some snow later on. Hope it don't mess up your trip," he said.

"Should be okay," said Charlie. "Not supposed to come until tonight. Be almost in New York by then."

A white step-van was parked in the lot and the library door was unlocked. The smell of fresh paint greeted them along with the sound of someone moving a ladder around on the second floor. Just inside the door, sat a half-dozen large boxes from Dell Computer. "You'll have to find some high-school kid to set these up," said Charlie with a grin, "beyond my capabilities."

"Mine too," Hank agreed.

In the main room, they sat side-by-side at the long central table. They were surrounded by stacks of heavy-duty shipping boxes all marked on the outside: *Westchester Library Association.* Charlie emptied the contents of the brown envelope on the table. There were three sets of shiny silver keys to the building, which he pushed over to Hank. Charlie thumbed briefly through two sets of legal documents. "This is to establish the *Red Bone Children's Library Trust,* with you as the trustee. Need to sign it a few places and send it back to the lawyers. Keep a copy for yourself."

Hank just grunted with a brief nod as he looked over the papers. Charlie opened another envelope and took out two checks, which he turned over and endorsed over to the trust. He pushed them over to Hank. "This'll keep you going for a while," said Charlie. Hank looked over the checks through the lower portion of his bifocals. The first check was the $317,000 payment Charlie had been given by Larry Tuthill. The second was a check for $200,000 from CanAmex Energy Ltd. "Half a million," said Charlie "Invest it in something safe, should last a few years anyway." Hank nodded, still staring at the amounts on the two checks. "One thing you'll have to do," said Charlie, "is hire a part-time librarian, fifteen, twenty hours a week, flexible schedule, you know, someone who really cares about having a children's library."

Hank cleared his throat without looking at Charlie. "Yeah," he said softly, "think I got someone in mind. Soon as she's ready."

On the table was a burlap sack that Charlie pulled over and reached into. He came out with the wooden base of the Charleston tournament trophy. "See what you can do with this," said Charlie absently rubbing the small brass plate with his thumb. "Something the kids should be able to take pride in." Hank took the heavy disc without comment.

Then Charlie took out of the sack, the large white envelope that Buck had given him because he didn't know what to do with it. He gave the envelope to Hank without opening it. "Nice picture of the team, from the tournament in Charleston," said Charlie. He didn't need to see it again, the image of a grinning, happy, beautiful, Natty Oakes with her arms around Emma and Brenda, laughing and proud, like the rest of the team around them. A picture from so long ago.

Charlie showed Hank the sprinkler and lighting controls in the basement, then with Hank waiting for him at the bottom of the stairs, Charlie took one last look around the upper floor. He stood at the expansive windows looking down on the new soccer field, the gazebo and the baseball fields beyond. With the beautiful still-green turf, the lighting and landscaping, the whole project had turned out even better than Charlie had envisioned it. *Yes, it was a complex that Darien or Riverside would be proud of, and with a little time to heal, so would Red Bone.*

Hank said he wanted to sit around for a while in the new library, so he wouldn't be walking back up the hill with Charlie. They stood in the parking lot looking down toward the soccer field, neither man wanting to start their goodbyes. Finally Charlie turned and looked up toward the fourth floor porch. "Left a check for you in the cribbage box," he said.

Hank shook his head. "No need for that."

"Did better than I thought," said Charlie. "Better than Alva Paine did."

"Had nineteen years to work on *him*," said Hank, his whiskers jerked up as he tried to smile. There was a long silence between them. Then Hank let out a long sigh. He turned to Charlie with his hand extended. "Well, you better get going Burden. You got a long drive ahead."

Charlie squeezed the old man's hand firmly. "Yeah, uh, well thanks Hank. Thanks for everything, thanks for . . ."

"Burden," Hank looked up into Charlie's eyes, "you, made a difference here. You made this a better place than it was when you came and ain't many men over the years can say that. Don't happen a lot around here."

Charlie released Hank's grip and smiled at his friend. "Well, I had a good teacher." Charlie gazed down over the soccer field and squinted with the pain of his thoughts, then shook his head slowly. "Keep thinking Hank, that maybe if I hadn't come here . . ."

"Can't blame yourself for any a what happened," Hank said firmly, "act of God, ever was one. You did a lot of good things for a lot of people here Charlie."

Charlie looked back at Hank and tried to smile. "Yeah, well, I just wish it didn't hurt so much." He stepped forward and the two men hugged. "Time to go," said Charlie slapping Hank's back lightly. He turned and trudged up the hill to Main Street for the last time and climbed into the Lexus.

Charlie drove down the hill, past the library but Hank was nowhere to be seen. On the seat next to him sat Pie's Yankees hat. *One more stop to make.*

The leafless trees and thin vegetation of mid-December, made the hand-painted sign wedged into the boulders at the base of *Oakes Hollow* appear even more ominous. As Charlie drove slowly up the rutted, stone-covered road, he had the distinct impression that the greenery of summer and the warm colors of autumn had masked from him the truly stark, cold-hearted nature of this place he had been living in for the last six months.

Natty's red Accord, covered with brown leaves, was tucked in front of the first trailer on the left. Light green paint was curling up on the side of the trailer revealing a rusting undercoat. A small wooden deck had been built at the door and was now listing at an angle showing that either the trailer or the deck had settled since its erection. Charlie pulled the Lexus in behind the end of the trailer so as not to block the road.

No one answered his rapping on the metal door and the inside of the trailer was dark. Charlie turned and looked up the hill toward the house. White smoke was wafting from the chimney and two dogs sat looking in his direction from under the porch. He looked down at the Yankees hat in his hand and thought about just hanging it on the door handle. He wanted to see Pie though before he left. Charlie hadn't seen him in a week, since he told him he was leaving soon to go to China. It was hard to tell if Pie was upset over the news – since the accident he had become more reserved and it seemed to Charlie, a little older. The accident had changed a lot of people.

A door slammed at the house across the road. Charlie looked up to see two young children clambering onto pint-size yellow and orange plastic vehicles. Then Natty's sister-in-law, Sally, the always talkative, flirtatious red head came out into the front yard. She lit a cigarette and pulled a bulky sweater close around her shoulders and stood watching the children. At the sound of Charlie's steps coming down from the deck, Sally turned and squinted at him and then noticed his car parked across the road.

Charlie stopped about twenty feet from her as one of the old coon hounds loped up and rubbed against him. He reached down and scratched the dog behind the ears. "What's his name?" he said, looking up toward Sally.

Sally stared at him blankly, and then down at the dog as if it were the first time she'd ever seen it. She hunched her shoulders against the cold and took a long drag on her cigarette. "Hell, we got a hard enough time namin' the *kids* around here."

Charlie moved a little closer and the dog started back up toward the house. With no make-up and her hair pulled straight back, Sally looked older to Charlie, with maybe the beginning of the hard scowl and sad eyes of most of the older women of McDowell County.

"I was looking for Pie," said Charlie, holding out the Yankees hat. "Wanted to give him his hat back, and to say goodbye."

Sally took the cigarette from her lips to speak. "*Heard* you were leavin'," she said. "Goin' today?"

"Yeah, I'm on my way out. Job's done here."

Sally took a long drag on her cigarette. "Yeah, well Pie ain't here. He's gone huntin' with his father. Buck and him left early. They're like best buddies now."

Charlie smiled and nodded at the thought of Buck taking Pie hunting. "That's good," he said. "Good for them."

"They'll be going' up to see Nat tomorrow, Buck and the kids. They go up a lot," said Sally, watching Charlie closely.

"How's she doing?" Charlie asked, even though he'd spoken to Natty's doctor the previous day.

Sally shrugged. "Comin' home 'nother week or so. Still can't remember nothin', 'bout the accident or the soccer team. Don't remember Emma." Sally shook her head angrily and threw the cigarette butt down and ground it into the dirt with her shoe. "Ain't the way it was all suppose to . . ." She shrugged without finishing the thought.

Large, lazy snowflakes began falling around them. Charlie held his face up to the gray sky for a moment breathing in the cold winter air of the mountains. "Looks like I better get going," he said. He reached the Yankees hat out to Sally. "Would you give this to Pie, and tell him . . . well, just tell him *thanks for being my best friend in West Virginia.*"

Sally took the hat without looking at it. "Yeah, sure, I'll tell him that."

Charlie walked back to the Lexus and backed it out onto the gravel road, pointed down the hill. Sally was standing next to the car. He lowered the side window and looked up at her quizzically.

"Just wanted to tell you," said Sally, "that Nat and Buck, well, they're doin' real good, like a couple of newlyweds, you know." Charlie just stared at her. "So," she continued, "maybe some good come out of it all."

Charlie nodded and smiled. He rolled up the window and drove slowly down the hill. He wasn't sure what Sally meant by *all* but it didn't matter. Now, none of it mattered any more. He was leaving, and all these people in Red Bone would be getting along just like they always did, and pretty soon they'd forget he was ever there, just another outsider who'd come for the coal. The way it's always been, for the last hundred years.

Epilogue

Spring came earlier to Red Bone, West Virginia, than it did to central China, or even Mamaroneck, and it felt good to Charlie, walking across the soccer field. The grass was soft and thick underfoot, just waiting to explode in growth with a few more weeks of warm sunlight. Ellen's heels sunk into the soft turf causing her to chuckle and lean on Charlie's arm as she concentrated her weight on the balls of her feet.

Up ahead of them, the PR woman from Charleston, carrying a large plastic scissors, and a photographer hefting several bags of equipment, walked quickly to keep up with the CanAmex man who had flown in for the event. Charlie lifted up his face to drink in the familiar pine-scented breeze that rolled down the north flank of Red Bone mountain and smiled to himself. He could tell that the CanAmex manager had drawn the short straw to see who would go down to West Virginia for some kind of library dedication, and couldn't wait to get it over with and get back on the black helicopter still hissing on the baseball field behind them.

At the top of the long cement stairway up to the library, Charlie could already see Hank, Eve Brewster, and a group of black women that would include Mabel Willard and Ada Lowe and several others from the Red Bone Baptist Church Social Club. Janice and Gus Lowe would be waiting there too. Charlie swallowed hard and took in a deep breath. Four months in China hadn't been long enough.

The photographer and the PR woman assembled Ada, Janice and Gus Lowe between the CanAmex man and the new Lead Engineer from Dietrich Delahunt & Mackey for the ribbon cutting. Zack and Sammy Willard, looking as uncomfortable as they could possible be, wearing suit jackets that were growing smaller on them by the minute and thin black ties, held each end of the wide red ribbon. Behind them, a plaque on the outside wall of the library displayed a reasonably good likeness of Emma Lowe holding a soccer ball next to an inscription carved in gold letters: *Emma C. Lowe Memorial Library.*

Charlie and Hank stood at the back of the small crowd watching the PR woman do her job – arranging the picture, eliciting smiles, instructing the photographer, and then carefully taking down the names of the locals in the picture. Hank frowned and emitted a low growl under his breath, knowing that they didn't have the right people in the picture. Charlie didn't care. The CanAmex man delivered his twenty second speech and everyone started making their way into the library for non-alcoholic champagne and doughnuts.

Hank led Ellen off for a tour of the new library stocked with books donated by the *Westchester Library Association* while the new superintendent of the power plant walked over to Charlie.

"So how's the new *big mule*?" Charlie asked with a chuckle.

His replacement laughed. "*Feel* like a donkey sometimes." They talked for several minutes about the progress of the construction and the typical union problems that never seemed to go away. Then there was a brief pause allowing Charlie to change the subject because he knew he only had a few minutes before the CanAmex man was going to be leading everyone back to the helicopter to make his escape.

"So, how's Buck Oakes doing? Job going okay for him?"

The other man squinted at him, surprised that Charlie even knew the *Chief of Security,* and then smiled. "Yeah, Buck's doing great. Christ, I wish every employee we had was as conscientious as Buck Oakes. Guy's there seven to seven most days and comes in to check on things on the weekend too. Guards respect him, and I think they're all a little afraid of him too 'cause he's tough as nails, so they work hard for him." The man cut through the air with his hand for emphasis. "One thing I *don't* worry about is security of the plant with Buck Oakes in charge." He looked past Charlie's shoulder and smiled. "Speak of the devil," he said.

Charlie turned to see a black *Chevy Suburban* with the silver CanAmex logo on the side turning into the parking lot. Buck Oakes and the Pie Man climbed down from the truck and walked toward him. Pie's *happy face* seemed somehow older, less of a child, but still the infectious image that Charlie would always remember him by. They pressed right hands together in a long *high-five,* and then Charlie pulled the boy close to him roughly with an arm around his head, making Pie giggle. "How's my little buddy, my best friend in West Virginia?" said Charlie.

"Chowlie, Chowlie," Pie said excitedly, escaping the headlock, "Papa and me, we go hunting in the wintwa, and I shot a deewa with my own wiffo." Pie was beaming.

"Wow, that's great Pie Man," Charlie said, offering up another *high-five,* "getting a deer, that's really something."

The remains of his happy face left the boy. He put his hands in his pockets and shuffled nervously on his feet. He glanced up at his father who just shrugged and smiled down at him. Charlie looked at Buck and then back at Pie. "What's up Pie Man? What's the matter?"

The boy squinted up at Charlie and then down at his feet. He spoke softly. "Chowly, I am not Pie Man any mowa." He looked up. "When I go to Mishgan to be a engineewa, like Chowly, they will laugh at me if I am called *Pie Man.*" He shrugged. "*Pie Man* is a baby name and I am not a baby any mowa. Tho now my name ith *Boyd.* Boyd Oakth."

Charlie looked inquiringly at Buck who shook his head and shrugged. "All his idea," said Buck. He put his hand on his son's shoulder. "Little boy's growing up, I guess."

The Pie Man's *happy face* was back. Charlie grinned and offered his hand to his friend. "Well *Boyd Oakes,* I'm glad to meet you." They shook hands. "*Boyd Oakes,*" Charlie repeated, "that's a fine name for an engineer."

Charlie turned to Buck. He looked taller and was noticeably thinner. He wore a dark blue uniform. Emblazoned in silver on the left breast of his jacket was, *CanAmex Security* and under it, *Chief, Buck Oakes.*

"How you doing Buck?" Charlie said as they shook hands.

"Okay Burden," Buck replied. "Good to see you again." Buck had shaved off the mustache and goatee, and looked like a different person.

"Understand you're doing great. Doing a great job at the plant," said Charlie.

Buck shrugged. "I'm tryin'" he said softly. He looked down at Pie and put an arm around the boy's shoulders. "I'm tryin'" he repeated.

Charlie nodded pensively. "Yeah, you sure are," he said. He wondered if he should ask Buck if Natty was coming to the open house, but Buck beat him to it.

"Nat was going to come," said Buck, "but her leg's been hurtin' her some and it ain't easy for her to walk, so . . ." Buck shrugged. "But she sure likes workin' up here at the library," he added quickly. "That's been *real* good for her. Can't do her nursin' stuff no more. So, library's been good for her," Buck said softly.

Charlie flashed a smile in appreciation of the news. "That's good," he said nodding. "Yeah that's good." Then there was nothing left to say. "Well," said Charlie, rubbing the top of Boyd's head. The boy's hair had grown back to a long fuzzy crew cut in the five months since the soccer tournament. "Better get some doughnuts and cider before the Willard boys eat everything," he said, motioning toward the library.

Buck and his son went up to the second floor where the refreshments and most of the people were. Charlie lingered in the entryway, chatting with a few of the women from the Red Bone Baptist Church Social Club, until they left him to find the doughnuts. Finally alone, Charlie moved over to the glass trophy case hung inconspicuously on the wall just inside the front door. On a tall pedestal sat the wooden disc from the Charleston tournament trophy. Hank had had the bolt holes filled in and the wooden disc refinished in a highly polished deep brown that shined in the glow of the small spotlights in the ceiling. The inscription plate on the front of the disc was also gleaming. Against the back wall of the case, was a huge enlargement of *The Bones* team picture from the Charleston tournament, with a caption added at the bottom, listing the players' names. Charlie took a step in closer to the glass case and stared at the picture. He looked one-by-one at each face of the boys kneeling in the front row, then the back row, before he allowed himself to look at her, in the middle of the picture with an arm around the shoulders of Emma Lowe to her right and Brenda Giles on her left, pulling them close to her, making them laugh like she was laughing, the smile that made his heart skip. He pulled in a deep breath and exhaled slowly. Ellen and Hank were coming down the stairs. Charlie stepped away from the case.

"Trophy looks great Hank," said Charlie.

"Yeah, came out okay," Hank said, glancing quickly toward the trophy case before heading for the front door. The CanAmex man and the PR woman with the photographer next to her, were coming down the stairs.

Ellen looked up at Charlie. "Time to go," she said. Charlie smiled down at his wife and nodded. Eve Brewster grabbed Charlie for the walk down to the fields while Ellen went ahead with Hank. They fell in behind Ada and Gus, and

Janice Lowe, going down the long cement stairway. Up ahead the women of the Red Bone Baptist Church Social Club were moving slowly down the stairs holding up the procession. The CanAmex man and the PR woman were halfway across the soccer field, heading for the helicopter. Charlie smiled. *They'll just have to wait.* He would enjoy his last few moments chatting with Eve.

They walked arm-in-arm slowly across the mushy sod of the soccer field while Eve brought Charlie up-to-date on the state of affairs in Red Bone. She told him about Mr. Jacks moving in with Natty and Buck; how Natty had gone up to visit him in the home in Beckley and took one look at the conditions and loaded him into her car and brought him back to Red Bone where they made a little space for him in the living room of their trailer. Eve's story made Charlie laugh. He could picture Natty doing that. And the best thing about it, Eve said, was that Buck was okay with it, which was a real change for him, she said, something he never would have done before.

The pitch of the turbines' whistle went up a notch as the helicopter's blades began to spin slowly. Beside the gazebo, the crowd was shaking hands, saying their thanks and goodbyes. Charlie could see Ellen hugging Ada and Janice Lowe. He and Eve stopped in the center of the soccer field. Charlie turned and looked up the hill toward Main Street, up to the fourth floor porch. The rear of the building was bathed in late-morning sunlight. Charlie took in a deep breath. "God, I loved living here. This is a wonderful place Eve with wonderful people."

Charlie felt Eve squeeze his arm. He looked down at her. She was staring off toward the road with a wry smile on her face. "Charlie," she said, "I'm going to go over and say my good-byes to Ellen now." She didn't wait for a reply before starting off for the gazebo.

Charlie looked over toward the road just as the orange Camaro rolled slowly to a stop on the sandy shoulder. He could see Sally Oakes in the driver's seat, arm extended out the window, a cigarette between her fingers. She glanced over at Charlie and then toward her passenger. Charlie waited in the center of the field while nothing happened for several seconds. He could feel the helicopter blades spinning faster behind him.

Natty finally opened the door. She held the seat forward to let Cat out of the back seat and they both came around the front of the car and started walking toward Charlie. Natty said something to her daughter causing her to run ahead across the field to her father and brother. The little girl took one nervous glance at Charlie, then put her head down as she went by him.

Natty moved slowly, with a noticeable limp, leaning on a cane in her left hand. When she got onto the field, the cane would sink into the soft turf, making her exert some effort to pull it out before her next step. She smiled over at Charlie then put her head down to concentrate on the placement of her cane in the wet grass. Charlie took a few steps toward her, conscious of the many sets of eyes watching the scene from behind him.

Natty stopped about eight feet away from him, took in a labored breath and rested on the cane. She looked around them at the new turf. "Used to have a nice field here, nice and hard, with a lot of stones. Easy to walk on." She spoke slowly. Finally, she looked up at him. "Hey Charlie."

Charlie smiled down at her. "How are you Nat?"

She shrugged and leaned on the cane to turn toward him. "Knee ain't so good, had to put some phony ligaments and stuff in there, but that's nothin'. Six months, maybe, I'll be fine, runnin' around again, all over the mountain."

Charlie used the few moments while Natty was talking to study her. She was wearing the blue warm-up suit with the collar pulled up around her neck. Her hair had darkened and grown out a little with a shock starting to fall across her forehead once again, and she had put on a little weight. Her face was fuller and a little paler, and under the warm-up jacket her shoulders looked rounder

She looked up at him and smiled. "I ain't complainin' though." She looked over toward the Gazebo where Buck was holding hands with Cat as the visitors were starting to board the helicopter. Charlie turned to follow her gaze. "Buck's been – like a miracle, you know, since . . . since the accident," she said softly. "All my daydreams come true now." She chuckled. "Got nothin' left to dream about up on the boulder anyway."

Ellen looked over and waved. Natty grinned and waved back. "Your wife still sticks out in a crowd don't she Charlie?"

Charlie glanced over at Ellen. "Yeah, she does that."

"How's she like her new house?"

"No," said Charlie, turning back toward Natty. "We're selling it this week. Came back for the closing."

"She okay with that?"

Charlie smiled. "Oh, yeah. She's got a bigger one to play with in China, and more money to spend on it. She loves China."

Natty continued to gaze over at Ellen. "Yeah, I heard you were in China," she said softly. "Like you always wanted, huh Charlie? Building something."

Charlie sighed and glanced quickly over at the helicopter, and then back at Natty. "Yeah, that's right. It's what I wanted to do."

Natty watched Ellen climb into the helicopter. "Looks like they're waiting for you Charlie."

"Yeah, I need to get going," he said. He took a step closer to her. "I'm glad you came Natty. I wanted to see you."

Natty flashed a nervous smile. "Got most all of my memory back by now." She turned her face up toward the library on the hill. "Not all of it thought. Don't remember *her* yet," said Natty. "I stare and stare at that picture up there and sometimes I get these quick flashes of her, kickin' a ball, or runnin' down the field, but they're gone in a second." She looked back at Charlie. "Remember most everything else though. Come back to me little bit at a time, mostly. But I'm remembering it all now, 'cept for the accident."

As Charlie watched Natty speak, surrounded by the green forest rising up around them, his time with her in this place all suddenly flashed back to him – their runs along the mountain trail, the soccer games, their night at the *Pocahontas Hotel* to visit Woody and Mr. Jacks, the lobster party, sitting in the warm sun up on the boulder watching her bare her soul to him and falling in love with her – and a cold shudder ran through him as he realized how much he wanted to stay here and not get on the helicopter that was whining impatiently for him on the baseball field.

Natty smiled. "Hear some music once in while from the show, from *Le Miz*, you know, and I think all about New York." She laughed. *"New York City*, wow, what a weekend that was huh Charlie?"

Charlie grinned down at her and nodded. "Yeah, yeah that was some weekend." Their eyes locked for a moment sharing the memory of what almost was, then Natty turned away towards the gazebo where Buck was holding Cat's hand. She could see Ellen in the helicopter watching them through a window.

"Well, looks like you're holding things up," Natty said softly.

Charlie glanced quickly back at the helicopter. "Yeah, gotta go," he said.

"Back to China," Natty said with a chuckle. Charlie just nodded and looked down at her.

Natty leaned on her cane and held out her right hand. "Thank you Mr. Burden, for everything," she said softly.

Charlie took her hand. He squeezed it softly. "Good bye Mrs. Oakes." He turned and started walking toward the helicopter, taking long purposeful strides, anxiousness to get into the air, his business here now concluded.

Natty stood in the center of the field and watched him as he shook hands with Buck and Hank, hugged Mabel and Ada, and gave her son a long *high-five* and then a brief hug. As Charlie went up the short stairway into the helicopter, Natty turned and started walking back across the field toward the orange Camaro, her cane sinking into the soft new turf of the soccer field.

Breinigsville, PA USA
29 September 2010
246307BV00002B/16/P